TILL
WE MEET
AGAIN

ALSO BY JUDITH KRANTZ

Scruples
Princess Daisy
Mistral's Daughter
I'll Take Manhattan

JUDITH KRANTZ

TILL WE MEET AGAIN

CROWN PUBLISHERS, INC.
NEW YORK

Grateful acknowledgment is given for permission to reprint lyrics from the following:

"Till We Meet Again" by Richard A. Whiting and Raymond B. Egan. Copyright 1918 by Warner Brothers, Inc. Copyright renewed. All rights reserved. Used by permission of Warner/Chappel Music, Inc.

Published by Crown Publishers, Inc., 225 Park Avenue South, New York, New York 10003 and represented in Canada by the Canadian MANDA Group.

CROWN is a trademark of Crown Publishers, Inc.

Manufactured in the United States of America

Library of Congress Cataloging in Publication Data
Krantz, Judith.
   Till we meet again.

   I. Title.
PS3561.R264T55   1988   813'.54   88-11857
ISBN 0-517-57026-2

10 9 8 7 6 5 4 3 2 1

First Edition

For the hundreds of women pilots, from more than a dozen countries, who flew in the British Air Transport Auxiliary from September 1939 through November 1945. These splendid women joined in the essential job of ferrying aircraft of the Royal Navy and the Royal Air Force throughout the British Isles, proving that women could fly anything with wings, from fighter planes to four-engined bombers with skill, valor and an outstanding safety record.

For Steve, once again, with all my love, yesterday, today and tomorrow.

Acknowledgments

I owe a great debt of gratitude to the people who helped me unearth the facts that are the necessary foundation of this fiction.

Lettice Curtis, British pilot and former First Officer in the British Air Transport Auxiliary. She was among the first women who joined the ATA and one of the last to leave, after six unstinting years of wartime service. Her later work as an aviation historian produced her book *The Forgotten Pilots*, which was an invaluable source of factual material on the ATA.

Claire Walters, American pilot and President-Owner of the Claire Walters Flight Academy in Santa Monica, California. Claire Walters is one of the great flight instructors. Her generosity, patience, dedication, warmth and good humor have no limit.

Ann Wood, American pilot and former First Officer in the British Air Transport Auxiliary.

Edna Gardner White, pioneer American pilot and member of the Ninety-Nines, Inc., the association of International Women Pilots.

Betty H. Gillies, pioneer American pilot and member of the Advisory Board of the Ninety-Nines, Inc.

Virginia Oualline, Archivist of the Ninety-Nines, Inc., resource center.

Monsieur Pierre Belfond, President of Editions Belfond, Paris. When I asked him for books on the Parisian Music Hall he sent me thirty-five rare marvels.

Mr. David Campbell of the Ritz in Paris. With his characteristic flair and kindness he opened the most important doors in Champagne to me.

Monsieur Alexandre Tolstoi of the French Consulate of Los Angeles.

Madame Marianne Bain of Los Angeles.

Monsieur Bertrand Mure, President and Director General of Ruinart Champagne.

Monsieur Edmund Maudiere, Chief Winemaker of Moët & Chandon.

Janey, Comtesse de la Boutetiere, of Moët & Chandon.

Mr. and Mrs. Anthony Hughes of Moët & Chandon, Château de Saran, Epernay.

H. Glenn Buffington, writer, aviation historian, and member of the Advisory Board of the Ninety-Nines, Inc., resource center.

Dr. Karim Valji.

Mrs. Edwina Lloyd. There could not be a better assistant.

TILL WE MEET AGAIN

Prologue

*H*OW could today possibly be her sixtieth birthday, wondered Eve, Vicomtesse Paul-Sébastian de Lancel, and the greatest lady in the province of Champagne, when, since morning, her spirit had been invaded by a sense of sparkling exhilaration, as festive as an orchard in full bloom, wind-tossed under a holiday sky?

Before breakfast she had slipped outside, as she did every morning, to inspect the vines that grew closest to the Château de Valmont, the home of the Lancels. The warm spring of April 1956 had caused an unusually large number of newborn bunches of grapes to emerge from the buds. Everywhere in the fruitful countryside, from the two-acre vineyards of the workers to the great holdings of the makers of the Grands Marques of champagne, such as Lancel, Moët & Chandon, and Bollinger, the news of abundance had spread from one freshly green hilltop to another.

Her happiness had nothing to do with the possibility of a large harvest, Eve de Lancel thought, as she dressed much later in the day for her gala dinner birthday party. Harvests were always problematical, spring bounty was no guarantee of autumn fulfillment. Today had unfolded with dancing steps because all her family had gathered at Valmont to celebrate with her.

Last night, at one minute before midnight, she had been fifty-nine. One minute later she had become sixty. Why was her age today not fifty-nine plus a few hours? Eve asked herself. Did you have to be sixty to know, absolutely, that sixty was a nonsensical number when it attached itself to you, no matter what foolishness it symbolized to the world? Was this a universal secret, shared by all those who reached sixty only to find that they still felt . . . oh, perhaps thirty-two? Or did she feel younger still, say . . . twenty-five? Yes, twenty-five seemed just about right, Eve decided, as she confronted herself boldly in the well-lit mirror of her dressing table. She made a rapid calculation. During her twenty-fifth year, her husband was serving as First Secretary of the French Embassy in Australia, her daughter Delphine was three years old, and her younger daughter, Freddy, christened Marie-Frédérique, was only one and a half. It had been a year of maternal worry she would choose never to live over again, she decided gratefully.

Freddy and Delphine were both at Valmont, grown women with children of their own, women who had arrived at the château this morning, Delphine from Paris, Freddy from Los Angeles, so surrounded by husbands, children, nannies, and baggage, that only now could they be expected to have finished unpacking. Eve's sons-in-law had promised to keep the children playing outside as long as possible. For the moment, no family members but Lancel women were in the château, and Eve felt an impulsive desire to be with her girls. She rang, and her maid appeared at the door of her bedroom.

"Josette, will you please ask my daughters to come to my sitting room, and ask Henri to bring up glasses and champagne, pink, of course, the 1947."

Neither of the girls would fully understand that a pink champagne from a superlative vintage year was the rarest sparkling wine ever produced on this planet, but it suited Eve's mood to offer it to them without explanation. Dinner would be served unusually early tonight, since every one of her grandchildren who could sit upright at a table was included. Now, at five in the afternoon, a restorative glass of champagne was quite in order during the half hour that could be expected before the noisy return of the men and boys.

Eve wrapped herself in a widely skirted, deeply flounced dressing gown of a special shade of pink taffeta, almost—if not quite—a flamenco pink that reflected all the slanting spring sunlight and returned her hair almost—if not quite—to the rare shade of blond it had been until a few years ago.

She had . . . aged—for Eve realized that she must not shy away from that irritating yet necessary word—brilliantly well. Her finely wrought body moved with the distinction and natural grace of a woman who had grown to girlhood in those last years of the Edwardian era, when posture was nearly as important as the irrefutable beauty her parents had been careful never to praise. Eve raised her eyebrows high, as a private, half-mocking smile crossed her lips at the memory of the long-lost innocence of those bittersweet days before the First World War.

"Mother?" Delphine's voice sounded at her sitting room door.

"Come in, darling," Eve called to her elder daughter, hurrying from her bedroom to the sitting room. Delphine drifted in, wearing a sumptuous white silk robe, ordered, like all her clothes, from Dior, and subsided gratefully into a deep brocade armchair.

"Oh, it's so wonderful to be here," she sighed, almost plaintively.

"You seem just a bit frazzled around the edges, darling."

"Oh, Mother, why do I have so many children?" Delphine exclaimed, obviously not expecting an answer. "Thank God the twins are ten and keep themselves busy—but the others! Paul-Sebastian and Jean-Luc have been fighting all day. If only this next one is a girl!" She patted her stomach hopefully. "Don't I finally deserve a girl, isn't that only fair?"

She looked up at Eve, as if her mother could guarantee a response to her question. Fatigue had not touched Delphine's transcendent beauty. Nothing

2

could mar the magnetic placement of her huge eyes, set so far apart beneath the calm shield of her wide forehead. Nothing could alter the way her lips turned up at the corners in an eternally mysterious smile, or the precise distance between her widow's peak and the deliciously small shape of her chin that created the heart-shaped face millions adored. Delphine was the most famous movie actress in France. At thirty-eight she was in the flower of her career, for the rational French find a woman more fascinating after thirty-five than she is in the unripeness of first youth.

"By now a daughter should be inevitable," Eve replied, touching Delphine's bell of brown hair in a brief, gentle caress.

Henri brought in the tray of glasses and champagne. "Shall I open it, Madame?" he asked Eve.

"No, I'll do it, thank you," she answered, waving him away. Tradition had it that the châtelaine of Valmont, the mistress of the house, should always be the one to open and pour the first bottle on any ceremonial occasion, and this private moment with her daughters was, for Eve, more ceremonial than the dinner tonight would be, no matter how gala.

"Where's Freddy?" she asked Delphine, who was groaning in a delicious orgy of relaxation, her shining head and fragile arms flung back in abandon on a pile of brocade pillows.

"Bathing her children. I can hardly believe that Freddy produced two little boys in less than two years. She's certainly making up for lost time."

"Couldn't their nanny give them their bath?" Eve inquired.

"Normally, yes," Delphine responded with amusement. "That poor woman was dragged six thousand miles from California, but now Freddy can't keep away from her own offspring."

"Who's taking my name in vain?" Freddy asked as she entered the room quickly, with the slight swagger that had always marked her springy walk. At thirty-six, her resemblance to a female Robin Hood was more vivid than ever. There was a spirited directness in her playful brigand's eyes, a carefree jubilation in the way she was ready to attack any challenge, a moonbeam insouciance in her smile. She brandished a hairbrush. "Delphine, take pity on me. Do something, anything, about my hair! You're so clever and you know I'm utterly hopeless."

Freddy dropped lithely into another armchair. Her legs, clad in water-splashed white linen trousers, swung high over its upholstered side, sketching a brief, exciting arabesque in the air. Just from the way Freddy moved, Eve thought, you might guess that she had been born to fly any airplane ever built.

Her daughter's hair was as red as an old-fashioned, well-burnished copper casserole, so brash that it drew all eyes to her wherever she appeared, hair so intractably rebellious that no hairdresser had ever been able to domesticate it.

3

Throughout Freddy's headstrong, headline-capturing career as one of the world's great pilots, during all her daredevil, glorious years in World War II, only an aviator's helmet had ever tamed that head of hair, and then only until the moment when she took the helmet off.

Eve surveyed her two astonishingly different but equally lawless, brave, willful, and outrageous daughters, whom time had blessedly transformed into women. "Will you join me in a glass of champagne?" she said, and bent to uncork the bottle of Lancel '47 with a quick twist of the blunt-edged tweezers that had been designed generations ago, especially for this task. She poured three inches into her own glass, gave the crystal an experienced twirl to wake the wine from its slumber, and watched the white froth vanish on the surface of the pale pink liquid. Eve took a sip, found it sublime, as she expected, deftly filled all three glasses, and handed one to Freddy and one to Delphine.

"I'll never forget my first taste of champagne," Freddy said. "It was here, outside on the terrace, when we all came over from California to visit for the first time. What year was that, Mother?" Unaccustomed nostalgia filled her gaze. Her eyes were of such an intense and unlimited blue that they seemed saturated with sky.

"Nineteen thirty-three," said Eve. "You were only thirteen, but your grandmother decreed that you weren't too young."

"What did Great-Grandmother say?" a voice asked from the doorway as Annie, Freddy's fourteen-year-old daughter, slipped into the room wearing jeans and a man's shirt, with the sleeves rolled up. "And why wasn't I invited to this party?"

"Aren't you supposed to be out with the others, Annie?" Freddy asked, taking a pass at sounding like a proper mother.

"Do I resemble a daddy or some sticky little boy?" tall, larkish Annie demanded with her seraphic, impudent grin. "I'm the only girl in my generation of this family and I wouldn't be caught dead hanging around with that crowd. I've been in my room. I actually fell asleep for a half hour. I intend to stay up all night—or I would if there was anyone here to dance with who wasn't a relative." Annie contemplated the three of them with delight. She considered herself far and away the most mature and wisest of all the Lancel females, even, in some ways, more grown-up than her adored grandmother.

"What are you going to put on for dinner, Annie?" Eve asked.

"I don't have a thing to wear," Annie said, shaking her curly head dolefully.

"You brought over two suitcases full of clothes," Freddy laughed.

"But nothing exactly right for the occasion. Grandma, may I go take a look in your armoire?"

"First have a glass of champagne," Eve suggested. There was nothing she could deny Annie, not even a Balenciaga, no matter how unsuitable.

Annie approached the wine with curiosity. She'd never had champagne before, but every time she tasted something for the first time, French tradition said that she could make a wish. She wrinkled her enchanting nose and took a large sip, tasted it thoroughly, as she had seen others do, and swallowed it thoughtfully.

"Hmmm." She made a silent wish and bent to take another sip.

"Did you notice anything special about it?" Eve asked.

"Yes. It tasted one way in my mouth, and then, when I'd swallowed it, there was another taste, a sort of glow at the back of my throat."

"That," said Eve, "is only possible because it is a perfect champagne. The taste is called the Farewell."

Annie took another big sip, put down her glass, and vanished in the direction of the biggest armoire in the bedroom.

"That child is the only one of you with a natural palate," Eve informed her daughters excitedly. "Neither of you has ever noticed the Farewell in all these years. Freddy—what would you think of sending Annie here next summer to let her start to learn about the creation of champagne? Somebody has to take over the House of Lancel someday."

"I think that she's going to be learning to fly next summer, but if she wants to—well, why not?"

Annie came back into the bedroom holding a hanger from which was suspended a red chiffon dress with tiny shoulder straps above a small, tucked bodice. The shoulder straps and the belt that was buckled around the small waist were thickly encrusted with rhinestones. They glittered with an unexpected freshness, as if a spotlight had just been turned on them. The skirt of the red dress flirted with the air, its layers of chiffon dancing into a flickering hemline that dipped in points of many different lengths. Even on a hanger the dress seemed magical, as if it had led a life of its own, as if it possessed a history and, somehow, a complicated personality, a thousand selves.

"Grandma, look at this! I've never seen it before—it's fabulous! And I bet it would just fit me," Annie said meaningfully.

"Where did you find that dress?" Eve asked, jolted.

"All the way at the back of the armoire. It winked right at me."

"I'd . . . forgotten it was there. It's an old dress, Annie—it must be— oh, more than forty years old."

"I don't care how old it is, it's better than new. What did you wear it for?"

"I didn't wear it, Annie—Maddy did."

Both Delphine and Freddy leaned forward with fascination. So this was the famous dress Maddy had worn, Delphine thought, a dress that was part of the family scandal she'd learned about years ago. She'd never laid eyes on it before, although she'd heard about it, far more, indeed, than she had ever wanted to. Freddy was intrigued. She knew about Maddy, of course, but she'd never imagined that a dress could be so alive, almost like another person in the room. She had an attachment to a certain red dress herself, she'd never throw it away, but it hadn't occurred to her that her mother would be that sentimental about Maddy's dress.

Eve filled all four glasses again. "I think we should drink to Maddy," she decreed, her eyes alight and playful, a faint blush rising on her cheeks. Whatever her daughters thought they knew about Maddy, they'd never be able to understand why she'd kept that dress. There were some things you could never totally communicate . . . nor did you ever intend to.

The Lancel women held their glasses high. "To Maddy!" they said.

"Whoever she is," Annie added, as she raised her glass.

1

EVE Coudert held out her five-franc note to the ticket seller. She gave him a nonchalant smile as she paid for a ride in the hot-air balloon that lay tethered on the huge field of La Maladière, outside of Dijon, where the great Air Show of 1910 was in its last day.

"You're alone, Mademoiselle?" he asked in surprise. It was rare to see such a young woman unaccompanied, particularly one so appetizing. He eyed her with interest, taking a rapid, knowing inventory of her charms. Under the brim of her straw hat, she looked up at him with gray eyes, dark enough to snare the devil, under brows that flew upward, as slanted as a pair of wings. Her heavy chignon revealed hair that was some unnamable but intoxicating shade between red and gold, and her full, smiling mouth was as naturally rosy as her cheeks.

"My husband is afraid of heights, Monsieur," she said, and added a delicate shade of meaning to her smile which told the ticket seller that she understood full well that he himself wasn't afraid of heights and that she admired him for his courage.

Oh ho, he thought with pleasure, this bewitchingly young bride of the provinces isn't as nearly innocent as she's supposed to be, and with a longing look, but without further question, he gave Eve the ticket that entitled her to a ride. Taking her gloved hand, he gallantly helped her step up into the basketlike woven wicker gondola that was big enough to hold five people.

She gathered her narrow white piqué skirt in one hand and, with the other, held on tightly to her fashionably wide-brimmed hat trimmed with floppy pink silk cabbage roses. Eve's pointed, laced-up low boots tapped nervously as she waited for the removal of dozens of sand bags that kept the huge red balloon on the ground. She took care not to look around at her fellow passengers. Eve turned her back on them, leaned against the waist-high rim of the gondola, and tucked her chin tightly into her high boned collar, so that its lace petals were articulated clearly against her delicate skin and almost hid her face.

It was Sunday, the twenty-fifth of August, a particularly hot afternoon, but Eve shivered with repressed impatience while the workmen ran about, shouting at each other. Suddenly the enormous red balloon rose in the air with utterly unexpected speed and silence.

Stunned by the magical upward soaring, Eve ignored the city below, the lovely old capital of Burgundy, about which King François the First had exclaimed, "Ah! The beautiful city of a hundred church towers." She looked directly toward the distant blue horizon, astonished by her first glimpse of the far line of green and yellow fields that grew wider by the second.

But the world is so *endless*, she thought, overwhelmed by the same childlike wonder felt by everyone in the gondola. Forgetting the caution with which she had resolutely held herself apart from the three men who had also bought tickets for the ride, Eve turned around and gazed enraptured at the panorama in which she was so miraculously encompassed.

Unconsciously, she opened her arms to try to embrace the sky. In that moment of irrepressible impulse, the balloon was caught in a sudden strong gust of wind. Her hat was torn free from the pin that held it on her head and was sent sailing away.

"Oh, no!" Eve exclaimed, and as she cried out in an incredulous tone, the men all looked at her. They saw a horrified girl whose inexpertly constructed chignon had been taken by the wind, so that her hair was now blowing about in as many directions as there are on a compass. The sight of her face and of her waist-length hair betrayed her age just as the hat had disguised it.

"Mademoiselle Coudert!"

"Eve!"

"Good day, Monsieur Blondel, good day, Monsieur Martineux," Eve said with trembling lips, attempting the polite smile with which she usually greeted these friends of her father's on those rare occasions when she encountered them, for Eve Coudert was only fourteen and had not even reached the age at which her mother would allow her to help pass the pastries at an afternoon tea party. "Is this not thrilling?" she added, reaching for composure in her most adult voice.

"Never mind that nonsense, Eve," Blondel sputtered indignantly. "What are you doing here? Where is your governess? Do your parents have any idea . . . no, of course they don't!"

Eve shook her head. There was no point in trying to explain that she had to go up in the balloon at all costs, that she had waited during the first three deliriously exciting days of the Air Show in mounting anxiety, that she had seized the minute when her father was called to attend a sick patient and her mother was taking her usual afternoon nap, to elude her governess, Mademoiselle Helene—no, somehow none of that seemed useful to tell him.

"I am here," she said calmly, now that she knew the inevitable price would have to be paid, "because everyone says that we French have finally conquered the atmosphere and I wanted to see it for myself."

Blondel's mouth fell open, the other two men didn't bother to repress their laughter. Doctor Didier Coudert's only child was unquestionably a pert minx, Martineux thought, but her presence added a particular charm to this extraordinary moment. He had an eye for a neat waist and a slender ankle, and these she already possessed, as well as the tentative but unmistakable outline of a young bosom under the short piqué bolero and tucked lace blouse of her very best costume.

"Blondel," he said with authority, "Mademoiselle Coudert can come to no harm here. When we return to earth, I myself will escort her safely home."

"Do you think, Monsieur, that first we could look for my mother's— for my hat?" Eve asked.

"I think the hat is still flying under its own power, Mademoiselle. It was headed south toward Nuits-Saint-George, if I'm not mistaken. Still, we will try."

"Thank you, Monsieur," Eve said, gratefully. If only they could find the hat, perhaps her mother wouldn't be quite as angry as she anticipated. But even if it had been eaten by a goat, it was worth it, oh, so worth whatever happened to her, just to have floated in the air and seen, at last, the greatness of the world.

She couldn't imagine what it would feel like to be one of the pilots who had come from all over France to participate in Dijon's great race meeting, pilots like Marcel Hanriot, just sixteen years old, who had already won most of the prizes. That national hero had actually flown faster than a kilometer a minute. Nevertheless, Eve reflected, as the balloon began its descent, and she looked down on the twenty-five thousand people who were milling about far beneath her, nevertheless, she too had mounted into the atmosphere, she too had seen beyond the familiar horizon of her childhood. She felt a link with all the buccaneers of the sky, if only for these minutes she would never forget.

Doctor Didier Coudert, Eve's father, was a busy man. He specialized in diseases of the liver, a well-chosen field in a country in which liver problems were four times more frequent than in any other nation in the world, since good living is never without its day of reckoning. He loved Eve, although he regretted having no son, but he was far too occupied by his practice to pay any attention to her education. That was the province of his wife, and if, after Eve's escapade at the Air Show, she felt it necessary to suppress Eve's unsuitable curiosity about the world by keeping all the books in his library under lock and key during the girl's next, dangerously impressionable years, he made no objection.

The Coudert family lived in a particularly handsome house on the Rue Buffon, a splendid street in the heart of the old city of Dijon. Doctor Coudert, a modern man, owned the first Dion-Bouton automobile in the city. However, he still kept a coachman and two fine horses so that his wife, Chantal, could pay her customary round of visits in the shining dark green coupé as she had since their marriage.

Chantal Coudert, heiress to a large fortune, ran her household with a strict hand. Long before Eve, at fourteen, became the subject of shocked gossip, it had been out of the question for her to go anywhere alone. Since her unthinkable adventure, her governess had not allowed her to so much as drink an unchaperoned cup of afternoon chocolate with a friend, during a visit arranged by their mothers. She was accompanied when she walked with another girl in the Parc de la Colombière, or the gardens of the Arquebuse; she was watched closely as she played a rare game of lawn tennis; she was even chaperoned when she went to confession in the neighboring Cathedral of Saint Bènigne. Eve was considered to be in constant danger from the excesses of her nature.

Like most girls of her class, Eve lived in a world of women. It was deemed unnecessary for her to study seriously at school. Her teachers came to the house, chief among them a Dominican sister who taught French and a smattering of mathematics, history and geography. She had a dancing teacher, a music teacher and a painting teacher, who all gave her lessons under the eye of Mademoiselle Helene. Only her singing lessons, with venerable Professor Dutour of the Conservatory of Music, took place away from the house on the Rue Buffon.

In the autumn of 1912, Chantal Coudert sat drinking hot chocolate in her luxurious, gaslit boudoir, discussing the always absorbing problem of her daughter, with her sister, the Baronne Marie-France de Courtizot, who was visiting from Paris.

Why was it, Eve's mother wondered in familiar vexation, that Marie-France, whose union had not been blessed with a single child, considered herself an authority on the care and upbringing of Eve, whom she referred to as her "favorite niece," quite as if she had chosen her for this honor out of dozens of contestants? Of course Marie-France gave herself airs—that was normal for a daughter of the wealthy bourgeoisie, who had managed to marry a baron and elevate herself into the aristocracy—airs could be expected of Marie-France, she had, indeed, a perfect right to them, but mere marriage did not entitle her to become an expert on matters only a mother could speak on from experience.

"You worry unnecessarily, my dear Chantal," the Baronne said, touching a fine linen napkin to her lips and reaching for another tiny cream puff. "Eve is a splendid girl and I trust that she has outgrown those ridiculously high spirits of her childhood."

"I wish I were as sure as you are, particularly since neither of us really knows what goes on in her head," Chantal Coudert replied with a sigh. "Did Maman know our thoughts, Marie-France? What a short memory you must possess."

"Nonsense. Maman was far too strict with us. Naturally we told her nothing—not that there was anything to tell."

"I have tried to raise Eve as we were brought up. One can't be too careful."

"Do you seriously mean, Chantal," the Baronne exclaimed, "that all you have ever told Eve about her future as a married woman is 'Do what your husband wishes you to do'?"

"Why should she know more? Was that not sufficient advice? You have become far too much of a Parisian, Marie-France."

The Baronne raised her cup hastily to her lips. Her prim older sister never failed to delight her with her prudish ways.

"When Eve is eighteen, will you let me give a ball in Paris for her?" she proposed.

"Of course, Marie-France. But not until she has a ball in Dijon or people will be offended. I must consider the Amiots, the Bouchards, the Chauvots, the . . ."

"The Gauvins, the Clergets, the Courtois, the Morizots—my dear, I know exactly who will be at that ball, indeed I can see each face now. I can visualize all the freshly scrubbed young graduates of the school of St. François de Salles, forming a phalanx of newly mustached masculinity. Then a winter of outrageous gaiety, such as only Dijon can provide, will follow. The Red Cross ball! The Saint-Cyr ball! Such mad abandon! To say nothing of the charity sales, the concerts, and even—since Eve rides so well—an invitation to join the hunt in the forest of Chatillon. How will she be able to survive so much excitement?"

"Laugh all you like, Marie-France. Most girls would give anything for her prospects," Madame Coudert said, feeling superior. Which of the two of them, after all, possessed a daughter?

"When should the child be home?" the Baronne asked, looking outside at the darkening sky.

"Any minute now. I told Mademoiselle Helene that Professor Dutour must allow them plenty of time to cross the city before nightfall."

"Does he still maintain that she has a remarkable voice?"

"Yes indeed, but since she will never use it except at a musical evening, or to entertain herself at the piano, I wonder if these lessons aren't just a waste of time. However, Didier insisted." Madame Coudert spoke in the tone of voice of a woman married to a despot, one which both sisters enjoyed using when talking about their well-disciplined husbands.

"Aunt Marie-France!" Eve cried happily as she burst into the room. As she gave her aunt a series of enthusiastic kisses, the Parisian noted that her niece's natural coloring was as high as that of any fashionable cocotte's; that her thick curly hair, that still hung down her back, was an inimitable color, a valuable color that would not fade like that of most redheads or grow dull like a brunette's; the hair of a strawberry blond; lustrous, naturally burnished, hair that would make even a plain girl fascinating. And her eyes! Their darkness was like charcoal on fire.

Eve had grown so rapidly that she was now a full head taller than her mother, Marie-France de Courtizot saw as she continued her observation. There was an intriguing immoderation, an unmistakable extravagance in the girl's sense of self. Eve carried her ankle-length skirt and simple shirtwaist with such natural assurance and style that she might have been a very young duchess rather than a child of sixteen. She simply *must* get Eve to Paris before she reached eighteen. Paquin should dress her with the wit and fancifulness she merited, and Worth should make her ball gown. Why should not Eve make a splendid marriage? Yes, one even better than her own. Decidedly she would be wasted in the claustrophobic, conservative society of old Dijon.

"My treasure," she murmured, returning the kisses. "You are such a pleasure to look at."

"Don't spoil her, Marie-France," her sister said warningly. "Eve, you may join us for dinner tonight since your aunt is here, but only this one time."

"Thank you, Maman," Eve said demurely.

"Now, Eve, you may sing something for us," Madame Coudert added, delighted to show off before her irritating sister.

Eve went to the little upright piano that her mother kept in the corner, sat down, thought for a minute, and then began to play and sing with a tiny, mischievous smile that she could not repress:

"Return to your Argentinian sky
Where all the women are divine
To the sound of your music so sly
Go, go dance your tango!"

"Eve! Is that what you learn from the Professor Dutour?" her aunt cried, as shocked at the throbbing, sensuous rhythm of Eve's husky voice, a voice of raw silk and dark honey, as by the words themselves.

"Of course not. He wants me to sing arias from *La Bohème*. But this is so much more droll. I heard it in the street, coming home. Don't you like it, Aunt?"

"No, not at all," the Baronne answered. She hated to admit it but perhaps Chantal was not wrong to be concerned about Eve. For a virgin to hear a tango was bad enough, but to sing it! And in such a voice, such an . . . *insinuating* . . . voice!

"And a dozen *dozen* handkerchiefs in the finest linen, embroidered with her future initials," Louise, the Couderts' parlor maid, enumerated, gloating, as she and Eve walked in the old botanical garden behind the Cathedral on a Saturday afternoon early in the spring of 1913.

"What if she never sneezes?" Eve asked to interrupt the recital of the details of the trousseau of linen that had just been ordered for the soon-to-be-bride, Diane Gauvin, daughter of the Couderts' neighbors.

Louise ignored her. She had been promoted to the post of Eve's chaperone when Mademoiselle Helene had left the household four months earlier, to everyone's surprise, in order to marry a widowed salesman from the Pauvre Diable, the largest department store in town.

"Six dozen dish towels, six dozen towels just for drying crystal, four dozen aprons for the servants, and as for the tablecloths, you can't begin to imagine . . ."

"I promise you I can," Eve said patiently. Louise had been her favorite person in the household ever since she had arrived ten years before. At that time Louise had been as old as Eve was now, almost seventeen, but she had lied and said she was twenty-four in order to get the job. She had a weathered complexion, a sturdy body capable of working a sixteen-hour day without tiring, and a round face with a severe underbite.

Eve had immediately recognized the soft heart and warm nature of the new addition to the staff, and from Louise's first days the two of them had fallen into the kind of friendship which was far from uncommon in a world in which children spent most of their time at home and saw little of their parents. They had become allies against the all-powerful Mademoiselle Helene, they had become confidantes in a house in which they were both constantly told what to do, and they had become intimate friends over the years, for each of them needed someone to whom she could speak her heart freely.

"I don't understand why Diane is getting married," Eve said, gently touching a switch of forsythia, which was the only bloom yet to be seen. "Her fiancé is so ugly."

"She's a sensible girl, Mademoiselle Diane, and she knows that the important thing is finding the right husband, not a handsome one."

"You too! I can't believe you said that, Louise. What makes him right except the size of his father's fortune? Are you going to tell me that any man with both legs, both arms, no big warts, and wealth to come is a desirable husband?"

"I wish I'd found someone, even with warts," Louise said, with a comic grimace, resigned to the fact that a poor parlor maid of twenty-seven had no possibility of marriage.

"I'm not interested in a husband. I want to be a nun, a nurse, a missionary, a suffragette, a . . . a . . . oh, I don't know!" Eve said violently.

"You'll get a husband whether you want one or not, because your mother will have you married before you're nineteen, and if she doesn't, your aunt will, so you might as well make up your mind to it, my poor Mademoiselle."

"Why? Why?" Eve cried, tearing the branch of frail yellow from the bush with a gesture that alarmed Louise by its ferocity. "If I don't want to be married, why should I? Why can't they leave me alone?"

"If you were one of a family of five or six, perhaps you could be allowed to do as you wished—every family needs an old maid aunt to attend to all the things no one else has time for—but you're the only child and your parents won't have grandchildren unless you marry, so why try to fight something that is bound to be?"

"Oh, Louise, I dread the thought of a life like my mother's—nothing but visiting and being visited, nothing changing except the style of my shoe. It simply isn't bearable, a future with nothing to hope for but making my parents happy by having children—is that why I was born?"

"When it happens you'll forget everything you're saying now and become a mother, just like most women, and more than content," Louise replied. "If I remind you, in three years, of what you've just

14

said, you'll refuse to believe me, and, in truth, you'll have completely forgotten it."

"It's not fair! If time makes you happy with the things you hate—then I say it's a *bad* thing to grow up! I must do something wonderful—something big and brave and exciting—something *wild*, Louise, wilder than I can even imagine!"

"I sometimes feel that way too, Mademoiselle Eve—but I know it's just because spring is in the air and there's probably a full moon tonight, and if we don't go home soon your mother will begin to worry."

"At least run back with me, let's race and see who gets there first . . . I'll *die* if I don't run," Eve cried.

"Can't . . . Madame Blanche and her husband just turned the corner behind us." Louise gave her warning to the air, for Eve had already flashed away, too far ahead on the path to hear her.

Eve's imagination was starved by the suitable books her mother gave her to read. The fashion magazine *La Gazette du Bon Ton*, which Madame Coudert permitted her to study, dealt with women from another planet, women as decorative and unreal as exotic birds in their soft Poiret and Doucet costumes of fantastic colors, which fell softly, with infinite charm, from high waists and tunics to feet that looked like those of harem girls.

However, she discovered that her father's copy of the leading Dijon newspaper, *Le Bien Public*, was always left carelessly in his study after he glanced at it each morning. This newspaper became her window into the world and she perfected a technique that enabled her to whisk it away every morning before his study was dusted, and to take it to her room to read whenever she had a few minutes of privacy.

In the high summer of 1913, Dijon was a merry, hospitable and prosperous place indeed, as it prepared for the celebration of Bastille Day on the fourteenth of July. The city resonated like one vast music box. Melodies sounded from all sides; from every street corner; from the singers and piano players inside the many dozens of cafés; from the restaurants; from the bandstands in the squares; from the racecourse called the *vélodrome*; from the permanent circus of Tivoli; and most stirring of all, from the public performances of the band of the 27th Infantry of the French Army, which was stationed at the Caserne Vaillant.

As Eve and Louise walked back and forth three times a week from the Coudert house to Professor Dutour's, they passed through zones of different music, and Eve's pace changed without her realization. Now she walked to a waltz, now to a martial beat, now to the rhythm of one of the songs that escaped from the terrace of a café, a song that, like all the others, had been born in Paris. She hummed as she walked, and only Louise's sternest efforts kept her from singing out loud the words she picked up so quickly.

Eve's fever of restlessness and her dissatisfaction with her life had grown steadily since the spring. Louise could hardly wait until Eve's eighteenth birthday would propel her instantly into a new world in which she would be overwhelmed with the attention of young men, thrilled by new clothes and captivated by new friends. The nervous, troubled, almost unbearable waiting of the last chapter of Eve's far-too-long-drawn-out childhood would finally come to an abrupt end. The girl was so close to being grown-up, Louise thought, that naturally she was in a turmoil, as edgy and fanciful as if there were a thunderstorm in the air.

Although she knew that her place in Eve's life would diminish, Louise's sense of responsibility lay so heavily on her that she almost wished Mademoiselle Helene were back in the house. Soon her duties would be over. A few more months, she told herself, and she could relax.

On the morning of July third, 1913, Eve rapidly scanned the front page of *Le Bien Public* and then she quickly turned the pages of the densely printed paper, looking for the column devoted to a chronicle of the amusements of the city. Finally she found the announcement of a long-promised arrival of a Parisian music hall troop at the Alcazar Theatre, the most important in Dijon. Eve gave a cry of relief. She had never been convinced that they would really come.

For months, posters had heralded this extraordinary visitation. Even a proper young lady, as sheltered as Eve, was aware that in Paris the modern music hall had claimed its place as the center of the entertainment of Europe. In 1900 the Olympia had been the first to open, and its enormous success had led to the Moulin Rouge, the Grande Hippodrome, the Alhambra and a number of other, less ambitious and less deluxe establishments.

Among these music halls of the second rank was the Riviera, and the Alcazar management had managed to attract the entire Riviera troop to Dijon for an engagement. Only the visit of Buffalo Bill and his circus, in the year of Eve's birth, had aroused such lively curiosity in the pleasure-loving citizens of the city.

Eve pounced on Louise, who was busy making her bed. "They're coming, they're going to be here in a week," she said, pink with elation.

"And I say what I said yesterday, and last week, and a hundred other times; your mother will never let you go. Last spring she said you were still too young when your father wanted to take you to the opera. But a music hall . . . never! Not for a girl of your class. Who knows what language the comics use, who knows what the songs may be about?"

"Louise, don't talk like that. You know perfectly well that I've heard all sorts of songs in the street," Eve said, shaking her friend fiercely.

"I'm only saying what your mother would say."

"But I *have* to go, I've told you that for weeks."

"I don't understand you, Mademoiselle Eve. You won't listen to reason. Soon you'll be a grown-up woman. When you're married, you will be able to do whatever you please, so long as you are attended by your husband, poor man, whoever he is, or another lady—if you can find one as capricious as you. You'll be free to go to the music hall every day of the week if that's your fancy, but right now you know as well as I do that it's impossible, so let go of me and let me finish this bed."

"So you won't go with me, Louise?"

"Isn't that what I've been saying ever since you got the idea in that head of yours?"

"I thought you'd change your mind when it was certain that the Riviera company was truly coming."

"I'm more positive than ever," Louise said without any hint of compromise in her eye.

"Then I'll go alone."

"Indeed? Just how, may I ask?"

"I don't intend to tell you," Eve said haughtily. "However, I ascended in a balloon three years ago when I was only fourteen. If I could do that, my poor woman, do you truly think that I couldn't manage to get myself as far as the Rue des Godrans, buy a ticket to the Alcazar, and walk right in? I believe you underestimate me."

Louise sat down on the bed she was trying to make, with a despairing look on her face. She knew that she had a choice to make. Either she would have to disobey every rule that Madame Coudert had made and many she hadn't thought of, and take Eve to the music hall matinée in secret, or she would have to resign herself to the fact that her charge would somehow manage, the Lord only knew how, to go by herself.

Of the two choices, the second seemed to her to be far worse. A beautiful girl alone at the Alcazar couldn't fail to be stared at, spoken to, perhaps even propositioned. No respectable female, even a girl of the people, would go to a music hall by herself. In fact, Louise realized, her choice was already made, as Eve understood perfectly well, judging by the measuring look in her eyes and the knowing, teasing smile on her lips.

They were seated half an hour before the brightly painted fire curtain went up, Eve's telltale hair caught up firmly in a tightly skewered chignon under a hat pinned on in three places, which Louise had been obliged to loan to her. Already the orchestra was playing the tune of *C'est pour Vous*, a song which they didn't know had been written by Irving Berlin and first called "Everybody's Doing It." Around them people were tapping their feet and buzzing in anticipation. Every seat of the hall was filled and Louise was somewhat reassured to see that there were many other women there, some of them with children.

Eve, so excited that her hands and feet were freezing in spite of the heat of the theater, studied the program that promised what she had dreamed of for so long; singers, all manner of singers.

Professor Dutour was in the habit of telling his wife that Eve Coudert had broken his heart. That a girl so gifted—a girl who could sing any aria written for the range of the contralto voice; an extraordinary voice, deep and rich, yet able to reach up into a mezzo-soprano without strain; a girl who could sight-read without a sign of effort—that such a girl should actually want to sing popular melodies, songs written for the ordinary public, went beyond his understanding.

It had seemed like sheer perversity to him, this weakness for the easy, obvious tune, yes, he said to his patient wife, waxing more and more indignant, for tunes that he could only call cheap. Not vulgar, no, Eve Coudert had never brought a vulgar song into his studio, but songs that cost her no more than the breath that she wasted on them.

Eve had long ago given up trying to explain her love for everyday music to her professor. He was the only audience she had, and somehow she craved an audience, even an audience of one.

The more she sang street tunes, the more her desire grew to hear the songs she'd picked up performed by professionals on a real stage, to see precisely how they did it, what expressions they wore, what they did with their hands and feet, how they dressed and how they communicated with the public.

At home she often sang to herself, when her parents were out, shutting herself away from the servants.

18

She took her voice down as far as she could, mining its treasures of warmth and intimacy, then pushed the tremolo to a point where she was barely in control of it. Finally Eve would lift the same melody up, octaves higher, into its resonating alto, until it seemed to beat with wild wings against the roof of her mouth. When she sang the songs of the people, she felt lawless and free, able to impose her own fantasies on the melodies since she was so ignorant of how they were interpreted by anyone else.

Now, as the program began, Eve lost all consciousness of the theater, she forgot Louise sitting grimly at her side, she didn't hear the eager responses of the audience, as she concentrated totally on what was happening on stage.

The rhythm of the music hall revue was deliberately organized in double time, so that if one act didn't please, by the time the public realized it, another act had taken its place. Four men on unicycles tossing golden circles to each other in a bewildering pattern were replaced by a thin woman, dressed in bright green, who half-sang and half-spoke two tragic and dramatic monologues in a voice of tattered steel; fourteen dancers in pink ruffles, top hats, fur collars and pussy-cat tails whirled through their paces and disappeared to give way to a fat man who sang dubious songs in a high, piercing voice, so rapidly that only the quickest of the spectators understood all of his double entendres, although he winked one eye to single them out in advance, and mopped his face with a large handkerchief after his most daring couplets. An acrobatic dancer, dressed in Egyptian draperies, went through a series of amazing contortions as one veil after another fell to the ground, leaving her in a flesh-colored leotard that had the citizens of Dijon gasping. She vanished from the stage to give way to six pretty girls dressed in soldier uniforms, who, in unison, sang patriotic songs while they pranced around showing as much leg as possible. The large orchestra never stopped, not even as the scenery was being changed.

Eve was beginning to feel disappointment and bewilderment. She had been to circuses before she outgrew them, but nothing had prepared her for the vaudevillian hodgepodge of the music hall from which she had expected . . . well, she wasn't sure what she had expected, but it wasn't this whirlwind of spectacle for the sake of spectacle, it wasn't this undigestible collection of acts put together for a maximum of gay, noisy confusion.

Suddenly the orchestra stopped playing and the curtain closed for a minute. When it reopened, a single spotlight shone on a piano standing on the darkened stage. From the left a young man walked out and sat down on the piano stool. He turned to the audience, bowed his head for a second, and gravely announced the name of his song.

"*Folie,*" he said, "one of my favorites, by the immortal Fysher."

As he began to sing the first slow, dreamlike line, "I only dream of her, of her, of her," in a baritone whose strength was embellished by emotion, the Alcazar fell silent. All the hullabaloo of the music hall disappeared as the spectators fell under the spell of that mysterious thing, one special human voice. Why this man possessed the configuration of the "inner face" which transformed Fysher's classic, but minor, lament of unrequited love into an experience that left no one unmoved, was beyond understanding, but it was as solid a reality as the piano on which he accompanied himself.

After *Folie* he sang *Reviens,* a slow waltz, with its plaintive refrain, "Come back, my heart, the joy I've lost, come back, come back, my heart." And then he sang, at last with a smile, "I Know a Blond," and the entire Alcazar exploded with applause. He stood up and bowed, impeccable in his dark suit, its vest buttoned, a gold watch chain just visible on its surface, below a high white collar and a dark tie. The sobriety of his clothes and the whiteness of his shirt only served to emphasize the darkness of his hair, short and brushed close to his head.

Eve and Louise were too far away to see the singer's face clearly; he was a study in black and white as the audience insisted on three encores, only allowing him to leave when the orchestra struck up a polka and a crowd of tumblers rushed onstage and rolled away the piano.

"Now that, even I admit it, Mademoiselle Eve, that was worth it. A moment to remember, yes, I'll have to give you that," Louise said in a tone she couldn't manage to turn into a grumble. She looked at Eve for assent. The girl's seat on the aisle was empty. "Eve!" Louise shouted in shock, but the intermission had begun and the audience had filled the aisles, rushing to seek a breath of air outside before the second half of the music hall was to begin.

Eve raced up the aisle, so filled with enthusiasm and determination that there was no room for hesitation when she found herself in front of the door that led backstage, as the first of the other spectators began to emerge into the lobby. She looked at her program once more, found the name she sought, pushed open the door, glanced around for someone in authority, and walked up to a likely looking man who held a clipboard.

"Monsieur Marais is expecting me, Monsieur. Could you indicate his dressing room, please?" Her voice, although she didn't realize it, was that of her worldly aunt Marie-France.

"Over there, the second door on the left, Madame—ah—Mademoiselle?"

"That does not concern you, Monsieur," she replied, somehow knowing precisely what words would assure him that she had the right to be backstage.

She tapped on the door.

"Come in," Alain Marais called, and she entered the dressing room in a rush, and then stopped dead, rigid in shock, the door slamming behind her. The singer, naked from the waist up, was standing with his back to her. His jacket, vest, collar, tie, and soaking wet shirt had all been stripped off and lay on a chair beside his dressing table. He was wiping his neck with a hand towel.

"Throw me a decent-sized towel, Jules. One more encore in that steam bath and I would have turned into a puddle. Christ, Dijon in a heat wave—the management should pay double."

"Monsieur, you are sublime!" Eve blurted out, her eyes on the floor.

He whirled around and gave a grunt of surprise. Then he grinned, found a big towel and continued to dry himself. Eve dared to look up, and only the door at her back prevented her from tottering at the sight of his bare chest, strongly muscled, with black hair that ran between his nipples down to his belt. His raised arm showed her the tuft of hair at his armpit that he was vigorously attacking with the towel. Never in her life had she seen a man's bare chest. Even in the hottest days of summer the working men of Dijon wore undershirts in the street as they went about their business. Nor had she ever been so near a sweating man. The authority, the raw sensuality of the smell of his sweat in the small room was as stunning as a blow. Eve felt attacked, in a profound way, but her knowledge of the attack was on a preverbal, preconscious level. All she knew was that she was blushing violently.

" 'Sublime.' As good as that? Thank you, Mademoiselle—or is it Madame?"

"Mademoiselle. I had to tell you—I didn't mean to interrupt, I didn't know you'd be changing—but oh, the way you sang! I've never heard anything so splendid, so glorious!"

"I'm not a member of the Paris Opera, you know, just a music hall singer, you embarrass me," he said, charmed by her praise, with which he secretly agreed. Alain Marais was used to backstage visitors, women who usually came in giggling groups, having bet among themselves that they wouldn't dare to do it, but this girl of Dijon in her terrible hat had an intensity that intrigued him. He shrugged quickly into a clean shirt, and took out a fresh stiff collar.

"Sit down, why don't you, while I finish dressing. Here's a chair," he said coaxingly, since she showed no intention of moving away from the door. He moved the second chair in the room close to his, which stood before the mirror on his makeup table.

Eve sat down, looking with fascination at the never-before-seen spectacle of a man fastening a collar onto a shirt. The intimacy of watching him struggle with the buttons was, only in degree, less than seeing him drying himself with the towel. He made short work of it, knotted a tie around his neck and offered her a drink of water, pouring it from a pitcher that stood next to a single glass.

"You'll have to use this, they don't provide much luxury in the Alcazar," he said, holding out his glass as if it were natural to drink from the glass of a stranger. Eve drank deeply and, for the first time, stared directly at his face. He had the blackest of hair, the darkest of eyes, and the expression of a highwayman with a sense of humor; an unconventional face, proud, even imperious, yet ready to break into laughter. But he was younger than she had thought from a distance, probably in his late twenties.

Her glance was avid in its passionate curiosity. A man who could stand unabashedly half-naked in front of a woman, who would give her a drink from his glass, who sang—oh, who sang as she had never dreamed of—she had to cling to every second of this encounter, she thought, frantic at the realization that the second act would soon begin.

"Take off your hat," Alain Marais commanded. "I can't see what you look like under that Black Forest cake." Judging by the hat and the light cloak she had been obliged to borrow from Louise, which she had kept on since she entered the dressing room, he guessed that Eve had come to the music hall on her afternoon off from work. Probably a salesgirl in a shop, Alain Marais judged.

Eve unpinned her hat, trimmed with a stiff, single aigrette feather, and dropped it on the floor. It had covered her hair to the tips of her ears, and much of her forehead. It was such a relief to get it off her head that suddenly the weight of the cloak was equally unbearable. She let it fall away, and sat gazing at the young singer with all her bold, fresh beauty revealed, yet without the deliberate presence of a woman who is conscious of her power.

Eve was as ignorant of the effect of the way she looked as a savage brought up without a mirror. Her looks had never been praised or made much of by her parents or the servants or her teachers. Time enough for such matters when a girl reached eighteen, was the way of old Dijon.

"My God!" Alain Marais exclaimed, and fell silent in astonishment. With Eve's gesture his musty dressing room disappeared and he saw a girl as unexpectedly lovely as a white lilac tree blooming around the corner of an ordinary street. He was enchanted by the surprise of this girl who belonged in a secret garden. He moved his chair closer, bent forward and tilted her chin up with one hand so that he could see her better and for the first time he looked directly into her eyes and met her gaze in which the light of innocence was so mixed with wild, bedazzled audacity that he was confused and speechless. His fingers traveled lightly from the curve of her chin up the edge of her jawbone to the tip of her ear and on up her cheek to the damp roots of her hair. Then, obeying an impulse too strong to resist, he lifted his other hand and plunged the fingers of both hands into the moist hair at her temples, clasping her skull tightly. Eve shuddered, but made no protest as she felt his hands where no man's hands had ever touched her. A prisoner, she couldn't have moved her head if she had wanted to.

"This is better, isn't it?" he asked softly, and she did not even nod her assent.

"Say, 'Yes, Alain,' " he insisted.

"Yes, Monsieur." Her lips felt numb as she whispered.

" 'Alain,' " he repeated, not understanding that for Eve to use his first name was almost as taboo as it was for her to have come to see him alone.

"Alain. Alain . . . Alain," she sighed, gathering courage. "Yes, Alain. It is better."

"But, Mademoiselle, how can you call me Alain when you haven't told me your name?" he said seriously, playing now with tendrils of her hair, pulling them loose here and there as he chose.

"My name is Eve," she said, and then jumped to her feet as the dressing room door was opened suddenly.

"Alain, Claudette is having one of her vapors . . . a regular fit, says she can't go on. I thought you could talk some sense into her," Jules, the stage manager, said anxiously. "Sorry to interrupt, but you know what she's like. It's this infernal heat. The trained seals are making so much noise that they sound like elephants."

"Isn't there anyone else, Jules, for God's sake?" Alain said angrily. "And will you ever learn to knock?"

"No one else she'll listen to. Come on, Alain, shake a leg. I need you or the intermission will last till dinner."

"Who is Claudette?" Eve asked.

"The tragic singer, damn her."

"The skinny old lady in green?"

"Precisely. Unfortunately she has decided that I remind her of her long-lost son. Eve, will you come again to visit me here tonight, in the intermission?"

"Yes."

"Good."

"Alain, will you get a move on!" Jules shouted.

"Until tonight," Alain said, and disappeared after the stage manager.

Eve looked around the dressing room in shock. She couldn't possibly have promised to come back here tonight. She couldn't possibly not have promised. Nothing that had happened could have happened. *It could not not have happened.* Her world was dissolving around her.

Tentatively she touched the objects on the dressing table: the brush, the talc, the straight razor, the tie pin, the watch and chain Alain had been in too much of a hurry to put on, and the face towel he'd been using on his neck when she first saw him. She picked it up and raised it to her face. It smelled of him, it was impregnated with his sweat. She put her lips to the damp fabric and inhaled deeply. The odor made her faint with longing, and more than longing. The first wave of pure physical desire she had ever experienced picked her up as if she'd been a swimmer in an unknown sea, and engulfed her, tumbled her over and over into the bottomless deep for sightless, shocking minutes until it left her as weak as if she had almost drowned.

With the instinct of someone fighting for survival, Eve picked up her hat, jammed it on, threw the cloak over her arm, ran out of the dressing room, rushed through the lobby of the theater and regained her seat before the intermission had ended. Two minutes later Louise arrived, puffing, flustered and furious.

"How could you, Mademoiselle Eve! How could you frighten me like that? I've been out of my wits, I looked everywhere—where were you, you impossible girl?"

"Oh, Louise, I'm so sorry! I began to feel sick to my stomach right in the middle of the last song—I had to run to the toilet, it was an emergency. Could we go home now? I still feel awful. There're too many people here. I can't take this heat. Come on, let's go before it starts again."

"You do look strange, all pale and shivering, and that's for sure. Up you get. This is no place for you, and now you know it. I hope this mad prank has taught you a good lesson."

"It has, Louise, I assure you it has."

2

ALAIN Marais was no stranger to backstage affairs. In every city in which he sang there was always an enraptured, willing female to satisfy his libertine appetites, but until he met Eve he had never known a girl who refused to so much as dine with him after the show.

"A stallion like you is wasting time with that one, Alain," Jules observed mockingly. "You've returned to your boardinghouse alone every night this week . . . I've never seen you go this long without a woman. Your new little piece doesn't even wait till the curtain has rung down on your last bow before she's out that stage door on the street at a gallop. I'll bet she's going home to a jealous husband, someone who works late. You'd better hope he doesn't follow her here one of these days."

"I'm not worried about that," Alain said with a wink. "She's never had a man."

"Tell me another!"

"It's true. She's completely inexperienced. Intact. A virgin, Jules. You have heard of that rare thing called a virgin, haven't you, pal? Or has your sordid life denied you the opportunity?"

"So that's what's got you all hot and bothered, is it? I was wondering at your patience. A virgin's not to my taste."

"My poor Jules, have you never had the chance of being the first man in a girl's life? It's worth waiting for, take it from one who knows."

"You have the gall of the devil, Alain, but something tells me you're not going to snare this particular filly."

"Would you care to bet on it, old pal?"

"Absolutely. Fifty francs says you fail before we leave Dijon."

"Done," Alain said, laughing confidently. His friend Jules had lost many such bets to him before. You'd think that by now he'd have been burnt often enough not to risk his money on a sure loss.

No wonder Jules couldn't understand the challenge of a virgin, Alain thought. Like most men, the stage manager was too crude, too much in a hurry. He had no idea of the power that was added to the simple act of sex when you knew that no man's hand or lips had been there before you. The idea inflamed him even in mere contemplation.

In the world of the music hall, virgins did not exist. Only when the Riviera troop traveled could Alain hope to encounter one, and then only rarely, for almost without exception the women who ventured backstage to admire him were married. They knew the ways of the world and what, precisely, they hoped for from him and what they would be expected to give in return. They provided variety, but there was no piquancy when the end of the chase was obvious from its first moment.

There were so few surprises in life, Alain thought, that you had to make the most of every one you came across. The mystery maid of Dijon was especially delicious in her palpable innocence, an innocence he had permitted her to retain so far, since it was evident that hasty action on his part would frighten her off and the game would be over.

Three days after his bet with Jules, Alain had not yet made his move, tantalizing himself with his own restraint. When Eve arrived to see him each night, the perfumed, dusty world of backstage vanished. The singer forgot that a few feet away a jostling parade of painted dancing girls, animals and acrobats all waited to take their place before the footlights. He didn't even hear the boisterous, muffled sound of the crowd of men and women with whom he had shared jokes and insults all day long. The little space in which he sat with Eve became the only reality; the hidden, dappled garden in which he had imagined her when he first looked at her closely somehow became tangible, and his desire grew painful in a way that gave him almost as much pleasure as satisfaction would.

If only, he thought, an experienced coquette could come close to arousing him as fiercely as did the tightly guarded virtue of this charming provincial demoiselle, how sweet life would be. Such unprecedented waiting was as stimulating, in its own perverse way, as any surrender could be. But the Riviera troop had only a few more days in Dijon, and there was the bet with Jules to be won. Alain almost wished he hadn't made that damn bet. He almost wished that he could go back to Paris and leave Eve behind, her ignorance unenlightened, her propriety untroubled. But she was entirely too desirable, and he had his reputation to maintain.

Heavy carved wooden gates, locked at night, protected the Couderts' courtyard from the street outside. During the day Emil and his wife, Jeanne, the guardians, who lived in a *loge*, a small house inside the courtyard, opened them whenever anyone drove in and out of the courtyard, but people on foot had only to ring at the little door set into the gates to enter or leave. The key to this pedestrian door, which was also locked at night, hung on a ring just inside Emil and Jeanne's own front door, which, in the history of the house, had never been locked. Why should it be?

The Coudert household went to bed by ten. Dr. Coudert rose before six in the morning to prepare to go to his hospital rounds, and Madame Coudert organized the rhythm of their domestic routine around him. In the summer months they often stayed home after dinner while the social life of the city slumbered in the heat. In any case, Eve was not yet included in any of their evening visits.

It had been a simple matter for Eve to pretend to go to bed, and then slip out of her room once the house was quiet, open the door of the *loge*, take the key to the little door, and flee on foot to the Alcazar. No precautions had ever been taken to guard her from this action, since the possibility of such freedom from convention did not exist in a world in which certain social rules were observed absolutely and without question.

Alain had instructed Jules to let Eve enter by the stage door in the side alley, so that she could watch the second act of the spectacle from the wings. On that first night she arrived at the Alcazar while the rest of the troop was going through its paces. Eve and Alain sat on the two chairs, which were the only furnishings of his dressing room besides the makeup table, and talked, Eve decorous as she perched in a way that made it plain that he was not to approach again.

"Why can't you go with me to a café after the show?" he had asked. "Why do you have to go home right away?"

"I don't live near here," Eve answered without hesitation, for she had prepared her story. "I work in a ladies' shoe store all the way on the other side of the city. The owner, Mademoiselle Gabrielle, gives me room and board as well as my salary. She's an old maid, awfully religious, very old-fashioned and impossible to please. She locks up at midnight and it's more than my job is worth if I'm not in by then."

"Don't you have a family?"

"I'm an orphan," she lied without a twinge of guilt. She knew, without knowing how or why she was so sure, that the less she told Alain about herself, the better.

Eve couldn't even tell herself what had happened to her. She was utterly confused, the connections between her brain and her body so overwhelmed with barely understood messages that her whole being was one tangle of frighteningly wild excitement.

Eating dinner with Louise, after they had returned from the Alcazar, had been like learning a new language. Knowing that she would go to the theater that evening, she had forgotten how to be herself, how to be a girl called Eve Coudert. She could manage her knife and fork, and pass the salt, but that was the limit of her capacity to deal with ordinary life. All her powers had fused into a tight ball of immeasurable intoxication, all her thoughts were concentrated on the source of that intoxication, Alain Marais.

The daylight hours of the next week passed in a blur. Sometimes there were games of lawn tennis with the boys and girls she had known all her life, twice there were picnics in the woods outside of Dijon, with entire families and their servants who drove out in their carriages or the family automobile called an omnibus, for a copious lunch served with less ceremony than usual, but Eve drifted automatically through them in a not-quite-visible daze, her thoughts locked into the evenings past, the evening to come. She stopped taking her lessons with Professor Dutour. It was out of the question to force herself to sing classical music when her mind beat only with the refrains of Alain's songs. Her long intimacy with Louise faded like a childhood memory since she couldn't speak of the one person who was on her mind. It was not so much that she became distant but that she became indistinct, a sepia version of Eve Coudert, gentle, obedient, and silent.

At night, after she had escaped through the little door, and dashed through Dijon to the Alcazar, she was so savage, so mad with anticipation by the time she knocked on Alain's dressing room door, that she had to fight to breathe evenly, struggle to make her voice sound almost normal. She would find him almost dressed for his second-act turn, the English clubman's vest and jacket that he invariably affected for his performance now hung from a rack rather than thrown over his chair.

Eve never dared to leave her house until her parents' gaslight was blown out at ten. Alain's second *tour de chant* began just before eleven, the last number of the show. Even though she ran every foot of the distance between her house and the theater, it was too far away to reach in less than fifteen minutes. That left them only a half hour to spend together each night, and the glib specter she had raised of Mademoiselle Gabrielle's locking her out by midnight had become as much of a nightmare to Eve as it was an obstacle to Alain, yet still she clung to it with the same unreasoning instinct that had led her to invent it.

Madame Chantal Coudert read the letter from her sister and then handed it to her husband with an enigmatic expression on her face.

"Take a look at this, my dear," she said.

He read the letter and handed it back. "It sounds wonderful. I could make the time. My assistant can handle the hospital work and I can postpone my appointments. Nobody ever died of liver disease in a few days. I think it would be good for us to get away—you married the wrong sort of man for proper vacations, I'm afraid, but surely I can be spared for a short one."

"Perhaps, but think of Eve."

"She's invited, what's the difficulty?"

"Oh, it's simply too complicated," Chantal Coudert pouted. "First of all, she doesn't have the clothes for Deauville. Everything she wears is made by Madame Clotilde, who's away until September. In any case there isn't time to run up anything at the last minute."

She looked through the pages of the letter with growing disappointment.

"Even if Eve did have the right clothes," she sighed, "I don't think we could consider letting her come with us. Marie-France writes that the group is entirely people of our age. It was kind of her to include Eve, but nothing spoils a party more than having to remember that a young girl with big ears is hanging about. The gentlemen don't know how to talk to her, or else they say the wrong things, and the ladies want to gossip in peace. She'd be out of place. You know that perfectly well. If there were going to be other young people . . . but no, we can't go." She put the letter back in the envelope dolefully.

"I think you're wrong, my dear. Let Eve stay here with Louise. She has tennis parties planned, I imagine, and a picnic or two? Well then, why should we miss a few days in the fresh air and sea breezes because of a girl whose life will soon be filled with nothing but appointments and new clothes?"

"It seems hard on her," Madame Coudert said, without conviction.

"Nonsense. Write immediately and say we'll be arriving tomorrow. I'll make the train reservations to Deauville immediately."

"If you say so, Didier."

"I do, and that's that." He gave her a kiss and pulled on his motoring gloves, in a high good humor. Chantal's scruples were becoming to her, no doubt, but just a trifle silly. Fortunately he liked silly women, always had and always would. They were a comfort after a hard day's work, as a clever woman wouldn't be.

"I don't have to rush home tonight," Eve said triumphantly, as she entered Alain's dressing room. She had taken her parents' unexpected

30

and sudden departure to be a clear sign that Mademoiselle Gabrielle had outworn her usefulness.

"Did the old crocodile have a fit and choke on an excess of sanctity?" Alain asked. "Or have you finally decided that you are tired of being Cinderella?"

"Neither. Mademoiselle Gabrielle is visiting her sister for a few days. She left me with the key to the house. I can't stay out too late or the neighbors might notice and tell her when she gets back, but at least the door won't be locked at midnight." Gleefully Eve showed him the key to the little door on the Rue Buffon.

Alain looked at it, his skeptical eyes lowered. For all Eve's skill in inventing Mademoiselle Gabrielle, he doubted her story, every word of it. As they talked together, evening after evening, he had soon known that she wasn't what she pretended to be.

Tonight for the first time since she'd come backstage, Eve was wearing a new hat, wide-brimmed and shallow-crowned, made of a fine pale straw and elegantly trimmed in a narrow band of black velvet, a hat she had borrowed as soon as her mother left for Normandy. She didn't realize, Alain thought, but this hat merely confirmed all the suspicions he had about her.

Eve was a rich girl, he had been sure of it, from the way she used her words, from every signal that upbringing unconsciously imparts to the air and attitude of someone brought up to privilege, no matter how sheltered. She was a member of the upper classes who didn't want to admit it, for some reason of her own, but now, in this expensive hat, this hat under which her face was exquisitely flushed, she looked it. If Eve had any experience of shoe stores, he thought, it was as a customer of a made-to-order *bottier*.

But he had not probed and he didn't intend to now. Let her keep her secrets—it was better that way. He feared nothing a woman could do to him, except involve him in her daily life. That, at all costs, was to be avoided. He never let his conquests tell him of their real problems, their husbands or their children, for even to listen was to risk being trapped.

"Can you come to a café with me after the show and have supper?" he asked, sure, for the first time, that she would agree, and high time too, for the bet with Jules must be won, and a quick, forced tumble in his dressing room, while it would satisfy the terms of the bet, would deprive him of the special pleasure he had been promising himself since he had first touched the hair of this mouth-watering girl.

"Only if we go somewhere very quiet and discreet. You know what a

31

small town is like—even with Mademoiselle Gabrielle away, it's a risk for me to be seen out late, her clients would be sure to tell her if they noticed me. Don't you know someplace tiny and very dark?"

"I'll find one, I promise."

"Is this what you had in mind?" Alain asked, looking around at the low-ceilinged, thick-walled room which had the advantage of being cool to balance its disadvantage of being as unprepossessing as any café he'd been in since he'd started working. He had secured a table in a corner in front of a shabby banquette as far away from the bar as possible, and ordered the best supper the menu could provide and the best bottle he could discover on a short wine list.

"It's perfect," Eve said. It was the first time she'd ever been in a café at night, the first time she'd ever been seated on a banquette with a man, the first bottle of wine ordered for her to drink in a public place. She looked around and realized that among the other customers there was no one who could possibly belong to the world of her parents and she relaxed with a sigh of relief.

"Drink your wine," he told her.

"Permit me to drink out of your glass," she responded, in a low voice, and he caught his breath as a wave of desire struck him. Did Eve have any idea what words like that could do to a man? Of course not, he thought, she didn't understand that her unpremeditated impulses could be so inflammatory or she'd be more cautious.

He offered her his glass and watched her drink the wine with as much pleasure as if it had been a *premier cru*, drink most of the glass without stopping, for, bold as she had been to come here, Eve felt the need of even more courage.

She knew the backstage Alain, the man who talked to her about Paris and how he had become the star of the Riviera without formal musical education and despite the disapproval of his working-class family; she had watched, from the wings, with an intensity that made her lose all feeling of self, the Alain Marais who sang ballads of love and held her captive with his voice; but suddenly she realized that there was a third Alain, a dapper, sophisticated man who wore a straw boater and a smartly checked summer suit and a soft shirt, a man so strikingly handsome, so Parisian, so worldly in his allure that women who didn't know him had turned to look at him in the street as they had walked from the theater.

He was the kind of man she would never have met in the ordinary run of events in Dijon, he was foreign here, out of place, as exotic as a traveler in a country more primitive than his own. She wondered what he could find in her that had made him willing to let her visit him every day, leaving a message with Jules that no one else was to be allowed to knock on his door. She felt suddenly inadequate to cope with this third Alain Marais, this stranger from another world. What would she find to talk about with him? The half hours in his dressing room had passed so quickly because they knew that promptly at a quarter to eleven Jules would appear to warn Alain of his second *tour de chant* and they would have to say good-bye, but tonight there was no such end to the evening.

"May I have another sip of wine?" she asked, and drank greedily.

"Mademoiselle Gabrielle, does she keep a good cellar, at least?" Alain asked. How far could she take this invention? For such an un-worldly creature, Eve took her wine with gusto.

"Oh, very. It's her one luxury. No, that's not fair. She keeps a good table too. I've never been hungry in all the time I've been working for her."

"Still, that's not enough in exchange for your youth. Don't you want anything better, Eve? You can't intend to spend the rest of your life selling shoes, can you?"

"Of course not," she answered, unguardedly indignant. Why hadn't she thought of something more grand, more high-flown, as her occupation while she'd been at it? "You understand," she continued hastily, "it is the most fashionable shoe salon in our part of town. We have only the best clientele, the nicest people."

"Don't you intend to get married? Or is Mademoiselle Gabrielle arranging that for you?" Her lies amused him so much that he continued to ask her more questions than he knew was wise.

"Oh!" Eve was breathless with the affront. Everything in her life had combined to make her know what a valuable tidbit of humanity she was, how carefully she was being groomed for some fine alliance. She didn't intend, by any means, to fulfill all the hopes and plans of her elders without asserting her independence, but nevertheless the thought that anyone might be supposed to have the right to dispose of her was out of the question.

"I'm sorry. I shouldn't have asked you that," Alain said quickly as he saw her outrage. "On the other hand I would like to know."

"Why? What difference does it make?" she bristled.

"Just curiosity," he answered casually. "We always talk about me. I don't know anything about you, nothing worth knowing. It seems very one-sided, this friendship we have."

33

"Oh." Suddenly Eve realized that an unfamiliar, fashionable suit had not caused the Alain she knew from the dressing room to disappear. She glanced at him sideways.

"So that's what you call it when a girl runs across most of Dijon to listen to you sing every night and then has to run back all the way home in the dark—a friendship?"

"What else could I call it when a girl spends night after night sitting on a hard wooden chair, looking as if she would jump up and run away screaming if I moved my own chair close enough to reach out and lay a single finger on her?"

"I don't know," Eve said slowly. She reached out, put her hand gently over his, and stroked it lightly. "I really don't know. But you're so much more experienced than I am, that if you say it's a friendship, then that's what it must be."

"Don't do that!" he cried, snatching away the hand she had covered.

"Do what?" she whispered.

"My God, you're worse than the damnedest flirt who was ever born." He grabbed her hand. "Do this! Here, feel my heart, feel it beating—do you think it beats like that all the time? Do you think that you can touch me when you please and never even let me kiss you?"

"I . . . might . . . have let you kiss me," Eve said slowly, "but you never tried."

"Of course I never tried. I don't try to kiss a girl who sits with her arms folded across her body and her hands tucked under her armpits and her feet crossed so tightly at the ankle that a crowbar couldn't get them apart, and her knees pressed together as if she were about to be attacked."

A tear rolled down Eve's cheek, but she didn't dare move to wipe it away. But oh, she thought, his heart, his wildly beating heart. He couldn't be so angry with her that he wouldn't forgive her. She felt as if her own heart were about to break. In one spontaneous, swift movement she slid toward him, turned her body so that she could put a hand on each of his shoulders, leaned forward and quickly pressed her lips to his. She drew back abruptly at the sight of a waiter passing their table. His tactfully avoided head had brought her, mortified, back to the realization that not only were they in public but that customers at other tables, less discreet, were watching them with open interest.

"Eve, let's go," Alain said, putting money on the table and taking her elbow, leaving the plates of food untouched. Silently she let him lead her out of the café into the crowded street where the citizens of Dijon were taking the night air. She saw none of them, for she was

34

spellbound, a girl who had just given her first kiss. All of her past life receded into the distance, she was thrown back into the dangerous sea of physical desire, the sea whose frightening undertow she had been so carefully avoiding from the first night she'd met Alain.

The two glasses of strong red wine, the lack of food to accompany it, had made Eve's head spin as never before in her life. The street seemed like something in a hallucination, a painted backdrop, the crowd around them seemed like phantoms, without life.

"I want to kiss you again," Eve heard herself say. "I want . . . I want . . ."

"This is impossible, ridiculous," he said roughly. "There's no place to go, no place to be alone. Come back to my boardinghouse with me. It's not far. I have two rooms, it's perfectly respectable."

Mutely she nodded her dazed assent. For a moment the thought of what her mother, her aunt or Louise might have said if they knew tiptoed through her mind. She was in unknown territory, Eve thought dreamily, and then forgot everyone as she and Alain hurried to the theatrical boardinghouse.

The second room, which Alain, as a headliner, rated when the troop was away from Paris, was almost filled with a complete suite of dark red Victorian plush furniture, and it was there, on a wide, long, swagged and betasseled sofa that Eve sat down, looking as if she had come to pay a call and feeling as if she were falling through space, falling in fear, falling in delight, falling faint with curiosity and apprehension.

Alain threw his boater in a corner and took off his jacket, looking at her on the sofa with a mixture of erotic excitement and irresistible amusement, for Eve was still wearing the gloves she had put on automatically when they left the café for the street. Yet when he sat down next to her and looked into her eyes he saw, beyond her obvious terror, the obstinate lawlessness that had brought her this far.

Quickly he took off her hat, unpinned her hair and spread it over her shoulders. Quickly he stripped her gloves from her fingers and quickly he undid the top buttons of the collar of her blouse. She said nothing, even when he bent down and slipped off her shoes with their high Louis heels and pointed toes, nothing when he put his arms around her seated figure and pulled her down so that she was reclining on the sofa. If it had not been for the increased speed of her breathing, he might have imagined that she wasn't paying attention.

Until he kissed her. The passionate innocence with which she met his kiss was like a slap in the face. Her lips were closed, yet they pressed against his strongly, with unconditional ardor and eagerness. There was

35

no doubting that she wanted kisses more than anything in the world, and no mistaking the fact that she didn't know how to kiss any more than did a child. Eve's arms were clasped so tightly around his neck that he had no room to shift from her lips to any other part of her face. Her eyelids were screwed tightly shut. Both of them were locked in a position on the plush sofa that threatened to dump them on the floor if they moved a single limb.

"Wait," Alain whispered, and in the moment in which she stopped kissing him, unwillingly but obediently, he gently disengaged her arms and drew slightly back. "Look at me, Eve."

She peeked at him, impatient to return to his lips, to close her eyes and just concentrate on feeling his mouth, so different to the touch from anything she had ever known, firm yet swollen, tender yet so muscular underneath.

"I want to show you how to kiss," he muttered, and he took one finger of his right hand and traced the outline of both her lips with as much care, as much attention as if his burning finger were a pencil and he were making a drawing that must be perfect. Then he drifted his finger back and forth between her lips, not trying to part them but caressing them by pressing downward on the lower lip and upward on her upper lip so that gradually they no longer were so adamantly fastened together.

"Now," he said, and bent toward her, "hold still." With the tip of his tongue he retraced the steps of his finger, outlining her lips twice, three times, until she fought for breath, but his arms held her so that she couldn't move her head. Then again with the tip of his tongue, as firmly pointed and hard as he could make it, he moved languorously sideways, straight across the tiny parting of her lips, sweeping across them only on their outside skin until he felt the moist inner edges of her mouth open to him. Now, with her mouth so sweetly relaxed under his, he returned to kissing in his own, educated rhythm, each kiss purposeful, each a conquest. Only when she stirred in his arms with an unmistakable fever of impatience did he finally use his tongue again, so gently that it was almost stealthy, an invasion that was so brief, so slight and yet so piercing that she cried out in rapture.

"Let me feel your tongue," he commanded. "I want it in my mouth."

"I can't! Oh, I can't do that."

"Yes, you can, just once. Here, I'll show you how," he insisted, and plundered her more deeply with his tongue, but slowly, carefully, retreating as often as he pushed forward, until he felt the tiny, timid flicker that told him that she had gathered the courage to do as he wanted. He made no sign that he had noticed until the little touch came again, stronger and bolder this time, and still he did nothing. The third time that Eve darted her tongue into his mouth he took it between his lips and suckled on it as if it were her nipple.

Alain was voracious, and yet he held himself severely in check. Only her lips, only her tongue, he said to himself, first only that, he thought with savage purpose as he felt himself reeling. An hour ago Eve had not known how to kiss. Now he could tell by the involuntary movement of her pelvis that there was nothing he couldn't do to her tonight. Gradually he made himself pull away from Eve, for she was faint with passion that she didn't understand was passion, mad with lust that she didn't know was lust, greedy with need that she didn't know was need.

"No, Alain," she begged, "don't stop. . . ."

"Wait here. I'll only be a minute." He disappeared into his bedroom. There was always one sure way, he thought, as he opened the buttons of his trousers and released his hugely distended organ, always one way to keep from finishing too soon. He stood in front of the washstand in the corner and rapidly handled himself, while he thought of Eve's still unseen body. In seconds it was over and he had gained time to enjoy in full the pleasure he had denied himself for too many nights. Trembling, he poured a little water from a pitcher, washed and dried himself, rebuttoned his fly, and returned to the other room where Eve still lay on the sofa.

Gently he took her in his arms and gently he began to kiss her again. It was possible to be gentle now. He was pleased with his self-control. The second time was invariably better, and took so much longer, even with a woman who knew what she was doing. His short absences from many a bedroom had gained him a reputation as a lover beyond equal.

Alain's deft, experienced fingers undid more of the tiny buttons that ran down the front of Eve's blouse. Soon they were all open and he freed her from the belt that was clasped so tightly around her waist. She lay passive in his arms as he gradually undressed her between kisses. Her lack of knowledge, and the wine she had gulped, rendered her as incapable of helping him as she was unwilling to stop him. She had no idea what he was going to do to her, but whatever it was, she knew beyond question that it was her destiny to obey him.

Eve was too modest to look down at herself, but she felt that her breasts had been freed from her lacy undergarments and now had no covering except the unbuttoned blouse that he still let her wear. The filmy material grazed her naked nipples and they rose without her knowing it. She closed her eyes as she heard her skirt and her petticoat

37

fall to the floor. Blindly she submitted as Alain gradually stripped her of everything but the blouse, taking time to slowly reveal each new and marvelous part of her young body, feeling himself grow steadily more excited with a focused, intent voluptuousness he could now prolong indefinitely.

He was careful not to stop kissing her lips at length, preparing her gradually for the removal of each piece of clothing. Any haste could cause him the loss of his pleasure. Alain knew that Eve was so uninformed that kisses would keep her hypnotized, and the years during which nakedness had been taboo could be forgotten. He let her keep the blouse on because it would reassure her, and even with it covering her shoulders and arms he could clearly see her surprisingly full breasts with their small, pink, excitingly puckered nipples springing out from between the wide open edges of the cloth. She was perfectly made, he thought, as he explored with his eyes the luscious curve of her lower belly, the blond hair that covered the meeting of her firm, shapely thighs, soft hair, and curly, yet thick enough to be to his taste, for he liked a well-covered mound.

"How beautiful you are, how beautiful," Alain murmured.

"Alain . . ." Eve whispered.

"Say nothing. I won't hurt you, I promise. Let me show you . . . I understand that you know nothing . . . I understand . . . just let me love you."

Alain glanced down at her thighs. Without knowing it, she was pressing them back and forth on the plush of the sofa and moving them so that they rubbed together. No, she could not be allowed to continue to do that, he thought, or again he could be robbed of his pleasure. "Lie still, darling," he muttered, and touched one hand to her thigh for a second so that she would know exactly what he meant. She went limp and he could see her blush mount into her cheeks. "You were made for love," he said into her ear. "How have you lived so long without it? No, say nothing . . . let me show you." He made his whole hand flat and rubbed it over her swollen breasts, taking care not to do more than pause slightly at the nubbins of her hard nipples and pluck them lightly between his fingers, enjoying his mercilessly self-inflicted restraint. Eve gasped each time he pulled. She doesn't know it, he thought, but she wants my mouth there. She doesn't know it yet.

He wet his fingers in his mouth and surrounded the pink points with a maddeningly swift caress, repeated over and over until he had to put his hand restrainingly on her thigh again. "Do you want me to kiss your breasts?" he whispered in her ear. "I won't do it if you don't want me to." When she nodded her bewildered, helpless assent it was almost with reluctance that he finally bent his dark head toward the virgin flesh.

Her mouth was sweet, her nipples would be sweeter, and if there were more time to remain in Dijon he would have chosen to postpone this next step for another day, chosen to drive them both to further heights of frustrated wildness, for once he fastened his mouth on her nipples he knew he would become so rigid himself that he could no longer retreat.

With one hand Alain supported Eve's right breast so that her nipple was captive between his lips, exposed to the ravishingly light and random attack of his flickering tongue, and with the other he slowly ran his fingers, as if they were wandering aimlessly, down over her belly from her waist to the top of the curly blond hair between her legs. He knew that she would be so mesmerized by his tongue that she wouldn't be completely aware of what his hand was doing, for this movement downwards must be gradual. She must become accustomed to it, tamed to accept it, or she might still shrink away, and, with her timidity, his pleasure could still vanish, even now.

He sucked, gratified at how much harder and bigger her nipple had grown, while the other hand indolently explored the delicate skin above and below the blond tangle, taking care not to encroach on the hair itself. At first, Eve had tightened her belly and thigh muscles at the touch of that deferential hand and squirmed slightly in protest, but now she was too absorbed in the strange and wonderful sensation of a hot, intoxicating heaviness that she felt between her legs to dream of doing anything that might make Alain withdraw his hand. She didn't know what its purpose was, but each time it touched her she wanted to open her thighs in unthinkable invitation.

Alain now turned his attention toward her left breast, and the new, piercing sensations in that nipple served to further distract her from the work of his lower hand, which moved with infinite leisure and touched her so lightly on the flesh of her mound that she wasn't sure it had done so before it had moved away. Craftily he waited for minutes before he touched her again, as lightly as before, but with a knowing precision of placement that enabled him to introduce his longest finger for a startling second to the center of her sensations. He withdrew the finger, certain that it had done its job, and waited, hovering, until he felt the mound of curly hair nudging unconsciously upward, questingly. Again his finger touched her, finding the expected reward of wetness, and this time he stayed a moment longer and rubbed her almost questioningly before he took his finger away. He lifted his head from her breast. Her eyes were still closed, her lips had fallen open, and for a second he thought she had fainted.

"I won't do that, darling, if you don't want me to," he whispered. She made no sign, which was, he knew as much an acquiescence as if she had been able to ask for it. He reached down, parted the curls and again found the exact spot in the heat between her legs that cried out for his touch. He caressed her teasingly but now maintaining the contact between his finger and her flesh, now he looked greedily at her face as his fingers moved faster and faster, now he watched her bite her lips, now he watched her pant for air, now he watched the contortions of her features as she strained toward she knew not what, now all five of his fingers had surrounded the delicious flesh because he wanted to feel every quiver, every jolt, every wild, unleashed contraction of the first spasm of a virgin's life. When, at last, she reached the moment she hadn't dreamed existed and madly, unknowingly screamed his name, he thrust his middle finger a few inches inside her so that she would remember, forever after, who was her master, so that she would be branded by his touch and would never forget him, for that was the ultimate pleasure he had been so determined to secure.

"Jules, for God's sake, you've got to help me," Alain said, grabbing the stage manager's arm and pulling him into his dressing room so that they could talk without being overheard. "Old pal, I'm in trouble!"

"What's wrong?" Jules had never seen Alain appear at the theater in his present unshaven, disheveled condition, nor had Alain ever shown up at the theater early in the morning.

"Christ, Jules, why did I ever make that bet with you?"

"Did I win or lose?"

"Neither—both—what difference does it make, here, take the damn money. Jules, I have to get out of Dijon on the next train to Paris."

"Calm down, Alain! You have a matinée and an evening performance today, and the troupe isn't leaving Dijon until Monday morning, you know that perfectly well. You can't leave here for four more days."

"I know all that—it changes nothing. I have to *disappear*, Jules, without a trace, before tonight. You have to cover for me with the management and with Eve."

"Come on! With the girl, perhaps, but the management—what can I tell them—don't be a fool, you're the star—I don't want to lose my job. What happened? You forced her, didn't you?"

"No. I didn't even screw her—I had her all ready for it, primed, I tell you, primed to perfection, when she burst into tears of joy, and told me that she loved me, that I was the wonderful, wild thing she'd wanted all her life. And then she told me who she really is. Her father's the most famous doctor in town—they'll ruin me, Jules, powerful people like that, they'll run screaming rape, to the management—who knows how far it will go? Rape, that's what they'll be sure to call it. Even you thought so a minute ago. They'd never believe she was willing. Oh Christ! Jules, for the love of heaven, help me!"

The stage manager sat down heavily and looked at his haggard friend. "You and your virgins. What did you expect?"

"I was crazy, Jules, what more can I say? I bundled her home just as fast as I could, once I understood what trouble I was in. Jules, this will end badly if I don't get out of here."

"Do you have a story I can tell, at least?" Jules said after a minute's reflection.

"I've been up all night fixing one up. Say that my mother died suddenly, that I got a telegram here at the theater, that you read it with your own eyes, and I had to go home immediately for the funeral. The management can't object to that. A mother's funeral—that's sacred. Tell them I'll be back at work the day you get back to Paris. Tell Eve only about the death of my mother. She doesn't know where I live in Paris. When she asks you how to find me, say you haven't any idea, that in this business people are always moving from place to place. Tell her I only had time to leave a message that I would never forget her . . . yes, that's what you must say to her, that I will remember her for the rest of my life. And believe me, I will!"

"What if she shows up at the theater in Paris?"

"No, that couldn't happen. She told me how closely guarded she always is during the day. She has no freedom—she has a chaperone— a chaperone, mind you!—wherever she goes. I knew she was lying about being a shopgirl, but I had no idea . . ."

"You have to do the matinée at least, Alain. There isn't a train until night—I'll tell the management that the telegram came during the matinée and I gave it to you right after the performance."

"Whatever you say. Jules. You're a real pal. What would I do without you?"

"Fall on your knees and pray for a miracle."

All that day Eve sat at the piano in her mother's boudoir. Wave after wave of severely erotic sensations attacked her and filled her with an almost unbearable sensitivity. She was consumed by thoughts of the undreamed-of ecstasy Alain had given her. She still didn't fully understand it, but it was the only thing that mattered in life. Alain, Alain, Alain . . . until she saw him again she wanted to tear things to pieces with her teeth, to run and run until she fell down, unable to move, to bite her lips until they bled . . . it was so long to wait until nightfall! She avoided Louise, knowing that the extraordinary thing that happened to her must surely show on her face. She played the piano for hours on end, picking out one after another of the popular songs she had learned in the streets, but not singing a note because she knew that if she did, she would break into tears of nerves. She didn't play any of Alain's songs, because her longing for him was so acute that she was terrified that anything that would aggravate it might drive her over the brink into a fit of animal howling.

Night finally fell on the endless summer evening, and Louise, strangely restless, took refuge in a good gossip with the cook, going upstairs to her room later than usual. It was almost ten-thirty before Eve could close the little door of the Rue Buffon behind her, and flee to the Alcazar.

She didn't even bother to knock on Alain's dressing room door, but opened it in the same wild, heedless rush in which she had run from home. The tiny room was empty, his clothes nowhere in sight. It was the wrong room, she thought, and turned back into the narrow corridor. On either side she saw the familiar dressing rooms that she had passed night after night, filled with the same performers she had grown to recognize.

"Jules!" Eve shouted, as the stage manager approached her. "Where is Alain? Why isn't he in his room?"

"He's gone. His mother died suddenly . . . a telegram came this afternoon. He had to go to Paris for the funeral—he didn't sing tonight. He left me a message for you."

"*Tell me!*"

"He said he'd never forget you, he'd remember you all his life."

"That's—all? There isn't any *more?*"

"That's all." Jules felt sorry for her. She wasn't the first woman to confuse the singer with his songs, but she was certainly the youngest and the most beautiful.

"Where does he live, Jules? Give me his address, oh please, you must tell me where I can find him!"

"I don't know myself . . . he never said, I have no idea."

Eve turned and ran out of the theater, moving without any realization that she was moving. Soon she found herself on the Rue de la Gare, which led toward the railroad station of Dijon. Within minutes she was inside the huge metal rotunda, looking around desperately for the placard that announced the departures and arrivals of all the trains that passed through the city. She knew that from late afternoon until night only one train for Paris stopped at Dijon.

"The train for Paris?" she asked imploringly as a porter hurried toward her.

"*Quai* number four, but hurry, it's about to leave," he shouted.

Eve raced toward the entrance to the long *quai* where the train still stood and leaped up the high step into the last car. Once she was safely inside, she stood almost too winded to catch her breath, listening to the train whistle, until gradually, it picked up enough force to move with a jerk. Only when it was smoothly chugging through the Tranchée des Perrières on the outskirts of the city did she recover enough strength in her legs to begin searching the length of the train.

She found Alain in a second-class carriage, far up the line of cars, standing in the corridor, his hands in his pockets and his head bent, looking gloomily at the iron rails of the roadbed. As soon as she recognized his figure in the distance she began to stumble toward him, the roughness of the roadbed throwing her so forcefully from side to side of the corridor that she couldn't call out. Eve pitched forward onto Alain with a final lurch, clutching at him to break her fall. He started violently.

"You're insane!" He shook off her arms.

"Thank God I found you!"

"You're getting off this train at the next station!"

"I'm never going to leave you."

"You must! Your family—"

"What have they got to do with it? *Nobody* can take me away from you."

"You don't understand anything," he said brutally. "I'm not a marrying man. I'll never settle down."

"Did I say anything about marriage? A single word?"

"No, but you were thinking of it. Do you imagine I don't know women?"

"I despise marriage, I despise everything about it," Eve proclaimed truthfully, and the unbanked embers of her eyes, the proud, willful turn of her head, everything that was intemperate and unharnessed about her, told him that she meant what she said.

"Does anyone know you followed me?" he asked, suddenly tempted beyond wisdom by tormenting memories of her body.

"Nobody. Nobody in my world even knows you exist."

"In that case—it's on your own head," he said rashly, and pulled her close. She was too necessary to give up now, not when he thought of the blood-stirring unfinished business that lay ahead.

3

VE'S first letter had arrived mercifully soon, two days after she had gone. Although it was addressed to her parents, Louise, frantic, had opened it immediately. It said only that she was safe, happy beyond belief, and, by her own incredible account, living with a man she loved. The parlor maid, too terrified even to hint at the catastrophe to anyone else in the household, had gone to the post office to wire the Couderts in Deauville, saying only enough to bring them home at once.

"Louise, you wretched creature," Madame Coudert had screamed, as soon as they arrived. "Tell me what you know, or I'll have you put in jail!"

"Chantal, be quiet," Doctor Coudert interrupted impatiently. "This letter says in three different places that Louise knows nothing, that she lied to Louise, that it isn't Louise's fault." Didn't his wife realize yet that no matter what Louise knew or didn't know, they needed her help in order to keep this matter secret until Eve came home?

"Now, Louise, think carefully," Doctor Coudert continued. "What man do you think Mademoiselle Eve has gone away with? You won't be punished if you tell us, I promise you, but we must find her before any harm is done. I beg you, Louise, tell us how she met this man, when did you see her talking to him? What did he look like? . . . Just tell us what you remember about him."

"There has never been a strange man who talked to Mademoiselle Eve. I swear it on the Virgin Mother. She's never been alone with a man in her life except when she went to confession, and even then I was always right outside, and so was Mademoiselle Helene before me. She never talked to me about men, never even asked me questions about what happened after a girl got married—except to say that she didn't want to marry, not ever." Louise broke into tears, remembering their walks in the garden only a few months earlier, in that cold beginning of spring. "She knew nothing, I swear it."

"Nothing," Chantal Coudert snorted. "Look at this letter! *She has run away with some man!* It's either one thing or the other. It can't be both!"

"Please, Chantal, try to calm yourself." Doctor Coudert took her

45

hand firmly. "If we're lucky, Eve will be back in a day or two. This is some kind of madness, some kind of adolescent problem to which girls of her age are prone. When she comes back we'll understand what happened and not before. But meanwhile, until she gets home, it's essential that nobody must know she's not here except the three of us. Louise, are you listening carefully?"

"Yes, Monsieur."

"Louise, you must tell the cook that Mademoiselle Eve is sick and that I believe that she is coming down with the mumps. I've left strict orders that none of the other servants go into her room. Tell them that she's in quarantine. You alone will carry her trays back and forth and dispose of the food. Bring her only broth and bread and honey. She will have no appetite. I shall be seen visiting her room four or five times a day. If any of the servants finds out the truth, I will have you dismissed immediately without any reference and make sure that you never get another job in Dijon. Do you understand?"

"Yes, Monsieur."

"Chantal, if for any reason Eve hasn't returned by the time Marie-France returns to Paris from Deauville, we will ask her to come here immediately. We need her advice. And by then, if it should come to that, we'll need her help."

"What do you mean, Didier? What are you talking about—her help?"

"Do you think that a doctor doesn't know what goes on in this world, my dear? Eve won't be the first girl to spend a few months outside of Dijon and return with no one the wiser."

"My God, how can you speak of your daughter so heartlessly? How can you talk about *months*, Didier?"

"I'm trying to be sensible and I advise you to do so as well. If we think ahead we can avoid a scandal, and that's the most important thing, next to getting Eve back. She'll thank us for this someday, you wait and see. Now, Louise, go to your room and try to stop crying. Wash your face and change your apron. It's only the mumps, you know, not the end of the world." He spoke as much for his own sake as for the parlor maid's.

On the same day that the Baronne de Courtizot arrived in Dijon from Paris, a second letter arrived. It was postmarked from Paris and told them little more than the first letter had. Eve had only sent it to reassure her parents about her well-being, for she knew too well what would happen if they found out where she was.

"Read this, Marie-France," Doctor Coudert said grimly. "And tell me what you think."

"You could always hire detectives," the Baronne said after she had read the few lines, "but I doubt that they'd be able to trace her. There's nothing to go on, no leads. Paris is so vast."

"Precisely what I thought. I'll hire them anyway, but I don't have much hope."

"What are we going to do?" Chantal Coudert cried in despair.

"If Eve hasn't returned by the end of another week, I can't keep on pretending that she has the mumps. They don't last forever. Marie-France must stay here until it's time for Eve to feel better, and then she will persuade us to let her take her niece back to Paris. Louise will pack Eve's trunks and they will leave, unexpectedly and without farewells to anyone but you, Chantal. I myself will drive them to the station, to catch the night train."

"And then, Didier?" Marie-France asked.

"And then, until she comes home, Eve will be remaining with you in Paris. What could be more normal? None of our friends will question it when we tell them. She will make a good recovery, as they will be happy to hear from us, and soon she will be well enough to enjoy the pleasures of Paris to the point that we will allow her to continue to live under your care and supervision until . . . until she comes home as she must, sooner or later."

"What makes you so sure?" his wife asked.

"Because the kind of man who would run off with a girl like Eve must be so fundamentally bad that she will have to discover it for herself. Or he will tire of her. But, mark my words, from everything I've ever learned in my years as a doctor, she will be forced to come back to the one place she belongs, as soon as her life becomes difficult. After all, Eve has no money, no way to make a living, no skills, no abilities. She's still a baby. She'll come back, and with her reputation intact, so long as we all remember to play our parts. For that we are indebted to you, Marie-France."

"Oh, my dear, it's nothing. I'll do anything, anything at all. My poor little Eve . . . oh, I thought all along that you were too strict, Chantal, but I was wrong. You can't be too strict, I see that now. Thank God I don't have any children, that's all I can say."

In a deliberate celebration of laziness, Eve stretched under the linen sheet and moaned in an excess of total well-being. Sleepily she glanced

47

around for Alain, although she had already guessed from the quality of the sunlight in the room that once again she had slept late and he had gone out to rehearsal without waking her. Getting up in the late morning was still a novelty to Eve, but the rhythm of her days since she came to Paris was as different from the pace of Dijon as her newly kindled awareness of the possibilities of her body was different from the days when a good game of tennis had been enough to satisfy her.

Eve was utterly enslaved by her sexual passion for Alain. Although in many ways he was a selfish man, he knew precisely how to take an inexperienced girl and train her appetites, an art few men ever had the leisure or the interest to perfect. Night by night, one deliberate, experienced, breathtaking step at a time, he led Eve down a pathway of erotic knowledge that most courtesans never trod in their lifetimes.

It was early in the month of October, an October in which the languor and perfume of summer still blew in through the windows on warm breezes; sunny days followed by nights untouched by more than the faintest hint of autumn; a blissful, heady, lovers' October that seemed as if it might last until spring; that final October of the *Belle Epoque*.

Eve almost fell asleep again, but just as her eyes closed she remembered that today she had promised to have lunch with a new friend, or rather a new acquaintance who might become a friend. She lived across the landing from them and called herself Vivianne de Biron, which Alain thought a good choice, neither too flowery nor too blatantly aristocratic. Scarcely any woman in the world of the music hall used her own name. Eve herself was known as Madeleine Laforet, because she knew that her parents must still be trying to find her.

Yawning, she slid out of the big bed and put on her peignoir of soft toweling. As she washed and dressed she realized that she was beginning to feel comfortable in this new skin of hers, no longer like a chick that has, just that second, pecked its way out of its shell.

Alain's small, fifth-floor apartment, on a side street just off the Boulevard des Capucines, the neighborhood of Offenbach and Mistinguett, was reached by an untrustworthy elevator. Indifferently but adequately furnished, it contained a salon, a bedroom, a kitchen, a bathroom and a little semicircular dining room in which Alain had installed his piano. Tall windows of the salon led out to a tiny balcony which soon became Eve's favorite place to stand, as she ate her morning *tartine*, the thickly buttered bread just slightly stale from being bought the night before, and drank her coffee, which Alain had brewed earlier. Sometimes she just gazed at the visiting peach and pink clouds that blew over Paris from the open skies of the Ile de France, or watched as the apricot light of late afternoon turned to violet, but often Eve found herself at the piano, playing and singing to herself for hours on end. Music was the one link with her past that she wanted to remember, although each week she wrote to her parents. Even if they were so angry at her that they did not read the letters, the sight of her handwriting would, she thought, let them know that she was still alive.

Eve's domestic duties were minimal. A maid who had worked for Alain for years came in every afternoon to make the bed and clean the apartment, accepting Eve's presence with a polite nod that clearly discouraged conversation. Eve's only concern was to select one of the splendidly cut shirts which Alain had made at Charvet on the Rue de la Paix, and lay out one of his three-piece British suits from Old England, the department store on the Boulevard de la Madeleine, so that he could dress before he left for his performance. Every other day she took his precious shirts to be hand-laundered and the suits to be pressed, for Alain set great store by his somber elegance.

He explained to Eve that he had had the inspiration to stand out from the crowd by the way he dressed, even when he had only been an extra in the crowd scenes at the Moulin Rouge. It was then, five years earlier, that he had bought two songs from the songwriting factory of Delormel and Garnier and, at his very first audition, been given a small turn in a minor café-concert. Eve couldn't hear enough of the details of his rise in his career. Every new fact he told her was touched with the flavor of first love, as impossible to describe as the scent of a gardenia. Everything, no matter how banal, was precious and embedded in layers of deeper meaning. Old England and Charvet became, to her, not the names of actual stores, but words that resonated with romance and mystery.

Eve knew no one in Paris. Alain's own days were largely filled with rehearsals, performing, and the free-spending entertainment which constituted the necessary professional elbow-rubbing of his metier. Eve joined him only after the performance, accepted by his dozens of friends without any sign of surprise. She was Alain's new girl, the little Madeleine, a lovely bit of fluff, charming enough, if a trifle silent and timid. That was as much as they needed or wanted to know about her, she realized, without surprise, since it was plain that she wasn't one of them, even as she joined them for those nightly feasts in boisterous cafés and brasseries, where a hilarious camaraderie took the place of conversation.

Although all her days were spent alone, Eve never felt solitary.

Downstairs lay the world of the Grands Boulevards, where everyone who was important in the world of the music hall lived. She explored the outdoor show of the wide streets, almost dancing along the pavements to the new syncopated rhythms that came from America, the beat of the maxixe, the bunny hug and the turkey trot, which were fast displacing the tango. She didn't dare to order a coffee on the terrace of a café, although she yearned to, because the sight of a young woman sitting alone in a public place might, Alain warned her, be misunderstood. Nor did she ever venture outside of the neighborhood for a walk on the Rue de la Paix or the Champs Elysées, or any of the other elegant promenades, because of the danger of being seen by Aunt Marie-France. No real woman of fashion ever walked on the Grands Boulevards by daylight, that much she could be sure of.

Now it was close to noon and Eve stood in front of the armoire that contained her new wardrobe, and tried to decide if today she should wear her best fall costume. So far she had only tried it on in the privacy of the bedroom. She was still not accustomed to the inconvenience of the hobble skirt, narrowed all the way down to her feet. To make it possible to walk, the skirt had been partially slit up the front, showing her new, "tango-laced" shoes. Difficult as this constraint was for a girl who was used to the freer stride of the fuller Edwardian skirts, Eve was wickedly pleased at how grown-up she looked in the skirt and its matching, pleated tunic, which, in turn, was topped by an angular, bolero-style jacket with a vee neckline over her bare neck, the vee that felt so free and playful after growing up in high boned collars.

She would wear the vivid green costume, no matter how warm the day, she decided, for Vivianne de Biron must be, by Eve's guess, thirty-five, and she dressed in the height of Parisian elegance. Eve needed all the assurance that her new clothes would give her, for this would be the first time since she ran away from Dijon that she had been alone with anyone but Alain.

Eve was more excited than she realized by the prospect. Alain gave her money to dress properly in front of his friends, he didn't ask her to do housework, but when he went off to the theater in the morning for rehearsal of the new show, he forgot her existence. Eve's unfamiliar and idle life revolved entirely around thoughts of him.

For his part, Alain Marais was pleased, indeed more than pleased, with Eve, for there was much she still had to learn before she became as accomplished a mistress as he intended her to be. It would only be then, as so often happened, that he would begin to tire of her.

Vivianne de Biron had been born Jeanne Sans, in a gloomy, lower-middle-class suburb of Nantes. Her superb body had gained her a first audition in a music hall, and although it turned out that she didn't possess even the ability to keep time to the music of the orchestra, she walked like an empress.

For twenty years she had carried the heavy, elaborately sequined costumes of the showgirl with magnificent dignity and remote allure. She knew that in the world of the music hall she and her fellow showgirls were like a maharajah's elephants, majestic, useless but indispensable. She prided herself on the fact that within her appointed role she "sold her salad" as well as any other "Walking Girl" and far better than most.

Now, honorably retired for five years, Vivianne de Biron had achieved one of the three possible ambitions of any veteran of the métier. Although she had not become a star (not that there had been any question of that), nor had she become the wife of some honest man (which certainly wouldn't have suited her), she had, however, acquired two middle-aged, not overly demanding yet solid protectors, whose advice had enabled her to make excellent placements of their generous gifts.

Her income was more than sufficient for a peaceful, quiet, luxurious life in the center of the only part of Paris in which she ever wanted to live. The music hall, Vivianne's world for so long, was her chief interest, and she never missed a new performer or a new *revue à spectacle*. Her knowledge of the life was vast since her quick mind had had little else to occupy it during thousands upon thousands of hours backstage. At forty-five she looked forward to the day, perhaps five years in the future, when she could bid farewell to her protectors and be assured of seven good nights' sleep out of seven. Meanwhile, the young woman who had moved in next door aroused her curiosity. She was so different from any other of Alain Marais's conquests. She had distinction as well as beauty, a naïve but unmistakable authority, for all her obvious provinciality.

"How do you find Paris, Madame?" she asked Eve as they began their lunch at the Café de la Paix, well placed in the large and sumptuous room with its celadon green *boiseries* and a ceiling painted as if to satisfy the taste of the Marquise de Pompadour.

"It's the most marvelous place in the world. I love it!" Eve's eyebrows flew upward with her fervor.

Vivianne inspected her new neighbor shrewdly. Eve was dressed in the very latest style. On each of her cheeks, under the little toque that came down over her hair, there was the spit curl that had just come into fashion, yet all her experience told her that the elegant Madeleine Laforet was as green as a country girl come to sell chickens in a market. If she were a "Madame," as politeness demanded she be called, she, Vivianne, was the mother of many children. And yet . . . and yet . . . there was the matter of the music.

"I have enjoyed your singing, Madame, more than I can say."

"My singing!"

"You didn't know that I can hear you in my kitchen?"

"No, I had no idea, none at all." Eve was flustered. "I thought, in fact I was sure, that I wasn't disturbing anybody, that the walls were thick enough—I'm sorry, it must drive you mad. I'm glad you told me," she apologized, deeply chagrined. To discover that the popular love songs she had picked up here and there, and sung to herself, had been overheard by a stranger who was probably trying to cook her dinner in peace and quiet was so embarrassing that she scarcely knew what to say.

"It's the way the walls are built in these apartment buildings. You can always hear your neighbors, but allow me to assure you, never has anything I've heard given me such pleasure. And I have heard Monsieur Marais too, many a time, just like a private performance."

"But you never said anything to him?" Eve asked.

"Certainly not. He has to try out new songs. That's perfectly understandable. And I admire his voice. But you, Madame, I feel safe in saying, are not a professional?"

"No, of course not, Madame de Biron. Anyone can tell from the way I sing, can't they?"

"Not at all. I guessed only from the fact that I've never heard of you, and if you were a professional I'd be sure to know it. I daresay the whole of France would know it. Nothing that happens in the music hall escapes me. I have little enough to occupy my days. The music hall was my life, now it is my hobby, my passion, if you will, and no one ever had a better one."

"The whole of France would know? Why do you say such a thing?"

"But it's evident! You must realize that your voice is enchanting— no, more than enchanting. And your interpretation! You've moved me to tears with silly little songs I've heard a dozen times. But I couldn't possibly be the first person to tell you this."

This was Eve's first frank, unconditional compliment. Professor Dutour in his grumbling way had always seemed to be not quite satisfied with her, and her mother thought of her voice only as a ladylike accomplishment, useful for making a good impression. She didn't know how to respond, and Vivianne de Biron, seeing this clearly, realized it was the moment to change the subject. "Have you been to many of the music halls, Madame Laforet?" she asked.

"No, unfortunately," Eve answered. "You see, Monsieur Marais sings at the Riviera every night except Sunday and I wouldn't feel at ease going out to a music hall alone. Is that very foolish of me?"

"On the contrary, it is wise. But what about matinées?"

"I haven't thought of a matinée."

"If I were to get some tickets—for me, you understand, the management always provides complimentary tickets—would you like to go with me someday?"

"Oh, yes, *please,* I'd enjoy that so much, Madame de Biron. It's strange, when I first met Monsieur Marais I felt it was all right to go backstage, but now, somehow, I don't feel comfortable hanging about when he's performing—I have no real place there—and . . . and I find that I miss it," Eve said wistfully.

"Ah, I know exactly what you mean," Vivianne answered. She had been in love with a young singer once, long, long ago. Give her two broken ankles, give her fifteen beestings on the tip of her nose, give her a never-ending itch, but, Dear Lord, never give her those days back again! That paradise, those torments, that final, bitter deception.

Thus began Eve's introduction into the world of the first-class music hall. When the sumptuous Eldorado had been built in 1858, it became the first true theater to replace the café-concert, that uniquely French mixture of singing and drinking that had grown too big to be contained within a mere café. Eve and Vivianne de Biron were soon on first-name terms as the older woman led the way from La Scala to the Variétes, from the Bobino to the Casino de Paris, pouring into the ears of the fascinated girl the lore and experience of twenty years.

"Now for Dranem. There are few singers who can make me laugh the way he does. He can fill a theater all by himself, but he's not much to look at, is he, with those enormous galoshes and that minuscule, ridiculous hat—a hat in gold, I tell you. He calls it his 'Poupoute' and there isn't enough money in Paris to buy it from him. And notice how he sings, without making the slightest gesture, rouge on his nose and his chin, with his eyes closed—he invented that specialty, and no one has ever done it better, although they have tried for years. Dranem, Polin and Mayol; they're the great originals, my dear, and imitated by a thousand young singers. Polin, sweet as he is, doesn't understand anything about publicity. He always used to say, 'The secret of success is to leave the stage five minutes before the public wants to see you go.' So he goes home every night, like a postal clerk, and you never read a word about him. I'm convinced that's why he doesn't make as much money as some who haven't half his talent. As for Mayol, that big, rosy creature, he would be more popular too if he loved women instead of men—the women in the audience can tell right away that he doesn't sing to them.

"Ah, look closely now, that third girl from the left, the one with the purple feathers and red hair. Yesterday someone whispered to me that she was four months pregnant by her impresario, but her stomach's flat as a board. It just shows you can't believe a word of the gossip you hear. Ah, I see you appreciate Max Dearly. I adore him—my old Max, I've always called him. He was the first comic singer who didn't paint his face like a clown or wear silly clothes—imagine the sensation he caused, a singing comic with chic, and he dances as well, which the others don't. The ladies are all mad about him, and he likes them almost as much as he likes horses. I wish I had the money he's lost at the track in his day."

Eve, captivated, followed every word of Vivianne's commentaries. It was not merely her knowledge that kept Eve riveted, but the new possibilities of human behavior, revealed by the older woman's words, that were the object of Eve's closely focused attention. Pregnant by her impresario—a man who loved men—losing money at the track—could anyone in the music hall have endured the colorless life she had led?

"Just look at young Chevalier," Vivianne said. "He took his inspiration from Dearly, in my opinion, but he's gone a long way since. Did you ever hear about the number that launched him? He and Mistinguett did a dance called '*La Valse Renversante*'—they knocked over all the stage props and ended up rolled up together in a rug. Naturally, one thing led to another and he became her lover. Just look, Madeleine! There's Viviane Romance, next on the bill. I still think she took her name from mine. She had guts, I'll say that for her. She actually dared to get into a catfight with Mistinguett after the Miss had her fined for laughing during a big tableau. She told the Miss that she was nothing but a grandmother and that one day she'd dance on her grave and got a good slap for her nerve. It took two men to separate them— I wish I'd been there to see it!

"Next week we'll go to see Polaire—you must have heard about her waist. No? It's so tiny that she can span it with a man's collar of only forty centimeters. To my taste her nose is too big and her skin too dark, she reminds me of a little Arab boy, but I have to admire her eyes. Enormous they are, almost frightening. Imagine, when she toured America they had the nerve to bill her as 'The Ugliest Woman in the World' and those crazy Americans liked her looks so much that they demanded their money back! She's on the same program as Paulette Darty. Now there's a true beauty, if you ask me. Big where she should be big and pink where she should be pink. 'The Queen of the Slow Waltz' they call her, and not without reason. She found Rodolphe Berger, a real Viennese, to write all her music—not stupid, eh?"

"Vivianne, I was wondering," Eve interrupted, "perhaps it's too hard to get tickets, but I'm really dying to go to the Olympia."

"Don't you want to see Polaire?"

"Of course I do, but I've been reading so much about the Olympia's new show. The Dolly Sisters and Vernon and Irene Castle and Al Jolson! All the papers say that no show has ever had such a wild success. Don't you want to see them?"

"Pah! A bunch of Americans. A novelty, that's all. My old boss, Jacques Charles, went to Broadway and hired everyone he could find. Not stupid either, I'll grant you, but not very patriotic of him. Personally, I'm boycotting it. No one will notice, but you couldn't drag me there," Vivianne sniffed, and the subject was dropped.

However, Eve was determined to go to the Olympia, Vivianne notwithstanding, and by now she felt enough at ease in the huge theaters to go alone. It was late November and the fragrant, mellow days of October had made way for an unusually cold and wet autumn, but she had a heavy new coat and a huge fur "pillow" muff and a head-hugging fur toque in which to venture forth. Alain had made some money at cards and had been more generous than usual with her. She hadn't dared to ask how much he'd made, for he didn't encourage questions about his life with his friends, but from the way he insisted on treating everyone he knew to oysters and champagne every night, she imagined that it must have been a great deal.

Indeed, now that rehearsals for the new show were over, Alain's afternoons, when he wasn't performing, all seemed to be spent playing cards, she realized, and then pushed the thought out of her mind. He worked so hard at his profession that he earned the right to any diversion, Eve told herself, as she dressed to go to the matinée.

Vivianne should have come, unpatriotic or not, Eve thought, as the curtain rang down on the Castles' ten curtain calls. To have missed them! To have missed that floating grace, that fresh charm! Her hands hurt from clapping, yet there was still one more number before the intermission, a singer named Fragson.

Vivianne had never mentioned his name in her many discussions of the stars, but nevertheless the audience had settled down into the clenched hush of excitement which Eve now knew preceded the appearance of a reigning favorite, a performer so established, so beloved that he or she had nothing to expect from the public except worship.

The curtain went up on a dark stage and then a powerful spotlight picked out a single figure; a tall, dark-haired man wearing a dark English clubman's suit, a high, starched collar, the chain of his gold watch just visible under the knot of his somber tie. He inclined his head unsmilingly at the avalanche of applause that greeted him. As soon as he sat down at the piano and began to play the first notes of *Folie*, the audience interrupted him with thunderous applause and it wasn't until he began to sing that they finally became silent. Eve heard the familiar words of Alain's signature song, "I only dream of her, of her, of her," in a nightmare in which she understood nothing. Did Alain *know* that someone named Fragson had stolen his song? How could this be allowed? How could the Olympia present this Fragson when only a few streets away, at the Riviera, Alain was singing the very same songs— the new one she loved so much, *Adieu Grenade*, and the droll song he'd just learned, *La Petite Femme du Métro*, and now, dear God, now even *Reviens*, Alain's most precious piece of music, the one he always sang at the last, just before *Je Connais une Blonde*.

She looked about the theater frantically, as if she expected the police to come in and arrest Fragson at any minute, but she saw only hundreds of faces nodding in delighted recognition as each song was performed, all so well known to them that they needed no announcement. The woman seated next to her knew the words to all the songs by heart, for her lips were moving silently as she sang steadily along with Fragson, Eve realized in cold horror. She forced herself to focus on Fragson as closely as possible, and she realized that he must be many years older than Alain, that he had considerably less hair and considerably more nose and that he sang with an English accent. Otherwise it might have been Alain Marais on the stage of the Olympia.

As soon as the final applause was over and the intermission began, Eve left the theater as quickly as possible, walking home in a trance. *Fragson*. Fragson, who was a greater attraction than even Polin or Dranem or Chevalier, for she had heard them all now and none of them had aroused the extreme fervor of the audience as he had. Fragson, who sang Alain's songs. Fragson, who sang in Alain's style, a style she had never heard anywhere else in the music halls.

Fragson, Fragson—the name filled her mind inescapably, like a drumbeat, until finally Eve had to admit the truth. It was Alain Marais who sang Fragson's songs, Alain Marais who sang in Fragson's style, Alain Marais who even dressed like Fragson. She was certain that if she looked in Fragson's shirts she'd see a Charvet label and if she looked inside his suit jacket she'd see that it had come from Old England.

Fragson's existence explained everything she had wondered about in silence ever since she and Vivianne had begun to go to the music halls twice a week. It explained why Alain was content to stay in a music hall that she had thought was second-rate, but now realized was no better than third-rate. Fragson's performance explained why a man with Alain's splendid voice had never auditioned for one of the great impresarios, for now that Eve's first shock at the sight of Fragson was lessened, she was forced to admit to herself that he sang with an extraordinary authority. He sang with the powerful presence of a grand seigneur, with a special charm of personality that could never—*should* never—be imitated. Fragson was the *real thing*.

Fragson explained everything about Alain's career except *why* he had chosen to become an imitation Fragson. Did he even possess the ability to be original? She could never ask him. She could never let him know that she had heard Fragson. Whatever had caused Alain to decide to live as a mere copy of one of the greatest entertainers in France was not for her to question. She could guess; she could imagine that perhaps it had been easier to get his first job that way and that, for some reason, he had never dared to stray from that first success, but she could never, *never* ask.

Eve's heart broke for Alain, as she remembered how he had told her how he had invented the Fragson way of singing; her heart broke for herself as she remembered how she had believed him. Was it possible that had happened only five months ago? She felt ten years older. No wonder Vivianne had tried to keep her away from the Olympia. With her encyclopedic knowledge of the music hall, she had known all along.

Automatically, Eve took the elevator upstairs to her landing. Vivianne, hearing her return, poked her head out of her door and asked, "Well, did the walk help your headache, little one?"

"Not really, Vivianne, but I'll get over it," Eve said. "A headache can't last forever."

The wet month of November began to seem like the tropics as December settled over Paris. Only the displays in shop windows lent a touch of color and cheer to a city where crossing the street had become a polar ordeal. Never, people told each other, had it been so cold, so windy, so dismal, so downright disgusting.

Everyone looked forward to Christmas as if it might bring a change in the meteorological factors that made Paris one of the least endurable cities in the world in bad weather. The fabled but always present sky pressed down on its low gray buildings with an almost personal vindictiveness that made wise Parisians keep their curtains drawn and their lamps lit from morning to nightfall.

Two days before Christmas, Alain caught the head cold that had raged throughout the Riviera troupe for several weeks. He went to the theater as usual that day and got through his *tour de chant* but, after struggling home on foot, he grew much sicker in a frighteningly short space of time. By morning he had such a high fever and was so weak that Eve, who had been up taking care of him all night, went across the landing in her peignoir to ask Vivianne if she knew a doctor in the neighborhood.

"I swear by old Doctor Jammes. He'll have him feeling better in no time. I'll call him right away, little one, don't worry. And you must telephone the Riviera to tell them that Alain won't be coming to work for at least a week. These Christmas colds are notorious."

Doctor Jammes examined Alain thoroughly and shook his head. "Perhaps the rest of the troupe had only head colds, Madame," he said to Eve, "but I'm afraid that this has all the signs of a case of pneumonia. He must be taken to the hospital at once. You can't care for him here by yourself."

At the word pneumonia, Eve was overcome by fear. How often had her father lost patients with mere liver problems to the dreaded pneumonia, for which there was nothing to do but cupping, and then pray that the patient had enough strength to live through the disease?

"Now, now, don't get upset yourself, that won't help, you know," Doctor Jammes said hastily at the sight of her face. "You must be sure to eat properly and keep up your own forces. This young man," he added, looking at Alain, "has been overdoing it, I'll wager. He's too thin by far. Yes, when he's over this, he must start to take better care of himself. Ah, that's what I always tell my patients, but do they take my advice? In any case, Madame, I'll make the necessary arrangements at once."

"Is . . . is the hospital very expensive, Doctor?" Eve forced herself to ask.

"Everyone complains that it is, Madame, but surely you have savings?"

"Yes, yes, I just asked because, well, any illness . . ."

"Don't worry too much, Madame. He's young and it's better to be too thin than too fat, I always say. But I must take my leave. I have five more patients to see before lunch . . . doctors don't have time to get pneumonia, and a good thing too. Good day, Madame, and call me if you need me for anything else. I'll see him in the hospital, of course, when I make my rounds."

"Vivianne, I know this makes me sound like a child, but I have no idea what Alain does with the money he makes. He gives me money for clothes, but he pays the maid himself and we never eat at home except for breakfast. I don't even know the name of his bank," Eve confessed to her friend. She had seen Alain settled in the hospital and there was no more for her to do for him.

"You shall just have to ask him, little one. Don't worry, he's been making good money for years and he's no fool," Vivianne answered, congratulating herself yet again on her own financial arrangements. She didn't doubt that the wives of her protectors were just as ignorant of their husbands' finances as Madeleine was of her lover's.

But for the next month Alain was in no condition to be questioned about the location of his savings, or anything else. He came perilously close to dying three times after he was admitted to the hospital. Vivianne kept Eve's health up with the nourishing meals she cooked, and if it had not been for the money she forced on Eve, Alain would have had to be transferred to one of the hospitals Paris reserves for the indigent.

Finally, in the last days of January he seemed to be on the road to recovery, and Eve, worn out but determined, asked him how she could obtain some money from his bank.

"Bank!" he laughed feebly. "Bank! There speaks a true daughter of the rich."

"Alain, I only asked a normal question. What makes you say that?"

"Because if you hadn't been born a rich girl, you would know that I spend every penny I make, I always have and I always will. . . . That's the life I chose for myself long ago. Any little bourgeoise would have realized that long ago. Economies! They're for the safe little man with

59

a safe little wife and, God help him, a bunch of safe little children. Pah! I'd rather lose it all in a good card game than hoard it in a bank. You can't complain, can you? When I had it I spent it and I didn't come complaining to you when I lost it all, either, did I?"

"Lost it all?"

"Just before I got sick. A bad run of cards." He shrugged his shoulders. "There would have been just enough for Christmas, but then I expected to get lucky again . . . or wait till payday, whichever came first. I never worried. I refuse to worry and I'm right, you'll see. I'll be back at the Riviera in no time now that this stinking pneumonia is almost over."

"But Alain, I asked Doctor Jammes how soon you could come home, and he said maybe in a few weeks but that then it would be . . . months, *months* of recovery before you could go back to work!"

"He's a pompous old fool." Alain turned away from Eve and looked out the window at the snow which so rarely fell on the city of Paris.

"Pompous, I grant you, but no fool. I think he saved your life," Eve said indignantly.

"Listen, I have some advice for you," Alain said bitterly. "Go home. Go back to Dijon."

"Alain!"

"I mean it. You weren't meant for this life and you must know it. You've had your adventure, but surely you see that it's over now? Go back to your parents just as fast as the railroad will carry you. You don't belong here. God knows, I never dreamed of asking you to come with me—that was entirely your idea, remember? My kind of life suits me, but I can't be responsible for anyone else for long. You invited yourself. Now it's time to go. Say good-bye, Eve, and get on that train."

"I'll leave you alone now. You're overtired. I'll be back tomorrow, darling. Try to rest." Eve fled the hospital ward without looking back, hoping that no one would notice her tears.

"And that's all he said?" Vivianne asked.

"Wasn't it enough? More than enough?"

"Perhaps he's right," the older woman said slowly.

"Do you really think that? You too?"

"Yes, my little one. Paris is no place for a girl without a solid situation of some sort, and that, Madeleine, is something that Monsieur Alain Marais can never give you. I think the more of him for realizing it. What he said—about returning to Dijon—is it possible?"

"No! Absolutely not! I love him, Vivianne, and no matter what you or even he says, I won't leave him. If I went back . . . home . . . they would expect . . . God knows what they would expect! It's unthinkable."

"Then there is an alternate solution, but only one."

"Why do you look at me that way?" Eve said, suddenly alert.

"I'm wondering. Are you capable of it?"

"Of *what*, for the love of God?"

"Of getting a job."

"Of course I could get a job. What do you take me for? I could be a salesgirl, I could learn to operate a typewriter, I could work at the telephone company, I could . . ."

"Madeleine. Hush. I'm not proposing to put you to work in some store or office for which a million other girls are just as well suited as you. No, little one, I mean a job worthy of your gifts. I am speaking of a job on the stage of the music hall."

"You can't be serious!"

"On the contrary, I've been thinking about it for months. Since I first heard you sing, as a matter of fact. I wondered why Monsieur Marais never thought of it himself, but then I realized that you never sang when he was home. Does he even know that you sing? No? I suspected as much. You were too much in awe of his . . . professionalism . . . to display your own unimportant, miserable squeak of a voice . . . that was it, wasn't it?"

"Make fun of me, Vivianne, I don't care. I didn't sing for him because I thought that perhaps . . . oh, I'm not really sure, perhaps he wouldn't like me to sing too, perhaps he would think I expected to sing duets with him or something stupid like that."

"Or perhaps you have a better chance to be a success than he does? Eh? Is that what you thought?"

"Never!"

"Why not, since it's true? Don't bother to deny it. I know it and I believe that you must know it too."

A complicated silence fell between the two women. Each one of them knew that they were skirting the boundaries of a subject they had no intention of ever discussing. At the same time, neither of them knew precisely how much the other was aware of. And yet this was no time for discretion. Finally Eve ventured to speak, leaving Vivianne's last question unanswered.

"Why do you think I could sing on stage? I've never performed in public, only for myself and . . . at home, and for you, once you found me out."

"There are two reasons. First, there is your voice. It has the strength that's necessary if you wish to be heard in the balcony of the biggest theater in Paris; it has a tone that conveys emotion as if it were joined by your lips to the heart of the listener; it has a special quality for which I can't find a name, that makes me listen to you sing over and over without ever tiring; and, most important of all, when you sing about love, I *believe* every one of the words. And I don't believe in love, as you well know.

"Second, you have a *genre*. You have a type. Mere talent, the possession of a voice is never enough in the music hall—you must have a type to succeed."

"What type do I have?" Eve asked with intense curiosity.

"*Your own*. The best of all, my little one, the best of all! I remember what Mistinguett said to me once: 'What is important is not my talent but the fact that I am Mistinguett. Any extra can have mere talent.' Ah, the Miss, how she likes to talk about herself. Little one, you are greatly talented and on top of that you are unique, you are Madeleine! With those two assets you can conquer the music hall."

"What if you're wrong?"

"Impossible. I am not wrong about such things. But you must dare to try."

"Dare—of course I dare. *I always dare*," cried Eve, her eyes alight.

"Then we must find the right songs and arrange for an audition. The sooner the better. Thank God I still have my contacts at the Olympia —Jacques Charles will always listen to you sing if I bring you to him."

"The Olympia?"

"Of course, where else? We start at the top, as any sensible person would."

Energetic, ambitious and imaginative, Jacques Charles was a veteran producer of the music hall at only thirty-two. He stood, stroking his neat black mustache, his eyes filled with a curiosity that never failed him, in his customary place for an audition, almost at the back of the second balcony of the Olympia. If a performer couldn't be heard from that position, so far from the stage, he had no interest in him, no matter how appealing the talent.

"What's up today, *Patron*?" asked one of his assistants, Maurice Appel, surprised at the morning audition on a day normally devoted to afternoon rehearsals.

"A favor, Maurice. You remember Vivianne de Biron, don't you, my lead Walking Girl at the Folies Bergère? What a marvel, that Vivianne;

never late, never sick, never pregnant, never in love and never tired. What's more, she was smart enough to retire before her breasts stopped pointing halfway to the ceiling. Since she left, there hasn't been one who could touch the way she paraded across the stage wearing nothing warmer than a ton of feathers on her head. She asked me to listen to a friend who sings. How could I refuse?"

"Her guy?"

"No, a girl, it seems. There she is now."

The two men looked at Eve, who had walked out on the stage wearing a copy of the newest dress in Paris, Jeanne Lanvin's navy serge chemise. But this history-making dress that had no waistline had been copied by Vivianne's dressmaker in a perfect red crepe whose singing color was reflected in Eve's strawberry blond hair, brushed out into two shimmering wings on either side of her face. On the dark stage she seemed like a flash of midsummer sunshine in which the brightness of the footlights had become entangled, a part of her own inner luminosity. Eve stood with composure, her right hand just touching the piano, at which an accompanist was already seated, with her music open in front of him. From her stance, so natural to one who had studied for years with Professor Dutour, it was impossible to tell that she was more nervous than she had ever been in her life.

"At least you can see her," Jacques Charles said.

"Shall we have a little bet, *Patron*? She'll have the *genre* Polaire."

"Why not the *genre* Mistinguett while we're at it?"

"Yvonne Printemps?" countered Maurice.

"You forgot Alice de Tender."

"Not to speak of Eugenie Buffet."

"That covers most of the possibilities. She can't intend to waltz in that skimpy dress, so Paulette Darty isn't in the contest. I'll go for Alice de Tender, and you, Maurice?"

"Printemps. I have an instinct."

"Five francs?"

"Done."

"Mademoiselle, if you please, you may start," Jacques Charles called.

Eve had prepared two songs. She had been frantic at the problem of finding new songs to sing at a time when every decent songwriter was working night and day for established stars, but Vivianne had proposed a solution to that problem.

"It's evident to me, little one, that you must *not* sing something original. It must not be the song that they notice, but you. Only you and your *genre*. I propose that you sing songs that are each famous as belonging, above all, to the women who launched them, songs that people think of as inseparable from Mistinguett and Yvonne Printemps —*Mon Homme* and *Parlez-moi d'Amour*. That way you will challenge them on their own ground and show that is it not the song that counts but the singer."

"Dear Lord, Vivianne, isn't that just going to make it harder on me? I'll sound as if I haven't an idea in my head," Eve had protested.

"Nobody cares about your brain power when you're standing on a stage, my dear. You are there to impose yourself. Make yourself *unforgettable*."

Unforgettable, Eve thought, as she stood with the footlights in her eyes. All I have to be is merely unforgettable. And I have five minutes in which to accomplish this. She took a deep breath and remembered the endless horizon as she had seen it from the big red balloon, remembered the moment when she had been at one with the reckless pilots of the great Air Show. Well, why not? she asked herself. After all, is it so remarkable to be unforgettable? I will, at least, *dare*.

Eve gave the accompanist the sign to begin, and as the first notes of *Parlez-moi d'Amour* sounded in the empty theater, Maurice held out his hand to his boss and Jacques Charles began to dig into his pocket. But as her voice crossed the distance between them, that contralto voice which was so intimate, so immediate, that voice which seemed to be singing directly into his ear, although the distance between the stage and the second balcony was great, he stopped and listened.

Jacques Charles listened to a voice that created a hunger in him where none had existed before, a voice that satisfied his hunger and then left him still needing more of the sound that was like the private beating of a beloved heart, a voice that seemed to hold some invaluable, yet still unlearned lesson. The impresario realized that he had grown so accustomed to hearing the pretty melody sung in Printemps's wistful soprano warble that he had never paid attention to the words. The "tender things" that the lyric begged for touched him with thoughts of tender things remembered, tender things hoped for, and, during the space of a minute, lovesickness brushed him amorously, born in the throat of the girl in red.

Maurice started to say something when Eve finished her first song, but the producer put his fingers to his lips. "Please continue, Mademoiselle," he called, and Eve began *Mon Homme*. She sang the lyrics of a song that both men knew, as an article of faith, *belonged* to the great and evil-tempered Miss as absolutely as her fabulous legs belonged to her, as completely as the young Chevalier belonged to her. Maurice thought that it was a lucky thing for them both that the Miss hadn't been here today to listen to this bold-faced and incredibly successful appropriation of her property. It would never belong to her again, not as it had before, and she would have been capable of murder. For his part, Jacques Charles thought that it was a shame that Chevalier, a good fellow, was not present to glimpse this opportunity to escape his stormy affair with the Miss. Or rather to escape it for another kind of enslavement, for no man who listened to this girl in red would leave the theater the same man he had been when he entered.

Eve finished singing, and both men found themselves clapping and shouting "Encore!" before they looked at each other sheepishly. It was not their business to scream for more like the customers. They were not civilians, after all.

Encore indeed, Vivianne de Biron thought in triumph. Madeleine would give them encores, but all in good time. First there was a contract to negotiate, and if they hadn't been carried away they might have gotten her on decent terms. Now . . . it was another matter.

"To work, Maurice," Jacques Charles muttered. "Perhaps la Biron will think we were just being polite."

"You can always try to say that, *Patron*."

"Not to Vivianne de Biron. I wouldn't even try."

"Because she was such a great Walking Girl?"

"Because she'd laugh in my face, idiot. I said she never got pregnant, I didn't say she was stupid."

4

HARD-HEARTED she might be, and undoubtedly a wicked woman, Vivianne de Biron reflected, but it was not a bad thing at all, in fact a decidedly fortunate thing, that Alain Marais had not improved as quickly as he had hoped. The doctors had insisted that he remain in the hospital until they were satisfied with him, and since the winter still continued wet and freezing and looked as if, in typical Parisian fashion, it might remain that way until Bastille Day in July, there was no danger that he might come home and discover his Madeleine in the process of being transformed into a debutante at the Olympia, the glorious Olympia, which he knew he could never hope to enter except as a ticket holder.

Vivianne had warned Madeleine to say nothing to him about her new job, and the girl had accepted her advice promptly, and without asking why. She must finally have heard Fragson sing. It was inevitable, since they were working on the same stage, in the same show, and Madeleine had been rehearsing new songs of her *tour de chant* every day at the theater. Yet she had said nothing, Vivianne thought. Some matters needed no comment, particularly between friends.

Vivianne shrugged her shoulders and thought about Maddy's future, for that was the name that the management had decided to give Madeleine. As Jacques Charles said, "Madeleine" had a decidedly religious ring to it, and if there was one thing you could say about Madeleine's singing, it was more inspired by Venus than by any virginal saint.

He had decided to launch his debutante during the first half of the current revue, since it wasn't destined to be replaced by a new show until summer.

"I don't want to wait till then," he had told Vivianne, once the contract had been signed and they were friends again, "because she's ready now—I'll make sure that the critics know she's appearing. A new attraction's always a good way to get them back into the house in the middle of the season. Maddy'll go on after the Hoffmann Girls and before the magician. Then Fragson sings, followed by the intermission. It's the perfect placement."

"How will you dress her?" Vivianne had demanded promptly, ready to go to battle if need be.

"In red, as you did, naturally. Your instincts were right. Just because you never wore clothes onstage doesn't mean you didn't understand them. With her hair she must always wear red, but not a chemise. No woman will ever dishonor my stage in a dress without a waist again. It's far less seductive than a pillow slip. Maddy has the body, thank God, that is promised by her voice. I intend to do her justice, as I did you, Vivianne, before you turned into a professional manager."

"Ingrate!"

"Ah, the classic stage mother," he laughed, and kissed her hand. "Too bad you never could keep step with the others, but now I see your talents lie in other directions. I am deeply grateful to you, Vivianne, you know that, don't you?"

"As you should be. I shall keep an eye on her costumes, *Patron*, don't think I won't."

"I have every faith in you."

"I shall also keep an eye on you," she said severely.

"And quite right you are. Why should you be the first person in history to trust a producer?"

"Now," said Jacques Charles to Eve, as she entered her dressing room on a morning in mid-March, the day after her first performance, "you're ready to begin work."

"But . . . I don't understand." She looked at him in astonishment.

"Yesterday Paris took you to its heart. The audience made a decision. They fell in love with you, my Maddy. Only an audience can confer that kind of love, and once they give it, they never take it away. It was victory, an unconditional victory. Look at these reviews—it's glory, Maddy, nothing less than glory. So I say you're ready to begin work."

"I still don't understand." After the ovations that had followed her first performance, Eve had half expected the flowers and notes with which her dressing room was already filled, she had anticipated the compliments she had received from the other performers, but his words didn't make sense.

"From the first time I saw you on stage, Maddy, I never thought of you merely as a singer. The *tour de chant* is the first step in your career. Absolutely necessary, of course. Without it you can't own the public. But it can also be a prison for a major talent. You have a potential I haven't seen in years. You could become a star, the kind of star around whom a revue is created, *for* whom a revue is created. That means you must dance and act as well as you sing. Lessons, my girl, lessons!"

"But . . ."

"Don't you want to be a star?"

Eve sat down on the couch in her dressing room and looked at the young impresario in confusion.

"I see," he said, "you thought that you were already a star. And no wonder, after that reception by the crowd. But Maddy, there are stars and stars. You are indeed a star now, not a great star, not yet, although you shine so brightly. You will never share your place in the sky with anyone who has not also held the public of the Olympia in the palm of one hand."

He looked at her closely and saw that his words had wounded her. "Don't misunderstand, Maddy," he said hastily, "you have every right to call yourself a star, if, to you, 'star' means being one name on a playbill, one name among many others. But if you have another dream, if you dream that one day people will flock to the Olympia just to see Maddy, never mind in what, because it is Maddy who matters more than any show, if you dream that one day Maddy will be known all over the world and tourists will fight for tickets to hear you, if you can see posters of Maddy on every kiosk in this city—then we have the same idea, you and I, of what it means to be a star. So! What do you say?" In his eyes Eve saw the unmistakable and utterly genuine excitement of a man who was offering her the world. This producer, who could engage any performer he chose, thought—no, he *knew*—that she had a chance. More than a chance.

"Nothing. For the moment. Thank you very much, *Patron*, but I have nothing to say."

"Nothing?" he said, incredulously.

"Please, don't think that I'm ungrateful or stupid. I . . . I'm still confused . . . I was so excited after last night that I didn't sleep at all . . . I . . . I just don't know what I want right now."

"I understand, Maddy—it's normal. Look, I'll give you all the time you need to think about it. Take a day, take two days—and when you're ready, come and see me in my office. We have a lot to talk about."

He gave her an encouraging smile and hurried off, thinking gloomily that not to know what you wanted was almost as bad as not wanting anything at all. If Maddy wanted to become a star, she shouldn't need more than half a minute to think about his offer. If she *really* wanted to become a star, she should have been pounding at his office door early this morning, the minute he'd arrived at the theater, demanding to know what his plans were for her.

Late that afternoon, with half an hour to herself before she had to dress to leave for the theater, Eve sat huddled in an armchair in front of the tall windows from which, only a few months before, she had been able to watch the slow setting of the sun of autumn. Now it was almost dark outside, but the day itself had been sunny, that one bright March day which keeps the spirits of Parisians from withering completely during the winter; the day on which the waiters in the cafés hastily set up tables on the sidewalk for a mob of customers, although they knew perfectly well that tomorrow they would have to take them inside again.

Eve shivered and held a cup of hot tea in her hands to warm them. All afternoon, during rehearsals with her accompanist, she had felt cold to her bones in spite of the stuffiness of the theater, and even now, wrapped in her coziest dressing gown, she couldn't get comfortable.

Why, she asked herself for the hundredth time, why had she been subjected to the words of Jacques Charles and why had she had to hear the sincerity in his voice and why, oh why, had she had to feel the leap in her blood when he talked about Maddy who could be famous, Maddy who could become a great star? The modest little stardom he had spoken of with such kindness—had she ever been guilty of hoping for more than that? Had she ever even allowed herself to dream of more? Wasn't it enough to dare to sing at the Olympia? Why should she be asked if she wanted more? Any success greater than that which she had achieved would mean that she would lose Alain. *Why should she be tempted so cruelly?*

Eve got up from the armchair and went to look for a warm scarf to wind around her neck. In the bedroom she stood for minutes in front of the huge armoire in which Alain's suits hung in an impressive row. She opened the door and inhaled the scent that came from the expensive wool, an odor that had seemed, for the last two and a half months, to be all that was left of her lover in the apartment. Although she visited him in the hospital as often as possible, it wasn't the same. The aroma of his tobacco, his cologne, his hair oil, and his body all blended into a marvelous smell that left her more desolate than before. She put her cold hand under her dressing gown and brushed her fingers lingeringly over her breast, trying to arouse a sense memory of his touch. She ached for him.

"Eve." A voice spoke from the doorway to the bedroom, and Eve screamed and whirled around.

"Alain! My God, Alain! Oh, you terrified me, coming in like that, what are you doing here?"

He laughed at her consternation, and held her tightly in his arms. "The doctors let me out an hour ago. I wanted to surprise you. Give me a kiss. Ah, that's so good. So good—in that hospital bed it never tasted like this—I was in danger of forgetting, I tell you. I'm so glad to see you, sweetheart. I'm glad you didn't let me chase you back to Dijon." He held her at arm's length and inspected her face. "You look different, Eve. I've never seen you put makeup on your eyes before. It makes you look older. I don't like it. Who taught you—Vivianne?"

Hastily, Eve nodded her assent. "Alain, darling, are you sure you're strong enough to be home? Did the doctors give you an examination before they let you go? You're so thin."

"You sound too much like my mother. I'll have to prove to you exactly how strong I am," he said, picking her up in his arms and carrying her to the bed. "Give me your mouth, first give me your mouth and then, then I'll take all the rest of you . . . you'll find out just how strong I am." His laugh was triumphant.

As he put her down on the bed and stood over her, taking off his jacket, Eve saw the time on the clock that stood on the night table. She had to leave for the theater in ten minutes or risk being late. She sat up. "Alain, my darling, not now."

"What do you mean, 'not now'? Is that the way to welcome me home?"

"I . . . I have to go out. I have an appointment . . . I can't be late. I'll be back . . . later . . . and then we . . ."

"Then we *what?* What the devil do you mean, an appointment? Since when have you been going out at night alone?" He thrust his arms back into his jacket angrily and stalked into the salon where he kept his brandy.

"Perhaps I should have let you know that I was coming," he shouted over his shoulder, "but it seems to me that whatever appointment you have is less important than . . . Eve, come in here! Come in here right now!"

Frantically Eve flew into the salon, her hands covering her mouth in sudden fear. Alain stood in front of an enormous basket filled with a bonfire of red roses that had arrived by messenger in the morning.

"Are you so rich that you're spending a hundred francs to buy yourself roses, is that it? And from Lachaume, no less. What the hell is going on here? Who sent you these things?" The muscles of his right cheek contracted and his mouth was stiff. His dark highwayman's face, that Eve knew in love and laughter, became that of a dangerous stranger. She was speechless as she watched Alain pick up the thick, cream-colored card that lay on the table in front of the roses. A card engraved with the name of the sender, Jacques Charles, his last name crossed out with a stroke of the pen to indicate that the roses had been sent on a first-name basis.

Thank you, Maddy, for last night.
It was even more than I had hoped for.
And tonight you will have no need to be nervous.
Until then. Jacques.

Alain read the words out loud. He crossed the space between them in one step, took both of her hands in one of his, and hit her open-handed across her cheek as hard as he could.

"Whore! You whoring bitch! Even more than he'd hoped for—I'll bet it was, after all I've taught you. How did you meet him? Vivianne. Of course, Vivianne! She was your pimp. I'll kill her and then I'll kill you." Again he hit her.

"Stop, it's not that, for God's sake, stop and let me explain," Eve screamed, struggling out of his grasp.

"Christ, you must really think I'm a fool. *Explain?* Do you think I have to read it twice? You fucked him, that's all. Maddy from Dijon, the newest whore in Paris," Alain grunted, the muscles of his cheek working, his breathing hard and fast as he prepared to rush at Eve and hit her again.

"I'm singing, last night was my opening, my *tour de chant!*" she shrieked desperately. At these insane words Alain stopped in his tracks, and lowered his hand.

"Get out. It's not even worth the effort to beat you up. A whore is one thing, a madwoman another. Get out and get out fast, while you can still walk."

"No Alain, no! I beg of you, listen to me. It's the truth. I should have told you but . . . I was wrong not to . . . I had to do something to get enough money for us . . . so . . . I auditioned for Monsieur Charles and I . . . it's not much, just a few songs . . ."

"*Your tour de chant?* At the Olympia? At the theater of Jacques Charles? Why, you don't know how to sing, you whore. You only know how to fuck. You make me puke. How stupid do you think I am? You have five minutes to get out." He turned away from her in disgust and walked to the buffet on which the decanter of brandy was kept. "What the devil? More flowers? Orchids this time. So you're really in the business, eh? If one, why not two? If two, why not a dozen? Who was this grateful customer?" he asked harshly, scornfully picking up a second card.

Eve knew what he was reading to himself; she had memorized the few words. "A thousand bravos, Maddy. I was proud of you last night. Your colleague of the boards." Helplessly she watched Alain's shoulders fall as the blow hit home. The name engraved on the card was that of Harry Fragson.

He did not turn around to look at her, but put the card down on the buffet and left the apartment without a word.

Weeping convulsively, Eve dashed into the bedroom to dress to go to the theater. What else was there to do, what else was there to do? she asked herself as she left the apartment to which she knew she would never return.

"Say, Maddy, do me a favor, all right? Take care of this little thing for me while I do my number? My maid didn't come in this morning," said Suzu, one of the showgirls, thrusting a baby into Eve's arms. She disappeared in a flutter of feathers before Eve could say yes or no, for everyone backstage at the Olympia knew that Maddy was a soft touch.

It had been two months since her debut, and not only had her head not been turned by her overnight success but Maddy was still the best of good kids, they agreed, who didn't put on any of the airs or graces of a star. She'd sit down and eat steak and fried potatoes at the café around the corner with anyone who happened to be hungry, from the dressers to the acrobats. She was the first one in and the last one out of the theater at night. No one could understand why she refused the invitations for supper in elegant restaurants, the invitations to galas, balls and nightclubs, that she received every day with baskets of flowers from her admirers in the audience. Maddy wouldn't even let them come to her dressing room to present themselves in person, the showgirls told each other, shaking their heads. Either she had a very jealous protector, which didn't seem possible since she had no jewels, or she didn't like men, which seemed even less possible.

Eve held the baby gingerly and contemplated it with alarm. It was sleeping now, but what if it should wake up and begin to cry during the show, before Suzu came back?

"Julie," she called, "come here quick and help me." But Julie, the dresser, who, with three others, was responsible for making sure that none of the showgirls went out onstage in a sequin too many, didn't respond.

"Julie," she called again, unable to get up and go to look for the woman, since she was sitting in nothing but the pale pink teddy that she wore under her costume. "Oh, Julie, where are you?" Hopelessly Eve listened to the brouhaha of backstage—the smothered laughs, the nonstop gossip, the ordered confusion—and realized that as long as the showgirls were performing their number onstage to the sound of the full orchestra, no one would hear her voice.

"Maddy, you decent? You have a visitor," Marcel, the assistant stage manager called out cheerfully, and pushed open her door without ceremony.

"You'll wake the baby!" Eve whispered, looking down at it in a panic.

"A baby," a woman breathed in horrified tones.

Eve jumped at the familiar voice, the baby opened its eyes and began to howl. "Aunt Marie-France!"

"A baby! It's even worse than I thought. Oh my God, what will I tell your poor mother?"

"Tell her it isn't mine," Eve said, beginning to laugh so hard that she had to deposit the baby in the young stage manager's arms. "You, Marcel, you're so smart that you don't even wait for me to say 'come in'—you take this kid to Julie and be quick about it, hear? And don't drop it. Suzu will want it back eventually, I suppose. Sit down, Aunt Marie-France, and make yourself comfortable. And Marcel, hey, Marcel, when you dump the kid, go and get us some coffee, there's a sweetheart."

"You still owe me two francs from yesterday, my angel," Marcel complained, using the familiar form of address that everyone in the company employed except when they spoke to the producer.

"Isn't my credit good with you, darling love?" Eve asked.

"Maddy, for you, always. Anything. Anytime. Do you desire my body as well as my heart? Just ask. Sugar too, Mesdames? And some little cakes?" He disappeared cheerfully, forgetting to close the door behind him, blowing them kisses and balancing the baby on one hand.

"Never mind him, Aunt Marie-France. He thinks he's irresistible. Why should I disillusion him?"

"Eve, will you please put something on over your underwear? I never saw anything so indecent. And saying *tu* to that frightfully impertinent young man, what could you be thinking of?"

"At least it wasn't my baby. Sit down, and tell me how you found me."

"Your uncle found out. He saw a caricature by Sem this morning, and it looked exactly like you. Underneath it said, 'La Belle Maddy, the newest pupil at the university of the Olympia,' so I knew where to come. I haven't said a word to your parents yet because I didn't want to upset them. Ever since you sang that tango in your mother's boudoir, I've been afraid of something terrible happening to you—but this is so much worse than I'd imagined," the Baronne wailed. "How will I ever break the news to them?"

"What, exactly, is so terrible? I'll give you tickets for the performance tonight—you'll see, I'm perfectly respectable. I sing fully clothed."

"You can call that respectable—singing in a music hall!" the Baronne said with incredulous contempt.

"Not *a* music hall, *the* music hall, the best in France, the best in the world. And I have my little moment of glory. You might try to be a tiny bit proud of me, Aunt Marie-France."

"Proud? You're *ruined*. Completely ruined! Don't you comprehend what that means, you stupid girl? You don't deny that you're living in sin?"

"No longer," Eve said coldly. "I live alone."

"That fact is of no importance—no one will believe it anyway. Now, when they see that drawing of you, by the most famous caricaturist in France, everyone will know that Eve Coudert, daughter of Doctor Didier Coudert, is singing in a music hall. For a girl from a good family to fall so low is worse than having a lover, far worse."

The door popped open. "Where's my brat, Maddy?" Suzu asked. "Oh, good day, Madame," she added, extending a hand to the Baronne, who shook it automatically, stunned at the sight of the girl's naked breasts.

"I sent it to Julie. She knows how to deal with that sort of object. And I don't understand kids. Please remember next time, darling."

"Sure, Maddy." As she spoke, the sound of a violent voice broke out in the corridor just outside the dressing room.

"Oh, the shits, oh, the stinking turds of the sidewalks, oh, I'll get them for this, I'll wipe their asses on sandpaper, I'll stuff their heads in the crapper! Maddy? Maddy! Did you see the bloody shits who did this?"

"Did what, Baldy?" Eve called.

"Nailed my shoes to the floor, beautiful. What do you think? They did it last week, in the same place. I'll bet you know who they are."

"If you didn't take them off and leave them waiting in the corridor until you're ready to go onstage, it wouldn't happen," Eve answered, shaking with laughter.

"You just wait, gorgeous, until you have corns. Then you'll understand. Julie, another pair of shoes and be quick about it. I'm on in two minutes, for God's sake!"

"Coming, coming." Julie bustled into the room, the baby under one arm. "Suzu," she shouted over her shoulder, "come here and give your nipper a tit right away or the *Patron* will hear it yowling." She handed Baldy his shoes and rushed out in a flash, to be replaced by Marcel, carrying the coffee and cakes on a round platter.

"*Voilà*, Mesdames. My treat, Maddy," he said gallantly, giving Eve a kiss on each cheek. "Since you have a guest . . ."

"You're a sweetie. Oh, I forgot my manners—just as predicted. This is the Baronne de Courtizot, Marcel." The young man bowed low in the direction of Marie-France de Courtizot's hand.

"I am enchanted, Madame la Baronne," he said with a flourish, "Allow me to present myself. I am the Duc de Saint-Cloud."

The Baronne could not bring herself to nod, much less to speak.

"Marcel, I'll see you later, all right?" Eve said, nodding toward the door. Understanding, he left them alone.

"Eve," her aunt said urgently. "It's not too late! If you go home *today* on the night train, I'll accompany you, and by tomorrow everybody who matters in Dijon will see that you could not be the girl in the caricature. If they should even mention it, you will know nothing about it, and your father and mother can say that there must be someone who looks something like you who performs on a stage. Nobody can *prove* otherwise. Thank God you didn't use your real name, and with all that makeup on your face no one will have recognized you. Oh, Eve, no one has to know!" Her tone was imploring.

"And why would I want to do that?" Eve asked.

"Why? Because if you don't, my girl, you're finished, that's why. You have made yourself completely *déclassé*, Eve, ruined, disgraced. But you don't *have* to be cast out from decent society! Don't you understand, there's still time, *just* enough time."

"It's you who don't understand, my poor Aunt. I'm not the same girl who left home last August. I've written every week, as you know, but I left out all the important things."

"Do you think your parents care now that you had a lover? Do you think that's the only thing that matters? If it's over, so much the better," the Baronne said angrily. "Forget it ever happened. You were always so protected that I'm not surprised someone was able to take advantage of you. Although how you were crafty enough to meet a man, none of us will ever understand. But don't be a fool, girl. Don't throw away your future."

"What if I feel that my future is here?" Eve said.

"Here? In this squalid, grubby little room? With these low, gross, vulgar people? In this *barnyard*? It's not possible. I simply will not allow it."

As she spoke the door opened, although again no one had knocked, and a showgirl, down on her hands and knees, her bare breasts swinging freely from side to side, scampered into the room, barking like a dog. She had started to sniff in an interested manner at the Baronne's feet as if she were about to lift her leg, when Eve jumped up.

"Enough! Morton, this time you have gone too far!" she yelled. "Get this girl out of here this minute, Morton, do you hear me?"

Sheepishly, the most famous magician and hypnotist in France poked his head into the room. "I thought you were alone, beloved. A thousand pardons, Madame. Alice believes she's a dog. Come along, Alice, there's a good doggie, come along and don't bother the nice lady."

"Sorry, Aunt Marie-France. Morton's a genius but he behaves like a child from time to time. He means no harm."

Marie-France's eyes were wide with shock. "Eve, I can't leave you in this . . . this abomination. You must come home with me."

"Darling Aunt, you 'can't leave me,' you 'simply will not allow it'— what do you take me for? I am not a little girl you can order around anymore. Do you seriously imagine that I could go back to Dijon and take my place among the eligible debutantes, and wait for some solid citizen to come along and do me the honor of making me his wife? Do you believe that now that I know the glory of singing on the stage of the Olympia I could be content with a life like my mother's?"

" 'Glory'? Vainglory! Conceit! It is odious and ignoble and contemptible, this glory of yours," Marie-France said violently. "In ten years you'll realize that you threw away all the important things in life for a momentary caprice. All you can understand now is the sound of cheap applause, the life of the . . . the gutter."

Eve rose, her face held tightly in icy fury. "I beg you not to speak of my friends in such terms. Perhaps you had better leave, Aunt Marie-France. It does not suit you to be out of your element."

The Baronne de Courtizot stood up and walked toward the door. "If you change your mind, if you become rational, Eve, I'll be at home for the rest of today and tomorrow. After that it will be far too late. Now I have to go back and decide what to tell your poor mother."

"Tell her the truth. Tell her I'm happy. Ask my parents to come to Paris to see for themselves. I have nothing to be ashamed of."

"You're worse than the fool that man took you for," the Baronne said, and left the room without a backward glance.

The next day, a morning in May, Eve made an appointment with Jacques Charles.

"Two months ago, *Patron*, you told me that I had the potential to become a real star," she said. "You gave me two days to think about it."

"I remember," he said grimly. "I'm surprised that you do."

"I wasn't ready. I can't explain it more honestly than that. But now, if it still interests you . . ."

"Well . . . ?"

"*I want it!* I'm ready to work with everything I've got, twenty-four hours a day, for as long as it takes. Months, years, it doesn't matter, if you'll just give me the chance."

Eve fell silent, looking at the floor, her whole body quivering with an excess of longing. This was what she had been born to do, and she'd probably thrown away her opportunity because it had come at the wrong time. She had still been in love with Alain, still trying to keep their life intact. And after he left her, her spirit had almost been destroyed by his words and his blows. His hatred.

She had failed to grasp the moment and she'd never forgive herself if the producer had lost interest in her because of her lack of ambition. From the instant that Aunt Marie-France had unwittingly shown her how much the world of the stage meant to her, she had realized how unthinkable any other life would be. She thought of nothing now but reclaiming the glowing, distant, infinitely alluring future that Jacques Charles had once held out to her. She belonged to the music hall, and the music hall *must belong* to her.

But the impresario hadn't answered her. She looked up to where he was seated behind his desk and saw him writing with concentration. Had she been dismissed? He finished writing, laid down his pen and handed her the sheet of paper.

"Here's your schedule of lessons," he said. "You're late for the first one already. Hurry!"

It was a spring of soft winds, a spring of soft clouds, a spring of soft rain, that last heedless spring of the Edwardian era. Eve was far too busy to pay any attention to the weather, much less to the winds of change, as she ran from her lessons in acrobatics, dance and drama to the theater, just in time to put on her makeup before her performance. She no longer had time to read the newspapers, no time for the camaraderie of backstage, the shared meals, the gossip and jokes. She ate what she could, wherever she could, just so long as it didn't take too long to chew, and after the curtain rang down she went straight home to her little furnished apartment and fell into bed, too exhausted to dream.

While Kaiser Wilhelm II spent twenty days of July relaxing on a pleasure cruise on board his yacht, the *Hohenzollern,* Eve, like everyone else, was wrapped up in her own life. The time bomb that had been ticking away for a month in Belgrade and Vienna went off on the twenty-eighth of July, 1914, when Austria-Hungary declared war on Serbia. For the next week the diplomats and military strategists of the great European powers worked at cross-purposes, in an insanely tangled web of downright lies, arrogance, recklessness, incompetence, duplicity, incomplete information and utterly differing intentions, until they finally managed to flounder and stumble, not inevitably but fatally, into a war that no one but a few extreme nationalists had ever wanted. On August fourth, Sir Edward Grey, the Foreign Secretary of Great Britain, said, "The lamps are going out all over Europe: we shall not see them lit again in our lifetime."

Marcel, the assistant stage manager, Jacques Charles, and Maurice Chevalier were merely three of the almost four million men mobilized by France in the first weeks of August. The business of the country was paralyzed as every able-bodied man was called up, and trains packed with ill-armed but gay and enthusiastic troops left for military positions every seven minutes.

After the Battle of the Marne, in mid-September, when the French threw back a German approach on Paris, the temporary national euphoria was marked by a reopening of all the theaters, cafés and music halls of the country. However, in that single month two hundred thousand Frenchmen had died, many of them wearing the bright red trousers that dated back to the uniform of 1830 and symbolized the lack of reality with which the country faced what it imagined would be a short, chivalrous and glorious war.

By the end of that first wartime September, both the German and the Allied armies began to dig in to rest and resupply along the Aisne river, in the province of Champagne, creating the trenches that were to become the first fortifications of the Western Front, a front that, for three years, would move back and forth within ten deadlocked miles, accomplishing nothing but the slaughter of millions of men.

On a low hilltop in Champagne lay the Château de Valmont, the family home of the Vicomtes de Lancel. It was located in the heart of the champagne grape-growing country, on the chalky, heat-retaining north slopes of the Montagne de Rheims, running roughly east to west between Rheims and Epernay, the two major towns of the province.

Valmont, unlike most châteaux in Champagne, had survived the Revolution, invasions and wars. It rose with a fairy-tale-like suddenness from a small but dense wood, proud possessor of three round towers with pointed, tiled roofs. Dozens of rooms with tall, many-paned windows looked out calmly on the semicircular stone terrace where topiary trees in carved stone urns stood as they had done for centuries. Valmont was surrounded by a treasure of vineyards, a portion of the tightly limited area of the world's surface whose grapes produce the only sparkling white wine with an undisputed right to be called champagne.

Each year the harvest of these grapes, the white Chardonnay, the black Pinot Noir and Pinot Meunier, proves the existence of one of the greatest mysteries in the history of winemaking, for although Noah planted a vineyard when he got off the Ark, even Noah could not have claimed that he could produce champagne.

Many châteaux throughout France were mere museumlike monuments to a family's history and, by the beginning of the Great War, had long since lost the vitality of their pre-Revolutionary days. Valmont, on the contrary, had always been a prosperous, bustling, hospitable dwelling. It had seen many changes since the days when the Lancels were loyal to the counts of Champagne as they strove to dominate the kings of France, a conflict that only ended in 1284 when Joan of Navarre and Champagne married the future king of France, Philip the Fair.

In the seventeenth century the Vicomtes de Lancel, like their neighbors, began to produce wine. Beyond the boundaries of their own large vineyards they were surrounded by the small holdings of farmers who sold them the grapes they grew. Soon they made enough champagne to begin to sell it. By the mid-eighteen-hundreds, the distinctive green bottles bearing the shield-shaped gold label on which the word *Lancel* appeared in large letters with *Château de Valmont* in smaller letters beneath it, had become a *Grande Marque*. Along with Moët & Chandon, Mumm, Veuve Clicquot Ponsardin, and a few other great names, chilled bottles of Lancel were a most desired sight at any festival celebrated by civilized men and women.

The present head of the Lancel family, Vicomte Jean-Luc de Lancel, had two sons. The elder, Guillaume, was destined to run the House of Lancel, the younger, Paul-Sebastian, had become a diplomat in the service of the Quai d'Orsay. At the start of hostilities he was barely thirty, the First Secretary of the French Embassy in London, and clearly a man who was bound to rise to the heights of the foreign service.

On August first, 1914, the first day of the call to arms, ignoring the opportunity afforded to diplomats to stay out of the fighting, he had volunteered. Now a captain, Paul de Lancel left behind his young wife, born Laure de Saint-Fraycourt, a frail Parisian beauty of twenty-two, who was awaiting the birth of their first child.

She had implored him not to leave her. "The child will be born in another five months and everyone says that this stupid war must surely be over before then," Laure de Lancel had said, weeping with weakness and fear. "I beg you, stay with me—I need you here."

However, Paul felt compelled to go to war at once. He knew that France would need every man she had in order to face the German armies that had been mobilized with massive efficiency and a staggering superiority in numbers as well as armament.

The weaving patterns of approaching battle had been observed by Paul de Lancel, from his diplomatic post. He knew that the French General Staff was riddled by a complex of superiority. The idea that the courage, dash and ardor of the French soldier, the ordinary, brave *poilu*, must count for more than mere fighting power, was an article of faith in the minds of professional army men. But Paul, unlike the average Frenchman, entertained serious doubts that élan alone would win the day. However, like every other human being in that unsuspecting summer of 1914, he had no suspicion of what lay in store.

Paul de Lancel was a complex man. He often wondered if he would have been happier if an accident of birth had made him the wine grower of the family rather than a diplomat. Certainly, as his mother, Anette de Lancel, often told him, he looked as if he should be out working in the vineyards rather than sitting behind a desk, for Paul was a massive man, both tall and wide-shouldered, with the powerful muscles of someone who worked with his hands. His blond hair looked as if it had been bleached by the sun while he labored. Although his dark blue eyes were the Lancel eyes, as deep-set as those in the family portraits that hung throughout the château, and he had the prominent Lancel cheekbones, the rest of his face was not marked by the fine Lancel bone structure, nor did he have any trace of the red hair that appeared, generation after generation, in the family. Paul's big and well-shaped nose lacked the Lancel slenderness, and his handsome mouth and chin had a vigorous and uncomplicated simplicity.

Nevertheless, Paul de Lancel's turn of mind was so questioning that he frequently wished he could deal with nothing more subtle than the simple preoccupations of the sun and the rain. Indeed, a grape grower and wine producer must wake up each day to worry about the weather, but since there is nothing he can do about it, a sort of resignation and philosophy is forced to reign in his mind, a condition that, it seemed to Paul, had a great deal that was blessedly solid and comforting to recommend it.

A diplomat, on the other hand, had an obligation to become a professional cynic, for without a cautious, double-thinking mind-set to protect him, he would be in danger of becoming a constant dupe, and worthless to his country. Paul de Lancel was not able to tell himself of any single verity in the world that he was absolutely certain of, except his love for France and his love for his wife. Of the two, he was forced to admit that his love for his country was stronger.

Eve, jolted by the mobilization, had decided not to return to the Olympia, which had reopened under the direction of Beretta, the former conductor of the orchestra, and Léon Volterra, who had saved an uncanny number of sous while selling programs in the lobby of the Olympia. Her personal ambitions would have to wait until this war was over, she decided.

If Jacques Charles could serve in the army, so would she, in her fashion. As soon as it was organized, Eve joined *Le Théâtre aux Armées de la République* and became one of the many entertainers who traveled to the various battlegrounds to give shows for the soldiers. Some of them, like Charles Dullin, performed in the actual trenches dug on the Lorraine front. Eve attached herself to a group founded by Lucien Gilly, one of the comics at the Olympia.

In 1915, a year after the Battle of the Marne, a new offensive began in Champagne. Joffre, the ever over-optimistic general, proclaimed to his troops, *"Votre élan sera irrésistible!"* and the men marched, in spite

81

of downpouring rain, to the sound of fifers and bands playing the *Marseillaise*. Ten days later a hundred and forty-five thousand Frenchmen lay dead and no strategic advantage had been gained.

Captain Paul de Lancel suffered a serious arm wound on the last day of the offensive. As he lay in the hospital he thought not of himself, but of all the death he had witnessed in the last twelve months. His men, the men of the First Army, had been among the first to die. His wife had not survived the birth of their son, Bruno, who was in the care of Laure's parents in Paris. Paul had been able to see the baby only once, during the brief leave he had been given to attend Laure's funeral, and the thought that he had a nine-month-old son made him neither sad nor happy. He felt only indifference. He knew that his own chances of surviving the war were so remote that they weren't worth a minute's consideration by a realistic man, and he found he minded not for himself, but only—and that was an intellectual, not an emotional feeling—for the mite who was certain to grow up an orphan. Paul de Lancel regarded himself as a dead man as much as any prisoner in a jail who is sentenced to be shot at dawn. He would live until he was well enough to lead other men to death. The prospect of death left him indifferent. He cared only for the men he commanded, men simple enough still to hope, men lucky enough still to love, men ignorant enough still to imagine that there was a future.

As soon as his arm had healed, Paul de Lancel rejoined his company, almost all of them replacements, who had been regrouped in the trenches just before the town of Festubert, midway on the Flanders front between Ypres and Arras.

Festubert was one of the towns over which the opposing armies fought during a year of unbroken stalemate. It was now late fall, and the spring would bring new and more savage warfare, but for the moment the soldiers of both sides found themselves in one of those comparative lulls that occur in even the most bitter battles: time in which to bury their dead, delouse their shirts, and even, on this cold autumn night in northeastern France, to group together in an improvised theater to roar at Lucien Gilly and his ancient jokes, to hum along to the tune of the accordionist, to applaud the six girls who danced with the six soldiers who volunteered to be their partners, and finally to listen to Maddy sing, Maddy who had already become a legend of the *Théâtre aux Armées*, in her brave red dress and her bright red shoes and her hair like the sunshine they all remembered from summer days, no matter where in France they had once been young.

Eve was growing worried. When she had left the lodging in Saint-Omer, now well behind the front, to be driven to Festubert, there had been adequate daylight. The others in Gilly's troupe had gone on just before her, in the series of soldier-driven military vehicles allocated to them. She had been delayed by the delicate but essential needlework necessary to repair a major rip in the bias-cut hem of her dress.

Now she and her soldier-chauffeur, a boy so young that she was astonished that he was of military age, had been driving for far too long, according to what Gilly had told her to expect, and Festubert was not in sight.

"Are you certain this is the right way?" Eve asked anxiously.

"It's the road my corporal told me to take, if you can call it a road," he answered. Indeed, the unpaved route seemed to be getting worse instead of better with each minute of approaching darkness.

"Why don't we stop and look at the map?" Eve suggested.

"Haven't got one. Generals have maps. And if I did, it wouldn't mean a thing, would it, without signposts?"

"Stop at the first farmhouse you see, and ask directions," Eve told him sharply. She had sung many times within sight and sound of enemy fire, and not trembled, but this lonely road, this desolate, almost tree-less countryside, this empty, unpeopled, destroyed land through which they were driving, unnerved her. If only she hadn't bothered about her hem, she thought fretfully, and tried to pull her heavy coat even more tightly around her.

"Look, there's a farmhouse down the road!" Eve cried.

"Bombed out, by the look of it," the soldier replied, and indeed there was no sign of life, no light, no smoke, no sound of animals or people. "Germans got it last year, I guess," the boy continued indifferently. As he spoke, there was a burst of flame in the field on their right, and a rending of the air as a mortar shell exploded.

"Jesus!" he screamed, and in the shuddering air a second shell exploded, fragments landing close to the car. The young soldier almost lost control of the wheel, but managed to stay on the road, and with as much speed as the vehicle possessed, he raced toward the farmhouse, screeching to a stop in a pool of water in the farmyard itself.

"Get down!" he shouted, but Eve was already out of the car and running, crouched low, toward the open door. They reached it together and dove inside on their hands and knees, looking for any object that might provide shelter. With a strange sharpening of all her senses, Eve saw in a split second that the room was empty except for bits of wood and pieces of crockery on the floor. It had obviously been heavily shelled; although the roof was almost intact, the stones of the walls had gaping holes everywhere. It could no longer be called a farmhouse, Eve thought, or any other kind of house. Outside they heard another mortar shell whistle pitilessly before it landed, but it was impossible to tell if it had fallen nearer to them than the others. For lack of any better place to put themselves, they huddled beside the empty fireplace. If it had been bigger, they would have hurled themselves inside the hearth.

"We'll never get there," Eve said, as calmly as she could. "You took the wrong road."

"Don't see how it happened," the driver protested in a pathetic voice.

"There isn't supposed to be any fighting on the road, for God's sake, or they would never have told us to come this way."

"Maybe," he said sullenly, "but just when it gets quiet, see, there're Germans waiting for you. And then they get you. That's what my corporal told me."

"I wish he were here now. I'd tell him what I think!" It was plain, she realized, that at best they would have to wait here until daylight and rescue. There was no point in considering the worst. She wrapped the skirt of her coat firmly around her ankles and eased herself down so that she was sitting on the stones of the hearth. In spite of her fear and her anger at this idiot *poilu*, she couldn't continue to ignore the fact that her feet, in her new pair of red shoes, undeniably hurt. If she was going to be killed by a shell, she might just as well be sitting down in comfort, comparatively speaking, than standing up in shoes meant for a *tour de chant* and nothing else.

"You got a cigarette?" the boy asked.

"I don't smoke. Here," she answered, handing him the packet she always carried for any soldier who wanted one.

"PUT OUT THAT MATCH!"

Eve screamed and jumped up. A group of soldiers rushed into the farmhouse. They had crept up so quietly that neither she nor the driver had heard them approach. Petrified by shock, she stood with her back to the wall, expecting to die with a bayonet through her heart, until she came to her senses and realized that if she could understand the command, it must be in French.

"Thank God, thank God, how did you know we were here? Oh, thank God you came to save us," she whispered.

"*Save* you? Who the hell are you? What the devil is a woman doing here?"

84

"I was going to Festubert . . . to perform . . ."

"You must be mad. *Mad!* What a damn fool woman! It's in the other direction. You're almost on top of the front, opposite Lens."

"Lens? Where's that?"

"Lens is on the German side of the front, last I heard," Paul de Lancel said brusquely, as he turned away from her and began to give orders to the men under his command. They had been thrown back by a surprise attack coming from one of the many fortified machine-gun nests that protected the German's artillery.

Four men were wounded, three too gravely to walk. The remaining three were unharmed. The situation was more serious then he had first realized, Paul discovered, as he moved among them, asking quiet questions. He judged that with the full moon that had already risen and the clear visibility that was expected, there was no chance of trying to transport the wounded men back to the trenches and medical help. In the first dim and confusing light of dawn he could send someone back with the news that they were trapped here. Meanwhile, he could only wait and do his best to help them live through the night.

"Can I help?" Eve asked, walking with caution between the men on the floor and coming close to the captain, before she spoke.

"Not unless you're a nurse." His voice was preoccupied, dismissive.

Eve retreated to the cold fireplace. She hadn't taken any of the Red Cross classes in which so many women were engaged. She had been too busy singing at various outposts along the front and, between trips, working at any theater that offered her a job for a few weeks, just in order to pay her rent.

In silence she listened to the few words that the men grunted, words so abbreviated and so weary that they might almost have been in a foreign language. Soon, whatever could be done for the wounded had been done by the able-bodied, and all eight men, including their captain, sat or lay on what, Eve mused, had once been a scrubbed and spotless farmhouse floor, its cleanliness some woman's pride.

There would have been a fine log fire, she imagined, to fight the darkness of this cold October night, and certainly children gathered cozily around, doing the homework they had been given in the village school. A thick soup would have been cooking, hams and sausages would have hung from the ceiling, and outside, the farmer would almost have finished his inspection of his animals, eager for the moment when he would come inside to the scene of comfort he knew so well. His harvest would have been in for weeks, and his relatively lazy winter would lie ahead, night after night of warmth and enough to eat, his wife's companionship and the joys of watching his children grow.

Once such a simple, ordinary life would have been all but unimaginable to her, or if she had been interested enough to attempt to visualize it, she would have disdained it as being brutish. A peasant's life, a life without possibilities of change, a life that could be written down, from birth to death, in three short sentences. No chance to dare in that life; no chance to meet the sky halfway in a big red balloon; no chance to run away to Paris with the first man she had ever kissed; no chance to walk along the Grands Boulevards to the rhythm of a maxixe; no chance to star at the Olympia. *To dare and to win.*

How lucky she had been! And she hadn't really known it, not known it fully, as she did now, just as the farmer and his wife didn't know how lucky they had been until the mortar shells of two great nations destroyed their farmhouse and laid waste to their fields.

As time passed and the moon shone more brilliantly into the pile of stones that sheltered them, Eve was able to see the soldiers more clearly than she had been earlier. None of them was asleep. The wounded were in too much pain to allow their comrades to close their eyes for so much as a minute. Their groans were muted, and came at intervals, but even without knowing the time, Eve was aware that it was still many hours until morning.

There must be something she could do, even if she knew nothing about nursing, she told herself angrily. She just couldn't sit here and watch them suffer without at least trying to take their minds off their pain. That unpleasant officer had said she couldn't help. Just because she didn't know how to roll a bandage didn't mean that she was worthless. After all, Vincent Scotto had just written the enormously popular song *Le Cri du Poilu,* with its rousing refrain, "Our soldiers at the front, what do they want, a woman! a woman!"

Simpleminded, perhaps, but clear and direct enough, Eve told herself, and without asking permission, she began to sing in her softest possible voice, in her voice of spring lightning that could be heard in the last seat of the third balcony, had she wished it, but which, tonight, only carried across the small space that separated her from the soldiers. She sang the first song that came to her lips, her good-luck song, her audition song, *Parlez-moi d'Amour.* At the sound of her voice the officer muttered an oath of surprise, but Eve ignored him and continued, following with *Mon Homme,* for good measure. "When he touches me, I'm finished, for I'm only a woman and I have him under my skin."

"Requests, gentlemen?" she asked as soon as she had finished with

Mistinguett's immortal hymn to the helplessness of a woman in love and the irresistible power of a man over her. And seven men answered her, some in voices so faint that she could hardly hear them, others eagerly, but each had a song he wanted to hear.

Eve sat on the hearth, and that whole night through she sang and sang, blessing the memory of all the melodies and lyrics she had heard once and never forgotten as she walked back and forth to her lessons through the streets of Dijon, for almost all the requests were for songs that went back to her girlhood. She could see the men only where the moonlight shone through the holes in the walls. Their faces were almost hidden, but those who weren't strong enough to speak up whispered their requests to their comrades. She even sang for the soldier whose hapless driving had brought her to this place.

Paul de Lancel, his officer's cap pulled down over his eyes, sat quietly, cradling in his arms a man whose legs were utterly useless. With every song this woman sang, he realized, some inner wound was slowly beginning to heal in him. Her voice expanded his heart, giving him back a glimpse, an intimation, of a place where love and laughter could be found. The elemental, caressing timbre of her voice, the rich humanity of it, that deeply feminine sound, a visceral warmth that existed nowhere on the front, that had nothing to do with the war, brought back the memory of so much he had forgotten. An impermanent vision? Unquestionably, but each of her songs, and their often banal words of ordinary human needs and hopes, of the deceptions of love, the joys of love, days and nights of love, began to restore the beginning of a belief in his own continued existence, a belief he had lost long ago. Would these hours be remembered? Would the long-dormant emotions she awakened, as he was enveloped in the magical world of her voice, endure in any form beyond this night? Probably not, he thought, but oh, how good were these moments of simple forgotten contentment, of tenderness.

Paul de Lancel never asked for a song for himself, for he was unwilling to take the place of any of his men. Finally there was a lull in their requests even though, to a man, they were still awake, and he spoke up. "Do you know any of the English soldiers' songs?"

" 'The Roses of Picardy,' of course, and 'Tipperary'—everyone knows them, even if they don't speak English."

" 'Till We Meet Again'—do you know it too?"

" 'Smile a while, you kiss me sad adieu' . . . that one?" Eve asked.

"Yes," he said eagerly. "Please."

"Smile a while, you kiss me sad adieu,
When the clouds roll by I'll come to you.
Then the skies will seem more blue,
Down in Lovers' Lane, my dearie . . .
Wedding bells will ring so merrily,
Every tear will be a memory,
So wait and pray each night for me,
Till we meet again."

Eve looked up as she came to the last line, and he said only, "Again . . . oh, just one more time." Before she finished the short, simple, unforgettable melody, she saw that the captain had fallen asleep, a smile on his lips.

5

TO think that some people have the luck to be born Swiss," Vivianne de Biron sighed pensively as she and Eve sat in her kitchen on a day in the last week of December of 1916, sharing a pot of herb tea.

"Swiss? You always said that it wasn't a country as much as a convalescent home," Eve retorted, disbelievingly. Two and a half years of war had made little outward change in her splendidly preserved friend. Vivianne was as irreducibly Parisian as ever, like a metal that cannot be further refined by any means.

" 'A calm neutrality,' that's what the Schultess has promised them. That and fresh cream in their real coffee, no doubt. No boring herb tea for them."

"Schultess?" Eve's winged brows rose higher than ever under the small black Persian lamb toque that almost covered her siren's hair. She was elegantly thinner than she had been when she first arrived in Paris three and a half years before, and when she walked down the street she strode with the inimitable confidence and panache of a woman who belonged to this city, a woman to whom the city, without question, belonged. "Who is Schultess?"

"The new president of Switzerland, as you'd know if you read the newspapers, Maddy. And our government finds nothing better to do than to raise the tax on adultery! Oh no, don't laugh, my girl, I'm serious. Before this miserable war, the fine for adultery was twenty-five francs. Today they've changed it to a hundred francs and a few days in prison! I ask you, is that reasonable? Is it logical, is it rational? Is it even French? That they've rationed our gas and electricity and food makes sense—but what could a little adultery take away from winning the war? In my opinion this new tax is positively unpatriotic."

Vivianne poured another cup of tea and regarded it without favor. "Reflect on it, Maddy. If a soldier is away from home and is able to take a little comfort with someone who isn't his wife—or if his wife misses him but in his absence finds a small pleasure to enable her to endure her loneliness—why should anyone have to pay a tax? And who is the voyeur who is going to be searching under beds for adulterers instead of being at the front where he belongs, can you tell me that?"

"It's beyond my capacities, Vivianne. I haven't got that much imagination," Eve replied, trying to repress her giggles.

"Ah, Maddy, you refuse to take anything seriously. Well, that's your privilege," Vivianne sniffed. "I suppose you think it's intelligent that the government won't allow the public to come into the theaters except in street clothes, too? No more evening gowns, no dinner jackets . . . as if that might impress the Germans enough so that they'd all swallow a few good mouthfuls of their own poison gas, and go running back to Berlin."

"It's worth trying," Eve said absently. She did read the newspapers and she was aware, as much as Vivianne, that the battles of the Somme and of Verdun, during 1916, the most frightful year yet known in human history, had taken a toll of lives so vast that it was beyond the power of the mind to comprehend.

Abruptly she pulled her thoughts back to join her friend's chatter. "Our allies are doing their best, even you must admit it, Vivianne," Eve said. "The King of England has vowed not to drink alcohol, not even wine or beer, to help win the war. Imagine, if the rest of the country follows his example. Think of it—all those English without their whiskey—what could it lead to?"

"A certain victory—for the Germans," Vivianne retorted. "At least no one is suggesting giving up the music hall. There isn't a seat in any theater in Paris, with all the soldiers on leave wanting to be distracted."

"I know. Since Jacques Charles got out of the military hospital and took over the Casino de Paris he's more dynamic than ever—at the Olympia we never had such sumptuous costumes, such elaborate decors. Just wait till you see dozens of girls, with nothing on but G-strings, climbing up and down ladders ten meters tall. The band is playing something from America that I've never heard before—it's called ragtime."

Vivianne looked unconvinced, not at all pleased to be told that the Casino de Paris surpassed the theater in which she had known her days of glory.

"And do you like to sing this 'ragtime'?"

"You don't sing it, you dance to it, more or less. But I must leave you, Vivianne, dear. Time to do a little work. At least now I can come and visit you since the coast is clear." Eve nodded in the direction of the landing, toward the apartment in which she used to live. Alain Marais, thanks to the weakness of his lungs after his bout of pneumonia, had noncombatant status in the army and was stationed at a supply depot far from Paris.

Eve got up to go. Vivianne thought she looked even more vivacious and alluring than ever before, in her coat of Parma violet wool, trimmed with an immense Persian lamb collar and cuffs, and a deep fur hem. As Eve turned toward the door of the kitchen she changed her mind and turned back to Vivianne.

"Let me ask you something, Vivianne. When you took me to the Olympia for my audition, didn't it occur to you that I'd have to see Fragson perform and then I'd discover the truth about Alain?"

"That was more than three years ago," the older woman protested.

"That's not the answer to my question."

"I suppose it should have crossed my mind. . . . Perhaps it did, and I didn't realize it . . . or perhaps . . . well, what if I had the notion that it wouldn't be such a bad thing for you to know how less-than-wonderful your Monsieur Marais was? Perhaps I hoped it might keep you from throwing yourself away on him for too long. In any case, I didn't do it from conscious malice—but I wouldn't be ashamed of myself if I had."

"I knew about Fragson months before that audition. I went to the Olympia alone one day."

"Ah."

"Precisely. Women in love are such pathetic fools, Vivianne. It's like a dreadful attack of willful stupidity. And once they're out of love, they ask themselves how they could ever have made such utter misjudgments, such obvious mistakes, but they never do find an answer. Since Alain, I've decided that it was much wiser never to fall in love —and I haven't, not even a little bit. He did me a favor, although it didn't seem that way at the time."

"Ah."

"That's all you have to say? 'Ah'?"

"You're almost twenty-one. When you're three times as old, you can tell me that again and I promise to begin to believe you."

"I thought you were a professional cynic, Vivianne."

"I am. About men—and a romantic about women."

"He says he knows you, Maddy. But he says you don't know his name. Shall I let him in?" The guardian of the stage door at the Casino de Paris was accustomed to mobs of soldiers trying to gain entrance backstage after the curtain fell on the show, and normally, war or no war, he told them to wait until Maddy came out. However, this one had obviously given him a good tip to induce him to approach Eve directly.

"What does he look like?" she asked, preoccupied. Her stage makeup had all been removed, and her arms were raised over her head as she brushed out her hair in every direction. Eve wore a light dressing gown of pale yellow silk, for it was warm in the month of May 1917. With the aureole of strawberry blond hair like a halo around her face she looked as positive as summer yet as tentative as spring, like a flower, ravished by the sun, with its open heart showing.

"He's an officer, lots of ribbons. Good looking, since you ask me."

"French, English or American?"

"French, of course, or I wouldn't have bothered you. The Americans just got here, after all. Although they do find their way to Paris quickly, I'll say that for them."

"Show him in," Eve decided. "Just give me time to put on my dress."

In a minute the guardian was back, closely followed by a tall, impatient figure in a colonel's uniform, carrying his cap under his arm.

"I hope I'm not disturbing you, Madame." The formula of politeness was at odds with the intensity of the way he said the traditional words.

"Not at all, *mon colonel.*" There was a question in her voice. She couldn't remember ever having met this big, blond man, with weatherbeaten skin and deep-set blue eyes, yet there was something disturbingly familiar about him, as if she had dreamed about him, forgotten the dream, and now was on the verge of remembering it again.

"I didn't have any idea who you were until tonight," he said, "and I didn't know how to find you—but then when I heard you sing—at the very first note . . . I . . . that night . . ." He fell silent, as if he didn't know what to say next, as if the urgent need to tell Eve something was too complex to put into words.

"That night?" she asked. There had been an eternity of nights since the war started.

"You can't have forgotten, even though it was almost two years ago."

"That night? *Yes, oh yes,* the night in the farmhouse! You . . . oh yes, of course—the officer—yes, I remember—naturally I remember— how could anyone forget that night? Now I remember your voice, I just didn't remember your face. You fell asleep while I sang."

"And I dreamed of peace," he answered. "A happy dream . . . it stayed with me for days. Two of my men would not have lived through that night if it hadn't been for you. I had to tell you that."

"What is your name, *mon colonel?*"

"Paul de Lancel. Will you dine with me, Madame?"

"It would give me pleasure."

"Tonight?" he asked, so hopefully that his deep voice almost cracked.

"Why not? As I remember, on the night we met we went hungry. And yet I sang for my supper . . . and almost for my breakfast as well. So I believe you owe me a dinner. But you must promise me two things."

"Anything," he said seriously. "Anything you ask."

"You must not tell me again that I'm mad or a damn fool."

"I'd hoped you'd forgotten how unforgivably rude I was."

"On the contrary, it was too memorable ever to forget."

In the past few years, Eve had been taken out to supper after the show night after night by military men from every part of France. Distraction was what they sought in a restaurant, a feverish bustle and brightness that brought its own gaiety.

Paul de Lancel, however, chose to take her to the dining room of the Ritz. It was an exceptionally formal room, high-ceilinged, with elaborate moldings, deeply carpeted and hung with brocades of a quality that would be justified in a queen's bedroom. The tables were placed far from each other, and one of its walls opened onto a semicircular garden where jasmine and trailing pyramids of geraniums surrounded a fountain. Each element of the service was attended to by a maître d'hôtel, waiters and busboys whose tasks were performed too silently to encourage bustle, the room was lit too discreetly to be bright, each table glowing in quiet invitation in a pool of light made by small lamps with pink shades.

Yet, for all its ornateness, the dining room of the Ritz was conceived under the spell of celebration and gaiety, and it had retained that mood throughout the war. Although the sum total of the details of the room made it the most splendid place to dine in France, Paul de Lancel was snugly and familiarly at home there. He ordered dinner without any unnecessary fuss, yet with an authority that was as complete as it was mild. As he spoke to the maître d'hôtel, Eve felt herself relaxing into a quietude of security that had nothing to do with the prospect of a peaceful meal.

In the soft light, Paul studied Eve intently. She sat with her normal serene confidence in the brocade armchair, her long earrings glimmering. Her hair was parted in the middle, and then brought forward so that it coiled, in the latest style, over her ears. Her dress had a low, square neckline trimmed in a band of lace, and two other broad bands of lace covered her shoulders, yet her strong, smooth neck and her slender arms were left completely bare.

He realized that this denuded style suited Eve, as it did few others, for it emphasized the exquisitely curved angle at the widest part of her jawbone, and the marvelously fresh tint of her skin. It was impossible for him to see into the depths of her eyes in the available light, but as she talked, the slow flutter of her eyelids under her upslanting brows was mysteriously important. The striking immoderation that her Aunt Marie-France had first become aware of seven years earlier had been sculpted and firmed by life, but not in the least tamed, so that now it appeared as a startling independence of spirit, a freedom and a composure that joined to give Eve a quality that was noble in its lack of conventionality. As they talked, he recognized the dancing lance of her intelligence, the teasing contagion of her inner playfulness.

"Who *are* you?" Paul de Lancel suddenly heard himself ask her.

"What do you mean?" Eve asked, although the beat of her blood in her veins knew perfectly well what he meant.

"You are somebody *other*, somebody else than the famous Maddy, Maddy with no last name, who sings at the Casino de Paris. I know I'm right . . . tell me who you really are," he commanded.

Eve considered her reply as she drank a few drops of wine. Since she had come to Paris four years before, she had not spoken of her origins, not even to Vivianne de Biron. Some deep instinct had told her not to share with anyone in the world of the music hall the knowledge that she came from a milieu that they sneered at, and were so profoundly scorned by in return.

But this man, this stranger, for all that she knew of his courage, his calmness and his endurance, this almost-stranger, Paul de Lancel, awoke a fearlessness in her and a curiously deep need, a thirst that literally compelled her to talk about herself. There was abandon in the feeling of challenge he aroused. She trusted him, she understood suddenly, trusted him so instinctively that it frightened her. She knew him so little. Yet, after that night in the bombed-out farmhouse, it seemed as if she already knew him too well to hide behind an identity that was only a part of her.

"I was born in Dijon," she said with a sigh of memory, "and my name is not Maddy, nor can I be addressed as Madame. To be precise, I am Mademoiselle Eve Coudert, a bourgeois name not considered suitable for the marquee of a music hall. As a girl I wanted—too much, perhaps—to see what lay beyond the horizon. I came to Paris—or rather I ran away from home to Paris—when I was seventeen, with a man I scarcely knew. I was utterly innocent and utterly reckless. In fact —quite mad. I had been brought up to be a lady and to make a good marriage. I hated that thought, but it was the only future my family intended for me. I was ridiculously in love as well as very foolish. Soon the man broke my heart—which was only to be expected. However, I disgraced my family, as well as myself. My parents have never even come to see me, although I write to them every week. My father is a celebrated doctor, my mother is one of the most respectable women in Dijon. And I . . . I am known as Maddy."

"He broke your heart, you said?" Paul interrupted, incredulous at the violent jealousy that had gripped him the minute Eve said those words. He had not paid attention to anything else from that phrase on.

"I thought so at the time. It felt that way."

"Has it mended?" he demanded.

"I'm sure it must have. Although for years it may only have been frozen . . . Don't all girls of seventeen have mendable hearts?"

"And since this man?" Paul insisted, with stern vigilance.

"I have been very careful not to give my heart away again."

"Are you absolutely sure of that?" Paul had a mad impulse to uncoil her hair, unplait it and pull it back from her forehead, so that he could see just how she would look as she woke in the morning.

"One minute, *mon colonel*—is this an interrogation?"

"Does it matter?"

"Perhaps not," Eve answered after a long pause. Her pulse beat visibly in her uncovered throat.

"You know it doesn't. Here, give me your hands to hold," he demanded.

"In public?" She had to lean forward so that he could hear her low tremulous question.

"You ran away with some wretch who hurt you, and now you won't even give me your hands?"

"I told you I have been very careful."

"You'll have to forget all about that now," Paul said sternly.

"Will I?" Her lips parted, her eyelids almost closed. A wave of emotion held her breathless, immobile, waiting for his next words. He had astonished her with his directness, his frank intensity, in a way she hadn't felt since she had risen over Dijon in a big red balloon and seen the great possibilities that lay beyond the blue horizon. The beginning of rapture made the dining room of the Ritz fade as if it were only a backdrop in a darkened theater.

"You know you will. You know it perfectly well, Mademoiselle Eve Coudert."

"You are very good at giving orders," Eve said, with the last resistance she possessed.

"You'll have plenty of time to get used to it."

"How . . . how long . . . ?" she whispered.

"A lifetime," he said as he took both of her shaking hands and raised them to his warm lips. "I promise you a lifetime."

The maître d'hôtel, who had been observing Paul and Eve from a well-disciplined distance, was not surprised to see Colonel de Lancel signal him for the bill halfway through the perfectly prepared and presented meal that he and his beautiful companion had virtually ignored. He had known the colonel since he was a boy, visiting Paris for the first time with his parents, who always stayed at the Ritz, but he had never seen the young vicomte in love before, no matter how many times he had dined at the Ritz since he became a man. In fact, the maître d'hôtel had made a bet with himself that they would not manage to get as far as their main course before they abandoned all pretense of eating. He lost his bet, for the colonel allowed it to be served, and managed to take one bite of it, yet he won, for the colonel tipped him five times as much as was normal.

Outside the Ritz, Paul hailed an open horse-drawn carriage. "Drive along the river," he directed the coachman as he handed Eve into the carriage. Cheerfully the man swung his horse around the Place Vendôme and down the Rue de Castiglione in the direction of the Seine at a pace that was at one with the lingering warmth of the May night, as if this trip down the *quai* were a voyage of discovery, leisurely, yet new in all its elements, rather than a circuit that he and his horse had made a thousand times before.

In the restaurant of the Ritz, Paul and Eve had been able to talk with a sense of freedom because they were surrounded by spectators whose presence put limits on their intimacy. However, the lack of privacy and the need to pretend to eat soon became unendurable, but now, alone except for the indifferent back of the coachman, they suddenly found themselves tongue-tied, awkward and confused.

He had promised her a lifetime, Eve thought. What did that mean? Was it a figure of speech? Was it a soldier's bravado? Were his words those of a man who wanted a brief affair before he returned to the business of war? Was Paul de Lancel the kind of man—and there were many such—who would use big words for that small purpose? In the course of the greetings he had exchanged with the maître d'hôtel at the Ritz, she had learned that he was a vicomte and a member of the Lancel champagne family. If a man from such a background promised her a lifetime, would it not be as his mistress, a woman he would keep in the background of his life? What exactly did he expect, this man whom she had allowed to take her to dinner—to half a dinner, to be precise —only tonight? This man who already knew more about her than anyone in the world?

He had promised her a lifetime, Paul thought. Did she understand that he wanted to marry her? Had he made himself sufficiently plain? No clearly defined plans had been discussed because a waiter had arrived at their table with the first course at the moment he uttered those words. Somehow they had been left suspended in the air, and with food set before them, the evanescent mood had changed in a maddening way that prevented him from returning to the subject. How could he reasonably expect that a woman who had never known him until a few hours ago would understand the way he felt about her? How could she possibly return his emotions? Was Eve the kind of woman who would let him declare himself and then play with him, enjoying her power? He knew nothing about her except the brief sketch of her life he had extracted from her, and she knew even less about him.

They sat silently, not touching, as the carriage turned left when it reached the riverbank and proceeded toward the oldest part of Paris, the heart of the city, where a tribe of riverboat fishermen called the Parisii made their first settlements on an island in the middle of the Seine. If the driver of the carriage had turned right, they would have passed the vast spaces of Imperial France, the Place de la Concorde and the Grand Palais, monumental symbols of an unequaled grandeur, but in turning left the coachman brought them quickly into humble, lively quarters where everything is scaled for humans and nothing is symbolic unless it is the tower of a church.

"Stop here, please, driver," Paul said as they reached the Pont Neuf. "Would you like to walk on the bridge?" he asked Eve.

"Yes," she answered. Anything to break this stiff trance of incomprehension in which she was caught, her mind bristling with a thousand questions and her lips incapable of expressing even one of them.

The Pont Neuf, the oldest bridge in Paris, cuts across the tip of that island, the Ile de la Cité, where the Parisii built their first huts, and it possesses a particular gentle magic that exists only where man has lived longest. Friendly ghosts seemed to promenade along the stone pavement, keeping up with Eve and Paul as they strolled to the middle of the bridge, joined only by his hand at her elbow. The wide bridge was almost abandoned, and when they reached its center they turned into one of the twelve semicircular bays that hang out over the Seine. Leaning on the edge of the bay, they had an uninterrupted view of the length of the river as it rushed with surprising speed through the city toward the ocean, the moonlight falling in such a broad path on the water that Paris itself seemed to have disappeared.

"Isn't it like being on shipboard?" Paul asked.

"I've never made a sea voyage," Eve answered.

They lapsed into a new silence, but the few words they had managed to exchange had eased their embarrassment and they turned toward each other at the same instant. Paul took Eve into his arms and kissed her lips for the first time.

She drew back and looked up into his eyes, which were so deeply set under his brows that she couldn't puzzle out his expression.

"Why . . . why did you want me to sing 'Till We Meet Again' that night in the farmhouse?" Eve asked, amazed that among all the complicated questions that crowded her mind, she had asked about an unimportant detail of an event that had happened when she hadn't even known Paul's name.

"Perhaps it was . . . foolish of me, but I knew none of the men understood English and I wanted to hear you sing something for me alone, something I could remember forever, without sharing it with anyone," Paul answered slowly. "I . . . I fell in love with you . . . while you were singing to the men in French. There were words in the song that I wanted to imagine you *saying* to me, and it was the only way I could think of—do you remember those words? 'Wedding bells will ring so merrily, every tear will be a memory, so wait and pray each night for me, till we meet again.' "

"Wedding bells?" Eve whispered.

"Even then. I knew it was the only thing I wanted. Wedding bells —Eve, *will* you marry me?"

She hesitated, frightened again by the way Paul de Lancel stripped her of all her hard-won self-protective instincts. And yet . . . and yet . . . could she *now* fail to dare? Could she draw back from adventure? Could she try to avoid . . . love? For that was what she felt for him, nothing less than love.

"It has been more than three hours since you came to my dressing room," Eve temporized, for one last earthbound instant. "Why have you waited so long to ask?"

"It took me two years to find you again."

"Ah . . . in that case . . ."

" 'In that case'?"

"Yes, *mon colonel,* yes!"

Vicomte Jean-Luc de Lancel, Paul's father, looked up from the letter he had just torn open.

"Wonderful news, darling!" he announced joyously to his wife, Anette, "Paul's getting married—in fact, from the date on this letter, I think he must be married already."

"Thank God! Oh, how I've prayed for this! After poor Laure died, I thought he'd never laugh again. Show me that letter. Who is she? Where did he meet her? When did they get married?" the Vicomtesse asked eagerly.

"Just a minute—let me read more. Ah—she's from Dijon, almost a neighbor, Anette! Eve Coudert—by God, Doctor Didier Coudert's daughter—he's the man everyone goes to for liver, darling. Your brother-in-law consulted him only a few years ago, don't you remember? They've known each other for—that's odd—he says that they met briefly the end of the first year of the war, and now, it appears, they met again—only last week! No one could get married in just a week before the war, but now they've changed the rules, eh? He writes that she's good and brave and beautiful—can't ask for more than that, can you? Of course, they won't have a honeymoon, but what does that matter? The important thing is they'll be in Paris now that Paul's working as liaison with the Americans. When can we go and visit them, Anette? I want to lay my eyes on my new daughter-in-law."

"Doctor Coudert's daughter, you said?"

"Yes. Why, does he have several of them?"

"Only one that I know of," she said grimly.

"You know of this girl?"

"*Everyone* knows of this girl."

"What are you talking about? And why do you look so sour? I've never heard of her."

"A year before the war started, no one talked of anything else—no one in certain circles. She ran away, decamped, disappeared, whatever you want to call it, with, I understand, some dreadful man or other, something thoroughly disreputable, something terribly *dishonorable* that the Couderts kept as quiet as possible for as long as they could. Marie-France de Courtizot, her aunt, was in on it too. My cousin Claire is a friend of Baronne de Courtizot's, and when it all came out—well! It was even more disgraceful than they'd thought. Oh, my poor Paul!"

"What do you mean, 'even worse'? Does she have a child?"

"Not as far as I know. That kind of woman makes sure not to have children. She's . . . she sings. She *performs* in a music hall. In Paris."

"A *music hall!* You're sure?"

"Absolutely. The Couderts never speak of her, but apparently she has become a great success—'famous,' they say. They mean *infamous.* There's no doubt about it. There was only one daughter, and this is the woman our son has married." The Vicomtesse began to sob.

"Anette, Anette . . . stop, I beg of you. Remember that Paul loves her. Think how unhappy he's been—isn't it more important that he's found someone to love?"

"A woman like that! Can't you imagine why she married him? It's a desperate grab at respectability, the classic last resort of a woman fallen so low. But she's wrong if she thinks that she can ever hope to be accepted here. Worst of all, after this war is over, his career will be ruined."

"Anette, how can you worry about that now? The essential thing is that Paul isn't at the front, that he will survive the war. What is this nonsense about his career? I prefer to believe in his judgment—that she *is* good, brave and beautiful. So what if she does sing? And in a music hall? Kings have married women who sang in music halls."

"And lost their thrones and been laughed at for the rest of their lives . . . and you know perfectly well that they never married those creatures, they *kept* them. This woman caused a great scandal. Her past will follow her all of her life. Do you honestly think that a diplomat with such a wife can hope to rise in his career?"

"A diplomat's wife is as important to him as his brains—perhaps more so," Jean-Luc de Lancel said with a profound sigh. Anette, as usual, was more practical than he was.

"This . . . person . . . he has married can never be the wife of an ambassador, you know that as well as I do. At the Quai d'Orsay he will never be forgiven for her. Our brilliant son has ruined himself for her, he has sacrificed his career."

"I wonder how much he knew about her before this sudden marriage?"

"As little as possible, obviously," the Vicomtesse said with visceral animosity.

"Perhaps not. Or perhaps he knew everything and believed that whatever it cost him, it was worth it," Vicomte de Lancel said, but his wistful words had no conviction behind them.

"He is a man in love, in wartime—that is to say, a fool," she retorted scornfully.

"Then he has been duped. He would never have married her in peacetime." Paul's father's voice hardened as he crumpled his son's letter.

"Now do you wonder that they got married so quickly?"

"No, now I understand it. Only too well."

"You cannot be serious, Maddy," Jacques Charles said, jumping up from behind his desk. "I refuse to believe you. How can you quit? If it were because some other producer had made you a better offer, I could see what you were trying to do . . . I wouldn't like it. I'd wring your pretty neck and have to give you a bigger dressing room and a good hard kick in the ass—but to quit the stage! For good! It simply doesn't make sense."

"Does your wife sing at the Casino de Paris?"

"Well . . . no, but what does that have to do with it? She can't carry a tune."

"And if she could? Every night, when you got home for dinner, would you be overjoyed to learn that Madame Charles had already left for the theater, or was still busy fitting her new costumes, or had a rehearsal of her new songs, or was being interviewed by a journalist? Would you enjoy waiting till after midnight for her to return, every night of the week but the one when the Casino de Paris is dark?"

"No. I would not! Damn you, Maddy!"

"So you do understand. In spite of yourself."

"Let's admit that I can comprehend the situation as a man who is no different from other men. But for you—*a star? Never!* Do you even begin to realize what you're giving up to be home for dinner? Why the devil couldn't you have had a love affair with the fellow? Who told you to get married? Do you think that stardom is something you can throw away this year and expect to find again, next year, when—and it is always possible, in spite of the way you feel now about your gallant colonel—you discover that you are horribly bored with being married and desperately miss the audience, miss the applause, miss the love of the people who come to hear you?"

"*Patron*, a week ago everything you're saying would have made absolute sense. I would have told someone like me the same thing. Perhaps even less tactfully. But now . . . when you speak of just being home for dinner . . . it's all I want."

"I can't stand how happy you look, God damn it!"

"You're too soft-hearted, *Patron*," Eve laughed gleefully.

"Get out of here. And, Maddy, when you're ready—*if* you're ever ready, I should say—will you come back? The audience is more faithful than any lover, any husband. A revue just for you, the revue I've been planning—well, I can't give you that again—but Maddy, if anything ever changes, you will come back?"

"Of course," Eve said, still laughing, and threw her arms around his neck and kissed him on both cheeks in farewell. What did the words cost her? It would never happen.

In 1912, when Paul-Sebastian de Lancel had married Laure de Saint-Fraycourt, the only child of the Marquis and Marquise de Saint-Fraycourt, his own family had been delighted. The Saint-Fraycourts were unhappily resigned. Laure, so dark, so fragile and already so elegant, was counted as one of the most beautiful girls of her generation. She was the only heir the Saint-Fraycourts possessed, and all of their fortune would go to her, a fortune as old as it was diminished.

However, to the Saint-Fraycourts, mere money was totally irrelevant. The *marquisat* of Saint-Fraycourt was a title so distinguished, so ancient, and so linked to the history of France that they considered it to be a vastly significant and powerful dowry. True, the title would die with the death of the present marquis, but Laure's children, no matter whom she married, would always be known as Saint-Fraycourts, before anything else. In the small circle of the highest aristocracy of France, the fact that their mother had been born a Saint-Fraycourt would gain them instant acceptance and the highest status. The Saint-Fraycourts knew that it was impossible to overestimate the absolute importance of ancient blood, and in the world in which they moved, where everyone knew everyone else, they were not wrong.

Of course, it had always been expected that Laure would marry exquisitely well. The last of the Saint-Fraycourts, she had grown up like an idol, cherished, prized, almost venerated. As she began to show clear signs of future beauty, her parents became as besotted as was possible for any French to be.

When she chose Vicomte Paul-Sebastian de Lancel, they were profoundly disappointed. Yes, he came from an ancient family, but he was not the eldest son. True, the Lancels were unquestionably aristocrats, of the old regime, but they were not of the transcendent quality of aristocracy that the Saint-Fraycourts expected. Their name counted for much in Champagne, but it was not that of a Duke and Peer of France.

Pre-Revolutionary Lancels had not spent their lives at Versailles, intimates of the King. Yes, Paul had a brilliant career, but it was largely in front of him. Eventually he would inherit half of the House of Lancel, no small fortune, but that was merely reasonable. However, there was nothing about Paul de Lancel they could reasonably oppose, they realized, no one thing serious enough to persuade Laure that she had made a mistake.

They could not find any saving grace in Paul's future possession of the world famous vineyards, which, one day, he would have to share with his brother. For their daughter to be connected to a château that had a name that appeared on the label of a bottle! The normal French esteem for wine-producing acres was not shared by the Saint-Fraycourts, who reserved their respect for direct, linear descendants of the house of Hugh Capet, first King of France, and those few whose ancestors had possessed high positions at court.

Laure had been happy in the first year of her marriage, and the Saint-Fraycourts might eventually have softened toward their son-in-law. However, he had the criminal insanity to throw himself into the army in spite of Laure's pregnancy. Their patriotism, like all their other emotions, took second place to Laure's welfare. Clearly, Paul's true and first responsibility lay with his wife and his child, and with no lack of honor, he should have waited to go off to war until after the baby was born.

He killed her, they told each other after Laure died, he killed her as surely as if he'd wrung her delicate neck with his brutal farmer's hands. Laure had never been the same after he left for the front; in her despair she had not eaten properly, she had not taken any exercise, she had literally pined away for him, and when the baby came, she had been too weak, too sad, to survive. He had taken away their only treasure and treated her with such cruelty that it amounted to torture.

Broken, and so far beyond bitterness that there was no word for their emotion, the grandparents took the baby, Bruno, and went to Switzerland, where at least there was the possibility that their priceless heir, Laure's one legacy, the child for whom she had given her life, would not be harmed.

In wartime as in peacetime, rumors travel faster than the mails, and by the time Paul's letter to the Saint-Fraycourts, announcing his marriage, arrived in Geneva, they had been informed of every detail, down to the particular shade of red in the costumes Eve wore on stage.

Normally, scandals involving the upper classes of the bourgeoisie, to which the Couderts belonged, would never have reached their ears, since no one they knew well would have been interested in discussing such people.

However, Baronne Marie-France de Courtizot existed on the far fringes of their world, for, in spite of the fact that her father had been nothing more than a rich merchant of cassis, she had managed to achieve acquaintance with certain members of the innermost aristocracy, the world of the Faubourg Saint-Germain.

Baron Claude de Courtizot spent a major part of his large income on maintaining his own hunt. The Courtizot horses and the Courtizot hounds ran over land on which deer abounded, and the baron was open-handedly generous with them, a fact that could not remain long unappreciated by members of the hunting-mad nobility whose purses had been restricted over the passage of time. Even when their ancestors had lost their heads and their lands, they had passed on their titles and their love of the hunt. The Courtizot title was newly minted, as far as they were concerned, almost worse than no title at all, given, as it had been, by that fellow Napoleon, but Claude was suitably humble about it.

But now! Throughout the salons of the Faubourg Saint-Germain a cloud of gossip rose over the teacups of the possessors of the oldest names in France. In 1914, when it had come out that there existed a Courtizot niece, a niece who, unthinkably, incredibly, performed in a dreadful common place, a vulgar music hall—the next thing to a *bordel* —in which she was doubtless surrounded by naked showgirls, if she was not actually one herself—or worse—the scandal that had been created had almost cost the Courtizots their small place in the world.

However, they had been forgiven because they simply weren't important enough to be treated as outcasts. But now! *That niece*, whom one kindly never mentioned to a rather pathetic Marie-France, had become the stepmother of the only grandson of the Saint-Fraycourts. Now the scandal reached directly into the heart of their own world.

Was it not, one bored and malicious duchess asked another, almost too good to be true? Yes, of course, it was a dreadful tragedy for the Saint-Fraycourts—those poor people, one simply had to feel sorry for them. Who would ever have believed that such a thing could happen to people who were so haughty, when actually their rank was no different from one's own? One had never been terribly fond of them, to be frank, but one had to grant them their right to their pride. They were people one had always known, no matter how cold and arrogant they were. Should one try to pretend that one hadn't heard about it, or should one, as tactfully as possible, of course, show the Saint-Fraycourts that one felt the most delicate sympathy? Should one write a note, just a few words? Or should one retire into a discreet silence, as if it had not happened? What a fascinating, what a downright—should one admit it even to oneself?—delicious dilemma.

"How are you going to answer Lancel's letter?" the Marquise de Saint-Fraycourt asked her husband.

"I'm not sure. As long as he was at the front, I prayed every day that I would hear that he had been killed." The Marquis de Saint-Fraycourt spoke dryly and concisely. "Millions of Frenchmen dead, and Lancel merely wounded. Indeed, there is no justice under heaven."

"What if he should send for Bruno, now that he has a wife?"

"A wife? He has thrown filth on the grave of our daughter. I beg you, my dear, do not speak of this person as his wife."

"Nevertheless, he may want to take Bruno back, now that he is settled in Paris."

"Paris is under attack. There can be no question of such a move."

"But one day," the Marquise said somberly, "the war will be over."

"You know as well as I do that Bruno belongs to us. Even if Lancel had married someone worthy of becoming Bruno's stepmother, I have never had any intention of letting him go back to that man." His voice was thinner than ever, like the sound of wind on a dead leaf.

"How can you be so calm?"

"My dear, some things in life are so evident, so right, that they leave no room for question. Bruno's future is one of these things. He is not a Lancel, he is a Saint-Fraycourt, and he will never be soiled by contact with that murderer and the person he has chosen to live with. I would kill Paul de Lancel myself before I would let him have Bruno. The less he understands us, the less trouble we will have with him. I believe I will answer his letter after all."

"What will you say?"

"Why, I shall wish him happiness in his marriage, of course."

"How can you bring yourself to do that?"

"To keep Bruno with us, I could embrace his . . . whore."

In late September of 1918, two months before the Armistice brought the war to an end, Eve gave birth to a daughter, Delphine, named after Paul's maternal grandmother. Paul was demobilized three months after the war ended, and on his return to the diplomatic service early in 1919, he was posted to Canberra as First Secretary of the French Embassy in Australia, the Quai d'Orsay's equivalent of Siberia.

Eve was overjoyed by the move to Australia because of Delphine. The baby was afflicted with the malady called croup, which attacked her without warning, signaled only by a sudden cough that sounded exactly like the barking of a dog, followed by anguished gasping for air. The only way to ease the croup was to hold Delphine in a cloud of steam until her throat expanded and she was able to breathe normally, but steam was a priceless commodity in France during the first year after the war. The shortage of coal was worse than it had been before the peace, and electricity was still so precious that the Métro ran on a wartime schedule.

Australia, with its plenty, was a blessing to the anxious parents. There, in one of the comfortable Victorian villas of Canberra, with its wide verandas and large garden, Eve could almost relax, secure in the knowledge that she could fill the large bathroom with hot steam in a matter of minutes. The best pediatrician in Canberra, Doctor Henry Head, examined Delphine and pronounced her perfect in every respect.

"Don't worry yourself too much about the croup, Madame de Lancel," he said. "There's nothing you or I can do that you don't know about already, and I can promise you that this young lady will grow out of it. There's a theory that it's caused by a baby's short neck. As soon as her neck grows longer, and it will, you know, all by itself, you won't hear that cough again. Keep a steam kettle going, night and day, in her room for three days after an attack and call me at any time if you need me."

On the ninth of January, 1920, not even a year and a half later, another daughter, Marie-Frédérique, was born to Eve and Paul de Lancel. Doctor Head, who had been called in by Eve's obstetrician to look over the new baby, hoped fervently that this little girl wouldn't be a victim of croup too. He knew how often Delphine had given her parents days and nights of tormenting worry, and in the privacy of his thoughts, he wondered why they had had another child so soon. It seemed to him that Madame de Lancel had more than enough on her plate, coping with the constant crises caused by the sickly baby, without the burden of another infant.

Eve had engaged a capable nurse for the two children, but in the year following Marie-Frédérique's birth she rarely slept for more than an hour or two at a time, waking constantly during the night to listen for Delphine's breathing, only able to return to the bed she shared with Paul after she stood listening, by the child's crib, for a half hour at a time.

At first Eve had been anxious for Marie-Frédérique too, but the baby demonstrated the kind of good health the British called "rude." Just looking at her was a reassurance. She had the red hair of the Lancels, and the blue eyes as well. She was as plump and sturdy and red cheeked and smiling as her sister was delicate and pale and given to crying for no reason anyone could discover.

Yet Delphine was of a rare and ravishing beauty, a beauty that had nothing childlike about it, a beauty so exceptional that her parents could take little pleasure in it, since it was so often threatened by that doglike barking cough in the night.

During the first four years after the war, until Marie-Frédérique's second birthday, Paul had been forced to agree with the Marquis de Saint-Fraycourt that Bruno should remain in Switzerland with his grandparents. During those two overwhelming years, when Marie-Frédérique was under two and Delphine was enduring the worst years yet of croup, Paul admitted, unhappily, that to burden Eve with the responsibility of a third child would be asking too much of her.

However, in 1922, when Bruno was seven, Paul wrote his former father-in-law and asked that his son be sent to join him as soon as possible.

"He writes," the Marquis de Saint-Fraycourt said to his wife, his tone as measured, as spare as ever, his concise, small lips set in their usual compressed lines, "that at last it is time for his son to join his daughters."

"He used those words?" the Marquise asked indignantly.

"Precisely. As if they were all part of the same pack, our Bruno and the two brats he has got from that person."

"How will you answer him?"

"I do not intend to answer this letter. It took weeks to get here, so presumably it could have been lost in the mails. It will be several more weeks before Lancel can expect my response. Then he will wait, believing perhaps that we are traveling, and after a month he will write again. Then you, my dear, shall answer, pleading my ill health. You will tell him that the doctors inform you that I have not many months to live, and you shall request that Bruno stay with us just a short while longer. Even a brute such as Lancel cannot deny this request. My illness will last and last . . . indeed, I shall *linger*." The Marquis permitted himself a brief smile. "You will, of course, write to him to report on my condition frequently. He must not be allowed to worry about our eventual intentions."

"And when shall you be forced to recover your health, my dear?"

"It is now almost March. Sometime next autumn, as late in the year as possible, I will send him a letter myself, explaining that although I am still extremely weak, I believe that I am on my way to recovery. However, I will throw myself on his mercy. I will tell him that my only joy during the months of my illness—I beg your pardon for saying this, my dear—was the daily visit of Bruno to my bedside. I will ask for a few more months in which to complete my recovery, just until the Christmas holidays are over, until the beginning of 1923, and I will promise to send Bruno out to Australia at that time."

"Then what?"

"I fear that you must be the next of us to fall ill. Far more seriously than I. And for a longer time."

"You can't expect Lancel to wait indefinitely just because one of us is sick," the Marquise protested. "This is the man who left for the war when Laure was expecting a child."

"That is *exactly* what I am counting on. He cannot have forgotten that our poor child implored him not to leave her. He cannot have forgotten that if he had only remained with her a few more months, as he so easily could have done, she would be alive today. And if he should have forgotten how guilty he is, you may count on me to remind him. He will not want another death on his conscience. Furthermore, I shall tell him, if he doesn't understand it by now, that Bruno has never known another mother than you. It is unthinkable that he could tear a child away from his mother when that mother is dying."

"For how long can my terminal illness be drawn out?" the Marquise asked, with a faint, superstitious quiver.

"Fortunately for a very long time. You have the best medical attention in Europe and you are a strong woman. You will have complications—complications upon complications—yet you will continue to draw breath, thanks only to the miraculous presence of Bruno, who gives you a reason to live. In this way we will gain—oh, at least a year and a half, perhaps two. By 1925, who knows what may have happened?"

"What if Lancel decides to come suddenly, without warning, and fetch Bruno himself?"

"Nonsense. He cannot come from Australia in a twinkling of an eye. It is a long journey. Like all First Secretaries, he has a heavy schedule of official duties—I have made it my business to keep myself informed of his affairs, and I assure you that my friends at the Quai d'Orsay will not allow him to take several months' leave for purely personal matters. But . . ."

"What?"

"One day, unquestionably, he will come."

"Bruno is seven now. Can we hope for more than four years' respite before Lancel demands his rights?"

"I am counting on no more than four. But by then Bruno will be eleven. No longer a child, my dear. And a Saint-Fraycourt in every sense."

In 1924, after almost five years in Australia, Paul de Lancel was posted to Cape Town as Consul General. The domestic upheaval caused by the new position forced him to postpone yet again a journey back to Paris, which he had long planned, in order to see the ailing Marquise de Saint-Fraycourt and arrange, finally, for Bruno to join his family. The frequent letters and photographs he received from the Marquis, and from Bruno himself, had done much to relieve Paul's mind on the subject of his son. Certainly the boy seemed entirely happy and busy in the Parisian life to which his grandparents had returned in 1923. He did not lack for friends or family pleasures, since he took his place, as a cousin, among the many grandchildren of the family.

However, it was growing increasingly difficult to realize that he actually had a son, Paul thought. The newborn baby he had seen only once during the first year of the war had lived more than nine years without being reunited with his father. If he were not a career diplomat, condemned to go to the ends of the earth at the command of his government, the boy would have been returned to him as soon as the war ended. The subsequent ill health of the Marquis and Marquise had created an impossible situation, but he felt he was too indebted to them for their care of his child during the war years to take Bruno away suddenly. It would be condemning to a tragic end people who had already lost so much.

With every letter from them he was reminded again of the loss of Laure. They wrote stoically, yet the letters were all the more powerful for a restraint he suspected they forced themselves to maintain so as not to reopen his own wounds.

But Bruno was his son. His place was with his father. The situation was unnatural in spite of its having happened so inevitably. No one was to blame. Everyone was to blame. And as soon as he had settled into the Consulship in Cape Town, as soon as the office was running smoothly, as soon as Eve and the girls had moved into their new home, he would return to Paris and not come back unless Bruno was with him.

Troubled, Paul de Lancel walked along the Rue de Varenne toward the entrance to Bruno's school. It was June of 1925. He had just arrived in Paris and immediately paid a visit to the Marquise de Saint-Fraycourt. What an effort she had made, he thought, actually to receive him in her sickroom. He knew that for such a proud woman to be forced to be seen lying helplessly in bed, with an embroidered bed jacket modestly covering her nightgown, must have been a humiliation, no matter how much she had protested that she must greet him in person. She had been so pale, so slow to speak, and obviously in pain, although she had insisted, as of course she would, that she was on the road to recovery. It must be cancer, he decided. In his letters the Marquis de Saint-Fraycourt had been unwilling to dwell on the exact nature of her illness in the way that, in Paul's experience, always meant cancer.

The Marquis still insisted that only Bruno's presence kept the Marquise alive, yet surely, Paul told himself, the Marquise must be putting the boy's future ahead of her own suffering. She had visibly repressed her unhappiness when Paul told her of his plans for Bruno to rejoin him, and she had not attempted to dissuade him from his intention. Could it be that she saw her own end near, and therefore was able to make this sacrifice? Was she so weary that she had no power left to try to keep the boy, or was she being ultimately unselfish?

He didn't understand her and he never would, Paul realized, as he approached closer to the school. The Marquise de Saint-Fraycourt belonged to this part of Paris, this walled, closed, secret heart of the *Ancien Régime*, where great houses stood like a maze of splendid gray fortresses, protected by their walled courtyards to which the uninvited could never gain entrance, their huge gardens hidden forever from view to anyone but their noble proprietors who lived in vast rooms with creaking parquet floors and sublime proportions. How different it had been for him, growing up in the open air of Champagne, running in and out of Valmont with his dogs, a part of ever-renewing nature. The Lancels had been too busy supervising the growth of the grapes, and the honor of the *Marque*, to make a ritual out of pure tradition, he mused, but in the Seventh Arrondissement, where the descendants of the highest nobility in France still lived, ancestor worship hung like incense in the air.

Paul turned a corner and stood on the curb, waiting. In a few minutes, Bruno would emerge from school. Bruno knew his father was going to be there, but Paul had not yet written him of his plan to be reunited with him. That, he decided, must be announced in person.

The massive doors swung open as the first group of boys rushed out into the sunshine. They were too young, Paul saw immediately. Bruno would not be among them. Paul was tense with suspense. He had thought it would be easier to first meet his son like this, in the open air, but now he longed for the formality of the Saint-Fraycourt salon, for the presence of other people, to blur the edges of this difficult, too-long-postponed reunion.

Another swarm of boys left the school, all dressed alike in their blue blazers and gray flannel shorts, the school caps on their heads, and heavy, brown book bags slung across their chests. They lingered in the doorway, joking in high animation before they disappeared in different directions, each boy giving his fellows the brisk, indispensable handshake of farewell.

The tallest boy of all approached Paul.

"Good day, Father," Bruno said with composure, extending his hand. Paul took it automatically, too surprised to speak. He had no idea that ten-year-old Bruno would be so tall, as tall as any fourteen-year-old Paul had ever seen. His voice, clear, high and even, was that of the child he still was, but his handshake was vigorous and his features were already well formed. Paul blinked with startled eyes at his son. Dark hair, well cut and well kept; dark eyes flecked with green that met his own with frank curiosity; a high, thin, arched nose, the Saint-Fraycourt nose; and, unexpectedly, a small smiling mouth, the only somewhat disappointing feature of a handsome face which otherwise was remarkable for its definition and purpose.

The moment had passed when he could have embraced his son, Paul realized in confusion, as he found himself walking by Bruno's side. Just as well perhaps, for the boy's poise was surely hard-fought-for, and a hug, certainly a kiss, might have destroyed it.

"Bruno, you can't know how happy I am to see you," Paul said.

"Do I look as you hoped, Father?" Bruno asked politely.

"Much better, Bruno, much, much better."

"Grandmother says I look just like my mother," Bruno continued calmly, and as he spoke, Paul realized that the small, full mouth was Laure's mouth. It was oddly shocking to see it on a male face.

"You do, yes, you do indeed. Tell me, Bruno, do you like school?" Even as he asked, Paul cursed himself for the banal question that every child must hear from every adult. Yet Bruno brightened, his grown-up composure becoming suddenly the enthusiasm of his age. "It's the best school in the Seventh, you know, and I'm at the head of my class."

"I'm delighted to hear that, Bruno."

"Thank you, Father. There are boys who have to study much longer hours than I do, but I get the best marks. I don't even mind taking exams. What's there to be afraid of, when you're really prepared? My two best friends, Geoffrey and Jean-Paul, give me a lot of competition, but so far I'm keeping just ahead of them. One day the three of us together will run France."

"What!"

"Yes, that's what Jean-Paul's father says, and he's president of the State Council. He says that only boys who start out like us can make it to the top. The future leaders of France are all destined to come from a few schools in Paris, so we've got every chance. It's my ambition to be Prime Minister one day, Father."

"Isn't it a little early in life to decide on your career?"

"Not at all. If I hadn't decided by now, it would almost be too late. Geoffrey and Jean-Paul aren't any older than I am. We know already how well we must do on the Baccalaureate—that's only a few years away. Then we have to pass the entrance exams for the Institute for Political Studies. But once we've graduated from 'Sciences Po,' well . . . we'll be in. Then it will just be competition from the other graduates. I'm not going to worry about that now."

"Good," Paul said dryly. In his years out of his country, he realized, he had almost forgotten the elitist mind-set of the French ruling class. There was an unquestioning acceptance of a system based on a combination of intellectual superiority and access to the very few select schools. The system effectively eliminated any other kind of person from participating in the government of France. It utterly rejected the outsider, although unquestionably it attracted the most brilliant minds and formed them early. Somehow, Paul had never expected Bruno to be part of this system. Certainly his letters had not indicated the ambition he so obviously felt, but then they had always been short and impersonal.

"Don't you have any time to have fun, or is it all study, Bruno?" he asked, worried at the image of a child spending all his time on schoolwork.

"All study?" Bruno laughed briefly. "Of course not. I have fencing classes twice a week, Father. My fencing master is very pleased with my progress, but the most important thing to me is riding. Didn't Grandfather send you a picture of me on horseback? I'm studying dressage already, because—no, don't laugh at me, Father, but I want to be on the French Olympic Equestrian Team someday. It's my biggest ambition."

"I thought you wanted to be Prime Minister?"

"You are laughing at me!" Bruno said angrily.

"No, Bruno, not at all, just teasing you." His son didn't seem to have a sense of humor, Paul thought. He must remember that he was just a child, after all, in spite of his grown-up talk about ambition. "There's no reason you can't do both."

"Exactly. That's what Grandfather said. I ride every weekend and during the school vacations. I'm too tall for ponies, of course, but my cousin François, Grandmother's nephew, has many wonderful horses, and he lives near Paris. I go there as often as I can—last Easter I spent the whole vacation at his château, and this summer he's invited me again, to stay as long as I like. His children all ride well. We intend to follow the hunt next winter, even though we're too young to join yet. I can't wait!"

As they walked the next few blocks, Bruno told Paul who lived in each of the great houses, which, to him, were familiar territory. There didn't seem to be one, except the embassies, which was not the home of one or another of his classmates, not one in which he had not played games in the secluded gardens and explored the attics and cellars. "This is the only part of Paris anyone would want to live in, don't you agree, Father?"

"I suppose so," Paul answered.

"I'm certain of it," Bruno said, with a conciseness that reminded Paul of the Marquis de Saint-Fraycourt. "Everything important is here. Even when I go to 'Sciences Po,' it's just right down that street."

"Bruno—"

"Yes, Father?"

Paul hesitated, drawing back for a moment from telling Bruno that next year he would be living in Cape Town. "I brought some photographs for you." He stopped on the street and took out the pictures he had taken of Eve and the girls in the garden of their house. "This one, these are your sisters." Bruno glanced at the picture of the two laughing little girls.

"They look nice," he said politely. "How old are they now?"

"Delphine is seven and Marie-Frédérique—she insists that we call her Freddy now—is five and a half. They were a little younger when this picture was taken."

"They are pretty children," Bruno said. "I don't know much about little girls."

"And this is my wife."

Bruno's eyes slid quickly away from the photo of Eve.

"Your stepmother is very anxious to grow to know you, Bruno."

"She is your wife, Father. But not my stepmother."

"What is that supposed to mean?" Paul demanded.

"I don't like the word *stepmother*. I had a mother, I have two grand-mothers, but I do not need a stepmother."

"Where did you get that idea?"

"It is not an idea, it is a feeling. I didn't 'get it' anywhere—I have always felt it, for as long as I can remember." For the first time, Bruno's voice trembled with emotion.

"That's only because you don't know her, Bruno. You wouldn't feel that way if you did, I assure you."

"I'm sure you're right." Bruno's brief, withdrawing words put the subject away on a distant shelf. Paul looked at his son's half-averted face, his features even more distinct and formed in profile than they were in full face, and put the photos back in the breast pocket of his jacket.

"Look, Bruno. I think that it is time for you to come and live with me," he said firmly.

"No!" The boy stepped back and his head snapped up.

"I understand your reaction, Bruno. I expected it. It's a new idea for you, but not for me. I'm your father, Bruno. Your grandparents have been the finest of grandparents, but they can't take the place of a father. You should be with me as you grow up."

"I am grown up!"

"No, Bruno, you're not. You're not even eleven years old."

"What does my age have to do with it?"

"Years matter, Bruno. You're mature for your age, but 'grown up' is something else. 'Grown up' means having a wider experience of life, so that you'll know more about yourself and other people than you do now."

"But *I have no time*! Surely you can see that if I went to live with you, even for a single year, I'd fall out of the race! Geoffrey and Jean-Paul would be ahead of me, and I could never get that lost year back. It would ruin my life! You don't think that they'd wait for me, do you?"

"I'm not talking about a single year. I'm talking about a different way of life."

"I don't want a different way of life!" Bruno said, his voice suddenly reaching a passionate pitch. "I have the best life in the world—my friends, my school, my plans for the future, my cousins, my grandparents—and you want to take me away from everything, just so that I can live with you. I'd lose everything I have! I'll never have a chance to lead my country," he cried hysterically. "I'll never even be able to ride in the Olympics for France, because suddenly you want me with you, as if you own me. I won't do it! I refuse to do it! You can't make me! You have no right!"

"Bruno . . ."

"Don't you care what it would mean to me?"

"I do, of course I do—it's only for your own good. . . ." Paul stopped, unable to continue. He heard his own words and he realized how unconvincing they sounded. What *did* he have to offer Bruno that could replace what the boy already had, aside from a father Bruno had apparently never missed? He would be tearing him away from the one place he belonged, from the one kind of life he knew, from all the ties and values and beliefs he had formed since he was born, from a world that existed nowhere else on earth. It would be like taking an animal out of a zoo and returning him to the wild. He would be miserably unhappy outside of the rarefied air of the Seventh Arrondissement.

"Bruno, we won't talk about it anymore now. I'll think over everything you've said. But this summer you must come and visit, for at least a month. I insist on that, at least. You may like it—who knows?"

"Of course, Father," Bruno murmured, suddenly subdued.

"Good," Paul said. A month of family life—that might make all the difference. He should have proposed that first. He should never have shocked the boy with such a new idea. He should . . . he should . . .

"Father, here's the house. Will you come in for tea? Grandfather will be there."

"Thank you, Bruno, but I have to get back to my hotel now. I'll come tomorrow, if I may."

"Of course you may—I'll take you to my fencing lesson if you like."

"Yes, I'd enjoy that," Paul said sadly.

"Well?" the Marquis de Saint-Fraycourt asked Bruno as the boy entered the salon.

"You were right, Grandfather."

"How did it go?"

"More or less as you expected. I said everything, just the way we decided. He wanted me to look at a picture of that person . . . that was the only part I didn't expect. I never thought he would dare to show me her photo. But I made him understand . . . I told you I could. There was no need for worry."

"I'm proud of you, my boy. Go tell your grandmother that she can get out of bed and join us now. We didn't know if he'd be coming back to tea, so we took no chances, eh? And, Bruno . . ."

"Yes, Grandfather?"

"Don't you think you should try to work harder at school, now that you are planning to lead your country?"

"France is led by functionaries and bureaucrats," Bruno said scornfully. "Not aristocrats. Isn't that what you've always told me?"

"So it is, my boy."

"But I really do intend to ride in the Olympics," Bruno said with a coaxing smile on his small, full mouth. "I was hoping that you might be thinking about giving me my own horse. My cousins each have one."

"The thought had crossed my mind."

"Thank you, Grandfather."

6

"OUR new posting might have been to Ulan Bator, think of it that way, darling," Paul said to Eve, to distract her from the view of the endless desert outside of the compartment window. Their train was the best that existed in this country in 1930, but its progress seemed imperceptible.

"Ulan Bator?" she asked, turning to him from the window.

"The capital of Outer Mongolia."

"Outer or Inner? Never mind, don't answer that. On the other hand, it could have been Godthaab," Eve retorted.

"Greenland? No, I would never have expected that—much too close to Europe," Paul answered with sardonic good humor.

"What about Fiji?" she asked. "Wouldn't you have liked that? It's so green, especially compared to this." She waved in dismissal at the glare of the desert sand.

"Suva has a nice climate, I understand, but it's a bit limited from the cultural point of view."

"Still, it is their capital. You would have been *Monsieur l'Ambassadeur*."

"Ambassador? I'm only forty-five. Still too young, don't you think?"

"Entirely too young. And much too good looking. It would have been unfair to the ladies of Fiji. I'm told they can't resist Frenchmen," Eve answered, squeezing his hand.

"What does that mean, 'can't resist Frenchmen'?" Freddy asked abruptly, her eyes, which she had closed in weariness only a few minutes before, popping wide open in interest.

"Ah . . . it means that they think Frenchmen are so charming that they will, oh, do anything a Frenchman wants them to do," Paul said laughingly, as he looked at Eve.

"Like what?" Freddy insisted.

"Like . . . well, I'm a Frenchman and that's why you're a good girl and do whatever I tell you to do."

"Daddy," Freddy said, giggling, "don't be silly."

"It wasn't a good example," Delphine said primly. "Freddy never does anything right, Daddy. I'm the one who can't resist Frenchmen."

She gave Paul the smile of a female who had been born to the uses of enchantment.

"I do so do things right," Freddy flashed. "Remember when you dared me to dive off the high diving board at the club and I did it and hit the water perfectly? Remember when you said I couldn't get on the new pony and ride him without a saddle, and I did and he didn't even try to bite me? Remember when you bet me that I couldn't win a fistfight with that big old bully, Jimmy Albright, and I jumped him and beat him up? Remember when you dared me to drive the car and . . ."

"Freddy! Delphine! Stop it, this minute," Eve said warningly. "It's almost time to arrive. There are bound to be some people waiting to greet us. Freddy, you have to wash your hands and wash your face and wash your knees and, oh, look at your elbows! How did you get your elbows dirty on a train? Good Lord, what happened to your dress? How did you get it so rumpled? No, no, don't tell me. I don't want to know. I'll try to do something about your hair myself. Delphine, let me look at you. Well, I suppose you could wash your hands, but it's not really necessary."

"They're clean."

"That's what I meant. How did you keep them so clean on a train all afternoon—no, don't tell me, I already know." Delphine was capable of sitting for hours, motionless and content, with only daydreams to occupy her, while Freddy rarely sat still for more than a minute. Eve looked at Paul, rolled her eyes and sighed.

The trip from Cape Town to Paul's new posting had taken them more than halfway around the world. Now, on the last lap of the weeks-long journey, they were confined in a train compartment where she and Paul had been exposed to more of their daughters than ever before since they had been small.

Surely parents and two little girls, one of twelve and one of ten and a half, weren't meant by any law of nature to be together for three solid days? No, it was unnatural, a thoroughly impossible situation, although less difficult to endure than the sight of the vast, almost frightening desert through which they had been traveling for endless hours. Was it possible that at their destination there would be anything that resembled civilization as she knew it? Canberra and Cape Town had not been metropolitan centers, true, but British tradition had been strong in both places, providing a feeling of continuity and establishment.

Eve had loved their big Cape Town home, with a superb view of Table Mountain, and a large, pleasant staff, but a career diplomat could no more refuse a new posting than he could not own a tailcoat, a suit of morning clothes, and three dinner jackets. She supposed she must regard this as a promotion. True, the city toward which they were traveling was only the fifth largest in this new country. True, Paul would still be Consul General, as far from an ambassadorship as ever, but nevertheless, he would be considered the head of the local French community, no matter how small. His philosophical, wry acceptance of his less-than-glorious career never failed him, but she knew, without any discussion of the matter, that he had been deeply disappointed to be posted yet again so far from the seat of any real power. Well, they would make the best of it, as they always had. The gentlemen who made these decisions had long memories and unbending rules . . . to them she was still that shockingly *déclassé* girl who sang on a music hall stage. But she and Paul had each other and the children, and that was all that really mattered to them.

The rhythm of the train slowed and, looking out of the windows, the four Lancels spied sign after sign that, after all, there was a city at the end of the desert. Shacks, small buildings, larger buildings of great ugliness, a few automobiles on a street, and finally, almost out of nowhere, a surprisingly large station could be seen in the near distance.

Three porters hurried through the corridor, carrying some of their dozens of pieces of baggage, while Freddy jumped up to stand on the seat, craning her neck in her characteristic impatience, so that her hat fell off, while Delphine checked the angle of her own hat, set precisely on her smooth hair, in the mirror that was attached to the flap of her small handbag. Eve felt a sudden apprehension as the train began to travel even more slowly, in the unmistakable cadence of arrival. Australia, South East Africa and now, of all places, this—surely as outlandish, as far from reality, as anything Jacques Charles could have imagined for a decor at the Casino de Paris.

"End of the line, folks," the porter said, coming in. "We're here."

"This is it, my love," Paul said, giving Eve his arm.

"Daddy," Freddy asked, "could I just ask you one more question before we get there?"

"Is it the same question you've been asking me the whole trip?"

"Sort of."

"Then why don't you ask the porter? You haven't asked him yet today."

"Sir," said Freddy, "do they really call this the City of the Angels?"

"Yes, miss, they sure do. Welcome to L.A."

Two months later, although Eve was supposed to be dressing for dinner, she found herself sinking down on the window seat in the bedroom listening to the doves begin to herald the approach of evening. The birds lived in the avenue of orange trees that lined the driveway that led to the entrance of their house, in the Los Feliz district, a gracious suburb northwest of the commercial center of Los Angeles.

The fragrance of the orange blossoms combined with the opening buds of climbing jasmine and the mingled scents of hundreds of rosebushes blooming in her garden. Was there, she asked herself in wonder, any other place on earth in which spring lasted so long or smelled so divine? Was Los Angeles the olfactory capital of the universe? She felt impregnated by the embrace of dusk, when trees and flowers released their drifts of aromas.

It had been spring when they arrived in February, a spring of piercingly sweet-smelling lemon blossoms, huge yellow and purple pansies, tiny violas, English primroses and spreading forget-me-nots; spring again in March, which brought the first irises and tulips, tall calla lilies pushing up even where they weren't wanted, and great gardenia bushes covered with small white flowers, just one of which could perfume an entire room; now spring had arrived for the third time in three months as the honeysuckle vied with the orange and jasmine for her pleasure; columbines, sweet peas, foxglove and larkspur grew in her garden, precisely as if it were spring in Sussex. Foxglove *and* palm trees? English cottage garden flowers growing in the shade of big-leafed tropical foliage? Blue-purple, otherworldly jacaranda trees—more than she had ever seen in Australia—sharing the same garden with the typically French hydrangea bushes? A spring with no end in sight?

It was almost too much. There was something that confused Eve's French soul about a land in which the combinations of flowers and trees were unrelated to any known botanical reality. Eve thought of April in Paris: the rain, the cold, the small, absolutely necessary comfort of a bunch of the first mimosa grown on a hillside near Cannes, bought at a Métro kiosk; rather pathetic and bewildered flowers with a blissful, nostalgic perfume and a powdery yellow bloom that would be gone tomorrow, flowers that were cherished for their bravery in existing at all. *That* was spring as she had known it. That was a familiar spring, miserable and miserly in its pleasures, spring during which only the dream of June kept you going. Was this land too good to be true?

Yet why should she question the gifts of the gods, Eve asked herself.

The first Frenchman to come to California in 1786, a visitor by sea, named La Pérouse, certainly hadn't troubled himself with the question, and when Louis Bouchette had planted his first vineyard on Macy Street in 1831, followed by Jean Louis Vignes a year later, they had not wasted their time in philosophical speculation on the ridiculous bounty of the climate.

By 1836 there had been a grand total of ten Frenchmen in Los Angeles. Now, less than a century later, the French community was two hundred thousand strong. An obvious affinity, she told herself, and stretched wearily, exhausted by her day with ladies possessed of an energy and enthusiasm she had never encountered anywhere in her life.

The two hundred thousand French residents might have been two million as far as Eve was concerned. She had spent a long morning in a meeting in the director's room of the French Benevolent Society to discuss the administration of the French Hospital, followed by another meeting of the ladies' branch of the Society of Saint Vincent de Paul. Her afternoon had been given over to a meeting of the *Société de Charité des Dames Françaises*. The only obligations she had managed to escape were the *Grove Gaulois*, which was the local chapter of Druids, the *Cercle Jeanne d'Arc* and the *Société des Alsaciens-Lorraines*.

If only the Druids, the Jeanne d'Arcians and the natives of Alsace could get together with the dozen or so other French organizations of Los Angeles to form just one huge club, her life might be less exhausting, Eve thought hazily. The joiner mentality and booster spirit of the American citizen, combined with the lively ability for endless conversation common to all Frenchwomen, made for endless duties for *Madame la Consule Generale*. Canberra and Cape Town had been the tiniest of provincial towns by comparison.

Yet she was as happy as she was weary. Paul was working hard every minute of the day, running the big Consulate on Pershing Square, and the girls, who both went to school at Sacred Heart, seemed to have adapted to the life of California even before they went to sleep the first night in their new home.

Eve suspected that their instantaneous transformation had been caused by the arrival of the Good Humor man, whose tinkling bell had sounded just as they stopped at their new home. He had presented all four of them with free Good Humors, and both Delphine and Freddy had discovered that they had won the coveted "Lucky Sticks" after they had consumed the vanilla ice cream bar covered with a splintery hard chocolate coating.

Lucky Sticks had been an omen of the days to come, a land in which each day that dawned was filled with infinite possibilities, even if they were merely the ripe kumquats on the trees on Franklin Boulevard, which Freddy popped into her mouth as she walked to the school at the corner of Franklin and Western. Delphine, with friends of her own age, sauntered sedately down the street, pretending that they were not sisters, while Freddy frisked and jumped and roamed until she looked as if she had not yet outgrown the long rope which Eve had been obliged to attach to her during her most rambunctious years in Canberra.

No question about it, Eve thought, Freddy was a child who was born to run away from home. Her first word had been "up," her first activity had been to climb whatever lay in her path and head outside the house. As soon as she could walk, she squirmed her way up and over every enclosure around the house and set forth to conquer the space around her. Only alert neighbors had kept her from trekking to the Outback, Paul said in despair, as he concocted a sort of harness that would allow her to go everywhere except into the street.

She takes after me, Eve told herself at first, secret delight mingled with mild public dismay. But it was soon apparent that Mademoiselle Eve Coudert had been a model of the most proper ladylike deportment compared to Miss Marie-Frédérique de Lancel. The child wanted to fly.

"She distinctly said, 'I want to fly,' " Paul told Eve, long before Freddy was three years old. "She said it five times and made a noise like those little sports planes from the Aero Club and ran around the room waving her arms."

"It's just an idea, darling. Perhaps all children want to fly, like the fairies in those stories you read her," Eve had answered him.

"She means she wants to fly a plane. You know her as well as I do. If she said it, she meant it," Paul said ominously.

"How could she have an idea like that, at her age? She probably means that she wants to ride in a plane."

"How does she even know that people ride in planes?" he demanded.

"Well, I didn't plant the idea in her mind, I assure you, darling. How does she know that people *fly* them, when it comes to that? It's nothing to worry about—she probably wants to *be* a plane," Eve retorted.

She dismissed the notion until, a year later, Freddy, who was supposed to be playing in her room, managed to grasp the four corners of a small quilt and jump out of a second-story window, hoping, apparently, that the quilt would serve as wings. She had been badly bruised, but her fall had been broken by thick bushes. Eve, terrified, rushed out to rescue her daughter, who emerged from the bushes by herself, disappointed but not frightened. "I should have jumped from the roof. Then it would have worked," Freddy said thoughtfully.

Eve was thirty-four, but she felt at once older and younger as she listened to the doves. Older because of her official day and its official duties; younger because she lived on a hilltop in a house that might have belonged to a Spanish hacienda, with its arches and balconies, courtyards and fountains, and red-tiled roofs on many levels. Older because she had two beautiful, fast-growing daughters who drove her mad, each in her own, utterly different way, and younger because she was going to a ball tonight, in a long, backless black satin gown from Howard Greer, as sensuous and naked as any evening dress that had ever been cut, with only strings of rhinestones to hold it up. Older, because she had to uphold a serious position as the proper wife of the Consul General of France, and younger because her hair, parted on the side, fell almost to her shoulders in soft, loose mermaid waves; because the style of the time demanded that she wear bright red lipstick and thick layers of mascara, and pencil her eyebrows, and darken her eyelids, and wear as little as possible under her clothes. Younger because she lived in a place—or at least everyone thought of it as a place—a place called Hollywood, where absolutely everyone was absolutely younger than absolutely everyone else in the world. Eve danced around her dressing room, not realizing that she was humming the tune of Le Dernier Tango, whose shocking, mocking refrain, "Go, go dance your tango!" had so alarmed her aunt when she had first heard it many years ago.

Greystone had been completed in 1928, a mansion that would never be equaled in Los Angeles. If it had been built centuries before in France or England, it would have been considered more than suitable as a fine residence that had no pretensions to being a castle. Its fifty-five rooms took up no more than 46,000 square feet, and the oil-rich Dohenys made do with a live-in staff of just thirty-six people. It was not a Newport Cottage or a Vanderbilt country house, but it rose less than a hundred yards north of the newly paved, almost unbuilt-upon country road called Sunset Boulevard. There the main structures were gas stations and a sandwich place called Gates' Nut Kettle. Classic Greystone, with its beautifully laid stone walls covered in thick slabs of Welsh slate, and its hundreds of terraced acres landscaped in grand

Renaissance formality, lacking only a moat, loomed large in the respectful attention of the community.

When Mrs. Doheny gave a ball, everyone came.

Eve clung to Paul's arm, feeling unexpectedly shy. It was the first major party that had taken place since their arrival in Los Angeles, and until now she had been so immersed in meeting the French residents of the city that she had had no chance to make other friends.

They didn't know the oil people or the newspaper people or the water people or the land developing people or the hotel people or the Hancock Park people or the Pasadena people—they didn't know the rich and powerful of the town, all of whom seemed to be at the Doheny's tonight. The only other guests Eve recognized were the few top movie stars who had been invited to mingle with the best society, and they, of course, didn't know her.

American informality, even in this distinctly European setting, prevented strangers being introduced to strangers, in a way that immediately indicated the particular place that each one held in the local hierarchy. It was all rather catch-as-catch-can, Eve told herself, as they descended the staircase that led to the swimming pool. There, on the roof of an enormous pool house, a full orchestra played for dancing on the wooden floor laid around the pool just for this evening's reception. It was entirely possible, she realized, that she and Paul would leave this important party knowing no one except the people they sat beside at dinner, whose names had meant nothing to them and who had seemed far more interested in greeting their friends at other tables than in getting to know a pair of foreigners.

When Eve had married Paul de Lancel during the war, she had had no time to wonder what the alliance would mean to him in the future. There had been no weighing life "after the war" in 1917. She had known almost nothing of his background, nor had she cared, and when she had impulsively given up the music hall for him, she had had no second thoughts about the limited domestic future she was choosing in place of the stardom for which she had trained herself, that great stardom Jacques Charles had destined for her.

Later, as the years followed, she had had ample time to realize that she and Paul had each given up something precious to be together. She had been received by Paul's family with bitter reserve and suspicion. His mother had spared no words in letting her know, in the special terminology of diplomacy, that Paul, because of their marriage, could never hope to "enter into his career," a term that indicated the path that must be traced by a future ambassador.

Eve had discovered that it was not just her deeply provincial and devoutly bourgeois family who felt themselves disgraced by her performing on stage, but the rest of the world as well—at least the world to which the Lancels belonged, and the world of the men who ruled at the Quai d'Orsay. In both worlds there was no meaningful difference between her *tour de chant* and the prancing of naked showgirls. A woman who worked in a music hall was little better than a streetwalker.

But Paul, she realized, had not been an innocent when he decided to marry her. He was a seasoned diplomat of thirty-one, wise in the demands and attitudes of the foreign service. He must have realized that she was just about as unsuitable a wife as he could have found, and he had chosen her anyway. Not "chosen," she would think, and tilt her chin proudly—but insisted, demanded, and implored her, overwhelming her with his passion and need. He had married her with his eyes wide open.

Eve felt—not precisely guilty, she told herself, but somehow—*responsible.* Never again did she sing in public, never again did she even mention the music hall years. She could not wipe out the past, but there was no need to insist on it, she decided, and in Canberra and Cape Town, as far as she knew, no one suspected that Madame Paul de Lancel, that young, devoted, proper and popular wife and mother, had ever performed before an audience.

But, oh, how she had missed it! Jacques Charles had been right. She yearned—from time to time—for the matchless thrill of walking out on a stage, for the applause, for the lights. And, more than anything, she missed the music itself. She sang and played to the children, but it wasn't the same, Eve thought, as she and Paul joined the Dohenys' hundreds of guests on the shining dance floor in front of the pool house.

Slowly they moved to the simple pace of the fox-trot that was the melody of the hour, surrounded by couples who were busy waving at each other, and talking over their shoulders even as they danced. The fun of the jazz age was over and the era of serious glamour had begun— the night air was thick with it, as heavy as the rubies that all but covered Mary Pickford and the diamonds flung over Gloria Swanson. Seven other women were wearing dresses exactly like Eve's black satin, but with far more jewels. Never had Eve felt so much like a green girl from Dijon in a borrowed hat.

"May I have the honor of a dance with your wife, *Monsieur le Consul?*" asked a familiar voice.

Paul glanced over his shoulder and then, with a smile of surprise, surrendered Eve. "Good evening, Monsieur," he said. "For a compatriot, I will permit it."

"So, *Madame la Consule Generale*, how do you like Hollywood?" Maurice Chevalier asked.

"Everyone asks me that question," Eve answered automatically. She had never met him before, nor had he met her, yet he seemed so at ease that it was as if they were returning to an old conversation.

"And how do you answer?"

"I say that I love it."

"And do you love it?" Chevalier asked, with genuine curiosity.

"Yes and no. It is . . . special. It takes time to accustom oneself . . ."

"Particularly when one remembers the lights of the Grands Boulevards."

"The Grands Boulevards . . ." Eve managed to make the words sound like neither a question nor an affirmation nor even a possible topic of conversation. She let them float in the air between her lips and the good-humored, absurdly famous face of her dancing companion as if they carried no associations for her.

"Yes, the Grands Boulevards," Chevalier repeated, "and the lights . . . Maddy . . . the lights."

"Maddy . . . ?" she said incredulously.

"But I have heard you sing. Once you have heard Maddy sing, you never forget her. Everyone said that, and everyone was right."

"Oh."

"It was in 1914, at the Olympia, that first time, before the war, and then again, still in 1914, but during the war, when you came to sing for the soldiers at the front. What a night that was! You in your brave, beautiful red dress and your little red shoes and your hair just the same color as it is tonight, as if someone took precisely three ripe strawberries and put them in a glass of champagne, and then held it up to the light . . . ah, Maddy, you made us poor soldiers happy that night. Sixteen years ago and I still remember perfectly."

"So do I—oh, so do I!" Eve cried.

"The night at the front? But you sang everywhere at the front. How could you remember one special night?"

"I remember them all," Eve said simply, tears welling in her eyes.

Maurice Chevalier, who had first sung for his supper in the slums of Paris at the age of eleven, understood her tears. He had been a star for twenty-two years and he had never ceased to evolve, until he had stamped his personal style on the century. He well remembered Maddy.

He realized that she must have disappeared into *Madame la Consule Generale*, and he knew, as clearly as if it had happened to him, what that must cost her.

"Do you know the words to *Mimi?*" he asked her, ignoring her tears.

"*Mimi?* 'My funny little honey of a Mimi'? Is there anyone in the world who doesn't know *Mimi?*" Eve asked.

"Would you rather we sang that, or would you prefer *Aimez-moi Ce Soir?* We could sing it in English. 'Love Me Tonight.' "

"Sing? *Here?* With you? No, I can't do that!"

"Ah! *Ça alors!* It's not every night that I get turned down. And so quickly."

"I . . . I didn't mean to be rude. It's just that I don't sing . . . anymore."

"Maddy would never say that."

"Maddy would never miss a chance to sing with Maurice Chevalier —never in a million years," Eve admitted, as much to herself as to him.

"Then *be* Maddy tonight, *Madame la Consule Generale!* Why not?"

Eve looked around at all the dancers who were openly watching her conversation with the greatest international star who had ever come to Hollywood. Strangers who had ignored her all evening were looking at her with fascinated eyes. Strangers, she realized, who had perhaps never entertained the notion that someone who would sing in a music hall was beyond the pale, an outcast forever; strangers who belonged to a new, odd, unconventional, unpredictable country in which entertainers were royalty.

"Mrs. Doheny asked me to sing, but I told her no," Chevalier continued. "However, if you consent to sing with me . . . I will reconsider."

"All right," Eve said quickly, before she could change her mind. She couldn't *not* dare. Not now. Not here. "But call me Eve," she said urgently, "not Maddy."

Arm in arm with Maurice Chevalier, Eve walked through the throng of dancers up to the pool house. The orchestra leader hurried down to meet them, for the dancers parted as they approached. Chevalier spoke to him quickly and then led her up the staircase so that they stood together on the roof of the pool house. He addressed the suddenly silent, expectant crowd.

"Ladies and gentlemen. I worked hard all day . . . singing. I worked hard all week . . . singing. In fact, I worked hard all month . . . singing. Tonight I came here only to honor Mrs. Doheny and watch you all dance. Not to sing. But then I did not dare to hope that tonight I would meet again a bright star, a compatriot, a colleague, who, when I first heard her sing, had all Paris at her feet, a brave and patriotic star who sang for us at the front during the war; a star so beautiful that I have forgiven her even though she abandoned her career for what? For marriage! I ask you, ladies and gentlemen, is that not a shame? And she has the audacity to tell me she is happy! I present to you Eve, the wonderful Eve, who has become Madame Paul de Lancel, wife of our new Consul of France. To sing with Eve I would even burn my hat and throw away my cane. Fortunately, she has not demanded that." He turned to Eve and whispered, *"Chantons, Maddy, chantons!"* Then he leaned toward the eager, excited crowd and cried, "So, Eve, *ma belle,* let us begin!"

"I won't be confirmed," Freddy announced, "until I get a plane ride."

"That's the limit!" Paul exploded. "Religious blackmail."

Freddy nodded in solemn agreement. After all, nothing else seemed to work. Each time she had asked for a plane ride, somebody or other had quickly promised it and then, just as quickly, forgotten. Her long-delayed confirmation could surely wait until she had obtained her heart's desire.

"I'll take you out to the airport this weekend," Paul decided reluctantly. He didn't approve of giving in to blackmail, but Freddy, at eleven and a half, was older than she should have been for her confirmation, and he wanted to see it over and done with, if only because the ceremony might have a much-desired sobering effect on his younger daughter.

Three times in the last year, local policemen had brought Freddy home after she had been caught roller skating at full speed straight down the center of the steepest streets, with a sheet firmly gripped by its corners, billowing out behind her like a sail. "The kid's a menace to traffic," the officers had said, "and she's going to get hurt someday." The Lancels' house was high in the hills of Los Feliz, and Freddy had been able to travel miles downhill before she'd been caught.

When her roller skates had been confiscated after her last brush with the law, Freddy had taken every last one of her dolls, shoved them unsentimentally into her doll carriage, and set up shop on the street corner, planning to sell them to the neighbors, among them Walt Disney and Cecil B. DeMille, so that she could buy new skates.

"She's just a tomboy," Eve said. "It's only a phase. She'll grow out of it." She couldn't even admit to herself that she liked seeing Freddy running wild as she had never been allowed to do. Some old and still-untamed emotion of her own was satisfied when she looked at her child and saw an unrepentant, happy outlaw.

Freddy was tall for her age, inches taller than Delphine, and already long-limbed. She was as nimble as an acrobat and intrepid enough to go over Niagara Falls in a rubber tire. Her arms and legs, under a network of scratches and bruises, were tanned, firm, and muscular, yet delicately rounded, as was her long neck. From Paul she had inherited exceptionally deep-set eyes, spaced unusually far apart, under thick brows that flew upward, like Eve's, toward her wide temples. Eyes of an unholy blue, they were so vivid that it seemed impossible that they belonged to a child.

Was it only her imagination, Eve wondered, or did Freddy truly see farther and better than everyone else? In Canberra and Cape Town she had always been able to spot birds in flight and animals approaching on the horizon before anyone else in the family, and even as a baby she would point and cry out to draw attention to her discoveries. She never had to brush her hair out of her eyes like other children, for it grew straight back from her forehead in an imperious mass of thick, tangled, turbulent waves of a shockingly aggressive red. Her nose was already straight and well formed, a distinctive feature that gave her face a look of unchildlike strength and purpose, until she laughed, and it wrinkled up in uncomplicated fun.

Her younger daughter was not, Eve suspected, going to be an indisputable beauty like Delphine, yet there would always be people who would judge her the more beautiful, who would be captured by her unruly allure, by a certain noble sternness that came over her face when she wanted something—as she so often did. She was an undomesticated creature, her Freddy, with a rakish, rollicking laugh and a swaggering walk, as if Robin Hood had come back to life as a young girl.

And, like Robin Hood, she held her father up to ransom. That night Paul telephoned John Maddux, who had first started an air service between Los Angeles and San Diego in 1927, with a single plane and a young pilot named Charles Lindbergh. The venture had prospered, and now Maddux had fourteen Ford Tri-Motor passenger planes, each boasting three engines, and able to make regularly scheduled trips on three routes: Los Angeles to San Francisco, to Agua Caliente, Mexico, and to Phoenix.

"What can I do for you, Paul?" John Maddux asked.

"I'd like to take a girl for a plane ride, Jack. Any suggestions?"

"Well, you're in luck. We've inaugurated a limousine service between the ticket office on South Olive and the airport. The lady should enjoy that," Maddux said, in a high good humor.

"She's only interested in the trip, I think, Jack. But thank you anyway."

"In that case, drive on out to Burbank and head for the Grand Central Airport. Let's see now—your best bet is the deluxe daily express flight to San Francisco—it leaves every day at two-thirty, and three hours later you'll be up there in plenty of time for drinks at a speakeasy, dinner in Chinatown, or maybe lobsters at the pier, spend the night in a suite at the Mark Hopkins, an early lunch at Ernie's, or maybe Jack's, and then you take the same flight back to L.A. You'll be home for dinner. Round trip will set you back seventy bucks per person, and it can't be beat for a good time."

"That sounds a bit . . . filling, Jack. The girl is my eleven-year-old daughter."

"Oh. Oh! I see. Well, in that case I suppose we're talking about a little sightseeing flight?"

"Precisely."

"No problem. I'll arrange it for you myself. How about Saturday afternoon, about three-thirty? The light's best in the late afternoon."

"Perfect. And thank you, Jack, I appreciate it." Paul de Lancel hung up, thinking once again that nobody at the Quai d'Orsay would care to know that men who had barely been introduced called each other by their first names in the City of the Angels, and that there was almost nothing that couldn't be arranged by a single phone call. It would shock them immeasurably if they suspected these facts, for if such sensible behavior ever became a world habit, it would eliminate the need for a Diplomatic Corps.

"Yes, sir, Mr. de Lancel," said the airline official. "Mr. Maddux made all the arrangements. Said to tell you the trip was on him, his pleasure. There's the plane, right out there." He pointed to a shiny new bi-motor plane standing on the tarmac not far from the single building that housed the air terminal on the great, wide field in Burbank. Six people were already waiting in line for the sightseeing flight.

Paul took Freddy's hand and started toward the plane, but she stood her ground and didn't move.

"That's a big plane and there are other people going on it," she said in a voice of utter disappointment.

"Now, Freddy, I didn't promise you a plane all of your own, did I? Just a ride. And this is the best time of day."

"Daddy, don't you understand? I want to go up *alone*."

"Come on, sweetheart, how can you go alone? You can't fly a plane by yourself."

"I know. There'd have to be a pilot. Just me and the pilot, please, Daddy, so I can imagine that it's just me, by myself."

She was all ardent pleading, her eyes looking into his. Paul seemed to see himself, and he remembered, for an instant, the flavor of his boyish dreams. Not the dreams themselves, but their urgency, their total lack of understanding of what it might ever mean to compromise.

"I'll tell Mr. Maddux that you were most kind," he said to the airline official, "but I believe my daughter would prefer to go up in a little plane. What do you recommend?"

"When you leave the airport, turn left and keep going on the same road until you get to a little town called Dry Springs. Turn off on the main street, drive through town, and pretty soon you'll see a sign for a flying school, the McGuire Academy of the Air. It doesn't look like much, but don't worry about that. Ask for Mac—he'll take her up for a spin. Best pilot out here. Flew in the war, I think."

"Thanks," Paul said, and led the way, with Freddy beside him, excitedly walking so fast that she kept up with his long-legged stride. The McGuire flying school, when they reached it some twenty-five minutes later, proved to be a low wooden structure that looked like a huge garage. There were a number of planes parked inside, but otherwise the big space was deserted. Eventually, off to one side, Paul and Freddy discovered a small office with its door open. Paul looked in and called out, "Anybody here?"

"Be there in a minute," a voice answered from behind them, and soon a man crawled out from under the plane on which he had been working. He was wearing mechanic's overalls over an open-necked workman's shirt. His brown hair, the pleasant color of gingerbread, was disheveled and he seemed, to Paul, to be no older than thirty. He had a good face, a strong, open face, what Paul thought of as a typically American face, self-confident, friendly and freckled. He walked with a markedly lithe assurance, almost as if he were a professional gymnast.

"I'm looking for Mac," Paul said.

"I'm Mac," the man answered, with a disarming grin, wiping his hands on a piece of clean rag and shaking hands with Paul. "Terence McGuire."

"Paul de Lancel." Unsmiling, Paul hesitated. He hated to entrust Freddy to a pilot in overalls.

"What can I do for you?" Mac asked.

"Please, I'd like a plane ride," Freddy said breathlessly.

"Just a minute, Freddy," Paul interrupted. "I understand that you flew in the war, Mr. McGuire?"

"Yes, I did."

"That's very interesting, isn't it, Freddy? Tell me, where did you fly?"

"In France."

"I meant with whom, with what group?" Paul probed, far from reassured.

"First with the Lafayette Escadrille in 1916—if I'd waited for our army to get the message that there was a fight going on, I might have been on the ground forever. Then, when the United States finally got into the war, I transferred to the American Air Service—the 94th Aero Squadron."

"Then you must have shot down some German planes?"

"Well, naturally, I bagged a few. Fifteen to be exact. The last four of them at Saint-Mihiel. We all had our share of victories. Eddie Rickenbacker got almost double my score. Are you a reporter, by any chance? I haven't talked to one for years. I didn't think anyone was still interested."

"No. Just an anxious father."

"I see. You didn't want your daughter going up with a mechanic? Can't blame you. You're right to be careful. She'll be all right with me."

"Oh, please, Daddy, don't waste all this time talking!" Freddy cried, at the end of her patience, dancing up and down, her hair bouncing, her eyes afire.

"Come on, kid. We'll take up the Piper Cub over there. I was supposed to be giving a lesson this afternoon, but it was canceled, so she's gassed up and all ready to go," McGuire said, pointing to the tiny plane parked outside the hangar twenty feet away. Freddy turned, without saying another word, and dashed toward it at full tilt, closely followed by the pilot.

Paul stood on the tarmac, feeling foolish. The man had been an ace, a triple ace, and had flown for France for two years. So this was what had happened to at least one of those chivalrous and romantic heroes once he got home and took off his shining boots, dashing jodhpurs and belted leather jacket. Paul sat down on a camp chair near the hangar

of the flying school and resigned himself to wait nervously for Freddy's
return. That Piper Cub looked dangerously small.

Terence McGuire buckled Freddy into the left-hand seat of the Piper
Cub, with a complete set of controls in front of her, circled the plane,
and climbed into the right-hand seat. No need to check out the plane;
he'd done it an hour before. He looked at the empty sky and started
off, taxiing toward the end of the unpaved, dirt airstrip. The afternoon
light at Dry Springs was as golden as any that had ever fallen in Greece,
the sky as thrillingly blue, the air as clear and beckoning, as if it
contained some splendid promise.

Freddy was silent, and he glanced at her profile to see if she was
frightened. It was rare that someone brought a young girl for a spin.
Mostly it was boys, and older than this kid, although, with the seat
pushed far forward as it was, her feet easily reached the rudder pedals.
No, she wasn't frightened, but it wouldn't be the first time that someone had decided at the last minute that he'd rather not go up after all,
thanks anyway. She looked, well, not excited exactly, but deeply intent, as if this joyride were something she was concentrating on with
every one of her senses. He held the Piper for a minute at the end of
the airstrip, and went through his pre-takeoff checklist. Then, before
he began his run toward the takeoff point, he took another peek at his
passenger. She'd gone white under her tan, and she looked as if she
were holding her breath.

"You O.K., kid?" he shouted over the noise of the motor. She
nodded briefly but didn't look at him. Her eyes were fixed on the
windscreen and he'd bet that she wasn't even blinking.

Once they were airborne, and had climbed to fifteen hundred feet,
McGuire leveled off and headed east, away from the brilliant rays of
the slanting sun, and flew straight and level, keeping an even airspeed.
First-time passengers had enough trouble just being off the ground, in
his opinion, without having to deal with any fancy stuff. Unlike some
pilots, he felt no need to show off at the passenger's expense.

"Like the view?" he asked Freddy. Now that they were up, he didn't
have to shout.

"It's great. It's better than great! When's the lesson going to start?"
she asked.

"Lesson? What lesson?"

"This lesson, *my lesson.*"

"Hold on, kid. Your father didn't say anything about a lesson."

"He didn't have a chance. You two spent the whole time talking

133

about the war. I'm supposed to be having my first lesson today. Why do you think we came to a flying school?"

"If I'd known it was supposed to be a lesson, we'd still be on the ground and you'd be learning how to check out this plane. This isn't the way to give anyone a lesson," McGuire protested.

"I'll do that next time," Freddy said, and smiled for the first time since they had left the airport.

"Damn right, you will. And not just next time. Every time. O.K., put your hand on the stick. Now, gently, push it forward. What happened?"

"We went down," Freddy said in rapture.

"Right. Pull it back toward you. Now what?"

"We went up."

"Forward takes you down, back brings you up. That's the first thing. And the most important. Everything's important, but getting up and down comes first, kid."

"Yes, Mr. McGuire."

"Call me Mac. All my students do. What's your name?"

"Freddy."

"Boy's name, huh?"

"Not in French. It's Marie-Frédérique, really, but no one's allowed to call me that. What's the next thing, Mac?"

"You've got your feet on the rudder pedals. They control the direction of the plane. You steer the plane with them, not with the stick. The stick isn't like the wheel of a car. The rudders *are* like the wheel of a car. So press—gently—on your left rudder. What's happening?"

"We're starting to turn left."

"How are you going to get back to flying straight ahead?"

"Right rudder?"

"Do it. Good. Now hold her straight. Just use your left hand. Relax your arm, this isn't an arm-wrestling contest. Good. Now look at this dial, Freddy. It's called an altimeter. It shows you how high up you are. And this knob is the throttle. If you push it in, the plane goes faster. If you pull it out, the plane goes slower. It's like putting on more or less gas. Got it?"

"Yes," she said and in that single second of sudden comprehension, all the power of her natural coordination shifted to the control panel of the Piper Cub.

"Look at the altimeter, Freddy, and try to take her up two hundred feet. You'll need to push in the throttle and pull back on the stick. Whoa! Not so fast. Gentle—gentle—gentle. That's what she wants, and don't you forget it. Try again, up another two hundred feet. Hmm . . . that was better. Now take her down—gently—four hundred feet so we'll be back where we started. What are you going to do?"

"Push the stick forward and pull out the throttle. Very, very gently."

"Right. Go."

Freddy's pealing laugh rang out. She could fly a plane! Mac's hands weren't on the stick. He was sitting in the cockpit with his arms folded and *she was flying the plane.* She'd known she could do it all her life, known with a knowledge that she could never remember not possessing or trying to explain. It was different from what she'd expected, more . . . more . . . *businesslike,* because of all the dials on the control panel whose meaning she didn't yet know, but the *wonder,* the wonder that she had known was waiting for her like a gift on the wind, the wonder, oh, yes, it was there!

"We'd better turn around and head back," Mac said. "I'll take over, but you keep your hand on the stick and your feet on the rudders and just feel what I do."

Reluctantly, Freddy surrendered the plane. "How old do I have to be before I can take her up alone?"

"Well, first you have to know how, and you don't yet. But you can't solo until your sixteenth birthday."

"What! Who says so?"

"The government. Regulations. The damn fools—I soloed when I was twelve, but that was back in the good old days. Before that, in the very beginning, there weren't any dual controls, so that first time you took one up you soloed—sink-or-swim-style."

"That means I'll have to wait four and a half years," Freddy wailed. "How can I wait that long?"

"No choice. You can learn to fly, but you can't solo."

"Four and a half years," Freddy said in misery.

"You take shop in school?"

"They don't have shop at Sacred Heart," Freddy said mournfully.

"Change schools, that's what you'd better do, and take shop. It's a start. And math, that's important. You good at math?"

"Yes," Freddy muttered numbly. "It's my best subject."

"Well, don't knock it. Without some math, how do you expect to navigate? And, believe it or not, there are people who can't do math to save their lives."

"Like my sister, Delphine," Freddy said, brightening a little.

"At least one of you has a girl's name. Freddy, can you see the airport from here?"

"Of course." She squinted into the sun and pointed out the precise location of the airport, all but invisible, and very far away on the floor of the San Fernando Valley. "I saw it a minute ago, maybe more."

"Hmm." He'd known it was there, Terence McGuire thought, because that was where it always was, but he wouldn't have bet a nickel that anyone else could spot it the first time up. And he'd only just seen it. The kid had good eyes. Better than good.

As they came in for the landing he asked, "Tell me what you feel, Freddy."

"What do you mean?"

"What you feel about the plane as I land it."

Puzzled, Freddy sat as still as if she were listening for a revelation from on high, as the Piper started on its final leg of approach to the airstrip, flying lower and lower every second. *"She wants to land,"* she shouted excitedly. "She wants to land, all by herself!"

"Yeah, and how'd you know that?"

"I felt it, I really felt it, Mac."

"Where?"

"In . . . on . . . in my seat."

"The seat of your skirt?"

"Right."

"Right. That's where you have to feel it. Next time you go flyin', wear pants." He landed the plane and taxied to a stop in front of his school. Paul rushed over to the plane as they were climbing out, furiously angry.

"Do you realize that you've been gone for an hour? I couldn't believe it! I've been worried out of my mind. Damn it, McGuire, where's your sense?"

"Hold on, now. A lesson lasts an hour. We're about three minutes early when it comes to that."

"A lesson?" Paul said incredulously. "A lesson? I asked you to take Freddy up for a ride, I never said anything about a lesson."

Terence McGuire looked at Freddy, who looked back at him with eyes that he knew saw farther than eyes could see, with a mouth set in a firm, proud line that said that she knew she was dead guilty of a lie, but that it had been worth it.

"I'm sorry, but I could swear that you'd said Freddy wanted a lesson," the pilot said. "Sorry about the misunderstanding. I hate to have worried you. This should be six dollars—four for the rental of the plane and two for the lesson—but I'll make it four since you only wanted a ride. Oh, and I'd better get a logbook for this young lady."

136

He hurried off to his office, found a logbook, and came back, carefully making the first entry. "Here's where you sign, Freddy. And keep this safe, now, don't lose it."

"I will," Freddy breathed, her gratitude shining from her face. "I will. And, Mac, I'll be back. I don't know when, but as soon as I can."

"Give me some credit, kid. I never doubted that. Not for a minute. See you, Freddy."

"See you, Mac."

7

I T was the summer of 1933 in Champagne, and on the terrace of the Château de Valmont, Vicomte Jean-Luc and Vicomtesse Anette de Lancel greeted the visit of Paul and Eve, accompanied for the first time by their daughters. It was a Lancel tradition that the châtelaine herself pour from the bottle when they raised the first glass at any gathering at Valmont, and today was a moment of more than sentimental or symbolic value. "Of course Freddy is not too young to drink champagne," Anette said, "especially on such a great occasion," and she filled thirteen-year-old Freddy's glass just as high as those of the others.

As Paul drank, he realized how much he'd missed Valmont, how carefully he'd trained himself not to think about his boyhood home. He'd almost forgotten that nowhere else that he'd ever lived had there been such a palpable sense of harmony between the land and the crop it produced, an invisible bond he felt he could reach out and touch. Well-being and lightheartedness and an extraordinary sense of hospitality were in every breath of the air of Champagne. No ocean he'd known had ever given him the sense of expanding beyond his own physical and emotional boundaries as did the lazy, open-armed sea of vineyards. Above each of them, during the weeks of harvest, the blue and red Lancel flag would be flown, just as at Pommery they raised a white flag and at Veuve Clicquot a yellow one.

Paul looked proudly at Eve, Delphine and Freddy, as they sat in the sun. They had just arrived from Paris by car, a trip of less than two hours. Two weeks earlier they had left Los Angeles by train, crossed the United States, and taken an ocean liner to France. Paul, with a two-month leave from his post, had decided that it was time at last to bring his family to the ancestral home they had never seen.

The flowering of the vines, accompanied by a perfume like that of the passionfruit flower, had lasted two and a half weeks in early June, blessedly free of the dreaded frosts of spring; the pollination of the flowers had taken place during weather that had been ideally warm and humid, with the moderate wind that grape growers pray for, and now the vines lay calmly filling out their grapes in the valley spread out below the château.

Valmont lay north of Hautvillers, the village where, in the 1600s, Dom Pierre Perignon had come to the thousand-year-old Abbaye of Saint-Pierre d'Hautvillers, and settled down to a monk's busy, regimented life during which, in the next forty-six years, between hours spent in devotion to God, he managed to find the way to turn the excellent local wine into champagne.

The château had once been surrounded by oak forests where game abounded and the seigneurs of Valmont planted vineyards and made wine only for their own pleasure and that of their friends. Now, looking down from the raised terrace of the château, where the family was seated before lunch, on a brilliant day in early July, the sight of great trees was rare in the valley beneath them. Vineyards were planted in a precise, infinitely pleasing patchwork as far as the eye could see. The tenderly rolling hills, on which great richness of ripening champagne grapes lay, created a landscape as rural, as secure and as peaceful as any on earth, yet in the past hundred years, two great wars that changed the history of Europe had been fought over these valuable and too-vulnerable slopes on the eastern frontier of France.

But war, even the thought of war, was impossible for Paul today. The bitterness with which his marriage to Eve had been greeted by his parents had finally been dissipated. During the previous winter his mother had written to him and apologized for the harsh words with which she had once told him that his marriage had cost him his career. "As the years go by," she had written, "I have come to understand that without Eve and your children, you could never have been truly happy —no, not even if you had been named Ambassador to the Court of Saint James."

Her softening of a long-held position was not due to the legendary but largely nonexistent mellowing effect of age. The passage of time normally makes patrician Frenchwomen more dogmatic and less pliable in their opinions than when they were younger, a condition they share with women of every social class in every country in the world.

If Guillaume, the elder Lancel son, had ever married and had children, Anette de Lancel might have felt the continuity of the family safe in his hands. She might possibly have continued to nourish her grudge against Eve. But Guillaume was an absolutely determined bachelor, who disliked children as much as he enjoyed the liberty of being wifeless. The Vicomtesse had finally accepted the fact that she would never have grandchildren who weren't Paul's children. Although she would always voice her disappointment at the undutiful, selfish and shortsighted conduct of her elder son, she knew that it was high time to make peace with her one, and almost certainly her only, daughter-in-law.

Now, as she saw her Paul and his family gathered around her, still wearing their traveling clothes, she was deeply glad that she had brought herself to arrange this visit. Guillaume and Jean-Luc were both bending attentively toward Eve, as she told them about the trip. She had slung the scrupulously cut, wide-shouldered, blue piqué jacket of her Adrian summer suit around the back of her cast-iron garden chair, taken off her small, tilted-brim hat and crossed her legs casually under her slim, mid-calf skirt, a picture of animation and ease. Anette de Lancel scrutinized Eve strictly, and recognized that, hard as it was for her to admit it, she was a woman of whom any mother-in-law could be proud. However, it was her granddaughters who inspired her immediate love, particularly Delphine.

Had there ever been such a lovely fifteen-year-old? she wondered. Delphine was not a peacock beauty, all immediate splash. There was something so delicate and touching about her creamy loveliness that each person who remarked on it felt as if he were making an original observation. Her huge, smoky eyes, of a mysterious gray that glowed like an opalescent mist on a twilight sea, were set almost too far apart under high, arched brows. She had a clearly defined widow's peak from which her brown hair curled in delicious softness down around her neck, with the gleam of valuable, highly polished wood. Her hands were exquisite, and all her dainty proportions so well made that they looked as if she'd been assembled with enormous care. Her widow's peak, wide forehead and small chin created the heart-shaped face that echoed those of a few of the noble ladies in the Lancel family portraits, the past châtelaines of Valmont. Delphine was of moderate height and so slender, so breakable looking, that her grandmother felt all her protective instincts aroused as she looked at her. She was that rare girl, the perfect *jeune fille*, she thought. She could have been brought up in France.

Marie-Frédérique, or Freddy, as they insisted on calling her, Anette de Lancel told herself, not without a stirring of the mildest disapproval, could never be mistaken for anything but an American. Although how that was possible when both her parents were French she couldn't fathom. It must be the California air, for no French girl of thirteen and a half would ever be *allowed* to be so rangy, so vivid, so *present* in every way. She obviously had inherited her height and the blueness of her eyes from Paul—she must be many centimeters taller than her sister—

and the extravagance of her self-possession from her mother. But her hair! All that bright, messy, ungovernable stuff! Beautiful, yes, she couldn't deny it, but so . . . so *unsuitable*, so flamboyant. *So red.* Of course there had been redheaded Lancels, from generation to generation, but had there ever been one with hair that so dominated the scene? Why didn't Eve try to tame it? Or, if that proved impossible, why couldn't Eve at least insist that her younger daughter achieve a more ladylike appearance? Still, Freddy was utterly lovable as she sipped cautiously at her first glass of champagne and looked around her in awe.

Freddy had known that her father had grown up in a château, but the reality of Valmont dazzled her. She counted the three romantic towers and wondered who lived in them. And what, she speculated, could they *do* in all the rooms behind the windows? How many fireplaces must there be, to account for so many elaborate brick chimneys? She hadn't understood before that a château would be a castle, and yet Grandmother insisted that it was only a small château, one of five in Champagne, and that the grandest of them, Montmort, had a moat, a much bigger park, and a spiral staircase so wide that a man on a horse could climb it. What a nifty idea!

Anette de Lancel glanced at her wristwatch. Only ten minutes until lunch would be announced, and the surprise she had planned hadn't yet happened. Well, lunch could wait, she thought.

Five minutes later, as they all relaxed while they watched Guillaume open the second bottle of champagne, a horseman at a gallop suddenly appeared from the wood that lay on the right side of the château, separated from it only by a stretch of well-raked gravel. Obviously the horseman had not expected to find anyone on the terrace, for he was looking away from them, toward the stables. When he saw them he threw his head back, and stopped abruptly only a few paces away. Expressionlessly, he loomed above them on an enormous bay horse. There was a moment of such silence that the faint stirring of the wind in the leaves of the vineyard seemed as loud as the slapping of the ocean at the side of a boat. Anette de Lancel's voice broke the odd, uncertain hush.

"Get down off that beast and greet the new arrivals, darling. When I promised you a surprise for lunch today, I didn't exaggerate, did I, Bruno?"

Quickly, yet moving with the suggestion of invisible armor that prevented his motion from seeming unpremeditated, Bruno, a tall and powerful eighteen, jumped from the horse and walked, with immediate composure, toward the group whose arrival his grandmother had so carefully concealed from him. As he came closer, everyone turned toward him with a different emotion.

Freddy and Delphine were simply agog with curiosity about the half brother whom they had never seen except in old photographs. Bruno! At last! Paul felt a rush of the bitterest resentment, and yet he couldn't prevent himself from thinking how magnificent the boy had become. Eve stiffened as if she had been struck in the face; this, then, was the son who had broken Paul's heart with his obstinate, incomprehensible ways, promising to visit every year, and each summer finding another reason why it wouldn't work out, until it became painfully evident that he had no intention of ever coming to see his father and his half sisters. Anette de Lancel felt an almost childlike glee in being the instrument of the reunion she had planned, without consultation with anyone except her husband, who had finally been persuaded that it was the right thing to do.

As for Bruno, whatever emotions he felt were concealed by a perfect and automatic courtesy upon which he could call in every situation, a courtesy that, in other days, had not failed gentlemen even as they made their way to the guillotine. He embraced Paul as if he had seen him last week; he kissed Eve's hand with a correct murmur of *"Bonjour, Madame,"* and he shook hands with Freddy and Delphine as if they were young ladies of his own age.

"You might have warned me," he said softly as he brushed his grandmother's cheek with his lips.

"Bruno, darling, I thought it best this way. So much easier for us all," she said, dismissing his words in a manner so airy yet so certain that even he had nothing left to say.

Anette de Lancel was well aware that Bruno had resisted the slightest acquaintance with his stepmother and half sisters. After Paul's shocking second marriage, she and the Marquis and Marquise de Saint-Fraycourt had found themselves of one mind on the subject of Eve Coudert. She was their common enemy. In becoming a member of their families, she had wounded them all deeply, and in a way that their families would have to endure forever. Time would never wipe out the stain of such a misalliance. Since the Saint-Fraycourts were willing to share Bruno fairly frequently with his Lancel grandparents, they had never tried to argue that Bruno be sent to join Paul.

As the years passed, and Guillaume remained obdurately but incontestably unmarried, Bruno's importance to them increased. Just as he was the last male with Saint-Fraycourt blood, so he was the last male

Lancel of their branch of the family. One day, far in the future, there would be no Vicomte de Lancel at Valmont except Bruno.

The grandparents often discussed the future, as they sat in their favorite brocaded armchairs before the fire, in the small sitting room they used after dinner. After they were gone, Guillaume and Paul would inherit the château and the vineyards equally. If childless Guillaume died before Paul, Paul would inherit everything. But then, when Paul died, his widow, if she were still alive, and his three children would inherit in equal proportions.

Their beloved Bruno would never be the sole proprietor of this family land. He would have to share these unique hectares with two diplomatic gypsies, two unknown foreigners who had not had the benefit of growing up in France, two girls who would probably marry other foreigners from dubious places and produce children, all of whom would inherit a portion of the estate until it was split into far too many pieces to retain any of that Lancel identity which was part of the very soil of Champagne.

As Bruno went to his room to change quickly from his riding clothes, and Eve took Freddy and Delphine to wash their hands before lunch, Anette de Lancel felt her heart lighten. Delphine and Freddy, who had always spoken in French with their parents, had perfect accents, and they had been so eager to meet their grandparents, so affectionate, so instantly beguiled by the Château de Valmont, that it seemed suddenly as if they couldn't be gypsies after all but true Lancels, back from wandering in the wastelands after many years. Oh yes, she had been so wise to invite them all at the same time. And even wiser not to tell Bruno.

Impenetrable, Eve thought, as she observed Bruno during lunch, utterly impenetrable, encased in a politeness that was as polished, as massive and as solid as the heavy pieces of family silver arrayed on either side of each plate. It was more plausible to imagine herself able to take up one of the knives between two fingers and lightly bend it backwards until the tip of the blade touched the crest than it was to believe that Bruno would ever smile at her with a true smile instead of just an inclination of the corners of his lips in an upward direction. Without the slightest gesture or word that would have been noticed by anyone else in the family, he had conveyed to her one absolute: she did not exist for him, she had never existed and she could never exist in the future. He didn't see her even when he seemed to be responding freely to words she had spoken. It was as if, under the lively surface of his brown eyes, there lived a secret blind man, icy and implacable. Was it just that false smile or was she right in not liking his mouth, in finding its deeply curved, almost plump outlines a contradiction in his firmly masculine face?

Yet what had she ever done to him, Eve asked herself angrily. In the context of her understanding of the standards of the French aristocracy, she could understand—at least try to understand—why it had taken the Lancels so long to accept her, but Bruno was of another generation, of the generation of her children.

Her own parents had long ago forgiven her for the old scandal. Her brilliant marriage had allowed them to hold their heads up again, and before they had died, both in the space of one year in the late 1920s, they had traveled to Australia and Cape Town to visit for weeks at a time.

Under the surface of the lunchtime talk, as lively as it always is when winemakers of any land are at table, Eve asked herself if she should try to find a way to communicate with Bruno, or whether it would be wiser to retreat and simply accept his inexplicable enmity.

Exciting, Delphine thought, as she watched Bruno talk in a grown-up way she had never heard before in an eighteen-year-old boy. None of the older brothers of her school friends carried themselves so erectly, as if the space they occupied was important, not even the ones who tried to act so high and mighty just because they had cars and could drive out to the beach, or to a drive-in movie, or to one of the Currie's ice cream parlors for a fifteen-cent hot butterscotch sundae, or a "Mile High" cone. Delphine had laughed at dozens of them and amused herself at their expressions when she refused their invitations, for Eve had decreed that she couldn't go out on dates until she was sixteen.

Delphine decided that Bruno looked as if he must be in his twenties. His dark, strong eyebrows were like a yoke under his broad, well-shaped forehead, and his face was dominated by his handsomely arched, masterful nose. It was such a different face from the American faces she was used to, so much more . . . more . . . she groped for a word and could only think of *civilized*. It was, she sensed, without ever having seen a family portrait before today, a face that belonged to a long line of ancestors, a face with a history. Do I have such a face, Delphine wondered. Already, with deep delight, she knew the answer.

A stranger, Paul said to himself. He found it impossible to recognize Bruno as the too-tall, too-thin, ambitious, eager boy he had met once eight years ago, a child with a high, enthusiastic voice who dreamed great dreams.

Bruno had grown still taller, but as his muscles developed he had grown into his height, just as his nose, once too highly arched for his face, had grown bigger and more dominant. He looked powerful, even commanding, as he sat talking, in his man's voice, his stranger's voice, with a cool and finished ease, teasing his doting grandmother, deferring to his grandfather and uncle Guillaume, being charming to Delphine and Eve and even, it seemed to Paul, to Freddy.

Surely he must be conscious that he had become the center of attention in spite of the visit of the four Lancels. It was as if they had all come to see *him*, and he was graciously allowing them to do so. He seemed to feel no embarrassment at meeting his father unexpectedly after so many years. He hadn't said a word, not even a perfunctory one, about their long separation, about the years of broken promises, and Paul suddenly vowed that he never would ask why it had been like that. Whatever the reason, he didn't want to know it, because it could only be painful.

"Tell me, Bruno, when do you do your military service?" Paul asked.

"This year, Father, right after the summer holidays. I'm going into the cavalry with a lot of my friends. It should be amusing."

"Take care you don't kill those military nags," Guillaume grunted. "They may not be as strong as my Emperor. He was exhausted when you brought him in today."

"I'm sorry, Uncle. Emperor hadn't been ridden in so long that I knew he needed a really good run, and I felt it would be cruel to restrain him—but you're absolutely right. It won't happen again, I assure you. Your stable boys aren't giving him enough exercise."

"I'll talk to them," Guillaume said, somewhat placated.

"The cavalry," Delphine breathed, impressed as she had never been.

"And after your military service, my boy," the Vicomte de Lancel asked, "have you made up your mind yet?"

"Not really, Grandfather. I'm still busy considering many things."

"You mean you've dropped 'Sciences Po'?" Paul asked sharply. "What happened to your plan to lead your country?"

"Just take a look, Father. Paul-Boncour's socialist cabinet lasted all of five weeks. The new Daladier government is filled with lamentable fools. Between his radicals like Herriot, weaklings like Laval, and the others, that bunch of liberals and labor leaders, we have a growing deficit and hundreds of thousands of men unemployed. Meanwhile, Daladier can think of nothing better to do than to try to raise the income tax. No, thank you, as an idealist, I prefer to keep clear of that mess."

145

"If you are so sure they are wrong, what would you propose in their place? It's easy to criticize, particularly as an idealist," said Paul, furious at the lofty tone in which Bruno dismissed the ambition that he had once convinced Paul was all-important to his future.

"A strong man, *one* strong man, instead of twenty-three cretins."

"As simple as that, eh? Where do you think this strong man is going to appear from, Bruno? And how is he going to achieve power?"

"We don't have to look far, Father. Hitler has done just that in Germany since January of this year, when he became chancellor."

"Hitler! You approve of that . . . that . . . *unspeakable* criminal?"

"Shall we say that I don't think of him in such simple terms? Of course I don't like him—what Frenchman could?—but I think we must grant that he is a political genius. He's taken over a country in a matter of months and made it stick. He's outlawed the Communist Party, he's putting the Jews in their place. His methods are strong and positive and he lets nothing stand in his way."

"Are you proposing that France needs a Hitler of her own?" Paul roared, half rising from his seat.

"Now, now," Anette de Lancel commanded hastily, "I absolutely forbid you to talk politics at the table. Especially not today. This is a great day for us, and you simply cannot ruin it! Jean-Luc, give Paul some more wine. And girls, I have a very special dessert for you." She rang for the butler, satisfied that the men had subsided into silence. "If you like it, I'll have the chef teach you how to make it. I always say that the mistress of a house must know how to cook, no matter how good a chef she has. Don't you agree, Eve? After all, how else can you tell when he does it wrong?"

"I agree entirely," Eve said quickly as she watched Paul's hands shaking with rage. Bruno's admiration, she reflected, was not, after all, something she'd care to win. How could he be Paul's son?

When the long lunch was finally over, Delphine and Freddy went to their room to change into country clothes.

"Isn't it exciting, having a brother, Freddy? I think he's absolutely marvelous, don't you?" Delphine said to her sister the minute they were alone.

"You're welcome to my half of him," Freddy answered.

Delphine turned sharply in disbelief. Just because Freddy had been too shy to say boo to Bruno didn't mean that she had to say something nasty about the handsomest boy either of them had ever seen. "What are you talking about?"

"He thinks he's hot shit," Freddy said defiantly.

"Marie-Frédérique! I'm going to ask Grandmother if I can have a room to myself. I don't want to share with you anymore. You're disgusting."

"Shit on a stick," Freddy repeated. "With sugar on it."

Several days later, early in the morning, while the night's coolness was still on the flowers, Eve went out to cut roses, carrying two long, flat, English trug baskets and one of the sharp pairs of secateurs that she had found in the flower room on the ground floor of Valmont, where three deep sinks had been designed to hold flowers as they waited to be arranged. Her mother-in-law had entrusted her with the task the evening before. "I always do it myself," she had said at dinner, "rather than allow the gardeners to do it—the Valmont rose garden has always been my special pride. I was wondering—would it amuse you to do the flowers tomorrow, Eve?"

"I'd love it," Eve had answered happily, knowing that this turning over of a job no one else was allowed to touch was a sign of just how much her mother-in-law had changed toward her.

"You do know . . ." the Vicomtesse said, and hesitated.

"To recut the stems underwater?"

"How did you know what I was going to say?"

"My mother taught me to do that when I was a child," Eve answered.

"Did she also tell you to put a few drops of bleach and a little sugar into the water to make the roses last longer?" Anette de Lancel asked.

"I've never heard of that. We used a centime in the vase. Does it work?"

"Not terribly well, but I do it anyway." The two women exchanged a look of camaraderie that mystified the men at the table, who had never anxiously eyed a cutting garden, trying to calculate whether the roses would be at their best for a party or whether they would be in one of their maddening interim stages, in which all the bushes would be covered with promising buds, but not showing any color, or, equally infuriating, whether all the flowers would be overblown the day before they were needed.

The Valmont rose garden was reached through a series of tall hedges, severely pruned into an almost mazelike design, in which Lancel children had played hide-and-seek for centuries.

Eve wandered about, secateurs poised, taking only the roses that were ready to be cut, for buds cut too soon would sometimes not open indoors. Nevertheless, both baskets were soon piled high with blooms, and although she knew it was taking a risk, she couldn't resist piling them over-high, for roses left on the bushes even a day too long would, in the heat of summer, open too quickly and be wasted. Holding one of the overflowing baskets at arm's length in front of her, and the other behind, she followed the narrow path back to the château. As she turned a sharp corner around a hedge, Bruno suddenly appeared, walking quickly on his way to the stables. Eve stopped abruptly, starting in surprise. The basket she held outstretched overbalanced and the roses all slid off onto the gravel path in front of her feet.

"Oh! You frightened me," she said in dismay, cautiously putting the other basket down. "I hope none of them is bruised." Eve knelt down and started to replace the dozens of flowers as carefully and quickly as possible. As she picked them up and replaced them, one by one, she saw that several roses had fallen on top of Bruno's riding boots, which were planted immovably on the path. She looked up at him, amazed that he had not yet begun to help her, and saw that he was standing with his arms folded tightly, his lips pressed together, staring straight ahead with an expression of impatiently withheld disdain, as if she were a maid who had splashed him with dirty water from a bucket, and was now mopping it up. Still kneeling, Eve mechanically continued picking up the roses, waiting for the wave of fury she felt to pass.

"Bruno! What are you standing like that for? Why aren't you helping Eve?" The Vicomtesse's voice rang out as she turned the corner behind Eve and came upon the scene.

Eve rose to her feet. "It's all right, Anette. I believe Bruno doesn't dare to risk the thorns. He seems quite petrified by them. Go on, Bruno, just run along and have your ride, like a good little boy."

That afternoon Anette de Lancel had arranged for Bruno to take Freddy and Delphine to visit the cathedral at Rheims. Freddy, however, insisted that she'd rather ride with Uncle Guillaume than explore any cathedral ever built. She would, in fact, have liked to have visited Rheims, but she couldn't face an afternoon of being captive while she had to watch Delphine admire Bruno. If he were a movie actor, Freddy thought in disgust, Delphine would certainly be the founder and president of his fan club.

Freddy loved Delphine with a depth of emotion, a feeling that was almost maternal, so primordial that she could never remember not feeling it. There had never been a time when Delphine hadn't been in the foreground of her life, closer, in so many ways, than her mother or father.

148

But when Freddy thought that Delphine was acting dumb, she couldn't keep from getting mad. She had the conviction that she had been born to protect Delphine, as if she were the older rather than the younger sister. Freddy *cherished* her sister. Except that Delphine was maddening, so bubble-headed, so stubborn, so obstinate and so accustomed to getting her own way that she didn't think that she needed protection and certainly didn't appreciate it when Freddy tried to force it on her. So then they fought, and since Freddy was much the stronger of the two, she had to use words instead of blows. She wished she could give Delphine a good swat, Freddy brooded, as she trotted along with her silent uncle. Just on general principles.

Her sister's absence pleased Delphine enormously. She would never have been able to try her first cigarette if Freddy had been watching, she thought gleefully, as Bruno showed her how to inhale, passing her a lit cigarette, as he drove slowly along in the car his grandfather had loaned him for the afternoon.

"I don't really like it," she confessed, disappointed by her acrid, incautious puff. "Still, it will make me look more grown-up."

"How old are you?" he asked indifferently.

"I'm almost sixteen," she answered, exaggerating by many months.

"Then you're approaching the dangerous age." Bruno gave a short bark of a laugh.

"Sixteen? Dangerous? My mother won't even let me go out on a date until my next birthday," Delphine protested. "Sixteen will only be the beginning."

"Well, your mother has good reason to keep you locked up. I suppose she's afraid that you've inherited her tendencies," Bruno said casually.

"Oh, Bruno, stop being so silly," Delphine giggled. Then she couldn't decide if she should be flattered or not. "What do you mean, 'tendencies'?"

"Surely you've heard . . . well, her background."

"Background? She's from Dijon. Is that what you mean?"

"Forget what I said. It isn't important."

"Now that's absolutely not fair!" Delphine said indignantly. "You can't drop a hint and then tell me to forget it."

"Never mind, Delphine. Let's just say that I think it's remarkable how your mother seems to have rehabilitated herself. It just shows you what the passage of time can do—that, and the shortness of most people's memory. Of course, your mother's past has been hard on Father. But, on the other hand, he's got you and Freddy to make up for it. I'm sure it was worth it to him."

" 'Past'? Bruno, you have to tell me!" Delphine demanded, blazing with curiosity.

"Ask her yourself, if you want to know so badly." Bruno lit another cigarette for himself, as if he considered the subject closed.

"I think you're just putting on an act," Delphine said in a scornful tone that she had learned never failed to draw fire. She drew a tiny puff on her own cigarette and studied the countryside with interest. "How far are we from Rheims?"

"I suppose you know where she started singing?" Bruno remarked after a few minutes of silence.

"In Dijon, of course. She used to have private lessons from the best teacher in the city. Mother sings to us all the time. Freddy and I know most of her songs by heart. Of course, she doesn't sing professionally anymore, but she's constantly asked to sing at the most important charity benefits in Los Angeles," Delphine answered proudly.

"Is she indeed? Charity benefits? How very respectable." Bruno gave a short laugh. "Did she tell you about running away from home to Paris?"

"Bruno, no!" Delphine squealed in delight. "*She didn't!* How exciting."

"It wasn't exciting at the time," Bruno said somberly. "It was totally . . . well, there's no other word than . . . sordid. She was only seventeen when she ran away with a cheap, third-rate music hall singer. They lived together in Paris—as lovers—before she met our father and got him to marry her. Everybody said that she had other lovers as well."

"Who told you such terrible lies!" Delphine cried, beating on his leg with her fists. He pushed her away.

"Both of my grandmothers, that's who. Grandmother Lancel told me it was the reason why our father has been as good as ignored in his career. With his war record and his name, he should have been an ambassador by now, instead of being exiled as far from France as possible." Bruno glanced at Delphine. Her face was averted.

"My own mother's mother, Grandmother Saint-Fraycourt," he continued in a conversational tone, "told me that no one in Paris would have received your mother because of the scandal of her living openly with a man she wasn't married to and working as a performer in a music hall—a place with clowns telling filthy jokes and parades of stark-naked girls. Then your mother came out to do her little turn, singing popular love songs in a bright red dress and red shoes—her signature outfit, I understand. She was known as 'Maddy.' That's why I say it's remarkable

150

how she managed to turn herself into a perfect lady after she married Father. You have to admire her for that."

"I don't believe one single word! You're making it all up!" Delphine shouted, in a fury of denial and shock.

"Then ask anybody. If you think I'm a liar, ask Grandmother. Ask Grandfather. Ask your own parents. Every word is true. I've grown up with the story. I'm amazed that they managed to keep it from you. It certainly explains why they waited so long to bring you back to your own country."

"We were posted abroad. We *had* to go," Delphine said, beginning to sob. Bruno pulled the car over to the side of the country road and stopped the motor.

"I'm really sorry, Delphine. Please don't cry. Listen, I really thought that you must have known all of that—it happened so long ago that it doesn't matter anymore. Come on, let me wipe your face. It hasn't been good for me, you know, never knowing my own mother and not having a father either because he's always been so far away. It was almost like being an orphan. How would you like to be brought up by grandparents?"

"If you wanted a father, why didn't you come to live with us?"

"I wanted to! But my grandparents Saint-Fraycourt wouldn't allow me to even come to visit. They're very old-fashioned. They were certain your mother would be a bad influence on me."

"That's the stupidest thing I've ever heard!"

"That's the way they are. You'd have to know them to understand."

"I'd never understand people like that!" Delphine said passionately.

"You'll never have to. Look, I shouldn't have said anything. Could we just pretend that you never asked me any questions, and I never answered any? Why bother about what a lot of old people think? Come on, Delphine, blow your nose. We're almost in town. We'll go to a café and have some lemonade and wander around. We might even take a look at the cathedral while we're at it. Keep Grandmother satisfied."

She'd ask her mother, Delphine thought, as Bruno started the car. She wouldn't believe Bruno or her grandmother. But what if her mother had run away from Dijon when she was seventeen? *What if her mother had had lovers and lived with them?*

She never talked about when she was young and going to parties and meeting boys and getting invitations to dances and how she met Father, the way you'd expect. There was . . . there always had been . . . *something*. Not secret exactly, but something . . . unspoken, mysterious

. . . something missing . . . something she couldn't even name . . . a gap . . . that informed Delphine's imagination that her mother was different from the mothers of her school friends. What if what Bruno had said was true? What if she had been . . . Maddy?

Of course she didn't believe him, but she wouldn't say anything to anyone. She didn't want to know a thing about it, Delphine thought defiantly. It was nobody's business. She'd never even think about it herself. It didn't matter. Even if it were true, it didn't matter at all.

After dinner, during the first week of the summer visit, Jean-Luc de Lancel asked his sons and Bruno to take a walk with him.

"You'll want to bring sweaters," he said. "It seems cool to me to-night." Paul and Guillaume exchanged a glance. Obviously, on this hot night, their father had an itch to visit his cellars, where, as in all of Champagne, the depth of the cellars hewn out of the chalky soil was so profound that from the hottest to the coldest day of the year the temperature never varied from a cool ten degrees centigrade.

"I'm not going to bother, Grandfather," Bruno said, and didn't no-tice as Jean-Luc picked up a heavy jacket that was hanging in the coat closet near the door to the château and threw it over his arm, along with the extra sweater he'd brought for himself.

So Bruno has never visited the cellars, Paul thought as the four of them walked along. I suppose he wasn't interested enough. Or perhaps Father didn't think he was old enough. After all, he didn't invite Delphine or Freddy or even Eve, and the Lancel cellars were certainly more fascinating than anything else on the property. They were not anywhere near as large as the sixteen miles of cellars belonging to the giant firm of Moët & Chandon, nor as extraordinary as those of Pommery, in which the connecting galleries were each arched in a different way, in the Roman, Gothic and Norman styles, yet Paul knew that the girls would have liked to see them.

A visit to any cellar of a major champagne-producing house was a revelation to anyone who thought of a wine cellar as merely dark, musty and cobwebby. The Lancel cellars were no exception. The four men found themselves inside an underground town, well lit and well ventilated and paved, with broad, walled access avenues leading to narrower, walled streets that were regularly crossed by other streets, until, within a few dozen feet, anyone but a habitué risked becoming completely lost between walls seven feet high, made of thousands of champagne bottles lying on thin strips of wood, built up layer upon layer, until they formed long, precise piles that were ten feet deep, protected at the edges of the cellar by chalk walls as smoothly finished as if by a mason.

With a grimace of thanks, Bruno put on the jacket his grandfather handed him. Guillaume and Jean-Luc walked between the walls of the champagne as if they were hedgerows, stopping every now and then to pull out a bottle of particular interest and show it to Paul and Bruno.

"Every one of our vineyards has been replanted since the plague of phylloxera first attacked them—there isn't an unhealthy vine left in all of Champagne, as far as I know," Jean-Luc said thoughtfully. "I suppose one shouldn't complain but it seems unfortunate that, with the Depression, the price of grapes should have plunged. People can't afford to drink our wine, it seems. Orders are way down, is that not so, Guillaume? Prohibition hasn't helped, either. However, we of Champagne have seen worse days and I have no doubt that we'll see better ones before long."

As he spoke, he stopped at a wall that marked the end of the cellars. Bruno looked back, unable even to guess at the location of the entrance to the cellars, dumbstruck by the size of the caves. He shivered slightly and took a step backwards, evidently unwilling to listen to his grandfather's discourse in the cold.

"Just a minute, Bruno. I have something to show you. Every Lancel must be informed of our family's safeguard, for who knows what the future will bring? Or how soon? Guillaume?"

The Vicomte pointed toward the wall, and Guillaume pressed firmly on a section of chalk no different from any of the others, except for a slight scratch on its surface. It swung away from the wall on a concealed hinge and revealed a metal lock. Jean-Luc de Lancel took a small key from his key chain and, inserting it into the lock, opened a door in the wall, made out of massive blocks of chalk many feet thick. Total blackness lay beyond the door. He entered the darkness before the others and switched on a battery of lights. Before them lay another vast cellar, filled entirely, except for the access streets, with gleaming ramparts of champagne. The wine, in piles of twenty bottles high, could almost have been bars of gold, so brilliantly was each bottle dressed in its two gilt labels with its upper neck and cork covered with festive gold foil.

"Most of these are normal-sized bottles," Jean-Luc said with a gesture, understanding their awed silence. "Over there are the Magnums, the Jeroboams, the Rehoboams and the Methuselahs, although the demand for the bigger sizes isn't what it used to be, I regret to say. The storage conditions are perfect, but nevertheless I remove the vintage bottles every twelve years and put them on the market, since even the best champagne is usually undrinkable by the time it is twenty years old. I make it an unbreakable rule to replace them as soon as there's another vintage year, no matter how that affects the profit of our house. When the harvest isn't good enough to be vintage, I replace the bottles from that year every four years. But this cellar is always full. *Always.* Even if we should have a disaster, a year in which the wine is undrinkable, I will never touch them—no, not even if several bad years come in a row—for it is the strength of the House of Lancel. This is our treasure. We call it *Le Trésor.*"

"What's the point of a huge cellar full of champagne you only sell and replace, sell and replace? What good does it do to hoard it?" Bruno asked, puzzled.

Jean-Luc de Lancel smiled at his grandson and put an arm around his shoulders. All this, after all, was for the family and he delighted in explanation.

"In 1918, Bruno, when the war ended, I came back to my home and discovered that the Italian general and his staff, who had used the château as their headquarters, had consumed all the stock of champagne in the cellars. Perhaps they had bathed in it, for every last bottle, of hundreds of thousands, was gone. The same thing has happened here before, in my grandfather's time, in 1870, when Valmont was occupied by German troops during the Franco-Prussian War. In 1918 our vineyards were in a pitiful state—many of them had been bombed to shreds during the last months of the trench fighting. It took three and a half years of unrelenting work and care, Bruno, and much of the family fortune, before we harvested our next full crop of grapes. We have, to a large extent, recovered, but now that our bank balance is healthy, many of our vines, alas, are middle-aged."

"Oh?" Bruno asked, not understanding as well as Paul and Guillaume what that meant.

"By the time a vine is ten years old, it is at its prime," Jean-Luc continued. "At fifteen years it is middle-aged. No vine is very useful after twenty years. Soon you must dig it up and replant it. Those vines planted in 1919 are at their best right now, but they have only a maximum of eight, perhaps ten more years of useful life."

"I still don't know why you keep these bottles here," Bruno interrupted impatiently, eager to leave the cold cellar. His grandfather continued, speaking with deliberation.

"Who knows what the future will bring? Who knows how easy it will be to replant as necessary? Who knows—and this is where I am most uneasy—what will happen if there should be another war? Germany is rearming. The first place the Germans march toward in France is Champagne—it has always been thus. We are blessed by our soil, and we are cursed by its location. I have no doubt that Monsieur Hitler already has plans for our heritage. So I have done all that I can do. I have kept back a large percentage of the best wine every year and stored it for as long as it was useful to do so. Should there be another war, after it is over, a Lancel will come back to Valmont and find a treasure that no one else knows about except for the Martins, three cellarmen —three cousins whom I would trust with my life. They brought these bottles here so that if necessary we will be able to rebuild, to replant, to restore the vineyards, by selling this champagne. There I have no fear—there will always be a market for champagne as long as civilization endures."

"Does Mother know?" Paul asked.

"Of course. Women have run vineyards as well as—sometimes better than men. Look back at the Veuve Clicquot and at the irresistible Madame Pommery. Today there is Madame Bollinger and the Marquise de Suarez d'Aulan at Piper-Heidsieck. Yes, your mother knows, and perhaps one day you will want to tell Eve. But the girls are too young to be bothered with my gloomy view of the future. Now, before we leave, let us drink a glass together—it will be quite cold enough without chilling."

The Vicomte turned to a table near the door to the secret cave, on which tulip-shaped glasses were standing upside-down, covered from any dust by a linen cloth. He pulled out a bottle of rare pink champagne, the most difficult of all to make, from the lath on which it rested, not disturbing any other in the pile, and, using the blunt-edged tweezers designed for the purpose, uncorked it gently. A spiral of smoke, as frail as a sigh, appeared and disappeared. Only then did he pour two inches of the champagne into his glass, twirling it to rouse it from its rest. Guillaume, Paul and Jean-Luc all looked approvingly at the snow-white, quickly vanishing froth on top of the wine. As the Vicomte held it up to the light they admired the incomparable pale pink tint of the liquid, and bent forward to inspect the many bubbles forming at the stem and jumping to the surface with an animation and a uniformity of shape that told them how good the wine promised to be. Only the Vicomte sniffed the wine, but he passed the glass to Bruno, and told him to listen to the bubbles, saying softly, "There are those who do not know that it speaks." Then he filled all their glasses, twirled his own glass, and finally tasted the champagne.

"To the future!" he said, and they all drank. As Bruno finished his glass, his grandfather asked, "Did you notice that the champagne tastes one way in your mouth and another way at the back of your throat after you swallow it?"

"No, to tell you the truth, I didn't."

"Ah, then you must pay closer attention next time, my boy. It is a glow, perhaps, rather than a definite taste, and only a perfect champagne has it. It is called the Farewell."

A few days later, on a misty afternoon in Paris, Vicomte Bruno de Saint-Fraycourt de Lancel, as his visiting cards introduced him, although he had not been baptised with the name of his mother's family, threw his cards down on the table in his club's card room and said to the friends with whom he'd been playing, "Gentlemen, that's it for today."

"Leaving us so soon, Bruno?" asked Claude de Koville, his close friend.

"My grandmother asked me to be home early for tea—she expects guests."

"The perfect grandson," Claude said mockingly, "and just when your luck was in. Too bad, Bruno. Maybe with you gone I can win a hand for a change."

"I wish you the luck of the draw," Bruno said, getting up and taking his leave. When he left his club he took a taxi directly to the Rue de Lille. Since his encounter with Eve he had found himself tense and irritable, and he refused to permit himself such emotions without relieving them.

"Good day, Jean," Bruno said to the butler who opened the door of the great house. "Is Monsieur Claude at home?"

"No, Monsieur Bruno, he's out for the afternoon," the man answered. He had been in the service of the Kovilles all his life, and he had chased both Bruno and Claude out of his pantry on so many occasions in years past that he spoke to eighteen-year-old Bruno as if he were still the schoolboy he had always known.

"That's a pity. I was hoping for a cup of tea."

"Madame la Comtesse is having tea now. She's alone this evening. Shall I inform her that you're here?"

"Oh, don't bother—on second thought, yes. Do that, Jean. I'm dying of thirst."

A few minutes later the butler led Bruno into the small second-floor salon where Sabine de Koville was sitting on a sofa in front of a tea tray. Her long legs were crossed under the skirt of her flowing, draped

156

Vionett afternoon dress made of almond green silk crepe. Its cross-cut bodice fell away from her white neck, and at her hip one fastening caught the dress to the side in a graceful, Grecian line.

Sabine de Koville was an elegant creature of thirty-eight, with a sleek helmet of dark, straight hair that turned under below her ears, and thin, curling lips painted bright red. Her eyes were long and lazy, with mockery in their corners, yet her low voice was characteristically impatient and restless, no matter to whom she was talking. She always dressed in the seductively feminine clothes of Vionett, for her firm flesh was just a bit too abundant to look well in the boyish Chanel styles and she judged that Schiaparelli was too easily copiable by the ready-to-wear, and perhaps too amusing to be worn by anyone seriously dedicated to the couture.

The Comtesse de Koville was considered one of the most intelligent women in Paris, in spite of the fact that she never made intimate women friends, or perhaps because of it. No one had ever been known to refuse an invitation to one of her parties, but she often took tea alone.

"If you're looking for my son, Claude, Bruno, I can't help you . . . he never tells me where he's going or when he'll be back," Madame de Koville said, as Jean left the room. Bruno approached the couch and stopped two feet away from her, his eyes respectfully lowered.

"I knew he wasn't at home before I came," Bruno said. "I left him at the club. I don't think he'll be back for hours." There was a pause as she inspected him, standing as if he awaited her orders. She raised one of her large, rather square hands to her lower lip and tapped it lightly, thoughtfully, as if she were trying to come to a decision. She uncrossed her legs, put down the cup of tea she was holding, and tilted her eyes up at Bruno as if he had just told her a particularly subtle joke. Her voice, when she spoke again, was as if the short exchange on the subject of her son had never taken place.

"So, it is like that, is it, Charles?" The question was asked brusquely.

"Yes, Madame," Bruno answered in a subdued tone, his head inclined in a manner that was utterly respectful.

"Did you put the car away, Charles?" she demanded.

"Yes, Madame." His voice was subservient, docile, and his dark eyebrows knit together in concern.

"Has it been washed and polished?"

"Yes, Madame, exactly as Madame ordered."

"Did you bring up all the packages I sent you for, Charles?"

"I have them right here. Where would Madame like them?" Bruno asked, his deeply indented upper lip more prominent than ever in his submissive face.

Sabine de Koville rose, in a swaying slither of silk, without a word or a smile, and led the way from the small salon to her dim bedroom, where her maid had already drawn the draperies. "You may put them down here, Charles," she said, and the restlessness in her voice deepened.

Bruno turned around and locked the door to the bedroom. "Does Madame need me any further?"

"No, Charles. You may go." Bruno took her hand, as if he intended to kiss it. Instead, he turned it over and pressed his lips to her palm, sucking the soft skin up into his plump mouth so that she felt his teeth and his warm breath. He held her hand prisoner and raised his head. Her eyes narrowed in sudden, almost unwilling pleasure. "You may go, Charles," Sabine de Koville insisted imperiously.

"I think not, Madame," Bruno said, and still grasping her hand, he pulled it forward and downward so that it rested on his crotch, where his penis was thrusting forward under his trousers. "Stop that, Charles," the Comtesse said, trying to pull away, but he held her hand mercilessly so that it was forced to cup him. She lowered her eyelids and held as still as if she were listening for some tiny, imperceptible sound while she felt Bruno twitch and harden, again and again, against her palm and long fingers, until he had grown enormous. Her thin lips parted involuntarily, she drew in her breath sharply, and an expression of gourmandise appeared on her severely sophisticated face.

"Madame must stand absolutely still. Madame must do whatever I tell her and nothing else," Bruno said harshly. "Does Madame understand?" She nodded gravely, feeling the hot, heavy congestion grow between her thighs as she looked at the boy's suddenly fierce features. A vein jumped in his temple, and his sulky-sweet mouth looked ugly in a way that made her long to kiss it, but she made no gesture in his direction.

"Madame must stand against the wall," he muttered. "Madame will not remove her shoes." She complied, her back straight and her breasts proudly high. He stood over her, only inches away, his hands roughly weighing her heavy breasts while his thumbs and forefingers sought her nipples under the thin folds of silk. He found them and pinched them, knowingly and repeatedly, with stern fingers that came perilously close to causing pain. Her hardened nipples sought the touch of his mouth that did not come. In spite of her resolution she pressed her body away from the wall, toward his, but he pushed her shoulders back. "I told

Madame not to move," he commanded in an implacable voice, and with one hand he continued to tease one of her nipples while, with the other, he moved with a scornful slowness down over the silk that covered her full, taut body until it reached the mound he sought. He stopped there and rubbed the firm protrusion with probing, adamant fingers. Again she tried to arch so that her pelvis could come into contact with the jutting ridge of his crotch, but Bruno forced her to stay immobile while his fingers gradually molded the silk until it slipped between her legs, stroking and pulling on her with a maddening touch, now light, now ferocious, now withdrawing, now venturing boldly. Her breathing became shallow as she waited, her head thrown back in absolute abandonment. The silk had grown wet. "Madame may kneel on the chair by the bed," Bruno ordered.

"I . . ."

"Madame will do as I tell her."

She crossed the room, her eyes cast down to the carpet, too excited to allow the boy to see her expression. Her gown flowed sinuously around her full body as she knelt on the armchair, holding on to its back. Bruno knelt on the carpet behind her and raised her skirt to her waist. Her rounded, proffered bottom was naked, her legs, still in her high-heeled shoes, were only half covered in silk stockings, her full white thighs were cleft by a thin line of black hair. For a long minute he looked and savored her position of powerlessness, until he bent forward and pressed his mouth, a mouth that might have been that of a beautiful woman, deeply into the hair between her legs. She moaned. "If Madame makes any sound, I shall stop," he threatened, and she nodded in absolute obedience, forcing herself to remain still, restraining herself from any response, so that all her senses were concentrated on the hot sword of his tongue, the biting, tormenting play of his lips and teeth, and the strength of his hands that held her apart so that he could use her freely.

She could hear Bruno opening his trousers with one hand, and she shuddered violently in abandoned anticipation. He pulled her to the edge of the chair so that her belly rested on its seat, with her knees on the carpet and her opening on a level with his straining, distended penis. She held her breath as she felt him mount her and plug its smooth, tightly engorged head into her hungry body. She knew enough not to try to push back on the length of him, but to wait motionlessly, her ferocity contained by her willpower, until he could endure his own torture no longer and jammed himself forward, filling her completely. His hands held her at her waist, pinning her to the chair so that she couldn't move, while he pulled himself out almost entirely before he plunged into her again, as brutally, as heartlessly as any animal. He thrust into her wide-open sheath without thought or care, in a bestial, murderous frenzy, until, in a long, violent spasm, with his face contorted into a silent scream, Bruno found his long, terrible, drawn-out release. Only when he had satisfied himself completely did he drag her off the chair and throw her down onto the carpet, face up. Roughly he plunged his face between her legs, and as she felt his lips sucking, she began to quiver and buck into a monstrous climax. For a moment they both lay silently on the floor.

"Has Madame any further need of me?" His voice was yielding, that of a willing servant.

"No, Charles. Not tonight," she said curtly. He got to his feet, buttoned his fly, and unlocked the door, leaving without another word. Sabine de Koville lay on the carpet without enough strength to get up, a smile on her long, curling lips, which Bruno had not once kissed. He knew better, she thought dreamily, far better than to try.

8

STRATOCUMULUS, Stratus, Cumulus, Cumulonimbus, Freddy said to herself, turning the words over lovingly in her mind, munching on them with a bone-deep pleasure she had never felt for any line of poetry. The meteorological terms for different types of low cloud formations were of absolutely no practical use to her. As a fifteen-year-old student pilot she would not be allowed to fly through anything but clear weather, but she hadn't been able to resist searching for the cloud names in the school library since they weren't in her basic ground-school textbook.

"Could you *please* give me that bag?" an irritated voice shrilled. Freddy whirled around apologetically, and handed over the half-pound of Woolworth's jelly beans. She tasted more lovely words—Altocumulus, Altostratus, Nimbostratus, the cloud formations to be found above 6,500 feet—and wondered who had invented them, while she poured a pound of chocolate-covered marshmallows into another bag. She worked absently but quickly, for she was the only girl behind the candy counter, and customers were waiting impatiently.

As she worked through the morning, Freddy began to calculate the state of her finances. When she had reached fifteen, last January, her allowance had been raised from a quarter a week to thirty cents, largesse in these Depression years. It was now early November of 1935, and her allowance had amounted to thirteen dollars and fifty cents so far this year.

Freddy shook her head over the thought of one personal extravagance that she couldn't resist, although it ate deeply into her allowance. She was a movie nut. She'd seen *The Lost Squadron* with Joel McCrea five times, and *Central Airport* and *Ace of Aces* six times each. She'd only been able to see the *The Eagle and the Hawk*, with Fredric March and Cary Grant, four times because of exams, but she'd gone to *Night Flight*, with Clark Gable, nine times during a school vacation. *Ceiling Zero* and *Devil Dogs of the Air* were coming to the movie house in the next few weeks, she thought with a sinking heart caused by the knowledge that she shouldn't, but would, spend the ten cents for each admission.

She had already wasted—no, not wasted, *invested*—three whole dollars on movie tickets this year. Another three dollars had gone on birthday presents for Delphine and each of her parents. If only she'd had time to make them presents at school, in shop class, instead of buying them, if only she'd even learned how to knit or crochet or sew, Freddy thought, angry with herself, as she contemplated the hoard of seven dollars and fifty cents she had saved out of her allowance. So much for unearned income.

The picture of her earned income was healthier. Her job at Woolworth's every Saturday paid thirty-five cents an hour, bringing in two dollars and eighty cents a week. Unknown to her family, she'd had that job for the past three months. She had been able to save it all except for the carfare to reach the downtown Woolworth's, the fifty cents she'd spent on a pair of men's Levi's to wear for her lessons, and the money for her sandwich lunch at work.

Her earned income now amounted to twenty-six dollars and fifty cents, which, combined with the seven-fifty from her allowance, made a total of thirty-four dollars. Thirty-four dollars was an awful lot of money, she thought ruefully—unless you were learning to fly. So far she had taken three hours of flying lessons, a half hour at a time each week, and they had cost her twelve of those precious dollars. Mac, thank heaven, had reduced his usual price of six dollars an hour to four, his "under sixteen" price, he'd told her. She still had twenty-two dollars in her kitty, enough for five hours more if she could continue to hitch rides out to Dry Springs and back each Friday. That would amount to eight hours of instruction in all. If she kept her job, she'd still be able to buy the essential Christmas presents for her family. Shouldn't anybody at all be able to know enough to solo in a total of eight hours? Maybe Mac would even let her solo with less time, she told herself hopefully, as she measured out jujubes.

After all, hadn't Mathilde Moisant learned to fly in thirty-one minutes? And become the second licensed woman pilot in America? But that was back in 1911, before all the annoying rules and regulations had been established to keep people out of the air. What's more, the early planes looked so simple that they must have been like flying bikes. They had no throttles, no brakes, no instrument panels; they looked like large pieces of weird gym equipment with a wheel somewhere in the middle; they had nothing in common with Mac's new, red, enclosed-cockpit Taylor Cub, than wings and the ability to get off the ground.

She really wished she didn't have to lie so much, Freddy admitted to herself regretfully, as she filled a bag with long strings of licorice. If she'd still been at Sacred Heart, under the inquisitive nose of Delphine, she couldn't have managed to get away with it, but her parents had allowed her to transfer to the local public school, John Marshall High, without too much of a struggle. The Sacred Heart education had been so good that, combined with a year of summer school, she'd been able to skip her junior year at high school.

Now, at fifteen, she was in her first term as a John Marshall senior. Three months ago, when school began, she had started to lie. To explain why she was away all day Saturday working, she'd invented a weekly day-long visit with an invented best friend who lived in Beverly Hills and had a swimming pool, in which Freddy said she was practicing to get on the school swimming team. This particular lie was readily believed, since Freddy was already a star on the diving team, the only girl in school to feel entirely happy as she launched herself from the high diving board. To explain why she came home from school so late each Friday of the past six weeks, after her flying lesson, she'd invented an extracurricular activity that kept her after school: painting scenery for the annual Christmas play. To explain to Mac why she only took a single half-hour lesson a week, although she was determined to solo on her sixteenth birthday, this coming January, she'd invented a mountain of homework, although, in reality, she was able to rush pell-mell through it all at school, during study period. To explain to her family why she spent so many hours after dinner studying for ground school with Mac, she'd invented determination to get very high grades. That was really only four lies—five if she counted hitching rides, Freddy decided. She'd never been told not to hitch rides *specifically*, but she knew what the answer would have been if she'd asked.

Cirrus, she sang to herself, Cirrocumulus, Cirrostratus—the clouds she would one day meet above 16,500 feet. The kings and queens of atmosphere. The only lie she hadn't been able to dope out was how to get out of school early on Fridays so that she could leave sooner for Dry Springs Airport. The teachers at John Marshall High School were the mighty Cirrostratus clouds of teachers. They'd heard every excuse known to teenagers, and only a note from home would make a dent on them. How many notes from home could she produce, even if she stole her mother's writing paper and was able to forge her handwriting? And what if a teacher checked on the phone with her mother? No, it just wasn't possible.

As she weighed out an enormous bag of gumdrops, Freddy wondered, not for the first time, if it wouldn't have been a better idea to tell her parents the truth right from the beginning, and as always, the answer

163

was the same. *What if they hadn't permitted it?* That chance was too risky to take. It was bad enough to lie about something that didn't officially exist. It would have been ten times worse to be forced to lie about something she had been formally forbidden to do. And the other choice —to give up the idea of flying until she was old enough to do whatever she pleased—was no choice at all. That would mean waiting five more years, until she was twenty-one. It was legal to solo on your sixteenth birthday, and on the ninth of January, 1936, she would—*must*—solo. Then, after another ten hours of instruction she could take the test for her private pilot's license. Then, and only then, could she start to build up the flying hours that would enable her to begin competitive air racing, or perhaps, one day, make a flight no one else had yet attempted. It was too soon to form clear-cut ambitions when she didn't know how she would get the money for those ten hours of instruction.

Other women had done it, Freddy told herself, firmly rejecting such gloomy questions. Last year, according to the *Aviation Yearbook* she'd found in the public library, over four hundred American women had held private pilots' licenses. They'd found a way, and so would she, Freddy promised herself as she moved briskly from the counter to the scale.

With relief, she saw that it was time for lunch. There was a sandwich counter in the Woolworth's where the counterman slipped her a free glass of milk with her tuna on rye. In return she gave him a grateful look, from eyes she had no idea were of a blue so saturated with color that they seemed locked into the sky.

As she ate her sandwich, Freddy turned her mind away from her money problems to ground school. Mac had warned her about it. "Sure, you want to fly, kid, but take my word for it, you're going to hate ground school," he'd predicted.

She *hated* Home Economics, Freddy thought, smiling, but she loved ground school. She doted on the Theory of Flight. *Lift!* Wasn't that one of the best words you could imagine? Of course, she'd known that a plane could fly—so had Leonardo da Vinci and the Wright brothers, for that matter—but until ground school she hadn't known why. Lift, glorious lift! And equally thrilling, *Angle of Attack*, the term for the angle at which the wings of a plane met the air—as essential as Lift, and something only the pilot could control. If her Angle of Attack was wrong, the plane, pointing too high or too low, could crash. It was something she thought about for hours. And what about Greenwich Mean Time, the time at that meridian of the planet where the Greenwich Observatory was located? It gave her a deep pleasure to know that everyone in the world of aviation, from the best pilots flying the most powerful planes, to Freddy de Lancel, sitting in front of a tuna sandwich, was willingly and dutifully subject to Greenwich Mean Time.

"I didn't order this, did I?" Freddy asked the counterman who had put another tuna sandwich in front of her. "Barbara Hutton's treat," he answered generously, wondering if she knew that she'd eaten her first sandwich in six big bites and still looked as if she were starving. How could such a *peach* of a girl be allowed to go hungry? He waited all week just to watch her eat lunch, but she must be in love, for she had that faraway look in her eye, and she never wanted to chat. Often, when he wasn't busy during the day, the counterman looked wistfully in the direction of the candy counter, knowing that he could pick her out immediately, for her long hair, like a pile of newly minted pennies, was a patch of brilliance in the busy store and she was tall enough that she stood out from the crowd of women.

As she bit into her second sandwich, Freddy's mind turned to Delphine, who, as she approached eighteen, was becoming even more beautiful than she had been, even to the eyes of a younger sister. The particular tender, almost heartbreaking fragility she had always possessed had not vanished with the years as it so often did as girls matured. The perfect bow of her lips, the upturned corners of her mouth, had been mysteriously accentuated in some way Freddy didn't understand, and which couldn't be explained merely by Delphine's moderate use of lipstick. Her sister's eyes had grown larger, her brown hair swung in a most enchanting bell-like curve, and her high cheekbones and small chin had become more defined. In family photographs she always seemed to be standing at the center of the group, even when she was only on its fringe, because the eye was immediately attracted to the extraordinarily interesting pattern of light and shadow created by her features.

However, Delphine could be just as annoying as ever. One day she had come upon Freddy reading a book on flying and had decided that her sister was pining away for a career in the air—as a stewardess. Delphine had found the requirements for girls applying for jobs as stewardesses and read them aloud to her with unconcealed glee. "You have to be a registered nurse, under twenty-five, under a hundred and fifteen pounds, not more than five feet four inches tall—that lets you out right there, poor thing—and single—well, that part isn't difficult. But what fun you'll be missing because you're too tall—it says here that you get to serve the passengers their food, help refuel the plane, assist in transferring the baggage, mop the cabin floor, carry a railroad timetable just in case the plane is grounded, and—this is the best of all—keep an eye on the passengers when they go to the toilet, to be certain that they don't go through the emergency exit by accident!"

"Funny, Delphine, very funny," Freddy said lamely, her face flushing at being caught with a book about the adventures of a young bush pilot in Canada, when she should have been reading *Anthony Adverse* like every other girl she knew.

She didn't know all the words to "You Do Something to Me" or to "Just One of Those Things"; she didn't spend her allowance to sigh over Greta Garbo in *Queen Christina* or weep at Katharine Hepburn as Jo in *Little Women*; she didn't buy Tangee lipstick or belong to the Joan Crawford fan club or pluck her eyebrows in secret or try on her mother's brassieres when her parents were out. And that was just the beginning of the list of things that she didn't do or care about that Freddy knew made her a willing outsider in her class at school, a girl who wasn't interested in dating or dancing or clothes. So be it, she thought philosophically, finishing her milk. It was no big deal. They didn't fly.

"How about a chocolate soda?" the counterman asked. "On the house?"

"Gee, thanks, but no thanks. I work at the candy counter—I've lost my sweet tooth," Freddy explained regretfully. She wished she had the nerve to ask him for another sandwich instead.

Terence McGuire sat behind his desk in his office, where he should have been paying his bills, and found that he was thinking about his fledgling, Freddy de Lancel. He had taught many men and boys the craft of flying, as well as one or two women, but Freddy was the first girl who had been his pupil.

The craft itself was teachable, he was convinced, to anyone with a grasp of basic logic and enough desire and patience to learn. Unlike some skills, it didn't require an inborn predisposition, for none of his pupils had flying genes, any more than he had.

Man was not born a flying animal, yet even if no birds had ever existed on the planet to demonstrate the fact of flight, McGuire was convinced that man would have learned to fly, just as, if there had been no fish, man would have learned to swim. Flight wouldn't have happened during his own century, more than likely, but sooner or later someone, one of the many who had cast their eyes questioningly at the skies since the days that man first stood upright, would have unlocked the secret of flight, just as someone had built the first wheel, someone had rigged the first sail, someone had figured out how to build the

Pyramids, and someone else had invented gunpowder. It was in the nature of the beast, he told himself, to keep pushing—regardless of whether it was a good idea or a bad one.

No question about it, you didn't have to be born a flying version of the young Mozart to become a pilot, and yet . . . and yet . . . a few, only a very few, people were *natural* flying animals—no two ways about it. The great majority of the people he'd taught successfully were not. But there had been, among his students, a few who had an immediate feeling of what he thought of as *rightness* in the air. It was as if they had an extra sense, a seventh sense, since the sixth sense was spoken for, that he, Terence McGuire, knew existed, even if he couldn't spread it out on a table and measure and weigh it. He had it himself, he had had it the first time he took up his first ship, and he believed that Freddy de Lancel had it too.

It wasn't just her eagerness. Eagerness, all by itself, was a bad thing in a game in which patience was as essential as the ability to tell your right hand from your left. It wasn't just her fearlessness. Too many pilots who crashed in training accidents had been fearless. No, there was something else involved in that seventh sense for which he had never found satisfactory words, a sort of *condition of energy* with which she entered into the flying process, so that the tall young girl who entered his office at a run, to let him know that she'd arrived on time, was a subtly different person as she walked out to the Taylor Cub to start her preflight.

Concentration was part of it. He always followed a few steps behind her while she inspected the plane, and he could see that a lightning bolt striking the runway would not have broken her concentration while she was checking the propeller for nicks or cracks both with her eyes and fingertips, looking as if she were positively listening with her skin for any defect in the metal.

You could tell a lot about someone just from watching them do a preflight, he thought. There were the people who did too much, too slowly, double-checking unnecessarily, because, in their hearts of hearts, they truly hoped to put off the moment of climbing into the plane. They shouldn't be trying to learn how to fly. However, with patience they could be taught, and eventually they might lose their fear.

On the other hand, there were the people who cut corners, as if they hadn't understood that they were entrusting their lives to a piece of equipment in which each bolt, nut and screw had an essential function. Those people shouldn't be *allowed* to learn how to fly, and after he'd given them one warning he'd refused to take them up again. Most mistakes a student could make were survivable, but improper inspection of the ship while it was still on the ground was not among them.

At this point, after watching Freddy make seven preflight checkouts, he'd be willing to go up in a ship she'd checked out without watching her do it with his own eyes. Not that he'd tell her, of course. Or do it, for that matter.

Damn, but he liked the way Freddy *used* the sky, Terence McGuire thought, getting up from behind the desk he hated. Students tended to bounce all over the sky, slipping and sliding, clawing and clutching, rearing up and plunging down, overcorrecting their mistakes and then overcorrecting the new set of corrections, as nervous and skittish as if they were unbroken horses. He made sure that there was plenty of sky for them to learn in, but so many of them approached it as if it were an enemy, as if they didn't trust it.

Sky liked to be treated with decent respect, combined with a calm, quickly responsive but determined hand on the stick, and dancing, dancing, *dancing* feet on the rudders.

As important was the fact that at each lesson he could see her precision improving. Precision was primary in this game . . . without precision, no other flying ability or combination of abilities was worth damn all. At each lesson, Freddy was achieving a higher degree of predictability and smoothness in the angles of her banks and turns, maintaining her airspeed and altitude exactly where he wanted them, more and more of the time. *Exactly*, McGuire was not backward about telling his students, meant just that: no room for any variance whatsoever.

With more and more frequency she was executing a perfect rectangle, that fiendishly finicky series of steps that set up a good landing, a procedure involving dozens of elements of coordination of mind and body. It was utterly elementary when you knew how to do it, McGuire reflected, and a nightmare of frustrating inaccuracy until then.

Freddy's landings were becoming more and more consistent as well: a steady floating descent toward the numbers painted on the end of the runway, and then a quick and gentle setting down, tailwheel touching simultaneously with the two front wheels, a merger with the ground in which an ordinary passenger wouldn't be able to separate out whether the plane had just decided to dissipate its speed and settle down on its own, or whether the pilot had put it down with a complicated knowledge as much in the body as in the head. It was all done through a series of totally unmagical and logical steps, yet, McGuire mused, no matter how many students he had taught or would ever teach, there would always be magic in a good landing.

Fortunately the kid didn't have a speck of passivity in her. A pilot with precision and accuracy down cold wouldn't be worth a hoot in hell if he weren't always on the alert, ready to react immediately to a change in conditions: a sudden gust of wind, a sudden drop in the wind, the appearance of another plane where it had no right to be; engine failure or any of the other devils that would always lie in waiting where man, machine and air came together . . . part of the price of flight. Or part of the challenge, depending on how you looked at it. If you ran out of lift and airspeed, you were in trouble, but if you ran out of ideas at the same time, you were dead.

McGuire ran his hands over the map box Freddy had given him for Christmas. Somehow she'd persuaded her high school to let her out of home economics and nutrition and managed to take shop instead, just as he'd told her to do four years ago. When she'd shamelessly fooled him into giving her a first flying lesson. He could still see the glory on her face that had caused him to tell her father that it wasn't her fault. The map box was a product of her shop class, a tall, long and narrow wooden case of her own design, with a number of deep drawers, each one with a metal pull and a place for a label on it.

The pile of maps that Mac was used to searching through now lay neatly in drawers that slid in and out with a smoothness that made it a pleasure to use. He'd given her two hours of air time for Christmas, and he didn't know whether he or Freddy had been the more delighted with the exchange of gifts.

Today it wouldn't be an exchange, he thought, whistling cheerfully in anticipation of the look on Freddy's face when he told her that today her birthday present was a cross-country flight, the destination her choice, the flight time his treat. Of course, they'd have to be back by sundown since the landing strip wasn't lit, and in the middle of the winter it would be dark very soon after five o'clock.

High school was still out for Christmas, so that she was due to show up for her lesson early in the afternoon, any minute now. After a week that had been spent giving lessons to would-be pilots, like the local doctor whose girlfriend thought he looked like Lindbergh, and the local banker whose wife hoped he looked like Lindbergh, and the local lothario who wanted to look like Lindbergh, and who persisted in wearing a helmet and goggles inside a closed cockpit, it was only natural, McGuire told himself, that he was looking forward so keenly to giving a lesson to someone who looked like a cross between the way

Carole Lombard must have looked when she was the same age and . . . what the hell, why not admit it, Amelia Earhart, before she'd cut her hair so short.

"Cross-country? Oh, Mac, I can't believe it!" Freddy fizzed with excitement, jumping up and down as if she were six instead of sixteen today. "It's the best birthday present I've ever had."

"But now you're wasting time," he said, shutting down his smile. "You can be as grateful as you want to when it's too dark to fly."

"Oh gosh," she said in the tone of voice of someone who has thought of an impediment to a priceless treat.

"What's the problem?"

"Nothing," Freddy said hastily. "It's O.K. I just have to be home at a decent hour tonight to get dressed up. My parents are taking us out to the Brown Derby for dinner, since I wouldn't let them give me a sweet-sixteen party. Can you imagine me and a sweet-sixteen party?"

"Frankly, no. So, where are we going?"

Freddy had been flying in and out of the many airports around Dry Springs for touch-and-go landing practice, and some of them appealed to her more than others. "Burbank," she decided quickly, picking the biggest and busiest and most challenging one first. "Then Van Nuys, then Santa Paula—then out over Topanga Canyon . . . and then . . ."

"Catalina?" He'd like to see her land at that tricky mountain airport, the shortest and least forgiving landing strip in the area.

"No, Mines Field—and then back."

"Mines Field? Are you planning to get a head start on the National Air Races?"

"O.K., Mac, so I just want to see it, I'm curious, I admit it, is there something wrong with that?" Freddy said in slight embarrassment as she busily took the necessary maps out of his box, so that she could plot her flight plan on paper.

In the air, Freddy realized how far she had progressed in three months. The terrain, which seemed to be fed toward her in a never-ending strip from the horizon to her wingtips, had once been bewilderingly unfamiliar. Now it was speckled with friendly landmarks: occasional farms; the scratch tracks of dirt roads; the deeper, darker scars of almost-dry riverbeds with the welcome olive green of the trees that grew along them; particular confirmations of the dry yellowish earth of the San Fernando Valley; and even the individual shapes of certain spots where the vegetation native to California grew in unwatered soil.

Freddy's eyes had been constantly roving through the sky and over the land beneath her, as Mac had taught her, her head moving from side to side so that her knowledge of what was going on in the sky and on the ground was as complete as possible at all times. Not watching for traffic was, in his book, as unsurvivable a mistake as not checking to make sure you had gas before you took off. Many experienced pilots had inexplicably failed to take these elementary precautions and died because of a moment of absentmindedness.

As she handled the controls he was quiet, letting her do as she pleased while he watched for mistakes. No question about it, she was a true flying animal, born to fly as some humans were born to ride horses and others were born to swim. He'd bet money he didn't have that one day she'd learn everything he knew and maybe more.

Although Mac wasn't issuing his normal instructions, Freddy heard his words in her ears. "The *earth's surface* is what you fly by," he'd said. "You mentally smooth it out and keep your fuselage *parallel* with the surface over which you're flying. The horizon isn't important unless there's a mountain on it. Always, at all times, you must be aware of the earth's surface."

The first time he'd said those words she'd been disappointed. Freddy had imagined that once she could handle a plane she would experience a kind of blazing burst into a state of exalted freedom from the earth. But the more she flew, the more earth and sky fused into one, so that her freedom existed *within* a great bowl, an inexhaustible bowl in which all things were important, a bowl whose edge was the horizon, everchanging as she approached it, luring her on and on, without end, because once the horizon was no longer ahead it disappeared and a new horizon beckoned.

She didn't agree with Mac that the horizon wasn't important. To Freddy's eyes, the sight of the horizon filled an elementary need, and caused a basic hunger to fly toward it and see what lay beyond. She knew it was the same for him, but that, as her teacher, he wanted her to concentrate on other things.

Casually, and so quickly that she didn't notice, Mac pulled the throttle back so that the plane's power went dead. "Your engine has just failed," he said in the sudden silence. "Where are you going to set her down?"

"There's an unplowed field by the right wing," she answered him.

"Where else? Forget unplowed fields. That's too easy. Pretend they're not there. Assume that this valley is covered with orange orchards. What's your second choice?"

"That road over to the left. It's wide enough and there's no traffic on it."

"Why wouldn't you want to put her down on that strip between those two imaginary orchards over there?" Mac asked, pointing, while Freddy, her eyes darting from the instrument panel to the ground, began to glide methodically down to the point at which she would begin an approach pattern for an emergency landing.

"I like the road better . . . there's no traffic in either direction. It's a bit wider, and I can land into the wind and stop quickly. Sooner or later I can hitch a ride to the nearest town and telephone for help."

"Hmm," he grunted in approval, sitting with his hands on the cowling of the cockpit while she cut a textbook-perfect pattern on the downwind and crosswind legs of the landing and, fifty feet above the road, glided straight toward the road on her final approach. At that point he pushed the throttle in and the power roared back on. Freddy pulled the stick back carefully to regain altitude without stalling, sorry as always that the simulated emergency landings they practiced so often could never be carried to their conclusion. Probably the highway department would frown on it, or the local farmers would complain.

She approached Burbank with caution. All the commercial airlines that landed in Los Angeles used Burbank, and while they could communicate with the control tower, she had no radio and had to depend on a visual entry into the busy traffic pattern. Something about taking her rightful place in the pattern, and finally working her way through it until she was next in line to touch down, reminded her of the formal etiquette of the dancing class her parents had tried to send her to, for a few miserable months. You had to be exquisitely polite, as if you had on white gloves and your best dress and were waltzing in a room full of other dancers, as you calculated your proper position in the sky. Van Nuys Airport, farther up the valley than Burbank, was much less crowded, and she almost felt that she had it to herself, as she touched down lightly and, without stopping, took off again in the direction of Santa Paula.

The Santa Paula airport was only five years old, a single grass landing strip bordered by a small river along which grew tall trees. "Let's stop here for a few minutes," Mac suggested. "The cafe has the best home-made pies in the valley."

After they had tied down the plane, Freddy realized that they were the only fliers on the field. It was startlingly quiet; no sound of engines or voices, only the wind that always blows at airfields rustled the leaves of the trees. It was so warm that she took off her blue pullover and tied it around her waist and stood, looking around, in her Levi's and a boy's white shirt. A heavy leather belt pulled the denim pants in as much as possible at her waist; still the man's trousers were baggy on her slender frame, but not too long since Freddy had cut them off at the tops of her tennis shoes.

Santa Paula looked like a rural meadow, yet even if her eyes had been closed, she would have known she was at an airfield, for an empty airfield is a waiting airfield, and rare is the flier who can stay away from one for long. It is as drenched with promise and excitement as the backstage of any empty theater before a performance.

Freddy and Mac each ate two slices of apple pie and drank coffee in thoughtful silence. The counter man read his newspaper as she impatiently tried to push her hair behind her ears and contemplated the next leg of the flight with almost uncontrollable curiosity. The Santa Monica Mountains, which lie between the San Fernando Valley and the Pacific Ocean, rise no higher than some four thousand feet. In the short lessons Freddy had taken so far, she had never had the time to spend crossing these mountains, and her experience of flight had been limited to the confines of the valley.

"Hey, Mac, are we or are we not goin' flyin' today?" Freddy asked as she finished her pie and looked up to see him looking as if he were thinking of something far, far away and long ago.

"You tell me, kid. This is your show."

Back in the air, Freddy quickly adjusted her compass heading due southwest and began to climb higher than she ever had before. She planned to cross the range of mountains at Topanga Canyon. The flat terrain she had become accustomed to changed with amazing abruptness as the mountains reared up quickly under the plane: wild, trackless mountains on which the evil-looking outcroppings of bare, jagged rock had nothing to do with California.

Looking around her, Freddy realized that she could have been over any rough, dangerous, uninhabited spot in the world. Nowhere was there any opportunity for an emergency landing, and she wondered if she shouldn't climb two thousand feet higher so that if Mac cut the motor she would have a longer glide path. She glanced at him, but he was looking calmly ahead, seeming bored. Better safe than sorry, she thought, and decided to gain altitude immediately.

"Don't bother. I promise not to do it," he said, smiling as he read her mind. Two minutes later the narrow mountain pass was behind her wings. As if the planet had decided to play some gigantic feat of magic, before her suddenly appeared an immensity of blue too supreme to have been imagined.

She had known that she was going to see the Pacific, it was plain on the map, but nothing could have prepared her for the sight of the wondrous, shining openness that stretched into infinity ahead of her. It was a new, unknown planet. A pack of sailboats, far below and far away, seemed to flow toward the edge of this endless world, and Freddy, as if she had fallen into a trance, flew toward them. They were venturesome, but not as venturesome as she, for she could overfly them and leave them behind, poor wingless creatures, dependent on wind. West, west she flew, until the sailboats lay directly beneath her, and still west, until they had been left far behind.

"Next stop Hawaii?" Mac asked.

Freddy's mouth fell open as the spell was broken. She was many miles off course and she'd been flying without thinking, flying heedlessly, enchanted, magnetized, straight into the horizon.

"I don't . . . how? . . . damn, I'm sorry," she sputtered, looking around and beginning to turn the plane back toward the coast.

"Take it easy. I let you do it." He watched as she immediately set about regaining a correct course in spite of being stunned by her own behavior. There were two kinds of pupils, Mac thought, those who saw the Pacific for the first time, gave it a quick look, and kept on course as if flying were a chore and the ocean a puddle, and there were those who lost their heads, like Freddy. Of the latter group, most of them were so upset when they discovered that they'd flown out to sea that they asked him to take over on the flight back to land.

Soon they were over the five hangars and the single runway of Mines Field, where the National Air Races would take place in six months. Bulldozers were already at work extending the runway, and bleachers were being built. Freddy circled the field, and then, looking at her watch, decided not to touch down there but to head back directly over the Santa Monica mountains in the direction of Dry Springs. She had lost precious time in her headlong embrace of the Pacific. She changed her compass heading and landed at her home base just after four-thirty in the afternoon of the winter day. The sun was low, but it was so clear that the air was still bright. As she stopped at the spot where the Taylor was always tied down, Mac spoke casually.

"I got you another little birthday present. I'll just go into the office and find it."

"You've given me my present," Freddy protested. She felt curiously empty of emotion. The cross-country flight seemed to have used up all her excitement.

"Don't complain. You're only sixteen once. And Freddy, while I go get it, take her back up, circle the field three times and come down." He opened the door, jumped out of the plane, slammed the door closed without looking at her, and walked away quickly.

For an instant Freddy sat motionless, watching McGuire's back as he strode toward the hangar. Had he said to take the ship up *alone?* No, he hadn't said "alone," but that's what he'd meant.

"YES!" Freddy shouted in victory to the empty cockpit. "Yes, yes, yes," she said out loud, unconscious that she was speaking in a serious, imperative undertone as she taxied to the end of the runway and raced toward her takeoff point, her throttle full open, in an ecstasy of thrust, passionately urging on the plane as she approached that miraculous and logical instant at which she would have enough speed and enough lift so that her wings would rise irrisistibly into the golden air, the beckoning sky, toward the setting sun.

As she took off, quickly rising, she was the archer, she was the arrow. She never glanced toward the empty right-hand seat. Time existed, but not for her. Freddy's hands moved calmly as she reached the right altitude and began to make the necessary adjustments for turns and banks, her heart beating madly with a joy she'd never known as the light plane responded to her touch as if it were her own flesh. The patterns she had cut so often seemed to be made of a new material as she flew alone, the landmarks around the airport registered on her mind with new import. There was a divinity in the moment, a divinity in the edges of her wings as they embraced the night, in the steady roar of the motor, in the knowledge that one machine and one human being, aloft together and alone, made more than one entity. She heard herself laughing and she saw the evening star in the deepening blue of the sky.

Below, Mac stood at the edge of the runway, gazing upward, his eyes never leaving the silhouette of the plane, his hands clenching and unclenching nervously in his pockets. Why the hell had he let her make that long cross-country flight before her solo? It was late in the day and she was tired and probably more emotional than he knew, after the flight over the ocean. Yesterday she'd been only fifteen, too young

175

to solo, and who would argue that the passage of twenty-four hours made her old enough today? What was wrong with his judgment? So what if it was her birthday—he could have postponed it to another time. Could have and, damn it, *should* have.

And yet . . . and yet . . . she was so *ready*. Watching Freddy fly today had caused him to relive the pure emotion that he had felt when he was a student pilot, an emotion that he believed he'd forgotten years ago. He'd thought that becoming a mundane teacher of what had once been his obsession had burned out his joy in the purity of flight, but today Freddy had made him relive the poetry, breathe again the air that lured him to leave the planet earth time after time. Christ, but the sky was getting darker by the second. It was almost the shortest day of the year. The temperature must have dropped twenty-five degrees since they'd been at Santa Paula. He was cold, but he couldn't dash into the hangar and get his jacket as long as Freddy was up there. He'd never known a plane take so long to make three circuits of any airport.

Freddy flew on. She saw the evening star again and knew it was sending her a message, a friendly and important message that she had already accepted as one she might never decipher, no matter how much it meant to her. How she longed to climb up into the heavens until she could see the stars of the constellation of Capricorn. The books said that they were far away, too far to be seen. She didn't believe it, would never believe it, for she knew that she flew now under Capricorn, the constellation of her birth.

Looking below, she picked out Mac's figure, a solitary dark shape on the runway. She waggled the wings of the plane to let him know that she'd seen him, completed the third circuit and, with a sigh of rebellion, but acceptance, prepared to come in.

Mac didn't move as Freddy made a perfect landing, the red plane set down sweetly on its front wheels, its small back wheel touching down at the same time. His hands were still clenched as she taxied over and came to a stop not far from where he stood, and they relaxed only when she cut the engine. The door opened and she hurtled out of the plane in one bound, almost knocking him over with the force of her rapture as she flung her arms around him. She burned in the night like a Fourth of July sparkler, her red hair whipped by the wind, her eyes so incandescent that they flung light wherever they looked.

"I did it! I did it!" she exclaimed, and kissed him all over his face. She opened her arms wide and looked up at the evening star as if she owned it. "I did it, Mac! Oh, thank you! Thank you!" He found he couldn't speak. He felt as young, as triumphant, as intoxicated as she;

the emotions he had long forgotten closed his throat with prohibited tears. He tapped his watch and shook his head warningly. "I know," Freddy said. "I have to go or I'll be late. I'm late already. Oh, Mac, I don't care. O.K., I'll go, I'll go. But Mac, I'll be back! There's so much to learn."

Forgetting to fill in her logbook, she gave him another huge hug and a last grateful kiss and ran out to the road to hitch a ride back home. Mac still stood on the landing strip. On his cold cheeks he could feel the warmth of her impulsive kisses. It seemed as if her strong arms were still wrapped around him, her wildly happy voice still rang in his head. He sighed and shook his head. As he started to tie down the Taylor he stopped and rubbed his cheek with a slow, meditative, half-astonished grin. Sweet sixteen, he said to himself, sweet sixteen—so that's what it was all about.

9

EVE would have preferred to hold Freddy's birthday dinner at Perino's, the most elegant French restaurant in Los Angeles, but Freddy had been to the Hollywood Brown Derby once before, and had fallen in love with the rough-and-tumble of its show-business atmosphere, with the corned-beef hash and creamed chicken and the bottles of catsup on each table, and the telephones that could be plugged into each table, an amenity that Eve still found unthinkable, no matter how often she visited the restaurant.

Eve wondered what her mother or, for that matter, her mother-in-law would have thought of taking young girls to such a place. Could either of those gentlewomen of the old school even have imagined a restaurant in which, as tonight, men and women in evening dress sat in the booths on either side of Tom Mix, who was dressed in an elaborate Western outfit and eating an enormous bowl of bouillabaisse; a restaurant where, every night, autograph hunters formed a permanent crowd on the sidewalk around the fringed canopy at the entrance, as they waited for the movie stars to appear; a restaurant from which, as tonight, many of the people in the room would leave for the prizefights at the Hollywood Legion Stadium only a block away, sometimes missing the notorious fistfights that took place regularly between some of the Derby's most famous customers?

How had she spent her own sixteenth birthday, Eve wondered. Surely there had been a special family dinner party; perhaps she had been allowed one festive glass of Dom Perignon; possibly there had also been a tea party with eclairs and petit fours for a few of her friends. She couldn't truly remember, for sixteen was not an age of which the French made much. At sixteen a girl was still considered a child; her own hair had still fallen girlishly to her waist, she had gone nowhere without a chaperone, she had never been to a public dining place.

And yet . . . and yet . . . at sixteen, had she not been more than a child?

Eve smiled secretly to herself as she looked at her daughters, sitting up so straight in the low-sided booth, gazing discreetly at the stars dining all around them, many of whom had greeted Paul and Eve as they went to their tables, for the French Consul and his wife were popular everywhere in Los Angeles. There had been many a glance of appreciation as they had been introduced to Delphine and Freddy, many a nod or a wink of congratulations addressed to Eve and Paul at the sight of their daughters.

Tonight they had both done her proud, Eve thought contentedly. Delphine, only seventeen and a half, looked startlingly sophisticated in her simple white chiffon evening dress, her only ornaments a string of pearls and pearl earrings. Even if she had been wearing inappropriate diamonds, no one would have noticed, Eve thought, because they would have been so occupied by the grace with which she held her head, and the outright beauty of her features.

Freddy, although she had come home late from school, tonight of all nights, had somehow managed to persuade her hair to fall into relatively disciplined waves around her flushed, happy face—Eve had always known that she could do it if she wanted to—and her first evening dress, made of dark blue velvet trimmed with a wide border of white satin, made her look more grown-up than she ever had before. This gala dinner must really mean a great deal to her, Eve thought, for Freddy radiated a kind of excitement that was new to her, an excitement of a higher intensity than any she had ever before displayed in a life full of noisy discovery and eagerly shared enthusiasms. In fact, Eve realized, Freddy was so excited that she had barely said a word the whole evening, and they had reached dessert. She touched Paul's hand and nodded lovingly toward their dazzling younger daughter, a blazing girl, all astonished blue eyes and bonfire hair.

"Where is she?" Eve said softly.

"We'll never know," Paul answered.

"Well, we know it's not a boy."

"Thank goodness for that," Paul said.

Delphine, a freshman at UCLA, went out on dates far too often to please him, and even tonight, after dinner, she was going to leave them to meet her best friend, Margie Hall, and dash off to some fraternity party. If Freddy was interested in boys, it had never yet been evident. Now, at sixteen, inevitably they'd have to let her go out when invitations came along, just as they had with Delphine. The French father in him objected, but after five years in California he understood the folkways of the country and knew that there was nothing he could do about it.

Delphine nudged Freddy. "Do you see what I see? Look who just came in! Marlene Dietrich and two men—that must be her husband

and Prince Felix Rolo of Egypt . . . they go everywhere together . . .
Freddy!"

"Huh?"

"Look, for heaven's sake, before they go into the bar. Oh, now you've
missed them. They'll be out in a few minutes—I'll poke you."

"Do you see Howard Hughes anywhere?" Freddy asked, in a distracted voice. Delphine could be relied on to spot anyone photographed
in the papers, movie star or not.

"No. Why would you want to see him anyway?"

"Just curiosity," she answered vaguely.

"You look peculiar," Delphine said critically. "Mother, doesn't
Freddy look as if she has a fever?"

"Do you feel hot, darling?" Eve asked. "Delphine's right . . . your
cheeks are so very red and there's a rather funny look in your eyes.
They're too bright. Perhaps you're coming down with something. Paul,
what do you think?"

"She's what is locally known as 'the birthday girl,' sweetheart—she's
just enchanted to be sixteen at last. That's not a fever, it's simply being
grown-up—more or less."

As the three of them turned to Freddy and looked at her with various
degrees of tenderness, she found that she couldn't endure keeping her
triumph to herself for another second.

"I soloed today," Freddy announced, her voice shaking.

"You what?" said Eve.

"You what?" Delphine asked.

"You what?" Paul shouted, for he was the only one at the table who
knew what she meant.

"I took up a plane in the air, circled the field three times and
landed."

"Alone?" Paul asked, although he already knew the answer.

"It had to be alone, Father. Otherwise it wouldn't have been a solo,"
Freddy said, trying to sound reassuring and mature.

"But it's just not possible, Freddy, just not possible!" Eve cried. "You
don't know how to fly. How could you go up in a plane without knowing how? How could you risk your life? Are you completely crazy?"

"Freddy, you had better explain," Paul said angrily, taking Eve's
hand to calm her down.

"It's perfectly legal," Freddy said hastily. "Anybody can solo at sixteen."

"That's not an explanation." Paul's words were angrier than before.

"Well . . . Mother, remember how many times you've told us how you sneaked away from home and went up in a balloon when you were just fourteen years old?" Freddy began.

"That has nothing to do with anything. Marie-Frédérique, I want the facts!" Paul said as loudly as he could without attracting attention in the crowded restaurant.

"The plane was a Taylor Cub with—"

"The *facts*! How did you learn to fly?"

"I took lessons. Eight hours."

"When? When did you have time for lessons?" Paul asked through tight lips.

"On Friday afternoons."

"But that's when you said you were painting scenery for the school play," Eve protested.

"I told you a lie."

Delphine gasped, Eve shook her head in disbelief, and Paul attacked again.

"How did you get the money to pay for the lessons?"

"I . . . I've been working at Woolworth's on Saturdays, at the candy counter. I earned the money."

"But the swim team, the friend in Beverly Hills . . . all those practice sessions in her pool?" Eve protested in outrage.

"I lied about that too," Freddy said, looking her mother in the eye.

"Where did you take these flying lessons?" Paul insisted.

"Out at Dry Springs."

"From the man who took you up the day we drove out there four years ago?"

"Yes."

"How *could* he, that bastard, without letting us know?" Paul's face hardened even further.

"I lied to him too. I told him you were paying for the lessons. It wasn't his fault at all."

"And just how, tell me *how*, you managed to get out to that little airport in the valley on Friday afternoons?" Paul asked, his voice pouncing on Freddy, who had still hoped that no one would ask that particular question.

"I . . . well, everybody does it, it's perfectly safe, I . . . hitched rides . . . but only with people who looked very, very nice."

"HITCHED?" Paul and Eve exploded together.

"There's no other way to get out there except by car," Freddy murmured, making herself as small as possible and looking at the table-cloth.

181

"Oh, Freddy!" Delphine breathed, finally shocked. Lying was nothing special, every kid did it about something or other, but hitching, that was really, truly *bad*. No nice girl would dream of hitching. She noticed Jimmy Cagney passing their table, but she didn't even follow him with her eyes. This was much more interesting.

There was an ominous, absolute, drawn-out silence at the table. Eve and Paul were too angry to trust themselves to speak.

"Eve! Paul! And the beautiful Mademoiselles de Lancel! Ah, what a surprise, what a delightful picture!" Maurice Chevalier stood before them, beaming down at the handsome family group.

"Oh, Monsieur Chevalier, it's my birthday, isn't that exciting? I'm sixteen today and we're celebrating," Freddy babbled desperately.

"Ah, but then I simply must celebrate with you! *Tu permet*, Paul?" He sat down on the end of the banquette next to Eve. "Waiter, champagne for everyone. Lancel, of course. Pink, if you have it. Yes, Paul, I insist." He turned to Freddy. "This is a great occasion, Mademoiselle Freddy. You must be so happy tonight. We expect great things from you, my little one, do we not, Paul? Is it not thrilling, Eve?" He turned to Eve and whispered in her ear. "Would not a certain Maddy have been delighted if she could have looked into the future and seen herself tonight, surrounded by such a gallant husband, such lovely daughters?" The waiter appeared with a bottle of Lancel in an ice bucket. "Good, here is the champagne. Now we must all drink a toast—to Mademoiselle Freddy de Lancel and to her future! May it be glorious!"

Freddy drained her glass. Whatever terrible thing happened to her now, it couldn't feel as bad after a glass of champagne. To fly with the evening star, under Capricorn—could there be a price too high to pay?

Eve lay awake after Paul had finally gone to sleep. Freddy's birthday dinner had ended soon after Maurice's interruption, and by mutual consent nothing else was said to her about her incredible behavior. The Brown Derby was no place to have a court-martial, and the matter would keep until tomorrow—only too well. She and Paul had been too weary and troubled to discuss it as they got ready for bed, but now, tired as she was, she couldn't fall asleep. She rose quietly, put on her robe, and went to sit on the window seat, where she could draw aside the curtain and look out at the garden.

How, Eve asked herself, could a child as straightforward, as honest and as uncomplicated as Freddy had always seemed to be, have calmly built up such a complex series of lies? She had led what amounted to a double life for months, since the beginning of the school year. How could she have lied to parents who had always, it seemed to Eve, given her the best things in life with open hands and unfailing love? She had managed to keep these secrets from Delphine, not an easy thing to do, and she had, apparently, even lied to the man who had taught her how to fly.

What could he possibly have been thinking of? What sort of irresponsible, reckless person would teach a fifteen-year-old girl to do such a dangerous thing, just for money? How dare he call himself a teacher? She drew her feet up under her and tied her robe more tightly around her waist.

It was bewildering even to try to sort this out because there was so much she didn't understand. There Freddy had sat, as bold as you please, looking proud of herself, no less, trying to compare her pack of lies to her mother's own harmless little trip in the hot-air balloon back in Dijon in—when exactly had it been?—in 1910, twenty-five years ago, only a quarter of a century as time is normally counted, but a date that belonged to another world, as long gone as Atlantis, that Edwardian world before the World War.

How old had she been then, Eve wondered. Fourteen, she realized as she calculated rapidly. So she had been as old as that . . . or had it been as young as that? But slipping away from her governess—Mademoiselle Helene, that martinet—and borrowing her mother's hat, was a far cry from learning, during months of deceitfulness and untruths, how to fly an airplane. Only a single detail, an unexpected gust of wind, had made her lose the hat. If it hadn't been for that, no one would have been the wiser and no one would have been angry. In any case, no harm had been done.

In the dark, Eve's lips curved in a smile she didn't know was on her face as she remembered the grandness of shock, the stunning, illuminating surprise she had felt when she'd opened her arms to the view of the countryside from the gondola of the balloon, and the pride she had felt in being one of the few who had actually managed to rise far above the crowd and see for herself what the great world looked like from the air.

She had to admit that she could feel some empathy toward Freddy, if it was only a question of wanting to see beyond the horizon. She had always understood that need, Eve thought grudgingly. It was quite normal to want to feel free and special, particularly at her age.

But actually to fly a plane by herself? There were women pilots, of course. Everyone had heard about Amelia Earhart and Anne Lindbergh and Jackie Cochrane. Their exploits were always news, but they were grown-up women, not young girls, and they were an unusual breed of woman, interested in achievements that belonged in the domain of men. Other women might admire them but didn't understand them.

Oh, it was true enough that Freddy had always wanted to "fly." She'd said so often enough, and demonstrated it with her daredevil antics, but that had been a childish whim, that a girl should put behind her just as she grew out of her escapades on skates or jumping from a window.

Sighing, Eve thought that she had rarely felt so much a failure. The Freddy she had found out about tonight wasn't the daughter she knew, and that must mean that she was an unobservant, careless mother. How ironic it had been when Maurice had sat down with them and insisted on celebrating, imagining that all was joyful with the family Lancel. What was it that he had whispered to her? She had paid no attention at the time, so deep was her shock and anger. "Would not a certain Maddy have been delighted . . ." *A certain Maddy.*

Eve jumped off the window seat, stunned by memory. She stood absolutely still, listening to the heavy beat of her heart. *Maddy!* Maddy who had, without thinking twice, caused a grievous scandal that had lived on for many years, a scandal that had brought great pain and shame to everyone in her family and, she had to admit it, caused Paul's career to come to a dead end; Maddy of the red dress and the red shoes and the amorous songs, the wild applause, the hot, incandescent, orange beacon of the footlights; Maddy who had finally craved every glory the music hall could bring her.

She had been only a year older than Freddy was now when she had deceived her parents night after night in Dijon, plotting to slip out of the house and run to the Alcazar to hear Alain Marais sing. Unthinkable—to meet him alone. Eve blushed deeply in the darkness as she remembered the night she had gone to his rooming house. Two glasses of red wine were no excuse for what she'd let him do to her there— and yet, and yet—he'd asked her permission each step of the way. No! She must not think about the events of that night, not deliberately, although she would never forget them.

She'd been only a year older than Freddy when she'd disappeared and gone off to live in Paris. To live in sin, as they must all have whispered in shocked voices . . . in blackest, deepest sin, although it had not seemed like sin to a carefree girl who called herself Madeleine and made the Grands Boulevards her territory; to Madeleine, who'd taken the dare and auditioned for Jacques Charles and made him sit up and take notice; to Maddy, again renamed, starring in a *tour de chant* at the Olympia, so sure of herself and of her right to do whatever she pleased that she had practically thrown her Aunt Marie-France out of her dressing room when she'd come to beg her to return home. Had she been seventeen still, or eighteen? Eve could still hear her own defiant words.

"I'm not a little girl you can order around anymore . . . How could I be content with a life like my mother's? . . . I have nothing to be ashamed of." Maddy, who was so utterly determined to become a star, come what may, and would never have left the stage had it not been for the war and Paul. When had she finally forgotten Maddy? When, at what moment in all these years, had she become *Madame la Consule de France*, who sang only for her friends at private parties or at black-tie benefits for the many charities of Los Angeles? When had she lost Maddy?

Back and forth in the bedroom, with only a little moonlight to show her the way, Eve walked in a daze of awakened memory. For many long minutes she was lost in the past. She came back to the present. Paul was still asleep, but somehow she knew that Freddy was not.

Eve left the bedroom and walked down the corridor to her daughter's room. There was a light under the door. She knocked and Freddy answered with a faint "Come in."

"I couldn't sleep," Eve said, looking at her daughter, curled up on her bed in her flannel pajamas, forlorn and diminished, clinging to a small book with a blue and red cover.

"Neither could I."

"What are you reading?"

"It's a student pilot's handbook."

"Any good?"

Freddy tried to laugh. "There's no plot and no dialogue, but lots of detailed description."

"Freddy, tell me, this person—this flying instructor of yours—is he a . . . young man?"

"Mac? I've never even thought about it. He flew in the war, with the Lafayette Escadrille, so he must be, oh, I don't know. I could ask him."

"No, never mind. I was only asking because I wondered . . . how much experience he had."

"More than anybody. He started flying when he was just a kid. He's taught hundreds of people. You know, Mother, it really isn't unusual to solo at sixteen. Lots of boys do it. Ask anyone."

"I'm sure you're right. It was just such a . . . surprise."

"You don't sound angry anymore," Freddy said cautiously.

"I'm not. I've been thinking about it. Flying means a great deal to you, doesn't it?"

"More than I can explain. I wouldn't have told so many lies if there had been any other way. I knew you wouldn't give me permission to learn if I asked," Freddy said earnestly.

"Hmm." Eve considered the question.

"Well, you wouldn't have, would you?"

"No, you're right. We would have made you wait."

"*I couldn't have waited.*"

"I know."

"How . . . how do you know?"

"I just do. I was young once too, remember?"

"You're still young," Freddy blurted.

"Not *that* young. Never that young again . . . and perhaps it's just as well. Yes, certainly it's just as well . . . and in any case, it's inevitable. Oh, what are we going to do with you now, my darling?"

"I have to get my pilot's license. I can't lie about that. For one thing, I promise not to lie anymore . . . and for another, I need your written permission to take the exam for the license. It's ten more hours of lessons, minimum."

"What had your plan been? To work until you could pay for that much instruction?"

"Yes. I was going to figure out some other . . . things . . . no . . . lies to tell you to account for the time I wasn't at home or at school."

"The tennis team? The Easter pageant? The Queen of the May?"

"They're all good ideas—except for the Queen of the May. If I hadn't been so proud of my solo and told you about it, I bet I could have done it."

"Even the written permission?"

"Forgery," Freddy said somberly. "I would have."

"I have no doubt," Eve murmured. "Still, now we know. All things considered, I think that it's better this way."

"Does that mean that you'll let me work at Woolworth's?" Freddy demanded eagerly.

"I'll have to speak to your father. But I believe I can manage to make him understand. However, there is to be absolutely no hitchhiking, Freddy. None. Whatsoever. Do you promise me faithfully?"

"Yes, of course, but how can I get out to the airport?"

"If you're good enough to fly a plane in the air, I must assume that you're quite capable of driving on the streets. Most of the boys get their licenses at sixteen, don't they? I remember when Delphine talked of nothing else."

"Oh, Mother!"

"When you learn to drive, Freddy, you can borrow my car."

"Oh, Mother—you're so good to me!" Freddy lunged at Eve and crushed her with a hug. Although she was bigger than her mother, she snuggled as close to her as she could, needing the comfort and reassurance that the contact brought. She hadn't been bad enough to be cast out of the family as she had feared during the last hours alone in her room. They both had tears in their eyes.

"Let's just say that I'm grateful for certain favors . . . big and small. Now you must go to sleep, darling. I'll see you in the morning."

"Good night, Mother," Freddy said, looking as if she were planning to stay up all night, dancing over her good fortune.

"Good night, darling. The solo *was wonderful*, wasn't it? I can imagine . . . no . . . I can . . . remember . . . yes, in my own way, *remember* . . . how you must have felt. Congratulations, my darling. I'm very proud of you."

"Come on, Freddy, it's time," Delphine said. Freddy looked out the window at the winter rain that had followed her birthday and had lasted for a week. Delphine had arrived that Sunday from her sorority house and announced that it was time to do the "make-over" she had promised Freddy for her birthday present. Freddy didn't see how she could reject the experiment politely, with the excuse that she had too much homework. Clearly she didn't, and clearly she had to accept this gift of Delphine's or be accused of being ungrateful, unsisterly and uncooperative.

"I'm going to drape a bath towel around you," Delphine said, once she had Freddy settled down in front of the dressing-table mirror in her room. "Did you bring your hairbrush?" Freddy handed it to her with a silent sigh of impatience, yet how many of Delphine's friends would give anything for this concentrated attention?

Delphine, absorbed and serious, turned Freddy around so that she was facing away from the mirror. She brushed all of her sister's waterfall of hair away from her face and held it back with big plastic barrettes. She took a bottle of cleanser, moistened a piece of cotton with it, and wiped Freddy's face with its high outdoor color. The cotton was as clean when she finished as when she had started, for Freddy used nothing on her skin.

"There," said Delphine. "Now I can start." She took one of the boxes of Max Factor pancake base she kept in a drawer and covered Freddy's strong features with a layer of thin, expertly applied base, turning them all one pale tint, several shades lighter than Freddy's natural coloring. She powdered Freddy all over in the same soft beige color and studied the result silently, circling round and round her sister.

Freddy looked as pure as a statue, she thought. A vigilant statue, with bone structure as resolute and inevitable as the vaulted ceiling of some great cathedral. But she was Freddy's sister, not a boy, and boys, normal boys or exceptional boys, simply didn't date statues with marvelous bones. That wasn't what they were looking for in a girl.

Although Delphine had never said anything to Freddy, she was concerned with the fact that her sister, at sixteen, was not being asked out enough. Enough? Practically not at all. If a girl hadn't become popular by sixteen, what possible kind of future could she hope for? Freddy stayed home on many a Saturday night, trying to seem perfectly happy to be left alone with her impossible books about flying, but Delphine knew that she must be deeply worried and too proud to admit it. Freddy danced masterfully, for they'd often danced together, practicing the latest steps, but who would ever know how light and rhythmic she was, if she never went out?

Delphine took out a puff and a round flat compact of rouge. Using the lightest of strokes, she applied the rouge delicately, blending it so that it looked absolutely natural. Then she took out a sharp eyebrow pencil and, with feathery gestures, drew tiny light brown lines between the coppery hairs of Freddy's eyebrows, darkening them just enough to make them a dramatic frame for the deep sockets of her wildly blue, unwavering eyes. Freddy stirred restlessly. "I didn't know you had all that stuff. Do you use it?" she asked.

"Of course. Everyone does."

"I never realized."

"That's the point. If it's too obvious, you've done it wrong. But it makes all the difference. Freddy, it's so easy to learn. I'll teach you exactly how to do it when I'm finished. I'll take it all off and then I'll do half of your face and you can do the other half yourself, and we can practice until you've got it just right . . . I don't care how long you take. You have to relax and have the courage to make a mistake. You can always wipe it off."

"That's . . . that's really sweet and generous of you, Delphine."

"You're only sixteen once. This is a big birthday and I had to give you something important," Delphine said with pleasure. She worked in silence for a while and then added casually, "High school boys are really drips."

"So I've noticed."

"You're lucky you skipped a year. You'll be at UCLA next fall, and that's another story. College men. Thousands of them. And a majority who aren't drips."

"Good news." Freddy gave her as innocent a smile as she could manage. Delphine could be so adorable when she was trying to be subtle.

"College guys know how to appreciate a good conversationalist. They'll go for you."

"That's better news."

"Only up to a point," Delphine said, using the words as expertly as a picador, as she took out a small box in which she kept cake mascara, her most precious possession.

"Oh?"

"Well, you know how men are. . . . They like to do most of the talking, even with a good conversationalist."

"That's silly. Isn't it a waste of the other person?"

"Not really. Good conversation is really making somebody else feel brilliant—you know—bringing him out, encouraging him to express himself, listening *creatively*." Delphine dipped a brush into a glass of water and rubbed it expertly on the cake of black mascara.

"If you're trying to say that I talk too much, I know I do," Freddy said.

"Oh, Freddy, it's not that at all. It's just that boys—even college men—can't talk intelligently about aviation. They don't know anything about it, and they certainly don't want to learn from a girl."

"Well, what else can I talk about?"

"Cars," Delphine said solemnly.

"I've tried. I really, truly have, but a car's such a ridiculous thing. I mean, where can the dumb thing go, for heaven's sake, except back and forth on some silly road? It's so one-dimensional! What's the big deal about cars?" Freddy asked in disgust.

"If . . . just *if* . . . you could not breathe a single word about planes and pretend to be interested in cars, just for a little while, cars could lead to other things. Most girls can't even be semi-intelligent about cars or engines, so you're in great shape there. Then . . . well, then the conversation will get around to other things."

"Like what?" Freddy was frankly puzzled but willing to learn.

"His fraternity, his classes, his professors, the football team and what he thinks about its chances, what bands he likes, what new movies he's seen, who his favorite movie stars are, what he's planning to do when he graduates, what he thinks about absolutely anything—even what he reads in the comics—oh, Freddy, there are a million things to get a man to talk about if you start with cars and keep asking questions."

Lash by lash, Delphine had applied the black mascara, managing, in her skill, not to make it too thick or too beady. Now she inspected Freddy's eyelashes, found them to her liking, and, slowly and dramatically, imparted her most important piece of insight to her sister. "If a man stops talking, and you don't know what to say next, just repeat the last few words he's said in a questioning tone of voice, as if you hadn't understood him, and he'll go right on talking, and tell you more and more. *It never fails.* I've never told another girl about it before, not even Margie."

Impressed, but not convinced, Freddy asked, "Just echo his last few words? That's all there is to it?"

"That's all. It's simple, but men just can't resist you if you do it right. You'll get a reputation as a terrific conversationalist, and with your looks, and your sensational legs—I'd give *anything* to have legs like yours—you'll be the most popular girl in the freshman class."

"My looks?"

"Don't look in the mirror yet. Wait till I've finished. I haven't done your hair." Delphine loosened Freddy's hair and brushed it until it lay as neatly as it ever would. She parted the bright tumble on the side and then, with the curling iron that she had been heating on the dressing table, she pinched a few cunningly placed waves into the long heap of hair until it rippled down on either side of Freddy's face and turned under at the ends. Finally she applied a coat of pink lipstick to Freddy's lips and, dissatisfied because the shade wasn't any deeper than Freddy's own, used a tube of light red lipstick to cover the pink. Delphine took out a big, black chiffon scarf from her dresser drawer, unpinned the sheet that she'd put around her sister, and draped the scarf artfully so that Freddy's triumphant shoulders and the deep cleft above her breasts were revealed in their nakedness.

Delphine caught her breath in delight. "Turn!" she commanded, like a fairy godmother, and she whirled Freddy around on the seat so that she faced the mirror.

Freddy looked at herself in astonished silence.

"Well?" Delphine breathed.

"I . . . I don't know what to say . . ."

"You're devastating! Freddy, you're simply breathtaking. I can't believe it's you!"

"Don't I look too . . . old?"

"You look like a movie star," Delphine said with reverence, bestowing the ultimate compliment. "I knew you could, if you just used a little makeup." Delphine bent over her creation and kissed Freddy on the top of her head. Her taste was faultless, and Freddy had turned out to be even more beautiful than she'd dared to hope. She felt a tiny twinge of envy, but a quick look in the mirror reassured her. They were such different types that they set each other off.

"Let's go show somebody," Delphine begged, tugging her sister's arm.

"No, I can't. I'm . . . well, it's a little frightening. Give me time to get used to it. Anyway, who can you show? Mother doesn't know you use all this stuff, does she? Dad would kill you. And me. Me first, I'll bet."

"You're right . . . I just got so excited that I forgot. Freddy, when you're at college I'll do your face for you any time you need it—that's the second part of my present." Delphine bustled about in satisfaction, putting away her battery of cosmetics, many of which she had first seen advertised in movie magazines and ordered by mail.

"Wait, let me look at those pictures," Freddy said suddenly, in abrupt curiosity, reaching for a pile of glossy photographs that she spied in the bottom of one of Delphine's cosmetic drawers.

"Never mind!" Delphine ordered hastily, but Freddy was already turning them over, photo after photo of Delphine and a variety of unknown escorts. They had been framed in pasteboard mats that bore the names of all the well-known nightclubs of Hollywood. There were unmistakable cocktails on the table in front of Delphine, and a cigarette in her hand, as she sat at the Coconut Grove, the Trocadero, the Palomar ballroom, the Circus Cafe, and Omar's Dome.

"But these men . . . they're not college boys, are they?" Freddy asked.

"Some are, some aren't," Delphine answered, flustered.

"Say, wait a minute . . . this character has to be thirty if he's a day. But not bad looking. Delphine, do you drink and smoke?"

"Not much. Only enough so that they won't think I'm a kid."

"How old do they think you are?" Freddy wondered, captivated by her sister in the photographs. She was a glamorous, older, poised, flirtatious stranger, smiling into the eyes of men no one in the family had ever met.

"Twenty-one."

"How do you get away with it?" Freddy asked in admiration.

"I have fake ID, of course. Everyone does," Delphine answered evasively, and, grabbing the photographs away from Freddy, shut them up into a drawer and slammed it shut.

"Just answer one more question," Freddy said to her older sister.

"One?"

"Those men? Do they take you out dancing in nightclubs and buy you orchids to pin on your shoulder and look at you the way they do in those pictures because you're such a terrific conversationalist? Do you spend the whole evening asking them what they think about the football team and the comic strips and what kind of car they own?"

"Not entirely," Delphine said carefully, "but it's a beginning."

It was a Sunday afternoon in June of 1936, the day after Freddy's graduation from high school, and she was off alone on a cross-country flight, the longest she had ever made, from Dry Springs to San Luis Obispo and back. The most direct route lay north and a little to the west, over Big Pine Mountain of the San Rafael Range, across the valley to the east of Santa Maria, past the Twitchell Reservoir, and over the Arroyo Grande, directly into the airport at San Luis. A far easier route would have been to simply follow the coast north and turn east at Pismo Beach, but it wouldn't have given her any practice in navigation, and during the months she'd been working with Mac toward her private pilot's license, which she obtained just over a month ago, Freddy had been studying navigation as hard as she could.

Navigation, *pinpoint* navigation of absolute accuracy and precision, was, once you could fly, the next essential key to becoming a true pilot. It wasn't as mysterious, Freddy thought, as she'd first expected it would be. Basically it meant flying with a knowledge of where she was at all times, knowledge gained by constantly reading the earth and its landmarks, instantly comparing that knowledge with the chart on her knee and resolutely staying on the magnetic compass headings she decided on before she set out. Winds aloft could push a plane off course in a few minutes of inattention, so Freddy watched with vigilance for checkpoints on the ground that should be coming up to the right, to the left or directly underneath her wings. If there was the slightest deviation, she immediately adjusted the compass to make a correction for the wind.

As she passed over the little town of Ojai, which was exactly where it should be, Freddy allowed her mind to turn to the future. Starting tomorrow, she would begin her summer job, working six days a week at the Van de Kamp bakery at Beverly and Western. The chain of bakeries, which had started with a homemade candy called "Darling Henrietta's Nutty Mixture," now owned a hundred windmill-shaped shops all over Los Angeles. Her job began at six in the morning, when the bakery opened, and ended at two in the afternoon, when the afternoon-evening shift took over. Because of the inconvenient hours and the six-day week, she was well paid, twenty-five dollars a week, as much as a trained secretary could hope to make. To Freddy it meant that she would be able to fly several afternoons a week as well as on weekends.

Freddy groaned. Her destiny was obviously bound to selling candy, cookies and cakes, all of which she loathed, but these sweet things seemed to be one of the few businesses that was Depression-proof. Still, daily suffocation in the smells of warm sugar became a minor matter when it meant money for her summer flying time and enough left over to begin, *just* to begin, *only* to begin, damn it to hell, to save for a down payment on a plane.

Today she was enjoying the pure delight of flying Mac's new ship, a bright yellow Ryan STA monoplane with a Menasco C-4 125-horse-power engine, a more powerful plane than the Taylor Cub, and one she'd only flown five times before. Her father had given her a string of real pearls for graduation, but her mother, blessings on her head, had come through with hard cash, enough to buy Freddy three of these long cross-country flights, of which today's was only the beginning. The pearls were the first valuable jewelry she'd ever owned. Maybe, Freddy speculated, she could pawn them.

She knew that she couldn't expect any future financial help from her father. He was perfectly willing to buy her a set of expensive golf clubs, or membership in a tennis club—even bridge lessons, if that had been her fancy. Thanks to her mother, he had finally agreed not to formally oppose her flying, but he'd made it plain that he wouldn't contribute a dime toward it, not even in the shape of a loan. He hoped, obviously, that by making it difficult for her, he'd hasten the moment when she lost interest.

There didn't seem to be any point in telling him that she was determined to own her own plane. The cheapest of the three leading low-priced planes, the Taylor, the Porterfield Zephyr or the Aeronanca Highwing, each cost almost fifteen hundred dollars, with a down payment of four hundred and fifty dollars. A fortune! Delphine had received a new, six-hundred-dollar Pontiac coupé for her eighteenth birthday, and it made her the envy of half the kids in the neighborhood. In car terms, wanting to buy an inexpensive airplane was like wanting to own a Packard, the most expensive car in America. Obviously, she had to find a second- or third-hand ship that she could put into shape, a ship that she could manage to get at a bargain price, on terms that would let her pay for it over a long time.

If she didn't own a plane of her own, Freddy asked herself, spying the peak of Big Pine Mountain right on course and beginning to gain altitude, what future was there for her in flying? More precisely, in racing?

Racing. She knew that she didn't stand a chance of being able to enter any of the speed dashes that covered a relatively short distance, with the planes going straight ahead full out, like racehorses. Nor could she enter closed-circuit races around fixed pylons. Only planes of far greater horsepower than one she could dream of owning stood a chance in any of the various speed races, and then only when they were flown by pilots with racing experience. During the past few years, interest in speed racing had grown so rapidly in the world of aviation that some records only stood for a few days before another pilot managed to surpass them.

However, there were cross-country races held around the Los Angeles area, in which planes flew from one refueling stop to another, toward a goal that might be hundreds of miles away. Each plane carried a handicap, based on its own best possible performance, so that the winner was the pilot who spent the least time in the air, the pilot who flew the smartest race, using the winds and the compass and the charts in the most astute way, the most precise pilot, the most ingenious pilot, the most resourceful pilot—and sometimes the luckiest.

Damn, but she'd been born too late! Amy Johnson, the British pilot, whose career Freddy followed with passion, had taken up flying in 1928. When the girl from Hull had only seventy-five hours of flying time to her credit, she had taken off from Croydon, outside of London, in a tiny, fragile, secondhand De Havilland Moth, and headed for Australia. A sandstorm had forced her to make an emergency landing in the desert; on landing at Baghdad she broke a wheel strut; she lost a bolt en route to Karachi; she ran out of gas at Jansi, where she had to land on a parade ground amid a group of fleeing soldiers; she flew through a monsoon between Calcutta and Rangoon, where she had to replace her propeller with the spare one she had brought along with her. On her last lap, past Indonesia, she fought a sputtering engine and bad visibility over the Timor Sea to reach Darwin, where she was acclaimed as the first woman to fly solo from England to Australia, and became an international heroine.

Now *that* was flying, Freddy brooded, and her hero-worship turned to wistfulness as she realized that Amy Johnson had accomplished her feat when she, Freddy, was only nine years old and had never even been up in a plane.

Amy Johnson had followed her first triumph by establishing a light aircraft record from London to Tokyo and then, when an unknown pilot named Jim Mollison became famous by flying from Australia to England in nine days, she had met and married him. Their two-day honeymoon had been followed immediately by Jim Mollison flying the Atlantic from east to west, breaking a number of records on the way, while Amy was busy beating his own London-to-Cape Town solo record flight by eleven hours.

What a glorious way to be married, Freddy thought with a sigh. She knew no one who would agree with her, but she was utterly beguiled by the idea of the two determined newlyweds setting off in different directions, each in pursuit of a new record to break. Lucky Amy Johnson, who'd met a man who understood the one thing she most cared about.

None of the boys Freddy had met and dated in this last year had been interested in planes. She'd put Delphine's advice to the test, and it had worked. However, being a good conversationalist had subjected her to too many dull life stories . . . it wasn't worth being popular, in her opinion. Sure, she'd been kissed; several times in fact. No big deal, Freddy thought, shaking her head in disappointed memory of timid lips on timid lips, clumsy arms around equally clumsy shoulders.

She'd allowed those kisses so as not to disappoint Delphine, but there were so many important things that she was too late for, Freddy grumbled to herself, as she scanned the horizon. It was all of six years ago that Ruth Nichols had broken the speed record of her friend and rival, Amelia Earhart; two years later, in 1932, Earhart had flown the Atlantic solo; in 1934 Marie-Louise Bastie of France became the first woman to fly a round trip to Tokyo from Paris; in September of 1935, Laura Ingalls flew nonstop from Los Angeles to New York, breaking Earhart's record for that route by almost four hours.

Oh shit, but hadn't everything been done? Amy Johnson had flown a smaller and far less powerful plane than this Ryan more than halfway around the world, and here, eight whole, long years later, where was she, Freddy, but right on course over the Twitchell Reservoir, a lousy

195

manmade body of water, not an ocean or a sea or a desert or even a big river. At this rate she'd never get out of California!

At the small San Luis Obispo airport, Freddy ate the sandwich lunch she'd brought along, and refueled, noting anxiously that aviation gasoline was twenty cents a gallon. When she'd finally earned her private pilot's license, her mother had insisted on taking out and paying for personal accident insurance for her as well as public liability and property damage. Without the insurance, which cost an additional hundred dollars, she wouldn't have been able to continue to fly, but Freddy had to pay for gas herself.

It was one hell of an expensive passion, this way she felt about planes, and Freddy envied the women who had someone who supported them in their flying. Floyd Odlum was behind his wife, Jackie Cochrane; Jean Batten, the great pilot from New Zealand, had been sponsored by Lord Wakefield, who had also helped Amy Johnson; Anne Morrow had her husband, Charles Lindbergh, to teach her to fly; and Earhart had the backing of her husband, the devoted George Putnam. Wasn't there a man somewhere, rich and preferably very old, certainly not one with romantic inclinations, who would like to advance the cause of American aviation by paying her bills?

No, there was not, Freddy answered herself. Perhaps there might have been, if she'd come along ten years ago, when women were first making their memorable marks in the air, but now the great days of the pioneers were past. Well, she might be too late for fame, but there had to be *something* left to do, and she was going to find it!

She knew it as surely as she had always known she was going to fly. She'd been right about that, she thought, looking around the unfamiliar little country airport that she'd never seen before and that she had found without wasting a mile of sky, as if there had been markers and arrows hanging in the air.

Last summer she hadn't even started to learn how to fly, and now she was a full-fledged pilot. If she had the time, the maps, and the money for gas and food, she would take the Ryan straight up to Alaska or way down to the tip of South America. She could start this very minute, knowing nothing more than what she knew already. *She knew enough to do it.* That was the essential thing. The rest would fall into place—she'd make it happen somehow. Freddy thanked the boy who pumped the fuel, made a pass at combing her hair, and climbed back into the yellow Ryan with a light heart.

Several hours later, Freddy was close to the approach to Dry Springs. The flight back had been so uneventful that she'd been tempted to take a few detours and stop at Santa Maria and Santa Barbara, just to enjoy the airport atmosphere and trade a little shop talk with whoever happened to be on the landing strip there, but she knew that Mac would have estimated how long her cross-country flight would take, and that he'd worry if she was late. She'd navigated so exactly, the winds had been so favorable, that she was a good twenty minutes before her scheduled time of return.

There was still time, she realized, with a tense plunge of excitement. It was the perfect kind of day, with unlimited visibility. And she was still far enough from Dry Springs so that nobody would see her. There was not another plane in her neighborhood. It was destiny, Freddy told herself, clearly destiny, that had provided her with this chance to try something she'd been studying for months in her cherished pilot's handbook by Jack Hunt and Ray Fahringer. She saw the introductory page to the "Acrobatic Phase" chapter of the book clearly in front of her. She'd memorized every word.

First of all the student must understand that he is always "a part of the aircraft" the moment he fastens his safety belt. From that time on, regardless of what position the ship may assume, upright or inverted, the pilot is always sitting in the same position relative to the airplane . . . and the controls respond accordingly. This being understood, it is obvious that the pilot need only to "observe" where he is going and "fly" the aircraft. He has been doing exactly this in all of his normal flying . . .

Well, what could be clearer than that? More reassuring?

. . . the loop is the easiest acrobatic maneuver to perform as it is the least complicated of all . . . set the throttle at normal cruising RPM. Now, ease the airplane into a gentle dive . . . as soon as sufficient speed has been obtained, ease back on the elevators and begin the upward arc of the circle . . .

She had flown a thousand loops in her mind, Freddy thought as she took the Ryan up to five thousand feet, an absolutely safe altitude at which to perform the maneuver. She could recite her handbook's list of usual student faults backward and forward in her sleep. The clear diagrams were engraved on her brain. She hadn't actually executed a loop. Not in a plane. But today she was flying the stock ship with the stock engine favored by Tex Rankin, the national aerobatic champion. Hadn't Rankin himself said that precision aerobatics made for a safer pilot? And didn't she owe it to herself to do something special to celebrate? Celebrate her graduation. Celebrate getting her pilot's license last month. Celebrate today's realization that she would not be intimidated by the towering figures of Amy Johnson and Earhart and Cochrane. *Yes!*

Freddy cautiously put the Ryan into a dive, and as soon as she'd reached a proper speed she began to pull the nose of the plane upward. Gradually she pushed the throttle until it was fully advanced, so that she obtained maximum power. A hundred and twenty-five inexhaustible horses were at her command, galloping forward at the lightest pressure of her hand. What bliss, after hours of meticulous navigation, with its pure, austere mathematical pleasures, to make this rushing, heart-pounding leap into the sky.

She held the Ryan in the arc of the circle, and as it reached the partially upside-down position, she threw her head back to observe the nose of the ship cross the horizon. She was a kid on a swing who *can* go over the top, who *can* escape the limitations of gravity for one blinding moment of elation. As the Ryan completed the loop and swung upward again, recovering, Freddy found herself laughing with the giddiness of a child, yet in total control of the ship. She did another loop. And another. And another. Only after a dozen loops could she persuade herself to stop, and then only by remembering how close she was to Dry Springs.

Soberly, flying like an elderly gentleman out for a Sunday drive, except for the uncontrollable grin on her face, she gradually lost altitude and made her usual immaculate landing. She looked around at the field. All was quiet. Several other fliers were fussing about, some of them taking off for a sunset spin, and others putting their planes to bed, but at the hangar of McGuire's school there was no one to be seen. She tied down the Ryan and started toward the office, swaggering like a pirate as she hummed "Till We Meet Again" in triple time. She was filling out her logbook as she heard the Taylor Cub land and its engine shut down.

"Just what the hell do you think you were doing!" Mac yelled as he burst furiously into the office, his hand raised to hit her. Freddy drew back, terrified, putting his desk between them, and he lowered his hand. *"Answer me!"* he shouted, violent in a way she had never believed he could be.

"I was practicing . . . loops," Freddy stuttered.

"How could you dare try a stunt like that! *You could have killed yourself,* you stupid, *stupid* kid, don't you understand that?"

"The book says . . ."

"What damn book?"

"My *Student Pilot Handbook* . . . Mac, it's all in there, everything, every detail. . . . I knew exactly how to do it, it's the easiest maneuver in the book, I took every precaution, and the ship is suitable for doing the toughest aerobatics. . . ." Her words were stopped by the look of murderous rage in his eyes.

"God damn you, Freddy. Nobody, *nobody* is ever allowed to start doing stunts without an instructor and without a parachute! You weren't even smart enough to know that every plane that was up this afternoon within fifty miles could see you clearly, *you dumb, arrogant kid!* I've never witnessed such an exhibition of criminal carelessness! You could lose your license for what you did. You could have blacked out and crashed, you damn fool! The Ryan goes 280 miles an hour at the bottom of the loop. Did you happen to know that detail, Freddy? *God damn you to hell!*" Mac folded his arms, his fists clenched, his lips tight, and glared at her while he waited for her answer.

Freddy looked around the bare office wildly for a place to hide, and not finding one, threw herself against a wall to hide her face. She was helpless to stop the tempest of wrenching sobs that overcame her. He was right, she was utterly wrong, and she had nothing to say for herself. All she felt was the most shameful, utter humiliation. It would be meaningless to say she was sorry. The crime was too big. He hated her. Crushed by most bitter guilt she wept harder and harder, beating her fists against the wall in useless, abject remorse. Finally, after long minutes, Freddy put her hands in front of her face and began to stumble out of the office as quickly as she could, needing only to get to the sanctuary of her mother's car.

"Back in here!" Mac roared. She didn't stop. She couldn't take any more of his rage. He pounced on her, turned her around, and forced her hands down from her face. "Are you ever, *ever* going to do that again?" he demanded.

She couldn't speak but she shook her head in a way that left no room for doubt and pulled away, moving in the direction of the car. He grabbed her again. "You're not going to drive anywhere till you get hold of yourself, for Christ's sake. Come on, sit down and stop it!"

She mopped her eyes and blew her nose, still quivering with diminishing sobs. He stood with his back toward her, looking out the window at the planes that were landing one by one. Sunday fliers reluctantly returning to earth. Finally she was able to speak.

"Can I go home now?"

"No, you cannot. Not until we have a clear understanding. Why did you do those loops?"

"I was feeling . . . happy."

"So you decided to stunt?"

"Yes."

"Why did you do so many loops?"

"It felt so good. I loved it."

"Do you promise never to do it again?"

"I promise."

"I don't believe you."

"Mac! I swear I won't. How can I convince you? I've learned my lesson—I'm not a liar, don't you trust me?"

"No, I don't. I don't think you're dishonest, I think that you truly believe you won't stunt again, but one day, somewhere safe, when you know that I'm two hundred miles away, the temptation will be too strong and you won't be able to resist it. Now that you've started, you won't be able to stop. I know a thing or two about that. It's bound to happen, no matter what you say."

"I can't stop you from thinking whatever you want to think," Freddy said miserably. This meant that he'd never let her use the Ryan again. She'd be back flying the slower, less powerful Taylor, if he even let her use any of his planes.

"Aerobatics is a science, Freddy, not a dumb-ass whoop and a holler. Recklessness is intolerable. Unpardonable. Unforgivable. Aerobatics requires more work, more repetitive precision practice, than any other form of flying."

"I understand. Mac, I wouldn't dream . . ." Freddy began hopelessly. He quirked a cynical eyebrow at her.

"*You wouldn't dream?* That's exactly what you'd do. I know you too well, kid. If there's one thing I can count on, it's that you'll dream. I'll teach you aerobatics. It's the only way to make sure that the next time you pull something like you did today, you'll know what the hell you're doing."

"Mac? . . . Mac?"

"Now, get the hell out of here. Go home."

As he watched Freddy drive away, McGuire thought that he had never come so close to hitting a female in his life. And when she'd cried so terribly, he'd never wanted to comfort anyone so much. Christ! That kid was more trouble than she was worth. But damn, those loops had looked good. And if he didn't teach her aerobatics, someone else would.

10

EVE riffled through the pages of the morning newspaper as she relaxed in the sunny breakfast room. Paul had left for the Consulate; her two daughters were at school; the efficient staff in the kitchen was already busy with preparations for the luncheon she was giving today for a number of the ladies of the French community; yesterday she had arranged the roses from the garden, and placed them throughout the house, so that, for the moment, she could give herself up to the idle pursuit of the news of the world, or at least that view of the world that the Los Angeles paper considered important.

It was May of 1936. France was paralyzed by strikes after the electoral victory of the Popular Front, whose members included a surprisingly large number of Socialists and Communists; Mussolini's war against Ethiopia was over, and an Italian viceroy ruled over millions of miles of North Africa; Hitler's Wehrmacht had occupied the formerly demilitarized zone of the Rhineland in defiance of the League of Nations, a move that was roundly condemned by Belgium, England, France and Italy, although nothing whatsoever was done to stop him. In Los Angeles, the front-page news was the marriage of Douglas Fairbanks, Sr., and Lady Sylvia Ashley.

With relief, Eve turned to the story of the wedding. Here was a woman who, according to rumor, was the daughter of a footman, a woman who had briefly been a "starlet," whatever that might have meant, in a London theatrical revue, and then managed to marry the heir to the title and fortune of the Earl of Shaftsbury. Now, eight years later, divorced from Lord Ashley, she had just picked off one of the greatest movie stars in Hollywood.

Eve bent in fascination over the newspaper photo of the civil wedding in Paris. Lady Ashley had supreme elegance, one couldn't deny it. Her pale wool coat was trimmed with a huge capelike collar of dark sable; the corsage of four giant orchids she wore was pinned below an enormous diamond and pearl necklace; her fingernails were painted as dark a red as her smiling lips. Under thinly plucked eyebrows her eyes were long and almost Oriental. In spite of her classic features she couldn't be called truly beautiful, and Eve saw a coldness in her face.

Next to her, a deeply tanned Fairbanks beamed with the unmistakable joy of a man who has obtained his heart's desire.

The couple was triumphant. They had risen effortlessly above the scandal of Fairbanks's divorce from Mary Pickford, cruised the world in his great yacht for a year before they married, and the wages of their behavior were adulation and envy. Eve wondered, as she studied the photograph of a woman so visibly wrapped in luxury and adoration, so coveted by men that they'd do anything to have her, just how many of the American housewives who would profess themselves shocked by this marriage would willingly trade places with her. Millions? Tens of millions?

She threw the paper in the wastebasket. Times had changed, standards had changed, and she, who had been so severely judged, must make an effort not to become too judgmental herself.

On the other hand, there were Delphine and Freddy, and if she need have no opinion on the Sylvia Ashleys of this world, she had a duty toward her daughters. Delphine had floated so easily through the years that had been, for Eve, full of repressed rebellion. Delphine was, she had to admit, something of a frivolous, self-indulgent child with the suppleness of a born coquette, but there wasn't a single mean element in her personality. She was a virtuoso in dealing with the male sex, yet she didn't seem to take an easy pleasure in making a man suffer because of her. She was an affectionate, mercurial girl; capricious, yes, but essentially good. Admittedly, Delphine didn't seem to have any strong moral convictions, but at her age, in this particular city, did anyone?

Eve missed Delphine, who had gone to live at her sorority house at UCLA. Paul had wanted her to live at home during college, but the campus was really too far away for daily trips back and forth. In any case, it seemed to Eve that her elder child would be much happier surrounded by girls of her own age. If she lived at home, she'd miss the chance to make really good friends, and, so they said, it was those college friends that you kept throughout life.

She was deeply glad that Freddy was still in high school. When her younger daughter went to UCLA next fall, Freddy too might join a sorority and want to live there, but Eve hoped secretly that she wouldn't. She hated the American system against which one couldn't protest that sent children away almost automatically, but at least Freddy wouldn't want to go to college anywhere too far from her precious Dry Springs airport.

On the other hand, she worried that Freddy was missing so much of the glorious fun of being young that Delphine was having. She couldn't think of a close girl friend that she had made during her school years—except, of course, that imaginary one in Beverly Hills. Her interests were just too different from those of her peers. She seemed so young to be driven by a passion for aviation, too young to be so single-minded. If only Freddy were a little more like Delphine, and Delphine more like Freddy. . . . You're a silly woman, Eve told herself, and went into the kitchen to make sure that all was proceeding properly. Thank heaven, she thought, as she began to inspect the finger bowls, the hostess at a luncheon wasn't required to wear a hat, unlike the guests. It was one less thing to worry about.

Delphine put out her cigarette and looked around the bedroom of her best friend and sorority sister, Margie Hall. The room, expensively and newly redecorated entirely in pink and white, was a temple to unsullied maidenhood. It didn't go with Margie's short, chrome-yellow curls, her voluptuous young body, or her sassy green eyes, but as Margie said, if it kept her mother out of her hair, she could endure the decor.

Margie's mother had just been divorced for the third time and married for the fourth. This was the third time that Margie's room in her Bel Air home had been redecorated since she and Delphine had become friends six years ago. It was the former Mrs. Hall's method of comforting her daughter for any emotional pain she might be feeling, and as far as Margie was concerned, it was certainly a more acceptable way to be treated than to be asked to sympathize. And perhaps the next divorce would bring a decorator more in tune with Margie's tastes.

Margie's mother was in Europe, on her most recent honeymoon; her father, according to rumor, was in Mexico, but he hadn't been heard from in years. The married couple who ran the house and asked no questions were, as usual, listening to the radio in their quarters over the garage. Delphine and Margie were settling down to one of their frequent "sleep-overs," for which Eve had given approval to their sorority's house mother.

Eve could hardly disapprove of Margie merely because of her disrupted home life or her lively coloring. According to the nuns at Sacred Heart, whom Eve had questioned, Margie Hall was obedient, punctual, polite and a hard worker who got acceptable marks. High-spirited, yes, but considering the mother, it was a blessing that she wasn't a child who was easily depressed. The hair? Well, it was natural, not dyed. Unfortunately noticeable, perhaps, but there was nothing that anyone could do about it.

If Eve had been given a guided tour of Margie's bower, she would have known that her uneasy instincts had been sound. Margie had ten times as much makeup as Delphine owned, stashed away in her fluffily draped dressing table. Her closets contained an astonishing number of elaborate and fashionable evening dresses, evening cloaks, and high-heeled shoes, all of them designed for a mature young woman, not a girl of eighteen. In a secret compartment of Margie's pink and white desk, there was a large hoard of cash, the proceeds of the many times the two girls had gone gambling with their male escorts in the illegal joints that flourished all over Los Angeles, under a city administration that grew more corrupt every year.

These two gorgeous creatures definitely brought them luck, a growing number of men about town used to tell each other. Margie and Delphine were highly decorative mascots, to whom their escorts slipped bills of large denominations with instructions to keep their winnings, and to come back for more if they lost. Delphine kept all the clothes she bought with her winnings in her friend's closets.

Bootlegging had ended with Repeal, and now that people could get a drink without risk, the gambling craze was bigger than ever. Anyone with the right connections could win or lose a great deal of money in dozens of places on the long strip reaching from the well-appointed clubs of Sunset Boulevard to the shacks at the beach and continuing right out to sea, where water taxis shuttled back and forth to the gambling ships *Monte Carlo* and *Johanna Smith*.

In the clubs where Delphine and Margie were familiars, champagne and caviar were on the house, and everyone who entered had to be in evening dress. There were whispers that the Eastern mob was taking over West Coast gambling, which only added to the allure of the forbidden activity.

Delphine had, of course, made arrangements to ensure her parents' ignorance of her nightlife. It was impossible to have her dates pick her up at the sorority house. The sharp-eyed, suspicious house mother, Mrs. Robinson, would have been on the phone to her mother in an instant if she had seen Delphine going out with anyone but college boys, fumbling, often penniless kids of Delphine's own age. These boys had quickly become far too young and too unsophisticated for her to bother about.

The two girls were inseparable. They were both able to keep their grades at an acceptable level by helping each other through exams, even though they went out dancing and gambling three or four nights a week. Only near dawn did they end the evening with scrambled eggs at Sardi's. Afterwards their dates deposited them back at Bel Air for a few hours' sleep before classes began. Frequently they cut classes, since they both had the ability to memorize easily, and could make up the work they had missed in a few days of studying.

On Saturdays, Delphine and Margie took their gambling money and made the rounds of the best department stores, gaily treating themselves to new clothes and lingerie, feeling superior, over a late lunch, toward the other girls in their sorority, whose idea of a good time was to go to a football game, and afterwards drink a cup of rum-and-fruit-juice punch in a fraternity house with a bunch of undergraduates.

The two friends held each other's heads when they'd had too much to drink; tested new hangover remedies together; never minded trading dates because one man was so much like another; gave each other advice on the newest hairdos and the latest slang; did each other's toenails; compared kissing and petting techniques, and warned each other against men who tried to get them to "go too far," for they were still "nice" girls and their virginity was important to them.

Their favorite topic, the one they couldn't seem to let alone, and the only part of their life that was less than ideal, was the unavoidable fact that they were merely extras to the central drama that took place nightly in the restaurants and nightclubs of Hollywood. They weren't movie stars themselves. No matter how pretty or well dressed they were, no one stared at them and asked for their autographs. They circulated with familiarity in the world that the rest of the country only read about in the movie magazines, on which so many people were fixated, but it was one thing to be recognized by the headwaiter at the Coconut Grove and another thing to be mobbed by fans and photographers.

"Try to look at it this way," Margie offered. "If a picture of you *did* appear in the papers, your folks would lock you up on bread and water."

"If I had my picture in the papers it would be because I was famous," Delphine argued, "and my parents couldn't do a thing about it."

They were both silent in the face of this indisputable reasoning. They both knew actors, but none of them were more than bit-part players. The men who had the money to take them dancing and gambling were young bachelors who were businessmen during the day— the actors were only invited along because of the aspiring starlets they brought with them.

"Cheer up, Delphine," Margie advised, taking five hundred dollars out of their stash and separating it into two equal piles. "Movie stars have to get up much too early in the morning and they're always falling in and out of love, which, you've got to admit, is a trap for anyone who wants a good time. Now, I don't know about you but I've got nothing to wear tonight, and we're wasting time sitting around feeling miserable because you aren't Lupe Velez and I'm not Adrienne Ames, or is it the other way around?"

"Your taste stinks, Margie. Myrna Loy for you, Garbo for me."

"Come on, hon, we have a big night ahead—after dinner we're going out to the beach—there's a new floating casino that's just opened twelve miles off Santa Monica Bay, and everybody who's anybody will be there. Delphine! Stop brooding . . . it's shopping time!"

Freddy was early for her lesson, but McGuire motioned her to stick around while he talked to his visitor. Freddy had met the man before. Swede Castelli was in charge of all stunt coordination at the relatively small I. W. Davidson studio out on Pico. Frequently he'd drive out to Dry Springs to consult Mac about the problems that presented themselves in making yet another World War flying film, for which the public had such an appetite.

Terence McGuire had been a twenty-two-year-old war hero when the Great War ended in 1918. He'd come home from France believing firmly that the future of transportation lay in the air, and had discovered, after making a number of disappointing attempts to start a small airline, that no manufacturer was even building planes with the capacity to make long flights between major cities and carry a payload of passengers. If people wanted to travel, they used the railroad.

Finally McGuire had faced reality and sunk every penny he had left into a Curtiss JN-4. He'd earned a bare living with the sturdy little ship, working at fairgrounds, where the landing field might be a baseball diamond, a racetrack or even a cow pasture. After doing an exhibition of aerobatics, he'd taken up passengers for a spin, at five dollars a head, but the day came when people were only willing to pay a dollar a ride.

The novelty had worn off aviation barely twenty years after the Wright Brothers had made the first powered flight. The army and the navy weren't interested in maintaining their air arms, and for a man who could not imagine working at anything other than flying, the only solution was to go to Hollywood and become a professional stunt pilot for the movies.

For years he'd worked out of the Fox Studios, where fifteen movie companies made their headquarters. There, his skill, his nerve and his youth had been freely and gaily expended in the company of men like himself, men who were willing to work for pay that ranged from a

206

hundred dollars to fly upside-down only inches above the ground to one thousand five hundred dollars to blow up a plane in the air and bail out of it. No stuntman ever made a dime unless his life was at risk, and they earned every cent they made with their bodies. McGuire had flown with Dick Grace and Charles Stoffer, with Frank Backer, Lonnie Hay, Clement Phillips, Frank Clark and Frank Tomick; with Dick Curwood and Duke Green, with Maurice Murphy and Leo Nomes and Ross Cook, and, by 1930, among the dozens of friends he'd made, only a few of them were still alive. Not one among them had died a natural death. They had lived gaily, valiantly, from day to day and died, almost as if by choice, in their youth.

It was then, with the opening of a new decade, when he realized how many of his bantering, uncomplaining friends had lost their wagers with death, that Terence McGuire had taken the money he'd saved and opened a flying school.

It was strictly a matter of percentages; all of the dead men had been superb pilots, and he knew that his turn had to come up sooner or later. He'd walked away from over three dozen carefully engineered crashes, but he'd had his share of broken bones.

Perhaps he was different from most of the others, but he wanted to live to see the future. Nevertheless, he'd never been able to turn his back finally on Hollywood, and although he no longer did stunts, he built a stable of vintage planes, hard-to-come-by antiques, much-repaired 220 Spads and German Fokker D.VII's and English Camels, which he rented to the movie studios to supplement the uncertain earnings of his school. McGuire's ability to plan and organize simulations of wartime dogfighting kept him in demand from film companies making war movies. But he couldn't deny that he missed the old days, the dangerous days, the bad, great old days.

Swede Castelli, like Mac, had been a stunt pilot himself before he retired, but unlike Mac, Freddy thought, he'd taken on the settled look of an executive, and an overly well fed one at that. Mac looked so young next to this man in a business suit who must be as old as he was. . . . Mac looked as if he belonged to another generation entirely, closer to hers than to Castelli's.

In fact, she didn't think that Mac had changed a hair since she'd first laid eyes on him, when she was eleven and a half, five years ago. She'd asked him how old he was after her mother had brought the question up, and he'd told her that he was forty, and explained how it was that he was much younger than her father, although they'd both fought in the same war. She'd been emboldened to ask if he was married, and he'd answered that all smart stunt pilots made it a point to stay single and unattached, and that once he'd passed the marrying age he'd been too much of a bachelor to change his ways. "End of inquisition, kid?"

That was as personal a question as she'd ever asked him, she realized, looking at him plotting out a six-plane dogfight, and yet he was her best friend in the world. Funny to have someone you consider your best friend who certainly doesn't think of you that way, Freddy told herself. Yet that was the way it was.

Freddy watched McGuire carefully, seizing a rare opportunity to observe her instructor. In his presence, during a lesson, she was too busy concentrating to actually see him, no matter how closely she listened to his words. He became simply part of the ship. Once they were back at the school, with her time so tight, she almost never had more than a few minutes to rehash the lesson before she had to drag herself away from the airport and head for home. As he spoke now, she could easily visualize the flight paths of each of the six planes he was flying through the air around his desk, so vivid and precise were his gestures.

Terence McGuire was Scots-Irish, as anybody would know by looking at his thick thatch of light brown hair with a ginger gleam in it, and his light green eyes fringed by unexpectedly long lashes. He had a charmingly good-natured face, on which the tan never quite covered the freckles. He was lean and fit, not quite six feet tall, with a gymnast's muscles. Freddy saw that his life had left a mark on him that would also tell anyone who was interested that this man had spent far more waking time in the air than on the ground. There was something so . . . so *free* about the springy way he moved and carried himself, a man ready for any challenge, something so free about the directness of his regard and the quickness and totalness of his smile. To Freddy, Mac's smile had always meant a promise that together they would turn their attention to the thing she loved best, and now that she considered it, he had never broken that promise. In spite of his open, easy manner he was a tough-minded man of self-discipline and self-control. She wondered if she'd ever meet another man with a smile like Mac's, a smile to which she could trust her life.

"Freddy, be a good kid and give us some more coffee?" Mac pointed to the pot that he kept going on a gas ring on the filing cabinet.

She brought the pot over to his desk. "O.K. if I have some too?" she asked.

"No, you're too young," he answered automatically.

"My mother lets me drink it," she protested.

"I don't."

Damn, Freddy thought, what am I, a two-year-old? I'm almost seventeen and I've been drinking *café au lait* for breakfast since I was in high school, and this creep treats me like a kid. In fact he keeps calling me "kid" and I don't like it.

Sulking, but silent, she listened to the conversation that had ceased to interest her. In the month that she'd been concentrating on aerobatics, she'd realized that all spectacular and complicated stunt maneuvers were based on a mere five simple basics—banks, rolls, loops, stalls and spins—combined in various ways.

Since many pilots crashed as a result of not being able to control spins and stalls, the hard and monotonous practice that she was getting was, no question about it, making her a far safer pilot. The practice was also increasing her ability to fly by the seat of her pants, since, once into a maneuver, mere precision couldn't substitute for a nearly inexplicable ability to capture and go with the "feel" of the plane. And, Freddy thought grimly, if that wasn't enough, there was a different ideal speed at which the Ryan would do each and every maneuver. For a single snap-roll she had to hold it down to ninety miles per hour, and for a double, increase the speed to one hundred and eighteen miles per hour. A vertical snap-roll was best done at one hundred and forty miles per hour.

So much for being a wild child on a swing in the sky! Freddy felt like slamming out of the office, leaving Mac and Swede Castelli to their fussing, and jumping into the first ship she saw and flying away. She ached, she longed, she yearned to take off for somewhere, *anywhere*, without worrying about navigation, precision, winds aloft, checkpoints, or any other thing that could get between her and the ecstasy, the wonderment that she remembered from her solo, when the evening star had called to her and Capricorn had beckoned. She knew that she couldn't just take off today, not realistically, but she would, damn it, yes she would, oh, and *how she would!*—if she only had her own plane.

"Wake up, Eve, wake up," Paul urged in alarm after he had answered the telephone at four in the morning.

"What . . . ? What time is it? What's wrong?" she asked sleepily, her eyes screwed up protestingly against the light of the bedside lamp.

"It's Delphine. She telephoned from the police station downtown— I didn't understand half of what she said, but I'm going there now to get her out. I'll bring her back as soon as I can, but I didn't want to leave you here alone to find me gone."

"The police station? Was there an accident? . . . She's not hurt, is she?" Eve asked, terrified.

"No, no, it's nothing like that. She didn't make much sense. She said she was only playing chuck-a-luck, whatever that is. But, darling, she sounded hysterical and something else . . ."

"Something else?"

"Drunk," he said grimly.

More than two hours later Paul returned with Delphine, now scared sober, her pitiful, unprotected face wiped as clean of makeup as she had been able to manage, but still dressed in the expensive black and white printed crepe evening gown and the matching, fur trimmed bolero in which she had been arrested on board the gambling ship, a luxuriously reconditioned freighter called the *Rex*.

She walked into the house with as much dignity as she could summon, but when she saw Eve, she burst into tears and sat down with a thump on a sofa in the living room, where Eve had been waiting for them.

Eve stared questioningly at Paul, but he just shook his head, disbelief and a deep sadness shadowing his eyes. Eve moved so that she could sit next to Delphine, putting her hands on each side of her daughter's desolate face, and holding her tightly. "Come on, come on, whatever it is, it can't be that bad," she said distractedly. To see Delphine, always so controlled and so self-confident, yet, to her mother's eyes, still so vulnerable and so fragile, in such a state, made her think of nothing but comforting her daughter.

"I'm afraid it is, my dear," Paul said quietly, and he made a gesture with his head that meant that he had to talk to her alone.

"Delphine, darling, go on upstairs and put on one of your old bathrobes, and when you're ready, come down to the kitchen. I'll make some breakfast," Eve said, pushing Delphine gently toward the staircase. She turned to Paul as soon as she heard the door close in Delphine's old room.

"What is this about, dear God?"

"There was a police raid on one of those gambling ships—Delphine and Margie were being held in a big cell with dozens of other women. All of them were dressed to the teeth, like her, and many of them were drunk as well. Some of them had passed out cold. The men were in another cell. It was a madhouse—lawyers, publicity men from the studios, photographers, reporters . . . If I hadn't been a diplomat I could never have obtained her release so quickly."

"But who could possibly have made her go to a place like that!"

"She told me the man's name. It didn't mean anything to me. I managed to get Margie out too. I had to take her home—there was nothing else to do. I doubt that she'll be sober before tomorrow. She kept assuring me that it was a really 'swell place'—roulette, it would appear, as well as dice, keno, faro, blackjack, and three hundred slot machines. Better than Tijuana, no less. She sounded like an expert. She insisted that there was nothing to worry about because the ship had hundreds of lifeboats, so it was perfectly 'safe.'" He tried to smile and failed.

"She was so drunk that she didn't realize who I was. She kept ranting on about the fact that she and Delphine had been a couple of thousand dollars ahead when the raid started and that the police stole their money. She insisted, all the way to her front door, that I must try to get it back. She wanted to kick the cops." Paul's disgust made his voice dry and expressionless.

"But . . . it's unbelievable, Paul, isn't it . . . isn't it?" Eve mumbled in utter confusion. "These college boys—going out gambling at their age—making the girls drink so much? What kind of house mother is Mrs. Robinson if she lets them go out with boys like that?"

"You don't quite understand, darling. But then you haven't had the advantage of listening to Margie rave on. Unless everything she said was a lie—and since she was much too drunk and far too angry to lie, I believe her—she and Delphine are members in good standing of the very highest nightlife of Hollywood, used to being treated with courtesy, as befits their position. They go only to the best clubs, which are protected from such indignities as a police raid. She couldn't believe that anyone had actually dared to arrest them."

"Nightlife? Nightclubs?"

"Gambling clubs, the most exclusive ones. To which college boys would most certainly not be admitted. They go with men, adult men, God knows who, men who give them money with which to gamble."

"Oh, Paul, not Delphine! Margie, maybe, but *not* Delphine."

"Yes, darling, the two of them. I'm afraid that there's no question about it. It's been going on all year, that much was very clear. Whatever has happened, they've been in it together."

"I don't believe her! Until I've spoken to Delphine I refuse to believe that girl. I've never trusted Margie, and I should have known better than to listen to the nuns." Eve resisted his account with a heart that had already begun to tremble with knowledge.

"We should have some breakfast first," Paul said, shrugging his shoulders wearily. "We can bring Delphine a tray in her room when we're finished. I don't want the servants to hear about this."

"I have to go and talk to Delphine now. I couldn't eat breakfast."

Eve found that her daughter had finished drying her hair on a towel, after a shower. She put on an old bathrobe of white chenille, and she sat in front of her dressing table, carefully parting her hair in the center so that now it fell, as always, in waves from her widow's peak to her small chin. Her face was paler than usual, but she looked restored to normal, for her gray eyes were as clear and calm as ever. There were no traces of tears.

"Darling, your father told me . . . Margie . . . he thinks . . ."

"I was in the car, Mother, and I know what Margie said," Delphine said quietly. There was a quality of apartness in her voice, as if she had removed herself from the reality of the situation.

"But darling, it's not . . . you didn't . . ."

"Mother, I really think that you and Father are making far too much of this . . . If I'd had any other way to get out of jail than to call you, believe me, I would have taken it. There's one chance in a million of the police raid, and tonight we were in the wrong place at the wrong time, that's all. We were trapped as soon as the police came on board. At least a thousand other people got away scot free. It's so *unfair*."

"Unfair?" Eve was incredulous.

"Most of Hollywood could have been arrested tonight. The heads of the studios were there, all the biggest stars, everybody who is anybody. Margie and I just had bad luck. The raid may be in the papers, but no names will be mentioned. They never are, so you can count on that. I was frightened, I admit that, and naturally I was upset actually to be thrown in jail, but it's not the sort of thing that I'd ever expect to happen again." She bent her head to examine a jagged fingernail, took up an emery board, and started to smooth it over.

"*Stop that, Delphine, and look at me!* Do you think anything you've been saying is what I want to talk about? What were you doing in a place like that? Are you a gambler? Who were the men who took you there? Where did you get that dress and jacket? What, *for God's sake*, is going on in your life, Delphine?"

"You make it sound so *sinister*, Mother. Margie and I know a lot of nice, amusing men who like to go out at night. They're boyfriends, nothing more," Delphine said dismissively. "It's all good fun . . . gambling is just as much a part of going out as having dinner or dancing or watching a floor show. Everybody does it. I simply can't see what harm it does—it's not as if we've lost money we can't afford. In fact, I've made enough to supplement my clothes allowance. And you know it hasn't hurt my schoolwork because you get my report cards."

"And the drinking?"

"I think that someone must have slipped me something stronger than I asked for tonight. I should have been more careful. Margie too." Delphine looked directly at Eve, her eyes, set below the wide, exquisite shield of her brow, as candid as ever.

Eve stood up, unable to endure her knowledge that Delphine was lying, that this was not the first time that Delphine had been drunk, any more than it was the first time she had been gambling.

"How old were the men you and Margie were with?" she demanded.

"Jed and Bob? Somewhere in their twenties, I guess," Delphine said casually, looking in her closet for something to put on.

"And how well do you know them?" Eve insisted.

"Pretty well. They're great guys. I hope they're out of jail by now," Delphine said with a rueful little laugh, choosing a pink cotton dress and putting it on the bed. "It's lucky I left so much of my old stuff here," she said, smiling as serenely at Eve as if their discussion were over.

"Delphine, I'm going to tell Mrs. Robinson that you no longer have our permission to sleep over at Margie's. There will be no exceptions. We can't stop you from being friendly with that girl, but I will not *tolerate* the kind of life you've been living. At least your father and I can make sure that you have to obey the sorority rules and get in at a decent hour at night."

"You can't do that! You'll ruin my life!" Delphine's face was distorted with sudden rage.

"You're ruining your life all by yourself, as far as I can tell," Eve said firmly, her mind made up. She walked toward the door of the bedroom and opened it. There was no use in further discussion. Delphine had to be brought under control.

Delphine ran to the door and held it so that Eve couldn't leave. She bent toward her and hissed, *"And who are you to talk?"*

"What?" Eve said incredulously.

"I have some questions, Mother, since you intend to treat me like a child. Just how old were you when you were living with a lover in Paris? Younger than I am now, weren't you? And just how many years was that before you married Father? And *how many* lovers?"

Eve apprehended the intention behind the words even before her brain was able to sort them out and try to make sense of them. No answer came to her lips, but she pushed the door shut with a quick gesture, so that no one would hear Delphine.

Delphine's lips took on a look of righteousness. "I learned all about it from Bruno, that summer we spent in France. *What a hypocrite you are, Mother.* Why don't you lock me up in my room here at home while you're at it? That way you could be absolutely certain that I won't do what you did. I happen to be a virgin, for your information, and I intend to remain one, but telling Mrs. Robinson that I can't sleep over at Margie's won't ensure that. Your parents couldn't manage to keep you from doing what you pleased, could they?"

How many lovers? thought Eve, appalled by the question. No matter what she said to Delphine, she could never make her understand the truth. The poison was in her mind, the harm was done. She forced herself to speak calmly.

"Delphine, I don't owe you any explanations about my life. I can't stop you from listening to any gossip that's still floating around, and believing what you want. It doesn't change my responsibility toward you. I intend to call Mrs. Robinson immediately."

"Hypocrite! Hypocrite!" Delphine's voice rose hysterically as Eve left the room.

She could never tell Paul what Delphine had said, Eve realized as she went back down the stairs holding on to the bannister as if she were an old woman. He would be too angry, too saddened by Delphine's suspicions. *How many lovers?* Delphine would never believe the truth—*would Paul?* There had been no one after Alain Marais until she met her husband, but it was a subject to which they had never returned after their first dinner at the Ritz. She had always thought that he had understood those careful, distant, unapproachable years. What if he had just been afraid to ask?

At the Château de Valmont there were ten large guest rooms, and by the time Anette de Lancel received her daughter-in-law's letter from California, most of them had been spoken for during every weekend of the summer. It was not a case of French hospitality, but of selling champagne, that caused the Lancels to entertain so often and so lavishly.

Centuries before French perfume and French fashion had properly organized their foreign sales, the seemingly natural human desire to drink as much champagne as possible, as often as possible, had been cleverly promoted by a group of young Champenois noblemen who owned vineyards at the time of the coronation of Louis XIV in 1666.

Forming themselves into a group, the Marquis de Sillery, the Duc de Mortmart, the Vicomte de Lancel, the Marquis de Bois-Dauphin and the Marquis de Saint-Evremond, among others, went to Versailles and deliberately set about making their own wines of Champagne the rage at court, for the court alone set the fashion for everything throughout France, from buttons to architecture.

After a triumphant success at Versailles, they spread out and conquered England, where the demand for champagne soon became so great that it commanded an enormously high price. Their equally enterprising sons and grandsons traveled thousands of miles, to sell champagne to the Grand Dukes of Russia and the founders of the new republic of the United States. Eventually great markets were also established in South America and Australia. A similar vision motivated Monsieur Moët when the armies of Russia, Austria and Prussia invaded Champagne after Napoleon's retreat at Waterloo. He encouraged looting of his bottles for the officer's mess on the basis that it would cause the occupying forces to develop a taste for champagne, and as the saying goes, "He who has drunk once will drink again." When the officers returned home, they became good customers indeed.

Along with this spirit of marketing and publicity, bred into the vineyard owners, there also developed a most untypically French attitude toward hospitality. There have never been many hotels in Champagne, so, for hundreds of years, the families of the region have received in their own homes or châteaux visitors from every place in the world where champagne is drunk. It is rare indeed that the maker of a great or small mark of champagne dines alone, except during the five cold months of winter.

"Just listen to this, Jean-Luc," the Vicomtesse de Lancel said, so excited that she only read every other sentence of Eve's letter out loud. " . . . important for Delphine to experience . . . a world in which tradition plays an important role, in which she has a place as well as a family . . . clearly impossible in a city as young as Los Angeles . . . both feel that she's still young enough . . . a visit to you could make a crucial difference in her somewhat immature attitudes . . ."

"A visit? Of course. When?"

"Right away! That's what's so amazing. The *Normandie* leaves from New York in three days, and apparently she can fly there in a day or less. It does seem a bit sudden but, well, these young people nowadays. . . . Eve wonders if we could keep Delphine over for the entire summer

215

—how can she doubt it! Of course it will turn our arrangements upside-down, but I'll manage somehow. Jean-Luc, we must telephone immediately. What time would it be now in California?"

"Eleven at night?" he ventured, calculating backwards, but his wife had already disappeared toward the table in the entrance hall where the telephone was kept, rearranging the occupants of the guest rooms in her head as she proceeded at a stately trot. Somewhat immature attitudes, indeed! What did Eve expect from that darling child?

11

VERY well-run private bank needs at least one or more bank officers of a particular and very special sort, men for whom a knowledge of the business of banking is their least important qualification. Like the most accomplished and cultivated of geisha girls in Japan, these bank officers serve to attract a rich clientele, and to keep them faithful by making sure that they continue to be amused and charmed.

When Bruno de Lancel completed his military service in 1935, he found that it had become necessary to have some sort of job, an annoyingly boring price he had to pay for not being one of his Saint-Fraycourt ancestors, whose only concern had been how to occupy their leisure most pleasantly. Shockingly, he did not seem to possess a private income and he was no longer willing to live with his grandparents.

However, he discovered quickly that the demands made by the position he soon accepted with La Banque Duvivier Frères were not too unlike those that might have been made on a Marquis de Saint-Fraycourt before the Revolution. It was necessary to hunt as frequently as possible during the season; important to play cards well—but not too well—with the right people in the right clubs; desirable to appear at the opera, the theater, the ballet and the openings of important art exhibitions; essential never to miss a major race meeting at the tracks of France, England, or Ireland; and, it went without saying, out of the question not to be seen at every meaningful social event of Paris society. The bank paid his expenses so that he could engage in these activities, and a small salary as well, plus a commission on any new accounts he brought in.

Even if Bruno had wanted, in this June of 1936, to spend more than a few minutes now and then at the Duvivier bank, it would have been difficult, given the demands of his position. The three Duvivier brothers were delighted with him. He was more than worth what he cost them; already he had attracted a number of new customers with whom they could not personally have hoped to make contact.

A bonus they had not anticipated to its fullest value in hiring Bruno was his bachelorhood. It doubled his worth, the youngest Duvivier brother reflected. "Tripled," replied the eldest. The middle brother, as usual, thought they were both wrong: "Lancel's worth is incalculable until he marries. Then we will have to reassess it."

Would he pick a girl whose relatives and connections would come from the same unfortunately reduced financial circumstances as the Saint-Fraycourts? Would he deign to marry money, but from outside his own world? Or, best of all for the bank, would he manage to make an alliance with an heiress who also came from a great family, an heiress whose parents might reasonably expect her to marry someone as rich as she?

While the Duviviers pondered the ultimate results of their investment in Bruno, they had, unknown to them, an ally in the Marquise de Saint-Fraycourt, who never spent a day in which she did not ask herself the same questions. The only party to Bruno's eventual marriage who had almost no concern about the success of the affair was Bruno himself. He was too certain of his entitlement to the ideal wife to worry about the future. Whoever she would be, since he was now only twenty-one, she would still be in a convent somewhere, learning whatever girls learned in convents.

Bruno knew the one essential thing about the girl he would marry, the only absolute on which he would insist: she must come to him with the assurance that she would inherit land. Money would never be enough. For enough land, a great deal of land, *family land*, Bruno would have been content to marry the devil's daughter . . . as long as the devil was French. The Saint-Fraycourts had lost their ancient lands and most of their income in the crash of the *Banque de l'Union Financière* in 1882. The Lancel land would be divided among Bruno and his father's wife and other children.

Although it was reassuring, from a financial point of view, to know that one day, in the far future—for Uncle Guillaume and his father both came from stock who lived to a great age—he would share in the income of Lancel champagne, the vineyards could never belong to him alone. Therefore, as some men must marry money, he must marry land. He hungered to possess forests and fields and a château of his own, hundreds and hundreds of hectares over which he would walk and ride as sole and undisputed master.

Meanwhile, there were such a pressing number of appointments in his daily life that he actually had difficulty in carving aside precious time in which to go to his shirtmaker and choose new cloth for his shirts, time to visit his shoemaker, time to have a new dinner jacket fitted.

Nevertheless, there were things that even the best of valets couldn't do for him, Bruno thought, as he stood impatiently while his tailor adjusted a shoulder seam. Sabine de Koville came into his mind, and he smiled faintly to himself. She was quite perfect in her way, once she had instructed him so precisely where her way led.

Yes, she had done him a great service when he was only seventeen and had not yet had a woman, Bruno mused, and he still continued to see her from time to time, for her needs were uncomplicated and direct. Perhaps he would take tea with her today. Perhaps not. There were many other women, less simple than Sabine in their requirements, equally gifted and equally . . . piquant. How he enjoyed each fresh surprise women could offer: the deliciously squalid fancies of a prince's daughter; the thirst for punishment of a high-minded mistress of a literary salon; and Sabine de Koville, who could only respond to the orders of a servant. Degradation was his hobby.

After Bruno's first experience with his school friend's mother, he had discovered in a short time that he was not just the classic case of an adolescent being seduced by a woman of the world. His deepest sexual preference, indeed his only sexual preference, was for women in their late thirties and early forties. He couldn't understand why a man would eat a green apple, if ripe fruit was available. A horse, perhaps, might, at the limit, be chosen unschooled, so that he could be broken in to one's own requirements.

But a woman? How much more agreeable to take them when they had already discovered what they craved most deeply and secretly. In ten cases out of ten they weren't satisfying their inadmissible needs with their husbands. How simple it was to give them their fantasies and watch them become utterly obedient, the proudest of them often the most submissive to his will.

It was a combination as undemanding as it was convenient, for, with the almost impossible demands of a job like his, Bruno reflected, he most certainly had not so much as a minute for courtship. Happily, his own unappeasable appetite, for well-tended flesh that was past the awkwardness and ignorance of youth, coincided with such a large and easily available supply. He couldn't understand his friends who spent time and money running after girls as if they possessed something worth having. How could any intelligent man prefer his meat unseasoned?

"Hello, Bruno," a voice said behind his back.

"Guy—I can't move. I should be finished soon," Bruno answered. He had an appointment for a lunchtime tennis game with Guy Marchant, a relatively recent friend. Now Guy, Bruno thought, would be able to try to explain the attraction of young women, for he was always

219

falling for one or another of them, but it was not a question Bruno could ask, for it would betray too much of his own private arrangements.

"What do you think of Schmeling beating Joe Louis by a knockout yesterday?" Guy asked, drawing up a chair. He was a tall and skinny young man with a pleasantly lopsided smile and clever eyes.

"I wasn't surprised, were you?" Bruno replied. "Actually, I don't much care about boxing. Next month I'm going over for Wimbledon—why don't you come along? Gottfried von Cramm, Fred Perry—you shouldn't miss it."

"I'll see if I can get away from the office," Guy answered. "It isn't always possible."

"Monsieur de Lancel, if you please, turn a few inches toward me," the fitter requested, reaching for more pins. Bruno turned and found that he was facing himself squarely in the mirror. He gave himself a quick, perfunctory glance, devoid of vanity. He knew perfectly well what he looked like, and he had no need to reassure himself by checking the mirror as so many men did. That women found him extraordinary was gratifying, but hardly surprising. The fact that something about the way his features were put together made men trust him—that, yes, *that* was important.

Bruno had found, to his surprise, that he liked the banking business, or rather that he liked making money, and certainly banking was among the few gentleman's ways to that end. When he started with Duvivier Frères he had done so because it was necessary to have an occupation. His first successes at attracting new clients to the firm had occurred almost by themselves; on a squash court, during a hunt weekend near Tours, after a thoroughbred auction at Newmarket.

The commissions from these clients had given him his first taste of economic freedom. He had found a flat to his liking in a vast private house on the Rue de l'Université. It belonged to a distant cousin who, like so many others, had recently lost most of his money in the Bourse and had been forced to convert half of his home into flats with private entrances. More commissions, which Bruno now sought with alert foresight, soon paid for a housemaid, the best of tailors, the services of a valet, and the first two horses he'd ever owned.

Now, in the year since he'd joined the bank, he had grown seriously ambitious. He realized that although there was a great deal of money to be made without venturing beyond his own class, there was far more money in that busy world which lay utterly outside the strict and immutable limits of the Faubourg Saint-Germain, in that wealthy bourgeois world of Guy Marchant, who sat tapping his foot, impatient to be on the tennis court.

Attracting that kind of money was a matter of accepting invitations, or rather of *provoking* invitations, that would not normally be extended to him because of who he was, Bruno thought, as the tailor, with maddening precision, pinned a perfect cuff. It entailed acting in a way that made him seem more accessible, a little less of a standoffish aristocrat, than people anticipated; in picking out older men who would never, under any circumstances, have set foot in his Grandmother Saint-Fraycourt's salon; and in unbending toward them ever so slightly, so that their wives dared to issue an invitation that they normally would not have tendered for fear of being rebuffed.

These first invitations were always, he noticed, for large, formal gatherings, the sort of invitations that could, in theory, be refused without making the would-be hostess feel as if she had presumed. When Bruno accepted them, his hosts were flattered and, encouraged by their wives, grew more bold.

His youth was a priceless asset. One could invite a twenty-one-year-old Vicomte de Saint-Fraycourt de Lancel when one would not invite, not dream of inviting, an older member of that aristocracy of the *Ancien Régime*. Bruno's commissions fattened. Of his many invitations, those he decided to encourage were for intimate dinners, yachting trips, weekends in the country; invitations that gave him the opportunities for which he was hunting. Soon Bruno's salary was ridiculously small in comparison to his income from his commissions.

Guy Marchant, whom he had met less than six months ago, was the only son of Pierre Marchant, who owned the most prosperous newsreel business in France, Marchant Actualités. It had worldwide distribution and was larger than Fox-Movietone, Pathé Journal and Eclair-Journal combined.

Bruno had first become acquainted with Monsieur and Madame Marchant at the Polo Club in the Bois. Soon he had met Guy, who was only three years older than he, yet already deeply involved in the day-to-day running of the vast family enterprise.

He was a fairly good sort, Guy, Bruno had decided, the kind of well-educated and shrewd product of the upper middle class who could eventually, by marriage—for of course that was the only way—rise up to the lower reaches of the upper classes. By the time he was fifty, he might expect to have a daughter who had married a man with a good title, even an excellent one, if that was what he wanted. His grandson could be born an aristocrat.

Guy Marchant was as much a part of the future as Bruno himself, and the two of them had become friendly, although not in the way Bruno would always reserve for the boys with whom he had gone to school. There had as yet been no placement of the Marchant funds in the Duvivier bank, and Bruno thought the better of the Marchants for this. Had they rushed to do business with his employers, as so many others had done, he would have found Guy less attractive, less worthwhile cultivating. The Marchants actually expected him to associate with them for themselves. That, in itself, was worthy of some grudging respect. It showed, if nothing else, a sense of self-worth.

"Bruno, how long will you be?" Guy asked, looking at his watch.

"Will you be finished soon, Monsieur?" Bruno asked the tailor impatiently.

"All in good time, Monsieur de Lancel," the tailor answered impassively. Another man who knew his own value, Bruno realized, and resigned himself to the expenditure of another quarter hour.

It was mid-July, and in her bedroom at the Château de Valmont, Delphine sat on the floor of the best guest room, surrounded by the contents of an enormous wardrobe trunk that had arrived only an hour earlier. Margie, faithful Margie, in a futile gesture of comfort, had packed up all of Delphine's evening clothes and sent them on by boat. Delphine ransacked the trunk, pulling out gown after gown, cloak after cloak, holding them lovingly up to her, and then placing them carefully on the carpet in a pinwheel of sumptuous colors and fabrics. In their hundreds of years of cultural superiority, the clever French had never managed to invent the closet; her armoire was already over-crammed, and there was no place to hang her dozens of evening clothes.

The trunk was completely unpacked now, and Delphine, filled with a growing grief, opened one of her evening bags and peeked inside. She found a lace handkerchief, a black and silver compact for loose powder, a pearl-headed pin that had once held a corsage at her shoulder, two quarters, a Coty lipstick, a book of matches from the Trocadero, and one of her many cigarette cases. Reverently, as if she were looking at relics of a dead civilization, she took out the objects and placed them in her lap, brooding over them as her melancholy grew. She opened the cigarette case and found a single wrinkled Lucky Strike. She rolled it lovingly in her fingers, sniffed it, and then, remembering that her door was locked, she lit the cigarette on a Trocadero match, inhaled deeply, and promptly burst into tears.

The familiar act brought it all back: the dance music that filled the air; the delicious flirting, always just on the edge of being dangerous; the first sip from a cold cocktail glass; Margie's conspiratorial wink; the sound of dice; the croupier's bark; and oh, the excitement, that breathless diet of excitement to which she had become accustomed, knowing that one wild, gay evening would be followed by another, that nothing would ever be humdrum or predictable.

She hated Champagne, she thought as the tears coursed over the curve of her cheeks, hated it! There was nothing to do here, nowhere to go, nobody to talk to except her grandmother, who seemed persuaded that she was interested in the remote details of the history of the family, and her grandfather, who tried to explain the mysteries of the vine to her until she almost fainted with boredom. And to be obliged to eat meal after meal politely with the many visitors, all too old to be interesting, who talked of nothing but vintage years and food, while she filled the role of the visiting granddaughter from America who must be asked several benevolent questions and then forgotten as a new bottle was uncorked. She hated it! And she was a captive here until it was time to return to college, and then what was there to look forward to but life at the sorority house, under the stern supervision of Mrs. Robinson?

Delphine put out her cigarette after that one puff, because she had to conserve it for further consumption. There was no tobacco in the house except her grandfather's pipe tobacco and her uncle Guillaume's cigars, and they never smoked until after dinner, taking themselves off to the smoking room, where she was never invited. It would have been unthinkable to them if she had bought French cigarettes—those vile things—in the village, and smoked in their presence.

No, she was expected to sit with her grandmother and learn gros point or read Balzac or listen to classical music on the Victrola until it was time to go to bed. It was essential, Delphine knew, to become a paragon of all the virtues in her grandmother's eyes, since she had realized that she had gone too far, much, much too far, in her last interview with her mother. She had made a major mistake in tactics, and only her grandmother's reports that she had become a model of decorum and goodness would, perhaps, cause some relaxation in her parents' plans for her next two years at UCLA.

Each night she went to bed, early and sober, in this big lonely room where the walls were hung in a delicately faded blue and white paisley toile, and the matching wings of fabric on the bed were slightly threadbare, and the highly polished wood floor creaked. No closets, Delphine wept, feeling more and more sorry for herself, no closets and creaking floors and faded fabric and probably not a drop of gin in the whole blasted grape-growing province, not that anyone would offer her some if there were.

Anette de Lancel, walking by in the corridor outside of the room, heard Delphine's sobs through the thick door. She paused uncertainly. She didn't want to seem to be snooping, but how could she just go about her business as if she hadn't heard her beloved granddaughter weeping her heart out? She was a little homesick, of course, that much had been evident from the first, but she had been so sweet and attentive and had shown such an interest in hearing everything about the château and the family and the vineyards, that it seemed that Eve had been right about Delphine's need to feel a deeper connection with her family.

She made up her mind and tapped on the door.

"Who is it?" Delphine's muffled voice called.

"Grandmother, darling. Is there anything I can do?"

"No. No, thank you. I'm all right."

"Darling, you're not all right. Please, let me come in."

Delphine dried her eyes on the little handkerchief, sighed, and opened the door to Madame de Lancel, who advanced into the room and stopped abruptly as she saw the carpet covered with its silky, satiny treasure heap of glittering long dresses.

"Where did they come from?" she asked in amazement.

"Los Angeles. My evening clothes . . . just look, Grandmother . . . just look how pretty . . . how pretty . . ." Delphine broke into a fresh flood of tears, clasping a white fur jacket to her breast and rocking back and forth in grief. Anette de Lancel took the girl into her arms and tried to comfort her, patting her as if she were a baby while she looked in astonishment at a larger collection of evening clothes than she had ever imagined anyone, even a Paris society woman, would possess.

"But Delphine, darling . . . do you *need* all that at home?"

"Oh yes," Delphine wept, "everyone does . . . we have such fun . . . oh, so much fun, Grandmother."

"But it must be so terribly, terribly dull for you here, darling. I simply never realized." Anette de Lancel was appalled at the realization that Delphine had been exiled from a life in which, as a matter of course, she went out so often that she owned such quantities of evening clothes. At the very least, Eve could have warned her . . . and how tactful and good Delphine had been about not letting them suspect that she must be bored.

"It's not that . . . not at all . . . it's just that I miss my friends . . .

224

I shouldn't cry . . . you've been so good to me," she said with a dolorous droop of her lovely head and a pitiful attempt at a smile.

"It's easy to be good to you, darling, but I should have realized that you needed friends of your own age. I can't forgive myself. But here in the country . . . the young people . . . frankly I'm not sure where they are. But I'll call all my friends and see if their grandchildren . . . Delphine, I'll try my best, I promise you."

"Thank you, Grandmother," Delphine said gratefully, thinking dourly of what the grandchildren of the neighbors must be like. "But truly, it's not important. The only thing is . . . do you think I could have another armoire in my room?"

"Oh, my dear! I'll have one brought up immediately. All those lovely things on the floor!" Anette de Lancel bustled off, glad to have something practical to do for Delphine. As for the grandchildren of her friends, they too must be produced. Surely there must be many suitable boys and girls, home for the summer. She would alert every family in Champagne, and find them and . . . and . . . give a ball! Yes, a young people's ball, a midsummer ball, such as had rarely been held, if indeed it had ever been held, in Champagne at the height of the growing season.

"Jean-Luc, I'm at my wits' end," Anette de Lancel said to her husband after a day on the telephone. "The Chandons' grandchildren are visiting in England, the Lansons have five, mind you, *five*, grandsons and not one of them expected home for weeks, the Roederers' children are all in Normandy—you know nothing can keep her away from her trotting-horses—Madame Budin at Perrier-Jouet says that her son is unfortunately too young, Madame Bollinger has two nephews but they're both away, all the Ruinarts are visiting in Bordeaux—finally I have four girls and two boys and I've called everyone I know. Everyone!"

"The proper time for balls is Christmas," the Vicomte de Lancel answered.

"That's an enormously helpful reflection, Jean-Luc."

"Anette, you're getting upset over nothing. If Delphine is bored, she's bored. She's a dear child, but remember that it wasn't our idea to invite her for the summer."

"How can you be so heartless? That poor girl, with all her splendid evening clothes . . . you can just imagine the gaiety to which she's accustomed."

"Too much, perhaps? Isn't that why Eve sent her here? To give her a little time for reflection? I seem to remember something like that in the letter."

"She's had six undistracted weeks for reflection. I must give her a party, Jean-Luc, even if it's not a ball. But four girls—five, counting Delphine—and two boys . . . no, that's just not possible."

"You could just invite the girls," he suggested. "The main thing is that she meet someone her own age, isn't it?"

"Jean-Luc, I wonder about you, I truly do. Do you remember nothing about being young?"

"As much as you do, I daresay, as we both approach our eightieth birthdays."

"Jean-Luc, it is not necessary to remind me. Anyway, I am a great deal younger than you."

"Three years and two months."

"Oh, why did I marry you?"

"I was the catch of the countryside."

"*I* was the catch of the countryside. Have you forgotten how many *arpents* of vineyard I brought with me?"

"Two hundred and sixty."

"Two hundred and sixty-one!"

"Your memory is as good as ever, my love. In any case, I telephoned Bruno before dinner. I made him promise to bring some young men whenever you like. Suitable ones. Now perhaps you will give me a kiss?"

"Bruno! How could I not have thought of him?"

"Vision, my dearest, is what makes man different from woman, broadness of vision, the ability to think beyond Champagne, to see an opportunity and to execute the plan with dispatch and . . . now, now, Anette, you know that I detest being hit with a pillow . . . calm yourself, act your age. . . ."

The Parisian visitors, for the dinner the Lancels gave for Delphine, were invited to spend the night at the château. Bruno had brought three of his invariably presentable friends, and among the six young Frenchmen who had been at dinner that evening, five of them had fallen in love with Delphine. Bruno had to admit that his American half sister had unquestionably become a credit to him. None among the five was as hard hit as Guy Marchant, who sat gazing out of the window onto the moonlit night, long after he'd closed the door to his bedroom, so unhinged by love that he hadn't even loosened his bow tie or slipped off his shoes.

Never had there been such a girl. Never would there be another. He would die if he couldn't spend the rest of his life with her.

He got up and paced around the room, ending up, after several circuits, back at the window, looking at the stars. Guy Marchant took an intelligent amateur's interest in astronomy, and on the drive to Valmont he had entertained Bruno with a philosophical reflection on the ups and downs of the state of the world, culled from a book he had read by the Englishman Sir James Hopwood Jeans. "Jeans," he had told Bruno, "estimates that, based on what can be seen of the universe from the great telescope at Mount Wilson, there are so many stars out there that if they were grains of sand and were spread over England, they would create a layer hundreds of yards in depth. *Hundreds* of yards, Bruno. Now then, our own earth is one millionth of a part of one of those grains of sand, only *one millionth*. Bruno, do you understand? One millionth of just *one* of the grains of sand that are hundreds of yards deep over England—which would be just as deep if it were in France—so you see, Bruno, nothing we do really much matters, does it, in that context? After all, aren't we basically ridiculous?"

But that was before he'd met Delphine. Now the size of the universe was not only forgotten, but utterly immaterial and irrelevant, and his own emotions were of the most essential and immediate importance to him.

As the hours wore on, he grew able to begin to think like the clever businessman he was. Clearly, he thought, he couldn't expect the Lancels to invite him to spend the rest of the summer with them. Clearly, he had to marry Delphine before she went back to the United States, where there must be hundreds of men trying to get her to marry them. Clearly, in order to win her, he had to get Delphine to himself without wasting any time, for he knew, with the sure instinct of a man in love, that the other four males at dinner had fallen under her spell.

What did he have that they did not, he asked himself, trying to be as rational as possible. Had she smiled at him more often than at the others? Had she danced with him after dinner more frequently? Had she told him anything about her interests on which he could build? No, she had been evenhanded with her smiles and dances, flirting with all of them in a way that was as frustrating as if she hadn't flirted with any of them.

But . . . but . . . she was from Hollywood. To be from Los Angeles was to be from Hollywood, no matter where in Los Angeles you lived —the worldwide newsreel business had taught him that. And of all the people at Valmont tonight, only he had even the dimmest knowledge of what it meant to be from Hollywood. Only he was aware that if you were from Hollywood you had to be fascinated by films, because, in some way or another, even the most remote, you considered yourself to be part of the world of films. Would Delphine be more interested in visiting Max's parents' celebrated château in the Loire or Henri's father's famous stables, or in Victor's family's yacht—or his own studios? And all the other studios, the big cinema studios he could show her at Billancourt and Boulogne? Yes, he had an advantage! Now all he had to do was to arrange it, he thought, finally calm enough to begin to get undressed. Tomorrow he would get it settled. At breakfast.

No, before breakfast, before the others got a chance.

Within days, the visit to stay with Monsieur and Madame Marchant in Paris had been confirmed, properly preceded by a long and persuasive discussion Bruno had with his grandmother and a letter from Madame Marchant to the Vicomtesse.

"No, Jean-Luc, I certainly do not think that Eve intended Delphine to remain here every single day until she returned to the United States, that's nonsense. She is not our prisoner, and you are far too Victorian, my dear," Anette de Lancel said tartly, delighted that Delphine was to have a bit of a whirl and a glimpse of the life of the capital. "In any case, what did you expect when you asked Bruno to bring young men for dinner?"

"You're convinced that she'll be well chaperoned?"

"Madame Marchant assured me that she would watch over her as carefully as she does over her own daughter, and, in any case, Bruno will be with her as well. Really, Jean-Luc, you amaze me."

"You don't even know Madame Marchant," the Vicomte grumbled, annoyed that he was to be deprived of the pleasure of telling Delphine more about the culture of grapes, with which he had spent many pleasant hours distracting her.

"Bruno says she's a delightful, cultivated woman, and entirely reliable."

"And is Bruno always right?" he asked sharply.

"What kind of question is that?"

"A foolish one, my dear. Perhaps I really am getting old. In which case I must take the only possible preventative that nature allows us, and have another glass of champagne. May I offer you some?"

"By all means, my darling, by all means."

228

Delphine's innate charm and tender beauty, potent though they were in combination, were amplified a thousandfold by a basic inner lack of effort. The French, accustomed throughout history to foreigners who tried to compensate for not being French, who labored to produce something from their personal bags of tricks that would make the French admit them to membership in the human race, were immediately entranced by the attitude she projected. She truly did not notice, or care, if the French in France approved of her or not.

Delphine had grown up in three countries in which Frenchness was merely something about her parents that made them distinctly different from the natives, but not necessarily better. Frenchness had to do with her father's job and the language they spoke at home, and the way her mother trained a new cook, but it was hardly sacred. Being a Lancel meant nothing to her if it were compared to being a Selznick or a Goldwyn or a Zanuck, and ten years of tutoring in the proud traditions of Champagne would not have changed that.

The Marchants were delighted by what they perceived as her lack of the stiffness that was only to be expected in members of the old aristocracy. They would never have believed that the only aristocracy Delphine was impressed by was a handful of families who had made their millions in the last few decades, and the actors and actresses who were to be found photographed in the pages of American movie magazines.

They were puzzled by Guy's plans for Delphine's visit. Surely she would prefer to go to the top of the Eiffel Tower, to Napoleon's tomb, to the Place Vendôme, to the Louvre? What was this talk of Gaumont, Pathé-Cinema and Kodak-Pathé? Tourists never went out to Billancourt, surely? Why would she want to visit places just like those she must be familiar with in Hollywood?

"No, Madame Marchant, I assure you, I'm really anxious to see them," Delphine said quickly. Several times while she was still in high school, some of her parents' movie-making friends had invited the family out to a studio, and the quick peeks she had at the sound stages —almost spoiled by her terror of getting in the way of all the important people rushing around so confidently, with jobs to do—had given Delphine a glimpse of the paradise she was condemned to only know as a stranger.

"As you like, then," Madame Marchant said with resignation. "Just give me a minute to put on my hat." She patted her blue hair with well-cared-for hands on which diamonds flashed.

"Maman, you don't have to come if you don't want to. Bruno is going to meet us there," Guy told her.

"As a matter of fact, in that case . . . I do have a number of things I could be doing," Guy's mother said, relief plain in her kind eyes. The prospect of a day spent watching people make films was boring beyond words. Once, years ago, she too had thought it would be amusing to observe the process, but several hours of it had cured her of that delusion.

In any case, the notion of herself acting as a chaperone was too utterly absurd. Guy, her youngest and favorite child, was a perfect gentleman and could be trusted with any girl . . . particularly one with whom he was so painfully in love. The Vicomtesse de Lancel's unnecessary concern for her perfectly self-reliant granddaughter came from another century. Provincial aristocrats were behind the times, although charmingly so. More important, if she did not have her third fitting on most of her new suits from Chanel today, they would never be ready for the beginning of the season. She saw them off with a vaguely benevolent smile, lost in happy reveries of tweeds, buttons and linings.

The drive from the Marchants' huge apartment on the Avenue Foch, out to the Gaumont Studio at Billancourt, seemed to Delphine to take forever. She said little, but Guy could sense that she was simmering with emotion as she sat beside him, and he dared to hope that it might be because she was glad to be alone with him. From time to time he stole a look at her profile, but although she felt his eyes on her face, Delphine decided not to notice. Today she could have been with Max, Victor or Henri, for they had all telephoned with tempting invitations after the dinner, but Guy's plan had worked, and she had chosen to take the bait he had set for her. Surely that was quite enough to keep him happy for the time being.

Bruno joined them at the studio, out of curiosity rather than from any sense of obligation to keep an eye on Delphine. The Marchants still had not become clients of La Banque Duvivier Frères, and after the enormous favors he had done for Guy, he found such a lack of gratitude utterly unacceptable. He had invited him to the home of his grandparents for dinner; he had interceded with his grandmother to allow Delphine's visit—did Guy not realize how much he owed Bruno? Or perhaps did he not have enough influence in his father's business to suggest a placement of funds? Either possibility was equally unforgivable. Perhaps he had been too quick to encourage Guy's friendship, quite possibly he had let himself be taken for granted. Guy was an upstart, he thought angrily. Bruno did not easily permit himself to be guilty of misjudgment.

He was glad to observe, as the three of them waited to be granted entry to the studio, that Delphine seemed remote, thoughtful, far less flirtatious than she had been on the night of the dinner at Valmont. He liked her incontestable elegance in a red shantung suit, trimmed in navy blue, which she had bought at Bullock's for visits to the track at Santa Anita, and he thought that she looked older than he'd ever seen her, with a small navy straw hat tilted down over one eye.

"Ah, there's my pal," Guy said, introducing them to a short, blond young man with a friendly grin who had arrived hastily at the main gate. "Jacques Sette, Mademoiselle de Lancel, Vicomte de Lancel—Jacques is the assistant to Bluford—he'll take us around."

"Sorry you had to wait, Guy, but you know how it is. Mademoiselle, Monsieur, follow me—Guy knows the way. We're not at all busy here today. Unfortunately, several films are being shot on location, and many are in pre-production, but Gabin and Michèle Morgan are working on Stage Five. René Clair's directing—I thought that would be the most interesting way to begin." He produced the great names casually, as if they belonged to him, and Delphine looked at him with envy.

There was a red light on above the small door on the blank, unexciting wall of Stage Five, and they had to wait until it went off to enter. Once inside, they found themselves in a confusingly vast structure. Some parts of the stage were in darkness and others were so brilliantly lit that the white illumination seemed to give off a noise like a low hum.

"Watch your step," Jacques Sette cautioned, and took Delphine's arm without ceremony, to guide her around the cables that led to banks of lights, and around obstacles created by props that rose up out of the floor. She looked everywhere at once, and understood nothing, until suddenly Sette brought them all to a stop just at the edge of an area in which the aura of concentration was as palpable as the lights were bright.

She could smell it, Delphine thought, her heart beating quickly, smell the excitement. They had stopped twenty feet from the set, the interior of a dining room, where Jean Gabin and Michèle Morgan sat at a table, their meal interrupted, with four other actors, none of whom Delphine recognized. A makeup woman circled the table, powdering down foreheads, touching up lips, rearranging a lock of hair. The actors sat patiently, in a kind of limbo; Gabin murmured one joking sentence and they laughed quietly, but for minutes they did not move, while two men, one standing, and the other in a director's chair, conferred. Finally the conversations ended, the makeup woman left the set, the standing man went to his camera and spoke to another man, and in

231

the deep silence that followed, someone unseen announced with aggressive authority, "Silence! On tourne."

Delphine shuddered with excitement. She had taken half a dozen silent, dreamlike steps forward before Sette noticed. He made a quick leap, grabbed her shoulder, and drew her back into the visitors' zone. She mimed an embarrassed apology. She hadn't known she had moved.

A minute later the scene was interrupted again. "Let's go," Bruno whispered into her ear. "This is no longer interesting." Delphine shook her head in refusal. The scene started again, and this time it continued for less than two minutes before René Clair, dissatisfied, stopped it with an abrupt "Cut." He walked onto the set and talked to the actors at length in a voice too low to be heard. Gabin nodded several times and Michèle Morgan shrugged and smiled, and to Delphine it was as if the gods on Olympus had deigned to manifest themselves to her in human form.

Lights were rearranged, the cameraman put a small object up to his eye, gave directions, spoke to his assistant, and now, with Bruno and Guy restlessly waiting, and Delphine as unmoving as if she were a garden ornament, the scene started one more time. Finally it came to an end. "Cut . . . and . . . print," René Clair said with some faint satisfaction. The lights went off, the actors rose and disappeared in all directions.

"About time," Bruno said, expelling a breath of boredom.

"They'll be at it again all afternoon. They broke for lunch. That was only the first good take," Sette explained. "However, I have the feeling that you've had enough."

"For the rest of my life," Bruno replied.

"I warned you," Guy said.

"Not vividly enough. Come on, Delphine, let's go."

"No," she said.

"What do you mean? There's nothing left to watch."

"I want to see them do it again."

"As you wish, Mademoiselle," Jacques Sette said, shooting a look of amazement at Guy. "But nothing will happen here for at least two hours. Lunch is sacred, particularly on a film. May I invite you all to join me in the commissary?"

"Oh yes! Please," said Delphine.

"You exaggerate, Delphine," Bruno remonstrated, but he was hungry after all that endless, dreary standing about, and he had not made another engagement for lunch. One had to eat somewhere.

———

The commissary, like all studio commissaries, contained a large private room that was reserved for studio executives and the more important actors. Delphine looked around avidly, imagining that she was about to see Jean Gabin and Michèle Morgan having their lunch, but they had both elected to eat in private in their dressing rooms after a morning spent before a dining room table.

Sette led them to a table, putting Delphine in the seat that had the best view of the room.

"First, a glass of wine," he proposed and ordered from the waiter.

"Please, tell me who everybody is," Delphine implored. He looked around, hoping to see a famous star who would make her evident wish come true, but except for the directors, Jean Renoir, Pierre Prévert, Marcel Carné, Nico Ambert and Autant-Lara, he saw no one except character actors who were unknown in the United States. Delphine cast a glance at each of the directors as he pointed them out, but they were only ordinary men, not movie actors, and her yearning was unappeased. Disappointed, she sipped her wine and gazed around the room, her huge eyes wistful yet alert.

At a table not far from Sette's, three men ate together.

"Take a look at that girl," Nico Ambert directed his two lunch companions. "The one with Sette." The three men turned slightly and examined Delphine from head to foot as if she were a sofa up at auction.

"Any idea who she is?" Jules LeMaitre, Ambert's casting director, asked.

"Not an actress," decided Yves Block, the cameraman on Ambert's production of *Mayerling,* which was scheduled to start production in a month. The three men had been meeting all day to discuss details of the film, which had advanced into the semifinal stages of planning.

"Why do you say that, Yves?" asked LeMaitre.

"She's too unselfconscious," the cameraman replied. "She's looking around like a tourist . . . no actress would allow herself to do that, even in a strange studio. What's more, I've never seen her face before. If she were an actress, don't you think one of us—*all* of us—would recognize her?"

"If she were an actress, she would have recognized me," Nico Ambert said matter-of-factly. The director, a sturdy man in his early thirties, was olive-skinned, with black hair and the typically warm-blooded look of a man from the south of France, more Italian than French. He had great vigor even in repose, an aura of authority, a prominent hawk nose, ferocious eyes and a relentless set to his mouth. He was a man who was accustomed to power and used it well; a man feared by many men and coveted by many women.

Delphine was aware that the three men were staring at her, but like everyone else in this letdown of a commissary, they were nobodies. She was so accustomed to being in the focus of men's eyes that she swam freely in their attention with as little curiosity about them as that felt by a gorgeous tropical fish, displayed to one and all in an aquarium.

"She's not French," Ambert said. "There's something altogether too neat and trim about the way she's put herself together, and look at her shoes . . . not possibly French."

"But she's speaking French, Nico," said Jules LeMaitre. "The shapes her lips make, the way she uses her hands . . . what do you think, Block?"

The cameraman was silently studying Delphine's face. He was an encyclopedist of the syntax of features. Why, he often asked, did people find it so wonderful that no two snowflakes were alike when no human face, even that of an identical twin, was the same as another?

Block didn't believe in beauty. He knew that the most flawless face could change into the flatness of a boring landscape under the lights. He had seen too many extraordinary eyes lose their power to project starlight when the camera was turned on them.

The banks of huge arc lights and the lens of his camera worked together in a diabolical conspiracy to reduce the looks of men and women who were, in real life, creatures of natural splendor. Yet some-times the lights and the camera seemed to regret their harsh verdict and made a compact to find the fascination in a face that had seemed only ordinarily beautiful. The most enchanting woman he'd ever tried to capture on film had possessed a nose that cast an ugly shadow, no matter how he lit her. He had filmed another woman whose prettiness was overwhelmingly banal, but in front of the camera, the arrangement of her features assumed the awesome mystery of a priestess vowed to ritual silence.

Block, without thinking, could read the essentials in a second: judge if the eyes were far enough apart, if the nose had any of the obvious and myriad inconveniences of most noses; gauge the volume of a chin, the length of a neck, the essential and absolutely crucial geometry of the placement of the mouth in relation to the eyes; but until the lights spoke, until the camera answered, he preferred not to be asked his opinion. "It's impossible to say," Yves Block finally answered, shrug-ging at the casting director.

"Do you want to test her?" Jules LeMaitre persisted.

"That's for Nico to decide."

"Yves, get that girl on film," Nico Ambert decided.

"For the part of Marie, Nico?"

"Who else?"

"We can have Simone," Jules reminded him.

"Only if we want her . . . nothing's signed yet. Jules, you know Sette, don't you?"

"Sure, Bluford's assistant."

"Go over and introduce yourself. If she doesn't speak with an impossible accent, tell her what we want. And arrange it for this afternoon. I'm seeing Simone's agent in two days."

"Wait a minute, Nico. Why would you even consider going with an unknown for Marie?"

"Actually I'd prefer it. *Mayerling*'s been done before, in films and on the stage; everybody knows the story of Marie Vetsera, Archduke Rudolph and their suicide pact at Mayerling. An unknown would add a touch of the unexpected."

"It won't hurt to see her, I suppose," Jules agreed without enthusiasm. The picture was definitively cast in his mind, and he didn't like any interruption once that constellation had been formed, but humoring the director was part of everybody's job. With Ambert it wasn't even humoring, it was obeying. He put down his fork and approached Sette's table.

"Well, Jacques, are you giving the guided tour today?"

"I have that honor. Let me introduce you—Mademoiselle de Lancel, permit me to present Jules LeMaitre, casting director with neither illusions nor scruples, in other words, one of the greats. Jules, our other guests, Vicomte de Lancel, and Guy Marchant—of Marchant Actualités."

As he greeted Delphine, LeMaitre heard, in the few words she said, that her accent was as French as his own, yet by nuances of attitude too subtle to be put into words, he knew that she was not French and not of the world of the cinema.

"Are you visiting Paris, Mademoiselle?" he asked politely, turning away from the three men after he had shaken hands with them.

"For a few days. Then I return to Champagne."

"You live in Champagne, then, and tend your most excellent vines?" he probed.

"I live in Los Angeles," Delphine answered, smiling. He was a smoothie.

"Ah. Then you must be in films."

"No," Delphine laughed, flattered in spite of the familiarity of his line. She'd never heard it from a casting director. "As a matter of fact, I'm a student at the university."

"So, an intellectual. Charming. I have another question, not too indiscreet, to put to you, Mademoiselle. My boss, Nico Ambert, the director, wondered if it would amuse you to do a little screen test for us. This afternoon, in fact, if you have a few minutes to spare."

"Damn! I knew you were up to something, LeMaitre," Sette said, annoyed by the poaching on his guests. What if Bluford, his boss, wanted to test her? He should have thought of that earlier.

"Delphine, it's impossible," Guy Marchant protested, instantly alarmed. "Bruno, tell Delphine that she absolutely can't do it. I'm sure your grandmother would be furious."

"Don't be an utter ass, Guy," Bruno shot back. "Why shouldn't she, for heaven's sake? There's nothing immoral about a screen test, as far as I know." Who, he wondered, did Marchant think he was, making decisions about what was right or not right for Delphine, telling *him* what his own grandmother would think. An inferior would always presume. It was something to remember.

"But, Bruno, just because some guy sees her and she appeals to him? There's something indecent about it—it's as if he just put out a hand and tapped her on the shoulder and said, 'Follow me.' It's not *comme il faut.*" Guy had risen from his chair in his agitation.

" 'Not *comme il faut*'? I think I can judge that for myself, Guy. Not *comme il faut*, indeed." Bruno mocked him.

"Guy, and you too, Bruno, may I ask what this has to do with either of you?" Delphine said calmly. "Monsieur asked me a question, and my answer is that it would amuse me very much indeed."

"Delphine, I beg you, think twice. It'll take all afternoon," Guy sputtered helplessly.

"My afternoon, Guy, not yours. Monsieur Sette, I enjoyed my lunch. Thank you for your hospitality." Delphine got up and looked directly at the casting director. "I'm ready for your test, or I will be after somebody does something about my makeup. Shall I follow you?"

"If you please, Mademoiselle."

"Just a second, LeMaitre," Sette demanded. "What stage will you be working on?"

"Seven. In about an hour."

"We'll all meet you there."

"I think," said Delphine, "that I'd rather do the test without an audience of friends and family. Guy, be an angel and meet me outside when it's over? Bruno, you really don't have to wait, you know. I'll be quite safe with Monsieur LeMaitre."

"I'm sure you will. I'll call tomorrow. Have fun." Bruno kissed her cheek and walked quickly out of the commissary, followed by Guy Marchant, still gesticulating in vain protest. Jacques Sette signed the lunch check gloomily. Bluford was sure to hear of this, and no matter how the test turned out, it would all become his fault somehow.

The makeup lady was fat and friendly and a brilliant professional. She addressed Delphine in the familiar form and admired her hat even as she took it off to rearrange Delphine's hair, releasing it from its polished waves with a brush so that it fell back from her face and almost clear down to her shoulders, dramatically revealing her widow's peak. She performed undreamed-of tricks with mascara and rewrote Delphine's cheeks, the bones of her jaw and the sockets of her eyes in dark shades of base, creating shadows that accentuated the natural contours of her face in a far bolder manner than Delphine would have believed possible or desirable. She explained to the protesting girl that on black-and-white film her work would look as natural as if Delphine wore only ordinary makeup. She crooned over the width of Delphine's forehead, the largeness of her eyes, and the perfect small oval of her chin. "A real heart shape, this little one, a true heart," she repeated, almost to herself.

At last Delphine's lipstick was applied and she was free to leave the makeup room. Outside the door she found LeMaitre waiting patiently for her.

"Good. Very good. Now come and meet Monsieur Ambert." He guided her in the twilight of Stage Seven toward the director's chair. Nico Ambert stood up, and as he extended his hand, he measured her again, sweeping her from head to foot with his unrelentingly open assessment, but his voice was gentle.

"I'm glad you accepted my invitation, Mademoiselle. I hope you're not nervous."

"Should I be?" Delphine heard herself saying teasingly, as if he were a boy back home. She only wished that Margie were here to see this. Only that could make it real.

Ever since the casting director had approached her at lunch she had felt as if she were in a feverish but miraculous dream. Every atom of reality was heightened by the heady surroundings of the studio, where the most ordinary door could open unto a world of wonders. She had scarcely spared a thought for the mechanics of a screen test, so stirred had she been by the sights and smells of what she thought of, confusedly, as being backstage. She was trying to absorb and remember everything around her, to fuse herself with it, just as she had lost herself in the scene with Gabin and Michèle Morgan.

"Should you be?" Ambert repeated. "No, of course not. Sit down here, next to me, and I'll show you what you will read. It's very simple, you'll just read the lines that are underlined in red, and I'll read the others to you . . . a little dialogue between us. You must not look at the camera, if you can manage that. Would you like to read it to yourself first?"

"I'm not an actress," said Delphine. "So what good would that do?"

"To orient yourself, perhaps?"

"You orient me, Monsieur. I think that would be better."

"Do you know the story of *Mayerling*?"

"Not really."

"Never mind. This scene is just a meeting between a young noblewoman and the heir to the Hapsburgs. It takes place at a ball . . . they are dancing together . . . and falling in love."

"Well, that sounds familiar," Delphine said, smiling. "Where do you want me?"

"Over there. Why don't you leave your jacket here? It will be hot in the lights."

Delphine shrugged off her red jacket and tossed it on the back of her chair, and wearing only the slender matching skirt and a simple white silk blouse, she walked fifteen feet to the high stool Ambert had indicated. As soon as she sat down the director gave an order and a bank of lights smashed on, making her throw an arm before her eyes with a cry of surprise.

"Tell me when you can see well enough to read," he said, speaking, across the distance that separated them, so clearly that he could have been sitting next to her.

Delphine waited, truly aware, for the first time, of the weight of many male eyes sizing her up with an avid yet professional interest. Like the lights, it was a blow, and like the lights it was utterly welcome, a primeval attention. She had never felt so alive, so much herself, so much in control.

In the minutes that it took her to grow accustomed to the glare she felt something growing warmly and alarmingly inside of her. It was not the heat of the lights on her skin. It was a glow that started in her belly and spread rapidly and irresistibly until it reached down and gripped her between her legs and made her cross her thighs so that they wouldn't reveal the involuntary and sudden fluttering of her lower lips. She sat pinned in the lights, holding on to the stool with both hands. The script fell to the floor as she was gripped by a powerful orgasm. She bit her lips, sat up as rigidly as she could, thrusting her breasts forward and her shoulders back, her legs pressed together with all her strength so that nothing would be betrayed to the watching men. Nico Ambert felt his penis fill and rise in response to her excitement. This hadn't happened to him in years.

There was utter silence on the set.

"Jules, give her the script," Ambert muttered when he saw that Delphine had recovered some of her composure. He was too hard to move.

LeMaitre handed Delphine the script. Nico began reading, a long speech that he had deliberately chosen to put an actress at ease.

Delphine listened, her eyes seeing but not comprehending the words, her breath coming too quickly in the aftermath of her orgasm to permit her to say her lines. The glow was still there, hot and urgent, and she knew that it would take little to set her off again. It must be the lights, she thought, it must be the lights.

"Mademoiselle?"

"Yes," she said faintly.

"Can you see to read?"

"I'll try." She took a deep breath and concentrated fiercely on the script. Soon the lines made sense and she read, unaware of the camera, unaware of the spectators, throwing all her being into the lines under-lined in red, because only then could she control her body. Ambert's voice responded to her lines. Who the hell, he wondered, had taught her how to fuck the camera? She continued to read, he answered, she replied, until *réplique* following *réplique*, in a dance of words, they had finished the short scene.

The director signaled for the lights to be turned off and in the sudden darkness he got up quickly and walked to where Delphine still sat, shocked by the abruptness of the ending. He took her by her arm, where it was bare beneath her short sleeve.

"You were splendid. I'm afraid it was difficult," he said in a low voice, and it seemed to her that the scene had started again.

"It was so . . . bright."

"I understand. You would like to sit down quietly somewhere before you join your friends."

"Yes."

"Come." He led her quickly off the set, around a corner, around a

239

forest of flats, and into his dressing room. He turned, with his back to the door, and pulled her toward him. He kissed her on her open mouth, a barbarous kiss, a rapturous kiss. "Do you know . . . do you know?" he asked her, his voice brutal.

"What?" she gasped, knowing perfectly well.

"What you did to me? Feel it." He pressed his body against hers so closely that the full, long, animal length of him etched itself on her belly. Men had tried to push themselves against Delphine dozens of times, but she had always eluded them. Now she almost fainted toward Ambert, her eyes closed, her mouth greedy for his brutal, necessary kisses. He carried her to his couch and lay her down, opening her blouse, hovering over her so that his lips never lost contact with her nipples while he flung off their clothes. Delphine had let men touch her nipples but never kiss them, much less see them, and now, naked, exposed, blissfully shamed, it was as if she were under the lights again. His relentless, experienced tongue made her madly liquid, but he knew too much about her already to allow her to have another orgasm. He pulled her hair painfully. "Not yet," he whispered. "Not yet, you little bitch, not again without me." As he opened her thighs he put down his head to inhale the scent of her readiness, but he was careful not to touch her anywhere near her pubic hair. She shoved herself upward, suddenly far, far beyond any modesty, but he just grunted in negation and knelt over her, taking his penis in his hand. He pushed it into her with the voluptuary slowness of a man who has been kept waiting for so long that he is cautious not to move too quickly. Slowly, slowly he entered her, with a vicious, selfish gourmandise that masqueraded as gentleness. She was so wet, so open and so wild to be taken, that he pierced the thin wall of her virginity before either of them knew it, and dug into her at full length. He still held her hair in his grip and only now did he release her so that she could concentrate on the voracious rod that filled her belly. Both of them scarcely breathed, feeling him grow bigger, impossibly bigger, inside of her. As he lay without moving he muttered, "Every man in that studio had his cock in his hand. And you knew it, you knew it, you little bitch." Delphine cried, "I can't wait, I can't," and she came in a great wilderness of exquisite tossing that touched a match to his own bucking, hurting, passionate explosion.

12

ON September third, 1936, Los Angeles was on the eve of becoming, for four days, the center of international aviation. Spruced up and enlarged, Mines Field had been renamed the Municipal Airport. The local organizers of the sixteenth annual National Air Races, which were being held for the first time in the City of the Angels, had resolved that if anybody could show the world how to put on a spectacle, they could.

Freddy had all but memorized the flood of newspaper stories on the events that were about to take place. She knew that Harold Lloyd, as grand marshal, would lead a long motor parade of floats and bands out to the airport; she knew exactly at what time a bomb, bursting in the air over the field, would announce the arrival of the crack Army, Navy and Marine pursuit squadrons, who would demonstrate formation and stunt flying in aerial attack and defense; she knew when in the day the motorcycle-to-glider transfer stunts would take place, and when to expect the mass parachute jumping contest. She knew that Mr. and Mrs. Douglas Fairbanks, Sr., and Benita Hume were planning to have a picnic before the races from a canary yellow basket filled with yellow cups and yellow plates; that Adrienne Ames, in brown tweed, was expected with her former husband, Bruce Cabot, that Carole Lombard and Kay Francis would be among the guests of honor. She even knew the names and faces of the Beverly Hills society girls who had been chosen to greet the service fliers as junior hostesses at the military and naval ball that would end the first day of the National Races.

And she didn't give a damn. It was all window dressing, fill, between the races.

Only three events commanded Freddy's passionate attention: the Bendix transcontinental speed dash from the East Coast to L.A.; the Ruth Chatterton Derby, for "sportsmen pilots," which had begun six days before in Cleveland, and was proceeding, in handicapped laps, on to Los Angeles; and the Amelia Earhart Trophy, a closed circuit speed race around pylons, the only race of the schedule that was limited to women, in which eight contestants would take part.

Of those three races, it was the Chatterton that had taken possession of her imagination, to the point where she yearned toward it in her mind, as she had yearned for nothing since her solo. It was a race that she could have entered if she had a plane. Could have entered. Would have entered. Might even have won. *If* she had a plane of her own.

There were thirty-two contestants, male and female, flying every kind of aircraft in competition against their own best possible speeds. The papers had been full of the Chinese girl, Katharine Sui Fun Cheung, who was flying a small Cessna, and of Peggy Salaman, the London society girl whose mother had smilingly told a reporter, "You really can't dance all day, can you? So Peggy took up aviation." Damn, but she *hated* Peggy Salaman, Freddy thought in a storm of envy, Peggy Salaman *and* her damned generous mother!

The Chatterton was so painful to think about that she walked around in a trance, trying to concentrate on nothing but the obviously, mercifully, self-evidently unattainable Bendix, with its band of famous pilots who were, even now, doing the last minute tune-up of their ships at Floyd Bennett Field, after weeks of rumors and counter rumors, stories of super-streamlined machines never seen before; secret wind tunnel testing of high powered designs; new and more powerful motors than had ever been known; desperate efforts, going on all through the night, to add speed to each plane by any means possible; mysterious last minute entries and hysteria in the press.

The Bendix was a free-for-all race, its only rule that the pilots had to leave Floyd Bennett at dawn on the fourth of September and arrive in Los Angeles by 6:00 P.M. of the same day. *Aviation Magazine*, Freddy's bible, had announced that the favorite was Benny Howard, who had won the annual race the year before in his famous ship, Mister Mulligan. *Aviation* had picked Amelia Earhart in her new Lockheed Electra as the best long shot, closely followed by Jacqueline Cochrane. Howard Hughes was cited by the magazine for the most sporting gesture; he had refused to enter the Bendix on the grounds that his own experimental aircraft was unbeatable by pilots with less money to spend.

Freddy, doggedly practicing Immelmans and Chandelles the day before the race, in Mac's Taylor Cub, which averaged ninety miles an hour at best, meditated on Howard Hughes and his hundred and twenty million dollars, and on Earhart in the plane on which Lockheed had lavished eighty thousand dollars. Decidedly she was in the minor leagues, she thought savagely, as she put the old reliable Taylor through its paces.

Most of her free afternoons of June, July and August had been spent mastering the basics of stunt flying. Eventually, with Mac sitting by her side, she had progressed to complicated stunts: the Oregon Sea Serpent, the Cuban Roll, the Cuban Eight, the Frank Clark Reversement Roll, and the Rankin Roller Coaster. All well and good, Freddy thought, but today she was no closer to her aim of saving money for a plane of her own than she had been before, since she hadn't been able to resist spending every penny she'd earned on her aerobatic lessons.

In two weeks her freshman year at UCLA would begin, Freddy thought glumly. She'd already received a copy of her class schedule. Her mother had taken her shopping for college clothes. When would she be able to fly except on weekends? It had been essential to make the most of the summer, even though it had taken all her salary.

Freshman year, she reminded herself in misery, would mean taking those required courses that were designed by a well-meaning university to give her a well-rounded education in the liberal arts. "Damn it to hell, I don't *want* to be well rounded!" Freddy raged out loud to the unimpressed altimeter, to the hapless airspeed indicator, to the stick that existed only to obey her.

Yet what else was there to do? Join the Navy and see the world? The Foreign Legion? Run away with the circus? Shit, any of them would take a boy, but a not-quite-seventeen-year-old girl? Fat chance. Her destiny led straight to a stuffy college classroom and English 101.

If Freddy could have taken her feet off the rudder pedals she would have stamped in such frustration that she might have kicked a hole through the floor of the plane. Instead she executed one last, flawless Chandelle, a steep, climbing turn of 180 degrees, and came in to land at Dry Springs.

Mac and Swede Castelli, who had come to the airport to talk more stunting business with McGuire, were both outside the hangar, watching her land. She jumped out of the plane, pulled her goggles off, unbuckled her parachute, slung it over one arm, and approached them, hair caught into a copper lariat by the wind, a rakish, slender figure with her Robin Hood walk, that slight, unconscious swagger which was accentuated by the jodhpurs and low boots she had bought when her Levi's wore out. She had rolled up the sleeves of the boy's shirt she always wore for flying.

"Hi there, little lady. That was a mighty pretty Chandelle up there," Swede Castelli said, in what she instantly decided was a patronizing tone. All old stunt pilots, she thought, were convinced that no one could ever fly as well as they had. Well, maybe not all, maybe not Mac. And she loathed being called "little lady."

"Purely decorative, Mr. Castelli," Freddy answered shortly. "A bagatelle."

"You looked O.K., kid," McGuire said.

"Gee, Mac, I just don't think I can handle all your lavish admiration. I may blush," she said acidly, and disappeared into the office. Mac too. They were all the same, she told herself bitterly.

"What's biting her?" Castelli inquired.

"She wants to be Amelia Earhart," Mac explained.

"Well, so do I. Doesn't everybody?"

"She's an emotional kid," Mac shrugged.

"Kid? Listen, Mac, that girl isn't a kid anymore. She's a dish, a dream, a—"

"*She's a kid, Swede.* And you're a dirty old man." Mac's voice was unexpectedly angry.

"It's not a bad way to go, don't knock it, McGuire," Castelli said, good-humored as ever, as Freddy reappeared on her way to her car. He waved at Mac and turned to leave. "Sure you won't reconsider?" he called back to Mac as he walked with Freddy toward their cars.

"Positive," Mac answered.

"It's good money," he shouted, visibly without hope that he could change Mac's refusal.

"No can do, Buddy. I told you, I'm out of that business."

"Ahh," Castelli said to Freddy in mild disgust, "he'd do it for me, I know he would, except he always had this thing against wearing wigs. But it was worth a shot."

"What was it?" Freddy asked indifferently. Mac was still turning down jobs that hopeful stunt coordinators continued to offer him, not believing that he could have finally retired from the business.

"A film called *Tail Spin*. I offered him his choice: Alice Faye, Constance Bennett or Nancy Kelly . . . he could have stunt-doubled any one of them. Roy Del Ruth, the director, asked for Mac specially. He never forgot how believable he was, doing Jean Harlow in *Hell's Angels*."

"But that was a silent movie—I remember it from seven years ago."

"They don't want him to speak, little lady, they just want him to put on a wig and fly. Is that too much to hope for? Is that an insult?"

"No," Freddy giggled, tickled out of her vile mood by the vision of Mac in a platinum blond wig.

"Well, I'm off to try to find three other guys. I'd do it myself, but I've lost my girlish figure. You going to the Air Races?"

244

"Every day," she said, suddenly remembering.

"Listen, little lady, maybe next year, or the year after, you'll be in them. You never know," he said kindly, as he looked at the cloud that had fallen over her face.

"Thanks, Mr. Castelli. But I don't think so."

"Say, wait a minute. What about you? You could be a stunt-double easy—Mac's told me how much you've learned—there isn't anything we've planned you couldn't handle. What about it?"

"Now *that's* impossible," Freddy said, laughing at his eagerness, "much more impossible than my being in the Air Races next year."

"Why? Just tell me what's stopping you?"

Freddy approached Eve's glossy LaSalle convertible. She reached inside, pulled out a pale blue cashmere cardigan and threw it around her neck. The sleeves, knotted hastily under her chin, caught her wind-whipped hair and tamed it into a flaming frame for her earnest face.

"I have to start college in two weeks, for one thing," she said, leaning on the door of the car. "I have a firm rendezvous with Beowulf, Mr. Castelli. In addition, my father, a very conservative man, would kill me, then my mother would kill me and if there was anything left of me, Mac would finish off the job." Freddy's positive stance, even more than the smart, expensive car, convinced Swede Castelli that he was barking up the wrong tree. This particular little lady was a society girl with an unusual hobby.

"I get it. No harm in asking, right?"

"Right, Mr. Castelli."

"So say hello to Beowulf. He's a lucky guy."

By the time the Air Races ended, on the ninth of September, on the day of Eve's big reception for Lieutenant Michel Detroyat, the only French flier at the races, Freddy was smoldering with so many emotions that she didn't recognize herself.

She had watched with a pounding heart as Louise Thaden flew over the finish line of the Bendix, at the wrong end of the field, so modestly convinced that she'd come in last that she'd taxied her ship almost off the field before a running, screaming mob of thousands was able to reach her and make her understand that she'd won. She had crossed the country in less than fifteen hours, leaving behind all the field of experimental, supercharged new racers. And she had won in a Beechcraft, thought Freddy, tormenting herself, torn between admiration and

245

new waves of the most poisonous envy, an ordinary little Beech Stag-gerwing, a plane *anybody* could fly, a plane anybody with a couple of thousand dollars could *buy*.

The night of the Bendix, Freddy had hung around the Egyptian tent put up by the Ninety-Nines, the national organization of licensed women pilots, and seen Thaden and second-place winner, Laura Ingalls, and Earhart and Cochrane, and dozens of other women pilots go inside to celebrate the victories, but she'd been unable to make herself join them, simple as it would have been. Freddy had found herself caged in by a paralyzing shyness that was far stronger than her desire to meet and congratulate her heroines. Her pilot's license was in her purse, but she simply couldn't force herself to walk in and introduce herself, although she knew, logically, that she would have been immediately made welcome. *I have nothing to show for myself,* she told herself miserably and listened to the merriment inside the tent for a few minutes more until she could bear it no longer, and fled.

The Chatterton, thank God, had been won by a man, and she'd put it out of her mind.

"Freddy, you do know that I expect you at my reception today," Eve said, walking into Freddy's bedroom, where Freddy sat looking at the walls. Eve felt the concern of a mother who had watched her child become more and more remote each day of the races. She had been confident that Freddy would be excited and thrilled by the aviation events taking place in their own hometown. They had filled the news-papers to a point where even Eve and Paul knew all about them. But no, Freddy spent every minute of every day at the airport and came home lost in her own thoughts, with strangely blurred eyes, which Eve attributed to the long days spent under the sun that beat down on the grandstands.

"Of course, Mother," Freddy said. "I'll be there." A good dose of the leading lights of the French colony would take her mind off herself and how inadequate she felt, she decided. Besides, she was curious to get a look at the famous guest of honor, king of the world's aerobatic pilots. He was as far out of the range of Freddy's envy as if he'd been Charles Lindbergh. Or Saint-Exupéry, for that matter.

Michel Detroyat had done France proud and become the undisputed star of the races, with extraordinary exhibitions in his Renault-powered Caudron, a racer that the French army had spent a million dollars to develop. It was the first completely streamlined plane ever built, and

246

in it, Detroyat had won the twenty-thousand-dollar Thompson Trophy Race, the international men's free-for-all, laughably far ahead of the competition. The superiority of his plane was such that he'd withdrawn from other races "to give someone else a chance to win."

"Darling, wear your new white linen," Eve instructed.

"But, Mother—" she tried to object.

"It's the most appropriate dress you have." Eve terminated the conversation in a tone of voice that she only used on days when she exercised her official diplomat's wife's capacity, and Freddy knew better than to pursue the matter.

Late that afternoon the gardens of the Lancels' home were filled with hundreds of guests. So many of them had waited in the receiving line to shake Detroyat's hand that Freddy had only been able to observe him and eavesdrop from her position behind Eve, who stood next to him. Not a handsome man, she thought, with his too-long, too-wide nose and double chin, but his eyes, under straight and unusually heavy black brows, made up for that. He looked as carefree as a happy boy, and visibly was accustomed to being lionized, for he answered the same trivial remarks over and over without losing his animation.

"Yes, Madame, I plan to return next year to defend the trophy, thank you, Madame, I am glad you enjoyed the exhibitions; yes, Monsieur, I find Los Angeles delightful, thank you, Monsieur; yes, Madame, you are right, my father is indeed the commander-in-chief of the French Air Corps, I will give him your regards, thank you, Madame; yes, Monsieur, you have the perfect climate here and I hope to return, thank you, Monsieur; yes, Madame, California is indeed a most beautiful place, thank you, Madame."

Small talk, thought Freddy, as the line dwindled and the guests fell upon the refreshments, would seem to be the price of fame. Finally, as always happens to every guest of honor, Detroyat found himself standing completely alone, while a horde of strangers, having paid their respects, forgot him in their interest in each other. She stepped forward, almost out of the shrubbery.

"Lieutenant Detroyat," she found herself saying in rapid French, "could you explain if your Caudron's two-speed, two-pitch Ratier propeller and air-operated retractable landing gear made possible your quick takeoffs?"

"What?"

"I said—"

"I understood what you said, Mademoiselle. The answer is yes."

"Ah, I thought so. Tell me, how many degrees of variation are there between the takeoff and high-speed positions of the propeller?"

"Twelve degrees, Mademoiselle."

"I wondered about that. Hmm . . . twelve degrees. No wonder you won all the time. What would happen if the landing-gear system failed? It is operated by compressed air, is it not?"

"Yes, Mademoiselle. Fortunately I have an emergency hand pump."

"And the tunnel carburetor scoop-ram—does it extend forward all the way to the nose of the Caudron?"

"Perhaps you . . ." He stopped, unable any longer to keep a straight face. Finally he recovered from his fit of laughter. "Perhaps you would like to inspect the ship, Mademoiselle?"

"I would," Freddy said. "But may I ask what it is that you find so funny?"

"The only person at this party who asks an intelligent question is a *jeune fille*. Oh, oh, that tunnel carburetor. . . ." and he went off into another irrepressible bout of laughter.

"I am a pilot, Monsieur, not a *jeune fille*," Freddy said with so much dignity that he stopped laughing and looked at her carefully.

"Yes, I should have known," he said finally, "I really should."

"After all, you couldn't have guessed," Freddy admitted forgivingly.

"But no. I could have. It's evident. You have a pilot's tan." He pointed to the wide neck and short sleeves of her dress, where the deeply tanned vee of her throat reached down and made a point on the whiteness above her breasts. "Even the arms," he said, looking at her tan arms, which abruptly became white halfway above her elbow, where she rolled up her flying shirts.

"I tried to point that out to my mother, but she insisted that I wear this."

"Even pilots have mothers. What do you fly?"

"A Ryan . . . when I can get my hands on it."

"*Tiens*, I know that plane. Tex Rankin and I once competed in two identical Ryans, just for the fun of it, and I almost failed to keep up with him."

"Have you done the Oregon Sea Serpent that Rankin invented? I've just learned it."

Detroyat looked alarmed. "That is not a maneuver for a young lady pilot, Mademoiselle, in fact it is most unwise. I must counsel you against it."

"I do . . . aerobatics," Freddy said, as modestly as she could, since she was speaking to the world's champion, but she could not prevent the pride that blazed out of her eyes. "I'm only a student pilot, but . . ."

"But one who has mastered the Sea Serpent?"

"Yes."

"I must congratulate you, Mademoiselle," he said seriously, visibly impressed, without a trace of mockery. "As one pilot to another, I salute you." He took her hand and was shaking it when Eve came up to him and unceremoniously swept him away.

"Madame de Lancel, who on earth is that unreasonably romantic-looking girl in white linen?" Detroyat asked. "I should like to invite her to inspect my ship."

"You don't mean my daughter, Lieutenant?" Eve asked, instantly alert.

"Your daughter? The pilot?"

"Yes, as a matter of fact. Amazing, isn't it, for a girl who is only sixteen?"

"Only . . . sixteen?"

"Only sixteen," she repeated firmly. "Still a child, Lieutenant."

"Ah."

"Come along, Lieutenant, the president of the French Hospital is so anxious to congratulate you."

"How delightful," sighed the gallant officer, "I can scarcely wait."

The night after the party for Detroyat, Freddy was unable to sleep, her blood rampaging with nervous excitement. "As one pilot to another, I salute you," he had said. One pilot to another! Not "little lady," not "kid," but *pilot*. Why was it that nobody seemed to think of her as a pilot? To Mac she was the eternal student. He'd seen her take her baby steps and he'd never forget it. Never let *her* forget it. She'd really like to hit him! To her father, she was daughter, first, last and foremost. Pilot only on sufferance, and he'd rather not think about it, certainly not hear about it from her. Her mother, once the car had been loaned, seemed to have forgotten where she was going in it, and what she was doing when she got there. Neither of them had any notion that she'd been mastering aerobatics, because they made it clear, without words, that they didn't want or expect progress reports.

And, to be fair, if she truly thought of herself as a pilot, why wouldn't she have marched right on into the Ninety Nines' tent and joined the only other women in the country who shared her passion? She was one of them, wasn't she? *Wasn't she?*

Damn it to hell, she had been selling herself short, accepting the evaluations and dismissals of the only people she cared about, not allowing herself to realize, except for a brief minute or two, how far she had come. *Pilot.* And a damn good one!

Was it because she was not yet old enough? Seventeen in just a few months—surely that was old enough to believe, if only inside yourself, in what you were?

Look at Delphine, not even a year and a half older, fragile, always-to-be-protected Delphine, who didn't know a spark plug from a potato, who could only navigate her way from one manicure to another, busy starring in a French movie without so much as an if-you-please. First, hysterical phone calls from Grandmother and then a letter from Delphine herself, who had been mysteriously unreachable by phone, a letter that had taken many days to arrive, containing the serenely happy announcement that she had signed a contract with Gaumont. She had begun work on the picture before they'd even received her letter. Somehow, everybody had decided that it was all Bruno's fault, but nobody could think of what to do about it, how to stop it.

So Delphine was launched off into the great world, while she, Freddy, was automatically turning down an offer to do some stunt flying that she knew she could handle, because the same parents who had stood by in frantic but futile alarm while Delphine turned herself into a movie actress had decreed that she was to remain a student. Well, to hell with that noise! It wasn't going to happen, not to this particular pilot.

Swede Castelli's office in the I. W. Davidson Studio was as untidy as Freddy had expected, but larger than she had thought it would be. As well as a desk, he had a big conference table, its surface littered with model airplanes; maps hung on all the available wall space, photographs of planes from the Great War were piled on the floor in the corners, and snapshots of Swede Castelli himself, from his stunting days, were propped up here and there.

"Nice," said Freddy truthfully, stretching out in the chair opposite the desk. "I like it here." She sat with her jodhpured legs square on the floor. She had worn her almost-knee-high riding boots today, although, for the sake of comfort, she never flew in them, but she knew the Prussian effect they made. She'd tucked an old black turtleneck sweater into her jodhpurs and cinched them with the biggest leather belt she owned. From the neck down, she thought with satisfaction, you couldn't tell her from Baron von Richthofen.

"Is your job offer still good?" she asked directly.

"You bet it is. But what about that date with Beowulf? What about your parents, little lady?"

"Let me worry about them," Freddy said. "And my name's Freddy, not 'little lady.' "

"This isn't some sort of prank?" he asked skeptically.

"Swede, I don't play pranks. I'm a pilot. You've seen how good I am. I've watched Mac plan a hundred stunts, and if there's one thing I know, it's that you can mount a camera on my ship one hell of a lot closer than you could on any guy's, since I don't get five-o'clock shadow. Put me in any wig and I'll look more like Alice Faye or Constance Bennett than anyone in the business. True or not?"

"True. Totally true. But Mac . . . you told me he'd object if you took a stunt double job. I don't want to cause any trouble, we work together all the time, and he's just about the best pal I've ever had."

"I've thought it over. Swede, Mac taught me to fly and he's like a mother hen with me."

"Yeah, Freddy, I kind of noticed."

"Does that mean that I have to live my life to make him happy? How many mother hens want the chicks to leave the nest? None of them, right? But do chicks stay in the nest forever? You know they don't. It's a law of nature. Now it's my time to get out, and Mac'll just have to understand that. *I need this job.* I really need it, and I'll give it everything I've got, I promise you."

"A rich girl like you? Ah, come on. What do you need this job for?"

"I worked the early-morning shift at the Van der Kamp bakery all summer to pay for my flying time. Now I have to have a plane of my own. *Have* to, Swede, not just *want* to." Freddy leaned forward, her elbows on her knees, her chin in her hands, and looked him in the eye with clear, untroubled power. She had grown up overnight.

"I had you figured for a rich girl."

"Rich means that I have money. Wrong. My parents are comfortable, but they don't give me a penny for flying. The car's a loan, if you were wondering. Look, Swede, if you don't want me, I know someone else will. They're making flying pictures at every lot in Hollywood. I came to you first because I know you, but if you have doubts, just say the word and I'm on my way."

"You've got the job, Freddy. Hell, you had it yesterday."

She laughed in glee. "Will I do Alice Faye or Constance Bennett?"

"Both of them, and Nancy Kelly too. I'm going to use you as much as possible."

251

"The money?" Freddy asked, standing up, her hands on her hips. "The money?"

"You said it was good, but you haven't told me how good."

"Fifty bucks a day, same as I pay Mac. You'll be working five, maybe six days a week once we start shooting."

"Extra for special stunts?"

"Freddy, I have the feeling that you know the stunt scale as well as I do. Extra, just like everyone else gets. A hundred for flying upside down, although that's not in the script, up to a thousand-two for a spin to the earth with smoke pots, and a thousand-five for a blow-up in the air with a bail-out—those you can count on. They're in the script. No crashes on the ground. I wouldn't let you do them anyway, no woman ever has. Tradition. As far as buying a plane—by the time this flick is finished, you can treat yourself to a fleet of them."

"Shee—it," said Freddy slowly.

"It's not exactly shit," Swede Castelli said, offended. "It's damn good money."

"I meant shit, as in 'shit, why did I wait so long?' "

They weren't going to like it whenever she chose to tell them, Freddy reflected, but maybe intelligent timing would give her an edge. The pleasantest minute of the day was before dinner, while her parents shared the better part of a bottle of champagne together in the living room. To open a mere split of champagne, her father maintained, was inconceivable unless three things were true: first, that you were alone; second, that it was lunchtime; and third, that you had not been born in the province of the noble wine. As was the custom, he had been given a few drops of champagne on his tongue as soon as he'd been born, and his mother had finished the rest of the glass, delighted that her new son, like all babies in Champagne, had immediately stopped screaming.

Nor would she mention the money, Freddy decided. If she was hired to work on merely a reasonable number of pictures every year, she'd be making more than her father. And of course she'd promise always to live at home, except when she had to be away on location.

"Well, darling, you look . . . exceptionally well tonight," said Eve, as her daughter joined them. She didn't believe in telling her daughters how beautiful they were, but it was hard, just now, not to use that word for Freddy. The child had evidently recovered from whatever malaise had seized her during the Air Races; that strangely anguished expression was gone, and the graceful, periwinkle blue dress she had

252

put on was reflected in the unlimited blue of her eyes, under the up-ward-lifting brows, so like Eve's own.

There was something strangely compelling in her purposeful, ener-getic pose, although she stood perfectly still, leaning on the mantel and looking at them with a smile Eve didn't recognize, a smile that hovered around her prominent, beautifully formed mouth, almost es-caping at the corners of her lips. It was an inner smile, scarcely sup-pressed, unmistakable, lighting her whole face with a kind of triumphant joy that was in clear contradiction to the gravity with which she was looking at them.

"What's the good news?" Eve couldn't resist asking. Freddy had always been so transparent. It was one of her most endearing qualities. "Not Lieutenant Detroyat, I trust."

"Hardly. Although I did like him. No, it's much better than that. I've got a job."

"Freddy, please be serious. You've been working all summer. You can't work at another job while you're in college, you must realize that."

"Your mother's right," Paul said. "We've discussed that problem and we've decided to finance your flying lessons on the weekends so long as you keep your grades up. We can't have you doing two things at once, and we can understand that you won't want to give up flying alto-gether."

"I appreciate that, Daddy. I know how you feel about it. But it isn't a part-time job. It's a real job."

"Just what does that mean?" Paul asked, putting down his glass.

"A full-time job."

"That's out of the question," he said heavily.

"Freddy, what are you talking about?" Eve cried.

"I'm not going to college, Mother. I can't possibly. I'd make a rotten college girl. I realized it last night. I should have realized it a long time ago, but I wasn't sure enough—not sure of myself, not sure what was best for me, not sure what was right for me."

"And what makes you think that you're old enough to know what's best now?" Paul retorted, holding back his anger as best he could.

"I know I am, Father. *I just know.*"

"Paul, wait a minute. Freddy, you haven't told us what kind of job you have."

"It's a flying job, naturally. It involves precision flying for the mov-ies."

253

"Oh my God! You've taken leave of your senses! What does that mean, 'precision flying'?" Eve's voice trembled in alarm.

"Special flying, the sort of flying I've been training to do, exhibition flying, if you will. I have a talent for it and I do it well."

"Not the sort of thing that Detroyat did?" Eve gasped.

"No, Mother. He's the best in the world. I'm good, but not that good. Not yet."

"God damn it, Freddy, I will not have it! I simply will not allow you to do such a thing. It's out of the question, absolutely, completely and once and for all, out of the question. You are not allowed, do you hear me, *not allowed. You do not have our permission,*" Paul thundered, standing up and looming over her.

"I shall have to do it without your permission," Freddy answered, stepping toward him fearlessly. "There's no way you can stop me."

"Marie-Frédérique, I'm warning you, and I won't warn you again. I've had enough of this sort of behavior from Delphine. I won't make the same mistake twice. If you think that you can do whatever you like and get away with it, you're mortally wrong. You will either do as I say or you will move out of this house at once and not return to it until you come to your senses. No daughter of mine is going to disobey me. *Do you understand?*"

"Yes, Father." She turned and started to leave the room.

"Freddy! Where are you going?"

"To pack, Mother. It won't take long."

Freddy hastily filled a small suitcase with basic necessities, leaving behind the shirtwaist dresses and the pastel sweaters and skirts, that pretty, expensive college wardrobe on which every item still had a price tag. She threw her leather flying jacket over her dress and took a last look around her room. It didn't feel like her room anymore; there was no emotion attached to leaving it. She knew that Eve would not come upstairs to try to stop her. In matters of discipline her parents had always hung together, and the only time she could remember her mother taking a basically different position from her father's was when she had understood why Freddy had soloed.

They were in the dining room as she quietly left the house, putting her door key and the key to Eve's car on the table by the front door. There was no irresolution as Freddy hitched a ride to the San Fernando Valley. She knew where she was going, and three-quarters of an hour later she found herself walking the last few hundred yards to the small house near the Dry Springs airport where McGuire lived. She'd never been there, but she'd memorized the address.

It was almost dark by now, yet no light showed in the house. However, the garage was brightly lit, and as she approached, Freddy could hear whistling and the sound of a hammer. Mac, his brown hair falling forward until it touched his long lashes, was busy rebuilding one of his latest finds, a rare, twenty-year-old Fokker D.VII with an Iron Cross painted on its tail and another on the long, delicate fuselage. War movies were often shot with Curtiss Hawks and M.B.3's disguised as Fokkers, but nothing equaled the real thing, and the genuine ships had become more and more valuable since Howard Hughes had used up most of them in *Hell's Angels*.

Mac's large collection of planes from the Great War, which had grown steadily in the past six years, was used and reused constantly, for no ship ever had to die, as long as all of its parts weren't in splinters after a crash. McGuire employed several assistants now, just to care for the planes, but on a difficult job he preferred to do the work himself.

Freddy put down her suitcase and slouched matter-of-factly into the garage, her hands nonchalantly thrust into the pockets of her leather jacket.

"Hi, there, Mac. Need some help?"

He put down his hammer with an astonished bang. "What the hell are you doing here?"

"The alternative was to check into a hotel by myself. That didn't seem like a swell idea."

"You've left home?" he said incredulously.

"I was asked to leave. Thrown out. 'Never darken my door again'— that kind of departure." Freddy spoke with bravado and a grin that would have fooled anyone else.

"Just a minute. What's going on? Your parents would never throw you out alone at night. What did you *do* to get into this mess?"

"I told them that I'd decided that I wasn't going to college. I couldn't cut it, Mac, I really couldn't. The thought of the whole thing made me feel as if I were buried alive in library dust. It's just not for me."

"Christ," he said disgustedly, "talk about overreaction. I can understand that they'd be disappointed, naturally, but to treat you like it was the end of the world—that's plain silly." He put away the hammer and turned off the garage lights. "Come on over to the house, kid, and you can tell me all about it. I'm sure that you can work it out with them without all this melodrama. Do they know where you are?"

"No. They didn't ask and I didn't tell them."

"Well, I'm going to let them know so they don't worry . . . but first let's talk about it."

He picked up her suitcase, led her to the dark house, and turned on the lights in the living room. "Sit down and make yourself comfortable. Want a Coke? No? Well, I'll have to drink alone, then."

"You wouldn't, by any chance, have a sandwich in this place?" Freddy asked as she watched him pour Scotch into a glass and add water.

"You left home *before* dinner? Bad timing. Come on in the kitchen and I'll see if I can find a crust of dry bread."

Freddy looked around with great curiosity. The house was immaculately clean and neat, almost impersonal. Mac's real life was lived in the air, but she'd expected something like Swede Castelli's office, a messy, masculine place, full of memorabilia. But there were no photos, nor were there pictures or plants. The bookcases were crowded with well-read books that she had never seen at the airport office, and the room was comfortably furnished, well furnished, actually, except that obviously it was never used. The kitchen was as neat as the living room, but here she could see signs that human life existed: a comfortable old painted kitchen table with a pitcher full of Queen Anne's lace standing on it; a good-sized stove, with an array of cooking utensils on the counter. A heavy pot stood on the stove, and Mac turned the gas on under it. "Stew. You're in luck, kid. I'll reheat it."

Freddy sat down on one of the four Windsor chairs placed around the table. She hadn't realized until this minute how tired and hungry she was. She was still so alight with her decision, so determined, so single-minded, that she hadn't given herself a chance to do anything but keep moving since the scene with her parents.

"Can I have some of that, please?" she asked, pointing to Mac's glass.

"Are you out of your mind, Freddy? That's whiskey. If you're thirsty, I have plenty of Cokes."

Freddy felt herself suddenly spark with anger. "I am getting so goddamned good and tired of being asked if I'm out of my mind, if I've taken leave of my senses, if I'm crazy. I'm saner than I've ever been in my life and I want a drink of whiskey, professor."

Mac whirled around from tending the pot of stew and looked at her narrowly. "Yeah, well, I'm getting tired of being called 'professor.' "

"I've never called you that before!"

"Once is too often. Cut it out."

"O.K.—old-timer."

"Oh. Looking for trouble, are we?" he asked mildly. "No wonder your father kicked you out. Did you call him 'old-timer' too?"

"No, not that it's any of your business."

"You've made it my business, showing up here. Now eat this stew and shut up. You're just hungry."

Ravenously, Freddy finished two helpings of one of the best beef stews she'd ever had in her life. Mac sat opposite her, sipping his whiskey and watching the top of her bright head bent over her plate. After she was fed, he thought, he'd talk some sense into her and get on the phone to her parents.

She had to go to college, he supposed, dumb as he personally thought it was, and a shocking waste of a great pilot. But even a great pilot had to fly constantly to maintain all the necessary skills—it wasn't like learning how to drive a car. Once Freddy was sucked into the life of the university, between her studies and her dates, she'd never have enough time. She'd turn into a weekend pilot, the kind he dealt with every day, and eventually she might stop flying altogether, as had the few other women he'd known who'd won their wings. She'd go to football games instead of chasing the clouds, chances were. Life would do that . . . a husband and, someday, children . . .

It was an obvious story, with an obvious ending. He didn't know why he felt such a personal sense of loss, of injury almost, even of something curiously like fear. It was for the best, after all. She had been born a flying animal, just as he had, but she was a female animal too, and there was simply no future in it for her. It was hard enough for a man to stick to it, to keep current, as he well knew. Them's the jokes, he told himself, and felt such a stab of total misery at the prospect of Freddy's inevitable future, that he had to hold his breath to keep from betraying his attack of emotion. This was the time, if ever there had been one, to sound avuncular and firm. And impersonal.

"Better?" Mac asked as she polished off her plate.

"Much. Where'd you learn to cook?"

"Starvation is the only other alternative for a man who lives alone. Like going to college for you, I had no option but to learn."

"Neat, very well put, but no cigar, Mac."

"Look, I know how you feel, Freddy, I really do, but you're in a bind, a serious bind, and being stubborn isn't going to make it disappear. How much money do you have in the world?"

"Three bucks fifty. In the world. And the clothes on my back and in my suitcase. Oh, and my toothbrush. I remembered to bring it."

"I don't know why you seem to think that's funny."

"I like the feeling of traveling light."

"How far can you travel on three bucks fifty?"

"We'll find that out, won't we?" She lifted her hands to her nape, under the weight of her hair, and pulled it back away from her neck in a lovely, proud gesture, thinking, Constance Bennett, Alice Faye, ready or not, here I come.

"Look, kid, you're just a little high on yourself tonight. I know the feeling. But tomorrow it'll be different. Tomorrow I'll go off flying and you'll be home making up with your parents and hammering out some kind of agreement . . . If you go to school, maybe they'll give you enough money to let you fly weekends. It's the only way and it's a damn sight better than nothing. You know it as well as I do."

"They've already offered that," Freddy said softly. "And I turned it down."

"The hell you did! After all these years of scratching for dough for lessons, you turned down some help from them?"

"Right." She got up and took the plate and the silver to the sink and rinsed them off. "Do you have a dishtowel, Mac? Or do you just let them drip? What's the option here? What's the bind?"

"Freddy, you're such a smartass tonight that I'm not going to waste my time trying to talk sense to you. You won't listen, no matter what I say. What's your home phone number? I'm calling your folks right now and put them out of their misery. No? O.K., I'll ask the operator." He picked up the receiver of the phone on the kitchen wall.

"Wait! Don't call them. Please, Mac?"

"Sorry, Freddy, no can do." He dialed O for Operator and she snatched the receiver out of his hand and hung it up.

"There's more . . . stuff . . . that I didn't tell you. Not just college."

"I should have guessed," he said, utterly without humor. "What kind of stuff?"

"I have a job. I can support myself."

"You're going to waste your life in a bakery or something like that? Oh no, you're not."

"A flying job."

"What do you mean, a flying job? There aren't any jobs in flying for a girl."

"There are now. I'm working for Swede Castelli. He hired me to double Alice Faye and Constance Bennett and Nancy Kelly in *Tail Spin*."

"*Stunt*-double?"

"Well you turned it down—"

"*Stunts!*"

"Nothing I can't do. If anybody knows that, it's you—"

"I read the script, Freddy. *You are not going to do it*—a spin to earth! A blow-up in the air with a bail-out—A BAIL-OUT—the fuck you are!"

"The hell I won't!" she screamed at him, her face a mask of absolute determination.

McGuire hauled off and smacked her as hard as he could across her cheek. "*Not while I'm alive!*" he shouted. Freddy rushed him, kicking his legs viciously with her shoes, and beating him furiously around his head with her strong hands. Finally he managed to pin her arms to her sides and held her in his grip, paying no attention to her kicks of fury until she stopped. Still he held her tightly, frozen, unable to let go. They stood for a minute, locked together, immobile, gasping, looking at each other with shocked, questioning eyes. Then Freddy, puzzled no longer, leaned forward and planted her mouth squarely on his lips. "I will *not* do this," he groaned, and kissed her with all the hungry, yearning, insane love he had tried not to face for so long.

They couldn't stop kissing each other. Each time they drew breath, the sight of the beloved face, the lips they had both refused to admit they had dreamed of, longed for, during more time than either of them guessed, brought them together again in a tempest of wildly aching kisses, so needy that it was the sweetest and most piercing pain. They couldn't get close enough to each other, they wanted to weld their skin together, to possess each other's lips, to be locked to each other, to own the other in a way no two humans can. They reeled and stumbled about, so dizzy with kisses that they could barely stand upright, in the middle of the kitchen floor, until Freddy moaned, "Please, make love to me," and he answered, "I can't, you know I can't."

"But I love you so much . . . I've always loved you . . . it's too late to say no . . . we can't stop now . . ."

"I couldn't . . . it's not right . . ."

"It's the rightest thing in the world. You love me as much as I love you."

"More, more than you can imagine, more than I thought it was possible to love. You're the love of my life. I'd die for you."

"Then how can it not be right?" she asked with such a look of implacable tenderness, with such exalted, insistent joy that he knew he didn't have the strength to resist her. Worse, he didn't want to. They were irrevocable.

In his bed he found himself clumsy, awkward, suddenly hesitant, until she led the way, her perfect innocence like the low note of a cello that played a melody only the two of them could hear. The rage to fuse into each other that had consumed them in the kitchen grew calmer now that they had confessed to each other the love that had been there for years.

It seemed, suddenly, as if they had all the time in the world, time to make, one by one, the discoveries they had panted and strained for only minutes before. There was time to touch each other with delicate wonder. Each hair on Mac's head was wonderful to Freddy, each bristle on his cheeks was precious. The shape of each of his ears had to be learned by her mouth, his eyebrows brushed in the wrong direction by her fingertips. She knew nothing about how a man's face was supposed to feel, and she was seized by a vast, yet unhurried curiosity. She was profligate with her untutored caresses, and Mac lay back and accepted her explorations, too happy to think beyond the miraculous moment. He looked up at her, leaning so intently over him, and willed himself to be patient, even as she ran her long, sensitive fingers up and down his neck and shoulders, until, almost shyly, she kissed his neck.

"Don't," he whispered. "Not yet." Her naked body was so exquisite that he could not risk looking at it for long. Her nipples, he saw in amazement, were already standing up, deeply pink and pointed on her magnificent white breasts, and he hadn't even touched them. Ah, but he had to now, didn't he? They were asking for it, he thought confusedly, and he turned and put Freddy down on the sheet and lowered his head over her.

Freddy froze with shock. She closed her eyes tightly. Nothing in her life had ever been this good. No intimation, no hint had ever reached her and made her wonder if a feeling so madly good was possible. She lay back, almost unable to draw breath, and willed him to continue, feeling, as he reverently caressed her, an electric current, as clear-cut and fiery as a bolt of lightning, shoot from her breasts downward until it informed her of things she had never guessed. How long could she lie still and endure this delight before she went mad, she asked herself, and then, as she felt his fingers move lightly and tentatively along her hips, she understood that there was no law that said she had to lie still. She pressed upward to meet him.

Time, that Freddy had thought so unlimited, so inexhaustible, suddenly vanished with her pulsing, passionate need to know him completely, to be completely known. Impatiently she opened her legs in a foreign signal of which she would not have believed herself capable. Mac understood, but he was reluctant, he hesitated, until she pushed so insistently toward him that he entered her. Suddenly he stopped. He had reached the barrier he had forgotten. "No, no more, I'll hurt you," he muttered.

"I want you to," she cried, consumed with love and desire. "I want you, I want you," she cried again, and when he still held himself resolutely motionless, she gathered herself together, roughly, impatiently, arching upward with all the strength of her back and legs and hips, so that the choice was no longer his to make. Now they strained forward, with a single will, a single need, and a single goal. The innocent girl and the experienced man reached it together, so deep was their love, so well did they know each other, so often had one taught the other what had been the most important thing in the world to them until they had turned to each other with the truth of their love.

13

PAUL de Lancel was not a man who had been formed by nature for rage. His upbringing in Champagne had been influenced, day by day, by the tranquility that rose like a mist from the gentle slopes of the fruitful countryside. He had come to maturity in the peaceful years before the Great War. He had been well trained in the artistic compromises of diplomacy, and he had lived in joy with the woman he adored for almost two decades.

Now, with Freddy's cool act of defiance, a state of rage, relentless, unreflective rage, had invaded him. It was an absolute rage, all the more unforgiving because he had never learned, as a naturally irascible man might, that it is unproductive to sustain rage at full pitch over a long length of time. He was so transformed by rage that Eve was unable to discuss it with him, because he would not even allow her to say Freddy's name. He dug himself into his rage with the same blind determination as a prisoner making an escape tunnel, for like a prisoner he had no other way to avoid the reality of the situation.

She must be taught a lesson. A lesson she'd never forget. Someone had to obey him! All his rage was contained in these words, as if he were a third-rate lion tamer rather than a reasonable member of a pragmatic profession. He allowed himself to think no further.

Freddy was paying for all the deflected, unabsorbed fury Paul felt toward Bruno, the son who treated him only with the politeness due a stranger, the son who had rejected him for reasons too painful to explore. Freddy was paying for all the recent bitterness of the disappointment Paul felt toward Delphine, the daughter whose conduct was so duplicitous and dubious, the daughter who had left him powerless to do anything to upset the *fait accompli* of her contract with Gaumont.

His impotence as a father, with all three of his children, was so ultimately maddening to Paul de Lancel that he could not bring himself to think about it consciously. It was easier to cast Freddy utterly out of his life, to reject her once and for all. She deserved nothing. She could do without her family, could she? Then so be it. *Someone* had to obey him!

Freddy became the focus of all his unutterable frustrations with Bruno and Delphine. Freddy's conduct—her unforgivable mutiny—

was the final insurrection against which he would stand fast, no matter what it cost.

Eve barely recognized her husband in the weeks after Freddy left. He woke up so early that he often departed for the Consulate before she went downstairs for breakfast, leaving her only a message with Sophie, the cook. He returned home and buried himself in the newspapers, scarcely speaking to her, until dinner. During dinner, he poured himself three times as many glasses of wine as she had ever known him to drink, which enabled him to maintain a meaningless conversation with her about the details of their separate daily routines, and after dinner he took himself out for a long, solitary walk, coming home only to inform her that he had slept so badly that he was going to go to bed. He hadn't laughed out loud since Freddy left, and he kissed Eve as if it were a duty.

Was he angry at her too, Eve wondered. She had to believe that he was, although he would never admit it. After all, it was she who had talked him into letting Freddy continue with her flying lessons after her solo; she had lent Freddy her car. Paul couldn't consider her blameless, but since he would tolerate absolutely no mention of Freddy, Eve could not shoulder her fair share of the events that had led up to Freddy's act of anarchy.

She was not even able to give her husband news of Freddy, for every week Eve received a brief phone call from her daughter at a time when Paul was at work. Freddy didn't give Eve details of her life. She didn't say where she was lodging, but she reassured her anxious mother that she was well and safe. Her happiness was evident in her voice. Eve had tried to pass the news on to Paul, but he had stopped her as soon as he realized what she was beginning to tell him.

"It does not concern me," he said, in a tone of voice so unyieldingly filled with a killing fury that she left the room without another word, terrified, for the first time in her life, of the man she had married.

Eve endured the misery of this life until shortly before Christmas of 1936. Paul could, at any time, have found out where Freddy was working, with a telephone call to any of his studio contacts. It was a call he would never make, she realized, even if he were willing to admit that he didn't know where his own daughter was. But she was beyond worrying about his pride after almost three months, she thought angrily, and made the call herself. She craved the sight of the girl, she needed to hold her child in her arms. A day later she had her answer, and she headed out in her car to the farm near Oxnard where the *Tail Spin* company was working.

"Yes, ma'am?" inquired the guard at the wire fence that had been built all around the fields on which part of the film was being made, to keep out the curious locals.

"I'm expected," Eve answered briskly. He swung back his gate without further questions. She left her car behind a group of sheds where she saw other cars parked, and walked toward the largest shed with a firm step. She felt no shyness about intruding on the surroundings of a movie on location. Someone who had starred at the Olympia was free forever of any trepidation about venturing into that area of the *spectacle* that was officially closed to the public. Backstage was backstage, wherever she came across it, and as much her world today as it had ever been in the reign of Jacques Charles.

"Is Freddy de Lancel around?" she asked the first person she saw who looked as if he might know.

"Freddy? You'll have to ask over there. I don't know the stunt schedule," the man answered, pointing at another shed that contained an improvised production office.

"The stunt schedule," Eve said, able to keep the surprise out of her voice.

"Yep."

"What about the precision flying? Shouldn't I ask there?"

"Same thing, lady."

"Like . . . aerobatics? Exhibition flying?"

"Stunts—exhibitions—six of one, half a dozen of another."

"Thank you." She turned toward the shed he had indicated. She wouldn't think about it until she knew more, she thought in dismay. The technical terminology of whatever it was that Freddy was doing was obviously so sloppy that one thing meant another or a third or a fourth.

In the production office they directed her toward another building, a hangar several hundred yards away. Eve walked toward it, feeling the dry wind of a Santa Ana wind whip the skirt of her smart dark green suit and almost lift off her soft felt hat. The sky was far away, unimportant, painted in the flat, cloudless blue wash caused by the wind that was to California as the Mistral was to the South of France. The field she crossed was the dry, slightly scruffy yellow of a California winter before the coming of the rains of January, that herald the spring. As she walked, as trim and elegant at forty as she had been at twenty, her gray eyes still fascinating in their darkness, her hair still a romantic strawberry blond, Eve aroused a wave of appreciative, curious glances from the busy technicians, who always managed to spare the time to eye a beautiful woman.

Eve looked into the hangar, dim after the sunlight outside. There were several people gathered around a plane that appeared as modern and powerful as any she had seen in newspaper photographs of the Air Races. As she approached them, she recognized Alice Faye, wearing a cream-colored shirt, tailored with so many flaps and pockets that it looked like a military uniform, tucked into a matching pair of the tightest slacks Eve had ever seen. A cream suede belt was wrapped around her small waist, a white silk scarf was casually flipped around her neck, and the unmistakable platinum blond of her long bob curled out from under her cream-colored leather helmet. Goggles were pushed back on top of the helmet, revealing her entire face, the familiar black eyebrows, the big eyes fringed in exaggerated black eyelashes, the brightly lipsticked, luscious lips that made such an intriguing counterpoint to her aggressive blondness.

Two men bent with her over the cockpit of the plane, one a plump, almost middle-aged man, and one a younger man, whom Eve recognized as Spencer Tracy. He was taller than she'd thought. Then, as she walked much closer, still unnoticed, she saw that he wasn't Tracy after all, just an actor who looked like him. The two men were in animated conversation about the shoulder straps that were intended to hold the pilot in the seat of the racing plane, the younger man plainly dissatisfied with them.

"I don't give a damn, Swede, if this is the best available equipment in the whole damn world. Make new ones. They've got to be three times as strong, or Freddy doesn't fly," he insisted as Eve approached.

"We'll lose a day," Swede Castelli protested, "maybe two."

"You heard the man, Swede," Alice Faye said. "Anyway, there's too much wind to fly today. The camera plane would bounce around."

"Freddy," Eve breathed.

Alice Faye whirled around. "Mother! Oh God, I'm glad to see you! Oh, Mother, Mother, how are you? Give me a kiss. How's Daddy? How's Delphine? Tell me everything! How'd you find me? Give me another kiss. Oh . . . this is Swede Castelli and this is Mac—Terence McGuire. Guys, this is my long-lost mother. Bet you didn't think I had one, did you Swede? Oh, I've got lipstick all over you, Mother. Let me wipe it off. Lend me your hanky, there's no room in this dumb outfit for anything but me."

Freddy was dancing around Eve in joy, hugging her and then holding her away so that she could get a good look at her, and then hugging her again. The child certainly wasn't starving, Eve thought in bewilderment, for she seemed not only to have grown taller but to have filled out so that her lanky frame had become that of the voluptuous screen star. Freddy saw her surprise. "It's padding, Mother, not me. I'm still your little girl inside this costume."

"You fooled me," Eve said breathlessly. "I didn't recognize you. I thought you were Alice Faye."

"That's the idea, Mrs. de Lancel," Swede Castelli said, beaming. "You should see her as Connie Bennett, she's a dead ringer."

"Swede, let's take my mother for a cup of coffee. We're finished in here anyway, aren't we?" Freddy asked.

"I've got to go and get that safety harness made, Freddy. I also have to talk to Roy Del Ruth about a few things. You and Mac take off. I'll see you here tomorrow morning if I have to sew it myself."

"Swede, what's your rush? You've got time for a cup of coffee," Freddy insisted as the four of them walked from the hangar to the temporary commissary.

"I'd better get going. Nice to meet you, Mrs. de Lancel. See you again, I hope." He went off hurriedly to find the director of the picture before he tackled the problem of the shoulder harness. With Mac rigging all of Freddy's stunts, Castelli estimated that days and days of production had already been spent meeting his safety demands and his redoubled precautions. On the other hand, once Freddy was flying, they saved far more time than they lost, and there had never been stunts in the history of the business about which he felt less anxiety. Nor had there been more convincing flying shots of a woman in the history of film.

As she drank her coffee and ate the Danish pastry that Freddy insisted she have, Eve felt herself struggling with a series of impressions that confused her. It wasn't just the garish makeup and the platinum wig that made Freddy seem so much like a stranger. There was something . . . she couldn't tell what . . . but something different about her. Her voice was the same, her affectionate attention was the same, but something basic had changed. It wasn't just that she had grown up, that she was making her own living and leading her own life—both topics that Freddy and Eve avoided by mutual consent—it was something else that Eve couldn't identify. Something new.

Eve ventured to ask Mr. McGuire a few questions to see if anything he said might give her a hint as to the change in her daughter, but his answers were just what she would have expected from the instructor who had taught her daughter to fly—measured, calm and reasonable. He explained the mechanics of several of the stunts to her in a way that she could understand. He was an exceptionally reassuring man, she thought as she listened to him, and if she had met him before, she would have been certain that Freddy was in good hands while she'd been taking lessons.

She'd come back another day, Eve thought, and see if she could talk to Freddy alone, when she wasn't wearing makeup that acted like a mask. But she was sure of the single vital thing she had come out to discover; Freddy was, indeed, all right. Perhaps she could figure out some way to get that reassurance through to Paul. Even if she failed, at least she and Freddy were back in contact.

Eve was very careful not to fall into an overly maternal attitude. Not only had there been a three-month break over the issue of Freddy's clearly declared independence, but Mr. McGuire, a stranger, was present. She would never discuss family matters unless she and her daughter were alone. She didn't ask where Freddy was living, or who cooked her meals, or how she got her laundry done, or what her plans were once this picture was over. She was content to just sit, in her vague but insistent confusion, and let her child's evident happiness wash over her. Freddy was working at the thing she loved and, according to Mr. McGuire, doing it brilliantly. That knowledge was enough for today, she thought, as she left to drive back home.

Eve concentrated on her driving as she zipped along the coast road back from Oxnard. She still felt a little shaky from the emotion of being reunited with her daughter, and she resolutely emptied her mind of thoughts of Freddy, so that she could cruise along and regain her normal mien before she had to go back and confront Paul, and not tell him where she had been all day.

She sang snatches of songs she had almost forgotten, and thought, in a scattered way, of the men of the music hall who had made them famous. For long minutes Eve disappeared and Maddy returned to life. She remembered Chevalier and one of his first hits, "I Can't Live Without Love." "Je n'peux pas vivre sans amour," Maddy sang, "J'en rêve la nuit et le jour." Memories, unbidden, almost twenty-five years old, touched and lingered. Suddenly, Eve pulled the car over to the side of the road with a screeching of brakes. She sat still in the smart little coupé, her heart thudding, her cheeks crimson, her hands shaking.

But, by God, she was stupid! It was as clear as if they had made an announcement. As plain to see as the lipstick on Freddy's mouth.

Those two were wildly in love. *Lovers*. Oh, but there could be no question. Plain. Plain . . . in every look they had not given each other, in every time that their hands had not touched, in every word they had not spoken. How could she have missed a passion so evident? So . . . solid. Unadorned. Incontestable. Had it been the mask of Alice Faye on Freddy's face that made her blind? Had it been because she still looked at her and saw only her little girl? Oh, but she was far deep into it, her daughter was, so deep, so gone, swept so far, far away to a land where mothers cannot follow. And he, poor man, he would never recover from Freddy. This was it for him.

Finally Eve started her car again, with a sigh as much of resignation as of experience. How it had happened wasn't important. What would happen was not something she or anyone on earth could control. Freddy was blindingly happy. And she herself . . . yes, she had to admit it, she felt a touch of envy. Admit everything, while you're alone, while you have time . . . envy for the remembered once-in-a-lifetime madness of a first passion . . . and even . . . yes, admit it to yourself, while you're still numb with the shock of realization, just a little normal female envy for the possession of that man. That enormously attractive man with his quiet, potent charm and his strong, muscular body, that exceptionally . . . desirable . . . man. Her daughter had chosen well.

La matinée grasse, Delphine thought in hazy pleasure as she lay half-dozing in bed, was not a uniquely French invention, yet giving a name and a kind of official status to the idea of a "fat," juicy morning, a totally lazy, worthless, good-for-nothing morning, made it seem less self-indulgent, more of a tradition. In any case, she deserved a *matinée grasse,* if anybody did, after making one film after another for month after month. She had instructed her personal maid, Annabelle, that she would be spending the morning in her room and was not to be interrupted, not even for an orchid tree, should one arrive.

It was raining in any case, on this tenth of April, 1938, but Delphine had grown accustomed to rain in her almost two years as a Parisienne and was indifferent to it. It never depressed her, for it never inconvenienced her. Her driver took her everywhere in her handsome, dove gray Delahaye; she spent most of her days at the studio where there was no weather; her house was always filled with offerings of flowers; and, unlike so many French homes, it was always warm and snug.

After Delphine's enormous success in *Mayerling,* she had looked for a place to live, while her new agent negotiated a far better contract with Gaumont than the one she had first signed. Off the Avenue Foch, in the Sixteenth Arrondissement, the richest section of the Right Bank, there are several little-known and particularly charming dead-end streets, known as "Villas," that had been built in the 1850s. The houses, in those un-French streets, are like those in English mews: small, cozy, intensely private, with a garden behind each one of them. Delphine had found one on the Villa Mozart which reminded her of a Victorian doll's house, built of pink, whitewashed brick, its woodwork painted turquoise. An old wisteria vine grew up the face of the house, shading its windows, and in the back garden there were pink hydrangea bushes and a weeping willow. Sun, whenever there chanced to be any, came in from the front every morning and from the back every afternoon. There were two rooms and a bathroom on each of the upper floors, a dining room, a salon and a kitchen on the first floor, and a small but well-insulated cellar. The heating system was new and effective. Delphine bought it immediately with the first money she'd ever earned.

Another eighteen-year-old who woke up to find herself a star, albeit one with only a single film to her credit, might well have spent her money on furs or jewelry or a car, or even been too overwhelmed to spend it at all.

Delphine wanted only one thing: a fortress. She had always lived in houses in which somebody older was in a position to hold her accountable for her actions. The house in the Villa Mozart was her guarantee that the growing demands of her body could always be satisfied in privacy.

There was no curious, officious concierge at the foot of the main staircase, as there was, by law, in all Parisian apartment buildings, to note the comings and goings of her visitors. In the Villa Mozart there were only a busy guardian and his wife, Louis and Claudine, who lived at the entrance to the street, several hundred feet away from Delphine's front door, literally out of sight, since the street curved away from their windows.

Whenever she notified them that she would be expecting a guest, they opened the gate that barred the cul-de-sac to casual traffic, as soon as her name was mentioned, without demanding any further information. She tipped them well and often. Although they weren't installed on her premises, she was already enough of a Parisienne to be aware of the necessity of their goodwill.

Delphine hired a staff, but required that none of them live in the house. Her driver, Robert, her personal maid, her cook and her *femme de chambre* all came to work early in the morning and left when their jobs were over. She paid them handsomely—far more than if she had provided room and board—but it was well worth it to her. Whenever any of them saw evidence, in the morning, that Delphine had not slept alone, they were far too pleased with their easy jobs to let her suspect that she wasn't leading her life in the complete privacy she had constructed so carefully.

To each other they had a good deal to report about Monsieur Nico Ambert and their young mistress. Louis, in admiration, announced to his wife that Ambert had spent the night five times last week. Yes, he even had his own key to the front door. Annabelle, the personal maid, who had the news directly from Claudine as she entered the street, whispered it with a wink to Helene, the cook. Claudine had installed her sister, Violet, as the *femme de chambre*, who did all the housework, so she knew each detail of the condition of Delphine's bedroom, and how many times clean sheets were required on the bed, and precisely why. He must be a hot-blooded brute, that Nico Ambert, she told them all, with an envious grimace. Not soon satisfied, and as rough as a stevedore, that was easy to see. Well, he was young.

Delphine, in her fortress on the Villa Mozart, was the center of a web of information more precise and more explicit than if she had chosen to live in Hedda Hopper's backyard, yet she would never be enough of a Parisienne to realize it.

Nico Ambert had lasted six months, until *Mayerling* was completed and Delphine had signed to star opposite Claude Dauphin in a film called *Rendez-vous d'Amour*.

Ambert had taught her more than he had intended, and Delphine, only hours out of his arms, would stroll slowly across a film set, as if she were contemplating her next scene, while she wondered which of the many men working there had begun to stiffen in arousal, as their eyes followed her passage. She would linger, from time to time, to greet a strong young assistant in any of the crafts and let her eyes wander down to his crotch, measuring his size with an imperceptible, practiced glance, as she asked a sensible question about his work. She would suck on her bottom lip in reflection as he answered while she looked steadily at his mouth, and only when she saw his face become flushed with desire would she quickly lower her eyes again to see how big he had grown, how far his trousers were bulging. Then she would bid him good-bye with a friendly smile, seeing in her mind the heavy, engorged member that she could so easily have drawn out from its hiding place, that marvelous hardness of blood-swollen flesh that she was utterly prepared to take, that she herself was now ripe to shove up deep inside her body.

But she never did. She fed gloriously on the lust of the crew, inflamed them without giving them a valid excuse to brand her a tease. Delphine became addicted to sexual need. She adored the blissful, giddy, pleasurable pain of her mounting tension, her maddened imagination; she gladly spent hours of excruciating desire, wet and needy, until the lights went on, until it came time for the cameras to turn, until the director unleashed her. Only then would she allow herself the orgasms she concealed so well.

She threw Ambert over for the director of *Rendez-vous d'Amour*. He had been reluctant to return the key to her front door, and she never made that particular mistake again. When she started her next film, *Affaire de Coeur*, with Charles Boyer, she moved into the arms of the producer. The director had not tempted her. She paid no attention to actors. They were too self-centered to interest her. The better looking they were, the less attractive they were to her. Their screen kisses never had the sensual reality of the sight of the big hands of a master electrician at work.

The passion that the camera captured in Delphine's most exquisitely romantic scenes of love was inspired by her certain knowledge that the crew, if they had half a chance, would have fallen on her and taken her, one after another. And, she thought avidly, still relishing her morning in bed, she would have been ready for them. More than ready. But they were forbidden. They would boast. One slip, one false move, and everyone would know. Directors, producers, composers, designers or writers were acceptable partners for a star, but she could not risk gossip about working men, no matter how their raw, rough masculinity made her quiver inside.

She hadn't so much as hinted to Margie. Her friend had come over to visit at Christmas and Delphine had imagined, before she arrived, that she might confide something of her new life to her old pal. What a bad idea that would have been, she thought wryly. Margie Hall had been so visibly impressed with Delphine's stardom that she was no longer capable of treating Delphine with the free-and-easy camaraderie of outlaws that Delphine still took for granted.

What was worse, Margie, at twenty, Delphine's age, had remained a virgin, continuing to live by the good-girl code that they had been faithful to in college. It was Margie's senior year at UCLA, and she was engaged to a promising doctor from Pasadena, and, it seemed to Delphine, she had been profoundly altered by the solemn prospects of a gigantic June wedding. After one or two trips out to the studio, she'd confessed that she'd rather spend her time in Paris fitting custom-made lingerie for her trousseau, buying gloves and perfume and ordering handmade table linen for her future dining room table. *Her dining room table*, Delphine thought in disbelief. Yes, Margie Hall was about to settle down and become a Pasadena matron in a few months. One day, not too many years from now, she'd find a strand of gray in her yellow curls, and she wouldn't even consider doing anything about it. One didn't, in Pasadena.

How was it possible to grow apart so totally, Delphine wondered. Margie in love was an utter stranger. Love. Would she ever fall in love? She hoped not. It changed people, and she had no desire to change anything about her life. Margie had as little in common with her now as the people who lined up at the box office to see her films. There had been seven of them since *Mayerling*, and each one of them a success. Her only equals in the eyes of the French public were Michèle Morgan and Danielle Darrieux.

The existence of those two actresses was the reason that she hadn't been tempted by the Hollywood offers she'd received. Both of them were making films in France at a rate equal to her own. They were older than she, ravishing both, and as ambitious as she was. If she took the time away from her triumphant career to make a movie in California, one or the other of them would be sure to pick off a role that should have been Delphine's. She'd been deeply upset when Morgan got the part she coveted opposite Gabin in *Quai des Brumes*. The Marcel Carné film was about to open and everyone she knew had been talking about it for months, using that infuriating word *masterpiece*.

Delphine picked up a copy of *Le Figaro* that Annabelle had put on her breakfast tray, and opened it to the page on which Carné was interviewed, a page she had already read from top to bottom. She had not yet worked with either Carné or Gabin, and until she did, she wouldn't be content.

She turned away from the interview with a frown of irritation. To take her mind off it, she scanned the front page. Ninety-nine-point-seven percent of the voters of Austria had cast ballots in favor of Hitler's "reunification" of their country with Germany—that number seemed insane, she thought idly. Otto von Hapsburg, she noted, hadn't been allowed to vote because he had been arrested on suspicion of high treason for demanding that the great European powers react against Germany. Well, the Hapsburgs hadn't been at all nice to little Marie Vetsera, had they? In France, Leon Blum was out, and Daladier was in

—who could tell one from another? What difference could it make? Who gave a damn? French politics were even more confusing than world politics, but she supposed that she should try to be aware of them since people seemed to talk about it all so much. It didn't do to look utterly ignorant. Tunisia was in some sort of uproar . . . but wasn't it always? There was a new way to travel—William Boeing had brought out a huge plane called the 314. It was the only really interesting thing in the paper. Apparently the passengers could walk down an interior staircase and meet in a bar. . . . Delphine wondered what Freddy was doing now. She'd gone to see *Tail Spin* and she hadn't been able to see any sign of her sister, try as she might, but she knew, from her mother's letters, that Freddy was going from work on one picture to another, just as she was. Only Freddy was not a star. Delphine threw the boring newspaper on the floor. A *matinée grasse* must never include newspapers. She'd instruct Annabelle.

Tonight she was having dinner with Bruno, Delphine remembered, and her momentary petulance vanished. It was wonderful to have a brother you could trust. Bruno and she had a relationship unlike one she could have with any other man. He never pried, never asked questions about her private life, never judged or tried to act as if he were supposed to be watching over her, yet she could ask him for any kind of advice and count on him to give her an unbiased answer.

Bruno understood the subtle nuances of French life in a way she had to admit she never would. He knew which tempting invitations she must never, under any circumstances, permit herself to accept; what dressmakers she should patronize; where to order her note paper, and which was the only correct way to have it engraved; and why it was necessary for her career to attend the Prix de L'Arc de Triomphe and the Prix Diane, but not to be seen at Monte Carlo. He'd stocked her cellar, recommended the *bottier* who made the best shoes in Paris, insisted that she throw out all of her American clothes, and picked out the perfect car for her position. Delphine knew that it was a blessing for her that everyone, from her agent to her servants to her producers, knew that she was under the protection of her brother, the Vicomte de Saint-Fraycourt de Lancel. God, but the French were impressed by a title.

In return she made herself available as a hostess for Bruno whenever he asked. "*Cherie*," he'd call and say, "could you do me a great favor and preside over my table next week? There is an elderly gentleman coming to dinner whom I shall put at your right—he has an enormous amount of money which he hasn't decided how to place." And she'd dress in her most alluring new evening gown and charm even herself by playing, in stunning balance, a dual role at one of Bruno's perfect little dinner parties; Delphine de Lancel, film star, and Mademoiselle de Lancel, daughter of the old aristocracy of Champagne, who depended totally on her brother's advice in everything. Only a glance now and then at Bruno would reveal his admiration for how well she carried out her role. He made a splendid partner. They were two of a kind, Delphine thought, and perhaps the best thing about Bruno was how emphatically he agreed with her about love. That utterly useless, *inconvenient* emotion, he called it, invented by someone with too much imagination and nothing better to do. Some petit-bourgeois unemployed troubadour.

Within a week of his dinner party, often sooner, she'd receive a magnificently jeweled trinket from Cartier with a note from Bruno, telling her that the gentleman had now decided—most intelligently— just where to place his funds. It was such great fun to have Bruno with whom to play these little games, Delphine mused, and the fact that they were family made their interests mutual.

After all, one day she and Bruno and Freddy would own the House of Lancel. Fortunately, he would know what to do with the vineyards, because certainly neither she nor her sister would want to shoulder that responsibility. Although . . . on second thought . . . it might be amusing to own a château. Michèle Morgan did not have a château. Nor did Danielle Darrieux. And even if either of them were to buy a château, it wouldn't be the same as inheriting one. Still, Valmont was too totally tedious to consider, Delphine decided, getting out of bed and stretching. She loved her little house, and when she left it, it was only for a suite in a great hotel at some resort, for a brief vacation between pictures.

As she rang for her maid she realized that her lazy morning was over. This afternoon she had the first meeting with the director on her new film, *Jour et Nuit.* His name was Armand Sadowski, and everyone in the world of the cinema was buzzing about him and his first three films. Brilliant they said, difficult they said, a genius they said, impossible they said. But what did he look like, Delphine wondered, as she waited for Annabelle. Would she want him in bed? How good would he be? Questions she could hardly ask her agent.

Normally, Delphine would first meet with a new director in a restaurant chosen by her agent, Jean Abel. Abel liked to control his business as much as possible, and the man who picked the dining place, ordered the wine and paid for the lunch became, if he did it well, in charge of the occasion. The negotiations for Delphine's participation in *Jour et Nuit* had long been over. There had, of course, been no need for an audition. The contracts were signed, but nevertheless there were bound to be conflicts in the course of the making of any film, and Abel wanted to start out on a strong footing with Sadowski. However, the director was busy supervising the editing on his latest picture, and he had refused to leave the set long enough for lunch.

Instead, he had given Delphine a rendezvous toward the end of the afternoon, all the way out at his own office at Billancourt, to which Abel had finally, and most reluctantly, had to agree, since Sadowski was finishing his current picture and starting Delphine's new film with only a weekend's break. Abel planned to pick Delphine up and escort her to this much-too-businesslike meeting, unwarmed by the consumption of food and wine, but she had told him that it wasn't convenient. She preferred to be driven out to the studio in her own car, since she needed it afterwards to go on to a long-planned fitting at her lingerie maker. He could meet her at Billancourt.

Delphine dressed carefully to meet Sadowski. The part in *Jour et Nuit* called for her to play a scatterbrained rich girl, suspected of murder, who falls in love with a police inspector. She knew already that the costumes, designed by Pierre Goulard, had been inspired by Schiaparelli's surrealistic, witty, often downright crazy clothes. Inspired? "Copied" was a more honest word, she decided. The clothes, strident and showily aggressive, would be right for the character, but wrong for the way she wanted any unknown director to first think of her.

Delphine had mastered the art of underdressing. The more famous she became, the more powerful she found underdressing to be as a weapon in any relationship. Everyone expected a film star to look like a film star. But that was too easy to do, too orthodox. *Obvious.* It was forgivable to be orthodox, perhaps, but never to be obvious. A film star decked out in the newest dress from dear Jean Patou, wearing Paulette's most extravagant hat, dripping silver fox from one arm—no, never. That was fine for public appearances, but not for the beginning of an uncertain skirmish in which all of her armament might have to be employed. Why alert the director's defenses so soon? She might, after all, detest the man. It had happened.

She picked out an absolutely plain, thin wool sweater in a shade of gray so misty, so insubstantial that it underlined the matte whiteness of her skin, even more than black would have done. She added a perfectly simple, supremely well-cut skirt in gray tweed, one shade

275

darker than the sweater; pale gray silk stockings; low-heeled, unadorned black kid pumps; and a classic, belted raincoat from England. Small jet earrings and a little black velvet beret, such as students wore, completed the ensemble. She could be anonymous, she could be nobody, she could be anybody, if one didn't look at her face, if she didn't happen to be one of the most beautiful women in the world, Delphine thought dispassionately. She was not vain. In her career, her looks had to be weighed and considered as coldly and seriously as the quarterly report of a large company. A diamond cutter in Amsterdam didn't judge a stone any more severely than Delphine did the angle of her nose, the perfect curves of her upper lip, the shadows below her cheekbones. Satisfied, she tightened the belt of the raincoat and pulled the beret down so that it covered the widow's peak that made her instantly recognizable.

At the studio she made her way toward the editing department. Abel should have been waiting for her in the parking lot, but perhaps he had been delayed; the traffic was snarled by the rain. She passed a number of people she knew casually, but none of them noticed her unless she deliberately caught their eye, smiled and nodded. This raincoat really managed to transform her into one of the masses, she thought, pleased.

Christ, but it felt good to be back at the studio. She hadn't worked in two weeks, since the last day of her last picture. She had needed the time to take care of the many details of her elaborate personal wardrobe, for which she never had a minute during a film. It had been like going on a two-week-long retreat into an overperfumed, overheated, worldly sort of convent, she thought, a world of giddy, chattering, excited women with only one thing on their minds. Now she was back in the world of men, thank the Lord.

Delphine lingered at the open door of a set that had just been struck. She could smell the distinctive metallic odor of the lights as they cooled down, and she watched the electricians, the grips and the prop men as they dismantled the massive set, observing, with a quickening of her breath, the brute strength with which they hoisted and pushed and pulled and lifted, and went about their work without noticing her, their loud, careless voices calling to each other, in a hurry to get the job over with, and go home. She backed away from the open door into the corridor behind her, to avoid being brushed by a large flat that was being carried off the set. Suddenly she was struck a heavy blow across her left shoulder from the hand of a passerby, who was gesticulating broadly, in conversation with a group of three other men.

"Hey! That hurt!" she exclaimed, shocked, and the man who had accidentally hit her, still moving fast and already several paces away, glanced back and shook a finger severely at her.

"Sorry, but that's a damn stupid place to stand and gape," he called, turning away as he spoke, to continue his animated conversation.

"Well, screw you too," Delphine said out loud in English. She looked around angrily for someone to whom she could complain about such rudeness, but the corridor was now empty. Abel's lateness was unforgivable, she thought, no longer pleased that she had managed to become invisible. She marched on down the hall, finally found the editing department, pushed open the door without ceremony, and spoke brusquely to a receptionist.

"Monsieur Sadowski, please."

"He can't be interrupted. What is it about?"

"I'm expected," Delphine said, annoyed.

"Your name, please?"

"Mademoiselle de Lancel," Delphine said coldly. The receptionist blinked.

"Excuse me, Mademoiselle, I didn't recognize you. I'll let him know at once. Will you have a seat?"

"No, thank you." Delphine stood, tapping her foot in impatience. She was not about to sit down as if she'd nothing better to do than to wait around at Sadowski's beck and call in a reception room. She should have been escorted into his office immediately. Abel would have seen to that, damn him.

"Mademoiselle de Lancel is here, Monsieur Sadowski," the receptionist said into her desk telephone. "Yes, I understand." She turned to Delphine. "He'll receive you as soon as he has finished his meeting, Mademoiselle."

Delphine stared at her, outraged. She looked at her wristwatch. She was late as it was. If she had been on time she would already have been kept waiting ten minutes. She looked a fool, she thought, standing like a supplicant. She sat down in an uncomfortable chair and glared at the door to the corridor, expecting to see Abel rush in, full of apologies, at any second. Five more long minutes passed in silence, while the receptionist read a magazine. Delphine rose to her feet. She didn't intend to wait another second. This had gone beyond the limit of possibility. Several men burst out of an office door, arguing, and walked past her out to the hall without a glance.

"He'll see you now, Mademoiselle," the receptionist said.

"You don't say," Delphine snapped. The receptionist looked confused, motioned her into a small office and disappeared, closing the door behind her. Inside, a man sat alone with his back to Delphine, holding up a long strip of film to the window and inspecting it closely. He swore out loud in a string of inventive obscenities while Delphine stopped in front of his desk. He was the man who had hit her in the hall. She could barely wait till he turned. He'd be mortified when he realized with what a lack of breeding he'd treated his star. She had the upper hand already—nothing could change what had happened.

Still looking at the film, he flung words carelessly over his shoulder, "Delphine, babe, sit down. I'll be with you in a minute. Lucky I didn't hurt you back there—you should be more careful. I only hit women on purpose. . . ." His voice trailed off as he looked at the film intently. "Damn! God damn that cameraman. The cretin, a Neanderthal. I'll tear his bloody guts out for him the next time I lay eyes on the bastard. No, no, it's really not possible, what he did, just not possible, and, of course, entirely too late to do anything but recut the whole scene. We'll be here all weekend. Shit!"

He put down the film, swung his chair around and, abruptly, smiled. The director half rose, leaned forward and extended his hand over the desk. Sadowski gave her a quick shake. "A filthy métier, isn't it, babe?"

He was very tall, Delphine saw, with an astonishing head. Masses of black hair, straight, ridiculously long, rumpled in every direction. He was young, not much more than twenty-five, and his face was like her idea of a hawk, all eyes and nose and alive with energy. There seemed to be more energy bursting from behind his desk than if he were fighting a duel. He wore huge horn-rimmed glasses, which he took off and placed on his desk, rubbing the place on his nose where they pinched him.

"Abel not here yet? Good, I didn't want him here anyway, but he insisted." He talked rapidly, intensely. Delphine was speechless. The director was using the familiar *tu* form of address with her, and calling her by her first name. That could happen between a director and a senior crew member when they knew each other well, but never otherwise. Absolutely never between a director and a star, unless they were old personal friends. Just who the hell did he think he was?

Sadowski sat back and studied her in silence through his glasses, making a tent of his hands, so that his own face was partly hidden, staring at her as if he were alone in a room in front of a painting he had bought in an absentminded moment and wasn't at all sure he liked. "Take off your beret and your raincoat," he said finally.

"I think not," Delphine replied stiffly.

"Are you cold?"

"Certainly not."

"Then take off your hat and coat," he said impatiently. "Let's see what you look like."

"Haven't you seen my films?" She emphasized the formal *vous*, but he took no notice.

"Sure. I wouldn't have hired you otherwise. I want to see what you look like *to me*, not to other directors. Come on, babe, hurry up. I haven't got all day."

Still sitting down, Delphine removed her hat and shrugged out of her coat, allowing it to drop to her waist, watching to spy his eyes widening in admiration. Sadowski's unconvinced, suspicious, grudging expression didn't change. He sighed. She waited, as impassive as he.

"Stand up and turn around," he demanded abruptly. His eyes, unshielded, were black, the irises huge, the pupils small, as if he were a hypnotist.

"How dare you? I'm not a showgirl!"

"You waiting for me to get down on my knees and beg?" He glanced at her face. "Something similar would be acceptable, wouldn't it? Ah —actresses! What else is new? Forget it, babe, you've come to the wrong place. I make films here, not pretty speeches. No brassiere?"

"I never wear one," Delphine lied.

"I'll decide that." He gestured for her to stand. Delphine inclined her head mockingly and decided to rise, knowing that her beauty was the ultimate reproach for his crude, offensive manner. She turned around by inches, offering him the time to become humble. She permitted herself no expression of triumph, not even the minuscule lift of an eyebrow, when she faced him again. He had taken down the tent of fingers and rested his chin on one hand, nodding negatively. "I don't know. I just don't know . . . maybe yes, maybe no . . . it's worth a try, I suppose."

"What are you talking about?"

"This whole little masquerade of yours, the schoolgirl shit, your skirt-and-sweater Shirley Temple number. It could just work. It's not as dumb as it looks, you may have something there. . . . We'll do a Chloe costume and makeup test and find out."

"I beg your pardon?"

He snapped his fingers. "Wake up, Delphine! Chloe, the character you're going to play, the rich bitch? Isn't that why we're here? Obviously you realized Chloe could decide to dress down to put the police inspector off the scent after the murder. It's an idea. Cute. Childish, I admit, and, of course, completely obvious to anyone with any brains, but yes, decidedly cute. It makes you look almost innocent. I like an actress who tries to make a creative contribution. Not too often, of course. Don't get carried away, honey."

"I'll . . ."

"Fine. O.K., we're done. You can go." He swung his chair around and resumed inspecting the strip of film, his back toward her again.

"You need a haircut," Delphine sputtered.

"I know. I've heard. It'll have to wait until I've made this fucking, rotten scene work. Bring some scissors and do it yourself if it bothers you. Be my guest."

"Asshole!" Delphine said in English.

Sadowski swung around and eyed her with a spark of genuine pleasure. "Right! Nice! I'd forgotten you were American. I have cousins in Pittsburgh—you from anywhere near there? 'Asshole'—there's just no perfect word for it in French, is there?" He waved, indicating the door. "See you Monday. Bright and early. And when I say early, babe, I mean early. Don't oversleep. Fair warning. And the last one you'll get."

"And if I should, by chance, oversleep?" Delphine asked, panting in fury.

"Don't worry about it, you won't. See, you don't want to give me problems, babe, because you know it won't work. Right? Now *go away*. Can't you tell I'm busy?"

14

FREDDY checked to make sure that her helmet was firmly fastened. The dark curls of the Brenda Marshall wig blew about her face, tickled her nose and got into her eyes, as she sat at the controls in the modified open cockpit of the little old Gee Bee. She knew better, after almost two years as a stunt pilot, than to try to convince the wardrobe department that no woman pilot would fly with her hair spilling fetchingly out of her helmet onto her shoulders. Anyway, in Freddy's opinion, the female jewel thief with a heart of gold and nerves of steel, who always escaped the scene of the crime by air, that she was supposed to be in *Lady in Jeopardy,* was capable of almost anything, including flying a plane in an evening gown, as she had done only last week.

She checked her altitude. She was exactly at four thousand feet, as she had planned. Freddy took her hands off the controls. She had trimmed the plane carefully; there was no turbulence aloft on this early August day of 1938, and the ship flew straight and level by itself, and could continue on in this way for a long time. There was a mirror sewn into the inside flap on the sleeve of her jacket, which Freddy now used to inspect her lipstick. It was as bright as when makeup had finished with her, an hour ago. Ready to start, she looked around for the four camera ships, one close to her left, and three below, each at a different altitude, flying in a tight formation that would guarantee complete coverage of her bail-out. She waggled her wings, in her signal that she was ready to start, and watched each of the four planes. This was not the sort of stunt for which you could afford a retake.

The big, sturdy camera ships all responded with the signal that meant the cameras were turning. O.K., Brenda, time to get a move on, Freddy told herself, and assumed an expression of alarm that changed quickly into one of decision. She grabbed the velvet prop bag full of jewels, jammed it into her jacket, quickly pulled up the zipper and hauled herself, parachute and all, to the side of the plane.

"So long, boys and girls, here goes nothing," Freddy shouted, dialogue she thought was as implausible as the plot. She could see the camera in the plane directly alongside, catching her mouth shaping the words that would later be revoiced by Brenda Marshall. She pressed a bright red button positioned on the side of the cockpit that would activate the dynamite in fifteen seconds, after she was well past it, so far away that none of the debris of the explosion could stray in her direction. The instant she pressed the button, she dove out of the plane, expertly clearing the side of the ship, careful not to let the wind catch her, and fell free. At the count of ten she would open her chute.

"One . . . two . . . three . . ." she counted, beginning to reach for the ripcord. Above her, twelve seconds too soon and far, far too close, the plane blew up. The shock wave of the premature explosion knocked her unconscious. Burning gasoline, in arching sprays of fire, and shattered, jagged fragments of the plane were thrown in all directions around her falling body. The heavy motor missed her by a yard, a burning wing by inches.

She fell, inert, a piece of motionless flesh in a flying suit, headed for the ground below. When Freddy came to, she had no idea how long she had been falling. Her instantaneous reaction was to pull the ring on the ripcord. Within seconds her descent slowed, as the great parasol of white silk opened above her. She wasn't on fire, she realized with a disoriented burst of relief. The gasoline had missed her. Swaying from side to side, she scanned three hundred sixty degrees of sky to see if any of the pieces of the plane were too close. The air around her was a mess of plunging fragments, but they were at an acceptable distance. The three camera ships still seemed to be holding their steady courses.

They got more than they had paid for this time, Freddy thought, as she looked upward to inspect the canopy of the blessed parachute that had opened so promptly. Leaping circles of flames, caused by drops of burning gasoline, rimmed large, gaping tears in many places all over the saving umbrella and were spreading rapidly, eating away at the silk that meant her life. She glanced down at the ground. She estimated that she had more than two thousand feet still to fall before she landed. In that time the parachute would burn to ash, the flames fanned by the air through which she was plunging. Even if it didn't burn up entirely, there wouldn't be enough of it left to slow her fall.

Opening a chute was easy—closing it in midair was fucking impossible, she thought savagely, as she pulled on all the shroud lines she could reach with both of her arms, grappling them toward her, fighting for her life with every ounce of her strength. Gradually the parachute, and the air that filled it, yielded, as she hauled the lines in together at the bottom, preventing any more air from entering the parachute. Faster and faster she fell. Now only the bulging top of the silk umbrella, where air was still trapped, slowed her descent toward earth. She refused to look up to see if the chute was still burning. All her senses were concentrated on picking the right moment to release the shroud lines that would allow the parachute to open in time to break her fall, and before it burned away.

"*Now!*" she shouted above the circled area where she could see the cameramen grinding on the ground. She could see Mac running toward the place where she would land. She opened her arms, letting all the straining shrouds escape her grip. With a jerk, the silk billowed out again, but still too fast, a deadly trifle too fast, the ground approached. She landed badly, her body meeting the field heavily. Her left arm and her right ankle broke at the same moment, and then, still fighting with her good arm to spill the air out of the chute, to keep from being dragged along the ground, Freddy passed out. When she recovered consciousness, Mac had fallen on top of her to bring her body to a stop, and the cameras were still grinding away. The last thing she heard was the director screaming, "Keep going, keep going, we'll write him into the script."

"Promise me you won't get soap in my eyes?" Freddy asked Mac anxiously, as she knelt on the floor of the bathroom, naked to the waist. Her ankle and arm were still in the plaster casts which she had been warned not to get wet, when she left the hospital a few days before. Mac had figured out that the only way he could wash her hair was if she hung her head into the bathtub, supporting herself on her knees, with her shoulders leaning on the edge of the tub.

"Why would I get soap in your eyes?"

"By accident . . . it's a mystery . . . no matter how hard people try to give someone a painless shampoo, they always end up getting soap in their eyes. There's nothing I hate more," she answered.

"You like to jump out of airplanes and you hate to have a shampoo?"

"You're beginning to understand me."

"Get your head down in there, close your eyes tight, and don't worry."

"Wait!" she said, alarmed. "It's not the soaping, it's the rinsing that's the dangerous part. How are you going to do it?"

"With this cooking pot. It's simple. I'll fill it with water from the cold and hot taps and pour it over your head. Jesus!"

"Go get a pitcher with a spout," she ordered. "A pot . . . only a man would try to use a pot."

"How about a watering can? That would give me perfect control, a drop here, a drop there . . ."

"Great. No, on second thought, it would take too long. Just a pitcher."

"Don't go anywhere, Freddy. I'll be right back." He ran downstairs to the kitchen, and found a pitcher. He was, he knew, trying unsuccessfully to keep from fussing over her like a mother, but he was just so damn glad to have her back in one piece, that he'd wash her hair for her a strand at a time with a wet toothbrush, if that was what she wanted. The heavy, lopsided casts emphasized the airy, exquisite delineation of her feet and wrists, but Freddy was so strong that he kept catching her trying to hop around in spite of his fear that she'd fall and break something else. She was so brave, so fine, so undefeatable, this precious girl of his—too much by half, he thought as he raced upstairs, three steps at a time.

After the hair wash, Mac picked Freddy up, over her protests, carried her back to their bed and started to dry her hair with a towel. It was, fortunately, cut shorter than it had been before she started stunt work, because she had to tuck it under wigs so often that she'd hacked away at it from time to time for the sake of convenience, but he still had difficulty dealing with the rebellious mass of tangled strands. Once her hair was half dry, he started to comb it out, dealing gently with each damp, snarled curl. She looked up at him with engrossed, dreamy eyes, half-child, half-woman, like a Da Vinci angel, he thought, standing by in an Annunciation scene.

"Where'd you learn your technique?" she asked.

"I had a big, smelly, shaggy dog when I was a kid."

"You never told me," she said accusingly.

"He ran away."

"That's the saddest story I ever heard," Freddy blurted, and burst into tears.

Stunned, for he had only been joking, Mac tried to get her to stop, but the more he cuddled her and told her it really hadn't happened, the harder she cried. Finally she subsided into little hiccuping sobs mixed with a wail of "Poor, poor little dog," until finally she lay silent, sniffling in his arms.

"What was that all about?" he asked when she had calmed down.

"I don't know," she said in muffled tones, into his chest.

"I think you're having a delayed reaction to the accident."

She sat up and gave him a fragment of her old smile, shaking her head in negation.

"No. It can't be that. I've figured out the accident completely," she assured him, as she had so often during the week in the hospital. "The riggers who packed the dynamite had to have miscalculated the lengths of the fuses, not that they'll ever admit it. That's the only thing it could have been. Everything else went perfectly."

"Understanding it is one thing, Freddy, but coming to grips with it emotionally, being able to accept that it actually happened to you, is another. You've had a big shock, even if you still refuse to realize it."

"I didn't say that it wasn't a shock. And I ruined my best chute. But I've had other accidents, I've broken bones before." Her bravado was intact.

"Not accidents like this," Mac said somberly. "Freddy, when are you going to give up stunt flying?"

"When are you going to marry me?"

A silence fell between them. Since Freddy's eighteenth birthday, over half a year before, she had mentioned marriage a number of times, but indirectly, lightly, glancingly, in a way that still had permitted McGuire to cock a sardonic eyebrow at her, to treat her words as if they couldn't possibly be considered anything but one of her impudent jokes, and to continue with whatever he had been saying. Now she had asked the question in a tone of raw, unblushing, absolute appeal that demanded to be answered. He'd been dreading this moment. It had been inevitable, looming larger month by month. He hesitated and finally, shaking his head, he said, "Freddy, look—"

"I don't like the sound of answers that begin that way. When, Mac?"

"Freddy, darling, I—"

"Look at me. When, Mac, when?"

"I can't," he said, in agony, "*I can't.*"

"You're not married. What do you mean, 'can't'? You *can*, nothing would be simpler, we could fly to Vegas today and be married before sunset. You mean you won't, don't you?"

"I mean I won't. It wouldn't be fair, Freddy. It would be unforgivable. You're only *eighteen*—I'm forty-two—we're generations apart—I'm too old for you!"

"And you know perfectly well how little difference that makes to me," she responded fiercely. "I've never loved anyone but you. I will never marry anyone but you. I swear I never will. *No matter how old you get, you'll never be free of me,* you know that, Mac. I'll be hanging around when you're a hundred and I'm pushing eighty. The older we get, the less difference there'll be."

"Freddy, that's the most ridiculous argument in the book, and it's nonsense. It skips over all the years in between eighteen and eighty. You're still a kid—I know, I know, but it's true—with all your life as a young woman still ahead of you, and I'm a middle-aged man who's lived most of the best years he's ever going to have in him. *That's real.*"

"You're not fair!" she said, passionately aware of injustice.

"God damn it, don't you think I know that! I wasn't fair when I made love to you the first time, because if I'd stopped it then, this would never have happened. I blame myself every damned day for being so weak, but I couldn't help it, I'd been in love with you for too long, I couldn't resist you, and I still can't resist you about anything . . . except this. I won't marry you, Freddy. It wouldn't be right."

"No wonder your dog ran away," Freddy said lightly. "I don't really want to get married anyway. I just thought I should make an honest man out of you, but you're such a moralistic old fart that I've changed my mind."

"I knew you'd see the light," Mac said, lying as fluently as she. So she still thought that he couldn't see through her, after all these years, did she? Freddy, the girl who'd never, ever, in her whole life, given up on anything she wanted, Freddy who thought he'd believe that she could run hot and run cold about marriage? "Ready for your sponge bath?"

"Nope. I'm still clean from yesterday's sponge bath. You can inspect me if you don't believe me. Go ahead, I'm not ticklish."

"Delphine asked me the strangest thing this morning," Anette de Lancel reported to her husband, and fell silent.

Vicomte Jean-Luc de Lancel sighed with the pleasurable resignation that only many decades of marriage bring. He knew that whatever odd remark Delphine had made, he was destined to hear about it in every detail, embroidered by speculation and comments on human behavior, as nonessential to whatever had actually been said as the illumination of a single letter on a long medieval manuscript, but not until he had shown himself worthy of the basic information by prying it out of his wife. He set himself to the familiar task, fortified by the well-iced champagne they were drinking as a cooling nightcap on an exceptionally warm night in August of 1938. Eventually, in less time than it usually took, he was successful.

"She wanted to know if, only hypothetically, of course, I'd ever heard of any sure way to fall *out* of love," Anette de Lancel revealed, in tones of fascination mixed with worry.

"What did you tell her?" he asked, interested in spite of himself.

"Jean-Luc, you're missing the point entirely. Obviously, if she wants to fall out of love, she must be in love with someone unsuitable. And

286

she must be at her wits' end to actually consult me. Someone as independent as Delphine wouldn't ask a mere grandmother's advice in any other circumstances."

"I shouldn't have thought her capable of falling in love," Jean-Luc said, mildly surprised.

"Jean-Luc!" Anette was truly shocked.

"I've never met a girl less likely to be carried away by an emotion, still less an unrequited one. Still, she has put on an impressive exhibition of moping since she invited herself to visit us. I thought it must be something about that theatrical career of hers."

"Not theatrical, darling—the cinema."

"It's the same thing, a lot of nonsense. I'm still waiting to hear what advice you gave her."

"I said to imagine that if someone, a hypothetical someone, was in love and didn't want to be, she should imagine, as graphically as possible, that the man in question had all sorts of utterly disgusting personal habits that she would only find out about when it was too late—and she just said it was a good idea, without, I could tell, intending to even try it—and I think it's not bad advice at all, as a matter of fact, don't you? She thanked me in that very sweet, sad way of hers, and took poor Guillaume's car out for a long drive all alone."

"Hmm." Jean-Luc took Anette's hand. Their oldest son, crusty to the last, had died of cancer only three months before, unmourned by the wife and children he had never had, but sorely missed by his parents and by all the workers in the vineyards, who had respected him even if they hadn't been particularly fond of him.

"Well, don't worry, my dear," he said. "With girls that age, love isn't a serious business. Delphine'll grow out of it, whatever it is."

"She's twenty, not fourteen, Jean-Luc. That's quite old enough for . . . oh, anything . . . and everything. I can't help worrying."

"Just don't let yourself get involved, Anette, I beg of you. The last time you got involved in Delphine's problems we gave a dinner party, and look what that led to," he warned, and prepared to climb into the high old bed they had shared for almost sixty years.

Delphine sat by the window of her room and looked out at the generous, pregnant moon of August, and cursed herself bitterly. Something like this simply could not happen to her! It went contrary to all her firm ideas of how to live her life with a maximum of pleasure; it went contrary to her years of training in how to achieve and maintain power over men; it went contrary to all the sophistication she had grown into, beginning at college and then expanding confidently, until she became genuinely worldly in Paris, under Bruno's guidance; it went contrary to everything she had learned about her body and how to satisfy it with a half-dozen lovers. It went against her will, a will she had felt so sure she could use to advance her interests. Worst of all, it went contrary to her deepest instincts of self-protection.

You don't fall in love with a man like Armand Sadowski! She pounded her fists on the window seat until the edges of her hands were bruised. You don't even *like* a man like Armand Sadowski. Oh, but she did! Oh, but she had!

When had this unthinkable thing happened? Had it been after the first weeks of the picture, when she realized that he was getting the best performance of her life out of her, and that her acting hadn't been a result of the welling up of unreined sexuality on which she had counted since that first test for *Mayerling* with Nico Ambert? Was it perhaps merely that—the knowledge that she truly could act, that she wasn't, as she had sometimes feared, without daring to admit it to herself, just a narcissistic girl who became so aroused by the crew and the lights and the camera, that somehow meaning poured into her performance from her own excitement?

From the first day they worked together, Delphine had forgotten the existence of the crew. They were there simply to carry out orders that others gave them. The lights were only turned on for purposes of illumination, the cameras turned merely as means of making a record on film. She hadn't been touched by a man since she'd started that film.

Yes, perhaps her feelings were purely professional, perfectly normal admiration for a man who could give her direction as no one else ever had. A form of the classic admiration of a Galatea for a Pygmalion? It wasn't unheard of for such admiration to feel like love. Transference, she'd heard it called by other actresses, and actors as well. Everyone knew that you had to be a little in love with your director. Directors were all highly seductive personalities in one way or another, or they didn't get jobs. It was part of the great game of making a film. A little in love, she thought, just a little in love. That would be acceptable. But if she were only a little in love, it should have stopped when the making of the film was over, months ago, in June. She would have taken a lover by now—if she were only a little in love—and cured herself.

Perhaps her feelings had sprung up when she realized that Armand Sadowski, of all the men she'd ever met, was the least impressed with

288

her. *Least* was not an accurate word, Delphine thought, correcting herself mentally. He wasn't just less impressed, he wasn't impressed in the slightest. Wasn't it human nature for someone who was as accustomed as she was to inspiring love, to become masochistically attracted to a man who was, as Margie Hall used to say, hard to get? Impossible to get? It must be that. If he had shown any of the signs of falling for her that she knew so well, her so-called love would have had a chance to disappear. Well, wouldn't it? She hadn't had the chance to find out. For a minute Delphine allowed herself to imagine Armand Sadowski displaying a romantic interest in her, and her head swam so dizzily that the moon swayed in the sky, like a kite on the end of a string on a windy day.

No, it had all started at some unmarked moment during the making of the film, as a direct result of his manipulative personality, she decided, looking hastily away from the moon. What else could you call him but manipulative? He knew just what psychological strings to pull, just the right words and attitudes to use to get people to do his bidding. She'd watched him with the other members of the cast. He'd bullied and jollied and persuaded and conned them one and all, using his brash energy to get what he wanted.

Then why weren't the other actresses on the film in love with him too? She'd spent hours in purposeful but roundabout gossip with them, showing a friendliness that came as a surprise to them. Everyone had discussed Sadowski freely. He interested them all, but as a director, no more, no less. They were pretty sure he wasn't married, they thought he didn't have any one particular girlfriend, they knew his family had come to France from Poland ages ago, and they assumed that he was Jewish, but who knew for sure with the Poles? He hadn't provided them with anything else to gossip about, hadn't shown any personal attention to any of them, so their interest went only so far, and then turned, to Delphine's well-hidden irritation, back to their own lives. Maybe Jewish, maybe unattached, of Polish origin for sure. Not much to chew on there.

Try to be honest for once in your life, she told herself severely. It started when he took his glasses off and looked at you. That's all he had to do to make you fall in love. Turn around in his chair and look at you. *Pushover.* A pathetic pushover, that's all you are. Now what are you going to do?

The casts on Freddy's arm and ankle were removed by the end of August, and it was evident that it wouldn't be long before she recovered her full strength. She hired a trainer to work with her every day, one of the tumbling team from whom she'd learned many tricks of equilibrium for various jobs. Now that she could get about without fear of falling, Mac was able to leave her alone at home, and return to his busy routine of giving lessons and managing his dual business, renting vintage planes and directing the flying stunts for Universal's Saturday matinee serial, *Ace Drummond*, which had originally been inspired by the adventures of Eddie Rickenbacker.

By the last day of September 1938, Freddy was able to fly her own plane again. She had made the down payment on the wildly extravagant Rider racer with the first big money she'd ever earned, unable to resist the beautifully designed new ship, one of the first completely streamlined planes, powered by a Pratt and Whitney 450-horsepower Twin Wasp Junior motor. It was painted entirely white, its low wings were cantilevered, and the landing gear was retractable. From its cockpit Freddy had more visibility than in any other plane she'd ever flown, and in it she won her first trophies at the International Aerobatic Competition at St. Louis in May of 1937. She competed valiantly in the Istres-Damascus-Paris Air Race in August of 1937, coming in third because of a delay caused by an unexpected storm over the Alps. In November of 1937 she flew the race from Vancouver to Agua Caliente, Mexico, in five hours and eight minutes, and came in fourteen minutes after Frank W. Fuller, Jr. That time was nothing to be ashamed of, but it had been fifteen minutes too many for victory. Still, she'd won the second-place trophy and she had won other, first-place trophies in a number of local races in early 1938. From early spring on, she had so much stunt work that she had not had time to enter any competitions.

Now, as she cruised up along the coast toward Santa Cruz, she tried to decide if she wanted to take time off from the film work that had been offered to her, and start trying for new racing records. She had missed the National Air Races because of her accident, and today she didn't care. So what if Cochrane had won the Bendix? Flying was enough, just in itself. She didn't need to prove anything, she thought, as she scanned scattered fields of daisies formed by the clouds on their wind-borne maneuvers, she didn't feel like scrambling for that extra winning minute, she didn't care if her navigation was sloppy, if she was lazily letting the Pacific, this morning sporting an overglaze of lavender, tell her where she was, without reference to any chart.

This joy was what all pilots meant when they left the hangar for their planes, saying only, "I'm goin' flyin'," those always casual words from which excitement was never missing. Freddy was astonished by the necessity of the contentment she had been granted. She had missed, more than she had let herself realize, the plain and simple physical contact with her plane: the solid sound of the engine, that was not a roar or a growl or a thrumming or a throbbing, but a sound to which nothing else can be compared, the sound of an airplane engine. She had missed her good-smelling leather seat and the feeling of the shoulder harness across her body and her throttle and her stick and her rudders. She had missed her *machine*.

She hadn't fully recognized until today the full duality of flying. She could fill pages with lyrical descriptions of the sky, more pages with infinitely detailed discoveries of how the earth appeared from above, but without her own personal contact with her machine, it wouldn't be more than what any passenger could see. *If she weren't at the controls, she wouldn't be free.* It was as simple as that. It was the only pure freedom she had ever known, and she must never be away from it for long.

For a time she flew mindlessly, automatically tending the controls, letting her reflexes take over, as she sank deep into the nameless, primitive emotion that bound her to her ship.

Eventually, Freddy realized that she was hungry, and she looked at her chart to find the nearest airport for lunch. She'd be at Santa Cruz in less than half an hour. The white Rider could make two hundred and fifty miles an hour whenever she chose, and the airport cafe at Santa Cruz was good. She wished she'd thought to bring a sandwich, as she turned the ship to head directly for the little coastal city. Even that tiny piece of navigation on a day like today was almost too much, but it was better than starving.

How happy she was, Freddy thought, as she prepared to lose altitude. It wasn't only because she had gone flyin', she realized. It was Mac. When had it not been Mac? But last night, after dinner, he had jumped in the car to bring home some ice cream because she had a sudden fancy for it, and when he'd returned, with more than they could possibly eat, she'd said, oh, very lightly, very jokingly, not hinting at all, that he'd make a wonderful father. He hadn't even frowned. He hadn't gone all hot and bothered or protested that he was too old or that it wouldn't be right, or brought up any of his other ridiculous scruples. He just said, "I don't need another baby when I've got you," but something had jumped in his eyes and she'd known that she'd touched a nerve. He was probably dying to have children but wouldn't let himself know it. She'd finally been convinced, right at that moment, that she'd manage to get him to marry her someday, if she had to get pregnant to do it. Someday soon.

On the last day of September 1938, Paul de Lancel read the evening papers with painful attention. All month long he had concentrated on nothing else but the crisis in Europe, a crisis most Californians regarded as just another one of the many ups and downs of faraway countries, whose endlessly quarrelsome business they were determined to ignore as much as possible.

Three times in this month of September there had been war scares. In early September, Hitler had finally demanded the absolute annexation of Czechoslovakia's Sudetenland to Germany, abandoning the former position that he only wanted to protect the rights of the German minority who lived in that region, so rich in mines, industry and fortifications.

Three times the British Prime Minister, Neville Chamberlain, had flown to Germany to appease the threatening dictator. The Czechs wanted to fight for their country, but they were the only ones in Europe who had the stomach for battle, except Stalin, who was ignored. Czechoslovakia's allies, Britain and France, had no fight left in them a bare twenty years after millions of their men had died for nothing in the Great War. On the thirtieth of September, Hitler and Chamberlain signed the Munich Agreement with the concordance of Daladier, the Premier of France. This time there would be no war. Common sense had prevailed.

"Thank God for that," Paul said to Eve.

"You really believe that there's nothing more to worry about?"

"Of course I don't. There's always more to worry about . . . but at least this piece of paper shows basic goodwill. Just listen, darling," he said, reading out loud from the paper. " 'We regard the agreement signed last night and the Anglo-German Naval Agreement as symbolic of the desire of our two peoples never to go to war with one another again.' I have to say, even as a cynical diplomat, that it sounds like a step in the right direction."

"What about the Czechs?"

"France and Britain are pledged to protect their integrity. The Czechs have always been a problem, but not one to start another war over. Well, now we can make our own plans again. What do you say, darling, shall we try to get passage to France at the end of October, or book it for early spring?"

"How much leave can you take?"

"I've had some time already this year. If we wait till spring we can take several months, but if we go next month it might be a little late in the year for Champagne at its best."

"I wish we'd been able to get away when Guillaume died," Eve said thoughtfully.

"So do I. But Father's letters make his feelings very plain. He won't hear a single word about my giving up the foreign service to help him with managing the business. He seems to feel that I'd be more trouble than I'd be worth," Paul said ruefully. "It's true I don't know much about making great champagne, or selling it, but it's never too late to learn. He says that his foremen can replace Guillaume without any problem. Their fathers worked for him too, and their grandfathers for his father, back as far as anyone can remember, just like the Martins, those three cellarmen he trusts so completely. Father's much too hale to give up running things his way, in any case, too hale and too set in his ways."

"How would you like to adjust to the agricultural life at fifty-three?" Eve asked dubiously. "In a place where the end of October might be uncomfortably cold and spring is five long months away, at best?"

"Are you hinting that California has ruined me?"

"It happens to the best of us. Even to the French. Something chemical changes in your blood when you live here long enough—it's like the tropics. One day—one day much too soon—the House of Lancel and Valmont will belong to you whether you like it or not. Or whether I like it either, for that matter. I rather dread the thought, to be honest. So why anticipate? I think we should wait till next spring. We could spend a month in Paris with Delphine and another month in Champagne."

"Done. May in Paris with Delphine, June in Champagne with my parents, learning exactly how a bee makes love to a grape blossom," Paul said briskly.

He had managed, Eve thought, once again to get through a conversation that had included everything but China and Japan, without any reference to the fact that they had another daughter, who lived, as she suspected he must guess, within a few miles of them. If he didn't want to know anything about it, she wasn't going to be the one to tell him. It was enough that she had Paul back, that he had recovered from whatever cruel emotion had dominated him in those early months after Freddy left, recovered to love his wife again, as much, as dearly as he had before. The subject of Freddy was like an unspoken, unwritten

293

Munich agreement—they had long ago decided not to go to war against each other over it.

Delphine started another picture early in September, starring opposite Jean-Pierre Aumont. She began the film hoping that something would happen on the set that would change the nature of her obsession, for obsession was what she had realized it must be, rather than love.

However, by the end of September she understood that she was in more trouble than she knew. She could still act. She could count on her true natural talent, and the technique she had absorbed in the last two years of almost nonstop work, to get her beautifully through one scene after another. No matter how complicated the scene, when another actor threw her the ball, she always caught it. She listened brilliantly, which was half the battle. The camera continued to discover far more emotion in her face than she felt. Her new director was delighted with her, and she found his direction satisfactory, if uninspired. Abel was working on setting up a film with Gabin, and the future smiled.

It was the present that stank. She went to bed too late and had trouble going to sleep because of thoughts of Sadowski. She woke up too early, with an abrupt exit from unconsciousness, thinking about Sadowski. During the day, whenever she wasn't saying her lines, she thought about Sadowski. It wouldn't do.

There was only one way to exorcise the man, and that was to confront him. Her obsession wouldn't stand up against reality, but first, to get rid of it, she had to expose it to the open air, let in curative daylight. It would be embarrassing, humiliating and ludicrous, and it went against all her principles, but if she simply told him how she felt, he would be so insensitive, so unreceptive, that she would finally be shocked out of her unnatural state. Best of all, he might actually feel sorry for her. Of course, he'd be low enough to let her know it. *Pity!* That should do it.

She telephoned him and told him she needed to ask his advice about her new film. Director trouble.

"Look, babe, I'm busy as hell, but sure, if you've got a problem I'll try to make time for you. Meet me at Lipp's at eight-thirty—no, I'd better eat on the set, we're reshooting something complicated. Come to my place at ten. If I'm not home then, it'll be because I killed an actor. You know where I live? Right, see you later."

Know where he lived? She had known for six months, she had walked by it dozens of times, hoping to run into him; she could get there by bus, by Métro, or on foot. She could crawl there if she had to, all the way across Paris. However, Delphine ordered a taxi, since she didn't want her driver speculating on why she would be going somewhere at ten at night and leaving a half hour later, like an unsuccessful second-story man.

There was no point in bothering to dress in any particular manner. Whatever she put on would make no difference to him. On the other hand, for an exorcism, only a black dress seemed appropriate. Something priestlike. Austere, severe. Her new Chanel, with just one string of pearls. The very, very good ones she had bought last year on Bruno's advice. Her second-best pearls would do just as well, but she'd be more . . . you're doing it again, you inutterable fool! Delphine scolded herself, her teeth chattering in spite of the warmth of the room, you're dressing to charm a man who can't be charmed. But the Chanel *would* do something for her own morale, she rationalized, as she slipped on the black, low-cut cocktail dress that had been the hit of the fall collection. Army officers wore their best uniforms in which to be court-martialed. Even Mata Hari had bothered to look nice at her execution, she thought, as she applied her makeup with trembling but adroit hands, and arranged her hair, until she looked even younger than twenty and twice as beautiful as ever, because her eyes were so frightened and her heart-shaped face was so sad.

She wrapped herself in Chanel's black, between-season coat and decided not to wear a hat, since it was late enough to go without one. As she sat in the taxi, crossing the Seine to the Left Bank, she wished above all that she had a script. An exorcism, a proper one, always had its script, a time-hallowed one, but she had nothing to guide her except her conviction that she had to end her obsession or something bad would happen to her.

Armand Sadowski lived almost directly above Chez Lipp, in an old and rather dilapidated apartment building that seemed to lean forward into the Boulevard Saint-Germain. Delphine looked wistfully at the crowds on the terrace of the Café Flore, across the street; happy people, drinking, calling the waiters, chatting, seeming to be full of good news as they enjoyed the last warm night of fall. She turned away from the pleasant, wonderfully ordinary sight, and forced herself to buzz open the heavy outside door, asking the concierge what floor he lived on, and climb the steep, uncarpeted stairs to the top of the building.

Armand Sadowski, looking strangely excited, threw open the door to his apartment, the second she rang the bell. He was in his shirt-sleeves, without a tie, and he needed a shave. She hadn't remembered just how tall he was, she thought, confused by the too-abrupt transition from the staircase to his apartment.

"What do you think of this?" he asked quickly, without a greeting, holding out the evening paper.

"I haven't had time to read it yet."

"It looks like peace. The Germans don't want to fight any more than we do. Hitler's finally signed an agreement."

"Maybe he didn't want to attack the Maginot Line."

"So even you know about the Maginot Line? Amazing." He grinned and waved her farther into the room.

"Everybody in the world knows about the Maginot Line. That's all the French ever talk about. Ah, why did I come?"

"For advice. You said you were in trouble with your new director."

"That isn't exactly the case."

"I suspected as much. More likely he's in trouble with you. Drink?"

"Gin, just pour it in a glass."

"Americans," he said, shaking his head. "Only Americans drink gin straight."

"So do the English," she responded wearily. She had no gumption left.

"Hey, babe, sit down. I forgot my manners." He gave her a glass and pointed to a big leather chair. She didn't even look around the big, disordered room but just sank into the chair and took a sip.

"So why'd you come? What's the problem?"

"I love you."

It was easier to say than she'd expected, because she spoke in French and that had always provided a mask, as any language but English would. The words, in English, would have been unbearable. She drained her glass and blindly fastened her eyes on its empty depths.

Sadowski took off his glasses thoughtfully, and regarded her silently for a minute or two. "Looks like you do at that," he said finally, his tone a confirmation of everything she had forced herself so slowly to understand.

"Aren't you even surprised! My God, what an ego!" Delphine's head snapped up in an unexpected anger, a welcome anger.

"It took you long enough to get around to it," he said, as if he hadn't heard her, as if he were continuing a conversation that had started differently. Perhaps with someone else?

"Have you been talking about me?" she asked suspiciously.

"Why would I?"

"Never mind. All right, now you know. Do you have anything to say?"

"You are *unspeakably* spoiled."

"I'm aware of that. Anything else?" Delphine said crisply. Being told she was spoiled wasn't going to exorcise him, anger or not. If only he'd pitied her. Damn him for taking off his glasses. She wanted to caress away the faint marks they had made on his nose between his eyes, those remarkable eyes, nearsighted or farsighted or whatever they were. She wanted to rub her face against the bristles of his disgraceful day-old beard, she wanted to take handfuls of his too-long, messed-up hair and pull him toward her and press him to her lips.

"You're appallingly privileged. You've done nothing to deserve it but be outrageously decorative. You always have been, and you always will be, and you'll always take advantage of it."

"That's not my fault. I can't help it."

"I didn't say it was, I said it was appalling." He fell silent, meditative.

"What does it have to do with my loving you?" Delphine forced herself to use the words again. He didn't seem to have paid proper attention the first time.

"For one thing, I've heard that you've done some painful things to a lot of guys."

"What can I do if people fall in love with me? I can't love them back on command," Delphine said, on the defensive. What exactly had he heard? How bad had she looked?

"I understand that you're a caroming renegade in sexual matters. They should put out storm warnings when you're on the loose, babe."

"I've never been in love before," Delphine said, hoping it was an excuse.

"That's no excuse."

"You sound like my mother."

"So what? I understand that you've specialized in directors, with an occasional producer for dessert."

"That's disgusting."

"But true. The word's out. I'm not interested in becoming a part of your fantasy life, another of the directors you've honored."

"I never asked you to! I didn't make a single move toward you when we were working together. I wish it were only a fantasy. You're not my director anymore. Don't you understand? I love you!"

"I understand, babe, only too well. There's a touch of the demonic about you. Frankly, you scare the shit out of me."

"Sissy! That's that. I'm going." Delphine rose to leave. He'd said

297

enough to start a good exorcism, and she couldn't take any more. It hurt too much to be here and not be able to touch him, even if he was talking about her, which was better, no matter what he said, than if he was ignoring her.

"Sit down. I'm not finished with you yet. Don't you wonder how I know that you love me?"

"I don't give a shit. How typical of you to try to analyze everything," she said bitterly. "It's your business to know how people feel. I probably gave myself away a dozen times. What difference does it make? Shall we now have a seminar on the portrayal of the emotion of unwilling love as perceived through the eyes of the brilliant director, Armand Sadowski?"

"Shut up, Delphine. You talk too much." He seemed to be buoyed up by a kind of secret joke.

"You're so pleased with yourself, it's sickening. I'm sorry I ever came here. I should have known better."

"I love you too," he said slowly. The joke vanished. "I love you more than I'm frightened by you. That's how I know you're telling the truth."

"You? Love me?" Delphine spoke quickly, in headlong disbelief. "You couldn't possibly love me. If you loved me you would have told me. I wouldn't have had to come here . . . and . . . throw myself at your feet."

"I hoped that if you loved me, you'd let me know in your own good time."

"*If?*" Where was her exorcism? Why were they talking, splitting hairs about a love that didn't exist, that couldn't exist, or he wouldn't have been able to conceal it? Why wasn't she angry anymore? Why was she listening to him as if her life depended on it?

"How could I be sure while I was directing you? It could just have been part of your well-known pattern."

"Oh."

"Exactly."

They sat facing each other, looking at the floor, enraptured, shy, elated, tongue-tied, the past wiped out, the future unknown, while the world turned and turned until it had changed forever around them.

"When?" Delphine demanded at last, falling back on the familiar to make sure of the bewildering present. "When did you fall in love with me?"

"Never mind."

"You have to tell me."

"It's too damn stupid."

"When?" She was inexorable. He owed her that.

"When I turned around and looked at you in my office that first day, that first meeting—I didn't know anything about you. Even Hollywood wouldn't go for something that simpleminded."

"I would. I'd go for that. But why? Why did you fall in love with me?"

"Now who's analyzing everything?"

"I have my rights," she commanded, blazingly certain that she did. "Why?"

"You've got me, babe. I don't know. No good reason, just love at first sight, God help me. Believe me, it was involuntary. Come over here."

"What's my motivation?" If she could tease him, she thought, the obsession must be exorcised. Now it was ordinary, simple, priceless, perfect love. Magic.

"Actresses!" He got up, took one big step and pulled her to her feet. He put his hands around her neck and unfastened the catch of her pearls. "Put these away somewhere, they're much too good to lose in this mess."

"Aren't you going to kiss me?"

"All in good time. First I have to undress you. Button by button. I've got to be careful of your dress, it's just too right."

"Right for what?"

"The scene where the girl goes to tell the guy she loves him, of course. It's such a clever dress, so severe, so uncompromising, so low-cut. So very low-cut. The poor sucker, he never had a chance."

Freddy had gone to sleep unusually early the evening after she'd taken her white Rider up for the first time since her accident. Mac sat at the kitchen table, in front of a sheet of writing paper, the newspaper he'd just finished pushed to the floor in weary disgust. He'd dueled in the air with too many fearless, wily German pilots to believe that they'd ever give up. The last twenty years had seemed like one long, uneasy half-truce to him, and Munich just another battle they had won.

Where would they attack next? And how soon? The pace had been getting quicker ever since '33, when, first, he had clearly heard the sound of approaching cannon. It wasn't a question of *if* any longer, now that the Sudetenland had been sacrificed, it was only a question of *when*. Any man, he thought heavily, who understood how the borders of countries vanish when you try to find them from the air, knew that Isolationism couldn't last. A year? Maybe less?

The news from Munich had only underlined the resolution he'd made yesterday, when Freddy had spoken of his making a good father. But it had come as a warning, pushing him over the edge of the line on which he'd been hesitating in heartbreak and self-hatred for the past few weeks. Freddy wasn't pregnant. He knew that. She wasn't yet, but, like the next war, it was only a matter of time. He took up a pen and started to write, searching with difficulty for every word he was doomed to write, finally leaving out all but the essentials.

Darling Freddy,

I have to leave you. It's the only thing for us. I know you want to get married. I know you realize that if you were pregnant I'd marry you. So I'm going away to give you room to live your life as you should. You haven't even started on your life yet. I can't clip your wings.

You know how I feel about marrying you. As unfair as I've been in the past, it would be worse to take that far greater advantage of you. I've told you that, as directly as I can, and I'd tell you again and again, but it won't do any good. You never believe I really mean it. And you'll never give up on me unless I leave. Everything I own is yours, the house, the planes, the business. Keep them or sell them, as you like.

The one thing you must never think is that I didn't love you enough. If I were a young man, I'd marry you tomorrow—I'd have married you long ago. It's because I love you so much that I'm letting you go. I am not your future, my beloved girl.

Mac

He reread the letter, put down the pen, took the paper, folded it in half and wrote her name on the outside. Then he weighed down a corner with the pitcher of wildflowers she always kept on the table, and went to the closet to take out the bag he'd packed while she was out flying. If there were any better way to do it, Mac thought, he'd have found it by now. But there wasn't. She would recover from the pain. He would not.

Many hours later, as he drove his car too rapidly north, he realized where he was going. His only thought, for hundreds of miles, had been to get far away before he changed his mind, his only destination a place without memories. Only as dawn broke did he feel safe, because soon she'd be reading the letter.

He could have used one of the planes, he thought. He would join up

300

in Vancouver, across the border. There was bound to be a Canadian Air Force base there. Or if not there, in Toronto. They always needed instructors, and didn't quibble about age. Nobody ever wanted that job, not once they'd learned to fly. At least he could lend a hand, at least there was one worthwhile thing left for him to do with whatever was left of his life.

15

FREDDY tore across the landing strip at Dry Springs, driving her car as fast as it would go. She came to a violent, skidding stop with a smashing of brakes, two feet away from her plane. She sprinted out of the car, untied the Rider, kicked the chocks out from under its wheels, jumped into the cockpit, punched the starter button, started the plane, and left the ground behind within seconds. For the first and last time in her life she neither checked out her ship before she got into it, nor went through the necessary run-up procedure to test the motor before takeoff.

She had found Mac's letter less than a half hour earlier, and she had known immediately that if she didn't get into the sky she couldn't live through the pain. She had no way to handle it. She had no capacity to exist with this all-obliterating plunge into intolerable suffering. She had to flee from it or go mad. She put the nose of the ship up as high as it would go and climbed at the top possible speed, up and up into the gloomy, overcast sky, her stall signal shrieking again and again, so that she was kept busy correcting the attitude of the ship to keep from falling into a nosedive. She panted through her mouth, like a dog, blinking constantly into the grayness that was lit by a white glare. She had forgotten her goggles, she had on only the Levi's, shirt and sweater in which she had gone down to breakfast, and soon she was shivering with the cold of altitude. Still she climbed headlong, on and on, height her only goal. Suddenly she burst through the overcast and found herself above the clouds. The blue sky struck the necessary blow she had been racing toward, like a runner straining for the tape at the finish line, and she slumped over the controls, all strength gone.

The Rider, uncontrolled, quickly assumed the configuration for which it had been designed and soon Freddy was flying level, a few hundred feet above a field of whiteness.

The sun on the cockpit warmed her, and little by little she stopped shaking. She lifted her head and took charge of her ship. Now, below her, there were scattered breaks in the clouds and she dove down through one like a porpoise, climbing up over the back of the next cloud, diving, climbing, diving and climbing, mindless motion her only focus. She saw a cloud with an unfamiliar shape and circled it meticulously, just at its edge, one wing in, one wing out. She found narrow, winding, brightly lit blue avenues between towering walls of white, and followed them wherever they led her; she entered clouds and stayed hidden inside them, unable to see more than fifty feet in any direction, until suddenly, at random, she charged out, seeking whatever lay beyond.

Freddy played with the clouds for as long as she could, crisscrossing, tracing edges, cutting them up, down and sideways, sometimes bullying them as if they were soapsuds, sometimes touching them as lightly as if they were made of old lace, never looking downwards. When, finally, she consulted her controls, she realized that she had almost no fuel left. She had no idea how long she'd been aloft. Now, some purpose restored, she dipped below the cloud level to find out where she was.

Beneath her, in every direction, stretched the desert. There were no roads, no trees, no landmarks of any kind. All pilots who know the San Fernando Valley know that only a few minutes away lies a vast desert no man has ever been able to chart. Freddy was as utterly lost as if she had been a thousand miles out at sea, except that, like all other mariners, she had a compass. Obedient to ancient laws that apply to all who wish to adventure, and all who wish to survive, she turned the Rider due west and found Dry Springs only minutes before she would have run out of gas.

On the ground she taxied to a far edge of the strip and came to a full stop. She turned off the motor, but she couldn't make herself get out of the plane. As long as she remained where she was, she thought she was insulated, safe. As long as she stayed in the cockpit, nothing bad had really happened. Even as the words came into her mind, she understood that reality had returned. Once she had realized that the plane was a refuge, it ceased to be a refuge. As lightly as a ghost, Freddy touched each of the controls, thanking them. Today they had been forgiving, today they had not made her pay any price for her insanely careless takeoff. Subdued by thoughts of what might have happened, she taxied the Rider and had it filled with fuel before she took it back to its parking space, and tied it down with reluctant thoroughness.

Now what, she thought, when the last knot had been tied and retied. Now what? She stood by her plane, touching its skin, a slim, tall figure with not a single idea of where to go or what to do. She folded her arms and leaned against the fuselage of the Rider, looking blindly at the dirt at her feet.

"Freddy, where's Mac?"

"What?" She looked up. Gavin Ludwig, one of Mac's assistants, stood in front of her.

"I don't know what he wanted me to do with the Stuka I've been working on," Gavin said. "Do I call Swede and let him know it's finished, or do I wait for Mac to check it out?"

"Are you satisfied with it?"

"It's better than when it was new, if I say so myself."

"Then call Swede and find out where he wants it."

"Nah, I'd better hold off on that. Mac's so particular about the planes."

"Mac had to leave for a little while. He's left me in charge until he comes back. Just call Swede."

"Well sure, Freddy . . . if you say so. When will Mac be back? He never mentioned anything about going anywhere."

"In a week or two. Family business. You know how it is."

"Who doesn't? So you'll be around the office?"

"Bright and early, Gavin, every day, bright and early."

"There's a bunch of messages on his desk that came in this morning. I guess they could wait till tomorrow, but if you're sticking around today . . . ?"

"Where else would I go, Gavin?"

"You've already been flyin'."

"So I have."

"Wasn't a great day for it," he said, looking up at the lingering overcast.

"Wasn't bad," Freddy replied. "Better than not goin' flyin', that's for damn sure."

On her way home from the airport, late that afternoon, Freddy stopped at the local market and bought all the ingredients for Mac's most complicated beef stew, made with red wine and seven vegetables. By the time he came back, she'd know how to cook it, she vowed. Why should he be the only one to master that dish? Why should she continue to let him relegate her to easy dishes like hamburgers and fried chicken? She hesitated in front of the butcher counter. Should she ask for soup bones and marrow bones and a cracked veal knuckle, so that she could make a soup from scratch? That was another of Mac's specialties that she'd never been allowed to try. Yes, she thought, as she talked to the butcher, this was the perfect opportunity to catch up with him in the kitchen.

When she got back to the house, Freddy dumped the bags of groceries in the kitchen. Mac's letter lay folded on the table. She took it, turned on one of the gas rings on the stove, burned the letter without unfolding it, and started briskly upstairs to make the bed she'd left unmade that morning.

When the bedroom had been put in perfect order, she turned to the bathroom. There was a hamper half full of Mac's shirts. She put them into a bag for delivery to the laundry tomorrow. When he came back he'd find every shirt he owned neatly piled on his shelves. She straightened their closet, making sure that all his shoes formed an orderly line, that his few jackets hung properly; she refolded his sweaters and put whatever socks and underwear of his she found near the sink, to be washed later.

By the time Freddy finished, it was dark outside. She turned on all the lights in the bedroom and went down to the living room, turning on all the lights there, noting that the bookcases needed her attention. Mac had never understood that books should be lined up neatly in the bookcases. This was her chance to work on them and make them as shipshape as they should be. She could even have some new bookcases built for the overflow. There wasn't nearly enough space for what he already owned, books were crammed together every which way, and when he bought more books in the future they'd end up on the floor, if she didn't do something about it while he was gone.

She poured herself a small shot of his whiskey and went into the kitchen to start to deal with the vegetables. Freddy was an expert at peeling, cutting and chopping. This was one of the jobs Mac had taught her to do when she first moved in with him. As she quickly scraped carrots, she wondered how long he could manage to keep himself from coming home. Certainly weeks, if she was any judge. Nothing less than two weeks would satisfy his scruples. Particularly after such a needlessly dramatic letter. If he slunk back in less than a few weeks, he'd just look plain silly and they'd both know it, no matter how careful they would be not to admit it to each other. A month? Possible. Even probable, now that she came to think about it. He was a hard-nosed bastard, and he was fully capable of letting this crazy situation go on for a month or even more, but not much more. He couldn't hold out longer than that.

There was no question, she decided, as she shelled peas, while the beef browned in a large skillet, that he'd be back by, oh, say, a little after Halloween. Last year they'd made a huge jack-o'-lantern and put it outside on the porch for the neighbors' kids. She mustn't forget this year, or the kids would be disappointed.

She went at the celery tops with a sharp knife and made short work of them. The kitchen could stand a paint job, Freddy thought as she started on the potatoes. In fact, the whole house needed to be painted, inside and out. That was the sort of thing that Mac invariably would keep putting off and putting off when left to himself. While he was gone, while she had the place to herself, it was going to get done. When he came home he'd have to admit that it looked a lot better. While she was at it, she'd pick out some fabric and change the bedroom curtains, maybe even have slipcovers made for the living room. It could look so much better than it did now. If it were a prettier room, they'd spend more time in it, instead of just shuttling from the kitchen to the bedroom and back. There was so much to do before he returned that she didn't know if she could get it all done on time.

It didn't really matter. Once the jobs were under way, even if he came home before they were finished, there'd be nothing he could do to stop her.

He hated change. That man really was a creature of habit. Since she'd known him he'd never even moved a single stick of furniture in his uncomfortable office, except to add the map box she'd made him in shop. Well, she'd make the office comfortable too, while she could. Not chintz, that would be going too far, but some carpet and a few decent chairs wouldn't hurt. It would serve him right for telling her to do whatever she wanted with the business. He'd learn not to give her carte blanche so easily when he was in a momentarily vile mood, for what else could account for a man as honorable as Mac sneaking out of the house in the middle of the night?

Somebody had to take over his private lessons on a temporary basis, while he was away, or he'd lose his pupils. She could get her instructor's license by the end of the week. It was just a question of making an appointment to take the exam. She didn't know why she hadn't bothered to get it before now. His students would have to be notified to wait until she took them over. And she could handle the stunt planning on the Saturday serial, so long as she didn't take on more flying work herself. All things considered, it would be better for her to watch the store than to accept another job. She wanted Mac to be forced to admit, when he returned to all the things he'd abandoned so hastily, that she'd been a good steward in his absence.

Freddy put all her vegetables into a tall cast-iron pot, along with a number of juicy, cut-up tomatoes, added the browned beef, three bay leaves and some homemade broth that Mac always kept handy in the icebox. Arms akimbo, she looked at the contents of the pot. She'd add the wine later, and the seasoning. There didn't seem to be anything further to do except wait for it to cook. She looked at her watch. Nine o'clock. How had it grown so late? Time flew when you kept busy. Dinner should be ready at . . . at midnight. The stew took three hours to cook. Worse, it was never, in Mac's opinion, ready to eat when first cooked. It had to wait until the next day or, better yet, two, and then be reheated, before its flavor developed fully. Well, she'd just eat it on the first night and to hell with deepening its flavor, she decided. This would give her time to start in on the books in the living room. She poured another small shot of whiskey and marched in to attack the bookcases.

During the period when Delphine had entertained a series of lovers in her little house, the women who worked for her had found her abandoned behavior a source of intensely pleasurable interest and vicarious entertainment. It was certainly no less than they expected from a film star. She had a series of liaisons, yes, without question, but in a proper manner, under her own roof, and as much as they found to comment on, they had no downright moral criticism.

However, now that Delphine spent all of her nights away from home, and they were left in complete ignorance about her whereabouts, their employer seemed worse to them than any common slut. Who knew, Annabelle, the cleaning woman, speculated with disdain, how many different men were involved? Who knew what kind of sordid neighborhoods Mademoiselle de Lancel frequented, suggested Claudine, the guardian's wife, sniffing with outrage. Who knew with what types of men she was making love, Violet, Delphine's personal maid, conjectured, her tone making it clear that she suspected Delphine of a variety of fascinating depravities, one more debased than another.

Delphine, they told each other in honorable indignation, was guilty of the sinful activity known as *découcher*, a verb that literally meant "to sleep elsewhere than in one's own home," but one that carried a specifically immoral overtone. In 1939 only those Frenchwomen who were utterly reckless about their sexual reputations behaved in a way that permitted others to use the term *découcher*, a word that came closest in meaning to "sleeping around" but was far more flagrantly pejorative.

The three women, as well as Helene, the cook, were as one in their new opinion of Delphine. They were personally insulted that Delphine had escaped their observation; they deeply resented the fact that they no longer possessed the knowledge that had, for so long, given them a feeling of power over her. Worse, there was the threat that her new liberty posed to their pocketbooks.

When Delphine didn't use her own house, they all lost money. She continued to pay their salaries, but many extras had disappeared, now that she no longer bothered to keep the house running as lavishly as before. They had lost the fat percentages each one of them had been accustomed to skimming from the household accounts, over which Delphine had never bothered to keep track, in her trusting, foolish, American way. In addition, she had been in the habit of giving them frequent presents and tips, treating these presumed keepers of her privacy with a careless and naïve generosity. This had vanished as well, now that she was never home. The natural envy the four women had always felt toward someone as rich, as young, as beautiful and as free as Delphine, surfaced and grew stronger as the months passed and she continued to spend each night in unknown beds.

Nobody in the world knows where we are, Delphine thought, suffused through and through with such happiness that it had to be unalterable, happiness so total that she had forgotten to be superstitious about it. She was complete, for the first time in her life, complete in a way she had never dreamed existed, she told herself as she lay snugly under a heavy plaid throw on the couch in the living room of the apartment on the Boulevard Saint-Germain, watching Armand read the script of his new picture, the most complicated of his career, that he had brought home from the studio. She was stripped of calculation, stripped of ambition, stripped of the constant observation of others, which had been part of her for as long as she could remember.

"What are you thinking about?" he asked, without lifting his eyes from the page.

"Nothing," she answered. "Absolutely nothing at all."

"Good. Stick to it," he said, and continued to read. He was incapable of spending as much as a quarter of an hour, no matter how immersed he was in his work, without making some contact with her. If she was near him he would reach out and touch her hand fleetingly; if she was across the room he would say something, and any answer would satisfy him. Delphine wondered if he actually listened to what she said, or just to the sound of her voice. She'd never asked, because it didn't matter. For her part it was enough that he was there and she was there. Hours could pass while he was busy with his reading, without her desiring any occupation other than being in the same room with him, and keeping the fire fed. When he left for the studio she puttered around all day, dreaming a great deal and dusting very little, in suspended animation until he came home.

The only thing she missed from her former life was the furnace that had kept her house so warm. The heat that was dispensed by any of the radiators of Armand's apartment was only evident if you stood no more than a foot away from the ancient apparatus itself. Delphine had a theory that the inhabitants of the lower floors were siphoning off all the available heat, preventing it from reaching them. Armand insisted that heat rose to the top of any structure and that they must be getting the best of it. This was the only subject on which they didn't agree, and now that it was late March the concierge supplied no more heat, giving them nothing to argue about.

"As soon as we get married, we'll find a place with better heat," he'd said often during the winter, but Delphine had decided privately that she'd rather freeze than ever move from this apartment, which more than five years of residence had marked with Armand's personality. Here, hung haphazardly on the walls, were the dozens of avant-garde paintings he bought from dealers in the neighborhood; here the grand piano on which, with equal enthusiasm, he played ragtime with vivid inspiration, and Chopin badly; here the worn, comfortable furniture he'd found in the flea market, and the rugs his parents had given him when he set up housekeeping for himself. Here was the room in which he'd told her that he loved her, and here was the bedroom in which they slept and made love, and no other home they would have in the future could ever mean as much to her.

She got up and put another log on the fire. Soon they would go downstairs to eat in a small neighborhood restaurant as they did most nights. Neither of them ever cooked. When they didn't eat out, they bought prepared salads, cheeses and sausages from one of the many delicacy shops in the neighborhood, and had a picnic in front of the fire that had been necessary almost every day since the beginning of October. Every morning Armand went downstairs and brought her up a croissant to eat while she still nestled in bed, with a cup of the *café au lait* he had somehow learned to prepare.

It was, thought Delphine, a life in which she no longer needed the clothes she had bought in the past, a life in which a lingerie maker had no place, nor a *bottier*. It seemed to her that the clothes she had brought over, bit by bit, from the Villa Mozart, would last the rest of her life, for she spent most of her time in her old, sailor-style trousers from Chanel and Armand's sweaters, often wearing two or three of them at once. When she returned for a few hours to the Villa Mozart, to pay her staff and make sure that the house was still there, she wore a proper suit and hat, but she never used her car or her driver to come from or go to the Boulevard Saint-Germain. She hadn't sold the house or the car, for she knew that their possession provided her with a façade it was still necessary to maintain.

Delphine was convinced that she had protected her life with Armand Sadowski from the eyes of the world. After he had spoken of his distaste at becoming another in the string of her lovers, she determined that their attachment must remain secret until she was ready to get married. She turned down all the films that had been offered her from the first night they spent together, giving her agent one ingenious excuse after another. She could not tell Abel the truth: that she was too emotionally focused on her love to spend her energy on acting, on learning lines and dealing with the complications of the life of a star. She had also refused to do the new film with Armand, knowing that she would give her feelings away to the entire studio if she worked with him. Make-believe held no further allure for her.

Nor did reality. Franco had conquered Spain and been recognized by France and England, but Delphine managed not to read about it in the same way that she managed not to read about the success of Marcel Pagnol's film *The Baker's Wife*. Katharine Hepburn's triumph in *Bringing Up Baby* was no less foreign to her than the reasons for Enrico Fermi's Nobel Prize for atomic reaction. *She didn't want to know.* Even marriage was an act that would involve coping with public reality. She managed not to deal with it each time Armand suggested that they get married.

All of Delphine's powers of perception were totally engaged in blocking out the world, in remaining invincibly safe within the cave of true love that she and Armand had created, in which the only subject for her concern was assuring the supply of wood for the fireplace, a matter of tipping the boy from the nearby wood-seller to carry it up the stairs.

She would cross the street to keep from walking by the kiosks of newsdealers, she never looked at posters plastered on walls, she picked restaurants where you couldn't overhear the conversation of the people at the next table, she never sat and had a drink at a café, all of which were filled with people talking politics, she never turned on the radio, and Armand knew never to bring home a newspaper.

All during the ominous winter and dire spring of 1939, Delphine kept the world at bay and lived a lifetime of joy with Armand Sadowski, who loved her enough to understand what she was doing, and too much to destroy her fragile structure of illusion by so much as a single word.

"Mademoiselle de Lancel," said Violet a week later, in early April, when Delphine next paid a visit to her house on the Villa Mozart, "Monsieur le Vicomte has telephoned twice in the past week. I told him you were not at home, and promised to give you a message that he had called. What am I to say when he calls again? He seemed worried that he had not heard from you."

"Never mind, Violet, I'll telephone him myself," Delphine said reluctantly. She had managed to avoid Bruno since September, finding for him a different, but equally clever, set of excuses from those she had concocted to avoid accepting film offers. However, Bruno was more persistent than Abel, and unlike Abel, his requests to see her had been personal, not professional. She knew that she couldn't continue to elude him any longer, even though her deepest instinct was not to let anyone, not even Bruno, break into the firmly constructed idyll of her existence. Nevertheless, her reason told her that in his case at least, she had to cope. Perhaps a lunch, she thought, as she called him at the bank.

"Delphine, I simply must see you," Bruno said. "It's been months and months."

"I'm miserable that I've neglected you so, Bruno, my angel, but this has been an absolutely crazy winter for me. Business without end, so many conferences, so many producers, all wanting something, not a second for myself, I feel as if I've been a prisoner. The cinema! But I do miss you. Can we have lunch? Dinners are impossible."

"How about the day after tomorrow?"

"Perfect. Where shall we meet?"

"How about my new little place? You haven't even seen it, and I have an excellent cook. I don't like to lunch in restaurants—I have to do it too often for business."

"You're on the Rue de Lille, aren't you? I have the address."

"At one, then. Until Wednesday."

Delphine hung up the phone with a sigh of resignation, and went to her closets to find something to wear to Bruno's. She had not bought any new spring clothes at all, but there were dozens of ensembles from last year hanging, perfectly pressed, in her wardrobe. She picked out a navy blue Molyneux suit with a white and blue printed silk blouse that matched the lining of the jacket. It had a tightly fitted waist, a flared

311

skirt that fell just below her knees, and the slightly exaggerated, puffed shoulders that were still the style of the day. Molyneux didn't date, she thought, and navy and white would always signal spring. Violet gathered together the wide-brimmed, saucerlike straw hat from Reboux, with a bow at the back made of the silk of the blouse, and the high-heeled shoes, the bag, the gloves and stockings that had all been bought to go with the suit.

"Could you please put these all together for me, Violet, and call me a cab?" Delphine asked.

"You do not have need for any other clothes, Mademoiselle? Only this outfit? Nothing, perhaps, for evening?" Violet asked.

"Not today," Delphine answered in a voice that silenced any other questions.

As she stood on the Rue de Lille, two days later, she was surprised to see that Bruno evidently occupied all of the good-sized private house. A butler in a tailcoat answered the bell and admitted her into a large entrance hall, with a floor of black and white marble. Suits of armor and tapestries of battle scenes were the only decoration of the severely masculine, museumlike room, which looked to Delphine as if it belonged in a medieval château. She was led up the wide central staircase into a magnificent red and gold library, where Bruno jumped up to greet her.

"At last!" he said, as he kissed her on both cheeks. "And more elegant than ever."

"Thank you, Bruno, angel. I'm so happy to see you. And this is your new 'little place,' is it, you joker? Things must be going well for you."

"They are, as a matter of fact, though no thanks to you, you wretched girl."

"When did you start to collect suits of armor?"

"They belonged to my Saint-Fraycourt ancestors. When Grandfather died, he left me everything. I finally found a home for them."

"Ah yes, I'd forgotten the sainted Saint-Fraycourt ancestors. It's too bad I never met your grandparents before they died."

"You know how ridiculously old-fashioned they were. They never could overcome their feelings about your mother."

"It was, perhaps, their loss," Delphine said lightly, refusing to be piqued by the absurd snobbery of people for whom she cared nothing. What could her mother have done that she hadn't done herself ten times over? She wished she could tell Eve, in one of the letters she wrote home, that she understood her now, but it would be too revealing.

"It was most assuredly their loss," Bruno replied, giving her a glass of champagne. "Shall we toast our mutual grandparents? To the Lancels!"

"To Grandmother and Grandfather," Delphine said, feeling guilty. She had neglected them for her love, as she had neglected everyone. From time to time over the winter she had telephoned them at Valmont, but she had not been back to visit since she had taken refuge there to try to get over Armand Sadowski. It seemed like another life, but it had only been last August, eight months ago. Too long, far too long, at their age, she thought, and vowed to drive out soon, even if it were just for the day.

Delphine ate, without appetite, a five-course lunch served by two menservants, while Bruno talked about his latest horses, his new passion for squash, his travels for La Banque Duvivier Frères. He was going to try to get her to do something for him, she knew, or else why the urgency, why did he have to see her? Still, until he came right out and asked, she was content to sit in her ravishing suit and her ravishing hat, and respond with her ravishing smile, while she wondered why an unmarried man would choose to live in such an elaborate way.

"You are a great beauty, Delphine," Bruno remarked suddenly, when they were back in the library, having coffee by themselves.

"There seem to be people who think so," she replied. So she was right, she thought. He wanted her help, and it was something to do with a man he needed to win over.

"A great beauty, and a true talent. What is more, you are a great charmer, which is more rare than beauty and as valuable as talent. In addition you are a Lancel, an aristocrat, from one of the oldest families of the provincial nobility. You have everything a woman can have. There is no man you could not subjugate."

"Bruno, are you about to try to *sell* me to somebody?" Delphine had to laugh at his solemnity.

"You must stop *wasting yourself*, Delphine. It's a crime."

"What on earth are you talking about?" she asked, puzzled. Did he know she hadn't made any films in months?

"I am talking about your affair with Armand Sadowski."

"Now *that* is none of your business, Bruno! How dare you? You go too far!" Delphine put down her cup with a crash.

"No, Delphine, you have to listen to me! It's for your own good. Everyone in Paris knows that you're living with him. I've heard it from a dozen different people."

"How could people possibly know?" She spoke in astonishment, her anger forgotten.

"You can't hide from anyone in this neighborhood. You live only a few streets from here—your apartment is in the heart of the Sixth Arrondissement, bohemian as it may seem to you. You eat in all the neighborhood bistros . . . you are not their only customers, I assure you. You buy food in the same shops that are patronized by everyone's cooks, you go in and out of an apartment house that's next door to Chez Lipp, where sooner or later everyone in the world of film and theater and politics has lunch or dinner."

"So what, Bruno? Do they spend their time looking at passersby? Have they nothing better to do?"

"People *recognize* you, Delphine, don't you realize that? You have a face so famous that you cannot cross the street without causing a stir. No matter how you dress, they know who you are the minute they lay eyes on you, and once you've gone out the door of a shop with your eggs or your cheese, they say, 'Did you see her, Delphine de Lancel, the film star? She's having a fling with Sadowski, the director, they were in here just the other day, acting like lovebirds.' The shopkeeper tells the duchess's cook, the cook tells the duchess's personal maid, and the following week the duchess teases me about it. It's that simple. As far as the world of the cinema is concerned, Guy Marchant knew about it months ago. He'd actually heard from three different people, all regulars at Lipp. He was the first one who told me."

"They can choke on their gossip! All the duchesses in the *Bottin Mondain* and all the Guy Marchants in the film world. Choke! And for that matter, Bruno, so can you!"

"God damn it, listen! If it were just an affair I wouldn't have bothered to try to bring you to your senses, but Sadowski, *that Jew*—how could you, Delphine?"

Delphine gasped at the cold contempt in his voice. She was as shocked as if she had just been smashed in the face by a piece of dung thrown by a boy in the street. Bruno could not possibly have said what he'd just said.

" 'That Jew'?" You don't mean those words, do you, Bruno?"

"Yes I do. He's a Jew, a Polish Jew, you can't deny it."

"Why should I? Of course he's a Jew. So what? As for his being Polish, his parents were born in France, and he feels a lot more French than I do. He's as French as you are, Bruno." Delphine was shaking with fury.

"He's two generations out of some Polish ghetto, but even if he had

314

ancestors who'd lived in France for hundreds of years, that wouldn't make him less Jewish," Bruno shot back.

"So, it's nothing but anti-Semitism that you have against him? Aren't you ashamed, Bruno? Aren't you sick inside to know that you feel like that?"

"I knew you'd misunderstand. I'm no more anti-Jew than the next man. If they stay out of my way, I'll stay out of theirs. But it's my duty to protect you. You're my sister . . . half sister . . . but still of my blood. If you're involved with a Jew, it's going to mean nothing but trouble for you. You must have read about the measures Hitler has taken against the German Jews. You must have realized that they're pouring into France from every country in Europe, not just from Germany, trying to find a place where they'll be safe. Some of them, the smartest ones, are leaving for the United States or Switzerland. Do you think that your Sadowski is going to become less Jewish because he's French? Do you think that the Germans will treat him differently because his parents were born here?"

"The *Germans* treat him differently? Why should he have to have anything to do with the Germans?" Delphine spoke in a voice in which fear was mixed equally with outrage.

"My God, Delphine, I can't believe how ignorant you are! We're going to have to fight Germany, and we're going to lose."

"*You're insane.* I'm going home." Delphine rose and picked up her handbag.

"Sit down and listen to me." Bruno put both of his hands on her shoulders and pushed her down into a chair. "Now stay there. Since you're . . . mixed up with a Jew, you at least owe it to him to know what's going on. Last month Chamberlain guaranteed that England would go to war for Poland. Daladier has joined his promise to Chamberlain's. That means that France too will go to war for Poland. War, Delphine, *war*—"

"Why Poland? Why do we have to fight for Poland?" Delphine cried, her eyes wide with horror.

"God knows. Six years ago we could have stopped Hitler. Now it's far too late."

"You just can't say that, Bruno. You're a defeatist, an alarmist. We have the Maginot Line and the greatest army in Europe." Delphine spoke wildly, forcing herself to discuss things about which she had fought so hard not to think.

"The Maginot Line won't stop him." Bruno shook his head with scorn. "Belgium is neutral, Luxembourg is neutral, Russia is neutral.

The Americans are convinced that war is coming and they're not going to get into it. Your Charles Lindbergh, who knows more about air power than anyone in France, has toured Germany and seen their Luftwaffe. He says Germany is so strong that no one can possibly beat it—"

"But the Munich Agreement—?"

"Delphine, spare me Munich." Bruno's disdain for her words was like acid. "Munich only gave Hitler *permission* to go ahead. There *will* be a war and we will lose it—"

"Are you a military genius—or perhaps a fortune-teller?" Delphine spat the words at him.

"And when we lose the war, my dear Delphine, your Jew boyfriend will be treated like the Jews of Germany. He'll have no work, no place to live, no citizenship, not so much as a driver's license. He'll be forced to flee France if he can afford to buy his way out. Do you want to share that with him? Because you will if you stay with him, I warn you."

"*You lie!* It won't happen. If there is a war, France and England will beat Hitler. You are a foul and disgusting coward, Bruno. I'm ashamed to be related to you." Delphine got up and walked to the door. "Why don't you go downstairs and crawl inside a suit of armor that belonged to one of your brave ancestors? Perhaps it might give you some guts. On the other hand, if Hitler ever does come looking for you, it would make a good place to hide."

"You gonna fly to New York for the World's Fair, Freddy?" Gavin Ludwig asked in May of 1939. He'd come into the office at Dry Springs for a Coke and found her at the desk, paying bills.

"I can't afford the gas," Freddy answered. He hooted with laughter. Only Freddy knew how true her words were. She'd been forced to hire three male pilots to give flying lessons. Americans were more interested in learning how to fly than ever before in history, but none of them, not a single one, was willing to accept a woman as an instructor. She'd only been able to hang on to Mac's pupils by promising them a man to teach them. In the eight months since he'd been gone she'd added two other instructors and been obliged to put a down payment on another plane, a Waco N&C, with a Jacobs motor and a comfortable backseat, which could be used for instruction as well as her own new aerial speciality, running an "elopement express" to Las Vegas and back the same night. She loathed the dullness of the work, but even being a matrimonial taxi driver was necessary if she wanted to eat.

Why would people trust her to get them to the church on time,

Freddy wondered, but not to teach them how to fly? She was one of the handful of women in the United States, a mere seventy-three in all, who held commercial ratings, yet any man, no matter how recently he'd won his instructor's license, reassured the students more than a woman who could make a plane do a hundred maneuvers he'd crash if he attempted. Did they think that you flew with your cock?

The three men who worked, in theory, *for* her had to be paid by the hour, the planes had to be maintained, Gavin's mechanic's salary had to be met each week, insurance cost a fortune, the hangar and office rent came due monthly, gas wasn't cheap—the school, Freddy reflected, only paid for itself and for the upkeep of her Rider. The occasional Vegas trips kept her in food, and allowed her to meet the payments on the new Waco. Otherwise she'd have had to close the school.

Restlessly she pushed away from the desk and wandered out into the hangar where the collection of vintage planes sat, each one of them burnished and gleaming, dust-free, rust-free and as recently painted as when they'd been new: the 1910 Curtiss Pusher, the Fokker D.VII, the two Nieuport 28's, the Thomas Morse Scout, the Garland Lincoln LF-1, and the Stukas. Why the fuck not keep horses and buggies, she thought wrathfully, as she tapped one of the wheels of the Nieuport with the toe of her boot. Or unicorns or unicycles? They'd have to be more useful than these old birds, for which the movies hadn't had any need whatsoever in the last year. The market for Great War movies had dried up completely as the shadow of a new war grew ever darker. Freddy did all the upkeep on the antique planes herself, teaching herself to maintain their engines, unable to pay anybody to do the delicate work properly, yet unwilling, in spite of their impracticality, to let them disintegrate into junk.

Wings of the Navy, a million-dollar production, had opened the past January, and the Navy had lent Warner Brothers some four hundred and fifty pursuit and training planes, as well as fifty PBY-1's, the giant Catalina flying boats. No, her poor old ducks most certainly weren't wanted anymore. This antique squadron of proud planes had as much relation to the films of 1939 as did the stars of silent movies. And she had as much relation to the Navy pilots who flew in the sequences that had been filmed in Pensacola for *Wings of the Navy* as she did to Lillian Gish. She might have been hired as a stunt double for Olivia de Havilland, who played the love interest in the film, except that the Navy obviously never let a woman get near enough to a plane to do anything but blow it a kiss. No question, business was lousy, and it wasn't going to get better. Even so, she could still go flyin', even if it was an expensive habit. But necessary. So very necessary.

Whenever Freddy was overcome with anger, more anger than even this sort of gloomy stock-taking could mask for more than an hour or two, she'd jump into the Rider and flee up toward the blue horizon, until she'd had enough relief from rage so that she felt that it was safe to put her feet on solid land again.

She had somehow managed to get through the first few months of Mac's absence in the belief that he would come back tomorrow, but on one morning of one of those empty tomorrows she'd suddenly realized that he wasn't about to show up, not then, and maybe not for a long time, and she'd been immediately strangled by the anger she'd been warding off with her frenzied activities.

It was a visceral anger, almost too strong for words. *How could he do this to me?* were the only words that came into her brain, repeated over and over, like a mantra of some Eastern religion that had taken possession of her mind until she feared that she'd go mad. Just those seven words, repeated with emotions that ranged from the outright depths of self-pity to murderous hatred of the man who had abandoned her, left her alone to struggle through life without the one person she had depended on. How could he do this to me?

It was a question Freddy had not been able to ask anyone, because she couldn't admit that he had gone. He'd said that he'd loved her so much that he had to leave her . . . Whatever that meant, it wasn't good enough, she thought, raw, flayed from head to foot with the anger that never disappeared or grew less. Whatever that meant, it could *never* be good enough, and her only wish now was that he would come back to her on his knees, so that she could tell him how much he'd hurt her, how much he'd failed her, how much she hated him, and then leave him forever.

When Freddy was home alone at night, she found some relief after dinner in sipping whiskey and studying newspapers and news and aviation magazines intently, as many as she could lay her hands on, until she had lulled herself to sleep. Perhaps she would find Mac's name somewhere in one of them, she caught herself thinking much too often.

She never did see his name, but she acquired a thorough knowledge of world events. Now, of course, aviation news had become of worldwide importance and she followed with fascination the rapidly increasing development of air power in the European nations as well as in the United States. The editor of *Aviation Magazine*, on his return from a trip of observation, had ranked Germany and Russia first in the number of military planes; Italy next; Great Britain and the United States after Italy; and France at the bottom of his list. In quality he had ranked Germany and the United States first. In production, Germany first again.

In Britain, the English had started a Civil Air Guard plan the day after the Munich Agreement, and begun to subsidize pilot training for women as well as men, open to anyone between eighteen and fifty, so long as he or she could pass a medical exam. Freddy followed this experiment with interest, particularly when a storm arose in the press over the use of women pilots, who were, it seemed, to be included in everything except the fighting services of the RAF, against many loud and furious objections.

C. G. Grey, the editor of *The Aeroplane*, the English counterpart of *Aviation Magazine*, wrote an editorial that allowed Freddy to feel fury that had nothing to do with Mac.

The menace is the woman who thinks that she ought to be flying a high-speed bomber when she really has not the intelligence to scrub the floor of a hospital properly, or who wants to nose around as an Air-Raid Warden and yet can't cook her husband's dinner.

What, Freddy wondered, would the two hundred English women pilots who were already members of the Civil Air Guard, and who had been told by Captain Balfour, the Under Secretary of State for Air, that they would be used to ferry aircraft in case of a national emergency, do to Mr. C. G. Grey if they could lay their hands on him?

The problematical fate of C. G. Grey had provided her something to talk about with her mother when they'd had lunch on Freddy's nineteenth birthday, the previous January. She'd been careful over the past months not to see too much of her mother, afraid that Eve, who'd obviously been taken with Mac, would ask questions about him that she couldn't answer, but her mother had kept the conversation light and general.

In fact, every time they met, her mother had refrained from probing into her private life, Freddy reflected gratefully. She could never speak to her of her misery or her anger—her mother would probably drop dead of shock if she knew that her daughter was not a virgin, much less that she'd lived with a man—but she hated to have to lie to her as she did to Swede Castelli when he telephoned or dropped in, as he did faithfully, too faithfully for her taste, every week. He took a fatherly

319

interest in the way she was carrying on the flying school, and he was obtuse or preoccupied enough to accept the story Freddy told him about Mac's protracted stay on the East Coast. Freddy knew that Mac had no family left anywhere, but she'd dreamed up an aged mother and father in Maine, for whom he had to care, and Swede, bless his heart, believed every word of it.

Swede Castelli was the only man Freddy could talk to without putting up her guard. She had to fire a number of the flying instructors she'd hired because they'd made persistent passes at her, which had led to a constant problem of replacing them. When Mac had left, she'd stopped looking in the mirror, but apparently the emotions that were gnawing at her insides, like snapping turtles, didn't show in her face, because only the most firmly married of the men who had worked for her in the past eight months had not tried to pull a fast one. What was she supposed to do—wear a paper bag over her head?

Freddy was still wandering about in the hangar, finding a little comfort from being near the venerable, aristocratic planes she loved almost as much as Mac had loved them, when she heard the sound of a car stopping outside of the flying school office. She walked outside, blinking as she emerged into the brilliant spring light, and shaded her eyes with her hand. Swede Castelli emerged laboriously from his old sedan, ponderously taking his time. He really should watch his weight, Freddy thought, he's moving awfully slowly for an ex-stunt pilot. Well, he'll be happy to see that all her three instructors were out giving lessons. If even one of them was hanging around waiting for his student to show up, it always looked as if business were slow.

She walked toward him welcomingly, her hair so whipped by the wind that it almost covered her eyes. She leaned forward to kiss him on the cheek.

"Hello, Freddy," he said, putting an arm around her shoulder. "Nobody around but you? Place seems awful quiet." He looked around noting the busy airfield and the deserted flying school.

"Don't sound so gloomy about it, Swede. My instructors are all out teaching. Earning a buck. Wait around and you'll see some dreadful student landings, I promise you."

"You wouldn't happen to have a cup of coffee going, would you?" he asked.

"How could you run a flying school without it?" Freddy answered, thinking that Swede looked as if he needed something stronger than coffee. The heavy, balding man was so pasty-faced that she felt sudden concern for him. He seemed to have grown years older since his last visit only a week ago. Perhaps he was in bad health—certainly his normally cheerful expression was entirely absent. "Come on into my magnificent office," Freddy said with a flourish, attempting to bring back his smile, "and try out one of the new chairs."

She gave Swede a big mug of the coffee she made constantly, so that there was always a full pot ready. Students asked for it shakily before they went up and as soon as they landed, always euphoric after an hour of the learning process. Among the students, the instructors and Gavin, Freddy estimated that she gave away more coffee than she'd sold pastries at Van de Kamp. She should charge for it. That might make the school a profitable paying proposition instead of a borderline operation.

Freddy settled in another of the inexpensive but comfortable armchairs she had bought to make the office more welcoming, and looked fondly at the unusually silent man who sat busily sipping her fragrant brew. He worked steadily at the mug until it was empty, and then put it on her desk with as much delicate care as if it were fine porcelain.

"Listen, Freddy, there's something I have to talk to you about." He took out a handkerchief and mopped his forehead with an unconscious sigh. "It's about Mac."

"Can't it keep, Swede?" Freddy said coaxingly, trying to hide her feeling of impatience. She wasn't in the mood to concoct another installment of Mac's devoted filial life in Maine.

Swede Castelli seemed not to have heard Freddy's question. "It's about Mac," he repeated heavily. "I've been . . . in touch with him, Freddy."

"You couldn't have!" Her words leaped out of her mouth without an instant of thought.

"Mac's telephoned me at home every week . . . since he took off. He . . . he had to find out how you were . . . had to make sure that you were making out O.K."

"You knew all along and you didn't tell me!" She jumped up and stood before him, accusation and betrayal glaring from her eyes.

"Mac made me promise not to say anything. I swore I wouldn't. I couldn't let him down, Freddy. We're old buddies—you understand what that means. He depended on me to keep my promise and I did, Freddy. Don't think it's been easy. I hated pretending I didn't know the truth—Jesus, Freddy, I felt so bad for you having to make up all those stories, but I had to keep coming over. When Mac called me, he would have been frantic if I hadn't been able to tell him that you were all right. Oh, Freddy . . ."

"*What's wrong?*" Freddy demanded, in alarm, without knowing why she used those words. She stood over Swede threateningly.

"Wait a minute, Freddy, let me tell you in my own way. . . . Mac . . . Freddy, Mac's . . . in Canada."

"WHERE IN CANADA?" she shouted. She'd go to him. She could be with him tomorrow. If she left right away and pushed the Rider, she could be with him in hours.

"Near Ottawa, at a Canadian Air Force training base," Swede answered. Freddy whirled and started for the door. Swede got up and put a restraining arm around her. "No, Freddy, no, listen to me. There's more."

"More?" she repeated, panic shooting through her at a new, fearful note in his voice.

"Mac's dead, Freddy," Swede said painfully, tears springing into his eyes. "There was a crash . . . he spun in, Freddy . . . it was over in seconds. I got a letter from his commanding officer this morning. Mac didn't have any next of kin so he'd given them my name, just in case. The letter said that it happened while he was instructing a kid who froze at the controls. At least it's what they think caused it. That, or something went wrong with the plane. They still don't know for sure. The general said they may never know. The . . . funeral . . . was yesterday. A military funeral . . . both . . . both of them."

"Funeral," Freddy repeated. "Funeral? Mac! *Mac?* My Mac? You're lying to me, aren't you, aren't you? Please say you're lying to me, Swede. Please, please say it." Her pleading voice broke as her shock turned into comprehension. Swede Castelli clumsily put both his arms around her, as if he could protect her from his words.

"Christ, I wish I was, Freddy," she heard him say. "The guy was the only brother I ever had."

"Oh, Swede," she cried out, almost inaudible through her savage sobs, "how can I live if Mac is dead? How, Swede, how? Why would I want to?"

"Oh, Freddy, I'm so sorry. It was . . . beautiful to see the two of you together."

"*You didn't have to leave me, Mac, you didn't have to go.*"

"He was certain he did, Freddy. He always told me that he knew he'd done the only right thing," Castelli said. "He loved you so damn much, it tore him apart."

Both of them looked up as they heard the voice of one of Freddy's instructors outside the office, his question answered by a student. A plane must have landed while they were talking. Hastily, Freddy locked the door of her office.

"Shouldn't you maybe go back to be with your family, Freddy?" Swede said anxiously, as her weeping grew more severe. "Remember I met your mother? It'd be good for you to be with her."

"Swede . . . how could I leave our house?" Through her primitive, annihilating heartbreak Freddy tried her best to respond to his efforts to comfort her. "Don't you know about our house . . . such a sweet little house . . . how could I leave it? It's all I have left of him."

"I understand," he said. "But when you're ready . . . promise you'll think about it?"

"When I'm ready? I'll never be ready, Swede, never, never for the rest of my life."

"Please, Freddy, you've got to let me do something to help you."

"Would you . . . come to the house tomorrow night and tell me everything Mac said to you? Everything that happened to him in Canada? Will you come and tell me again . . . how much he loved me?"

That night, after it was dark, Freddy returned to the hangar where the great old airplanes were kept. One by one she rolled the fragile, magnificent, beloved ships outside onto an open, grassy space on the other side of the runway. Each one of them could still be flown, each one could carry a man—or a woman—far, far into the blue horizon.

When they were all grouped closely together, she half-pushed, half-piled the lightest of them onto the heavier ones. Then Freddy brought out a can of gasoline and poured it carefully over and around the ships. She circled the planes slowly, caressing their wings and their struts and their fuselages for the last time, giving each propeller a final spin, saying their legendary names out loud, names Mac had loved to speak. There was not a ship over which he had not spent hundreds of hours of labor to bring back its original glory.

At last, reluctantly but resolutely, she lit a match and touched it to the edge of the nearest plane. When the blaze was at its height, when the noble ghost squadron had almost taken off to join him, she said only three words before she turned away.

"Good flyin', Mac."

16

D O you give your chilblains names, Jane, or do you number them?" Freddy asked her roommate, as they inched reluctantly out of chilly blankets into a far colder room early in the morning of the sixth of January, 1941. She pinched a hole in the curtains, peeked out on a black, frozen, British predawn, and shut them hastily.

"Oh, names, pet, names . . . boys' names, only the ones who proposed of course." The Honorable Jane Longbridge yawned, managing to sound cheerful as she staggered to the washbasin. "Numbers would be too depressing. Does one really want to know how many one has?"

"But you've never complained," Freddy said, sleepily indignant. Chilblains, those painful raised inflammations, red, hot to the touch, itching and throbbing, which were caused by cold weather, took the form of something between a callus and a wart. They grew and flourished on her toes and fingers in winter, in spite of several pairs of wool socks she put on under her flying boots, or the lined gloves she wore whenever she went outside.

"I used to at school. Complained madly, but it never did any good. Matron only cared when they got ulcerated. That was nasty, but it got me a few weeks' excuse from games. Made it almost worth it. Hated games." Brown-haired Jane hastily splashed her face, brushed her teeth vigorously, and looked at herself approvingly in the mirror, briefly admiring, as she unabashedly did every morning, her straight hair, straight teeth and straight nose, all of which, combined with her naughtily unastonished, big brown eyes, and her wicked, easily provoked smile, made her one of the prettiest girls, as she often complacently but correctly remarked, from John o'Groat's to Land's End.

"It's sickeningly Dickensian," Freddy protested, as she took her turn at the basin.

"Chilblains?"

"Sending kids to schools where they get them. What's the point in being a baron's daughter? Didn't you tell your mother?"

"Didn't bother. Waste of time. Mother's keen on games. Her chilblains were probably points of pride." Jane set her teeth and shed her heavy pajamas, one half at a time, and hastily struggled into a set of precious prewar woolen winter underwear. Freddy slept in her own woolies, as well as in the voluminous teddy-bear cloth lining of her Sidcot boiler suit, the only way she knew to attain a body temperature on the verge of comfort in the virtually unheated bedroom of the lodging she shared with Jane. It was one of the worst winters in history. For the last month, even the German air force had had to call off the Blitz. The massive night bombing that had begun after the Luftwaffe failed to knock out the RAF in the Battle of Britain the summer before, was temporarily halted by the impenetrable weather over Britain.

Freddy had been in England for almost a year and a half, since late June of 1939, when she had wound up her life in California. With Mac's death, there no longer existed a reason for her to keep the flying school open. When she asked herself what she intended to do, only one answer seemed possible: find a way to join the cause for which he had died. The United States was neutral, and in any case there was no place for a woman pilot in any of its forces. However, there was the British Civil Air Guard, with its four thousand new recruits who wanted to learn to fly.

Mac had left Freddy everything he owned, in a will that Swede Castelli had in his possession. She sold their house and all the school training planes, including her lovely white Rider. Before she went off to Britain to volunteer, she said farewell to Eve and Paul, making peace, at last, with her father. Freddy had immediately been accepted as an instructor in the pilot-training program.

Three months later, on September first, 1939, Hitler invaded Poland, and two days later, England and France, pushed over the line they had waited years too late to draw, declared war on Germany.

On January first, 1940, a small group of highly experienced women pilots who were, like Freddy, instructors in the Civil Air Guard, had been carefully chosen to sign contracts with the Air Transport Auxiliary. The ATA was formerly an all-male civilian organization reponsible for ferrying planes throughout Britain for the RAF, flying them from the factories in which they were built, to the airfields at which they were so desperately needed.

Now, a year later, the number of women pilots in the ATA was growing, relieving more and more men for aerial combat. The women had proved that they could fly in the same highly rigorous and hostile conditions as the men: working thirteen days in a row before they were given two days off; picking up and delivering planes in weather so risky that no fighters ventured aloft; piloting without radio or any navigational aids except a compass; dodging, twisting and turning above a countryside covered by tens of thousands of barrage balloons, whose steel cables were traps for any plane, friendly as well as enemy. Over the island that was Britain, the utterly unpredictable weather could change without warning to conditions in which a pilot found himself lost within seconds; the landscape was dotted by RAF fields, protected by ack-ack guns that shot first and asked questions later, for the country was in a war where the enemy was so close that an ATA pilot about to land was never surprised to see Messerschmitts diving over the landing strip for which he was heading.

In winter the sun rose at nine o'clock and set around five, since England maintained the optimistically named "British Double Summertime," or daylight savings time, all year round during the war. It was still dark outside by the time Freddy and Jane arrived at their base in Hatfield, in the battered MG in which Jane had once terrorized the countryside. Today was an anniversary, marking a year after the first ferry trips by women pilots, and Pauline Gower, their commanding officer, had arranged a celebration party for that night.

Yesterday had been frightful—icy, snowy, foggy, rainy and cloudy, "the whole bloody lot," Jane had said good humoredly, squinting at the sky—and at Hatfield all flying had been canceled shortly after noon. Both Freddy and Jane had spent the afternoon back at their rented digs, brewing tea, napping and reveling in their rare unexpected leisure. Nevertheless, from other bases a few pilots had made the decision to take off, among them Amy Johnson—now divorced from Jim Mollison—who had joined the ATA soon after Freddy. The world-famous pilot, Freddy's heroine for so many years, had left Blackpool on the Lancashire coast, ferrying an Oxford twin-engined training plane, the same plane Freddy and Jane flew most often. Her destination was not far, Kidlington, an air force base near the Somerset coast.

Freddy and Jane hurried from the MG into the comparative warmth of the Operations Room, where they picked up the chits that told them what planes they were supposed to fly that day, if weather conditions allowed. Clutching their chits, they made for the Mess, a wooden hut which was the source of endless coffee, tea, and chat, with a dart board, a billiard table and copies of the daily newspapers. A few pilots even brought chessboards and backgammon boards to the Mess, and there was talk of a bridge school to be established in the Flight Captain's room, a school Jane and Freddy had pledged each other not to join. Jane's game of choice was darts; Freddy's was pitching cards into her cap, which she insisted required more coordination and skill than any of the others. Actually, when she was on standby, she was too keyed up to concentrate on a game of any complication.

"Oh, oh, there's trouble," Jane said the minute they walked into the Mess. Pilots were grouped together, coffee abandoned, as they talked intensely, in low voices, expressions of shock on their faces.

"What's up?" Freddy asked Helen Jones.

"It's Amy Johnson. She crashed into the Thames Estuary yesterday."

"Oh God—no!" Freddy cried.

"She was long overdue by late afternoon," Helen said. "She must have been out of fuel and lost above the clouds because she was one hundred miles beyond Kidlington. It's official now . . . they recovered her flying bag from the water. She bailed out above cloud cover and landed in the drink. She was almost rescued . . . a trawler on convoy duty saw her Oxford sink and tried to pick her up, but she disappeared under its stern."

Freddy turned away abruptly from the others and went to stand at a window. She looked out, seeing nothing, in a state of deep shock. Amy Johnson, who had survived sandstorms, monsoons and dozens of forced landings when she became the first woman to fly solo to Australia, the daredevil about whom millions had sung "Amy, Wonderful Amy," crazily courageous Amy, whose endurance knew no limits when she established a light aircraft record from London to Tokyo, dashing Amy who had set a solo round-trip record from Paris to Cape Town dressed in a Schiaparelli suit and a matching coat—it was impossible that Amy Johnson, *her* Amy, the most experienced woman pilot in England, should be the first of them to die.

"I know, Freddy," Jane said, putting an arm around her.

"When I was nine, she flew all the way to Australia in a little old Moth, and now I'm almost twenty-one and she's dead trying to fly a steady twin-engine from Blackpool to Kidlington. She was only thirty-eight. I just can't believe it. How could it happen?"

"We may never know. Freddy, come on, let's pitch cards into your hat. Winner pays for dinner," Jane said briskly.

"If she hadn't been over water . . . if it hadn't been so icy . . ."

"No *ifs*, poppet. It was up to Amy to decide if it was safe to take off yesterday. She could have stayed in Blackpool. We all have the choice at every moment we're flying. We can land whenever it looks bad and stay on the ground until it clears. You know that and she knew that. She made the decision to fly yesterday. Almost everybody else didn't. That route is well inland—we've both flown it dozens of times. She went over the top, Freddy, she went above the clouds, and got lost. Otherwise she wouldn't have been over water. We're not supposed to go over the top . . . ever. It was character as much as the weather, pet."

"Character," Freddy repeated thoughtfully.

"Doesn't every one of us fly her particular character?"

Freddy looked around at the many women in the room, her eyes pausing at Winifred Crossley, who too had been a stunt pilot; at Rosemary Rees, who had been a ballet dancer as well as an explorer of new air routes; at Gabrielle Patterson, married and a mother, who had been a flying instructor as early as 1935; at Joan Hughes, who had started flying at fifteen and was no older than she and Jane; at Margie Fairweather, daughter of Lord Runciman, whose brother was Director General of BOAC and whose husband was also an ATA pilot. They were the most splendid and honorable company of women pilots to be found anywhere in the world, and yes, each of them had her own flying character, each approached every new takeoff with a different combination of courage and caution, of competitiveness and humdrum adherence to rules, of precision and chance-taking. Which of them would have taken off from Blackpool yesterday? Quite possibly none of them . . . or one . . . or even two. Impossible to say, impossible even to guess.

She turned to Jane. "I'm beginning to understand why you were Head Girl at your awful school, games or no games."

"Are we going to pitch cards or are you going to fawn over me?"

"Let's play. From the looks of this so-called sunrise, we may not fly again today. Did I ever tell you about sunrise in California? We have them every single day, believe it or not, even in winter. Did you know England is on the same latitude as Labrador? Odd place to settle."

"One more word, and I get another roommate."

The ATA anniversary party that night was canceled. Freddy, Jane, and a few of the others gathered at their local pub in Hatfield, drank one drink to the memory of Amy Johnson, and quietly returned to their lodgings through the icy, dark streets of the blacked-out town.

On the ninth and tenth of January, 1941, Freddy and Jane's schedules gave each of them two days off, and for the first time since they had known each other Freddy was able to accept Jane's standing invitation to visit her family at their manor house in Kent. Longbridge Grange was the home of Jane's father, Lord Gerald Henry Wilmot, the fourteenth Baron Longbridge, and Jane's mother, Lady Penelope Juliet Longbridge, born a Fortescue.

Under their heavy navy greatcoats they wore their well-tailored, strict, masculine-looking uniforms: navy trousers and a navy blue jacket, known as a tunic, with two buttoned breast pockets and two large pockets, also buttoned, below the brass-buckled belt. Above their right breast pockets they wore a pair of gold wings four inches wide, embroidered in heavy gold bullion, and sewn onto the tunic. On their shoulders were the two gold stripes of a second officer, one broad and one thin. On Freddy's arm was a red, white and blue insignia that identified her as an American. Under their tunics both girls wore RAF blue shirts and black men's ties. Because of the cold they had decided to wear their slacks and their flying boots, which, strictly speaking, were never supposed to be worn anywhere but at the airdrome. Each girl had packed the navy skirt and sensible black shoes and stockings that were official dress for all times when they were not flying, and tilted her navy forage cap rakishly over her forehead.

They managed to get a ride in a sturdy Anson, one of the indispensable, workhorse taxi planes that flew ATA pilots out to pick up planes for ferrying and, once they had completed their missions, brought them back to base. Both Freddy and Jane occasionally piloted an Anson, which was big enough so that fifteen pilots carrying their parachutes could be crowded inside. The loss of a single Anson would have been a catastrophe, so the job was reserved for the most reliable pilots.

After a short hop they were dropped off at an airfield in Kent, where Jane's mother, who had been saving her gas ration for the long-planned visit, picked them up. Lady Penelope hugged her daughter and put out her hand to shake Freddy's hand, when suddenly she changed her mind and hugged Freddy as well.

"I'm so glad you're here at last, my dear. Jane has written about you incessantly. I think she's finally found a good influence," the handsome, auburn-haired woman said, with a covertly proud look at her daughter.

"Actually Jane's a good influence on *me*," Freddy protested, laughing.

"Nonsense. Impossible. We know our Jane. She's unredeemable . . . but she can be rather sweet from time to time. Now get into the car before you freeze. We don't want to be late to lunch."

She drove rapidly and expertly, pointing out the many spots where bombs had fallen on the now snow-covered fields during the worst of the Blitz. "I'm sure they weren't actually aiming at us—we're not dangerous, after all—but the house is almost directly under the flight path between London and the Channel ports. Such a nuisance . . . one of them brought down all the plaster in the drawing room . . . Of course, the tennis court was ruined by that incendiary bomb last autumn, and there's still that tiresome unexploded bomb on the road to the village. I do trust that someone will remember to come around and defuse it by the time the snow melts. Too silly. However, all the fuss does manage to remind me to make sure that the house is properly blacked out every night."

"Who's the warden, Mummy?" Jane asked.

"Really, Jane! I am, of course. I couldn't count on anyone else, could I? Your poor father can't see in the dark, try as he will, although Small, the new gardener—seventy-five if he's a day—is rather clever. He makes Molotov cocktails in his spare time, in case of invasion. We have a most impressive stockpile of them. I've told him that the invasion scare is over—it is, Jane, isn't it?—but he's too deaf to pay attention." She turned around to look at Freddy. "Jane wrote us that your parents are in London, my dear. Have they had a bad time?"

"No, not so far. Inconvenient and a bit frightening, but nothing worse than that. I went to London to see them the last time I had leave, and a house had been bombed out at the end of their street, but otherwise they're fine."

"Your father came to join General de Gaulle, I understand."

"He left Los Angeles as soon as de Gaulle broadcast from London in June of 1940, and joined the Free French here. He's working with Gustave Moutet and a group of journalists who've founded a daily newspaper called *France*. My mother's working as an ambulance driver. . . . She's on duty this weekend."

"Good for her," Lady Penelope said, careful not to ask for news of Delphine, for Jane had written that no one in the family was sure what had happened to her since Paris had been occupied. The car passed quickly through a small village and slowed down as it came to a large gate. "Well, my dears, welcome. Here we are."

Lady Penelope drove up a long, oak-bordered driveway, and stopped in front of a house that seemed to have welled up out of the snowdrifts, so closely was it married to the bare but beautifully shaped trees and still-green yew hedges with which it was surrounded. The house was half-timbered, with thick walls made from stout oak beams and creamy brick, both materials native to the countryside with its chalky soil and wooded hills. No one had ever been able to count the various levels of roof of Longbridge Grange, nor the different styles of tiled and bricked gables and the ingeniously contrived multitude of its chimneys. The many and asymmetrical windows had rows of tiny panes of glass, most of it so old that it was lavender in color. The last time Lady Penelope had had some plaster removed in the smallest pantry, the workmen had found two coins minted in 1460. Time had been strictly selective at The Grange, preserving nothing that was not indescribably pleasant to the eye.

Longbridge Grange had five wings, all built in different periods, and reflecting the fortunes of the family. In spite of its size, nothing about the marvelously rambling building suggested the classic formality of a stately home. It had always been a manor house, and always the center of a large, prosperous group of farms owned by the Longbridges, possessing an important cider mill, a large stable block, a carriage house, a dovecot, and any number of outlying barns and buildings. As Freddy entered The Grange, she felt as if she were walking into a welcoming, fragrant forest. Branches of pine trees decorated each doorway and lay on the mantles of the many fireplaces, and Christmas mistletoe still hung in the entrance hall. Dogs barked and bounced everywhere, in welcome.

Jane Longbridge was the second oldest of seven children. Her two younger brothers were away at school, but the three youngest, all girls —twins of nine, and the baby of the family, who was seven—were still at school in a nearby village. They had been kept out of school today in honor of Freddy and Jane's arrival, and they shyly shook Freddy's hand before they climbed onto Jane, almost knocking her over in rapture.

"Come along, all of you. Lunch in the kitchen," Lady Penelope interrupted, looking at her leaping offspring and animals with detachment, as if she couldn't imagine how they happened to be there at all.

"The kitchen, Mummy?" Jane said, surprised.

"It's the warmest room, darling. I've closed off most of the house and just left it to molder quietly away. When we've won the war there will be the devil's own dusting to do, but I'll worry about that when the time comes."

Jane and Freddy played with the little girls for much of the afternoon, reveling in their sweetly awed attentions. Finally, Freddy went to her room for a nap before dinner, first drawing the blackout curtains. She slept soundly for an hour, thinking gratefully as she drifted off that she had actually been almost, if not totally, warm since she'd entered The Grange. Five whole hours of comfort . . . or was it five hours and a half . . . ?

A knock on her door woke her. Jane came in wearing a bathrobe and heavy socks and bedroom slippers. "I've drawn you a bath," she said in a low, conspiratorial whisper.

"A bath?"

"A hot bath. A real bath. A prewar bath. Strictly illegal. I count on you to say nothing to anyone else. It must remain a secret, just between us."

"You mean . . ."

"It has more than three and a half inches of water in the tub," Jane announced solemnly.

"Oh, Jane, how could you?" Freddy cried. "You know you shouldn't have. It's against every regulation."

"Don't ask silly questions. Just follow me. Quietly . . . everyone's busy in other parts of the house. I don't want to hear a peep out of you."

She put her fingers to her lips and, handing Freddy a toweling robe, led the way down a corridor to the door of a large bathroom in which a vast Victorian tub mounted on brass lion's feet held pride of place. Freddy tiptoed to the tub, looked in and gasped. There must have been fully fifteen inches of water steaming in its depths. She hadn't seen a bathtub with that much water in it since war had been declared. At their digs, she and Jane were allowed, by their complaining landlady, one tepid weekly bath of the required three and a half inches. All other bathing was done bit by bit in front of the basin in their room. Here were riches!

Freddy stripped naked and quickly lowered herself into the water, finding that it came just above her waist. She took the bar of soap that Jane held out to her, lathered her hair and scrubbed and rinsed it thoroughly before she started to scour herself with a huge sponge that sat on a chair placed alongside of the tub.

"Oh God, that's good. Good, good, good! I'm going to stay in here until it gets cold. Until it freezes over. Nothing will ever get me out!"

"Is the water cooling off, pet?" Jane asked anxiously.

"Well . . . actually . . . yes. Just a bit. No, Jane, whatever you do, don't turn on the tap. It isn't fair to the others. I feel terribly guilty enough about this already. How can I ever face your mother?" Her wet hair was slicked back from a face suffused with pleasure. Her body was pink from rubbing.

"Don't be silly. Mummy still has mountains of wood." Abruptly, Jane went to the bathroom door and threw it open.

"HAPPY BIRTHDAY!" came a chorus of voices, and Jane's three little sisters marched in, each one of them carrying a steaming kettle of hot water. They were followed by Lady Penelope, smiling broadly, lugging a huge kettle from which more steam rose. They surrounded the tub and, led by Jane, sang a chorus of "Happy Birthday to You" while they ceremoniously poured more hot water into the tub. As the last line, "Happy birthday, dear Freddy, happy birthday to you," began to fade away, a male voice joined in the singing. "Stand up, stand up, stand up and show us your face," the voice rang out and all the five female Longbridges dropped their empty kettles with a clatter and shouted, "Tony!" forgetting their guest as they wrapped themselves around their older brother.

Cowering under the water, almost bent in half, Freddy watched the scene, shaking with giggles. Had Jane planned this too? Could anything so typically Jane be an accident?

"Tony, come over here and say hello," Jane commanded. "Second Officer Marie-Frédérique de Lancel, may I present my brother, Squadron Leader the Honorable Antony Wilmot Alistair Longbridge. Freddy, Tony."

"You're absolutely sure?" Freddy asked her friend suspiciously, her arms securely tucked over her breasts.

"Oh, quite. I remember him well," Jane said.

"Good evening, Squadron Leader Longbridge." Freddy managed to nod graciously, without lifting her head.

"Good evening, Second Officer. Out of uniform, I see."

"On leave, sir."

"They always say that."

"I assure you, sir, it's true."

"Can you prove it?"

"No."

"Then I shall have to take your word."

"Thank you, sire."

"No need to go so far. A simple 'sir' will do. At ease."

"Antony, come out of the bathroom this minute!" Lady Penelope said. "Let Freddy finish her bath in peace."

"But it's her birthday, Mum, don't you think she wants company? I'll just sit down here and chat with her. Jane, you may leave us. Kiddies, go get the second officer more hot water."

"Antony, you try my patience," his mother said warningly.

"Oh, all right, me old Mum, since you insist," he said reluctantly, not moving away from the edge of the tub. "You do know there's a war on, don't you? Old standards must make way for new, and all that. Now, Mum, no need to pinch me, damn it. I'm coming."

Muttering what sounded like Druid incantations, Jane rummaged through her closet, picking through her rows of prewar evening dresses.

"I didn't think people still dressed for dinner," Freddy said as she watched.

"Did you imagine that you were going to be allowed to eat your birthday dinner in your uniform?"

"Since my public bathing exhibition, I don't know what I thought . . . or what to expect." Freddy brushed her hair, trying to make it lie down, but today, because of the snapping cold air it had more of a mind of its own than usual, and although she kept it cut to standard ATA length, so that it cleared her uniform collar, she could hear it crackle and feel it sparking up so vigorously that it tickled the backs of her hands.

"Such luck, Tony showing up," Jane chortled. "I think he rather liked you."

"I hope that with all that steam he couldn't really see me. I certainly couldn't look at him."

"Are all Americans so proper?"

"Are all Brits so fresh?"

"Tony? He's absolutely harmless," Jane replied, over her shoulder, with the judicious air of a younger sister's appraisal of her twenty-five-year-old brother. "He didn't climb in with you, did he? Now that might have been fresh, or impudent, possibly rude—it might even have indicated a lack of basic good manners. He was just hoping to make a new friend. Our Tony's a gregarious chap, good-hearted, salt of the earth. He'll give you no trouble, poppet. Unless you're looking for it . . . or unless you're a German pilot stooging around upstairs in a Messerschmitt or a Junkers 88, in which case you have indeed found trouble, serious trouble. Ah-ha! Here it is. I was wondering where it had got to."

Jane emerged from the closet holding up a hanger on which was suspended a dress of cloth of silver, a strapless dress that splintered the light in the room with darting arrows of brightness. It had a skirt so full that it looked as if it could take off and waltz by itself. Its waistline was marked by a wide black velvet sash with a bow on one side, from which streamers of velvet almost touched the ground. On another hanger there was a black velvet wrap in the form of a huge draped bow, bordered with silver. "Festive enough, I think," Jane said, holding out the hangers, "and, should you feel chilly, there's the wrap. Try this on and see if it fits."

"It will, it will! Nothing will stop me from wearing that dress." Freddy was breathless with a sense of almost incommunicable delight. Everything that had happened since she had walked into Longbridge Grange seemed like a picnic on the grass, impromptu, spur-of-the-moment, and so gloriously inappropriate to the realities of England at war. She felt giddy, indecently excited, inadmissibly pleased with herself. Even her chilblains didn't hurt.

"Shoes!" Jane said, slapping her forehead, and darted back into the closet, returning with silver shoes and a handful of filmy chiffon underthings. "What else have I forgotten?"

"No tiara?"

"Not absolutely necessary for dinner. Although . . . although . . ."

"I was kidding."

"They're in a vault anyway. No tiaras for the duration. Pity, that . . . We'd better dress. Papa should be home by now, and if he doesn't get his drink before dinner he's apt to grumble. Shout if you need any help. Otherwise, downstairs in half an hour?"

"Oh yes. Thank you for finding that dress, Jane."

"I was proposed to five times in it . . . a lucky dress . . . but, of course, not for them, poor things. I *do* feel sorry for them."

"That was their hard luck," Freddy said, whirling around and around, watching the skirt of the silver dress billow. "Screw them, Jane."

"I did, poppet, I did."

By the time Freddy had managed to dress herself in the unfamiliar garments, put on her lipstick and make a fruitless attempt to tame her shiningly clean red hair, which foamed back from her face in celebratory disorder, the adult Longbridges had just gathered in the library in front of a large fire, all of them talking quickly and, it seemed, simultaneously, while Lord Gerald, armed with a silver cocktail shaker, had started to make martinis.

Freddy hesitated just outside the door, unseen, feeling a confusing combination of emotions. They were a family, she was an outsider, yet she had been welcomed today as she had never been welcomed before by any group of strangers. She felt that she knew Jane better than she'd ever known her own sister, but she'd never met Jane's father and she'd only glimpsed Tony as a looming figure in an RAF uniform. She felt unquestionably shy—an emotion she hadn't felt for years—but she couldn't feel *timid*, not in this dress of sublime theatricality that, as she had known it would, fit her perfectly. This was her twenty-first birthday. She was the guest of honor. And, dear Lord, they were all waiting for her.

That thought—Jane's father was shaking the gin and vermouth and she could tell from the sound alone that in a second he'd be ready to pour—propelled her into the room in one long, fluid step. Then she stopped, shyness again gaining the upper hand, because all four people in the room had stopped talking and had turned to look at her. There was a moment of utter, stunned silence that Freddy didn't realize was an ultimate tribute to her loveliness, and then Lord Gerald Longbridge put down the cocktail shaker and advanced toward her.

"Happy birthday, Miss de Lancel," he said, taking both of her hands in his and looking, startled, into the victorious blue of her untamable eyes. "My son tells me that I missed the high spot of the day, indeed of the year. I call that downright unfair. I don't know how you're ever going to get on my good side after such wretched treatment. I suppose I'm going to have to make an exception for you, or, better yet, you could repeat the performance tomorrow, but give me fair warning so I won't be left out again. I wonder if, by any chance, you happen to drink martinis?"

"Yes, please, Lord Gerald. And will you call me Freddy?" she laughed, shyness banished by the gray-haired, handsome charmer whose eyes were as wicked as Jane's.

"Freddy it is," he replied, offering her his arm. "Now come over to the fire. I must pour those drinks before they get watery." He led her across the large, dim, high-ceilinged room to Jane, far from demure in sweeping scarlet satin, and Lady Penelope, magnificent in brown velvet and old-ivory lace. Tony had retreated, rapidly and unnoticed by the women, to the ornament-frosted Christmas tree in the corner, and pretended to fiddle with a string of lights, so that he could watch Freddy before she greeted him.

From the moment she entered the room, it had seemed to him that she walked within a nimbus of light. There was something almost celestial in her sudden, silent, silver apparition in the doorway, something that made him think of the first, always surprising, always somehow dangerous, always heart-stabbing glimpse of the evening star. Could she be the larky, joky seal of a girl in the tub? Was metamorphosis so easy? Would she turn into a glade of flowering trees before dinner was over?

"Tony, give me a hand," his father asked. "Take Freddy a martini, would you?"

As he carried the chilled glass over to the fireplace, Squadron Leader Antony Longbridge almost tripped over his feet on a rug that had been in the same place for five generations before he'd been born. Freddy looked up. "Good evening again, Squadron Leader," she said. "Out of uniform, I see."

"Oh, this." He looked down at his dinner jacket. "I thought . . . well, a special occasion . . . my tunic needed pressing . . . this seemed, well, more comfortable . . . after all, at home . . . on leave . . ."

"They always manage to have an excuse, don't they, Jane?" Freddy shook her head disparagingly.

"Shocking. No morale, these RAF types. Dress like billy goats. Think spit and polish is for everybody else. He probably didn't even shave before dinner," Jane agreed.

Freddy stopped herself from lifting her hand to find out. She'd have known Tony had to be English if she'd so much as caught a split-second glance at him in Sumatra or Antarctica, she thought, as she accepted her drink. He had that unmistakable fine, clean facial structure, that unmuddled sweep of bone, that clean, long, almost knifelike purposefulness that permitted no neutrality of feature. His forehead was high and his plain brown hair, parted sternly on the side, swept straight backward with a slight wave. His eyes were pale, pale blue under light brows, his nose as pointed and distinct as a Crusader's, his mouth wide, firm and thin, his cheeks flat and ruddy, his ears big and set close to his head. There was nothing relaxed, nothing frivolous to his lean, imposing head. Tony was big-boned, yet he seemed, for all his height, almost slender. He bore himself with the habit of authority and the presence of command. No British overbreeding here, Freddy decided, and smiled at him as she had smiled at no man in almost three years.

"I did manage to shave," Tony said, ignoring his sister, "although the water was not as hot as it might have been."

"I'll take your word for it," Freddy replied lightly, and, inspired by the most totally calculated flirtatious move of her life, turned away from him so that she could ask Lady Penelope a question about the provenance of her lace.

———

Dinner, in a room warmed by two huge fireplaces, was served by an elderly woman assisted by a fourteen-year-old boy, both of whom lived in the nearby village and were still available to assist the cook on special occasions. This odd assortment of domestic help was the only reminder, throughout the blithe and playful meal, that England was at war. Everyone at the table blessed the crushing freeze that had brought hostilities to a temporary halt, but no one mentioned the weather, as if to notice it would be to break the spell.

If the Wright Brothers had been strangled in their cradles, if the descendants of George III still reigned over the New World and the descendants of Louis XIV held sway over France, it would have made no difference to the conversation around that civilized, candlelit board. But if champagne grapes were no longer growing in Champagne, if Mozart and Gershwin had never lived, if horses were not bred to swiftness and strength, if Bloomsbury had never bloomed, or Fred Astaire not bought his first pair of tap shoes, they would have had to find other things to talk about.

As the leisurely meal ended, Lord Gerald disappeared into the kitchen and returned with a Jeroboam of Dom Perignon. He opened the bottle almost as expertly as Freddy remembered her grandfather doing, and served them all, with Tony's help.

"This is a very special toast," he said. "Today Miss Marie-Frédérique de Lancel—Freddy to her friends—has reached a most interesting age. Alexander Pope wrote of 'the brisk minor' who 'pants for twenty-one' . . . Samuel Johnson spoke of 'towering in the confidence of twenty-one' . . . Thackeray wrote of 'the brave days when I was twenty-one.' Everyone else in this room is past that magical age, perhaps by only a few months, like you, Jane, or by many years, like me, but no matter. The important thing is that Freddy need no longer pant for twenty-one —she is living in brave days, and she deserves all the joy of them. May the joy be great and may it grow with every year that passes. To Freddy!"

Freddy sat blushing while they all drank her health. Her blush deepened when Lady Penelope rang the bell and the young boy, who had obviously been just behind the kitchen door, walked out with several gaily wrapped boxes and placed them in front of her.

"Oh no," she protested. "You've all been so good to me already. That fantastic bath was my present."

"Nonsense, my dear. These are just improvised—we couldn't get to the stores, but you have to have souvenirs of such an important occasion," Lady Penelope said.

"Go on, Freddy, open them," Jane echoed eagerly.

Lady Penelope's present was a thick, soft, sky-blue turtleneck sweater that she'd knitted herself and that only Jane knew had been intended for her daughter. Lord Gerald had contributed a monogrammed silver flask that he always took with him when he hunted, and a bottle of precious malt whiskey to fill it. "Carry it at all times," he explained, "in case of shipwreck or being charged by a rogue elephant." Jane herself had found, in her Ali Baba closet, a black chiffon and lace nightgown she had decided was too divinely indecent to be worn except for a special occasion, which had inexplicably failed to present itself before she joined up. "Believe it or not, pet, you'll find this will come in handy, now that you're old enough," she whispered to Freddy.

Freddy was wise enough not to dare to remember the last time she had been so happy.

It was hours after midnight before she finally found herself in bed. Officially, it was no longer her birthday, but a gala spirit still fizzed like wine in her blood, and Freddy was far too keyed up to sleep. Nor did she want to. This jubilation of emotion was too welcome to allow it to taper off into mere dreams. She lay under the covers with her eyes wide open in the darkness of the room, wearing her black chiffon nightgown, the blue sweater and a pair of woolen socks, smiling up at the unseen ceiling.

A light tap sounded on her door. Jane, she thought, wanting a postmortem chat about the evening. "Come in," Freddy called, and the door opened to reveal Tony, carrying a candle in a short candlestick. By its flickering light Freddy could see that he was still dressed in the trousers and shirt of his dinner clothes, but a cardigan had replaced his jacket. He didn't enter the room, but stood in the doorway.

"I brought you a birthday present," he said. "I didn't know it was going to be your birthday today, and I didn't know you were going to be here, so I wasn't prepared at dinner . . . perhaps you'd like it?"

"Could it wait until tomorrow morning?" Freddy suggested.

"It's a strictly nighttime present." He held out an oblong object tied up in many ribbons with Christmas tree ornaments attached here and there, so that there was no way to guess what it was. "No good in the morning."

"Then I guess I'd better have it now."

"That's what I thought . . . much better right away." He walked over to her bed and put the sparkling object into Freddy's hands. It was very warm and it moved when she touched it.

339

"My God . . ." she gasped. "What . . . ?"

"It's my hot-water bottle," he explained, pleased with her surprise. "I filled it two minutes ago. It was the wrapping that took a long time."

"Oh, Tony . . . not your very own hot-water bottle? I can't possibly deprive you of it."

"I do have a strong sentimental attachment to the thing . . . we've been together through many long cold nights . . . but now it wants to belong to you. I'll have to find another one and tame it . . . shouldn't be too hard to do. They generally come when you whistle. Please keep it."

"If you're sure—I'd love it. And I'll think of you every night when I fill it. Now I'm going to sleep. Good night, Tony."

"Good night, Freddy," he said, taking a chair, placing it next to her bed, putting the candle on the floor and sitting down. "There was just one other thing . . . since you're not actually asleep yet . . . if I might have a word with you . . ."

"*Only* a word," she said, pulling the clumsy wrappings from the hot-water bottle and putting it next to her, under the blankets she pulled tightly up under her chin.

"You see, I've just been transferred, made commander of a new squadron, of a bunch of chaps I've never met before, chaps . . . well, I thought you could explain how I should get along with these chaps."

"Explain to an RAF commander how he can 'get along' with his pilots? Ha! Good night, Tony."

"They're Yanks, the Eagle Squadron, been over here since September, but they haven't seen much action yet . . . there was nobody to train these glamour boys during the Battle of Britain . . . they've been standing by since the bad weather started, and their squadron commander's gone sick . . . anyway, these blighters are my squadron now and I thought that you, being a Yank, more or less, could advise me how to get off on the right foot. I'm completely cheesed as how to approach them. I feel rather dim about it . . . a bunch of foreign types, these chaps, you can understand why I need help."

"Just call them 'guys' instead of 'chaps' or 'blighters' or 'glamour boys' or 'foreign types' and you'll do fine. Good night, Tony."

"Guys? That seems awfully rude. You're sure, Freddy?"

"Guys. Or 'fellows,' or 'boys,' or gang, as in 'hey, gang, let's put on a show'—that should be enough linguistic adaptation. For everything else, count on them to pick up RAF slang or teach you theirs. Good night, Tony."

"I'm very grateful, Freddy. You've made me feel a lot more secure."

340

He got up from his chair and sat on the edge of her bed. "Awfully good of you to take the time, Freddy."

"Always glad to help. Good night, Tony."

"Good night, Freddy," he said as he leaned over and kissed her full on her laughing mouth. "Oh, Freddy, you darling, beautiful Freddy, we'd better try that again, I believe," he murmured before he took her in his arms and kissed her over and over, both of them dangerously athirst for each other's closeness, each of them filled with an imperative impulse to touch, to hold, to grasp, that had been inevitable since Freddy had entered the library earlier that night.

They were as surprised by the long-pent-up explosion of kisses as if they hadn't been marvelously inescapable, a supreme necessity, postponed to the point of pain. Tony groaned out loud, transported by felicity, as he lay on top of the blankets and wrapped his arms around Freddy's sweater so that he could hold her pressed to his chest. For long, delicious minutes they surrendered to the rapturous discoveries of wordless kissing, separated by so many layers of wool that it might have been a bundling board, only able to catch glimpses of each other by the small light of the candle on the floor.

"Tony . . . are you comfortable?" Freddy whispered at last.

"Not frightfully . . ."

"You could . . . well, take off your shoes."

"They're off."

"Your sweater . . . your shirt . . . your trousers . . ."

"But then I'd freeze."

"I'll keep you warm."

"You're sure? I couldn't . . . I shouldn't . . . oh, darling, if I get into this bed . . ."

"Are you positive you're a pilot?" she asked artfully, finally understanding that he was too much of a gentleman to make love to her under his own roof without unmistakable encouragement.

"Quite positive."

"Then stop dithering around like a deadbeat," she said, using the RAF term for non-flying personnel.

As she spoke, the candle that Tony had put on the floor went out, plunging them into total blackness. "Blast!" Tony muttered as he groped for it. His movement was so eager that he heard the candlestick fly to a far corner of the room. He tried to find another candle on Freddy's night table and only succeeded in toppling over the lamp by her bed, which fell with a loud crash and the sound of broken glass. "Oh shit," he muttered, standing up carefully and ripping off his clothes as quickly as possible, letting them fall to the floor. Naked, he jumped hastily into Freddy's bed and reached out for her.

"OUCH!" she yelped as their foreheads cracked together loudly.

"Did that hurt?" he asked anxiously.

"Damn right it did—what about you?"

"I think I broke my nose. Here, feel it—what do you think—no, damn it, that's my ear."

"I don't want to feel your nose, I might put out your eye," Freddy protested.

"Don't you have any night vision?" he grumbled, trying to pull off her sweater.

"You're tearing my nightgown! Watch it! Oh, you brute, let go of me! You ripped a shoulder strap. And take your knee out of my stomach."

"I think that's my elbow."

"What are you doing down there? Come back up here right away! You're too tall . . ."

"Don't you have a match?" Tony begged, his neck caught under Freddy's armpit. She crumpled with laughter.

"Tony! Lie still! I know where I am! I'll take my clothes off, and if you don't move for a minute I'll feel around and sort you out."

"O.K." He lay motionless as she pulled her sweater off over her head and slithered out of her nightgown and pushed off her socks, listening to the sounds each piece of clothing made as she tossed them aside. Then he submitted to her questioning, warmly triumphant hands as he breathed the air in the fragrant cave under the blankets.

"Good lord, Squadron Leader, what have we here? Oh, it's the hot water bottle—for a minute I was worried—now what could *this* be?"

"Don't—touch—that—yet."

"Why not?" Freddy asked, all innocence. "It feels . . . friendly."

"Let—it—go," he implored.

"Why? Don't you know there's a war on? Waste not, want not." She flung one long leg over his hip in a prodigal, irresistible movement.

"What do you know?" Freddy whispered. "I happen to have just the place for it."

There was only broken sleep for Freddy or Tony that midwinter night, as they dozed off together to wake and discover that their need had grown again. They found all the warmest and most private places of each other's bodies, a pair of patient, dedicated explorers with fingertips and tongues and nostrils for eyes. They murmured bits of praise

342

and gratitude to each other and fell asleep again, waking disoriented, until they had touched enough to establish new boundaries to cross, new rules to break. Their last sleep seemed to Tony to have lasted a long time, and he forced himself to get out of bed and pull the blackout curtains aside an inch. He jumped back from the window and dove under the blankets.

"Blast!"

"What's wrong?" Freddy asked, alarmed.

"The kids . . . they're all right outside . . . they've just finished making a snowman under your window, and it wasn't there yesterday. Christ knows what time it is."

"Look at your watch, darling."

"I left it in my room last night."

"Well, they'll just think we slept late."

"Not Jane," he said with sure knowledge.

"I don't care," Freddy declared. "Kiss me, you fool."

"I want them all to know! I'm going to tell them!" he said exultantly.

"No! Don't you dare!"

"What's your parents' address in London?" Tony demanded.

"What are you going to do, ring them up and tell them you've just spent the night with me?" Freddy asked, suddenly alarmed. He seemed capable of anything.

"I'll be there next week. I want to go and see your father."

"Why on earth . . . ?"

"To inform him of my intentions, of course. To ask his permission," Tony said with as much dignity as anyone in his rumpled, sticky condition could muster.

"My God," Freddy said softly, visualizing the scene. "I don't think that's a good idea . . . it might . . . startle him."

"But I intend to marry you. I mean, you're aware of that, I assume. So I have to talk to him."

"Don't you have to talk to me first?"

"I will. All in good time. But first, surely, I have to present myself. Will he mind dreadfully that I don't speak much French?"

"No," giggled Freddy, "I shouldn't think so. You really mean to . . . ask for permission to . . . ah . . . pursue me?"

"Certainly. Unless you object."

"Not strenuously, no. I don't have the strength."

"So I'll go see him, all right?"

"Now that I think about it . . . he does deserve a nice surprise after all these years."

"What does that mean, Freddy, darling?"

"Perhaps one day I'll tell you. Or perhaps I won't."

"One day you'll tell me everything," he said in a confident tone.

"Only after a long and persistent courtship. And possibly not even then. I'm afraid that recent events, Antony, may have led you to take me for granted."

"Oh, Freddy, I do adore you—absolutely and forever. Do you love me?"

"A little."

"Not more than that?"

"Much more than that."

"How much more?" he demanded greedily.

"I'd tell you . . . but the hot-water bottle's leaking."

17

DELPHINE stood dazed in the doorway of the apartment on the Boulevard Saint-Germain, listening to Armand's footsteps as he descended the stairs. A minute ago she had been encircled by his arms, still almost protected, still half-shielded by the bulwark of his love, even as the truth of his departure crept toward her faltering heart. Now she was truly alone, for in the instant of leaving, he had become just one among millions of Frenchmen who had left their homes for an unforeseeable period, ordered to rejoin their military units in the general mobilization of September second, 1939. For a few desolate, disbelieving hours, too sad to weep, she wandered numbly about the apartment, picking out melodies on the piano, and huddled under the plaid coverlet, trying, without success, to pretend that at any moment that she would hear him climbing back up the stairs, hear his key in the lock, see him enter the room.

The moment Armand left, Delphine's ability to fend off reality vanished. For many months it had sustained her, a balancing act, as reliable as if she had spent her life as a performer on the high wire. However, her equilibrium had depended on his presence, for she had created it to fend off a day she had refused to believe would come.

Now, her sense of self-preservation came to her rescue and Delphine recognized that it was time for her to return to her little fortress on the Villa Mozart, time to take stock of the new situation, amid whatever weapons of possession and position she had amassed in the years before she met the only man she ever loved.

The first thing she did, after she had locked her bedroom door in her pink and turquoise Victorian house, was to go to her desk, unlock the drawer and open her strongbox. There, amid other documents and the many velvet cases that held her collection of jewels, lay her blue French passport and her green-covered American passport. Years earlier, when it became apparent that their stay in Los Angeles was to be a long one, Paul de Lancel had taken the steps to ensure that both his daughters would have dual French and American citizenship. Although they had been born French, of French parents, they had always lived outside of France, and as a diplomat, he had never underestimated the power of an American passport.

She had a decision to make, Delphine understood, as she balanced her two passports on her palms. She could leave Europe, as most Americans in Paris were hurrying to do, even as she sat there, and go home to neutral America. Within a short time, perhaps in less than two weeks, she would find herself back in Los Angeles. She would stay at the Beverly Hills Hotel—she could call and reserve a suite just by picking up the phone on her desk. She played with the idea for a moment, clearly visualizing herself ordering a Cobb salad at the Hollywood Brown Derby, lunching with an agent, discussing a choice of movie scripts. Nothing about the scene was in any way implausible or the product of wishful thinking. On the contrary, every detail was practical, feasible, attainable, needing only a visit to a ticket office to make it come true. Yet she rejected this vision of the future with every one of her deepest emotions, even as she saw it so clearly in her mind's eye.

What was her alternative if she didn't buy that steamship ticket? The French film industry had shut down tight, like most civilian businesses, on the day of the mobilization. Actors, technicians and crews had all disappeared, just like Armand. Twenty films in the middle of production had been closed down. She had no job, no one depended on her, and she had no useful function in a country at war.

Yet she simply could not leave. Armand Sadowski was somewhere near her, his feet planted on the same French soil as hers, breathing the same French air she breathed. For the moment there was no way to know *exactly* where any soldier was, but surely things would soon settle down. At any moment he might be able to telephone her from his barracks, assuming he was in a barracks and not a trench. He might even get leave in two or three months, since, so far at least, there had been no active fighting anywhere. Any day now, she expected to receive Armand's first letter—he had promised to write as often as he could. As long as she remained exactly where she was, as long as she stayed put, unmoving, unmovable, right here in Paris, they were linked, they shared their future. How then could she even consider putting six thousand miles between them?

Delphine put the passports back into the strongbox with a sense of relief. There really had not been any decision to consider, after all.

During that winter of 1940, the *drôle de guerre* or the "Phony War" in which no French army moved, and even the RAF dropped only leaflets, Armand Sadowski remained in his army unit on the north-western Maginot Line. In April the Germans invaded Norway and Denmark. On the tenth of May, Hitler ended the "Phony War" by attacking nonbelligerent Holland, Belgium and Luxembourg on his way to conquer France. The French army, disintegrating and demoralized, fought the advancing enemy alongside English troops. Within two weeks, both allies were in full retreat toward the beaches of Dunkirk.

The miracle of the evacuation of Dunkirk, during May, rescued most of the British forces to fight another day, but the French found themselves defeated on the shores of their homeland, cut off, with no possible retreat except into the waters of the English Channel. Armand Sadowski, with hundreds of thousands of other Frenchmen, found himself a prisoner of war. Within days he was sent to work in an armaments factory in Germany.

During the battle of Dunkirk, Delphine stayed on, waiting for news. She continued to wait during the occupation of Paris; she waited through the day in June when an armistice was signed between France and Germany and what remained of the French army on French soil was demobilized; she waited, steadfast and stubborn, through all the chaos of July and August. Late in September she was rewarded. A postcard arrived from somewhere in Germany, which told her that Armand was alive, and had enough to eat.

Now that Germany was no longer at war with France, it became important to avoid civilian unrest in occupied France. Prisoners of war were allowed to write postcards home every two weeks. Delphine soon understood, as did every French citizen who received these postcards, that they were merely to be taken as evidence that the prisoner was alive and could still hold a pencil, but she, like so many thousands of other women, counted every day that passed between the postcards that arrived with diabolical irregularity.

Now, in the fall of 1941, there were nineteen postcards in all in the priceless bundle that Delphine kept in her strongbox. In June of 1941, four months earlier, the world of French filmmaking had come back to life, as thirty-five new films started to be produced in less than four months, under an organization called COIC, which had the unified support of the industry in its dealings both with the Vichy government of France and the German occupiers.

Delphine saw all too clearly that there no longer were any Jews to be found working in the cinema, but the awakening of the film industry coincided with negotiations that resulted in the return of a number of prisoners of war. Even if Armand couldn't work as a director until the

Germans were defeated, she told herself, there was now the possibility that he would be sent back to France. This hope was enough for her to live on.

The strongest, best financed and most active producing company in France was a new company called Continental. Such major directors as Marcel Carné, Georges Lacombe, Henri Decoin and Christian-Jaque; such top stars as Pierre Fresnay, Danielle Darrieux, Jean-Louis Barrault, Louis Jourdan, Fernandel, Michel Simon and Edwige Feuillère had all signed contracts with Continental. Now Delphine de Lancel also signed, as ignorant or as apolitical as all the others, who neither knew nor cared that Continental was entirely controlled by Germans, and that its head, the autocratic Alfred Greven, who oversaw all the activities of the company, reported directly to Goebbels and was a close personal friend of Goering.

Zany, lighthearted mysteries and fast-paced, sophisticated comedies were favorites with Continental, made to replace the American films that had proved so successful before they were banned. Continental also produced police films, written by Georges Simenon about his immortal Inspector Maigret, as well as elaborate and painstakingly made classics adapted from Zola and Balzac.

In the grand old tradition of filmmakers everywhere, Continental produced the movies the audience wanted to see, the wartime equivalent of the films Hollywood had made during the Depression, when movies about the rich had been so popular. In Continental's films there was no pro-German propaganda, since the war had never happened; everyone had more than enough to eat, tobacco was not rationed, alcohol was plentiful, no one was ever cold, and German was never spoken. The time frame of most of their product was an idealized mid-1930s, in a France inhabited solely by the French.

Delphine was grateful for the requirement to go back to work, the obligation to keep busy that allowed her so blessedly little time in which to think. She threw herself into a wildly popular series copied from *The Thin Man.* She played a character named Mila-Malou, the girl Friday of one Inspector Wens, played by the great actor Pierre Fresnay. Delphine, who had never truly envied another woman, envied lighthearted, silly, frivolous Mila-Malou. The madcap girl Friday reminded her of herself, only three years ago.

When Bruno's elite tank corps, which had seen no action, was demobilized after the Armistice, he returned to Paris as quickly as possible. He took no comfort in having been right about the outcome of the war—the problem was how to make his future, which he did not doubt for a minute would be lived under the Thousand Year Reich, as pleasant as possible. Of course, he reflected, a truly clever man, who didn't mind being bored, would have settled in Switzerland years ago, but there was no use regretting that missed opportunity. La Banque Duvivier Frères had not reopened its doors, and in the monumental confusion of the early post-Armistice days, Bruno could not foresee the future of any private bank.

What, he asked himself, would any sensible Frenchman do in such circumstances? What did every Frenchman and Frenchwoman know was the best place to live during an upheaval of the political order? Where was the natural haven in which to remain until matters sorted themselves out and it was safe to return to normal life? Where was there always something to eat and something to sell? On the family farm, if one had a farm, or at the family château, if one had a château. *Land.* It was the only thing that mattered in the end, after all, he thought as he made his way to Champagne.

By the time Bruno arrived at Valmont, a Führer of Champagne had already been appointed by the occupation authorities: Herr Klaebisch, a member of a prominent Rhineland winemaking family. When Vicomte Jean-Luc de Lancel told his grandson that Klaebisch's office in Rheims had ordered that between three and four hundred thousand bottles of champagne must be sent by the province to the German armed forces each week, Bruno merely shrugged. It was only to be expected, he thought, and certainly indicated that the Germans had a large stake in continuing to keep the people of Champagne productive, and the vineyard owners in business. He resolved to learn everything he could about a business that had never before interested him. The fortunes of war, he told himself, as he set his mind to mastering viniculture, must, of necessity, include the good as well as the bad.

Within a year, Bruno, always keeping in mind that the Wehrmacht was his biggest customer, had managed to learn an impressive amount about the making of champagne. He toured the Lancel vineyards vigilantly, mounted on a fine horse for which he never lacked fodder. Nor, as he had foreseen, did he ever go hungry. Even before the invasion of May, Anette de Lancel, remembering the Great War, had given orders to turn the rich soil of her rose garden into a vegetable garden, and several of the older servants were entrusted with keeping chickens, rabbits, pigs, a bull and several cows in outbuildings erected in hidden clearings of the small forest that belonged to the château. The domestics at Valmont attacked these tasks with zeal, for they knew that the

Vicomtesse would not let them suffer hunger, even if they couldn't look forward to the kitchen feasts of prewar days.

Jean-Luc's invaluable triumvirate of cellarmen, the Martin cousins, were all well over the age of automatic mobilization. Because they were essential in their specialized jobs, they had been allowed to remain on the land. Twice a year, many of the other skilled workers in the vineyards, who had been taken prisoner when the enemy entered France through Champagne, and were now working in Germany, were sent home for the vital pruning of the vines in March and the gathering of the harvest in September. Nevertheless, like all the other wine producers, the House of Lancel now relied on a sadly depleted labor force, and, as in the Great War, the women and children and old men of Champagne became workers in the fields. Under Bruno's watchful eye, these strong peasants, highly motivated and loyal to the Lancels, managed to keep the vineyards productive. The old Vicomte had grown infirm overnight, with the outbreak of war. They looked to Bruno to replace him, and did not question his orders.

Why, Bruno asked himself as he rode about on his tours of inspection, should he be so stupid as to assume that the German character was monolithic? Surely human nature, in all its fascinating variations, operated amid the ranks of the victors as it had among the rich of Paris when he had entered the world of banking. True, his own personal currency had been devalued; no longer did his title and his family command instant respect, no longer was his acceptance of an invitation enough to bring him a social advantage that could be turned to a business end.

Yet, was it not possible that among the conquerors there were men who would respond to being treated without the covert hostility of most of the population? They would be suspicious of any attitude that smacked of over-friendliness from a Lancel, or indeed from any Frenchman, but surely *civility* . . . merely civility, purely civility . . . might be the opening wedge that would lead him to some . . . opportunity. There had to exist an opportunity, he told himself, an opportunity that it was still too soon to envision clearly. There were always opportunities for a man who was on the alert for them, in wartime as well as in peacetime, and now, in this time of Armistice, in this ambiguous, unsettled period, there should be more opportunities than ever. France had lost the war, but Bruno did not intend to lose the Armistice.

The Führer of Champagne's office sent out regular inspectors, in their shiny black Citroëns and their well-polished jackboots, to make sure that the champagne firms were doing everything necessary to meet their quotas. The mighty Luftwaffe and the mighty navy had a priority on a constant supply of champagne—as well as a mighty thirst—and it was well known that the wily Champenois had to be closely watched. These inspectors, therefore, were frequently men who had been in the winegrowing business themselves, for it only made sense to send men who could tell the difference between a bunch of properly tended Pinot Meunier grapes and a turnip.

How, Bruno brooded, did one show civility to one's conqueror without falling into servility? You could hardly invite a man to taste a particularly fine glass of a wine that belongs, to all intents, to him. You could be polite, yes, but politeness had little value when a lack of politeness could cost you your life.

But could you not, without arousing suspicion, reasonably ask *advice* of these experienced winemakers, especially when you were not a Champenois yourself, when you had not been bred to the soil? And in asking advice, you could, even as you did so, convey the sense that you were confiding your own personal problems as if to—not a friend, no, perhaps not that, perhaps never that—but to an equal. How many men, he asked himself as he looked at his trust-inspiring features in the mirror as he shaved, did not enjoy giving advice? How many men did not take some hidden pleasure in being treated as an equal by an aristocrat, even a vanquished aristocrat?

Within a surprisingly short amount of time, it became known by certain of the major representatives of the Führer of Champagne's office in Rheims that young Lancel, out at Valmont, was understandably ignorant about certain fundamentals of the culture of the vine. He was, so he had explained as he accompanied them on their inspections, holding down his position of responsibility only because his grandfather was too old to properly run the business, certainly too old to patrol the vineyards on horseback as tirelessly as he himself did.

A Paris banker stuck here—well, they certainly didn't feel sorry for him; they were stuck in Champagne themselves—but, on the other hand, he was not as difficult to deal with as were so many of the others, not by a long shot. What's more, Lancel was smart enough to ask for advice when he needed it, which was often, and not too stiff-necked to take it and use it. If more of the French were like Lancel, their own jobs would be made considerably easier. And, come to think of it, more pleasant. They didn't enjoy being away from their homes and families, they didn't enjoy living with the infernal paperwork from Berlin, with the pressure to supply the quotas of wine, or with the studied invisibility with which most of the population of Rheims and Epernay treated them.

With Bruno de Lancel, not one of the inspectors was treated as an occupier, none of them ever suspected his well-hidden pride or his normal arrogance. Yet Bruno's policy was undetectable by any Frenchman who might bother to observe him. It lay purely in a crucial nuance of manner, in an agreeably neutral shading, in his naturally pleasant voice, in a willingness to look at them directly, to venture a small and harmless joke, to make an assumption that they shared a common humanity, all done with the bred-in-the-bone graciousness with which he had gone fishing for banking commissions not many years ago.

Within months of his arrival at Valmont, Bruno had obtained an *Ausweis,* the paper that let him travel to Paris. Authorization for his trip had not been difficult to arrange, since his previous residence in Paris gave him every explanation for an absence of several days to make sure that his house was intact.

As he approached his front door he saw a German soldier standing guard. Cautiously he went around to the delivery entrance and rang the bell. Georges, his old butler, opened the door and exclaimed, with surprise and happiness, "Monsieur le Vicomte, thank God!"

"How did you get back, Georges?" Bruno asked after he entered the "office," a sort of catch-all pantry outside the kitchen. "When I came through Paris after the Armistice I found the house empty."

"We all fled Paris," Georges answered, "and after we managed to return, we learned that you had gone to the château. We understood, of course—your duty lay there."

"Who lives here now?" Bruno demanded, noticing in a swift glance that Georges had been polishing his best silver when he had arrived. From the kitchen came the smell of roasting beef, and every surface of the office was shining with cleanliness.

"The house was requisitioned by a General von Stern. He works for General von Choltitz, in the bureau of cultural affairs, and speaks excellent French. We have been fortunate, Monsieur le Vicomte, the general has kept everyone on, even your valet, Boris, who is convinced that von Stern has never had the services of a valet before. He is, thank God, a very quiet man, interested in antiquities, a great admirer of your collection of armor and books. Nothing has been changed, Monsieur, the house is exactly as you left it."

"He has no wife, no children?"

"I doubt it. There are no photographs of them, and that's a sure sign, in my experience. Often he brings home a woman of the streets, but he never keeps her overnight."

"Does he entertain?"

"Occasionally a few other officers, quiet men like himself. They discuss painting and architecture, not the war." Georges shrugged. "The dinners are far from brilliant, Monsieur, but they eat heartily and they enjoy the best bottles from your cellar."

"A small price to pay, Georges. You reassure me. Perhaps it would be prudent, for the sake of all of you, if I showed this general the courtesy of thanking him for taking care of my treasures?" Bruno murmured.

"Purely temporary care, would you say, Monsieur le Vicomte?" Georges asked in a low tone of hope.

"Naturally only temporary, why should you even question it?" Bruno responded. He gave his card to the butler. "Present this to von Stern. Ask him if I may come by tomorrow at his convenience to thank him. I should like to see for myself what kind of man is sleeping in my bed."

"I understand, Monsieur le Vicomte. What is the news of Mademoiselle de Lancel? And of Madame your grandmother and Monsieur your grandfather, if I may ask?"

"Sad, Georges, sad. Mademoiselle Delphine seems to have shut herself away from everyone . . . even I have no news of her . . . and my grandfather is finally showing his age. Only my grandmother still has retained any of her old spirit."

"We all count on you, Monsieur le Vicomte. You are much in our thoughts."

"Thank you, Georges. Leave word about my meeting with your general at my hotel."

"Never 'my general,' Monsieur le Vicomte," Georges protested as he let Bruno out.

"A joke, Georges. We must still laugh, must we not?"

Within minutes Bruno had taken the measure of General von Stern. A Prussian of the most minor aristocracy, he judged, from a long-impoverished family, a man who no more fit the title of general than Bruno himself, a scholar in early middle age, who, because of his specialized knowledge, was one of Goering's handpicked experts, spending his days seeking out the greatest works of art in France, to be sent to Germany for the Marshal's personal collection. A mild enough man, von Stern, Bruno realized, not unattractive and sufficiently well bred to be faintly uneasy with Bruno, as if he knew that, conqueror or not, he had no right to the magnificent house on the Rue de Lille. Bruno was quick to put him at his ease.

"I had heard horror stories of houses, General, historic houses, that have been treated like barracks—you can imagine how relieved I am to see that you love and understand beauty," Bruno said, looking around his library with an air of the perfect guest, as if he had no proprietary connection with the room, yet felt free to admire it as it deserved.

"It is one of the most beautiful houses in this most beautiful of all cities, Vicomte," von Stern said, pleasure, well-hidden yet still visible, in his eyes.

"It was built while Louis Quinze was a young man. I have always maintained that those lucky enough to live in it are only caretakers, like the fortunate curators of museums."

"You are a museum-goer, Vicomte?"

"It was my passion, my reason for living. Before the war I spent every free hour in museums, every vacation was devoted to travel—Florence, Rome, London, Berlin, Munich, Madrid, Amsterdam—ah, those were the days, were they not, General?"

Von Stern sighed. "Indeed they were. But they will return, I am convinced of that. Soon, under the Führer, all Europe will be at peace."

"We must hope for peace everywhere, General, or else all the beauty in the world will be destroyed. I think we can agree on that without any problem."

"Shall we drink to peace, Vicomte?"

"Willingly, General, most willingly," Bruno agreed. Rules against fraternization with the enemy were meant for German soldiers and French whores, not for gentlemen who might have something of mutual interest to offer each other. Von Stern was not a man who was alone by choice, of that he was certain, he thought as he relaxed in his armchair, waiting for the invitation for dinner that he knew would soon be forthcoming.

I love you, I love you, thought Freddy in rapture. I love every one of your one thousand two hundred and fifty fierce and mighty horses, I love the clear bubble of your perspex canopy, I love your tapered, ellipse-shaped wings and your noisy, don't-give-a-damn exhaust and your snug narrow cockpit and your crazily crowded instrument panel, I even love the too-long cowling of your sublime Merlin engine that blocks my forward view on landing and takeoff, and your nose-heaviness that means I have to brake you like a baby carriage, I love you ten times more than any reliable, Hawker bloody businesslike Hurricane I've ever flown, and I'd give anything to throw you around the sky, to battle-climb you all the way upstairs at full throttle with two thousand eight hundred and fifty fucking wonderful RPMs and then put you into a screeching, diabolical power dive, until we'd both had ourselves a bit of well-deserved fun, and, for dessert, trim you off at four hundred and sixty miles an hour and fly your lovely ass off, because I know I could do it, and, God knows, everybody knows you can, because once you're off the ground you're a snap to fly. A pussycat! Just a simple, forgiving love of a pussycat. I'm talking to you, my Mark 5 Spitfire. What do you have to say for yourself?

"Bloody bugger," she said out loud, as the sight of a familiar chalk pit far underneath, in the toy landscape that was England, reminded her that she was routinely delivering a Spitfire from the Vickers Supermarine factory in Eastleigh to an airdrome at Lee-on-Solent. From her altitude she could clearly see across the Channel to the green fields of France, where the German raids were daily launched against England.

Today, in September of 1941, the day was made for flying. No fog, not even any haze over England, and only a few big scattered clouds out over the water. The late-afternoon sun, sharply angled and unusually bright, warmed the back of her neck between her helmet and her collar. On this rare day, after two other ferry jobs, Freddy had been given much too short a trip for her taste, one that took only a half hour. Worse, the new Spitfires were flown by the ATA at their two-hundred-miles-per-hour cruising speed, to break in their powerful engines, a procedure that, to Freddy, was utterly frustrating, no matter how accustomed she was to it.

She now flew Spitfires every day, for she and Jane had been sent to temporary duty at the 15th Ferry Pool at Hamble, to work clearing the Vickers factory of the sleek, sophisticated warplanes they were making with greater speed each succeeding month. There was great danger in allowing any group of new planes to sit on the field outside the factory, providing a natural target for a hit-and-run German bomber, so they had to be moved as quickly as possible.

When Freddy handed the Spitfire off at its new base, it would be painted with identification numbers, armed, perhaps fitted with special fuel tanks for long hops, or cameras if it was to be used as a spy plane; it would receive the painted insignia of the nationality of its pilot, and if he was a Squadron Leader or Wing Commander, his initials would be inscribed on its rear fuselage. It would become some lucky fighter pilot's very own kite, his most prideful possession, which no one else would fly unless its master was sick or dead. Now, only now, was it hers, totally hers.

She had just glanced to the left to see how far she was from her coastline destination, when, from out of a particularly large cloud mass over the water, two specks appeared on her newly polished canopy. Something about them drew Freddy's instant attention and she looked hard, with all the extraordinary power of her vision. There was an abnormality there, even at this distance. Like half of England, she was no stranger to observation of aerial combat from the ground, but now, aloft, the relative positions of the two planes told her instantly that one of them was chasing the other.

She should lose altitude and get out of the way, she told herself, even as she gained altitude so that she could observe them. She was invisible, with the sun at her back. The planes had rapidly reached a place in the sky, perhaps a mile away, where she could recognize them. The first machine, fleeing for its life, was another Spitfire, one wing lower than the other in an attitude that meant its aileron controls had been hit. The second plane, a Messerschmitt 109F, whose performance rivaled that of any Spitfire, was gaining on the English plane, clinging to its tail. The Spitfire was jinking violently to avoid the bullets coming from the Messerschmitt, bullets now clearly visible to her, since they were tracers used to inform pilots when they were about to come to the end of their ammunition.

"No!" Freddy screamed as the Spitfire's oil tank was hit and the flames started spreading backward from the engine toward the cockpit. The hood of its canopy popped open and its pilot tumbled out. She held her breath until she saw the chute open. The victorious Messerschmitt, flaunting its Maltese cross and its swastika, circled the area. Making sure of the kill, she thought. But then, instead of heading for home when the Spitfire hit the Channel, it continued to circle, without opening fire, in descending spirals around and around the dangling Spitfire pilot. The bastard's going to shoot him while he's in the air, she realized, and since he's low on ammo, he's taking his time, waiting for the perfect shot.

Immediately, Freddy opened her throttle to the maximum and charged ahead, her engine responding instantly. As she did so, all that she had ever learned about dogfights from Mac, all the RAF lore that Tony had taught her, all the flying stunts she had planned for the movies, fused in her mind into one piece of absolute knowledge: the only hope lay in a head-on attack.

She had exactly one chance, in an unarmed plane, to drive off a Messerschmitt. She had to pounce at full speed directly into his cannon. He had to be convinced that she was approaching to blaze away at his windscreen and that she intended to wait until the last second to fire.

He saw her coming now, she realized, as he stopped circling and veered about, presenting his windscreen head-on. They were about three thousand yards apart, Freddy estimated automatically. An accurate shot was made at two hundred and fifty yards. She held her reckless, relentless course as the two planes sped toward each other, in an instant that hung in the air, like a static painting of a war dance. Some three hundred yards away, at the last possible split second, the Messerschmitt swerved, made a tight, climbing turn, and fled east.

"Got you, you fucker, got you!" she screamed, bounding in her seat in victory as she started chasing after the German fighter. It took her minutes before she came back to her senses and realized that she was acting like a maniac. Pulses pounding, higher on adrenaline than she'd ever been before, she reluctantly listened to the voice of reason and turned back to the west, where she could see the pilot of the Spitfire just about to hit the water.

Wearing his Mae West life jacket, he struggled out of the harness of his parachute, and while she throttled back and swung protectively over him, he inflated his single-seat "K" dinghy, the tiny, puffy, oval rubber boat that had saved the lives of so many Allied airmen. The pilot brandished his double-bladed paddle reassuringly at her, but Freddy continued to circle low over his head until she spotted one of the Air-Sea Rescue launches, leaving from a station on the beach, and approaching him. She couldn't resist slowing the Spitfire down to its lowest speed, just above the sixty-four miles an hour at which it would stall. Impulsively she pushed back the hood of her canopy and leaned out to try to exchange some sort of greeting with the pilot, bobbing about in a brisk current. Only the blur of his tanned, grinning face was clearly distinguishable.

Freddy could see that he was trying to shout something at her, over and over, but she couldn't hear him. She pushed back her helmet so that her ears were uncovered, and a few strands of her hair blew free in the wind, but she was still going too fast to catch his words. The launch had nearly reached him now, and she no longer had an excuse to linger, she realized, expelling her breath. Regretfully, Freddy shut the hood, eased the stick forward, and prepared to head for her destination over a countryside so familiar by now that she could tell when an individual farmer was cutting his hay.

"Freddy, do you know anything about this?" Captain Lydia James, the commanding officer of the women's ferry pool, asked her, holding up a copy of a newspaper. Freddy inspected the page in question. MYSTERY SPIT SAVES RAF PILOT the headline read, over a story of her feat, written by a reporter who had been at the air-sea rescue station when the pilot of the downed Spitfire was brought in, wet but unharmed.

"I don't understand, Lydia."

"I've been queried about this incident . . . this 'mystery Spit.' You were flying in that area yesterday. Did you see anything unusual?"

"No, Lydia. I must have missed it."

"Strange, I can't seem to find anybody who witnessed anything. That pilot claims he didn't make out any identifying markings on the plane that saved him, but that the pilot had red hair. They think it may have been one of our lot."

"That would hardly be likely, an unarmed plane taking on a Messerschmitt. Who would do anything as crazy as that . . . unless it was one of the men? Why did they ask you? There are three male pilots to every woman. To say nothing of its being against every ATA rule? That RAF pilot was probably in shock."

"That's what I've told them," Captain James said with normal ATA formality. "Well, Freddy, good luck tomorrow. Or isn't that exactly the right thing to say to a bride?"

"I think it's utterly appropriate, Lydia. Thank you—and thank you again for the week's 'compassionate leave.' "

"Normal, under the circumstances, wouldn't you say?"

"Normal but wonderful." Freddy turned to leave the office, her back to her commanding officer.

"Oh, Freddy—one more thing . . ."

"Yes?"

"If you want to stay in the ATA . . ."

"Yes, Lydia?"

"Don't do it again."

Longbridge Grange lay dozing, all its inspired sprawl redolent of the scent of late-blooming yellow climbing roses, in the lazily lambent

September sun of Freddy's wedding day. Eve and Paul de Lancel, and Tony's two schoolboy brothers, Nigel and Andrew, had arrived the night before. With all the Longbridges, they were waiting impatiently outside the front door when Freddy and Jane finally drew up in the MG, driven on the gas denoted as a wedding present by some of the other ATA pilots.

It had been a long courtship, as Freddy had warned Tony, for she was not about to leap into matrimony without a thought for the consequences. She was not infected by the feeling that it was her duty to make some fighting man happy, as were so many noncombatant women, for she was desperately needed at her job, as few women have ever been in the history of warfare.

Although Freddy's schedule of thirteen days on duty, followed by two days off, rarely coincided with time when Tony could get a day's leave, they were able occasionally to catch a few hours together at night, when flying was over for the day. Eventually she had capitulated to his determination and his passion. She had fallen reluctantly in love, with many an internal question, many a secret backward glance, which became, in Tony's perception, a captivating elusiveness.

To cheers and kisses, she emerged with difficulty from the MG, her progress impeded by the arms of the three little girls around her legs.

"Where's my Antony?" she asked his mother, surprised not to see him.

"Only just on his way. He rang up ten minutes ago . . . it's too silly, my dear, but it would seem that you're going to have a stranger for best man . . . Patrick's down with the mumps, today of all days!"

"Better today than tomorrow," Jane exclaimed. "Who did Tony say he was bringing?"

"One of the boys from his squadron, I imagine . . . the connection was bad and he was in a rush."

Freddy turned to kiss Eve and Paul, who both looked perfectly at ease amid the swarm of Longbridge children. They had visited Longbridge Grange a number of times before, coming out from London by train during the spring and summer of 1941, at Lady Penelope's invitation, and the two older couples had grown into a warm, easy friendship, motivated just as much by mutual liking as by their hopes that Freddy and Tony would manage to get themselves married, as they quite obviously should be.

"Is it all right for a bride to be starving?" Freddy asked no one in particular. Paul put his arm around her shoulders, tipped her chin up and kissed her forehead. Thank God for this child, he thought, and exchanged a quick glance with Eve. Where was Delphine? Their eyes asked each other the question that had tormented them for so long. They had learned to speak of her as little as possible, for inside Occupied France she was as unreachable as if she were on the dark side of the moon, but the question was never far from their minds. Eve turned away to concentrate on Freddy.

"You'll need your strength," she advised her daughter. Eve had been part of all the arrangements, from the wedding in the village church, to which every soul in the neighborhood was invited, to the reception at The Grange, at which they expected only family, restricted by wartime travel problems to some sixty people, which seemed to Freddy an enormous number.

Accompanied by the little girls, Sophie, the youngest, and Sarah and Kate, the twins, Freddy and Jane ate sandwiches in the pantry, warned not even to think of going into the kitchen, where several women from the nearby farms were helping Lady Penelope and Eve put the finishing touches on the wedding feast.

Traditionally, the wedding should have taken place at noon, but since neither the bride nor the groom could guarantee to get there in time, it had been arranged for three in the afternoon, to take advantage of the daylight and still enable all the reception guests to arrive before dark and the blackout.

"I don't think this is such a hot idea," Freddy muttered to Jane, as she swallowed the last of her sandwich.

"What's wrong . . . stomachache? You ate too fast. You're excited, that's all."

"Excited, shit, I'm in a panic. I'm terrorized. I can't do it, Jane. It's a mistake. I hardly know Antony. I should never have let you talk me into it."

"Me?" Jane was indignant. "I never said boo. Do you think I *want* you for a sister-in-law, you half-assed Yank? My brother could have had a duke's daughter . . . and here he's throwing himself away on just another fairly pretty face. You'd never have had a chance with him in peacetime. What's worse, you're really a half-assed Frenchie, when it comes right down to it, and in my family we've never forgiven William the Conqueror. Should have stayed on his own bloody side of the Channel and left Britain to the Anglo-Saxons. Look, if you like, I'll go tell Mummy to cancel the whole show. We've already lost the best man, so why not the bride too? The wedding presents weren't up to much anyway . . . nothing we'd mind sending back. People would un-

360

derstand . . . since the war everybody's had to learn to be flexible. If Antony weren't my brother I could marry him myself so as not to disappoint the guests, but just say the word and we can be back at Hamble before they know we've gone. Better yet, we could drive on to London and pick up some cute, hot-blooded, sex-starved enlisted men for a really good time."

"All right, all right, I'll come quietly," Freddy said gloomily.

She dressed in Jane's bedroom, with Eve and Lady Penelope hovering about. The Longbridge attic had been ransacked for wedding dresses, but nothing that fit Freddy had been discovered, for she was taller than any of the Longbridge brides of past generations. Wartime restrictions and lack of clothing coupons made buying a new wedding dress impossible, yet Lady Penelope had been determined that her oldest son was going to have a bride who looked like a bride.

Wartime had turned her talent for petit point into an almost professional dressmaking skill. For the bodice, Lady Penelope had taken the top of a late-Victorian gown with a low, wide, ribbon-trimmed neckline and balloon puffed sleeves, that began just at the end of Freddy's bare shoulders. Ruthlessly, she cannibalized two dresses from the period of George III, one of them possessing a pleated, full satin cloud of a skirt, held at the waist by a wide belt. It wasn't long enough to reach the floor, but served beautifully under a split overskirt, made entirely of lace, from which trailed a four foot lace train. Sophie, Sarah and Kate had spent the morning weaving a garland of tiny white rosebuds that held in place a shoulder-length veil, a family heirloom that had been carefully preserved for more than three hundred years, from the time of Charles II.

As Freddy, unresisting, looked at her ongoing transformation in the mirror, she thought that it was getting a little easier to go through with the wedding with each added layer of this extravaganza of time-mellowed, multi-centuried ivory, for the less and less she recognized her out-of-uniform self, the idea of marriage became slightly less implausible. The only familiar sight in the mirror was her hair rising like a fireworks display from the ivory clouds that enveloped her.

Lots of people got married, she told herself. Her mother was married, Lady Penelope, whom she was now supposed to call just plain Penelope, but never Penny, was married . . . she knew hundreds of married women who didn't seem to find their condition abnormal or onerous. Why then did getting married seem so strange a thing to be doing on a lovely afternoon? It was, on the other hand, just the right time of day to go flyin'.

"Is Antony all done up too? Uniform pressed and all that?" she asked Jane, out of idle curiosity.

"Antony?" Jane looked vacant, too busy zipping up her pale green maid-of-honor dress to pay much attention.

"Your brother Antony. The groom, or so I've been told."

"Oh my God!" Jane ran off to check and returned in several minutes, stammering hysterically. "There's no sign of him. Nobody knows anything!"

"Just what was that you were saying earlier about enlisted men, Jane?" Freddy inquired.

"Jane, calm yourself," Eve said soothingly. "He called to say he was on his way, did he not?"

"Hours ago!"

"Perhaps he's changed his mind," Freddy mused. "It does happen, you know, in even the best families."

"I talked to him," six-year-old Sophie piped up.

"When, you devil?" her mother demanded.

"A few minutes ago. I was downstairs and the telephone rang so I answered it and it was Antony. He gave me a message."

"Why didn't you tell us?" Lady Penelope almost whispered, so that she wouldn't scream.

"He gave *me* the message. He didn't say to tell anyone else," Sophie answered importantly. "He has a flat tire and he'll be late. He said to meet him at the church."

Lady Penelope looked at her watch. "Sophie, Kate, Sarah, go put on your bridesmaids' dresses. We'll leave the house in exactly twenty minutes."

"What if we have to wait at the church, Mama?" Sophie asked, in portentous tones, sashaying to center stage.

"Sophie Harriet Helena Longbridge . . . you . . . are . . . beginning . . . to . . . try . . . my . . . patience." At these ultimately ominous words, the three little girls vanished in a squeaking flurry of white stockings and Mary Janes.

The wedding procession, in horsedrawn carriages, followed by the entire village and all the county neighbors on foot, on horseback, and in other carriages, had arrived in time to see the groom's car speed up to the church. Tony and his best man managed to duck into the vestry and hurry to the back of the church, just before the bell in the tower struck three.

Once she started walking down the aisle on Paul's arm, Freddy became a figure woven into a tapestry. She moved through that familiar, noble march, the center of a stately saraband, to music that no one in the church could listen to without also remaining, in some part of the brain, alert for the sound of bombers overhead.

"So that's your girl," sighed the best man, Jock Hampton, as he caught his first sight of the regal, tall, heavily veiled figure who approached from a distance. Only a few hours ago he had been about to leave for London on an overnight pass. "Now I understand the mad rush."

"Shut up," Tony said out of the side of his mouth, not wanting the sound of a human voice between himself and the sight of Freddy, although she was unrecognizable. As tall and straight as he was, Tony was still a good two inches shorter than the lanky, blond Californian who had been with the Eagle Squadron from the beginning, months before Tony himself had become Squadron Leader. The two young uniformed men in RAF blue waited silently, while the organ played until Paul brought Freddy to the altar, and put her hand in Tony's.

Jock Hampton fell a pace back and watched them repeat their vows. He could barely make out Freddy's veiled face in the dim light of the old church. The heirloom lace was so thickly encrusted that it covered the color of her hair, and it wasn't until she threw it back, after the ceremony, so that she could kiss Tony, that he got his first real look at her. The hair stood up on his scalp even before he had a coherent thought. Not just because she was beautiful, surpassingly beautiful, but because he had seen her once before and he knew already that he could never forget her face. The first time he'd laid eyes on her had been twenty-four hours ago, when she had pushed back her helmet and waved at him, twenty-four hours ago, right after she'd saved his life.

The largest room of the oldest wing of Longbridge Grange had been thrown open for the wedding party. Freddy danced with every one of her new relatives, before Jock Hampton felt it was proper to cut in on her, as she did some sort of teenaged box step with her new brother-in-law, Nigel.

"I was trying to say thank you," he said, as he took her in his arms.

Freddy's veil had long ago been laid aside and now her hair was flung in shafts of brilliance about her face, from the exertions of dancing with so many men, aged from twelve to eighty, each one of whom claimed close kinship with her. The best man was the only male here she hadn't expected to make any demand on her confused brain.

Puzzled by his words, Freddy looked up at Jock Hampton. A Califor-

363

nia face, was her first thought. She'd gone to high school with types like him, the campus football heroes, standing taller than anyone around them, athletic heroes, golden boys, not much younger than this character, whose scorched blond hair flopped over his forehead in a way that was both against regulations and the fashion of the day, which made men use some kind of goo to keep their hair neatly plastered to their skulls. He looked tough, she decided, as she realized with relief that he danced marvelously, tough and insubordinate, and there was a curiously laughing light in his clear blue eyes, around which the sunburst of squint lines were deeper than any man's but a pilot's would ever be. This chivalrous Viking, who had appeared unexpectedly at her wedding, was undomesticated and unsubduable, she was sure of it. All his strong features were blunt, as if he'd kept a lot of rough edges. He was a bit of a thug, Freddy thought. Where had Tony found him? She looked at him questioningly. What was he talking about?

"The other day," he explained. "I was trying to say thank you for saving my life . . . the guy in the dinghy . . . don't you remember me? Do you do that every day?"

"*You?*"

"Yep. Mighty nice flyin', Mrs. Longbridge."

"Why, you bastard! You bigmouth! You *cretin!* You damn near got me kicked out of the ATA with your story. Why the bloody hell couldn't you keep the details to yourself, jerk? Creep! No, you had to go and blab about it to some reporter . . . of all the stupid, moronic . . ." She stopped dancing abruptly, and almost slumped in his arms, too amazed by her outburst to go on.

"You do have a definite gift for expressing yourself," Jock said as he held her up. "I'm glad you haven't got your guns loaded today."

"I didn't have any the other day, either. We fly unarmed, wise guy."

"You were *bluffing* a Messerschmitt?"

"I didn't give it much thought, to tell you the truth."

"My, my, Mrs. Longbridge, I'm not sure I envy my splendid Squadron Leader. Does he know what kind of maniac he married?"

"Oh, fuck off, smartass! I had to have a little fun for a change! You fellows grab all the action, and we just get to creep along with our delivery service. How would you like to have to do that all the time? What's your name again, anyway?"

"Jock Hampton, ma'am."

"Well, Jock Hampton, don't you ever dare tell Antony what I did. Don't you ever even think of mentioning it to anybody else on the face of the earth, do you hear? Or I'll get you, and I'll get you good. And when I get someone, he stays got."

"You have my promise. I'm too terrified of you even to remember . . ."

"Remember what?" she asked, eyes narrowed suspiciously.

"I don't remember whatever it was that I wasn't going to remember."

"Maybe you're not as incredibly thick as I thought," she said.

"I believe it's time to cut the cake, Mrs. Longbridge."

"Stop trying to change the subject."

"No, it really is. They're waiting for you. But could I just say one word of explanation, extenuating circumstances and all that? And then I'll never say anything again, ever?"

"Oh, all right, get it over with."

"I didn't tell the reporter you were a girl. I only said red hair. I saw right away that it was too long for a man."

Freddy thought over his words.

"I guess you didn't, at that," she replied slowly. "Does that mean I should apologize for all the mean things I said?"

"A bride never has to apologize for anything."

"I will anyway. I shouldn't have told you to fuck off. Not on my wedding day."

Oh, but I want this girl, Jock Hampton thought. *She should have been mine.*

18

THE poster that had been plastered all over the walls of buildings throughout France, in early 1943, showed a monumentally well-muscled and well-nourished young Frenchman, dressed in blue overalls, standing boldly below an orange sky, in front of a group of tools. Far in the distance could be seen a tiny Eiffel Tower, and the lettering on the poster, in tall red, white and blue letters, announced, BY WORKING IN GERMANY, YOU ARE THE AMBASSADOR OF FRENCH QUALITY.

French quality, Bruno reflected, whenever he passed that particular poster, would always be a desirable commodity, in whatever form it was found . . . although he congratulated himself that he did not personally have to demonstrate French quality in the form of the forced labor in Germany that the poster presented so glowingly. His duties at Valmont provided him immunity from such work. Since 1942, when his grandfather, Jean-Luc de Lancel, died of pneumonia, Bruno had found himself master of the House of Lancel, of the Château de Valmont and all its vineyards. After her husband's death, Anette de Lancel, heartbroken, had retired permanently to her rooms and taken no further interest in running the property.

In spite of the relative goodwill that Bruno had cultivated and maintained with the Führer of Champagne's representatives, he could not change the basic fact that his champagne was treated as spoils of battle. True, the Germans had finally permitted the growers to sell almost twenty-five percent of their annual production of wine to civilian sources in France, Belgium, Finland and Sweden, but that concession merely made it possible to continue to produce the crop and allowed for no luxury.

What a damnably unprofitable business champagne had become, Bruno thought wrathfully, after his grandfather's funeral, looking out over the ocean of vineyards in the rolling valley below the château. French quality, yes, he didn't deny it, but he might just as well be a butcher looking at a counter covered with offal—tripe, liver, brains and sweetbreads—for all the sense of aesthetic pleasure the sight gave him. After the past two years he knew quite as much as he needed to

366

know about how to oversee the cultivation of the grapes of champagne, and far, far more than he had ever intended to learn.

He had no intention of remaining in this infernally boring corner of France after the war ended, and end it must eventually, when all the countries of the world had exhausted themselves. Yet who could guess how many years in the future the end would be? Who could be certain where the new centers of power would lie? They knew little of the progress of the war in Paris, and even less here in Champagne, far from the fields of battle. He assumed, like millions of others, that eventually France would be somehow attached to Germany and, with luck, would be treated as a junior partner in the Reich rather than as a defeated territory.

Bruno fingered the key to the vast cellars full of hidden Lancel champagne, which had lain untouched since the war began, their existence unsuspected by the Germans, and now known only to him and to the three Martins, who had last brought in bottles of the vintage of 1939. Only the day before his death had his grandfather finally allowed him to take possession of that sacred key.

When he had first been taken to visit the cellars, in 1933, Bruno remembered, his grandfather had said that in case of war a Lancel, returning to Valmont, could restore and rebuild the vineyards by selling this great stock of champagne. As far as he was concerned, Bruno mused, the château could tumble into ruins, and the chalk soil of the vineyards be used to grow cabbage—he would be perfectly content never to lay his eyes on another vine, never to oversee another harvest. French quality be damned!

Would he love this land if it were all going to belong to him some-day, untainted by the equal inheritances of his half sisters? No, he thought, never, not even then. He'd be . . . gratified . . . by its possession, but he could never love land that demanded so much from its owner. Land should exist to be enjoyed, not to be served. A château should be renowned for its richness in game, its horses and hunting, for the magnificence of its art objects and architecture, for the visits of long-dead kings and the pomp of centuries, as the Saint-Fraycourt châteaux had been before they were lost. Valmont was not splendid enough; its art consisted of family portraits and good but unspectacular furniture. And this land of Champagne was resolutely agricultural, no matter how much was made of the specialness of its soil, the nobility of the grape.

If he were its sole owner, he would hire a manager to wring the last drop of profit out of each hectare, and only come to Valmont to make sure that he wasn't being cheated. What was the point of being an aristocrat, when, at Valmont, he had the same worries as if he were a peasant, one of the many workers who owned their few *arpents* of champagne grapes?

But that hoard of champagne in the cellars, ah, now that was another matter entirely. It was riches, better now than gold, and it must be made to yield itself to him. The death of his grandfather had freed him to sell it, and the arrangements must be made soon, for each day that the green bottles lay sleeping, festively dressed in their glittering foil labels, brought the end of the war one day sooner. With that inevitable cease-fire, no matter if the Germans became the undisputed masters of all Europe, there would be a period of uncertainty and confusion, as there had been after the Fall of France.

But this time, Bruno promised himself, he would be better prepared. The champagne would have been converted into a safe currency and deposited in a stable country so that he could seize the best opportunities that peace would offer. He was already twenty-eight, and three years had been wasted here. French quality indeed!

Bruno went to pay a call, as he had done with as much frequency as could be managed, on his pleasant friend, General von Stern, who, by now, felt entirely at home in the house on the Rue de Lille. It did not take them long to reach a gentleman's agreement as to the fate of the many hundreds of thousands of bottles, lying in piles twenty feet high, that were the hard-won strength of the House of Lancel, its heart's blood, its future.

The general had acquired, in the course of his search for works of art, a far larger knowledge of who was selling what to whom, in Occupied France, than was strictly necessary for his mission. He understood Bruno's problem immediately, and with several phone calls, a meeting, an agreement on the division of the spoils, he solved it to their mutual satisfaction.

Arrangements were made for a steady diversion of an inconspicuous convoy of trucks that were at the general's disposition, to make the short night run to Valmont. Well-disciplined German soldiers lifted the bottles of Lancel champagne in their arms and onto rolling carts, filling the trucks as carefully and respectfully as they moved paintings and sculpture. There was no breakage, no looting, no vandalism, no disturbance that would attract the attention of a soul at the château. Nor were the officers from the Führer's office any the wiser, for they did not linger in Champagne cellars after dark.

The hidden cellars of Valmont bled their treasure, month after month, until the strength of the Lancels disappeared forever into the black market, and Bruno, through banking connections in Switzerland, had laid a sound basis for his fortune. No one was harmed, except for the three Martin cousins, the loyal cellarmen, who were unfortunate enough to know of the existence of the wine. Bruno judged it only prudent to dispose of them and their inconvenient memories. They must never see the empty cellars of *Le Trésor*.

The next time an officer from the Führer's office in Rheims came to inspect the Lancel vineyards, he found Bruno deeply troubled, again needing the advice he had so often sought.

"I feel it is my duty to tell you that I have reason to be sure that three of my most trusted men have joined the Resistance," Bruno admitted to him. "I don't know what to do—my grandfather loved these men—but I cannot, in good conscience, shield them, for to shield them would be, in effect, to join them."

"Vicomte, you have made a prudent and patriotic decision. Give me their names and think no further about it. I will turn the matter over to the Gestapo office in Rheims."

He would miss their experienced labor, Bruno reflected, when he heard that the three Martins had been executed. However, he had to admit that even the Gestapo had its uses.

She'd give a lot to hear Cary Grant utter his ironic laugh, or watch Fred Astaire tap his insouciant way up a staircase, or see Myrna Loy wittily make an idiot out of some man, Delphine thought, as she held her head steady so that the hairdresser could hide all her own hair under a wig that would turn her into the Empress Josephine. But American films were only nostalgic memories, since they had been banned in 1940. Today she was being made up for yet another of the formal, lavish, historical and biographical dramas that had become so popular with the producers of French films in the last few years.

"Prestige" and "high art" were now the key words in filmmaking, and producers sat in the commissaries debating the values of a script on the basis of whether or not it sufficiently glorified French culture and tradition. Occupied France was isolated from the world, but it would always own its sublime past. Backward the cinema turned, backward toward the proud nationalism of that former grandeur, backward toward a vision of past splendor.

Many producers claimed that they used epics to offer hope and inspiration to the French people in this period of defeat; others, openly resigned to the new regime, admitted that they took a welcome shelter in the safe refuge of history, as well as in the timelessness of myth and legend, since no breath of the tragic reality of the present could ever be presented on the screen. The conqueror was far too shrewd not to understand that the show must go on, particularly for the people of a defeated nation who crowded the cinemas as never before.

Delphine had worn period wigs and floor-length costumes in her last five films, all of which had been shot in châteaux that the Germans had made available for location work, or on elaborately decorated sound stages. Her scripts were full of high-flown literary language, and the action of the pictures took place within a strictness of form and a search for perfection of sentiment, a return to classicism that left no room for the spontaneous fun and sophistication of the early Continental films.

Delphine searched her face with the cruelty of a professional in the mirror of her dressing room. Yes, she could still take the scrutiny of a close-up, although how this was possible, when she had not had a single postcard from Armand in almost four months, she could not understand. When she was at home alone, without makeup, she could see the traces around her eyes that were the residue of long nights of weeping, of trying to fight despair and sleeplessness. If she could see the marks today, the camera would see them tomorrow, she thought with concern, for, like everyone else, she could not afford to be without work. She had to get advice, had to talk to someone, Delphine realized as a diamond and emerald tiara was pinned onto the wig, or she would crack under the weight of her growing fear for Armand's safety.

But whom could she approach? She had kept up a constant correspondence with her grandmother at Valmont since 1940, finding the same comfort in pouring out her heart to the old woman as she would have felt if she had kept a diary. She received increasingly infrequent answers to her letters—it was almost like posting them in a bottle—yet it gave her a small, utterly necessary sense of family that was as comforting as a hand warmer carried in a muff by some Victorian lady. Certainly Anette de Lancel, in her eighties, could no longer find an answer for her granddaughter's problems, as she once had, when she gave that midsummer dinner party almost seven—or was it seven hundred?—years ago at the château in Champagne, and changed Delphine's life.

Reluctantly, Delphine realized that the time had come to seek out Bruno. He had been right about the war, he had been right about the way the Germans would treat the Jews of France, and she wished, too many times to count, that she had possessed the common sense to listen to him. Now, with hindsight, it was almost impossible to believe how blindly she and Armand had continued on with their lives—and yet they had acted with as little foresight as almost everyone else, except for a wisely pessimistic handful—Robert Siodmak, Max Ophuls, Boris Kaufman, and Jean-Pierre Aumont among them—who had left France in time.

When Delphine telephoned Bruno at Valmont, she discovered that he was spending a few days in Paris. She reached him at his hotel, surprised to hear in his voice as much pleasure as if their last encounter had never taken place.

"Of course I have time to come and see you, you goose. How could I not?" he exclaimed, and they set a meeting for the next day, at the house on the Villa Mozart. Delphine dressed and applied her makeup carefully for the encounter, and when she was finished, she evaluated her image and decided that she looked not too different from the girl he had last seen almost four years ago. She must not appear to be filled with the panic that all but overwhelmed her, for her instincts counseled her against any display of weakness.

She's as exquisite as ever, Bruno thought, as he greeted her. Delphine was now twenty-five, and her poise, always formidable, had grown from that of a girl to that of a woman. The bewitching charm of her heart-shaped face, the placement of her huge, uptilted eyes, had a magical quality that time had only embellished. What, except actual privation, could rob Delphine of the power she possessed, he wondered, until he looked into her misty gray eyes and knew immediately that she was terrified.

She gave him an aperitif and they chatted about nothing of importance for a few minutes, during which Delphine satisfied herself that Bruno was as unjudgmental, as easy to talk to, as he had been in the days when they had been so close, when they had done each other favors without asking reasons.

"I'm worried, Bruno," she said abruptly. "Armand was taken prisoner at Dunkirk and sent to Germany to work in a factory. Until four months ago he wrote me postcards to say that he was well . . . now there is only silence."

"What have you done to find out where he is?" Bruno asked in a businesslike way. So, he thought, it *was* still that damned Jew. How unfortunate, and how foolish. *How unnecessary.*

371

"What can I do, Bruno? I don't know where to start."

"But you must have friends . . . people who would take an interest . . ."

"I have friends in the studio, pals, more than real friends, but how could they help?"

"I don't mean them. Delphine, *cherie,* I assume that you are invited to the salon of Obetz, the German Ambassador, and that of Herr Epting of the German Institute . . ."

"Invited—of course—but go? I've never considered doing so."

"Now there is a mistake, little goose, if you'll permit me to say so. You've cut yourself off from potential friends, from important contacts, from people who might be able to help you."

"The Germans?"

"Who else? They control Europe—who else but the Germans?"

"Why would any German help me find a Jew?"

"Ah, Delphine, you see everything in black and white, just as you used to. It was a charming quality in peacetime but unnecessarily naïve in our present circumstances. You heard from Sadowski regularly for years—to me that indicates that he was considered a Frenchman of Polish origin, who was treated as any other prisoner of war. Was he circumcised? No? Well, that was his good luck. It would be clearly most unwise to run about in these times seeking news of a Jew named Sadowski, but of a French citizen, the well-known film director Armand Sadowski, why not? You would naturally be expected to use your influence to try to get news of him."

"My influence? What influence?"

"You are far more famous today, Delphine, than you've ever been, don't you realize that? And fame *is* influence, if it is properly managed. To leave such influence unused is like burning good money, my dear girl. It doesn't keep forever, like gold bars under the floorboards."

"I wouldn't know how to start."

"Isn't that why you called me?"

"I . . . I wanted to get your advice . . ."

"Put yourself in my hands, Delphine."

"Oh, Bruno, do you really believe there is hope?" Delphine cried, unable to conceal the precariousness of her emotions.

"Of course there's hope," he said reassuringly. "I'll have to consider where best to start, but if you cooperate with me, if you follow my advice, you will be doing the maximum possible for Sadowski, wherever he is today."

"Oh *yes,* Bruno, yes, I'll do whatever you say!"

As he walked at a rapid pace back toward his little Left Bank hotel, Bruno hummed in a glow of satisfaction. Delphine's departure from his life had left him shorn of an important asset. The possession of such a sister had been valuable in the past, and now it might well prove even more valuable. Obviously she needed to believe that the Jew was still alive. A pity—she would be far more useful if she had the intelligence to realize that he must be dead. Yet, if she were deprived of that hope she would be worthless. Well, he could give her hope—hope cost nothing—but what could she do for him?

He wanted no favors from the German Ambassador to Paris or from the representatives of German culture and arts, Bruno thought, as he crossed the Seine. It didn't matter that Delphine hadn't cultivated Obetz and Epting or even Greven, her boss at Continental, which would have been so ridiculously easy to do.

His own General von Stern, on the other hand . . . yes, von Stern was another matter. The man had shown amazing dexterity in the matter of the champagne. Why should they not do more business together?

As he walked along the pavements of Paris, Bruno considered the news, or rather the rumors, for the press presented almost no news, of the defeat of a vast German force at Stalingrad only a few months ago, in the early winter of 1943. Was it a sign, he wondered, that there was a possibility that the Germans might not emerge as the only power in Europe, or was it one miscalculation among many victories? After all, even Napoleon had not been able to conquer the Russian winter.

It didn't matter that he could not read the lesson of Stalingrad, Bruno decided, for whatever it meant, it only reinforced his conviction that the time to build his fortune was now, before the end of the war. Von Stern was too subtle a man not to agree. They both wanted the same thing, guaranteed wealth in the future.

But von Stern wanted one other thing, that thing which every conqueror of a great and glamorous city has always wanted: acceptance. He had grown in power and position, and now his dinner parties were no longer confined to quiet fellow officers. He invited certain Frenchmen and women, just as did the Ambassador and the President of the Institute, and some—although certainly not all—came and dined with him at the Rue de Lille. He had often hinted to Bruno that he would like to have the honor of being presented to Delphine. Bruno had been forced to make excuses, embarrassing at the time, which now seemed fortuitous. How much better to be able to produce Delphine after von

Stern's past disappointments, than if he had done so earlier, when his cellars at Valmont were still full.

Yes, Delphine could be controlled by hope. She would put on her most beautiful jewels and her most elegant evening gown and sit at von Stern's table and he would say those few words that would permit her to hope. Each of them would get what each wanted . . . nothing more . . . but quite enough to be as valuable to him as *Le Trésor,* which now lay locked away and forgotten, as if it had never existed.

She loved Freddy more and more, Lady Penelope Longbridge thought, as she bustled about in her flagstoned kitchen on an unusually hot Sunday in early May of 1944, organizing a picnic lunch for her family, but wasn't she just a little too caught up in the business of flying huge bombers all about the countryside? It had been an entire year now since Freddy and Jane had both been trained to fly four-engined aircraft at Marston Moor, and you'd think that in that year Freddy would have grown accustomed to an adventure that, in her private opinion, was just a little . . . unladylike. It gave her an uncomfortable feeling to think of either girl at the controls of a bomber, even if they did have a Flight Engineer along, and sometimes a copilot.

It was splendid for a woman to fly a one-seater Spitfire from the factory to the airdrome, delivering it to a fighter pilot, just as a stable lad would mount a racehorse and gently trot him out to the jockey waiting to ride the race, but, and this was something which she would never breathe to anyone except darling Gerald, it was, well, a trifle *unbecoming* for the girls to be flying the giant Stirlings and Halifaxes and Lancasters, to say nothing of those enormous Boeing B-17 Flying Fortresses they'd been zooming about in since last summer. She'd never thought she'd spend an entire breakfast listening to her daughter and her daughter-in-law arguing about the boost pressure of an "electronic turbo-supercharger"—whatever that meant—while they devoured the scrambled eggs made from the absolutely splendid powder that Jock brought with him yesterday, when he'd arrived for the weekend. They'd sounded like two old mechanics in a grubby garage.

What would Freddy do after the war, when she had to live an ordinary life, she'd like to know? The invasion of the Continent couldn't be far off, to judge by the expectancy and tenseness she saw on the faces of Tony and Jane and Freddy and Jock. It had been ages since all four of them had managed to be here at the same time, Penelope Longbridge realized, as she sliced heaps of the rare and fabulously luxurious treat of tinned corned beef that had also been the gift of Jock Hampton.

And why was she worrying about Freddy's adjustment to the future, and not her own daughter's? Was it because Freddy would be facing a new kind of existence entirely, while Jane would be returning to a life she'd been bred to? On the other hand, she didn't expect Freddy to turn into a model Englishwoman overnight. She was too much of a pirate, with her flamboyant hair and her swaggering walk and her vivid gestures, for one to imagine her sliding without a problem into the role of lady of the manor. Yet . . . yet . . . one day she would become the mistress of Longbridge Grange, the wife of the Fifteenth Baron, and, in their part of Kent, the woman to whom others looked to set standards.

It couldn't be denied that Freddy didn't have a clue as to what would be expected of her—although, of course, she was only twenty-four. The darling girl would simply have to learn to take more than a passing interest in the church fête and the Hunt Ball and the Ladies' Guild and the hospital and the garden fête and the local horse show and the coming-out balls in the county—oh, after the war there was going to be so *much* to bring back to life! Did Freddy have any idea of the time and planning that went into giving a proper dinner party? Would she even know how to make out a shopping list? And was she prepared to learn bridge? She couldn't flip cards into a hat that would be worn to Ascot! Surely she must understand that when she and Tony lived here in the country, bridge would be *essential*. Penelope Longbridge sighed without knowing it.

As for Jane, she was so outrageous that a mother just had to fling up her hands in amusement, or she'd go mad. There was no point in being shocked—oh, she knew about Jane and men, although not even dearest Gerald suspected it, but somehow it didn't disturb her. Every good family produces its legendary Jane from time to time—that naughty, *naughty* girl would marry well yet, never fear, very well indeed, and have half a dozen happy children—yes, Jane was a phenomenon, but not worrying, like Freddy.

Time enough to think about it all when the war was over, Penelope Longbridge told herself briskly, as she contemplated her preparations. A basket of Milky Ways for dessert, a bottle of whiskey to drink before lunch, plenty of corned-beef sandwiches on thin slices of wartime bread, redeemed by the tinned butter spread on them, a salad of cold sliced boiled potatoes, Brussels sprouts and onions in her own dressing, which made up for its lack of oil by its vigorous use of pepper; it was a meal that, except for the bread and salad, had been made possible only by Jock's largesse. Now that the Eagle Squadron had been turned over to the American Eighth Air Force, he never visited Longbridge Grange without a hamper of food supplied by his Mess Sergeant, to whom nothing was good enough for his Squadron Commander, Lieutenant Colonel Hampton. Darling Jock, thought Penelope Longbridge, what would they possibly have done without him?

He loved Freddy madly, Wing Commander the Honorable Antony Longbridge thought, as he deposited a pile of moth-eaten blankets and pillows under one of the flowering pear trees near the dovecot for the picnic, but somehow she'd changed from the girl he'd married. Or, to be fair, could it be that he'd changed, since this fucking sinus condition had developed? The thing didn't bother him at all except when he was climbing to twenty thousand feet, or diving from twenty thousand feet, but it had made him unserviceable, landed him at a desk, commanding a wing of thirty-six fighters, instead of being allowed to pilot his own kite. If you couldn't fly to the limit, you were no damn good at all. Sinus! Christ, what a bloody bad show! To be fair, to be scrupulously fair, even over-fair, was it perhaps the difference between the earth-bound, like him, and the freedom of the pilot, like Freddy, that caused him to feel a difference in her?

And what was that difference, exactly? Surely she hadn't always had the aura of . . . was it *command?* . . . that she had now. She looked so damned dashingly on top of the world in that uniform he was planning to burn the second the war was over. Burn her uniform, weigh her black shoes with pebbles and sink them in the river, cut up her forage cap into a million small pieces, take her wings and hide them for a thousand years, make her grow her hair down to her knees and wear dresses that showed her tits right down to the nipples, to hell with what people would say, and give her a good spanking to let her know who was boss—he couldn't wait! Surely she hadn't always been so utterly enchanted by what she was doing, so that on the occasions when they managed to spend her two days off together, she rattled on about her bombers until he was tempted to tell her to shut up? He was proud of her, damn it—who wouldn't be proud of a wife as brave as she was?—but a bomber was just a bloody lumbering big bus on wings, didn't she realize that? Didn't she understand that the messiah hadn't come when they'd invented the Norden bombsight? Wouldn't you think that she might be a little more . . . tactful . . . about the kick she got out of her work, considering that he couldn't properly do his, not the way he wanted to?

In fact, thought Tony, sitting down on one of the blankets and folding his arms around his knees, wouldn't it have been normal if she'd retired from the whole show two years ago, when Annie was born? The ATA was a civilian organization, after all, and Freddy could have left without any criticism from anyone, but no, she flew every day right till the beginning of her sixth month, when she couldn't squeeze into her uniform any longer, no matter how cleverly she eased her waistbands. Only then did she stay put here at The Grange, probably driving his poor Mum as crazy as she'd driven him—true, he admitted it, they hadn't planned on having a child in the middle of a war, but when you got married these things had a way of happening; what was he supposed to do, apologize? Then she'd produced the kiddie at the end of eight months as if she didn't intend to wait a second longer than necessary, and three months later she'd gone back to the ATA, as strong, as lively, as much of a buccaneer as ever, leaving darling little Annie with his mother and Eve and Sophie and Kate and Sarah and anyone else who felt like taking care of her, which, naturally, they all did, so that Annie probably thought that she had six or seven mothers, poor little bugger.

The thought of Annie made Tony smile. She was an inquisitive elf, who never walked if she could run; already she knew every vegetable in the walled kitchen garden, every tree and every yew hedge around the house, every rose and every dog and every horse that had ever come near the house. She took a serious, almost precocious interest in these living things, which she far preferred to toys. She was so delicately balanced on her little feet, as graceful as a larch on her slender legs and as fastidious as a kitten, his little Annie was, and she didn't fly anything, not even a balloon, and if he had his way, she never would. No, she'd grow up as demure and dainty as she was now, deep in a peaceful green countryside, learning to ride and do needlework as well as his mother, and to speak French, of course, which she already did with Eve, who came out to Longbridge Grange to see her whenever she could. Ah, his Annie would be a proper English gentlewoman. And as soon as the war was over, the minute peace was declared, he'd get Freddy pregnant again, and then when she'd had that baby, he'd start all over until she had enough children so that she'd wonder what she'd ever found to fill all the long, lazy hours she'd wasted during the war.

Bombers? Fighter planes? What were they, she'd ask? How could any machine ever built interest the mother of so many children . . . especially when she had to put her husband first, as any good wife would?

She loved Freddy, she really loved her, thought Jane, as she helped her mother carry out the food for the picnic, but the longer she knew her the more she realized that there was something about Freddy that just resisted giving itself up and blending into the unity that made up a proper family. Sometimes she thought that the two of them had talked about everything two females possibly could talk about, particularly when they were sisters-in-law and fellow pilots, and then Freddy would suddenly drift away with a look as if she were seeing something Jane had never seen, as if she were thinking about something Jane could never understand. She'd never asked Freddy about those moments, but she knew that there was a mystery in her past—about a man, of course, what else could it possibly be?—that meant too much to her to ever be revealed. The eternally surprising blue of Freddy's eyes would grow dim, and her quick, sporting smile that wrinkled her nose would disappear, and for just a moment she'd seem not to be there at all.

Whatever the mystery was, it explained why flying meant more to Freddy than it ever would to her. In a way Jane envied Freddy her constant passion, the way a married woman, not unpleasantly bored with her husband, would envy young love in its first wildness. When the war was over, Jane didn't think that she'd ever want to look at an aircraft again. Soon it would be five years of climbing in and out of the blasted things—oh, it had been wonderfully exciting and challenging to be able to do the job, especially as it grew more complicated—and, without question, it was still the most direct possible way of replacing a man for battle that any girl would ever know. On occasion, it was just as good sport as ever, especially when you drew a bomber to ferry. Freddy was dead wrong about that bloody Yank Minneapolis-Honeywell Supercharger—it was much more reliable to use the standby screws, one for each engine, but who could win such a theoretical argument? Come to think of it, did she really give a good goddamn, or had she just bickered about it to be companionable?

Jane put down the platter of corned-beef sandwiches and covered them carefully against potential attack by insects. She glanced at Tony, sitting lost in thought, and thought that he looked the way she felt. Some of the heart had gone out of her when Margie Fairweather, who had started with them back in the earliest days, was killed when the Proctor she was flying had engine failure. She'd managed to land it safely in a field but it had blown up in a hidden ditch before the engine could be stopped. There had been other deaths in the ATA, many others, but Margie's had been the saddest of all, for she'd left behind a small baby. Her husband, Douglas, also of the ATA, had been killed on a volunteer mission over the Irish Sea in bad weather, four months earlier. Did Freddy never think of little Annie when she took over the controls of the heaviest planes that had ever been flown in this war? It wasn't something you could ask her, somehow, any more than you could ask Jock why he kept on flying with his squadron when he'd had so many missions that he could have chosen, with honor, to fly a desk ten times over. You had to accept the fact that Freddy was willing to take the risk, baby or no baby.

Where was Jock, she wondered. Probably, on this rare day that found them all able to come back to The Grange for a few days, he was talking to Freddy about—what else?—the bombing of Germany that would soon, very soon now, prepare the way for the invasion. All of England seemed, when she flew over it, to have become one vast staging ground for the combat to come. Men and materiel were collected so thick on the ground and at the seaports that it was a wonder the whole island didn't sink under their weight. And after the invasion, after the victory that they all prayed must come, what would Jock do with himself?

Unquestionably, Tony and Freddy would live down here in the country, leading the life led by fifteen generations of Longbridge landowners and gentleman farmers. She herself would go to London and have a series of fabulous escapades, one after another, each one more thrilling than the last, until she had her final fling and found the man she could settle for, and did the right thing by her Mama.

But Jock? Jane Longbridge sat down on a blanket with her back to her brother, so as not to seem to want to interrupt his thoughts, and contemplated the question of Jock Hampton. Perhaps, after all, she was lucky that Freddy's sneaky, ingenious attempts to throw her and Jock together had failed. What if he had fallen in love with her, as Freddy had intended him to do? Now she'd have to be worrying about going back to California with an American husband and adapting to a new country and a new way of life. Another war bride.

No, she was fortunate indeed that it hadn't worked out that way. She had—Jane prayed—almost stopped being in love with Jock. If anyone had ever told her that she'd do something as girlishly banal as caring for a man who didn't love her, she'd have hit him over the head with a bottle of whatever was handy . . . but she loved him, alas, with an absurd, passionate, painful intensity, although no one, not even Freddy, knew it. The cure she chose was as humiliating as it was trusty.

She had only to look at Jock and Freddy together, only to see that the beautiful blond fool of a Californian—whose face Jane ached to touch, ever since Tony and Freddy's wedding—was still in love with her sister-in-law, only to see that Freddy still didn't know it, to feel her heart harden a little more against him. Soon, very soon, the shell around her heart would have grown as tough as a crab's, and thoughts of Jock Hampton and his eyes and his lips, his Viking face, would no longer trouble her nights and darken her days.

As for Freddy, Jane congratulated herself, she could honestly say in her heart of hearts that she'd never been jealous of another girl, and she didn't intend to start now. Poor Jock . . . when the war was over he'd undoubtedly leave England, and although he'd become an honorary member of their family, who knew how often he'd be able to come back again? And when he saw Freddy after the war, a Freddy in a twin set and a tweed skirt, with a bunch of children and a house to run, would he still be in love with her? She'd be a bit plump then, probably, and perhaps her hair would have started to fade—even to gray a bit— and she'd be preoccupied with the new baby or a sick dog or a cook who hadn't worked out—yes, in a few years, inevitably that's the way Freddy would be. She'd grow out of some of her piss and vinegar . . . England would get to her yet. On the other hand, Jane thought approvingly, she herself would still be enjoying her flings. Ten years of lovely flings would hardly be enough to compensate for the deprivations of thirteen days on duty and only two off. How soon, she wondered, would decent stockings come back after the war?

He was still more or less fond of Freddy, Jock Hampton thought, as he leaned on the windowsill of his room and looked out at Tony and Jane sitting in what looked like a comfortable silence on the blankets under the flowering pear tree, but why the fuck couldn't she stop singing "Till We Meet Again" to his goddaughter? When the Eagle Squadron had still been intact, for a year after her marriage, she and Tony had joined them at the squadron's favorite pub as often as she had leave. Each night, as they sat drinking and smoking and trying not to think about the men who hadn't come back from the latest sortie, she'd sung to them for hours on end, songs of today and songs of World War I that she'd learned from Eve. The evening had never been over for anyone until Freddy had sung that last lovely line, those last words, "Till we meet again," which Jock had always believed, against all logic,

380

was a private promise made directly from her to him. She didn't know it—but he did, and that was what mattered.

Annie's room was right next to his, and even through the thick walls he could hear Freddy's lilting voice as she waltzed the little girl around and around. Didn't Freddy realize that it was the kind of tune that got stuck in your mind and didn't stop driving you crazy for months? Why couldn't she sing "Mairzy Doats" or something forgettable like that? He could always tell her to stop, he supposed, but how can you tell a mother that the sound of her singing to her child is a torment? How could you explain to her that you'd find yourself hearing that old tune when you should be concentrating on one of the dozens of pretty, willing girls you had to beat off with sticks in London? They didn't call pilot's wings "leg spreaders" for no reason . . . they even worked for Second Lieutenants, but rank sure had its privileges.

He could always go out and sit with Jane and Tony, or else find Lady Penelope in the kitchen and give her a hand—the cook was getting too old to be much help—but something had made him unable to move from his observation post. It must be the weather. Everyone in England said it was the hottest May in memory—back home, in San Juan Capistrano, California, U.S.A., it would just have been another nice day, the sort of day on which you'd have a hard time trying to decide whether to surf or play tennis, so you'd end up doing both. Or maybe it was the kind of day on which a guy like himself, in love with speed, in love with danger, in love with excitement, in love with flying, might just hear one word too many about a big show going on overseas in England and manage to dig up the train fare to Canada and get enough flight training so that he could join the Eagle Squadron.

It was exactly on this kind of day, four years ago, that he'd said good-bye to his family and set off—maybe that was why he felt so restless. Not just restless . . . moody. In fact, he was pissed off for some inexplicable reason . . . unquestionably pissed off, which was damn peculiar, for he hadn't had an opportunity to come to The Grange for months now, and he should be enjoying every second of it. Didn't this beat leading his squadron through the hostile air toward Germany, escorting the slow-flying bombers, protecting them from the German antiaircraft guns and fighter planes until they approached the target? Didn't this beat flying back through a sky shit-full of flak, until you could see the coastline below and all you had to worry about was being shot down in water that was never anything but very fucking wet and very fucking cold? And yet, when he was doing his job, he never felt pissed off like this. He might feel bored or terrified or furious or insanely victorious, but one thing about that Mustang P-51, that fucking brilliant fighting machine, that glorious gun platform with wings, was that its pilot never had the time to feel pissed off. Pissed off, in his book, was as maddening as a constant low fever, an aggravation, an irritation, an itch you couldn't scratch, a thirst you couldn't satisfy, no matter how much you drank.

One of the reasons he kept on flying was that he knew if he let them bump him up to Headquarters he'd feel pissed off all of the time, instead of just some of the time. Group HQ grounded him every once in a while, saying that he was due for a rest, but they couldn't keep him on the deck for long. If you wanted to fly and you weren't sick or loony, they just had to let you go and do it, Lieutenant Colonel or not.

When he'd left home to join the Eagle Squadron, he'd just been another wild, sky-mad, inexperienced college kid of twenty who couldn't stand the idea of missing the fun. Now he was twenty-four; he'd learned that fun and war weren't the same thing during his first mission, but he was deeply glad that he'd come to the right place for the wrong reasons. Before the Eagles had been transferred to the United States Army Air Corps, they'd shot down the equivalent of six Luftwaffe squadrons, and that was way back in '42, two centuries ago. Not too shabby. And they hadn't even had their Mustangs then.

Shit, why was he sitting up here waxing philosophical when he could be doing some good in the kitchen? Naturally, Freddy wasn't there— she probably didn't even know how to put together a decent ham sandwich. What a hopeless wife she'd make for Tony after the war—it really made him feel sad just to think about it. A great guy like Tony deserved better. He deserved a girl who'd been brought up to do things graciously, a girl with his own kind of traditions in her blood, a girl who'd sink into the pleasures of peacetime with nothing more on her mind than making him happy. His best friend—the best friend he'd ever had in his life—had every right to a wife who put him first in everything. That was the only kind of girl he'd even *consider* marrying, himself, that was for damn sure.

Instead, poor old Tony was stuck with Freddy, the bossiest bitch a man could imagine. *Everything was wrong with Freddy.* She was too stubborn, too spunky, too aggressive, too determined to have her own way, no matter what. So what if she'd once saved his life? It only went to show what a thoroughly *unreasonable* female she was. How poor Eve and Paul had put up with her all those years, when she was learning how to fly, was beyond him. They might just as well have had a boy like him instead of a tomboy like Freddy, who didn't seem to know she was a mother, much less a wife.

Jock looked down on the lawn and saw Freddy and Annie emerge at a gleeful run. She'd dressed the kid in a pair of tiny blue overalls—now wasn't that typically dumb of her—did she want to turn his goddaughter into a tomboy too? Wasn't one enough in the long-suffering Longbridge family? And look at her; what did she think she was playing at, all done up in a strapless flowered sun dress as if this were the fucking French Riviera? Shit, she even had on red high-heeled sandals—she must have been raiding Jane's closet again. Well, at least it made a change from that navy blue uniform she usually sailed about in like some sort of damn corsair, looking as if she expected him to salute her, with that big smartass smile and that infuriatingly friendly look in her eyes.

Without knowing that he'd done so, Jock got up from his seat by the windowsill and followed Freddy downstairs and outside, no more able to resist being close to her than he'd been able to pull himself away from the sound of her voice while she sang to her daughter.

Freddy lay full length on one of the old blankets, a slim version of one of Renoir's luscious redheads who had happened to borrow her dress from Matisse. She had crossed her bare arms over her eyes to shut out the brightness of a sun to which she had become unaccustomed, and kicked off her shoes so that she could wriggle her bare toes in its warmth.

Whiskey, corned-beef sandwiches and Milky Ways made a mysteriously satisfying combination, she decided; each one was a form of perfection in itself, yet, when taken one after the other, they turned into a total treat that couldn't be explained by the individual parts. Was she feeling this deep contentment because so many of the people she loved were within touching distance? In a few hours her parents were expected on the train from London, and that would make it complete . . . if only Delphine were here. As the thought came into her mind she felt the same unexpected plunge of her heart that attacked her each time she realized how long it had been since any of them had had news of Delphine.

France lay so heartbreakingly near. Barely a day passed when she didn't see its coastline from a cockpit, and yet there might as well have been a concrete wall built around the country, reaching up into the clouds, an impenetrable prison wall that allowed no one to see what

383

was going on inside. Her father would have been notified, through the headquarters of the Free French in London, and their network of radio communications with the Resistance, if anything out of the ordinary had happened to Delphine, and he'd had no news in years. They all had to reassure each other that Delphine was managing to get along somehow, but the lack of any contact was increasingly painful. It was something that she and her parents only talked about among themselves; it wasn't fair to lay another burden on the Longbridges, who had so many children of their own to care for, to say nothing of Annie.

Darling little Annie, she thought, listening to Jock and Tony and Gerald all vying to tempt her into their laps, had probably caused less worry than any baby ever born. She looked a little like Delphine; she had the same perfect little chin, and lips that tilted up at the corners even when she wasn't smiling. She'd been named after Anette de Lancel, much to her grandfather's pleasure, but to Freddy, Annie would always recall the nickname that everyone in the ATA used for the faithful taxi Ansons that had flown them to and from the aircraft they'd ferried some forty million miles within England since the war began. She opened her eyes to see Annie sitting on Gerald's shoulders, her arms wrapped around his neck.

Near him, Jock lay frowning at the sky. What was wrong with Jock anyway, she wondered fleetingly. If only he hadn't been so busy making out like a bandit, he and Jane might have made a couple, as she'd plotted they should. Then they'd all truly be one happy family. She lay back and closed her eyes again, thinking that some people—including Jock, she suspected—didn't approve of her decision to return to flying so soon after Annie's birth, leaving her at Longbridge Grange with her mother-in-law and her bevy of prepubescent aunts. But she had come to England in 1939 to do a job—never mind what had brought her here, never mind if she had been following in Mac's footsteps rather than thinking for herself—and that job would not be over until the war was won. As one of the only thirteen women in England who had the training to fly four-engined aircraft, how could she even consider retiring to spend all her time on one small infant, particularly when Penelope was so willing to take Annie into her practical and experienced care?

Whenever she had her two days off, or even overnight, if she could get a lift from another ATA pilot to the little airport recently built near The Grange, she came home to her daughter, so long as she could report back, without fail, to White Waltham the next morning.

In what other country in the world were the airdromes so close to each other that they were like subway stops, she wondered? There was one less than every ten miles now, many of them on the vast lawns of great homes, on cricket fields, polo fields and soccer fields, many of them so new that they weren't included on any maps, so that, like every other ATA pilot, she put in a lot of time at the Maps and Signal Office, memorizing the positions of the latest landing fields on her route and their surrounding landmarks.

Stirlings delivered to Keevil, Spitfires delivered to Brize Norton, Warwicks to Kemble, Mosquitoes to Shawbury, Halifaxes to Yorkshire, she thought in a sleepy litany—so went her days. The only plane she hadn't been trained to fly was a Flying Boat, and she bet she could handle one if she had to.

Lying here with her eyes closed, Freddy visualized the island that was England as one vast, complicated map, crisscrossed by the many pathways that were so deeply engraved in her mind: the railroad lines, the roads, the forests, the factories, the rivers, the castles and manor houses, the narrow corridors created by thousands of barrage balloons that protected the big cities, the church spires and even the traces of the old Roman roads that still could be seen from the air. Would it ever become a three-dimensional countryside to her, turn into no more —or was it no less?—than this home, with its many rich acres clearly surrounded by boundaries and walls, or would it always remain a two-dimensional map?

Why wonder? Whatever happened after the war wasn't worth bothering about, because the only thing that mattered now was winning. When? When would the invasion come? Baking here lazily in the sun made her feel as if she were goofing off, although the weariness of the last thirteen days was deep in her bones and she knew that she must take advantage of this respite. Jane was as tired as she . . . or was she restless? She'd been awfully snappy at breakfast. Did she just need to get laid?

And if only Tony too looked happier. That weary, tight, almost angry look he had on his lean, lined face seemed more set each time she saw him again, after the long absences their jobs imposed on them. It must be due to the weight of responsibility he had now. What could it be like to send thirty-six planes up every night, after spending all day making plans with the officers responsible for arming and fueling and maintaining each flight, and then sleeping only fitfully after the flight took off, for what wing commander could really sleep when his men were over Europe? Before they were due back, he'd be up, sweating out the return of his planes early the next morning. No wonder he looked so drawn and far away. She tried to chatter enough to take his mind off his preoccupations whenever she could, for ferrying was such a simple job compared to his, but it didn't seem to help somehow.

Thank God they had The Grange to come back to from time to time. She lived with Jane and a bunch of other girls in a cottage they'd rented near White Waltham, while Tony lived at the base. It was a rotten way to conduct a marriage, but war was a rotten way to conduct a world, and until one was over, the other would have to be endured.

"Annie," she said, half-opening her eyes, "do you think you could leave those nice men alone long enough to come and give your mother a little kiss?"

19

DELPHINE stepped resolutely out of her house on the Villa Mozart, but when she saw the huge black Mercedes parked on the cobbles of the narrow street, she stopped moving abruptly, as an involuntary prohibition rendered her incapable of entering the automobile that General von Stern had sent for her. She had been carrying a black chiffon wrap, bordered in silver fox. Now she flung it quickly over her shoulders and clasped it tightly around her with both hands, as if the flimsy garment could protect her.

"If you please, Mademoiselle," the driver in his Nazi uniform said politely, opening the door. Only the familiar, courteous formula enabled her to force her legs to carry her into the car. During the drive to the house on the Rue de Lille, she sat rigidly, as far back in the seat as possible, so as not to be seen through the windows, yet unwilling to allow her back to actually rest against the cushions of the automobile. She breathed shallowly, her gaze riveted, in a trance of loathing, on the helmets on the heads of the driver and the armed soldier who sat beside him.

She had been obliged to allow the general to send his car for her. Delphine had had no car or driver since the Occupation began; there was no fuel for taxis in the spring of 1943, no transportation except by bicycle or foot or Métro—how, in her long, bare-shouldered evening dress and the diamonds Bruno had advised her to wear, could she otherwise have reached the formal dinner party? Bruno had promised her that the cultivated and surprisingly decent general who had requisitioned his house would listen to her fears and set in motion the search for Armand. He had further assured Delphine that she must not be nervous, for she was to be the guest of honor, and she would find herself among people of her own world.

Once she entered the house on the Rue de Lille, Delphine found that although everything should have conspired to make her feel at home, she remained numb and cold with disgust. It was not nervousness that made her awkward, but revulsion. Although Georges, Bruno's butler, whom she had known so well in former days, greeted her with unsurprised warmth as he took her wrap, she could not meet his eyes, and she surrendered the wrap with reluctance. Although Bruno himself, smiling with the success of his plan, was waiting in the entrance hall to offer her his protective arm as she mounted the steps to the salon, her feathery black chiffon gown weighed her down as if it were chain mail. Although General von Stern greeted her with old-fashioned courtesy, bowing correctly over her hand, her lips were incompliant, and her thin smile owed everything to her training.

At dinner, as Delphine sat as stiffly upright as an Edwardian princess, in the chair that she had occupied on so many other occasions, she looked around the table in bleak, profound astonishment. Was there nothing short of downright cannibalism that could mar the worldly surface of a Parisian dinner party, she asked herself?

Arletty, the charming, dark-haired actress, was holding forth in her droll and witty way about the pre-production problems of her next film, *Les Enfants du Paradis*, which was scheduled to be shot in Nice in a few months. At the other end of the perfectly appointed table, Sacha Guitry, who had directed Delphine in one of the several Napoleonic films she had made, *Le Destin Fabuleux de Désirée Clary*, was vainly trying to turn the conversation in his direction, while Albert Préjean, Junie Astor and Viviane Romance, who was about to star in *Carmen* with Jean Marais, all listened, fascinated, to Arletty's description of the plans for the most expensive film that had ever been planned in the history of French filmmaking.

It could be 1937, Delphine thought, drinking from a wineglass that had once been Bruno's, a glass whose very weight and shape were familiar to her hand, if the charming young officer whom everyone in Paris knew was Arletty's lover had not worn a Nazi uniform. She could be having a gay dinner with a group of colleagues if Junie and Albert and Viviane hadn't been among the small group of Continental's many stars who had gone to Berlin last year, and met with Goebbels in a show of Franco-German unity. Only the thought of Armand kept her from rising from her seat and running down the stairs and leaving this house in which the "people of her own world," whom Bruno had promised her, were the most notorious collaborators of the cinema.

After dinner, Bruno guided her to the library where General von Stern sat apart, sipping cognac. He rose as Delphine gathered the folds of her skirt in one hand and sat down next to him, in the chair he indicated.

"I am a great admirer of your art, Mademoiselle," he said eagerly, leaning forward to offer her a cigarette.

"No, thank you, General, I only smoke in films, when the script demands it."

"You are under contract to Continental, I believe. Bravo, Mademoiselle." He measured the tops of her breasts with his eyes, so swiftly that she almost missed his glance.

"Yes, General. I work for Continental," she replied dryly.

"Greven is a good friend of mine. He has done wonders, has he not?" he asked pleasantly, touching her bare arm lightly.

"I imagine the films are as good as can be expected," Delphine answered, swaying gracefully toward the far edge of her chair and folding her hands tightly in her lap.

"General," she began abruptly, unable to endure the small talk, "my brother told me—"

"I explained to the general that you have a certain concern, Delphine." Bruno cut her short. "He understands your position."

"As you know, Mademoiselle, we have always encouraged talent in the cinema," General von Stern said with an expansive gesture. He smiled directly into her eyes.

"*General, can you help me find Armand Sadowski?*" Delphine exclaimed, her voice too loud, her question too specific, her manner too abrupt, for the delicate transaction that Bruno had planned.

"I should like to be able to relieve your mind, Mademoiselle, if it is in my power," the general said, his smile losing none of its insistence.

"My sister means that she would be deeply grateful for any information that would allow her to hope, General," Bruno interjected, gripping Delphine's shoulder.

"You do understand that such . . . hopeful . . . information is normally impossible to obtain?" the general asked. "Even for me?"

"My sister is aware of the problem, General. She realizes how much she would owe you," Bruno answered. "She understands that what she asks is most unusual, most irregular."

"But will you try to find out where he is?" Delphine demanded brusquely, shaking off Bruno's warning fingers with impatience. "*Can I hope?*"

General von Stern pursed his lips thoughtfully as he inspected Delphine openly, from head to toe. He was pleased as he measured the depths of her desperation, and he allowed time to pass without a word, as noncommittal as if she were a shopkeeper and he was turning a piece of antique silver over in his hands, inspecting its hallmarks and trying to make up his mind if—at a certain price, to be sure—it might prove to be an interesting purchase.

"To be sure, nothing is impossible," the general agreed at last, his smile returning. "It's a question of time . . . most careful inquiries . . . a matter that demands tact . . . delicacy . . . my personal attention. I should have to ask favors . . . important favors . . . favors that would have to be repaid. Hope does not come easily in these days, alas. But then you are a woman of the world, are you not? My friend, your brother, has surely made that all quite clear to you. Meanwhile, it would please me a great deal to receive you here often, Mademoiselle de Lancel. Very often indeed. You illuminate every room you enter. You grace my home."

"Thank you, General, but about Monsieur Sadowski—"

"I won't forget our conversation."

He touched her arm again. Dismissively. Commandingly. Caressingly.

"Do have a drop of this cognac. You haven't touched your glass. Did your brother tell you that I have seen every single one of your films? No? Well, he was at fault. I'm one of your greatest fans. Perhaps . . . who knows? . . . I may have some news for you soon . . . if matters proceed as they should. Now, Mademoiselle de Lancel, what do you say to being my guest at the theater next week? Raimu is opening in *Le Bourgeois Gentilhomme* at the Comédie-Française. I have excellent seats —I hope I may count on you?"

Delphine made herself nod in false assent. No, she thought, no, you may not count on me, General, any more than I may count on you.

Bruno volunteered to escort Delphine home, and rode back with her, across the Seine, in silence. He told the driver to wait while he saw her safely into her house.

"Just a minute, Bruno," Delphine said as she turned around, just inside the open door.

"I should be on my way. I don't like to be out this late after curfew."

"I won't keep you long. What foul and filthy business are you doing with that general, Bruno?"

"How dare you! I do no business with him."

"He treated me as if I were for sale. No, as if I'd already been sold and he was awaiting delivery."

"General von Stern was perfectly correct. How did he offend your overdelicate sensibilities?"

"Bruno, you saw and you heard. Don't pretend you don't know what he expects from me."

"Do you imagine that he would go to the trouble of finding your Jew for nothing? Are you that naïve? Are you so special that hope is *due* you? Of course you have to give him something in exchange."

"Is that what you meant when you spoke of using my influence?" she said in such bitter contempt that he grew furious.

"You don't deserve my help. You think that you can afford pride in times like these? Well, I have news for you, you stupid bitch, pride is for the conqueror, not for the vanquished. Do you think that your cunt is too precious to use to get what you want? You asked me to help you, you came begging to me, you were ready to do anything—'Help me, Bruno, help me, is there hope, Bruno, is there hope?'—and when I offer you a chance you'll *never* get again, *never*, you throw it away. Let me tell you something, Delphine—if you want help, be prepared to pay for it! If you insist on hope, peddle yourself while you have a good customer!"

"His price is too high." She threw the words in his face. "I'll manage without it. But no price is too high for you, Bruno, is it? You still haven't told me what stinking business the two of you are up to. You can't merely be his pimp. What currency does he pay you in that's so precious that you'd bring him your sister for his bed?"

"You're insane! I won't give you a second chance."

"That's the only good news I've had in a long time." Delphine looked up at the darkness of Bruno's handsome, vicious face and laughed tauntingly before she pushed him with all her strength so that he stumbled backward as she slammed the door in his face.

In her defiance of Bruno, Delphine found a temporary exultation that carried her through the next few days, but soon her brave words haunted her. She'd said that she'd manage without hope, she'd even believed it while she said it, but hope could not be cast off like an unbecoming dress. Hope was her torture and it had to be endured like a fever, a constant, capricious fever that rose and fell without warning, an irrational, harrowing fever that no medication could control.

She would wake abruptly in the night, as if someone had called her name, and feel the unwanted infection of the hope she'd thrown away, flaming so high that her hair was wet with sweat, her neck and forehead dripping. The next morning, while she was having a costume fitting, she would feel the residue of that fragile, stubborn, foolish hope drain out of her like a hemorrhage, as if the fitter, with pins in her mouth, had suddenly been endowed with the power to condemn her to death. A song—Chevalier, on the radio, jauntily singing "The Symphony of Wooden Soles" in a bow to the fact that there was no more leather for shoes—could cause a forfeited, uninvited flare of hope to mount so high that she felt as if she could rise like a spark from the window of her bedroom and float over Paris. Yet, the same night, listening to Charles Trenet melodically lamenting "What Is There Left of Our Loves?" her heart would be invaded by a wave of vast, unexpected and total desolation, anguish such as she had never known, and she would pay ten times over for every moment of unreasonable, unbidden hope that had had its way with her.

Unsought, a sunrise or a new moon could sweep her into a moment of agonizing, groundless hope, yet she smelled despair in every dead flower, heard it in the cheep of a bird, saw it in dust on a staircase. Helplessly she was ground between the unreasoning welling-up of the hope she had vowed to do without, and the reality of bone-dry hope-lessness, as peaceful as a grave, that she knew she should accept, but that she could not maintain.

Delphine became superstitious as she had never been before: she stopped reading newspapers, and while American troops debarked at Anzio and the Russians liberated Leningrad, she consulted a dozen fortune-tellers; she sought out astrologers as the Germans occupied Hungary and the Luftwaffe lost four hundred and fifty planes in just one week in February of 1944. When General de Gaulle was named commander-in-chief of the armies of the Free French in April of the same year, Delphine was hunting throughout Paris for palmists and clairvoyants. The only hope she could endure was one she knew was clearly artificial. Only false prophets could ease the pain of her heart's inextinguishable hope. She grew steadily thinner and more beautiful. She was on the border of madness.

In all the long history of Paris, no plague, no coronation, no revolution, no wave of popular adulation, no reign of terror, could compare to the mass hysteria and frenzy that gripped the city by mid-August of 1944. Only wild rumor and uncontrollable uncertainty were free to race like a pack of rabid dogs through the streets that lay electric with possibilities under the summer sun. Bridges were barricaded by German troops, movement should have been impossible, yet people swarmed everywhere, they knew not why, and disappeared as quickly as they had arrived. Anticipation, fear and bewilderment were on every face.

Liberation was coming! More than two months after the Americans, the English, the Canadians and the Free French had landed on the beaches of Normandy, at last liberation was coming! No, there would be no liberation! Eisenhower would bypass the city, intent on chasing the Germans toward the Rhine. Nothing could stop liberation! General Leclerc would disobey Eisenhower and march toward Paris!

From mouth to mouth the rumors spread; everything was believed, nothing was believed, yet exultation and the confused beginnings of insurrection were everywhere. The railroad workers went on strike. The Métro workers went on strike. The police recaptured their own headquarters even as a thousand people were routinely deported to a German concentration camp. Teenaged Frenchmen, newly armed with rifles, were massacred on street corners where they had played as children. The crack of gunshots—German or French, no one knew—was heard from roofs, from windows, from the street. Blood pooled on the sidewalks, on the street corners. Delirium bloomed unchecked in the summer air. What was happening? Did anyone know?

On the twentieth of August, General Dietrich von Choltitz negotiated a surrender, promising not to destroy Paris, as Hitler had ordered him to do, in exchange for an orderly withdrawal of his men. Yet the irrepressible uprising continued, heavier than before. Islands of German troops were attacked by untrained snipers. Resistance newspapers that had been printed underground for years were sold in broad daylight to venturesome passersby, while a thousand yards away the French Forces of the Interior battled for control of the City Hall.

Continental had been taken over by the *Comité de Libération du Cinéma Français* on the nineteenth, and all production shut down. Delphine, who lived so close to the Gestapo headquarters on the Avenue Foch, where a furious battle continued, kept to her house, and found herself utterly alone. Violet, Helene, and Annabelle, too prudent to risk the streets, had deserted their jobs, and the neighbors, who knew no more than she did, had retreated firmly behind the closed shutters of their windows. When she looked out of her own windows she saw no sign of life at all on the empty street.

By the twenty-second, except for a few bottles of wine, there were no provisions at all in the house, not so much as a piece of stale bread. Late in the afternoon of the following day, Delphine was so hungry that she decided she had to chance a trip to the nearby market street and try to find something to eat. She hadn't shopped for food in years. She wasn't even sure where the bakery was. She looked for the most inconspicuous clothes she owned, and found a forgotten prewar blue cotton skirt, belted in red, and an old sleeveless white blouse. Instinctively wary of being recognized, she used no makeup and brushed her hair so that it fell in shadowy wings over her face.

As she passed the empty, inexplicably closed guardian's house, and turned into the main street, she felt exposed and imperiled by the unnatural, surrealistic silence of the neighborhood. Could everyone have left the city, she wondered. Were they being sensible and staying home to wait and see what would happen? Surely they too must have run out of food, or had they had the wisdom to lay in some provisions, no matter how meager?

On the market street, only two shops were open, and Delphine, armed with her ration book, was able to buy two withered turnips, an onion, and three hard rolls. She chewed one of them hungrily as she scurried home, keeping to the shelter of the buildings and walking as fast as she possibly could without running. Thankfully she turned into the relative security of the Villa Mozart, now frankly racing toward the protection of her own walls. Out of breath, she took the key to the front door from her pocket and had almost inserted it when two men suddenly stepped out from around the side of the house. Fear struck to her heart, for they were tramps, clad in rags, bearded, desperate and terrifying.

"No, please no, don't," she whispered, too petrified to scream, looking around frantically for the help that she knew was not to be found. She held out her shopping bag, trying to ward off their menace with the offer of food, but they advanced steadily toward her. She could smell their filth.

"It's all right," one of the tramps said hoarsely.

"What?" Delphine shrank away but she knew they had seen the house key in her hand and it was too late.

"Your get-up," the tramp said, his voice breaking, "simple, patriotic —just right, babe . . ."

"Armand!"

". . . to welcome a soldier . . . to welcome him home . . ." He fainted into her arms.

On the twenty-fifth of August, General Omar Bradley ordered two divisions into Paris: the French 2nd under General Leclerc, and the 12th Regiment of the American 4th Division, accompanied by the American 102nd Cavalry Group.

Weeping and cheering, on a flood tide of such ecstasy that it surpassed any individual rejoicing, the citizens of Paris poured out of every building and took to the streets. Bells rang constantly in every church tower, while, at the City Hall, when he was asked to proclaim the existence of the Republic, de Gaulle answered, "The Republic has never ceased to exist."

Colonel Paul de Lancel was a member of the group that accompanied de Gaulle. He had helped to implement Gustave Moutet's inspired idea to use the maps from his 1939 *Michelin Guide* to assist in the D-Day operations, maps which gave the Allied Forces invaluably detailed information. Paul was unable to get through to Champagne by telephone, for it was still occupied by the Germans. Three days later, as soon as he learned that Patton's Third Army had liberated Épernay, he borrowed an American jeep and set off to find his parents.

He had been able to snatch only a few hours with Delphine. When she flung open the door in answer to his unannounced ring, the power of her welcome had all but knocked him off his feet. Her emotion was absolute, yet somehow secondary, and when she led him quickly upstairs to meet Armand Sadowski, Paul looked no further for the reason for her happiness.

Delphine was as light and fragile as swansdown, yet he could see that she was nursing her returned soldier and his friend, a Norman named Jules, tirelessly, sending the women of her household scurrying everywhere in the neighborhood to unearth ingredients to make soup that she fed spoonful by spoonful to the tall, terribly thin, terribly weary man who lay a prisoner in her bedroom, not allowed to do anything but eat and rest.

"Was she this bossy at home?" Armand Sadowski had asked Paul de Lancel, insisting, as one man to another, that, weak as he was, he had the strength to shave himself.

"Yes," Paul had answered, "but her basic intentions were always good." He fell at once into an easy relationship with this man of whose existence he had just learned. Delphine had wanted Armand to tell Paul of his escape, but the only thing Sadowski could say was, "We had dumb luck . . ." before he drifted off to sleep. Later Delphine told Paul the meager details Armand had given her of his escape from the vast Schweinfurt ball-bearing factory, where he had worked for years, preserved from death by the German need for slave labor. During one of the repeated American bombings of the enormous factory, Sadowski and his pal Jules, who, like Armand, had picked up a smattering of the German language, dressed in the uniforms of dead German guards and made their perilous way by foot through Germany and across the border into France.

They had been almost invisible, protected by the vast confusion of war and the presence of mobs of millions of refugees made homeless by round-the-clock Allied bombing. Once back in French territory, they had been helped by peasants and bands of local Resistance members, who gave them clothes to wear.

Passed from one link of the Resistance chain to another, they had made a painfully slow trip toward Paris, hiding from German patrols that might have demanded their nonexistent papers. "It wasn't luck, Father, it was a miracle," Delphine said, towering in her love for Armand, and Paul had realized that his frivolous, flighty, willful daughter had disappeared forever into a woman of twenty-six whose strength he had yet to measure.

Paul managed to get a brief message to Eve in London that Delphine was safe and well before he set off, very early, on the road to Champagne. The journey took longer than he had expected, for at every village his jeep was stopped and acclaimed by excited crowds, as if he were a fairy-tale hero riding on a dragon. It was afternoon before Paul found himself at the great door of the Château de Valmont. He hesitated a minute before jumping down, remembering a conversation with Eve in 1938, after Munich, when he had decided, as casually, as foolishly as if the world had nothing but time, to wait to visit France until the next spring. Consular business had forced him to postpone that intended spring visit for a few months, and then, while the world stood by in helpless disbelief, his country had plunged into the long, dark, terrible night of the Occupation.

It had been more than a decade since he had last stepped onto the soil of Champagne, but Paul knew there must be something seriously wrong at Valmont, for he had driven past the unimaginable sight of empty vineyards in which no one, not even a child, was at work. The front door hung open on its stout hinges, and not a soul had come forward to see who had driven through the gates.

Paul crossed the threshold of his childhood home, and ran directly to the kitchens, the heart of the house, without finding anybody. Rapidly he searched the reception rooms and finally the bedrooms, without success. The château was as silent and empty, as untouched and unchanged, as if it had been bewitched, yet all the rooms showed signs of recent human habitation. Clearly it had not been occupied by the Germans. He returned to the front door and had been standing there for a minute, deeply disturbed, when he saw a long line of black-clad men and women approaching slowly on foot. An old woman detached herself from the file and ran clumsily toward him.

"Monsieur Paul, is it you?" she cried urgently, her creased face turned up toward him, almost as if she were hoping it would be someone else. "Is it truly you?" He recognized Jeanne, the housekeeper, who had been a plump young maid in the house when he was growing up, more than forty years ago.

"Jeanne, Jeanne, my dearest Jeanne, of course it's me! What's happening, why is the château empty? *Where are my parents?*"

"We come from the churchyard. We buried your mother today, Monsieur Paul," she said, and burst into tears.

"And my father—where, Jeanne, where?" he asked, although he knew the answer from her streaming eyes.

"It's more than two years since he left us, may God rest their souls."

Paul turned away. The empty vineyards, the deserted château, had already whispered the truth to him. It was ever thus when the entire population of Valmont was burying one of its number. But he had dared to hope that it was not one of his parents. Jeanne plucked at his sleeve.

"Monsieur Paul, at least Monsieur Bruno is alive, remember that," she said, trying to comfort him.

"Bruno . . ." He turned and searched the crowd who stood around, waiting to greet him, their sorrow mingled with surprise at the novel sight of a French officer in uniform. "Yes, Bruno—why is he not here?"

"He left right after the funeral. He said he had business in Paris but he'd be back tonight. He's fine, Monsieur Paul, he's been here in safety since the Armistice began. It was a cruel time, such an evil long time . . . the worst time I can remember . . . I can't begin to believe it's over. Come inside, Monsieur Paul, and I'll find you something to eat, you must be hungry."

"In a while, Jeanne, thank you. First . . . I must go to the churchyard."

After Paul returned from a silent hour's vigil by the graves of his parents, he spent hours driving around the roads that bordered the Lancel vineyards, stopping whenever he saw workers to greet them and ask about their welfare. At fifty-nine, in the uniform he had worn since he joined de Gaulle in 1940, Paul de Lancel was a fine-looking man; his thick blond hair was now gray, but his carriage was upright, his massive body as vigorous as ever, his glance resolute and skeptical at the same time, calmly commanding. Many of the workers had never seen him before. Paul had not been back in Champagne, except during a few vacations, since the First World War began, thirty years earlier. However, many of the older workers remembered him as a young man, and every one of them of every age gave him a hero's welcome, for he was a Lancel returning to his home, and none of them had ever worked for anyone but a Lancel, nor had their fathers or their fathers' fathers.

Paul picked up scraps of news as he talked in the vineyards: the managements of Moët & Chandon and Piper-Heidsieck had been completely taken over by the Germans in early 1944; during the past years, many employees and heads of other houses had been arrested by the Gestapo for anti-German activities; several hundred local Resistance members had been murdered or deported; massive Allied bombing at Mailly had destroyed the entire Von Stauffen division that had been concentrated there before the invasion of Normandy; there had been even more destructive Allied bombing at Rilly, where the Germans had stored V-2 rockets in the tunnel that ran through the Mountain of Rheims. Only ten days ago an entire train, heavily loaded with champagne, had left Rheims, bound for Germany. Now throughout the province of Champagne a shortage of bottles had developed, but, as each of the workers was quick to tell him, during the past three years the district had produced harvests of exceptional quality. They all agreed that the vineyards had greatly suffered during the war, the invasion had damaged many vines, no replanting had taken place, but look, Monsieur Paul, just look at the ripening grapes—were they not a fine sight? The Liberation harvest would be a good one.

Yes, by God, yes, Paul thought, Champagne had survived another war, for its people were utterly indomitable, with a strength to which he responded so deeply that he found tears filling his eyes as he watched them busily weeding by hand around the delicate stumps of the vines, uncomplainingly completing the next-to-last of the twenty-seven obligatory tasks that ensured the harvest. Yesterday they had been liberated, this morning they had buried his mother, whom they had loved all of their lives, but this afternoon, as always, the cultivation of the vines came before all else. They were obstinate, determined, courageous, the only vine tenders in France to have continued to persevere so far north. Without their attachment to the land called Champagne, the wine called champagne would have long since ceased to exist, for it can only be produced in a cold climate.

Paul had dinner with Jeanne in the kitchen, and afterwards he spent hours alone, smoking, ruminating, wandering about the château that now, with the death of Anette de Lancel, had become his responsibility.

He had never dreamed that it would be Bruno who would be the strength of the family, Bruno who must have been staunch and valiant indeed to have stepped into the role his grandfather had filled for so

398

long, and to have managed to hold the vineyards, the House of Lancel, and the château on a steady path throughout the difficulties of the past four years. He owed his son a great deal, he realized with rising happiness. How could he have so underestimated the boy? Was it now possible that he and Bruno, at long last, united as father and son, would work together in the great job of rehabilitation of the vineyards which lay ahead?

They were the only male Lancels left; to succeed in this effort was their duty as well as their heritage, and they must shoulder the task for the sake of the family, for the House of Lancel, as well as for every loyal worker in the vineyards. Paul knew that hard years of rebuilding lay ahead, but he felt himself filled with energy and a sense of absolute rightness. He had much to learn—everything!—but champagne making was not a mystery, it followed strict laws that had been laid down, one by one, since Dom Perignon became cellarer at Hautvillers in 1668. His father's key workers, the *chef de cave*, the vineyard foremen, were still alive, hale and active, ready to teach him everything he needed to know.

He strode up and down the long salon, growing more elated with each step. A new life, by God, after all these years of foreign service! He welcomed it with all his heart, this life that would demand all his still-abundant strength and the fruits of his intelligence. He and Eve would grow young together in Champagne! What a magnificent châtelaine she would make! Four years of ambulance driving in bombed-out London had proved that there was nothing she couldn't tackle—not that there ever had been. With Bruno, they would restore that life of grace and dignity and productivity which the Lancels had led century after century.

Paul realized, slow shock growing at the same time as his unforeseen excitement, that he, Paul de Lancel, had totally lacked foresight. Busy with his own problems, far from France for decades at a time, he had not dreamed intelligently of this possible future. He had not planned for the day on which he might suddenly find himself the sole owner of the ancient House of Lancel, the sole proprietor of the vineyards that stretched as far as the eye could see around this well-loved château, the lord of the forest, of the stables, of everything that surrounded him down to the last egg laid by one of the chickens out in their hidden coops, of which Jeanne was so proud. He had left Champagne too young, too unfinished a man to dream of a future that now presented itself to him with the allure and mystery of a bride.

Minute by minute, Paul became more jubilant, more exultant.

Carrying on the House of Lancel would give meaning to the rest of his life. He too was Champenois-born, and although he had been absent too long from his native soil, it was not too late to come home. Paul resolved with all his heart to answer the challenge he had just come to recognize fully and embrace. With this resolve, as is often the case with a true Champenois, grew a thirst, and Paul went in search of the finest bottle of champagne the province could provide.

A while later, in the darkest time of the night, an hour before the early dawn of August, Bruno returned to Valmont from Paris. He had made the trip in order to see how matters stood on the Rue de Lille. General von Stern had left his house as he had found it; all was in order, and Georges, his butler, was already directing the servants in anticipation of Bruno's return.

Of course, the general was now in the hands of the officials who had accepted the surrender of the German garrison of Paris, but Bruno did not fear for his future. The man was as resourceful as he was philosophical, and together, during the past year, he and Bruno had joined their wits and connections to make a series of fortunes together on the black market. The failure with Delphine had not blinded von Stern to the profit motive, and now his money was as safe in Switzerland as was Bruno's own.

As he entered the château in which he had spent the war, Bruno wished he had not had to return, even for a few weeks, but the current atmosphere in Paris was uncomfortably explosive. Various factions of the Resistance were embroiled in fighting among themselves; accusations and counter-accusations filled the air; arrests of known collaborators were taking place; groups of young hotheads were roaming the streets, conducting kangaroo courts, and, most dangerous of all, every hour brought fresh denunciations of anyone who was so much as suspected of having been too friendly with the former conqueror. Four years of frustration and fury were erupting all over Paris. *Les réglements de comptes*—final accounting for actions during the war—were the order of the day. He had nothing to fear, surely, for he and von Stern had been utterly discreet—yet could one ever be entirely sure? People had an inconvenient way of knowing more than one expected. Ordinary men were envious of their betters, they always had been, and denunciations were one way in which they could avenge themselves for the inequalities of circumstances. Why, Bruno asked himself, should he take even the slightest chance if reason told him that a measure of caution was still desirable? No, it was not yet safe to move back to his fine Paris house, not yet time to leave the protection of this country-side.

But oh, how he thirsted for the moment when all would be normal! The glorious future lay just a few short weeks away. Paris, as always throughout history, would become itself again and he would be there to revel in its revival. He, Vicomte Bruno de Saint-Fraycourt de Lancel, would take his place once more in the only world he had ever known that was worth living in and living for. Now he would never need to grub at a job, never be obliged to do anything except allow his money to make more money while he enjoyed a gentleman's ease and sport and splendor, moving as it pleased him from salon to salon of the Boulevard Saint-Germain, entertaining in his beautiful house, collecting new women—Parisian women again, after a necessarily limited, yet far from uninteresting diet of provincials—as he would collect great paintings and splendid furniture and precious objects from the stupid new poor whom the war had ruined. He would buy back one of the Saint-Fraycourt châteaux and live in it as if history since the Revolution had never happened. Yes, Bruno thought, as he strode quickly upstairs to his room in Valmont, yes, all things considered, he had had a very good war, and in weeks, just weeks, he would return, triumphant as a prince on his coronation day, to the world of the old aristocracy, which was, when all was said and done, the only love of his life.

He walked into his room, turned on the light and froze, every muscle contracted in alarm.

"What the devil!" he exclaimed.

Paul's tall figure rose from the chair in which he had been sitting in the dark, waiting for his son.

"My God!"

"Did I frighten you, Bruno?"

"But it's *impossible* . . . how could you be . . . where . . . when?" Bruno babbled, shocked into immobility.

"I got here this morning."

"But that's fine—yes, wonderful, a great surprise, you came almost as quickly as Patton—you've seen Jeanne, then? She gave you a good dinner, I hope." Bruno's good manners, which never let him down, rallied to carry him through this moment with the father he had not seen, or cared to see, for eleven years.

"An excellent dinner. Aren't you going to offer me a glass of champagne, Bruno?"

"You mean Jeanne didn't open a bottle? It's late for champagne, almost morning—but of course, to toast your return—why not? Like

401

everybody else, we had to sell almost everything we produced to the Germans—I'm sure Jeanne told you—but I can still find something fit to drink."

"Why not a pink champagne, Bruno, a pink champagne from a vintage year, the kind your grandfather took such pride in? Will you not offer to open a bottle of the best Lancel?"

"You sound strange, Father, not yourself, not at all. I understand . . . the shock of Grandmother's death . . . a sad homecoming . . . I should have realized sooner. Perhaps you should try to get some rest."

Paul took a key on a gold chain from his pocket. "My father gave me this when I left for war in 1914, to remind me of Valmont, wherever I was. I used it tonight, to open *Le Trésor.*"

Involuntarily, Bruno took a step backward.

"I don't have to tell you what I found."

"No," Bruno said coldly, "don't give yourself the trouble."

"There used to be half a million bottles there, Bruno."

"I used them, as would any intelligent man. While you had your soft war in London, far from your country, tagging after your courageous, talkative general, never seeing a German, I did what I had to do."

"For whom did you do it?" Paul's dry voice was empty of emotion. He might have seemed merely curious.

"For myself."

"Not even for the Germans?"

"I repeat, for myself. I have no intention of bothering to lie to you." The primitive contempt in Bruno's voice cracked like a lash on tender flesh.

"It was the black market, of course."

"If you say so. A market is a market—the only difference is who sells and who buys."

"And the money you made?"

"Safe. You can never find it."

"What makes you think you can get away with this?"

"Think? *I have.* It's done. Finished, over. You can't retrieve those bottles, can you? And you can prove nothing. Nobody in this world except the two of us knows that they were ever there."

"Your word against mine?"

"Precisely."

"Leave Champagne," Paul commanded.

"Gladly."

"Leave France."

"*Never!* This is my country."

"You have no country from this time onward. If you do not leave France, I will expose you, and I will be believed. *I promise you dishonor such as you cannot imagine.* You dishonor your name, you dishonor your family, you dishonor your tradition, you dishonor our dead. No one in France will ever think of you without horror. We have long memories. Your country is lost to you."

"You won't be able to make people believe all that." Bruno still sneered.

"*You don't dare to risk it.* The man who could sell the heart's blood of Valmont on the black market did not stop there. What other crimes did you commit during the war? All criminals leave a trail, particularly when they do not act alone. Do you imagine that the government of a free France will fail to deal with men like you? I offer you no choice."

Bruno whirled and lunged toward the desk, where he kept a revolver. He plunged his hand into the drawer but found nothing, for Paul had searched the room while he waited for his son's return.

"*You would do that too, would you?*" Paul cried. He raised the riding crop he had taken from Bruno's night table and, with the unnatural strength of a man who is forced to kill a vile and deadly snake, lashed out and laid open Bruno's upper lip so that his teeth showed white through the blood.

"*Go!*" he said, keeping his voice low. "*Go!*" When Bruno held his ground, Paul used the riding crop again and again, until Bruno turned and started running down the stairs, with Paul, his arm raised, following closely, ready to rip Bruno's face apart if the foul traitor did not leave the land he had desecrated.

20

"THE thing I do outstandingly—everyone agrees—is sell cakes," Freddy said to Delphine, her smile wide with enthusiasm. "I had so much valuable experience at Van de Kamp's, back in Los Angeles, and the knack of pastry selling is something you never lose. My mother-in-law was terribly pleased —she said they'd never had such a successful cake sale at any winter church bazaar since she could remember—there wasn't so much as a single soggy scone left on the table, and the apple pies I baked myself were the first to go. We made twenty-five pounds for Doctor Barnardo's."

Delphine lay back languidly on the cushions of a sofa in the sitting room of the roomy new apartment she and Armand, married at last, had rented on the Rue Guynemer, opposite the Luxembourg Gardens. Freddy and Tony Longbridge were staying with them for a few days, before going on to visit Eve and Paul at Valmont, on their first trip outside of England since the end of the war, a year earlier.

"Who's Doctor Barnardo?" Delphine asked in idle curiosity.

"He runs orphanages—the money goes for Christmas presents for the kids. I was also involved in the jumble sale to raise money for a new roof for the village church. Every Sunday morning we sit there, singing hymns as softly as possible, waiting for the old one to come crashing down. A really rousing sermon would mean disaster."

"What a dreadful way to go, after all those years of not having a bomb land on your head," Delphine murmured in indolent agreement.

"Precisely! That's why I volunteered to help run the sale," Freddy said fervently. "Since gas is still not to be had, even if you have the ration coupons, I hitched a horse up to a cart and drove it absolutely everywhere—you can't imagine the stuff people gave me! They turned their attics upside down; heaps of bric-a-brac, old books, china they didn't even remember they had, old clothes—you name it. I didn't turn down a single donation—you never know what's going to appeal to people—and we had a near sell-out. It's amazing what you can accomplish with only one ancient horse . . . Tony was so proud of me."

"As well he should be, Honorable Freddy," Delphine agreed benevolently.

"In June the summer church fête will be held on the vicarage lawn. Everybody tells me it's incredibly colorful," Freddy said, sparkling with anticipation. "There's going to be Maypole dancing and pony rides and a pet show, but the main attractions really are the contests for the best flowers and the best vegetables. The competition can be very heated, I hear. So much prestige is involved! I haven't decided yet whether to concentrate on peonies or tomatoes, but I'm beginning to wonder if I shouldn't do both. I have to make up my mind as soon as we get back, and start working. It's more of a challenge, don't you think, Delphine, when you don't specialize in just one area?"

"Oh, absolutely. I couldn't agree more. Personally, I'd go in for the Maypole dancing."

"Oh, Delphine! That's for the children, not for old married ladies like us."

"Be careful who you call an old married lady," Delphine growled lazily, patting her belly complacently.

"Old married, very, very pregnant lady."

"Leave out the 'old' and I'll agree to the rest."

"You were always so vain . . . I guess you're entitled to that much of a concession . . . twenty-eight isn't really old."

"Twenty-six isn't either," Delphine observed wryly. "Even if you do have little Annie."

"Oh, I never think about age," Freddy said gaily. "There's just too much to do at Longbridge Grange. I've got my bridge lessons, and now that some of the staff have come back to work, Penelope is teaching me all the fine points of dinner parties, and I'm learning to embroider so I can make tray mats and how to knit so I can make tea cosies and egg cosies for the next bazaar—apple pies are too easy—and of course there's my Sunday school."

"Your *own* Sunday school?" Delphine asked, manifesting as much surprise as her supine position permitted.

"Absolutely. It's a Longbridge tradition, every Sunday afternoon from three to four—just for children up to ten years old. After that, they go to the vicarage to prepare for confirmation. I keep the attendance books, and if a child shows up for six consecutive weeks I put a pretty stamp in it, but if any of them miss even one single week they have to start the six weeks all over again *from the beginning* to get the stamp."

405

"That seems rather drastic," Delphine objected.

"Consecutive must mean consecutive," Freddy insisted with ardor. "It's excellent character training. Penelope plays hymns on the piano, and the children sing and I read them Bible stories. I'm getting rather good at it."

"Somehow I never thought you were the religious type . . . still, people do change, don't they? And we haven't seen each other in so long . . . you're getting to be the perfect English gentlewoman."

"I hope so . . . after all, I married a country gentleman, didn't I? Oh, I almost forgot to tell you the most exciting thing of all—I'm making my own potpourri! Penelope has a secret recipe—it's been in the family for hundreds of years—so I decided to invent my own. I started with lavender and roses, naturally, and then I just went plain crazy: marigold petals, cornflowers, heather, salvia, larkspur, pinks, lemongrass, lemon verbena, thyme, feverfew, peppermint leaves, sweet woodruff, mace, chamomile flowers, powdered orrisroot—just a touch —violets, geranium leaves, a dash of powdered nutmeg—let's see, did I forget anything? Heavens! Cinnamon sticks! Don't even *try* to make it without cinnamon sticks. Of course, the secret is in perfect timing in the picking of the flowers for drying—only in the morning after the dew has evaporated, and only when the flower is *perfect.* Then you mix, very, very carefully, and add essential oils at the end. The whole process is far more complicated than it sounds. My potpourri is going to be wonderful when it's aged properly. Right now it still smells a little . . . unfinished . . . but my mother-in-law's very optimistic. I'll send you some when I'm satisfied with it. Delphine . . . Delphine? . . . are you asleep?"

An hour later, when Armand came back from his walk with Tony, he found Delphine brushing her hair before dinner, refreshed by her nap.

"Did you have a nice, intimate, sisterly talk with Freddy?" he asked.

"Fascinating. And you with Tony?"

"Highly informative. I know more than I ever wanted to know about the stupidity of the Labour government, shortages, lack of funds, price controls, low productivity, high taxes, and the all-over impossibility of ever getting anything done in England. I kept wishing I was back here, listening to the two of you wallowing in low-down, sexy girl talk."

"Don't feel left out, you didn't miss much. Unless you enjoy watching a very bad actress at work."

"What bad actress?"

Delphine yawned luxuriously. "My little sister, you oaf. I was brilliant, pretending to believe her."

"As brilliant as usual?"

"You bet your ass, Sadowski. I think I'll let you stick around, after all."

Freddy looked up from her embroidery frame as she heard Tony tear sheets of airmail paper into tiny bits and throw them into the small fire that burned ineffectively in their bedroom at Longbridge Grange, against the bone-chilling damp of a rainy April afternoon in 1946, an austere springtime of tiny, unopened buds and increased rationing.

"Wasn't that from Jock?" she protested. "I wanted to read it too."

"I didn't want to waste your time," Tony said, clearly irritated at his friend's letter.

"More about his relentless love life? I rather enjoy all the disgustingly sordid details. Makes a change from Trollope."

"Not even that, darling. He's got another of his mad ideas. Now he wants to lease a bunch of surplus planes and start an air cargo business."

"That must mean Jock still hasn't got a job," Freddy said thoughtfully. "How long does he expect that the fortune he won at poker is going to last?"

"Not long, if he goes on like this. He's dead keen on the notion—he says he can rent DC-3s for four thousand dollars a year, a special veteran's rate—'only four thousand,' mind you—and he proposes that *we* pull up roots and move to Los Angeles and go into partnership with him. Us! Just like that! He says the place is crowded with demobed pilots and ground crew who will work for practically nothing to get a job in aviation. He says we'd be getting in on the ground floor of a whole new industry. I say he's a piss-artist."

"Some things never change," Freddy agreed. "Did he say what kind of cargo he was talking about?"

"You know Jock—he's thinking of fresh produce—can't you just picture a DC-3 full of vegetables? Jock says the plane holds three and a half tons of cargo. It's a classic Hampton cock-up . . . the flying greengrocer."

"As a matter of fact, oddly enough," Freddy said thoughtfully, "somehow it rings a bell."

"How so?" Tony asked, surprised by the unaccustomed pensiveness of her tone.

"On the West Coast we grow so much stuff that's out of season in the East, and too perishable to go by train . . . there has to be a market for it." Freddy had put down her embroidery frame and was looking into the fire with dreaming, visionary eyes that saw a country Tony Longbridge had never believed really existed.

"Now hold it, darling. In the first, second and third place, if it were a foolproof plan and we wanted to do it, which it isn't and we don't, we can't possibly take any money out of this country to go into a partnership, not even with Jock, the silly blighter. Currency restrictions, remember? We couldn't have gone to Paris if the Sadowskis hadn't put us up."

"You know perfectly well that I have fifteen thousand dollars in Los Angeles, gathering interest since 1939."

"That's your private nest egg."

"It's my dower, my wedding portion . . . you did not marry an empty-handed bride."

"I've never agreed with you about that. It's your own money—nothing to do with me."

Freddy paid no attention to his familiar protestation. "If," she said, "and I'm just saying 'if,' Tony, it's only a 'for instance,' so don't jump on me—*if, just for instance,* we did use that money, we could lease a couple of planes and still have plenty left over for living expenses before we started to make a profit. If Jock leased another two, maybe three planes, *only for instance,* so we'd have five all together—"

"Steady on!"

"Just let me finish my thought—I wonder what Jock means when he says guys will work for practically nothing—how much 'nothing' would that be exactly?"

"Freddy! What the bloody hell are you raving about? A fleet of five cargo planes! You're not taking this seriously, are you?"

"Hmm . . . just turning it over in my mind, only for fun, merely letting it simmer . . ."

"Are you indeed?"

"How does it hurt to imagine it, Tony, just to *imagine* those DC-3s, loaded to the gills, taking off for New York or Boston or Chicago—but of course I'm being whimsical, it's not as if we could possibly leave The Grange."

"I should damn well think not."

"You've lived here all your life. How could you begin to consider pulling up stakes and moving to a strange place where the sun shines every day of the year or they give you your money back?" Freddy had walked over to the window and stood looking out at the funereal, inexorable rain that had been falling for weeks, during the English spring. "I wonder what it's like above the weather?" she murmured. "Is the evening star still there?"

"What was that, darling?"

"Nothing." She smiled at him gently. "Jock doesn't need us anyway if he wants to get into air cargo. As he said, California is swarming with pilots. And we have our life here—you have the land to manage, and I have Annie and my bazaars and my bridge lessons and the Sunday school. Still . . . if neither of us took a salary . . . no, never mind."

" 'Never mind'—two of the most irritating words in the English language, as well you know. If neither of us took a salary, then what?" Tony demanded.

"I was just wondering about . . . well . . . profits. There wouldn't be any, not for a while. It wouldn't be a piece of cake. First we'd have to get there, find a place to live, buy a car, rent an office, arrange for hangar space, pay office staff, interview pilots and crew . . . it would cost a bundle just to gas up five DC-3s . . ." Her voice trailed off as she looked at the dripping yews below their window. She seemed to be insulated from the firelit room by a haze of yearning so palpable that it quivered in the air.

" 'Five DC-3s'? Are they that real to you already?" Tony asked, with an enigmatic note in his voice.

"I'm just remembering all the financial problems I had with my flying school."

"It was rough, wasn't it?"

"Yep. Real rough." As she turned to answer Tony's question, a passionate, wild, hopeful child looked out of Freddy's eyes for just a second before she lowered her lids, but it was too late and Tony had seen it.

"Was it more difficult than the cake sale?"

"Not on the same level."

"Rougher?"

"Considerably."

"But you did it well, didn't you?"

"I managed."

"Was it as thrilling as making potpourri?"

"Stop teasing, Tony. That's like comparing . . . oh, flying to . . . to . . . there's nothing you *can* compare it to, is there?" With a resolute set to her jaw, Freddy buttoned up her cardigan, sat down and took up her embroidery again.

"Darling, who do you think you're kidding? You're *perishing* to try this air cargo caper. Do you think I don't see you stop whatever you're doing and listen hard every time a plane passes overhead?"

"Habit, mere habit," Freddy said, blushing angrily.

"Rubbish! If your ears could flap, they would."

"Well, even if Jock's idea did intrigue me," Freddy cried, "how could we ever consider taking such an enormous step? It would mean moving away from your family, it would be a complete change of our way of life. You'd hate it, Tony, I know you would. So let's just not talk about it anymore."

"But you're dying to give it a try, aren't you? Try to tell me that isn't true."

"I'm not any good at lying to you, am I? But times have changed. The war's over, Tony. I've . . . settled down in this sceptered isle . . . this other Eden . . . this demi-paradise."

"Bullshit, sweetheart. What's more, you forgot 'this earth of majesty' and 'this seat of Mars.' That will never do. Oh, you put on a bloody marvelous act, I grant you, but what did the war ever have to do with the way you feel about flying? My poor grounded baby, reduced to one fucking horsepower, and an old farm nag at that."

"I've never complained," Freddy said tonelessly.

"No, and that's the scary part. It's so unlike you to be docile—it makes me nervous. Look here, Freddy, I honestly, truly wouldn't mind a bit of a change. I get in Father's way a hell of a lot. He's much less impatient than I am with red tape, and a damn sight more experienced. If he really needed me here I couldn't even consider it, just couldn't, you know that, but it's not as if it were forever—I mean, why the hell not? Old Jock's not stupid, got the spirit of enterprise, that boy does. And when we blow all the money, and come back with our tails between our legs—"

"It'll be *my* nickel?" Freddy exclaimed, still not believing him. Tony nodded at his wife, withholding nothing.

"YIPPEE!" Freddy catapulted out of her chair, so high into the air that her wide-flung fingertips brushed the beams of the ceiling.

A tiny knock sounded at their door and Annie slipped in, dressed for bed in a long, flowered flannel nightgown. "Yippee what?" she asked.

"Guess what, little Annie, we're all going to visit your pal Jock in the place your Mama grew up in—the City of the Angels, she used to call it," Tony said.

"Like in Sunday school?" Annie asked, wary, but ready to be enchanted.

"Nothing like that at all. Like a summer day, like a big, warm, blue trip to the seaside, and do you know the best thing about it? Your Papa won't have to play bridge with your poor Mama any more because—don't tell her I told you—but she still hasn't figured out the difference between trumps and spades, and odds are she never will."

"So what are we going to call it?" Jock asked, as he poured himself a beer in the backyard of the tiny house Freddy and Tony had finally found near the Burbank Airport.

"Something confidence-inspiring, I should think," Tony answered. "What do you make of 'National Airfreight Express Limited'?"

"A bit windy, old chap, if you don't mind my saying so."

"Undoubtedly you have a better suggestion, old buddy?"

"I kinda like 'Fast Freight Forward.' " Jock grinned proudly at his inventiveness.

"I wouldn't give my business to an outfit with a name like that," Freddy protested. "It sounds like a football play on a high school team . . . a second-rate high school."

"Why Freddy, I think that Jock's name is just plain fabulous," protested Brenda, Jock's latest girl and their volunteer office manager. "You could even call it 'Fabulous Fast Freight Forward'—I bet I could get Hedda Hopper to use it as an item."

"Brenda, you don't exactly have a vote here," Jock said hastily. "Brenda knows a lot of people in show business," he explained, turning to Freddy and Tony.

Freddy inspected Brenda with wonder. Her dark hair was so long and shiny that she looked as if she had puddles on her shoulders. Her astonishing tits indicated full female maturity, yet could she possibly be old enough to have graduated from high school? Where did Jock find them? He had sworn that she could type, take dictation, file and answer phones, but she looked as if she'd never even done her own long and perfect dark red nails. And why did she have a Southern accent, when she said she was from San Francisco?"

"Darling, any ideas?" Tony asked Freddy.

"Eagles," Freddy said promptly.

"Eagles? What kind of name is that?" Jock objected immediately. He was still smarting over the fact that Freddy had spent several days teaching him and Tony how to fly the big, unfamiliar, twin-engined

411

planes, after she checked out in one herself, with a mere half hour of instruction. Six years in Spits, and he'd actually had to take hours of instruction from her, as if he were a kid.

"Look," Freddy said patiently, "you guys are heroes, and you met because of the Eagle Squadron, so it makes sense if we try to get a little mileage out of it. Eagles—short, to the point, easy to remember, no confusing initials."

"It does have sentimental value," Tony agreed. "Send your cauliflower to market by Eagles—memorable, that."

"Jock?" Freddy asked. "What do you think?"

"Looks like I'm outnumbered. 'Eagles' is O.K., I guess."

"Jock, honey," Brenda drawled, "what exactly was the Eagle Squadron?"

"And where's Our Lady of the DC-3s this morning?" Jock asked Tony as they sat in their cramped office, plundering copies of the Los Angeles Yellow Pages for prospective cargo clients, while, in their reception room, Brenda ineffectively explained to a crowd of would-be employees that they hadn't started hiring yet.

"Missing."

"It figures. Now that you've got a good live-in gal to take care of Annie, she probably went shopping. Freddy could use some new clothes, or haven't you noticed? Maybe she's getting her hair done, or having a girlfriend lunch . . . maybe a matinee, maybe a little game of gin rummy . . . women can accomplish less and spend more in any given time period than you'd believe possible. Is she coming in this afternoon?"

"She's away for a few days." Tony was tight-lipped.

"Yeah? Where to?"

"Frankly, I don't know. Take a look at this note that she left me." He held out a piece of paper and Jock read it out loud.

" 'Darling, please supervise Annie's supper and sit with her, Helga will prepare. Bathe Annie, read to her from red book on night table, not more than twenty minutes, put her to bed, night light O.K. if she wants it. Helga will have dinner for you by seven-thirty. Please check on Annie several times during evening, keep your door open in case she wakes up. Morning, make sure Annie finishes her whole breakfast, Helga will walk her to kindergarten and pick her up. Let Helga know what you want for dinner before you go to office. Don't worry about me. See you in a few days. Annie understands. Love you, darling. Gone flyin'. Freddy.' "

"I found it this morning when I woke up," Tony said furiously. "This gets on my tit."

"You notice she said 'please' twice? Damn decent of her. What does she mean—'gone flyin'?"

"If I knew, I'd gladly share the information with you."

"What'd she go in?"

"Not one of our planes, I checked first thing. Maybe she talked someone into lending her a kite," Tony answered grimly.

"Or stole one," Jock said thoughtfully.

"She'd never have done this back home . . . not in a million years. It's *unthinkable* to decamp like that. It must be this fucking place! She hasn't been the same since she set foot in California. I can't put my finger on it, but she's just . . . different. As if she owns the whole bloody world. Sweet Jesus, I'd like to smack her!"

"Brenda's scared shitless of her. Says she makes her feel inferior."

"Brenda's not as stupid as she looks."

"Come on, Tony, she is so."

In the swift racing plane she'd rented, Freddy hopped down to make a number of stops in the Imperial Valley in the Colorado Desert, the southernmost of California's great farming areas, and then headed north toward the wet delta lands where asparagus and tomatoes grew ten months a year; from there she skipped on to Salinas, with its hundreds of thousands of rich acres, zipped back to Fresno for figs and grapes, setting down many times in the lushness of Imperial County, Kern County and Tulare County, the nation's top areas for farm produce. Everywhere she went, she passed over vast farms and orchards that had only grown larger and more profitable since she'd last seen them.

She followed a gloriously erratic flight plan that depended only on whim and mood. She strayed, she wandered, she hedgehopped, she zoomed and dove and chased her tail, and danced the plane from one end of the state to the other. She never bothered to calculate, so long as she had enough fuel, and her navigation was based on instinct and memory and meandering, rambling, arbitrary fancy. She was fancy-free and free for anything fancy, she sang to herself, as she lost herself in the delirium of flying again, flying without rules or regulations, flying in a rapture of freedom that she had given up seven years ago, liberated again for brazen adventure and high old times with the winds and the sky and the clouds and space. *Space!* God, how she'd missed space in England. The ATA routes had been so constricted that it was like

413

snaking your way through a maze to deliver a plane, but California was an ecstasy of bright, endless, flowing space, space that again belonged to her. How had she lived so long without this direct connection with the horizon, she wondered. How had she held out, how had she fooled herself into believing that anything could replace the sublime astonishment of sky?

Whenever she spotted the main buildings of each enormous agricultural holding, she looped a couple of spectacular loops, added a few showboating Immelmanns and spine-chilling Chandelles to announce her arrival, before she set the plane down elegantly in a half-filled parking lot or, failing that, a field, under conditions that anyone in the ATA would have regarded as laughably easy.

As she swaggered into the office, looking for the boss, she carried an official-looking notebook and a fine new Parker pen, with a fat gold nib. She wore a uniform of her own confection, consisting of her trim ATA skirt and RAF blue shirt, tieless and unbuttoned almost to her bra, with her four-inch-wide wings sewn above her right pocket. Her combustible hair was pulled back in a businesslike way and fastened with fraudulent severity at the nape of her neck, where it kept escaping conveniently from its inadequate velvet bow. Her skirt had been shortened four remarkably attention-getting inches, and belted in red patent leather, tightly enough to warrant a court-martial. Freddy had traded her sensible ATA lace-up shoes and black stockings for sheer nylons and a pair of the highest-heeled red shoes she'd been able to find in all of Los Angeles. If the boss didn't happen to be in, he soon arrived, as word reached him of the visitor.

In four days, Freddy managed to make warm and admiring friends with the largest shippers of farm produce in the major growing area of the entire world, as she announced to them, with the most delicately outrageous divergences from the truth, the formation of a major air cargo company. She made judicious and frequent references to its large corps of American Eagle Squadron pilots, who had all, each and every one of them, been among the heroic Few to whom the Many owed so Much. Eagles could handle as much farm produce as the farmers could grow, she told the interested men, as she leaned earnestly forward, her breasts straining the fabric of her shirt, her sales pitch almost landing her in their laps. Her notebook grew fat with potential orders, with valuable facts and figures and the names of major big-city wholesalers all over the country who were clamoring for California fruit, vegetables and flowers, which they could sell at premium prices, enough to include

414

the cost of air shipping, if the cost of air shipping were not pegged too high.

The hungry New York City flower market alone, dependent on greenhouses, could absorb incalculable tons of fresh-cut flowers every week if the right connections were made, Freddy realized as she sat in the cafe at the Santa Paula airport, just before the final short hop home, and meditated over two pieces of fresh peach pie. How many tons of fresh peaches could they sell in Chicago? And if the peaches were made into pies here by, say, Van de Kamp, what could a chain of East Coast bakeries charge for them in the middle of winter? How would you ship peach pies without breaking them? *Stay out of baked goods, you dumb broad! When will you learn?* Well, then, how would you ship peaches without bruising them? How would you ship grapes, strawberries, tender Bibb lettuce, fresh salmon from Monterey Bay? How would you ship *orchids*? Eagles could change the face of the college prom corsage.

All that's a secondary problem, she said cheerfully to herself, as she set about worming the recipe for the pie from the owner of the cafe. Let Tony and Jock worry about the details. They'd be so thrilled when she came back with all this information—but it had been absolutely necessary to go alone. Her husband, to be sure, had flown all through the Battle of Britain, but the Honorable Antony Wilmot Alistair Longbridge wasn't exactly a Yankee Doodle Dandy. Jock was as American as an all-night crap game, but he had just missed flying in the Battle of Britain and it would have cramped her style to have had to misrepresent . . . only slightly . . . the mighty pilot corps of Eagles if the two of them had been standing there listening. Or, God forbid, talking.

"Where's the new Brenda?" Jock yelled desperately as he clasped two phone receivers to his chest so that the pair of grape growers he was trying to talk to simultaneously wouldn't hear him. "I need some help here, pronto!"

Freddy, trapped behind her desk, telling three disappointed but still eager ex-bomber pilots that two hundred and fifty dollars a month was the maximum Eagles could offer for the time being, shouted over their heads. "She quit yesterday—I haven't had time to find another." Why was she in charge of finding Brendas, she asked herself in irritation? There had been four changes in office manager in the two weeks since the original Brenda had broken her last fingernail and left in tears of rage, that fate had so conspired against her. Brendas did not thrive on hysteria, Brendas couldn't handle panic, and Freddy's trip had started an avalanche of premature customer demand that they couldn't possibly control without a half-dozen competent office people.

"Who's answering the phones in the reception room? It sounds like a New Year's Eve party out there," Jock said wildly. "I could almost swear I hear Annie's voice."

"You do, Squadron Leader. Helga's taking the phones, Annie's with her."

"Where's Tony, for Christ's sake?" Jock screamed.

"The Wing Commander's on his way back from Newark. He delivered those three and a half tons of carnations. Colonels Levine and Carlutti delivered the strawberries and tomatoes to Detroit and Chicago—they're on their way back too."

"Any joy?" Jock asked, using the two words with which, after a sortie, RAF pilots had asked each other if they'd shot down any enemy planes.

"Nope," Freddy answered, her brief reply meaning that none of the three Eagle pilots had been able to scare up cargoes for the return trips, the essential backhaul without which there would be no profit on the deliveries. The three planes were all returning to L.A. as "deadheads," the most awful word in the business except for "wreck."

"Fellas, could you just wait outside for a minute?" Jock asked the pilots who were following their conversation with interest. "I need a quick meeting with my partner here."

"This isn't going to work," he said frantically to Freddy, when the room was empty. "How can we be turning away business and operating at a loss at the same time? How? How long do you think that can go on? How long? Here we are, grounded ten feet under a ton of office work, when the original idea was that the three of us would be flying without salary; those Brendas of yours disappear overnight; we still haven't hired enough mechanics; I have a full load of ripe peaches waiting to leave from Bakersfield—do you have *any* idea how perishable they are?—but I can't turn even one single plane around without more pilots than Tony, Levine and Carlutti, and today I got orders for three more loads for tomorrow—oh shit! Me and my big ideas! In another few weeks we won't be able to meet the payroll. We'll *owe* money!"

Freddy tipped her desk chair back so that she was almost reclining in it, hoisted her sublime legs up onto the desk, lifted her skirt a few inches above her knees, and crossed her spike-heeled red pumps at the ankle. She seemed to be silently consulting the ceiling while Jock drummed violently on his desk, waiting for her to say something. She groped in her handbag for her compact and carefully applied a fresh layer of bright red lipstick, looking at her image approvingly. Then she swung her legs to the floor, got up, and started, light, lissome and larky, toward the door.

"You can't leave me here alone! Where the hell do you think you're going? Flying again? That'll finish us for sure!"

"Squadron Leader Hampton," Freddy said with a deliberately, unfairly, unrighteously jazzy smile, "*do* try to calm down, I hate to see you in such a flap. You'll get an ulcer. Take deep breaths. Think good thoughts . . . even *your* mind must be capable of a good thought from time to time. Actually, you don't look terribly well, do you?" she crooned, ruffling his hair and tweaking his ears casually. "Have you been eating right, Squadron Leader? Getting enough vitamins? I know what, you can have Annie's lunch . . . yum, yum, eat it all up. I'll take her with me and feed her."

"You're really leaving?" he said in incredulous fury. "I don't fucking believe it!"

"Helga will watch over you. I'm going—to buy a mink coat."

"Bitch, bitch, bitch!" Jock roared as his two phones and Freddy's two phones all rang at once. "Now I know why you didn't let me die when you had a chance. You were saving me so you could kill me yourself!"

"Aren't you getting a little paranoid? I didn't even know you then," Freddy said sweetly, as she closed the door softly behind her.

Jock let the phones ring on, not trying to answer them. He shook his blond head from side to side, an expression of consternation subduing his untamed features. Why did he suddenly feel so fucking *lonesome?* Why did he feel as if he'd been abandoned? "Paranoid"? He only prayed that was the answer. He'd settle for merely paranoid any day.

Swede Castelli's familiar office was filled with photos and model planes and flying relics as ever, but Swede himself looked, it seemed to Freddy, less cheerful than she had ever remembered seeing him. He had greeted her surprise visit with delight, but his face seemed forlorn under his pleasure. He swept Annie up, and regarded her small perfections with wonder, shaking his head over the passage of time. "Now, little lady, you sit right here," he said, putting her down carefully.

"Oh, I'm not a lady," Annie said gravely. "My Grannie Penelope is a baroness and my Grannie Eve is a vicomtesse, and my Auntie Jane is engaged to marry a marquess, which means she'll be a duchess someday, but I'm just plain little Annie."

"Why, you poor kid. That's a crying shame. Maybe a prince will come along for you."

"What kind of prince?" Annie asked, interested.

"Annie, don't you want to play with the model planes?" Freddy said hastily.

"I'd rather talk to Mr. Castelli, Mummy."

"Later, Annie." Freddy shooed her away.

"I was wondering when you were going to get around to coming to see me, Freddy. You've been back for weeks," Swede said, mildly reproachful.

"It's been too complicated, Swede, you old honey bun. I can't begin to describe it."

"Don't bother, I can imagine only too well. No work to be had, no matter how hard you try, just like here. Remember those years when we were so busy planning stunts that I almost had to sleep in the office? Remember when you went from one film to another without a weekend off, and so did everybody else? Remember that great little organization I ran? It's finished, Freddy. Nobody's making movies with flying in them anymore. During the war I had lots of business with films about the Air Force, but now, kiddo? Forget it. It's picket-fence time, rose-covered cottages, love in bloom, and nobody, but I mean not a single studio, wants to know from that old wild blue yonder. I just sit here looking at the walls and wishing the phone would ring. Not a peep out of it for months and months. Maybe I'll rip the thing out."

"It's been that bad, Swede? I'm really sorry."

"Or that good, depending. I mean, kiddo, I never thought you could have so much money and so little fun. There's something wrong about it." He slumped despondently in his desk chair.

" 'So much money'? With no business? How come?"

"Boy, have you been away a long time! Everybody made money during the war, and some of them hung on to it. Like me. Everything I invested in turned to gold. I'm rich, kiddo, really rich. Seems I've got a touch for making a buck. But I'm not the type to sit still and visit my money. I wish there were some kicks in it, but I guess I really can't complain. I've had my fun."

"I've come just in time," Freddy said. "Have I got a job for you!"

He raised his brows. "Where? Not in that air cargo outfit of yours? Freddy, do you have any idea of how many little bitty companies like yours have already been started and gone bust in L.A. in the last year? Hundreds."

"I've learned that. As it turns out, Jock Hampton wasn't the only veteran to have an idea about air cargo. But a few of the companies are going to survive and get bigger. It's inevitable, it has to happen, it's the future. Eagles will be one of them."

"What makes you so sure?"

"*Because I say so.*" She ambushed him with her smile and the flag-blue certainty of her eyes.

"Same old Freddy. Bossy, pig-headed, stubborn, mulish, obstinate, domineering—if you weren't so damn beautiful you'd be impossible." Swede sighed reminiscently. "Some things never change, thank God."

"We need you, Swede."

"Doing what? I don't see myself hustling freight, even if you should ever get any. I'm too old and too rich for that, kiddo. And probably too fat."

"I want you to *run* Eagles, take over operations. Our problem is too much business, too fast. We have six phones that ring all day long. *It's mouth-watering.* Oh, Swede, it's your kind of picnic, the kind you thrived on. You'll have more damn fun straightening out our mess—I almost envy you. First you've got to decide how many *more* planes we should be renting and how many *more* pilots we need, because if we don't grab the business they're throwing at us now, somebody else will. Then you have to solve the backhaul problem—you should have done that *yesterday*—find a guy to run maintenance and engineering and another to handle contracts. You'll have to hire office help immediately, take a good look at our charter rates to different cities—"

"That's all?" His round face had lost its gloomy look, and he sat up straight.

"That's just the beginning. You could also answer phones in your free time, but you're not going to have any free time."

"What do we use for money?"

"I've got a few bucks left. And of course, as our chairman of the board, you'll want to be in for a piece of the action, since, as you said, everything you touch turns to gold. Also—we'll make a lot of promises."

Castelli looked at Freddy sharply. The kid was wearing thousand-league boots. She was in the mood to jump out of a plane without a chute and fly under her own power—and he didn't doubt she could. Well, what the hell, he never had been able to resist her, and she'd made him a lot of money in her day. What was the worst thing that could happen? He'd lose some of his no-fun bucks. He'd risk more than that for a bunch of ringing phones.

419

"Ah, what the hell . . . count me in. I'll need a few days to wind things up here—"

Freddy hugged him tight and kissed him loudly on both cheeks. "You won't be sorry, I promise. Oh, Swede, you're going to *love* it. We have nothing but problems!" She picked up a sign that read "Back in Five Minutes" and shook it thoughtfully. "I'm double-parked downstairs. Come on, Swede, we've got to get out of here fast! I'll hang this on the door. You don't want me to get a parking ticket, do you? And I have to fly a load of peaches to New York in an hour. When I get back, I'll help you kick ass."

Taken by surprise, the ex-stuntman followed Freddy as she cantered out of his office, with Annie running at her heels. It wasn't until they were halfway to Burbank that he realized Freddy couldn't get a traffic ticket on a studio lot, but by that time he was too excited to care.

The worst thing about Dior's New Look, Freddy thought as she descended gracefully from the Buick, was that it was so long that it hid her legs above the ankle. On the other hand, it emphasized her small waist and exaggerated the volume of her hips and breasts. But legs, face it, Monsieur Dior, legs were what males were fixated on. Still, when you came to think about it, once any woman was lying down in bed, what did legs have to do with lovemaking? You could wrap them around a guy, but unless he was some sort of knee fetishist or calf-and-thigh freak, why legs?

She walked slowly, conscious of the elaborate scaffolding under her violently fashionable suit, which had a tightly buttoned jacket of natural silk shantung and an immensely full black shantung skirt. First came the tulle corset that also served as a low, strapless bra, a deceptively fragile-looking garment that had an implacable will of its own, owning to dozens of supple, narrow bones hidden in the layers of tulle that encased her like an iron maiden from the tops of her breasts to below her hips. Then came crinolines of different thicknesses, to hold out the skirt to its proper dimensions; a skirt that was itself lined three times, once in tulle, once in sheer organza and finally in silk pongee, so that the other linings wouldn't scratch her stockings. She wondered if her grandmother had ever been so shaped and molded and restricted by anything she wore? If she dared to draw a deep breath, Freddy reflected, she'd probably pop a half-dozen buttons. As for reaching her arms over her head, it was out of the question. She should be grateful that she could still bend her elbows. No, in this suit she had to sway and mince, not prance or caper.

Such was the price of elegance in 1949, and Freddy understood why Dior himself, on his first tour of the United States, had been met in city after city by mobs of angry women with posters that said "Christian Dior Go Home" and even "Burn Mr. Dior." When she discovered that there was no other direction in new clothes, aside from the New Look, she had accepted it reluctantly, but she had drawn the line at a hat. She hadn't worn a hat since she'd been out of uniform, and she wasn't about to change that now. Her hair had been carefully cut and shaped and set and combed out by an expensive stylist, but now, a day later, it had rejected whatever he had tried to do to it, and reclaimed its own unpredictable and unnamable shape, a combination of wave and curl and tumble and bumptiousness that was, if nothing else, familiar. She shook her head reproachfully at her hair's disobedience to fashion, and it was as if a giant bright copper dahlia shimmied in the sunlight.

"Mrs. Longbridge? The front door's over here, Mrs. Longbridge," said Hal Lane, the real-estate salesman, trying to move her along. This was his second day of showing Freddy around, and he was still not willing to believe that, unlike his other clients, the last thing on her mind seemed to be buying a house. However, the important thing about Mrs. Antony Longbridge was that she absolutely *had* to move; she wasn't just a lookie-look, like some women he'd wasted time on. She had to get out of that dump she and her husband had rented three years ago. It simply wasn't fitting for two of the partners in the biggest air cargo outfit in the country to be living in those rundown, cramped quarters. Leaving aside their own comfort, they couldn't possibly entertain there. Imagine inviting people to dinner in a place that wasn't as nice as even the cheapest tract house. The Longbridges, in his opinion, were well overdue to go for something that would reflect their position. He just couldn't understand why they'd waited so long.

"This is probably one of the finest dwellings in Hancock Park," Hal Lane announced as they approached the front door. "It has a very special Old World quality."

Freddy looked up from her frowning contemplation of her billowing hem and halted suddenly on the paving. "Mr. Lane, I told you yesterday when we started out that I had only two days to devote to finding a house, and I warned you that fake English was absolutely out of the question. Why are you wasting my time?"

"But . . . but . . . this isn't fake English, Mrs. Longbridge, it's real . . . ah . . . Queen Elizabeth. Just wait till you see the interior. It's exceptional. A master bath to die for."

"I see half-timbers that don't have any purpose, nasty little red

421

bricks, tiny windowpanes that shut out the light. Sorry, but there's no point in even going inside, Mr. Lane." She looked at her watch. "We have another six hours."

Well! he thought as he helped her back into his Buick. Maybe a good-natured, chatty lookie-look would be preferable, after all. What was her hurry? He riffled through his listings, discarded half of them—Mrs. Longbridge obviously wasn't sophisticated enough in the language of real estate to understand that in Los Angeles an English house, preferably Tudor, commanded instant respect and conferred immediate status—and started his new car.

Freddy sat back, not even seeing the tree-lined streets with their bright winter flowers, sprinklers playing on the lawns during this November day. She had mixed feelings about this move away from the poky little house in Burbank in which so much had happened. She'd never forget those elated, crazy, twenty-hour days, after Swede Castelli had taken command of the office, when they'd hired fifteen new pilots in the middle of the worst of the postwar housing crisis. Between delivery trips the guys hunted for trailers or motels into which they could move their families, meanwhile bunking on the floor of her living room—except for the lucky one who'd managed to share a bed with Helga—and Freddy had cooked big stews for them every night that she wasn't flying herself. Annie had been in charge of milk, cookies and paper napkins. Tony had tended bar, and Jock had run the poker game.

Those were the early days of catch-as-catch-can backhaul: the tragedy of the three valuable planeloads of live Maine lobsters that had died of fright, as far as anyone could figure out, during a thunderstorm; the thrill of the hundreds of shipments of dresses and blouses, hot items that sold out in minutes, sent straight from the factories of Seventh Avenue and delivered without a wrinkle in them, for they had flown cross-country on hangers attached to racks that had been hastily installed inside the planes; the weekly loads of *Life* and *Time,* to which they had gradually added a dozen other major magazine clients; the "dearly beloveds" as the Eagles referred to the many carefully crated dead bodies that were rushed to their former hometowns to be properly coffined and given funerals; the racehorses that recovered so much more easily from a plane ride than from a long trip by train or truck, that Eagles pilots took to betting their entire salaries on them; and most important of all, the charter flights.

Without human bodies—living, breathing human bodies—they would never have made it, Freddy knew. It was the chartering of entire planes that had allowed them to weather the very early days: the football teams, the conventioneers, the church choirs going to competitions; the servicemen on leave, the student groups, the stranded circuses, animals and all; the marching bands; the nuns and nurses, none of whom could wait until the postwar log jam in transportation was solved. They'd switched from the DC-3 to the four-engine DC-4, discovered the right kind of collapsible seating and the right kind of sandwich box lunch, and sold space at ninety-nine dollars per person cross-country to countless groups willing to endure an austerity flight to get where they wanted to go cheaply and safely.

Hal Lane pulled up in front of a white-columned house. "Mrs. Longbridge, I believe this major residence will be well worth your time."

"Lord have mercy," said Freddy, "I'm back home at Tara."

"Tara was *copied* from this mansion."

"I'll take a look," she said as cheerfully as possible, since the house was within the circle she'd drawn on a map to show Lane the distance from the airport beyond which she wasn't willing to live. As she walked through the many grand, empty rooms, blocking out Lane's commentary as automatically as if he were engine noise, Freddy wondered how long it would take her to get used to living in this vast amount of square feet. She'd gone from her bedroom at home to Mac's little house, and from there to the half-dozen crowded ATA digs she'd shared with Jane, to the comfortable bedroom and small sitting room that she and Tony had been given at Longbridge Grange, and finally to the tiny house in Burbank. Could she ever feel as cozy here as she had in her past twenty-nine years?

Did Jane, she wondered, have that problem of adjustment when she married her marquess, the adorable Humphrey, and moved to that venerable Tudor pile in Norfolk, that exalted feudal sprawl? Never fear, not her Jane. She'd probably turned half the rooms of the castle into closets, and now that she had produced an heir to the dukedom, to the admiration of all England, and was regally pregnant again, she'd undoubtedly requisitioned a wing of her own for nurseries, nannies and worshipful attendants of all sorts. Jane had always been to the castle born. The Grange had only been her launching pad.

"Mrs. Longbridge, may I call your attention to this powder room? Exquisite fixtures, aren't they? As I'm sure you're aware, a hostess is judged by her powder room as well as by her guest list."

"Why don't we take a look at the basement?" Freddy suggested. Reluctantly he led her down a flight of tricky stairs and watched her carefully circle the furnace, giving it a number of well-placed kicks before she unbuttoned her jacket and gingerly investigated the pipes that led upstairs. "Heating system's shot," Freddy said. "I'm not interested, I'm afraid. Sorry about that, Mr. Lane. What's next on your list?"

"I have a trend-setting contemporary classic. Something tells me that you're going to love it."

The modern house was cold and institutional, in spite of the sunlight that came in from the skylights, Freddy decided, staring pensively into the only comfy room in the house, a walk-in, cedar-lined closet. But it had acres of space. Perhaps that was what was wrong with Tony . . . not enough living space? Could that be even part of the reason that he'd become so . . . remote? When had she first noticed his growing distance, she asked herself. Had it started, without her paying much attention, during the two-year trauma of the merciless rate war with American Airlines? They'd all been so preoccupied, trying to keep aloft as they lost money month after month, to worry about nuances in personal relationships, Freddy reflected ruefully. There had been so little time to be a family, with a monster payroll to meet each Friday.

Swede had poured all his personal resources into Eagles, but the major reason they had been able to survive the first two years had been a providential contract with the Air Transport Command to fly military personnel from California to Hawaii, Guam and Honolulu. When the Civil Aeronautics Board, moving with its infernal, heart-murdering slowness, finally ended the rate war in April of 1948, Eagles was one of the few independents still in business, out of more than two thousand such ventures that had been started by veterans after the war.

Freddy blinked, walked out of the cedar closet and toward the front door. "Onward, Mr. Lane, onward," she said with a patient look, rustling down the long, stark corridor in her panoply of skirt and crinolines. The next house was pleasantly Colonial and unthreatening, and she walked through it paying as much attention as she could, while she sought the exact moment when it had come to her that Tony didn't only tend bar when they got together with their pilots, but propped it up every night, even without guests, and often slid under it.

The years between 1946 and 1949 had included a struggle known as the Air-Freight Case, during which Eagles had attempted to win a CAB-certified route of its own. That last and most important battle the company faced had not been won until three months ago, in August of 1949, and of the thirteen companies that had applied for certification in 1946, only four companies besides Eagles were not bankrupt by the day of victory.

When, Freddy wondered, just when during those long, tense years, without a penny of profits to show for all their hard work, without a dime to spend freely in spite of millions in contracts, at what precise point in those years during which they had all continued to operate by every means possible, often hiring themselves out for charter work to other established lines, had Tony's drinking become serious? Desperate and serious beyond her understanding?

Until three months ago they had all been hanging on by their finger-nails, fingertips long since gone. She couldn't remember the first time she had been forced to realize that the only way Tony could calm down and stop raging at the CAB was by having far too many drinks. When was the first time he had stayed home, too hung over to fly or even go to the office? A year ago? Two years ago?

Nothing could change his intrinsic decency, but there was a weary accusation in his eyes now, day as well as night, that glazed over and hid his good nature and gentleman's gallantry and sense of humor. The worst of it was that now that the fruits of their struggle had been harvested, now that a public underwriting had made all of them instant millionaires, Tony was still drinking as heavily as ever—or was he drinking more heavily now? "Drop it, Freddy, just drop it," he'd say whenever she tried to open the subject with him and there was some-thing in his opaque eyes, into which memory seemed to have eaten too deeply, that silenced her.

"Well, Mrs. Longbridge, what do you think?" Hal Lane said. Freddy took off her jacket and folded it over his arm, eased her blouse up at the waist, opened a window of the Colonial house, hitched her skirts up to her knees, climbed up on top of a radiator, leaned forward and reached far outside. A few seconds later she dropped back into the room, waving a long chunk of metal gutter that had broken off into her hand.

"The whole roof's gone," she said. "And who knows about dry rot I can't see? Let's get on with it, Mr. Lane." She took her jacket back and headed out of the house and back to the car, tucking her blouse down into her waistband as best she could.

After a short ride the Buick drew to a stop. "A gated estate, Mrs. Longbridge, recently redecorated from top to bottom. A dream prop-erty."

"I hope so," Freddy breathed, moving impatiently forward. It wasn't English, that much could be said for it, but it was altogether too French. To be fair, she hadn't told the salesman not to show her anything French, she reminded herself as she entered the house. She didn't object to fake French with the same intensity as Tony loathed fake English.

"*Regardez* that jewel of a staircase," Lane said. "You have a daughter, don't you, Mrs. Longbridge? Just imagine her descending that staircase as a bride. This exceptional residential property was meant for weddings."

"Annie's only seven," Freddy said.

"Ah. Well, in that case, shall we proceed to the family room and wet bar?"

"A wet bar in the Petit Trianon? What next, Mr. Lane?"

"After all, this is California, Mrs. Longbridge—wet bars, family rooms, powder rooms, master suites with walk-in closets and his-and-her baths—that's what we're all about, aren't we?"

"If you say so, Mr. Lane. Where's the kitchen?" Freddy stuck her head in the ovens, inspected the refrigerator, and watched the flow of water from the sink. "Hmm. I'll go flush a few toilets. Don't bother to come." She returned in three minutes. "The plumbing needs a total overhaul, Mr. Lane. I wish they'd done that before they painted those murals in the guest john. I'm afraid we don't have much time left."

"Shall we just look at newly built abodes, Mrs. Longbridge?" he sniffed. "At least that would eliminate any minor construction imperfections."

"I doubt that. Postwar building isn't as good as prewar. They cut every corner they can."

Freddy walked through a replica of a Bavarian hunting lodge, a Palladian villa and a Moorish fantasy, methodically checking out their vital systems, while Hal Lane silently clutched her abandoned jacket. As she climbed down and up into places he'd never seen a woman investigate, bundling the froufrou of her skirts unceremoniously under one arm, as she kicked and peered and lifted and knocked and poked and turned things on and off, she found herself strangely unable to imagine herself living with Tony and Annie and Helga, and their yet-unknown servants, in any one of these places.

Yet she had to decide on a house today, Freddy reminded herself. The rest of the week would be devoted to the interviewer and photographer from *Life* who had come out from the New York headquarters to do a major story on Eagles. They'd had a lot of publicity during their years of struggle, and they'd always welcomed it because it meant more business.

Reporters tended to concentrate on Freddy, because she was a woman in a man's world, because of her racing trophies, her Hollywood stunt-flying background, and her Lancel birth. Could Tony be upset because she go so much publicity, Freddy asked herself, and turned the thought over in her mind only once before she dismissed it. Such pettiness wouldn't be like him. Could he possibly be disturbed that he was now worth millions in his own right, yet he had not been able to invest any actual cash of his own? Could that technicality be bothering him? His pride had never allowed him to make total peace with the situation, but she didn't believe that, in itself, could be responsible for his drinking.

When they'd learned of their victory, Jock had gone out and blown ten thousand bucks at poker in one game—he must have been *trying* to lose—Swede had flown to Tijuana and disappeared for a week; she had wandered into Bullock's custom department and ordered a dozen new dresses and twenty pairs of shoes . . . but Tony hadn't done anything special to celebrate except to go into the backyard and empty most of a bottle of whiskey, so preoccupied as he sat there, sipping steadily from his glass, that even Annie hadn't been able to get his attention.

Freddy had gone outside, poured herself a drink and dropped into a deck chair near him, stealing a glance at Tony from time to time, unnoticed by the man who was sunk in a profound sadness while he watched the long sunset of the hot August evening. The fine, long structure of his head was as noble as ever, his Britishness had not been tempered by any Californian ease, but something more basic had changed. When Freddy had first met Tony, he was the undisputed master of that crucial moment in the world's very existence. Had it not been for the RAF and fighter pilots like Tony, there could be no question now that Hitler would have won the war. None of them had been thinking historically during that time, for they were all too caught up in surviving each day, yet Tony had been certainty itself; his was the essence of pure courage, his the joy of a warrior's skill and dauntless domination of the skies, his the dedication to a great and dangerous duty, gladly undertaken.

But now? Something vital had gone slack, the sense of purposefulness had all but vanished, yet nothing had replaced it. He was a fighter bred who saw no adversary, a gladiator without arms, a commander with no troops. Was she just being romantic, Freddy wondered, or could he be still remembering the glory of leading his wing in combat? Had anything in his life ever lived up to the magnificent narcotic of those heroic years? He never talked about them, not even with Jock, unlike most of the dozens of wartime pilots she knew who loved nothing more than a detailed reliving of those air battles with other men who had shared their experiences.

Was he feeling nostalgic about the family he'd left behind in Kent? Even in 1949, England hadn't recovered enough to allow its subjects to travel abroad except on business, and Tony hadn't seen his parents or his brothers or sisters in more than three years. Or was it possible that he was brooding over his fantasy of the children they didn't have? Freddy squirmed uneasily as she watched his expressionless face, his dulled eyes, his sunken regard, the lethargic set of his fine mouth. She had no idea what he was thinking about, and he'd had so much to drink that it was not possible to try to find out.

She wasn't thirty yet, Freddy reminded herself, and now, at last, with the future of Eagles secure, they could try to have that family she'd always known he wanted. Finally she could allow herself the time to have another child—even several children. For the first time since the day she had determined to preserve Mac's flying school until his return, she wasn't *needed* at one job or another. She could become that creature so foreign to her, a lady of leisure.

Delphine and Armand had twin boys and a third son, yet Delphine was now the leading movie star in France. Children didn't have to mean the end of a career.

But to get pregnant you had to make love. And she and Tony had not made love in months. Many months. So many months that she didn't dare count them. Would moving to a new house change that? Could it be the sheer overfamiliarity of their tiny, crowded bedroom that made him fall asleep so quickly every night that there wasn't even time for a good-night kiss that might have led to something more? Or was it just the booze? Had he met another woman during one of the many cargo flights, while one or the other of them had been away?

Somehow that just didn't feel like the answer. Tony was *absent*, but not in a way that could make her believe that he was concentrating on someone else. Was she just being naïve? Or had she, all unknowingly, become unappealing to him in some way she couldn't remedy? Tony had not failed to notice each of her new dresses, so feminine and romantic in their complicated, elaborate allure, and he had commented on each one of them with mild, faraway, gentle admiration that made her want to weep or hit him, for in it there was all the slow, nonviolent disintegration of their life together. She couldn't blame his lack of interest in making love on the bell-like skirts that covered her legs down to the ankle. The problem predated the day when she could afford to buy the New Look.

If there was the smallest chance that a new house would help them grow close again, she had to grab it.

"Stop here!" Freddy said to the real-estate salesman excitedly. "At that 'For Sale' sign."

He pulled to the curb. "I don't have the listing on that house," he protested. "We can't go in, I'm afraid. It's just a . . . house, Mrs. Longbridge, not an estate or a residence or an important property, just an ordinary . . . well, house . . . big, I grant you, but not exceptional. It does have a nice garden, but you can see that it's been neglected. I don't particularly recommend this neighborhood for investment purposes. It's still good, but not far enough west. I'm sure I can show you something far more suitable, a dwelling that's more representative of your position in the community. This—this *house*—was built so long ago that it probably doesn't even have a wet bar."

Freddy stood and looked at the house for a few minutes, without moving toward it to check out its condition. "I'll take it," she said. "Phone me with the price tomorrow. I'll make a counter-offer, of course, but I intend to buy it."

"Mrs. Longbridge, you haven't even been inside!"

"I know what it looks like," Freddy said. "I grew up in it."

GET the employment agency on the phone, Miss Kelly," Bruno told his secretary as he walked into his imposing office at the Beecham Mercantile Trust, a powerful private investment bank that had been firmly established in New York City for more than a hundred years.

"Yes, sir. Here are your messages, and your mail's on your desk."

Bruno gave her his overcoat to hang up in his closet. It was windy and cold in Manhattan on this day in early December 1949, but he made it a practice to walk to work from his Sutton Place house in all weather but driving rain. He was thirty-four, and his important position at the bank frequently meant that he had to cancel his daily squash game in favor of a business lunch. At least the walk, from 57th Street and the East River down to Wall Street, ensured a minimum of exercise.

"Mrs. McIver's on the phone, sir."

"Good morning, Viscount de Lancel. What can I do for you, sir?" asked the owner of Manhattan's most expensive agency for domestic help, in an optimistic tone of voice.

"Mrs. McIver, send me more people to interview. Butlers, chefs and valets."

"Sir, I supplied you with the best people I could find, only two weeks ago. Haven't any of them worked out?"

"There isn't one of them who could get a job in Paris. You'll have to do better than that, Mrs. McIver."

"Viscount de Lancel, I assure you that I have personally placed each of those men before in positions in which they remained for years. There wasn't one I wouldn't be happy to have working in my own home."

"As far as I'm concerned, they're not good enough. Try again."

"I'll do my very best for you, sir. As you know, it's never easy. I'll get on it right away and I'll call Miss Kelly to arrange the interviews."

"Do that." Bruno hung up abruptly. On the other end of the line, Nancy McIver smiled lovingly at the telephone. If all her clients were as insanely hard to please as this Frenchman, her gold mine of an office would be producing pure platinum. Each time he had a problem with

some member of his staff, she collected a commission on the replace-
ment, and no one had lasted more than two months at Lancel's in the
three years she'd been doing business with him. Yet he had nowhere
else to go but her agency, for no one in New York handled such
exclusive help, the cream of the crop, the ultimate in every kind of
domestic worker, from hand laundresses who would barely condescend
to wash any but heirloom linen, to majordomos who wouldn't consider
a job with a family that didn't have at least three fully staffed homes.
The names of the people she placed, and the names of the families with
which she placed them, formed a stately principality of its own, that
moved regularly from a few square blocks of Manhattan to Sea Island
to Palm Beach to Saratoga to Southampton, depending on the season
of the year.

"Lancel's on the rampage again, Genny," she said cheerfully to her
assistant.

"What's with him? He's the most difficult man in the city. There
isn't a single dotty dowager on our books who gives us as much trouble
as that one bachelor."

"Who knows? Remember, Genny, when there's no turnover, we
don't make money. Give me his file, please."

"But he's had just about everybody on our available lists already.
We've scraped the bottom of the barrel for him, over and over," Genny
protested as she pulled out the bulging folder.

"If I have to send him people he's already fired, he'll never notice.
His house is run like a subway turnstile. When a client can't keep good
help, it's invariably his problem, not yours. That's the golden rule of
this business. Never forget it."

"I wonder what he's really like?"

"Take my word for it, you wouldn't want to know," Nancy McIver
said scornfully. "The real question is, who does he think he is?"

"Bruno de Lancel? Marjorie, that's a ridiculous suggestion," Cynthia
Beaumont said to her secretary.

"I thought that with Larry Bell canceling dinner at the last minute,
it was worth a try," Marjorie Stickley replied.

"Damn Larry Bell! A strep throat is no excuse. Is he incapable of
making a little effort? How does he expect me to get an extra man at
such short notice? Nobody would have noticed—I wasn't planning to
look down his blasted throat with a stethoscope."

"Perhaps he was afraid he'd be contagious," Marjorie ventured, as
her employer, Cynthia Beaumont, raged back and forth in her sitting

431

room, looking wrathfully at the ruined seating plan for her carefully planned, black-tie dinner party.

"Not him! He'd give people leprosy if he knew they'd never find out. He's just worried about his own precious health, the selfish wretch. What does he care about my dinner?"

"Oh, Mrs. Beaumont, you know it's going to be the party of the season," Marjorie said as soothingly as possible. She knew, after years of being a social secretary to a number of New York's most important hostesses, that nothing could so upset even a highly sophisticated and secure woman as the last-minute defection of an extra man. There wasn't one of them who could face up to the dreaded prospect of seating two women next to each other, although, in her private opinion, men added little gaiety or charm to a party as they sat back and waited to be entertained, while any vivacious and interesting extra woman could be counted on to sing for her supper.

"What to do, Marjorie? What to do? It's a catastrophe! And we only have a few hours left. Do you suppose that Tim Black might be—no, he just announced his engagement. Cross him off my list permanently, I never liked him anyway. What about—never mind, I swore I'd never ask him again, after he got so revoltingly tipsy and made an indecent remark to Mrs. Astor at the last party. Oh, why do I ever try to give a dinner in December? I should know by now that from Thanksgiving to New Year's Day there isn't a single halfway presentable extra man who has a free night."

"But it's Mr. Beaumont's birthday celebration," the social secretary protested. Even in busy New York society, this particular annual occasion was sacred.

"Well he'll just have to change it next year, that's all. I won't go through this hell again. Now, Marjorie, be creative!"

"I'll go to my office and ring up every single warm body on your emergency list."

"Try all our doctors and our dentist too. Maybe one of them is single, or getting divorced. I'll call James Junior at Princeton myself."

"He's in the middle of final exams, Mrs. Beaumont."

"Surely he could make a little sacrifice for his mother? Oh, it's too utterly maddening to have five sons, and four of them married right out of college. What's the point! Why did I bother to give birth to those ungrateful brutes? Just think, if none of them had married, I'd have my hands on the four best-looking young extra men in the city—five, when James Junior graduates. But no, not even one of them bothered to consider me or my problems. Ingrates! All they care about is their own happiness. Today's young people have no sense of duty, tradition, family. You're lucky you have no children, Marjorie. You've been saved a lot of pain."

"Maybe I'd have had a girl, Mrs. Beaumont."

"An extra woman? God forbid! I'll try to dress while you phone."

"I'd still like to try Bruno de Lancel."

"Marjorie! How could I possibly ask him at the last minute—I plan a party *around* that man. One thing I'll say for Bruno de Lancel, he'd never cancel at the last minute unless he were on his deathbed. He's too well bred to dream of it. What marvelous manners he has."

"You did ask me to be creative, Mrs. Beaumont."

"Creative in a reasonable way. I didn't expect your Christmas list. And anyway, he'd be insulted to be asked for the same night, to fill in when someone else has dropped out."

"He's been here so often that surely he'll understand. Any good friend would. It should be quite all right."

"He's not that kind of friend. If he were American, I'd say yes, he'd be glad to lend a hand, but you know how . . . cold . . . he is. I've never felt I knew him better than the first time I met him, yet I've seated him on my right more times than I can count. His marvelous manners don't include talking about himself. However, one can't deny that he's absolutely divine looking, very, very rich, and unmarried— plus the title, of course—so he can be as uncommunicative as the Sphinx for all I care, as unapproachable as the Pope without an audience, as formal as the Queen of England . . . wait a minute . . . the Pope . . . perhaps Cardinal Spellman? What do you think, Marjorie?"

"As an extra man at the last minute—no, somehow I shouldn't think so, Mrs. Beaumont."

"Oh, I suppose you're right." Cynthia Beaumont sighed in vexation, but it was just these little nuances that Marjorie Stickley was so terribly good at. It paid to have the best social secretary in town, even if she earned twice what any other secretary did. Even if the Cardinal were free, and she'd bet he was, it wouldn't be fitting.

As Cynthia Beaumont emerged from her bath, and began to put on just enough makeup to cope with the florist who was arriving to start decorating the house, Marjorie returned, brimming with triumph. "I've got Bruno de Lancel. He said he'd be delighted to come."

"How fantastic! What a treasure you are! You've saved my dinner. What did you say? How did you put it?"

"Ah, that's just my little secret, Mrs. Beaumont. Now I must go and tell the florist that you'll be with him in a few minutes or he'll have a nervous breakdown."

As she vanished down the corridor toward the dining room, the social secretary reflected on her own Golden Rule: The worst someone can say is "No, thank you." She'd built a long, satisfactory career and a comfortable nest egg on making phone calls her employers were basically too timid to make for themselves. Society women—sometimes she could almost feel sorry for them. But not often. As for Bruno de Lancel, his reputation for being stiff and standoffish had made so many hostesses terrified of him that it had been an even bet he'd be free tonight. It was all right for him to be a snob, society understood that, but not with people who were just as good as he was. Who, she wondered scornfully, did he think he was?

Bruno left the bank early on Friday afternoon and walked up to J.M. Kidder Inc., for the fourth fitting on a new riding jacket he had ordered months ago.

"So you'll be going down the Main Line to hunt, Viscount de Lancel?" Allensby, the ancient head fitter, asked pleasantly.

Bruno grunted noncommittally. He couldn't understand why a tailor could possibly consider that his comings and goings were any concern of his.

"We take care of a lot of gentlemen from the Main Line. Always have. Good hunting there, they all tell me."

Bruno snorted. If you considered good hunting going out with a bunch of dull, pompous stockbrokers, lawyers and businessmen from a collection of tedious suburbs, men who knew nothing of noble sport, men who had never spent an entire day chasing over their own lands, then he supposed it must be considered good hunting. In any case, it was the pitifully best hunting within a few hours of New York—Fairfield was a joke—and life without hunting was unthinkable.

"The collar still isn't cut right, Allensby."

"Now, now, sir, I recut it after your last fitting. This is an entirely new piece of cloth. Look how well it hugs your neck."

Bruno moved his neck backward and forward and twisted his head from side to side, managing to make the brilliantly cut collar gape a fraction of an inch as he pulled away from it. "No, it won't do. It simply won't do at all. Rip it off and start all over again." He struggled out of the jacket and threw it on a chair. "Call my secretary when you're ready for another fitting."

"Yes sir," Allensby said agreeably. As he took the coat away, he thought of his own Golden Rule: Only a certain kind of man would ever take out his temper on his tailor, and that kind of man wasn't worth worrying about. The Frenchman, with a title he seemed to think mattered here, could have as many fittings as he wanted; such contingencies were built into the price of the jacket from the beginning. The old firm had survived generations of difficult customers, although never one with such a fine torso. He'd be a pleasure to fit, Allensby thought scornfully, if he weren't such a bastard. Just who on earth did he think he was?

As he left the tailor's, Bruno looked at his watch. He still had almost two hours before he had to begin to dress for dinner. A short walk away, there was a woman waiting for him, curled with the proud grace of a rare and valuable cat, in front of a fruitwood fire. There would be low music in the air, and on her face, with its pouting, full mouth that drew the eye as if it were a barbaric ornament, there would be a look of impatience. She was lazily lush, with creamy, marvelously abundant flesh, dark brown nipples as large as quarters, a mouth that would rather suck than talk, and a full bottom that had been shaped to invite the delicious punishment Bruno was so expert in inflicting. She had urgent, vicious, inventive hands, this woman who was one of the great ladies of the city, not quite forty, and enormously rich in her own right. She had belonged to him for three months.

Bruno considered the fact that at this very minute the woman was ready for him, ready to let him do anything to her that he pleased, for earlier in the day he'd phoned and told her in explicit detail how he wanted her to caress herself before he arrived. He could see the way her thighs must be spread apart so that she could reach down easily to touch herself, with the moist and knowing fingers she had been licking. He knew that she would be stretching restlessly and biting her lip to keep from reaching any premature spasm.

If he entered that room and flung himself down on the couch and said that he was tired, that he wanted nothing more than for her to bend her head over him and bring him to slow satisfaction with only her wide, waiting mouth, she would do so. If he lay on the couch and didn't touch her, if he just waited until she made him hard with her clever hands and then told her to straddle him and take him into her body, and if he gave her harsh orders to raise and lower herself until he obtained the release he had come to her for, she would obey without a word. If he told her to lie on the rug and pull up her skirt and raise her knees and spread her legs for him, and if he then entered her and took her as quickly and selfishly as any schoolboy, she would be grateful. If he told her to stay in her chair while he stood in front of her and opened his trousers and shoved himself into her mouth, she would give him exquisite pleasure and never protest. If he merely sat on the edge of a chair, a spectator, and told her to touch herself until she writhed with her own pleasure, she would comply.

She was that kind of woman. She was at the age he had always preferred. She knew what she wanted, and what she wanted was to be treated like a whore. No other man in New York had ever dared to treat her as he treated her, and as yet, Bruno had only begun to do to her all the humiliating things he knew she craved. She was his creature.

That was precisely the problem, Bruno thought as he turned away from that scented room where the woman was waiting, and walked toward his own house. He could predict every one of her secrets. They weren't new to him. He had almost reached the age of those experienced women he had always preferred, and as each year passed, it became more and more difficult to find a woman whose most private and forbidden fantasies weren't twice-told tales. Seldom, now, was he excited for long by any new woman, particularly among the society women of New York, whose attitudes toward sex were so often tame and banal, without subplots, lacking the dark and forbidden scenarios that were to be discovered among the women of Paris.

Yes, he blamed them, these richly glittering American women with clean-scrubbed, disappointingly hygienic imaginations, for his lack of desire. He felt no welcome stirring in his groin at the thought of that woman who was waiting for him at this very minute, ardent, avid and wet. He envied her arousal. At least, tonight, when she realized that he wasn't coming to their rendezvous, she would find some way to relieve the lust that had been welling in her since his phone call this morning. She was lucky, she'd enjoyed hours of itching excitement, hours that, for him, had been as barren of anticipation as his whole day, as the predictable dinner party that faced him.

What could there possibly be to look forward to in this city, he asked himself as he walked unseeing through the thrilling streets of New York before Christmas, where, for everyone else, a dozen promises zinged through the snapping air; where, for everyone else, brightly lit windows competed with each other for attention; where, for everyone else, there was a rush of energy and vitality to be discovered at the crossing of every street.

New York. An ugly, ugly city, without charm, without intimacy, without history. The buildings were too tall or too short and, in all cases, too new. All their proportions were wrong, uninteresting, clumsy. The streets were too straight, too narrow, too regular, a grid of boredom. There were no trees—even that excuse for a park was enclosed within a severe rectangle—there were no hidden courtyards, no unexpected cul-de-sacs, no places where you could turn a corner and be forced to stop dead in your tracks by the power of a view. There was no necessary riverbank winding through the city, without which any urban landscape was only half-alive. People who considered themselves elegant were content to live in apartment houses on a dark, too-wide street called Park Avenue, where anyone who was curious could gape at their windows, for there were no walls to protect their privacy.

New York society. A perfect reflection of the city, too noisy, too gaudy and too giddy, without charm or history, open to anyone who could afford the entrance fee. A society that would never comprehend and pay proper attention to the claims of family, to heritage. A society he could not even relate to the word *aristocracy*. An elaborate joke that had the pretension to take itself seriously. He wondered if any of his overanxious hostesses had the slightest idea of what he thought about them. Probably not—they were too stupid to expect his utter scorn, and his manners were too automatic to hint at it. Just as well, for they were the only people available. The French colony was made up of hairdressers and headwaiters.

The only redeeming quality about New York was that it was not a European city. He could not have endured living in the second-rate, self-absorbed, yet provincial Europe of Rome or Madrid, with Paris only a few hours away, forbidden to him. At least here, in this completely sterile exile, the main topic of the city was money, and money, unlike sex, would never cease to fascinate him, never grow predictable and stale; its pursuit could never become devoid of interest. Even as he accumulated more and more of it, he never asked himself for what purpose, when it couldn't even buy a decent valet, for money was totally good, in and of itself.

As Bruno approached his house, to which he never invited anyone, a house that he had decorated in exactly the same manner as the house in the Rue de Lille, he wondered if there would be a letter from Jeanne.

The housekeeper at Valmont had remained loyal to him. She wrote regularly, from her retirement cottage in Epernay, to tell him the news of the family, and he responded faithfully, for she was his only means of knowing what was going on in Champagne. Paul de Lancel was only sixty-four, and the Lancels were a long-lived family. His Lancel grandparents had both been in their eighties before they died. Yet accidents

437

happened every day to people with equally good genes; car accidents, riding accidents, neglected infections, even a fall in the bathroom. Disease could strike without warning. His uncle Guillaume had died relatively young.

Yes, he knew that soon—if not today, then soon, for it would drive him mad to think otherwise—there had to arrive a grieving letter from Jeanne that would give him back his life.

Freddy perched on Tony's desk on a Friday afternoon in March of 1950 and looked at him hopefully. "Tony, let's go for a drive. Jock and Swede are nailed to their desks, but there's no reason why all the bosses have to be in at the same time. It's such a lovely day."

Tony looked up from the empty blotter at which he'd been frowning when she came into his office.

"Go for a drive? Where to? What scenic wonder lures you? The amazing view of the Hollywood sign? The flat beige sands of Santa Monica? Don't you really mean that you'd like to hop into your new Bonanza? Don't you mean go for a plane ride, not a drive?"

"No, I mean a drive," Freddy said patiently. He was in a vile mood. Too much whiskey at lunch or just general bloody-mindedness? It was impossible to say for sure this early in the day. "Come on, we can put the top of my car down. I'm dying to get out of this place. It's not that much fun anymore, with everything running smoothly and business so good. Do come on, darling."

Tony sighed reluctantly, but he got up and followed her out to the parking lot of their new main office building at the Burbank Airport, and sat listlessly as she drove back from the San Fernando Valley over the hills into the Los Feliz neighborhood.

Freddy drove straight up a street that she seemed to have picked at random, and parked in front of a house at the top of the hill, a typically Californian version of a Spanish hacienda, that rambling old house with balconies and two courtyards which she'd bought in November, not quite five months earlier. She'd insisted on a short escrow, and the day after the escrow closed she'd had a contractor with two crews working overtime putting the house back into perfect order, while a decorator was busy full-time, working on the furnishings. The avenue of old orange trees that lined the driveway was in fragrant blossom, and a landscape architect had finished pruning every tree and restoring the garden that Freddy remembered so well, turning over and enriching the neglected soil, planting wide beds of English primroses and tiny purple violas. Pansies were everywhere, their yellow, white and dark ruby faces mingling with the smaller blue dots of the impertinent forget-me-nots. In another month the bushes of the rose garden, on which the buds were already swelling, would be in their first bloom; all the lawns were green with newly laid turf. The house had been entirely repainted, and the red tiles of the roof were in perfect condition. She turned off the motor.

"I thought you wanted to go for a drive," Tony said. "We haven't been on the road for fifteen minutes."

"Do you like this house?" she asked.

"Actually, yes. This is probably the only kind of house that looks absolutely right in California. I've always said that, as well you know."

"We need a new house, don't we?"

"I certainly can't disagree about that."

"Something like, as an example, this one?" she asked eagerly.

"I assume that means that you've already bought it?" Tony glanced at Freddy's face. Her eyes were downcast to hide her expression, but from her heightened color and the carefully neutral look on her always mobile, readable face, he knew the answer. "It looks very pretty indeed, and in good condition, I imagine," he continued, without waiting for her reply. "Shipshape from top to toe. All systems working, checked out and ready to be lived in."

"You're not surprised." Freddy felt flat with extinguished excitement. Every day, while the contractor and the landscape people had been working on the house, she'd managed to sneak away from the office and drop in and oversee their progress, bullying and cajoling, threatening and vamping shamelessly, until it had all been done exactly to her specifications and in less time than anyone would have anticipated. She'd been on the phone to her decorator a half-dozen times a day, and had met with her to make final choices every week, without anyone at Eagles knowing what she was doing. She'd been filled to the brim with her wonderful secret.

"Well, in point of fact, how could I be?" Tony answered. "Now that we're filthy rich, a new house was only a matter of time. You do like to get things done, don't you, Freddy?" He spoke with a gentleness of tone that touched her as uneasily as would an unfamiliar chord in a well-known tune. It wasn't a gentleness she'd ever heard before from this essentially gentle man. There was something new about it, something forced, as if gentleness were covering up another feeling she couldn't identify.

"Even if you're not surprised," she said, hiding her childish disappointment at the way he was taking her achievement for granted, "aren't you dying to see what it looks like inside?"

"I'm certain it's perfectly charming. And I know I'm going to get the grand tour, so push on," Tony said, getting out of the car and starting toward the front door.

In all the times Freddy had played this scene in her head, trying to picture Tony's response to the new house, imagining his delight at the new vision of daily life that it offered, the new possibilities it opened up to them, she had never thought of such a low-key, almost resigned reaction, as if he were being offered a dish that he had to eat out of politeness, even though he wasn't hungry. Maybe he had a hangover, she thought as she followed him, digging in her purse for the key to the front door. Maybe he was being as nice as he could be with a terrible headache and a dry mouth. It was impossible to tell with Tony. He held his liquor far too well. His drinking was deceptive. Sometimes it was only after he passed out that she realized how drunk he'd been.

Freddy led Tony through all the main rooms of the house. There were palms and flowering plants in baskets everywhere; the floors were covered in large squares of Mexican terra-cotta on which soft-toned rugs had been placed; the furniture, beautifully made but uncomplicated in design, was an illustration of the deepest meaning of the word comfort, and the fabrics were mellow linens and cottons, hand-printed in unfussy patterns. There were so many windows that in each room, people could spend hours of tranquility watching the light change. It was, deliberately, a house without grandeur, in spite of the generous scale of the rooms and the high-beamed ceilings; just as deliberately as it was a house in which a man would feel as much at home as a woman.

As they went from one room to another, Tony paused in each doorway and murmured, "Charming, really charming," until she wanted to punch him. He sounded like a well-bred visitor, not like a man seeing his own house for the first time. He hadn't peered into a closet or opened a single drawer or demonstrated as much curiosity about any single detail as a person entering a new hotel room might show the bellman. "Charming." But she hadn't bought the house and fixed it up to charm him. She'd done it to make him happy. Or, at the very least, happier.

"Where's the bar?" Tony asked as they sat down at last in the living room, where six arched, floor-to-ceiling doors opened out on three sides to the beckoning gardens.

"Over there," Freddy said, pointing out a long, hospitable-looking table on which were placed crystal glasses of every shape and kind, a gay array of bottles, club soda, ginger ale, jars of nuts and olives, and a silver bowl of lemons.

440

"What does one do about ice?" Tony asked, pouring himself a whiskey.

"One brings in an ice bucket from the kitchen," Freddy answered, forcing a smile. It was the first question he'd asked. "But you don't use ice, do you, darling, so we'll only have to do that when we have guests," she added, feeling like a saleswoman pushing a product on a reluctant buyer.

Tony drank his whiskey in one gulp and poured another. "Do you fancy a wee dram?" he asked.

"Please. Same as yours."

"Cheers," she said, as he handed her her glass and sat down on the other side of the coffee table. Never, she thought, had she spoken that word in such a curious atmosphere. It was so . . . tentative . . . yet he knew the house was definitively theirs, even if he lacked the enthusiasm she'd been so sure he'd feel.

He hoisted his glass a few inches, in a vaguely sketched salute, but he didn't say anything before he drank half of it.

A silence fell. Freddy inspected the contents of her heavy crystal tumbler as if there might be informative tea leaves lurking at the bottom. Nervously she finished her drink. He must be getting the feel of the house, she told herself, just letting it seep into his pores. Perhaps he'd actually been far more surprised than he'd seemed, and didn't quite know what to say.

"You don't think it's too big, do you, Tony?" Freddy asked, breaking the silence. "Because when we have more children and when we entertain and have houseguests and later, when the kids bring their friends home, it won't seem nearly as big as it does with just the two of us sitting here."

"So you have all that planned already, do you? You're a bloody wonder, you are, Freddy. I should never underestimate you. I know you can't have conceived a child, but you may well have sent out invitations to a house-warming by now, isn't that so?"

Freddy felt herself bristle. What was wrong with him? Why this disapproval? What was he blaming her for?

"Of course I haven't sent out invitations," she said as lightly as she could, ignoring his tone. "The house was only finished yesterday. The paint's barely dry. Anyway, what's wrong with my dreaming about the future? How about another drink?"

"No, thank you."

"What?" she said, startled.

"I have to be sober for this," Tony said, and Freddy's blood froze.

441

Now his voice had a truly chilling edge, as if he were restraining himself from anger.

"Sober?" she asked.

"Sober, stone cold sober. Frequently I am not, as you may have noticed. I hoped I could do this drunk, but as it turns out, Dutch courage never works for me. Particularly not for this."

" 'This'? Don't you like the house? Are you trying to tell me that you don't want to live in it?"

"It's a very nice house. It also happens to be exactly the sort of thing you do that I *cannot endure*. Here's a house for you, Tony, all ready to move into. Here's a future for you, Tony, parties, houseguests, a big family, oh, but you're going to have such fun. Here's a business for you, Tony, you can call yourself a vice-president, here are millions of dollars, Tony, here's your whole cocked-up life, Tony, on a silver platter! Freddy will give it to you!" He took his glass and threw it straight against the stone of the fireplace. "Sweet Jesus, Freddy, your dreams are tomorrow's facts! When you want something, nothing stands in your way until you get it. On your own. I'm incidental, I'm your fucking consort! *We're wrong together, Freddy.* That's what I've had to tell you for a long, long time. I had to stay sober to spit up that bare fact. We're dead wrong. I want to get out of this marriage. I want a divorce. I cannot be married to you anymore."

The brutality in Tony's voice stunned her as much as his words. He sounded as agonized and as determined as an animal that was biting off its own paw to free itself from a trap.

"You're crazy! You *are* drunk! I don't care if you say you're not. You've probably been drinking since you woke up, you bastard!" Freddy listened to herself from some distant place, even as she jumped up and screamed at him. *"If you could hear yourself, you'd be so ashamed."*

"I *am* ashamed. I've been ashamed for years. I'm almost used to it— but not quite, thank God. Look, Freddy, just listen to me, hear me out. It doesn't matter if you think I'm drunk or sober. That's not the issue. The fact is that you took over our lives from the minute we moved here, five years ago. Damn soon, you became the whole show. You were invincible, unbeatable. *And I hadn't a clue.* If it hadn't been for you, we'd have been bust and back in England in a few months. You made Eagles work. Jock and I couldn't have done it without you. You needed Swede, but *nobody needed me.* I haven't contributed a damn thing except to fly cargo—any pilot could have done that. I've been excess baggage right from the beginning, and you—"

"Tony, stop! How can you be so horribly unfair? I couldn't possibly

442

have lasted all these years without you, I'd never have had the guts, I couldn't have hung in there when it was so tough—"

"Bullshit. You could and you would. You would never have given up, you'd have found a way. I kept selling myself that same face-saving lie, I told myself that you needed me. That Annie needed me. It was the only way I could keep from facing up to the truth . . . that and the booze. Now that we're a big success, there's no excuse left, no way to keep on kidding myself. The big struggle's over. But don't try to make me believe that you're ever going to stop running the show. That's not the way you're made. I can't compete and I won't live this way. It's *killing me*, Freddy. *I have no self-respect left.* Do you realize what that means?"

"Tony, look, I'll go back to England with you, I'll stop working, we can go back to the way it was before, only now we'll have money— remember, coming home was only an experiment, nobody ever said that it was forever." Freddy spoke as collectedly as she could. He couldn't mean all the things he was saying. If she stayed calm, if she didn't get upset, if she reasoned with him . . .

"Poor little Freddy. You really believe you can fix everything, don't you? Even change your basic character? Do you honestly think you could ever again play the part of the lady of the manor? You were so utterly miserable then—though you were such a damn good sport about it when we didn't have any options that I didn't guess what it was doing to you. But now—it would be a ridiculous charade, like a great race-horse at the peak of its form, pretending to prefer to pull a cart along a country lane. Didn't you hear what you just said—'coming home was only an experiment'—home is right here in California for you, just as home is Longbridge Grange for me. I miss it *dreadfully*, Freddy. Rain and all. We—you and I—are not to blame. Neither one of us has the stuff to be a happy expatriate. You're too American, I'm too British. It was never meant to work. If we hadn't moved to California, you wouldn't have been able to keep on living in England without stamping out all the things in you that made you . . . the girl I used to love."

"But—but—what went wrong?" Freddy asked. Tony was sober, she realized in anguish, and even in her great pain she couldn't deny that her country gentlewoman years had felt like a bad joke. There had to be words to explain this, words that would take them back to the beginning and let them start over, words to stop this nightmare, to change it, to make it not be true. "Tell me—please, oh please, *tell me*, Tony."

"When we got married we only knew a part of each other," Tony said. "Don't you remember how all we ever talked about, when we weren't making love, was flying and fighting? We were in the same game, you and I, we had the same passions. I loved that fighter in you, but how could I have guessed that when the war was over you'd still be dashing off to do battle? To run the world? I never understood what kind of woman you really were, until we started Eagles. I admire you, Freddy, I always have, but you're not a woman I want for my wife. We have nothing truly in common except Annie and the old glory days. It's not enough. I'm sorry, but it just is not enough."

Freddy looked at him hard. Tony looked ten years younger than he had when they'd walked into the house, and the look of relief on his face was too obvious for her to doubt the truth of his words.

"You have a girl, don't you, Tony?" she said with sudden certainty.

"Yes. I rather thought that would be understood. What could you have imagined when I didn't touch you all this long while?"

"I don't know. Not that. Who is she?"

"Just a woman. Quiet, pliant, pleasant, relaxing, the kind of woman you'd suppose I'd have."

"Do you want to marry her?"

"Good God, no. I don't want to marry anybody. I just want out, Freddy. *Out.* I want to go home."

Delphine read Freddy's letter and handed it across the breakfast table to Armand. He scanned it quickly, then more intently, and finally studied it at length while Delphine watched his face. As soon as he put it down, she pounced. "Are you surprised?"

"I'm stunned. Who would have expected a divorce? Eight years of marriage without any terrible trouble, at least none we've known about, and then this, out of nowhere—it's over, finished, and she says it's *nobody's fault?* When two decent human beings stay married for eight years, when they have a child together, a life together, how can they possibly get divorced without reasons, without fault? Is this some bright new American idea?"

"No, that's Freddy's shorthand for letting us know that she's never going to talk about it in the future and doesn't want to be asked questions. It's her pride, poor baby. She's infernally proud about exposing her emotions. She has no vanity, I don't mean that, it's something different—a sense of privacy that's almost—savage. You remember the first time they visited us, when they were still living in England? She never even hinted to me how unhappy she was, in fact she tried to persuade me that her life was a dream of bliss, but if she couldn't tell

444

her own sister she was having trouble, who could she tell? She's never learned how to let people help her. She's stiff-necked and stubborn."

"And are you so different, babe?"

"No, I'm a tough customer too—except with you," Delphine answered slowly. At thirty-two she still had three years to go before her vast French public would consider her to have arrived at a really intriguing age, and she was enjoying every second of her youth. "That's why I understand Freddy. You got my number the minute we met. I've never been able to hide anything from you for a second. I may even stop trying someday. Tony *never* had Freddy's number, didn't you sense that?"

"My newly ex-brother-in-law was always a mystery to me . . . there's something about being the heir to fifteen generations of British aristocracy that I'll never comprehend, vast as is my knowledge of human nature. That's one of the reasons I haven't tried to direct a film about Anglo-Saxons at play or in love—I don't understand their games as well as they do."

"I don't know why, but this makes me think of that love affair Freddy had when she was a kid."

"What are you talking about?"

"Last summer, when we were at Valmont with the children, Mother and I were having a heart-to-heart talk, and she told me that when Freddy was sixteen she fell madly in love with her flying instructor and actually left home and lived with him for years. Nobody guessed, but Mother happened to see them together and she knew. She said it was a grand passion, the real thing, for both of them . . . but, after the war, when she asked Freddy what had become of him, Freddy only said that they hadn't been in touch for years, and changed the subject. I'd never have believed it, if Mother hadn't been so certain."

"So that's what mothers and daughters talk about when they're alone together."

"Naturally. When we're not complaining about our husbands. You still have a lot to learn about women, Sadowski. Stick around. Little innocent, tomboy Freddy, living in sin with a man in his forties . . . and I thought I was the red-hot scandal of the family. Well, it's obvious to me what happened. She got tired of Tony and all that British restraint. Fed up to here. She finally faced up to it and ditched him. I'll bet anything that Freddy has another man waiting in the wings, and we'll hear about him when she's good and ready to tell us. That's the subtext of this letter. Still, I feel sorry for her . . . those eight years weren't easy. I feel sorry for Annie. I particularly feel sorry for Tony, poor guy. It's bad enough to go through a divorce without feeling as if you've been rejected. It's a kick in the teeth."

At Valmont the mail didn't arrive until noon. Eve put Freddy's letter aside to read at her leisure, for she was too busy arranging a lunch for a group of buyers to give it close attention. She circled the long oval dining room table, its wood gleaming, heavy lace-encrusted mats before each chair, as she set out place cards, a task she never entrusted to anyone else. Here she put the wine buyer for a growing chain of British hotels; there, Eve decided, was the place for the buyer from the Waldorf Astoria in New York and his wife; and right here, at her right, in the place of honor, she put the wine buyer for the Ritz in Paris. His wife would sit on Paul's left. As for the couple from dear little Belgium, where more champagne per capita was drunk than in any country in the world, he would sit on her left and his wife on Paul's right, next to the *chef de cave,* who always joined them. Thank God, Eve reflected, she'd been a diplomat's wife for so many years that these delicate decisions could be made almost automatically, for her week included at least four such lunches and almost as many dinner parties.

Hospitality, which had always been a part of the life of Champagne, was now more than just a tradition, it was their most potent selling tool, and Eve was the leading practitioner of the art. In 1949 the growers of Champagne had sold as many bottles as they had sold annually during the first decade of the century, which had been their most successful period in history, and now, in 1950, they clearly were going to break that record.

"Girls, please come on in now," Eve called, and two young English university students appeared from the doorway where they'd been waiting for her to finish placing the guests. They were both living at the château for an entire growing season in order to be introduced to the lore of viniculture, and they helped her as well with the flowers for the château. As always, when she had finished with the place cards, they brought her trays of small vases filled with flowers, their stems cut as short as possible, which she had taught them how to arrange. Eve could never understand why so many hostesses used tall flowers in the middle of a table, preventing people from seeing each other clearly, and impeding the flow of conversation. She dotted the center of the table with small bouquets until it looked like a lilliputian flower bed around which the taller glasses bloomed in their waiting pride, four at each place.

In less than an hour, a group of strangers would meet over her table, and with only champagne as their mutual interest, they would have as lively an interchange as if she'd planned the guest list for weeks. Perhaps it was the pre-lunch tour that put them in such a cordial mood; first the ritual trip to the church at Hautvillers where Dom Perignon was buried, and then, after their return to Valmont, the tour of the press-house and a glimpse of the cellars while Paul answered their questions. In the anteroom of the cellar, he would open a bottle and fill their glasses himself, to sip from as they strolled back to the château on the paths above the vines, which now, in May, were covered with embryo bunches of grapes, growing bigger each day.

Her table ready, Eve went to her dressing room to change for lunch. She retouched her makeup expertly, without thought, seated in front of her dressing table, until something, some fugitive scent of spring in the air, made her pause and look at herself in the mirror. Had she really become la Vicomtesse de Lancel, châtelaine of the Château de Valmont, she inquired of her reflection, tilting her chin in a way that concealed the faint lines on her neck. She remembered a night in another May, a night in 1917, when she had been twenty-one, not fifty-four as she was now. She had taken off all her makeup at another dressing table, backstage at the Casino de Paris, and a gallant officer had come a-calling on a girl with strawberry blond hair parted in the middle and coiled over her ears, an impetuous, free-spirited girl, a girl who called herself Maddy and who had many secrets, none of which included a knowledge of the disposition of place cards, or the way to make a table of strangers feel like friends, or how to run a château with twelve servants and many guest rooms, which sheltered buyers from all over the world for seven months of the year.

Eve sighed philosophically, recalling the panic of her well-meaning aunt, Marie-France, who had been convinced that she would never make a respectable marriage because she sang in a music hall. She was far more than merely respectable now; "distinguished," the wine writers always called her when they wrote about their visits to Valmont. Her brows still slanted wildly upward as they always had, her eyes were no less gray, no less quick to kindle, she still hummed bits of all the tunes she'd ever heard as she walked about the château, she still chaffed at the conventions of life when they restricted her impulses—but she had to admit that the face she saw in the mirror was more suited to a château than to a stage. Would she have it otherwise? No, never. In thirty-three years of marriage she had not once regretted her choice, for longer than those normal periods of questioning the very existence of the matrimonial condition that every woman must expect to go through, given the essential nature of the male animal.

From Dijon to Paris, then Canberra, Cape Town, Los Angeles, London—and now Epernay. She had almost traveled in a perfect circle. Doctor Coudert's naughty runaway daughter had ended up within a hundred miles of her birthplace. As Vivianne de Biron, now nearing eighty, and as tart as ever, had remarked when she paid them a visit last year, what luck that her Madeleine had not married a mustard prince and settled in Dijon, although she still had not brought herself to approve entirely of the way in which her protégée had thrown away a great career.

Eve put on one of her Balenciaga suits, a thin wool in his most Spanish mood, as black as a mother superior's habit and twice as chic as all of next year's Dior collection. She thought of them as her "suits of lights," as chosen for effect as the theatrical vestments of the great toreros. If she was to be considered distinguished instead of bewitching, she'd give them their money's worth.

With only five minutes until her guests arrived, she gazed out the window at the vivid promise of the vines, and she gave thanks for the amazing recovery of the House of Lancel. When Paul had told her that nothing remained in *Le Trésor*, that Bruno had sold it all on the black market, and that all that was left in the cellars were the vintages of the war years, still aging "on the yeast," her heart had plunged in pain for him in his humiliation and shame.

Survival seemed impossible, not just at Valmont, but throughout Champagne. But she hadn't appreciated the dedication of the people of Champagne, nor had she realized that the war vintages, although small in quantity, were, as if to compensate, superlative in quality. By 1945 all the prisoners of war had returned home, and the workers in the vineyards, most of whom owned their own tiny patches of grapes, had rallied around the new proprietor and sold him whatever remained of their small reserves of wine, much of it successfully squirreled away in hard-learned Champenois manner, throughout the Occupation.

Nevertheless, the past years had been a time of greater struggle than they had ever lived through, as every centime they made was put back into the land, replanting the oldest vines, restoring and rebuilding. Until last year there had been no new clothes, no trips to Alexandre in Paris to get her hair done. In fact, not a single worn-out casserole in the château had been replaced, but she had managed to entertain as soon as the first buyers returned. They were still deeply in debt to the banks at Rheims—perhaps they would never be out of debt—but the House of Lancel, like the other *Grands Marques*, had triumphed.

The postwar years had taken a heavy toll. Paul had aged more rapidly during the first years of his sixties than she would ever have expected. He worked in a demonic, exhausting way, and when he sat down for a rare minute after spending hours over the accounts, she'd often looked up to see his face wracked with bitterness and sadness, yet he never mentioned Bruno's name again.

Eve looked at her watch. Time to go downstairs. She left Freddy's letter—a disappointingly thin one—on her dressing table, and found no time to open it until after dinner, when she and Paul had finally been able to bid their houseguests good night and retire to their own part of the château.

Paul was getting into his pajamas in his dressing room when she appeared in the doorway, holding the sheets of paper in her hand.

"Freddy and Tony are getting divorced," Eve cried out in disbelief, tears standing in her eyes.

"Let me see that," Paul said, reaching for the letter. He read it and reached out and held her close to him and kissed her hair. "Darling, don't cry, I know how you feel, but it's not the worst thing that could happen," he said.

"But I simply don't understand! What can she mean—that it's nobody's fault? That's ridiculous! You know that can't be true."

"Of course it isn't. And I do understand," Paul said slowly.

"What do you mean?"

"Last winter, when we went to California to see our buyers, I spent a lot of time with Tony. He was more than a heavy drinker, he had become an alcoholic. The signs were clear to me, although he hid them well. I imagine that it started during the war—the British have always been able to consume staggering amounts of whiskey and still fight like madmen the next day. Unlike us, they must possess livers of solid copper. I didn't say anything to you because you weren't aware of it and Freddy was so anxious for me not to notice. I prayed that he'd pull himself out of it, but I honestly didn't have too much hope. Obviously his drinking got to the point where she had to make this decision. I don't expect her ever to tell us about it, but it's clear to me that she had to leave him, for Annie's sake as much as her own."

"My sweet Freddy," Eve murmured, almost to herself.

"Yes, but it's better that she pull herself out of an impossible situation than let it degenerate totally. She'll survive, darling, I promise you. Freddy's so strong. I pity Tony. To have fought so heroically, to have survived . . . and now, to end as a rejected husband."

22

BETWEEN the two of us, Swede, don't you think that we've got to know damn near everything there is to know about women?" Jock Hampton asked, as the two men ate lunch together in February of 1951. "Wouldn't you bet that there aren't any odds on broads that we couldn't handicap if we put our heads together?"

"Remind me never to go to the track with you," Swede grunted.

"How many girls have you had? Dozens? Hundreds?"

"Too many to even remember how many."

"Me too. But you're older, more experienced, and you've known her longer. So you tell me, what the hell is wrong with Freddy?"

"I thought you were talking broads in general. Broads in general I know a thing or two about. Freddy—I wouldn't want to try to figure."

"Look, I know she's special, I'm not a total lout, give me credit for knowing the difference between broads and Freddy, but she's still a woman, a female, a *girl*. So she's got to be more *like* other women than she's *different* from other women. Right?"

"Maybe. Maybe not."

"You know, Castelli, I'm really glad I brought this up. You're a hell of a lot of help. For Christ's sake, she isn't the Holy Grail, she's flesh and blood and *I miss her*! I want Freddy back, the way she used to be before the divorce. Remember?"

"You better believe it."

"She always left us gasping didn't she? Shit, Swede, didn't we have fun with her nipping at our heels, keeping us off balance, strutting her stuff, surprising us, always ahead of the pack, making us hustle to keep up? And laughing at us while we tried? She made every day seem like the Fourth of July. One gorgeous burst of fireworks after another. God, but I like a difficult bitch. Every great broad I've ever met was a difficult bitch—and Freddy made them all look like they were bucking for sainthood. What happened to her, Swede?"

"She got—ladylike. That's about as close as I can put a name to it."

"I've known a lot of divorced women, and going all over ladylike isn't the normal drill. Usually they bust out, start to date, buy sexy new clothes, get their friends to introduce them to guys—maybe not right

450

away, but eventually. Freddy and Tony broke up a year ago, her divorce is practically final, and she's still sitting at home in that big house every night, having dinner with Annie. Helping an eight-year-old with her homework is the high point of Freddy's social life. I happen to know because I drop in now and then, just to see my goddaughter, and it's always like that. Don't tell me that's normal."

"That's the way she wants to conduct her private life, Jock. It's not any of our business."

"Agreed. No argument. But she also happens to be our partner. We've got a bunch of money to lose if Freddy doesn't get her ass back in gear pretty soon. When's the last time she dragged in a fat new account, kicking and screaming a little bit maybe, but unable to resist her? I haven't got what it takes to melt hearts, neither do you, and we're losing business to the Flying Tigers because she's so screaming ladylike she won't even bat her eyelashes anymore. She doesn't even walk the way she used to! When's the last time she had one of her bossy fits, and vamped and needled us into doing something we had no intention of doing, and we ended up making buckets of money out of it? Sure, she shows up at the office and sits in it all day and she puts in a full day's work, but she's not giving us her old stuff. She doesn't even go flying anymore, and that's when she gets her best ideas. It's as if we'd bought a big, fancy, bright roller coaster and it turned into a little dinky kiddie-cart when we got it home. It's not fair to us, and I think you should talk to her seriously about it."

"How did I get elected?"

"Because you knew her when she was a kid. She'll listen to you. She'll just tell me to stick it."

"No, thanks. If you want a job done, do it yourself, Jock."

"You chicken?"

"You bet."

"Well, I'm not. I think it'd be more appropriate coming from you, Swede, but since you have such dainty ways, I'll tackle it myself. What's the worst that can happen? So she tells me to stick it? At least I'll get her thinking along the right lines. Nobody has to go into mourning for a divorce for the rest of her life."

"Gonna put it that way?"

"Nope, I'll be more tactful. First thing is to get her out of the house and away from the office."

"Go with her when she gets her hair done. That's the only time she isn't at one place or the other," Swede Castelli grinned. The day he poked his nose into Freddy's personal life would never dawn. He knew

451

her too well. Who else knew about the rotten luck she'd had with the only two men who'd meant anything to her? If she wanted to shield herself from the world, who could blame her? Anyway, Jock Hampton was the one who was all hot and bothered. As far as he was concerned, and he should know if anyone did, their business was going just fine.

"I'm going to invite her to come to the reunion of the Eagle Squadron. Yeah, that's it. She can't refuse—she'll be the only girl there who'll know what it's all about, the only one who deserves to be there."

"Think she'll come?"

"If she doesn't come willingly, I'll tie her up and throw her in the back of my car. I'll kidnap her."

"You sure you wouldn't prefer it that way?"

"You're a pervert, Swede. A disgusting, filthy old man. I'm going to make you pay for lunch."

Freddy frowned at herself, irritated beyond measure that she'd been forced to go to this evening's party. From the moment that Jock mentioned the Eagle Squadron reunion, she'd known that if ever there was one event at which she would be a no-show, this was it.

Of all of Jock's ideas, this was the worst. It was so utterly insensitive, so incredibly tactless, that she just hadn't believed it when he'd proposed that she go with him. How had he even dared to ask? Didn't he have enough basic empathy to realize that the men of the Eagle Squadron would remind her inescapably of everything that had been so high-hearted and was now so lost? The glory days, Tony had called them in his last, terrible speech, of which she had not forgotten a word. The days when she'd been in love with her job and in love with Tony, until the two loves had somehow seemed like one. She'd been filled with a sense of mission that had lifted her to heights she could now remember only with sick envy of her own former self. Jock had asked her to go, with such utter incomprehension of why there could be no question of her walking into a room full of people who were a part of her dead happiness, that he left her speechless with her mouth all but hanging open, while he spilled out his pathetic little story.

"I just can't hack it unless you come with me," he'd said, absolutely abject. "Every one of those guys has a wife and two and a half kids, and at the last reunion you wouldn't believe what they were saying—poor old Jock, how come you haven't found a single woman who would put up with you, there has to be something basically wrong with you, maybe you're too attached to your mother, I bet you'll never get married, you'll end up a lonely old bachelor trying to fill your empty life,

452

and, worst of all, have I got a girl for you! Every one of them tried to fix me up with his sister. I love those guys, Freddy, but I won't go to the reunion again without some sort of a female companion, and I can't take any of the girls I know, they'll stand out like sore thumbs and have a terrible time. How could it hurt you to just spend one evening helping me out? You could just stick around, protecting me, like a wingman, and when they start attacking me—especially the wives—change the conversation, get them off my tail. It seems to be a crime against the American way of life to be an unmarried thirty-one-year-old man in this country. I'd do the same for you anytime you had to have an escort for something, you know you could count on me." And on and on, practically whimpering.

She'd run out of excuses quickly, since the one reason that would have shut him up was the one she'd never admit to: that since Tony had fled, his only salvation lying in getting far away from her as quickly as possible, she'd been paralyzingly at war with herself, unable to move in any direction. On the one hand, she was utterly shamed by the words Tony had said, infinitely mortified by his accusations, which she accepted as a true picture of the way she'd been to him. Her self-reproach crushed her. On the other hand, she was angrier than she'd ever been in her life. What kind of spineless man would dump the whole burden of his decline onto his wife? Yet no sooner did rage come to her rescue than memory insisted that he was right, that back in England he'd been content, that he hadn't started to go downhill until they'd moved to California.

Night after night Freddy sat at home, once Annie was in bed, obsessively putting herself on trial, acting as prosecutor and defender, judge and jury, accusing herself and excusing herself, going back and forth over the last fifteen years of her life. Mac would never have run away from her if she hadn't been so transparently manipulative. If he'd believed that she would listen to reason, he would never have gone to Canada and never have died there. As for Tony, why *couldn't* she have been content to live at Longbridge Grange? It was a life so many women would have loved to lead. Why *couldn't* she be more adaptable? More feminine? More like Penelope and Jane and Delphine and her mother? They put their husbands first; their children weren't touched by divorce, and they had good, full, satisfying lives.

But, damn it, didn't she have her own rights too? Weren't her dreams and her passions valid? What was wrong with wanting things if you were willing to go out and work for them? Only within the walls of her house could Freddy approach, at times, a kind of exhausted truce in which shame and fury balanced each other out for a time. At least in the world outside, no one could guess at the facts of her divorce, at the disgraceful truth of how Tony had cast her aside, of the mistress she hadn't even dreamed he had. She'd lost all faith in herself, all self-confidence. However, Freddy realized, none of this was the kind of excuse you can make for not going to a party.

And then there had been Annie. Jock, the sneaky bastard, had actually said, "Annie, wouldn't you like to see Mommy go out and have a good time? Wouldn't it be good for Mommy to get all dressed up and go out with me for one night?" How had he coached an eight-year-old to look as wistful and hopeful and hungry as Oliver Twist? Had he trained her to say, "Oh, you've got to go, Mommy! I can do my homework by myself and I love to eat in the kitchen with Helga. You haven't had any fun at all in such a long time," with a catch in her voice that made Freddy realize that it might not be such a good idea for Annie to think that her mother was an object of pity.

No, Freddy told herself grimly, she'd been forced into it. Jock Hampton had seen to that. She checked her image in the mirror. Everything seemed to be in order. The exquisitely made black silk dress, high-necked and long-sleeved, fit too loosely, as did all her other clothes. She'd lost her appetite after Tony had left her, and she could only force herself to eat a decent dinner by telling herself that she had to set Annie a good example.

Freddy added a wide black belt that pulled the expensive silk in severely at the waist. It was utterly appropriate: inconspicuous, not aggressive in any way, the kind of dress in which a woman melted into the crowd. Only its price, which no one would recognize, set the dress apart from what the other women would be wearing. She'd had her hair done that afternoon and it looked suitably disciplined. For once, thank heaven, it had decided to behave. She put on a touch of lipstick, but no mascara or eyeshadow. The wives of the former pilots were bound to be a bunch of busy, happy souls who spent their energies in having happy babies and making their homes into happy places for happy husbands—more than likely they wouldn't use eye makeup, even if American fashion magazines were just beginning to show it for the average woman. She certainly didn't want to look too Hollywood. A small pair of earrings and black pumps finished her ensemble.

When Jock arrived, Freddy had been dressed for a half hour. However, she couldn't seem to make up her mind to leave her room. She hung about, hanging things up and checking out her handbag for the fifth time. Jock and Annie were having a lively conversation. She could hear them all the way upstairs. Why hadn't he invited Annie to his stupid reunion? Now it was too late to suggest that solution. Finally she forced herself to go downstairs, listening to them laughing together. She entered the living room and their voices stopped abruptly.

"Mommy!" Annie wailed.

"Freddy, we're not going to a funeral!" Jock said. "What the hell have you got on? Go change to something else right away. We're going to be late anyway, a few more minutes won't matter."

"Oh, Mommy, you look terrible!" Annie cried.

"Black is always appropriate, always chic—what do you two know about clothes? This happens to be a Jacques Fath."

"I don't care what the hell it is, put on something pretty—and not black," Jock roared.

"You look like a widow!" Annie added, her enchanting face woebegone.

"All right, all right." Freddy shot a glance of fury at Jock. With all those Brendas of his, she could imagine the kind of flashy, bad-taste, sexpot dressing he was accustomed to. And that peacock had never told her that he was going to wear his uniform. The male ego! She dashed up to her bedroom and reviewed her dresses, sliding them past her on their hangers in a rage.

"Something pretty"—that shithead! *Pretty.* That just went to show his idea of what a woman should look like. Pretty—a word she'd always hated. A namby-pamby word, a girly-girly word, a ruffled and beribboned word, a trifling toy word, a gewgaw bibelot of a word than which the only worse thing was *cute.* At least nobody'd ever accused her of being cute.

She snatched a hanger from the rack and held the dress up against her. It had been too tight when she brought it home, just before Tony had left her, a dress she'd intended for the housewarming that had never taken place. She'd never bothered to take it back to have it fitted properly. But it was the only thing in the closet that wasn't in a dark color, and by now it would fit. She stripped off her black silk and stepped into the dress. It zipped up perfectly. But she'd have to change her shoes to the shoes that matched the dress, and she'd have to use another bag and different, brighter, bigger earrings. And she'd have to wear more makeup or the dress would overpower her. And she'd have to do something about her hair because it looked too tight, too schoolteacherish to go with the dress. Shit on a stick!

In a flurry, Freddy attacked her makeup with a deftness she'd almost forgotten. She went at her hair, brushing it out with great whacks of her hairbrush until everything that had been done to it was undone and it balanced, in its audacious, cocksure, ungovernable turmoil, the dress she had chosen, the strapless bright red chiffon dress with a closely fitted, almost nonexistent bodice and an outrageously full skirt, a dress made for dancing all night, and seducing the moon, and luring the stars down out of the sky. She paused in front of the mirror, completely transformed. She didn't look exactly pretty. She looked . . . well . . . *better* was probably as good a word as anything else.

But there was still something missing. Freddy went to her jewel box and opened one of its drawers and took out her ATA wings. If Jock was all done up in his uniform, his full colonel's dress uniform no less, with every ribbon he'd ever won, she guessed she could wear these. Fortunately the bodice of the dress was so securely attached to its built-in underpinnings that the wings could be pinned on and not drag the dress down over her naked breast. Yes, that splendid black and gold spread, those two wide wings of heavy gilt bullion framed in black, with the oval in the center bearing the ATA insignia, gave the dress just the finishing touch it needed.

Freddy tromped downstairs, as indignantly as any woman can tromp in a thin pair of high-heeled sandals.

"I hope you two are satisfied," she announced belligerently.

Jock and Annie jumped up from their chairs and gaped.

"This is as good as it gets," Freddy snapped.

"Oh Jesus, Freddy!"

"You're so—oh, wow—so *beautiful*," Annie breathed.

"Thank you, Annie darling. I'll be home early but promise me you'll go to bed on time. I'll tell you all about it in the morning."

"Oh, wow, Mommy, oh, the way you look! How old do I have to be before I get to wear a dress like that?"

"Old, very, very old, Annie," Freddy said.

"Thirty-one, Annie, like your Mommy," Jock said. "Very, very young. Come on, gorgeous. Let's not be the last ones there."

"Jock, don't, and I mean DO NOT call me 'gorgeous' in that cocksure tone of voice or I'm not setting foot out of this house. I'm not your date, I'm your *wingman*, or I wouldn't be here."

"Yes, sir!" He threw her a salute. "No excuse, sir. Deeply sorry, sir."

"That's more like it," Freddy said testily. Jock wrapped her in her new mink jacket and offered his arm. She raised her eyebrows at his unnecessary gesture.

"I think I can manage by myself, thank you," she said as she stepped quickly toward the front door, swaggering ever so slightly.

Freddy stopped transfixed, unable to put one foot in front of the other, outside the room from which she heard the strains of "The White Cliffs of Dover."

"Jock," she said, imploringly, "that music . . ."

Jock, immeasurably pleased with himself, didn't hear her. He'd organized the whole reunion himself, auditioned the orchestra, given them the list of the music he'd chosen, hired the small ballroom at the Beverly Wilshire, planned the dinner menu, and hunted up all the pilots of the Eagle Squadron. Those who didn't live near Los Angeles had all been flown in with their wives, courtesy of Eagles, and each couple had been put up at the Beverly Wilshire, again courtesy of Eagles. It had been Jock who decided that they should wear their uniforms. He'd figured that the six weeks' notice he'd given the guys was fair warning to let them diet off any pounds they might have put on since the end of the war . . . he hadn't gained an ounce himself.

If anything had been left out that would make Freddy able to resist this invitation, he complimented himself that he'd anticipated it. Funny that, try as he would, he hadn't been able to think up any other way to take her out, short of asking her to this particular do. Somehow, Freddy and he, for all the years he'd known her, didn't seem to be on the kind of comfortably casual terms that would permit him to invite her to dinner alone for no special reason. There was an unspoken barrier that he was damned if he could understand, which prevented him from feeling free and easy with her. Without Annie as a reason, he'd never dare to drop in on her at home from time to time, and he was always careful to phone first. If he didn't know better, he'd almost have to think he felt a little shy with Freddy. Could you know somebody *so well* that it became counterproductive?

"That music," Freddy repeated, "it's so—"

"Great, isn't it?" Jock beamed.

"Awful!" Freddy exclaimed. "I loathe wallowing in all that manufactured nostalgia."

"Can I help it if the guys make requests?" Jock asked, gripping her under her elbow and moving her relentlessly along.

"Bathos! Maudlin!"

"Sickening stuff. You're right. But we can't just stand here. You're a real sport, Freddy, I appreciate this. Remember, when they start in about their sisters, you say, 'Jock has a very lovely steady girlfriend but she couldn't make it tonight.' "

"That's utterly impossible to say with a straight face."

"So laugh, crack up, it won't matter if you just get the words out—emphasize the 'steady' part."

The music had changed to "Waltzing Matilda," which was too bouncy to be sentimental, and it was on those rousing strains that Freddy let him push her into the ballroom, where they were immediately surrounded by uniformed men pummeling Jock and hugging Freddy, and pummeling Freddy and hugging Jock.

They must, Freddy decided, have started this party yesterday. It was noisy and crowded and confusing and high-spirited, and all the wives were as dressed up as she was. This wouldn't be as bad as she'd thought. By the time Jock grabbed her and dragged her out on the dance floor, with the band playing "Long Ago and Far Away," she'd cheered up enough not to reflect on the last time she'd danced with Tony to this song, or the next one, "Spring Will Be a Little Late This Year." She realized that she'd forgotten what a good dancer Jock was. She was almost having a good time. The music changed to "You'd Be So Nice to Come Home To."

"Will you stop singing in my ear?" she hissed at him.

"I know all the words," he objected.

"That's no excuse. You're no Bing Crosby."

Blessedly, old friends started cutting in, and for the next hour Freddy was whirled from one eager pair of arms to another, with Jock unable to keep her to himself for more than a few steps at a time. Maybe this wasn't going to be the ideal setting for a little chat with her about her rotten attitude, he realized, his cockiness diminishing. She was the belle of the blasted ball, an exquisitely footloose devil, kicking up her heels in a killer dress he should never have let her leave the house in, a demolition expert who was about to cause a few major fights between husbands and wives when the party was over. And who had told her she could wear her wings? They made all the other women look so . . . underdone.

Dinner passed in a bubbly hubbub of toasts and jokes and seat-switching, and tall tales of great deeds that had really taken place, and then the dancing began again. Freddy had been hearing the music for several hours, so that it had been defanged of its memories and turned into mere background melody. Even "When the Lights Go On Again" had lost its power to throw her backward in time. She felt as if she were out on a spree, deliciously mellow, yet at the same time more cheerful than she had remembered she could be, and the wine that the waiters never stopped pouring had its effect.

The bandleader approached Jock and whispered to him. Jock hesitated, and then responded with a nod of his head. Jock climbed up on the bandstand, and with a fanfare to bring the crowd to silence, he made an announcement.

"Guys—remember how we used to fall out of our kites and drop our chutes and race each other to the Blue Swan, and drink warm beer and sing till we fell down, to give us the strength to do it all over again the next day? Remember that sometimes a girl would be there who sang songs from World War I and taught them to us? Let's all gather around and listen to her sing again. Freddy, where are you? Come on up here, First Officer de Lancel."

A great cheer went up, and Freddy heard a roomful of men calling out requests, and realized that she had been set up. Not one soul had said a word yet about introducing Jock to his sister, and Jock had not told her that she was expected to sing. She fixed him with the deadliest of her inventory of glances, but he just kept waving her up to the platform, where the band had already struck up the tune of "Hello Central! Get Me No Man's Land," music that they couldn't possibly have had in their regular repertoire.

Get it over with gracefully, Freddy told herself, and found herself all but passed from hand to hand to the bandstand, where she was helped up by Jock.

"Cute," she said to him.

"I knew you'd want to do it for the guys."

She turned to the bandleader. "We've got all the music," he assured her, "from Mr. Hampton. Been practicing for days. You just sing, we'll follow right along."

Freddy shook her head. Trapped was trapped. Jock had even put a barstool on the stage for her. She climbed up, and when she looked out on the ballroom full of waiting men, her heart turned topsy-turvy with memory and she launched into "Tipperary," her voice rusty for a moment before she and the musicians caught each other's beat. Immediately, Freddy could feel an emotion collecting in the room that was different from the emotion that had been elicited by the songs of the last war. These old songs were soldiers' songs, not the romantic longing ballads of separated lovers that they had all danced to in the forties, but the songs that frightened, brave men had sung to themselves in the trenches twenty years earlier. The pilots of the Eagle Squadron who hummed along with her words were joined by the music to another generation of warriors, their brothers-in-arms. She swung smoothly through "Tipperary" and then launched into "Pack Up Your Troubles in Your Old Kitbag."

Freddy's contralto voice, though untrained, was so much like Eve's, tawny and irresistible, burnt-sugar sweet in the high notes, with a tough little tickle of wryness in the middle register, and an unhallowed lure hidden under its bottom octave. She lost herself in the music, feeling power growing from verse to verse. She flew from "Keep the Home Fires Burning" to the "Blue Horizon Waltz"; she soared from "Good-Bye Broadway, Hello France!" and into the skylarking of "I'm Always Chasing Rainbows," her head thrown back, as she sat flinging the songs down like valentines to the listening men. She became Maddy, in another red dress, singing by moonlight to wounded French soldiers and one officer, on a night that had been her destiny. She was herself, ten years younger, singing in a packed pub to men who knew—and dismissed the knowledge—that some of them would die in the air the next day, but who demanded a song tonight. Freddy was phosphorescent, not needing the spotlight to glow on her own, a self-luminous girl who sang the songs she'd learned from Eve when she was a child, as freshly as if she'd just invented them.

Freddy came to the end of the great old songs, although the audience was bound together in a mood of entrancement, and she could have sung on for hours. She slipped off the barstool and she signaled to the bandleader to play something else while she looked for a way down from the bandstand. But Jock, who had stationed himself near her, started singing the one song she didn't want to hear, because it meant too much to her. All the men in the room took Jock's voice as a signal to join in. Freddy couldn't even move her lips as the simple, unforgettable melody enfolded her.

> *"Smile a while, you kiss me sad adieu,*
> *When the clouds roll by I'll come to you*
> *Then the skies will seem more blue,*
> *Down in Lovers' Lane, my dearie . . ."*

"Come on, Freddy, sing!" Jock urged her. "You never stopped before until you'd given us this one." Some of the men of the Eagle Squadron had clambered up on the stage and she felt their arms around her waist as they swayed from side to side, roaring out the words.

> *"Wedding bells will ring so merrily,*
> *Every tear will be a memory,*
> *So wait and pray each night for me,*
> *Till we meet again."*

They started singing the song over again from the beginning, and Freddy, unable to prevent them, felt the tears rolling down her face. Oh no! I can't take any more, she thought, and nimbly she slid out of the arms that held her, hopped down to the dance floor, wove her way rapidly through the crowd of singing pilots and their wives, and fled out of the ballroom and down the wide hallway, carpeted in wine and gold, to Wilshire Boulevard, to hail a taxi.

"Wait up! You forgot your jacket!" Jock skidded to an abrupt halt behind her, and put the fur around her shoulders. He took out his handkerchief and swabbed inexpertly at the tears on her cheeks. "Christ—I'm sorry you're upset . . . I just didn't think."

"Well, you certainly thought of everything else," she accused him. "Those old songs . . . where'd you dig up that music?"

"Come on, Freddy, you were fucking sublime! Aren't you glad I got you to sing?"

"I have to admit . . . it wasn't as awful . . . as I'd expected. I didn't even know I remembered all those words," she said, forgiving him with her glance.

The doorman brought Jock's Cadillac convertible around, and he drove her back to her house in silence, echoes of immortal tunes filling the car so loudly that there was no room for words. It was so late that there was no traffic, and he drove, depending entirely on bone-deep reflexes, with a pilot's usual speed and disdain for rules and regulations, in spite of all he'd had to drink. He parked in the driveway of Freddy's house, with a wide-flung swish of gravel.

"So, the reunion's over. Guess we won't do that for another ten years," Jock muttered. He sounded so regretful, she thought, more regretful than the occasion deserved.

"Maybe you should never do it again," Freddy suggested. "Maybe there should just be this one night and then . . . let it go . . ."

"But then I'd never hear you sing again . . . and I'd miss the hell out of that, Freddy, you were just the way you used to be . . ."

"Nothing stays the same, Jock, everything changes, and not always for the better," Freddy said, with a note of finality in her voice, gathering up her bag and gloves and preparing to step out of the car.

"No. Wait. Stay here for another minute, can't we just talk? We never just talk, except about business . . ."

"Just talk?" Freddy was puzzled.

"Yeah, about—oh, anything—the way people might talk when they've known each other for ten years but don't really know each other all that well and—maybe they should."

"Should we?" Now she was frankly amused. In all the years she'd known him, she'd never seen Jock affected by liquor, and certainly he'd never struck up an aimless conversation between the two of them. "Haven't you had a little too much to drink, Squadron Leader?"

"Damn right I have. I'm smashed. *In vino veritas,* whatever the fuck that means."

"Don't you think you should go home and sleep it off? We can talk another time," she said, repressing her laughter. He seemed so serious, not like Jock at all.

"My God, Freddy," he cried indignantly, "you don't even know the first thing about me, do you? You don't even want to know."

"Jock," she chided him, as entertained as if he were Annie's age and making one of Annie's elaborately exaggerated statements. "You were Tony's closest friend, the Longbridges consider you a family member, we've been business partners for five years, you're Annie's godfather, you were even the best man at my wedding, for heaven's sake—of course I know you."

"The hell you do. To you I've always been a member of a group— you just proved that. Don't you think I have an existence of my own, a life—a whole damn life of hopes and dreams and feelings that doesn't have anything to do with the Longbridge family or Eagles?" Smashed or not, Freddy thought, she heard an unmistakably honest outrage in his unexpected words that silenced her. And there was truth in what he'd said. He turned to her, and the outline of his head and shoulders suddenly seemed unfamiliar.

"Jock . . ." She put out her hand as if to touch his arm in tentative apology. He saw her gesture and, with a groan, reached out and pulled her toward him. "Damn it, Freddy, has it ever for one second occurred to you that I'm so much in love with you I can't take it anymore?"

"Jock." Astonished, disbelieving, laughing at his absurdity, she pushed him away. "Come on! It's the liquor talking—that and tonight, the old friends, the music, the memories, the . . . glory days . . . not love. Look at all the ladies in your life." Freddy's voice grew droll, just thinking of them. "How can you even be sure that you've ever been in love?"

"God damn it to hell, will you listen to me! And stop snickering in that repulsively superior way. I had the bad luck to fall in love once in my life—in a church in England, five seconds after you went and got married, when you pushed back your wedding veil and I saw your face. Stupid bastard that I am, I fell in love for keeps and I've spent the years in between trying to get out of it—trying to make it go away, disappear, change, fade—but, just my luck, it won't. I don't *want* to be in love with you! Do you think it's fun to be in love with someone who treats you like wallpaper—funny wallpaper at that—someone who thinks of you as something that came along with the wedding presents?"

"But . . . but . . ." Freddy floundered. She'd never heard Jock talk with this kind of blundering, unstoppable intensity, all his cool, tough-guy attitudes abandoned.

"Don't 'but' me, I know all that shit by heart. I got there too late in your life, you were taken, your love's been elsewhere, I'm just a pal, I'm part of your history and nobody can rewrite history, it's too late to think of me this way—spare me the no hearts and no flowers, and no thanks—there isn't a single 'but' you can pull out that I haven't thought of a thousand times. But listen, Freddy, listen to me, I know what's over is over, but we can rewrite *the future.* Do you know how many times I've rewritten the past—what if we had really met when we *should* have met? No, don't try to stop me. Sure, I'm a little plastered—that's how I finally dug up enough courage to tell you this, you've got to listen! Oh, Freddy, what if we'd gone to high school together, or college, it could so easily have happened that way, we grew up only a hundred miles apart, we were born in the same year, the same *month,* for Pete's sake! I would have taken one look at you and asked you to go with me to the class prom and we would have talked about nothing but planes and forgotten to dance, and by the time I took you home, you would have known that I was meant for you. Maybe you would even have let me kiss you good night. We would never have looked at anyone else again for the rest of our lives. We just missed each other *by inches,* Freddy! Damn it, can't you even imagine how happy we would have been?"

"I suppose . . . it wouldn't have been . . . utterly impossible . . . if you believe in time travel," she admitted, unable to quite put her finger on a flaw in his reasoning. Her mind wasn't working as logically as usual.

"I was just about to ask you something real stupid," Jock said, his eager heart seesawing as he heard the first unaccustomed note of conjecture in her voice.

"Ask me what?"

"Only a jerk ever asks a girl's permission," he said. "Don't you remember that from school?" He slid toward her and took her in his arms, and before she had a chance to protest, he kissed her on the lips, respectfully, tenderly, sweetly, but with the unmistakable dignity of a man who knows that his kiss will not be entirely unwelcome.

"Stop it," Freddy squeaked in surprise. It had been so long since she'd been kissed that she stiffened in alarm.

"Put your arms around me, Freddy," he said. "Go on, just try it, if you don't like it, I'll stop."

"What the hell do you think you're doing, Jock Hampton?"

"Kissing. That's all, just kissing," he said, and kissed her again.

"You said you wanted to talk," she protested wildly, utterly unnerved by the warmth and completeness of his lips and the inadmissible beginnings of a delicious comfort that came from the strong, sure hug of his arms around her. He was so big, he smelled so good, like roasting chestnuts, his arms were so safe. Who could have guessed he'd have such lovely lips?

"Later. Kiss me back, Freddy, darling Freddy, please try to kiss me back when I kiss you. Yeah, that's better, much better, don't be bashful, you're so beautiful, I love you, I've always loved you, you don't have to love me right away but please let me try to make you love me, promise me you will, it's been so long, and I've been so lonely for you —I've been lonely for you all my life—I've wondered forever what it would feel like to kiss you but I never thought it would be this good." He buried his face in her hair and both of their confounded hearts reeled as they clutched each other for balance in a world that had suddenly slipped its moorings with no more reason than the touch of lips upon lips.

Jock took Freddy's face in his hands and kissed her, with slow, exploratory kisses along the edge of her hairline, down the side of her hot cheek to the lower corner of her ear, and then, tilting her head upward, he started to kiss the delicate skin of her neck, pushing aside the fur collar that still wrapped her closely. Freddy made herself draw back, although she was quivering with pleasure at the delicacy and lightness of his questing mouth, although she wanted to sink into the marvelous security she felt in his arms. She tried unsuccessfully to search out his eyes in the dimness of the car.

"Jock, wait! You're going so fast, I don't know how I feel, back up, give me a chance to sort it out, pretend it's after the school prom, go slowly, Jock." Freddy's damaged self-confidence, wounded and sore, warned her that she was too vulnerable, too needy, that she must cling to whatever reality she had fashioned in long, self-questioning nights and not be carried along by the confusion of unexpected feelings his words and kisses had released in her.

He let her go, and drew her head down on his chest, against his uniform. With one arm he held her lightly and with the other he smoothed her hair as if she were a child. "It's after the school prom, Freddy, and all I want is to hold you here next to me for a long, long time. I can't believe my luck. I can't believe that there's a beautiful, redheaded, blue-eyed girl who wants to fly as much as I do. I'm wondering if there's a chance that one day we'll go flyin' together. That's about as far as my imagination will let me go, because I'm only sixteen." He laughed joyously. "I'm much too young to think that I could ever dream of doing anything else with a girl as perfect as you."

Freddy relaxed against him, feeling a willingness to let him talk on and on as if every word were a tiny assurance that she still had her whole unblemished life in front of her, as if enough of his words could be added together and they would somehow make it true. Jock was so beautifully, unexpectedly sweet, she thought dreamily, so earnest in his clumsy way, as straightforward as a little boy. She'd thought he looked like a chivalrous Viking when she'd first laid eyes on him . . . perhaps she hadn't been wrong. There was such naked longing in his voice—if he'd loved her forever, it would explain why he'd always seemed a little angry at her—anger that would have armored him against showing his love. *If he'd loved her.* Suddenly every doubt vanished. She recognized the voice of love when she heard it again after so many years without it. Freddy reached up and twined her arms around Jock's strong neck, lifting herself up so that she could press her willing lips on his, giving him the first kiss he hadn't taken on his own, an impetuous, wholehearted, passionate kiss in which, for the first time, she held nothing back.

"Jesus!" Jock gasped. "How could any man be fool enough to leave you? I told Tony he was out of his mind! Every time I saw him with that girl, I warned him he was nuts—thank God he didn't listen to me."

Freddy felt as if she'd jammed a fistful of pointed pins into her eyes. "You . . . *saw Tony with her—you told him!*" Her arms fell rigid to her sides.

"Well . . . you know . . . guys, friends, naturally they—uh—communicate."

"My God, the two of you sat around and talked about me!" Freddy choked with horror. "You *conspired* with him—you went out and sat around with my husband and his mistress, and when you were having your sniggering little heart-to-heart chats, no doubt he confided in you, didn't he, all the ugly, sad, *private* details of what was going on between us—you knew everything all along and I never dreamed—never dreamed—" Violently she wrenched open the door of the car. Before

Jock could move, Freddy had scrambled out of the front seat, run up the pathway, unlocked her front door, vanished inside and slammed the door behind her with a sound whose finality he could not doubt.

During the few hours that were left of that night, Freddy sat, sunk in an easy chair in her bedroom, locked into a circle of fury and hatred. At one point she grew cold enough to get up to strip off her dress and put on a warm robe and socks, but otherwise she didn't move from the chair except to run into the bathroom and vomit until there was nothing left in her stomach but bile.

Obsessively she repeated every word of the conversation with Jock in his car. A target of opportunity, that's what he'd taken her for, she told herself over and over again. A disabled plane, out of ammunition, separated from its companions, left behind to straggle back alone over enemy territory, the pilot praying only to get home before he was spotted and shot down—a helpless, pathetic, defenseless target of opportunity, the kind of kill that even the greenest pilot wouldn't boast about, a target that a boy on the ground with a rifle could shoot at and hope to hit. Nothing better. Nothing finer. Nothing *easier*.

How could she have allowed herself to believe him for even a few minutes? Freddy raged at herself in such impotent humiliation that she welcomed the bouts of nausea as a relief. She couldn't even fool herself. She had believed him. She had actually believed him when he told her that crap about loving her and she had, oh God, how often could a woman be as pig-stupid, *she had liked it.* Oh yes, she had liked it so very, very much that she would never stop hating herself for those minutes. Yet she knew Jock Hampton, that foul-mouthed bastard, she knew the kind of women he went for, she'd seen enough of them come and go, right back from the first days of her marriage to Tony. British Brendas and American Brendas, they'd all been the same girl, but one minute of sweet talk—drunken sweet talk, at that—and she was ready to fall for his line.

She must be so desperate that it was branded on her forehead. "Please, mister, throw me a mercy fuck"—that was what a man must see when he looked at her. Even a hug was enough to make her melt. Just one lousy hug. He was the only person in the world, except Tony, who knew that she hadn't been made love to in far longer than a year. He knew how vulnerable she was, and he had taken advantage of it the first minute he could.

Or—wait a minute—was Jock the only one who knew? Had Tony told Swede? Had he told anyone else? Maybe everyone knew! Maybe it was common gossip, Tony Longbridge and his mistress, Tony who'd dumped her, Tony who'd wanted out so badly that he couldn't stand to touch poor old Freddy.

Nobody had said a single word to her about Tony tonight. There she was, all dressed up like an idiot, parading her wings, no less, and miracle of miracles, everyone had had the supreme tact not even to look the least bit curious or embarrassed. Yet they *must* all know about the divorce, she didn't kid herself that in a small world like that of the Eagle Squadron, such news wouldn't have spread quickly, particularly since they all had had so much publicity. Obviously everyone—certainly every man—must have been sure that she was Jock's girl. Otherwise there would have had to be some sort of recognition—a gesture, a word of sympathy—something. Tony had gone back to England right after they'd signed the divorce papers . . . it would have been only natural if even one person had said something, but nobody had. *Jock's girl.* Oh God, they all thought she'd fallen right into Jock's bed . . . a bed that would still be warm from the last girl who'd been in it. Easy pickings.

When would it be dawn? When? Even in California, in winter the dawn came late. Before the sun rose, Freddy was dressed in her warmest flying clothes, leaving a note for Helga and Annie in the kitchen, and as it rose she was at Burbank, pulling her Bonanza out of the hangar. She had rarely flown it since the day she'd shown Tony the house. It was the top of the line, the plane she had thought that they would all go out in, she and Annie and Tony . . . the family plane that had never had a family in it.

During the last year Freddy had made several attempts to gentle her heart out of the whiplash of misery her divorce had aroused, by taking the Bonanza up for an afternoon's spin, but, disappointingly, she hadn't been able to recapture the bliss of flight that healed. More and more often she'd found temporary forgetfulness only in burying herself in work at the Eagles office, where her loneliness was peopled with fellow workers and a constant stream of problems that needed solving. She'd needed the sound of human voices, the contact with secretaries and accountants and marketing managers and all the other human beings she dealt with in the course of a day, to balance the roiling solitude of her evenings after Annie was asleep.

But this winter morning there could be no question of going to the office, of risking an encounter with Jock or Swede. Jock had robbed her of Eagles too, she thought, as she started to check out the plane. She'd sell her stock and get out of the air cargo business. She couldn't remain in a partnership with him. It was unthinkable. But she'd deal with ways and means to put Eagles behind her later, when she came back from her flight, for if ever there had been a time, since she'd returned to California from England, when she had to drink the solace of sky, it was today.

Freddy glanced overhead. There was almost no visibility. The low, foglike winter clouds of California's rainy season thinned out a little bit at the end of the runway, but on the ground it was dark, dank and miserable. Not a tempting day, a nonpilot would think, to take up a plane. But once above the clouds, once she'd broken through into the sunlight, it would be as good a day as any other, except that she wouldn't be able to see the earth. And that was just as well, Freddy thought, as she walked watchfully around the Beechcraft, it would be better not to be reminded that no matter how high she flew, mankind still crawled below. Just sky. Just horizon. And most important, clouds to play with. She craved that more than anything.

The Bonanza had been maintained by one of the Eagles' most experienced mechanics, but Freddy took extra care in her visual and physical inspection of the exterior of the plane, since she hadn't personally checked it out in several months. She forced herself to be particularly meticulous because she was so anxious to be off. The airport was quiet at this early hour of the morning, and because of the weather, there were no other private pilots landing and taking off. She taxied out to the end of the runway, heart beating with a captive's eagerness for escape, as she sped efficiently through the preflight checklist, saw that none of the needles on her instrument panel was in the red, and finally, released from discipline, let loose into the oblivion of the elements, headed down her home-base runway toward the beckoning promise of sky.

Once above the overcast, it was a day of overwhelming brightness. The cloud cover below was squashed so flat that it was like a lid on an endless can. The alluring cloudscape that Freddy had hoped to find was absent. Even the smallest peak and valley had been compressed into the lid, above which everything was the clear, unambiguous blue of morning, a blue without mystery or variety. A boring blue, Freddy realized in hostile disappointment, a blue that contained nothing that could help her to clear her mind and diminish her anger, the kind of blue a pilot could only drone through impatiently on the way to someplace else.

She headed north, hoping for a wisp of cloud that might have detached itself from the mass below, even a very small cloud, just big enough to tangle with, to tango with. If only she could catch up with a thunderstorm, the sort of storm every sensible pilot flew around, a vulgar, obvious storm, gaudy with menace, a vow of danger lurking in its turbulence, risk the unspoken covenant in its lightning, a storm that would throw her around in the cockpit and demand every ounce of her ability and experience. There probably wasn't even a rain shower from here to Chicago, she thought in disgust. The day was all zero visibility and no action.

Freddy looked around the spacious, comfortable cockpit with sudden loathing. What a characterless plane! Its leather was immaculate, its instrument panel shining with newness, the metal of its brake pedal, which didn't bear the traces of a single foot, so new and unmarked that she scuffed at it in anger. She'd flown thousands of new planes before, right from the factory to the airdrome, that was what the ATA job was all about, but she'd never resented one for being new as she resented this Bonanza.

This plane was not only too new, it was exceedingly uninteresting, Freddy decided grimly, wondering why she had been so eager to buy it. The model had been introduced to the market only a few years ago, the first single-motor plane ever designed to carry four people at a cruising speed of one hundred and seventy-five miles an hour, a highly crash-worthy plane built with great attention to quality in each of its details, a plane that everyone called incomparable. She called it a fucking bloody fat cow, Freddy thought furiously, a flying cow that could carry Ma, Pa, two kids, a picnic basket, overnight bags, a couple of slobbery dogs—why not a potty seat too, while they were about it?

She flipped the Bonanza around the empty sky, ripping through some aerobatics and noting, with a bleakly unimpressed eye, that the cow could stand up to pressure. And why not? She'd certainly paid enough for this airborne limousine, Freddy thought in contempt, filled with an acrid longing to be flying some beat-up, honorable old crate, some ancient kite with history stored in each of its fabric-covered wings, a plane with individuality and valor invisibly engraved on each of its instruments. She'd fallen in love with a lot of planes in her day, and not one of them had ever betrayed her, not one had turned on her and made her into the worst kind of laughingstock, a plane didn't spy out the fact that you were a woman, with a woman's weaknesses, and use them to sucker you, to treat you as a victim, easy to mock, easy to gull —easy, easy pickings.

There was a small break in the cloud cover to her right, and she flew over and dove through it to see where she had wandered to. She realized that she didn't really know where she was, and her watch told her that almost two hours had passed since she'd left Burbank. She was out over the ocean, a gray ocean with a horizon that was only one shade less gray. A dense fog was rolling in toward Santa Monica. Every airport for many miles around would be closed to all but instrument traffic, or maybe just plain closed.

This might as well be Lapland, Freddy decided, shaking her head in bitterness, remembering the day she had first flown over the Pacific, so sky-loony that she would have chased the sailboats over the edge of the horizon if Mac hadn't stopped her. So young, so wild . . . *so happy*. It had been that day that she'd soloed. January ninth, 1936—in a few days it would be sixteen years in the past. Half of her lifetime.

Don't look back, Freddy told herself, don't *ever* look back. She must be hungry, she decided. She hadn't had breakfast, she'd thrown up dinner, so even if she didn't feel hungry she probably needed food. The quickest place to find something to eat was at the airport on top of Catalina Island. She'd been there many times, an unkempt little strip without a tower but the only place to land in the neighborhood with the distinction of being fifteen hundred feet high, on top of a rocky desert island with a romantic name and a harbor that had been a gambling haven in the thirties. There was a coffee shop in permanent operation at the airstrip, for day trippers made Catalina a popular and simple excursion in good weather. She'd have it all to herself today, which fit in with her mood, Freddy thought, as she headed toward the familiar, flat-topped lump far out in the ocean.

On a clear day, as real-estate salespeople always point out, you can see Catalina. But not today, she realized, as it began to disappear. She looked at her compass, adjusted her heading, and pointed the Bonanza directly toward the island.

As she came near Catalina, a pouncing sponge of fog, dense and disorienting, moving much faster than she had estimated, unexpectedly slopped over her windshield. Her nose and wings disappeared. She was, it seemed, flying a magic cockpit. So what, thought Freddy angrily, so what. A California fog was nothing. She could always head upstairs and punch through to sunlight but, damn it, she wanted her coffee, she *owned* this territory, it was her personal sky, claimed when she was a kid, won and rewon time after time, and she was damned if she'd let a little shitty fog snatch it away from her. She was the only person in her sky, and she knew the approach to Catalina so well that she could fly it blindfolded. She checked her altimeter. She had plenty of altitude, which was the only thing to worry about as she started to plan her landing.

Moving dexterously, handling her plane with supreme confidence, her coordination unaffected by either her emotions or the fog, Freddy flew the perfect invisible rectangle that would bring her, in a minute, smoothly settled onto the landing strip on top of the boulder-strewn, treeless bluff. The Bonanza was slowed down to its precise landing speed, the landing gear extended, the flaps down.

Too low, were the only words Freddy had time to think as Catalina, like soundless thunder, came at her out of the fog, a wall of rock, inescapable. There was a second left, only time enough to pull the nose up sharply, so that when she crashed she was at an angle to the side of the mountain. The shattered Bonanza still climbed the mountainside for yards and yards until it skipped and slid and fell into a ravine where it split apart and the noise stopped.

23

MARIE de La Rochefoucauld could be a young czarina, she could be an Infanta of Spain, Bruno thought. And yet she was so miraculously French. He had never imagined that anyone in this barbaric circus of Manhattan could possibly be so flawlessly, consummately French, so imprinted in every detail of her carriage and appearance and speech with the essence of a high-born Frenchwoman, that it was like a fragrance in the air around her, that moved when she moved. She carried France—old France—with her as she entered a room, so unassumingly that she barely displaced the atmosphere, yet with such quiet presence, with such mild and absolute dignity that heads turned toward her, glances flickered from eye to eye, and people signaled questions at each other, already envious, already acquisitive. They had to know who she was, these hard citizens of this tough stone city, because she was everything they could never hope to be. Even to be able to identify her would lend them some distinction.

Bruno had been one of the first people in New York to meet Marie de La Rochefoucauld, one of the many daughters of the most prolific noble family in all of French history, a family whose members, under the notation "House of La Rochefoucauld," occupied more than a full page in that bible of aristocracy, the *Bottin Mondain*; a family of inter-related branches adorned by three dukes; a family so large that many a La Rochefoucauld heir had married a La Rochefoucauld heiress throughout the parade of centuries; a family allied to all of the great names of France; a family whose origins, as *Debrett's Peerage*, with an editorial bow, would occasionally note about an English duke, were "lost in time."

Bruno had known one of her brothers at school, and it was through him that Bruno had met Marie soon after she arrived to earn her master's degree in Oriental art at Columbia University. Why she would want to do that was only one of the marvelous mysteries of her supremely self-contained personality.

How could he have not expected that he would fall in love someday? Why had he been so sure that he was so different from other men, Bruno asked himself, yet, had he known, had he even suspected what love was like, how would he have been able to endure the years of waiting until he met Marie? In this spring of 1951, he was filled by an astonishing emotion that spread its branches through every one of his limbs, until he imagined himself looking like a chart of the circulatory system, each artery and vein and blood vessel a rushing thoroughfare of first love, all the more painful because he was thirty-six years old and Marie was only twenty-two.

Yet Marie didn't treat him as if she thought he was too old for her, Bruno mused as he sat, immobilized by love, in his office at the bank. Of course, she did not know yet how he felt about her. She behaved toward him with beautifully simple but faintly reserved friendliness, the same friendliness, he had to admit, with which she acted toward everyone else she knew.

Marie was living in the John Allens' vast stone town house. For many years the Allens had been friendly with Marie's parents, the two couples linked by a common passion for the Chinese ceramics that they collected to the benign lack of interest of their acquaintances. The Allens had invited Marie to stay with them during the two years of her studies, and had put several rooms at her disposal. She had a sitting room where, from time to time, she received her new American friends for tea or sherry, although her days were rarely long enough to permit her to spend time on such matters, for up at Columbia she plunged deeply into her studies.

As brilliantly made as a crown jewel, Marie was tiny and slim. She had long, straight, shining black hair that she wore hanging down almost to her waist, pulled back from her untroubled white forehead and tied behind her nape with a silk ribbon. Her eyes were gray, under thin black brows, so lovely in shape that they might have been designed by Leonardo, and her fine nose had a delicate arch. Her mouth was gentle, excellently formed, and untouched by lipstick. She had little color in her exquisite face; the fascination was in the contrast of the blackness of her hair, the whiteness of her delicate skin and the clear, exceptionally light gray of her eyes.

Marie dressed innocently, almost childishly, in simple sweaters, blouses and skirts, artlessly thrown together with a lace scarf or a velvet vest or an embroidered jacket, in which she looked enchantingly old-fashioned in a city where tailored suits were the rule. She might have found her clothes in the attic of one of her family's châteaux, Bruno thought, as he longed helplessly to buy her sumptuous clothes and great jewels. On her birthday he had gone to the best dealer in Oriental antiques in the city and bought her a bowl of Ching-te-chen whiteware of the Sung Dynasty, unequaled in its simple shape and its unadorned glaze, and she had taken one enraptured look at it and refused to accept it, because she knew the value of the seven-hundred-year-old work of art. If she had taken the bowl it would have been as if she had allowed him to give her a sable coat. Now the rejected ceramic was placed on his bedroom mantelpiece to remind him not to behave like a besotted nouveau riche with Marie de La Rochefoucauld.

She had such purity that it drove him mad. Marie never mentioned it, but Bruno, who had become the sleuth that every man in love discovers within himself, found out that she went to early mass every morning. One day when he had arrived a few minutes too early for tea and found himself the only guest, alone in her sitting room, he looked through a partly opened door and glimpsed a corner of her bedroom where a worn prie-dieu was placed before a crucifix. He had not dared to open the door any farther, and the image of her unseen bed had become a holy mystery to him, a mystery about which he knew he was unworthy to speculate.

When he woke up in the middle of the night, as he did now with increasing frequency, Bruno found himself wondering how it could have happened that he had fallen so completely and unexpectedly in love with an inexperienced, religious, intellectual, virtuous girl, whose young life had passed tranquilly in convents and classrooms and museums; who cared nothing for society or intrigue or position or possessions; whose desire, if what he deduced was true, was to spend most of her life in pursuit of scholarship, for the pure joy of learning; a girl who was, from the sensual point of view, a blank page, waiting without impatience for the destiny that would or would not bring her a husband and children.

Was it merely a turn toward an idealized virgin that had overtaken him, after so many years spent living out the most hidden, shame-laden fantasies of mature women of the world? Was this an aberration, born of sexual satiety? Could it be explained as an infatuation with her quality of being entirely French that made him, the homesick exile, believe that Marie, and Marie alone, would rescue him from the wasteland of his life?

None of these rational explanations ever lasted more than the time it took Bruno to form them. They vanished as soon as he thought of Marie, turning her little imperial head toward him, and laughing at one of his jokes, or letting him take her out to dinner and to a movie, for she adored American movies, the sillier the better, and she thoroughly enjoyed New York, making him ride on the subway and take the Fifth Avenue bus all the way down to Washington Square Park. They would watch the chess players in the park and then walk to Bleecker Street and find a cheap student coffee house where she liked to sit and watch the bohemian life swirl around her. He had this happiness only occasionally during a weekend, for on weekday nights Marie ate dinner with the Allens and studied until she went to bed.

There were other men around Marie. The Allens had presented her to some of the most eligible young bachelors in New York, but to Bruno's watchful and jealous eye, she had not shown a preference for any of them. Above all, not one of the other men who claimed her time was French, not one could even speak decent French, and he was certain, as certain as he could be of anything, that Marie had no intention of spending the rest of her life in the United States. Much as she was amused by New York, much as she felt rewarded by her studies, she had confided in him that she deeply missed her big family. Bruno had known Marie de La Rochefoucauld since Christmas of 1950 and now, in the late spring of 1951, she was eagerly anticipating the summer in France.

"I'm sailing on the *Ile de France* the day classes are over, and I won't come back until just before the beginning of the fall semester—three whole months," she'd said happily. "You'll be in France for your summer vacation, won't you, Bruno? Even New York bankers must get a few weeks off."

"Of course," he'd answered because he couldn't think of an explanation for any Frenchman not going home on his vacation. It was so traditional, such a basic thing to do, that to say he had made other plans would sound strange. Frenchmen didn't travel outside of their own country if they could avoid it.

Marie had invited him to come and visit at the château near Tours where her family spent each summer. He'd told her that he'd try to come, even as he had known that he would be separated from her all summer long, and that every day of that summer would bring the possibility that Marie might fall in love. His worst fear was that Marie might not even come back to New York to finish her work at Columbia, for it seemed impossible to him that she should remain heart-free during the gay, pleasure-filled, hospitable days and nights of an entire summer.

Yet Bruno dared not return to France, not even to visit Marie for a few weeks. The La Rochefoucauld château was not in the neighborhood of Valmont, but the jungle drums of the French aristocracy would immediately sound with the news that Bruno de Lancel was back in his native land, after his long and remarkable absence. His father would inevitably learn that he had returned, and Bruno knew that Paul's interdiction and Paul's threats could not have changed in six years. He would do what he had said he would do. Bruno fingered the scar that still remained over his upper lip.

Why couldn't he ask her to marry him now, before she left, Bruno asked himself for the thousandth time, and as usual the answer was the same. Marie was not in love with him, and so she would refuse him, as charmingly and certainly as she had refused the Ching-te-chen white-ware bowl. Then he would be unable to see her frequently, unable to claim her free evenings, unable to win her love. The rules Marie lived by, rules he respected, for they were part of the world they shared, would prevent her from encouraging false hopes. She would be scrupulously careful not to spend time alone with him once she knew how he felt. She would most gently and firmly ease him out of her life, for Bruno de Lancel was not a man she could relegate to the position of a mere friend.

He had to run the risk of losing her over the summer, since the only alternative was to lose her now, once and for all.

Jeanne's letters still came. All was well with his family, she was happy to assure him. "Yes, Monsieur Bruno, you will be glad to know, all is as it should be at Valmont."

"Mr. Hampton, it doesn't make sense for you to stay here any longer," Doctor David Weitz said to Jock, who hadn't left the corridor outside of Freddy's room at the Cedars of Lebanon Hospital, since she had been wheeled into it on a gurney eighteen hours earlier, a grotesque mummy encased in a sarcophagus of white, with only the valiant strands of her hair to identify her. "I promise to phone you the minute there's the slightest change in Mrs. Longbridge's condition."

"I'll just hang around," Jock said stubbornly, for the tenth time.

"There's no way to tell when she'll come out of the coma. It may be days. It may be weeks. It could be months, Mr. Hampton. You're not being reasonable."

"I know." Jock turned away, feeling another wave of intense, illogical hostility toward David Weitz. The man was too young, Jock insisted to himself, to be in charge of anything. He'd telephoned Swede and had him run a check on the guy.

Weitz was forty-two, enormously respected, and the youngest Chief of Neurology the great hospital had ever appointed. There was no higher authority at Cedars to whom he could appeal for an older, wiser, more experienced doctor. Every doctor Swede talked to said they were fortunate to have Weitz supervising Freddy's case.

The information reassured Jock for only a minute. Here was this fellow, only forty-two years old, ordering around a flock of residents, calling in the specialists he needed, making dozens of decisions that he relayed to Freddy's round-the-clock nurses, none of which he had time to explain to Jock except in a doctor's typical shorthand-for-civilians.

Meanwhile, Freddy lay where Jock couldn't see her or help her, smashed up, injured in ways he didn't understand, in ways even *they* didn't seem to understand, or surely they could be more accurate about her condition. Here was this stranger who had suddenly become the most important person in the world, because it was up to him to pull Freddy through, make her all right, and he didn't even know her, had never met her or heard her talk or laugh or watched her walk, he couldn't have any idea of how . . . how essential . . . how *necessary* Freddy was.

Freddy's life lay in the hands of this man, which meant Jock was totally dependent on Weitz, and hated him for it. He wanted to take the tall young doctor by the shoulders and shake him, until that confident, controlled, intense expression left his face, until his glasses fell off and broke, he wanted to scream at him that he had to make Freddy well, perfectly well . . . he wanted to put the fear of God into the bastard, let him know how much was at stake, that if Weitz didn't do his job he'd kill him with his bare hands . . . and at the same time he didn't dare to offend him.

Jock walked up and down the corridor, thinking in a rage of the nurse who'd tried to tell him that it was a miracle that Freddy'd lived through the crash. What did that woman know about it? Naturally she'd lived. She hadn't crashed, for Christ's sake, didn't they know better than to use that word? She'd had a bad landing, a rough landing, she'd come in with too much speed. People don't die from bad landings, they get shook up, they break a leg or a collarbone, or even a bunch of bones, but bones mend eventually, nobody dies from broken bones. What had Weitz meant by a "closed head injury"? If her skull wasn't broken, what was the problem?

There were chairs in the corridor, and Jock tried to make himself sit down for a minute. He'd walked so many miles that his legs were almost too heavy to lift, but sitting down was worse, because as long as he kept moving, he felt as if he were accomplishing something, not just waiting helplessly. He perched on the couch, in the same falsely relaxed position he used to settle into, near his plane, when his squadron was on two-minute standby, waiting to be ordered to scramble for a combat sortie.

Damn the incompetent, criminal idiots at the Burbank Tower, he thought, for not having closed the airport yesterday. Nobody should have been permitted to take off in that weather. Damn even the well-meaning, clumsy idiots at the Catalina airport coffee shop who'd climbed down to rescue her. God knows how much more damage they'd caused, carrying her back up to the top of the mountain like a sack of potatoes, or bumping her around in the winding drive down to the harbor or on the boat trip across to the mainland. Christ, what a place for a bad landing in a fog! Damn to eternal hell the Catalina airport for existing at all. Fifteen hundred feet high, without a tower, without radio communication—it should be bombed into rubble, so no one would ever be tempted to land there again, not that he thought for a minute that Freddy was trying to land there in zero visibility. Obviously she'd been off course, lost in the sudden fog, that was the only possible explanation for her being near that treacherous, murderous rock. Freddy was a careful pilot. She'd never bent a blade of grass in six years in the ATA, much less a kite.

But what had possessed her to go out flying at dawn yesterday? What kind of crazy idea had that been, Jock asked himself in desperation, thinking of all the things he had promised himself he was going to explain to Freddy, all the words he had rehearsed during the long, sleepless night after the Eagle Squadron reunion. He had been planning to go over to her house at breakfast time and force her to listen to him, force her to understand, to forgive him. And she would have, he was certain of it, because you couldn't tell him that Freddy wasn't ready to love him, at last, as he had always loved her. You couldn't . . . lose . . . true love, just when you'd almost found it. Could you?

The ceiling light fixture had a dead fly caught inside it, Freddy thought, dimly aware that she had had the same thought before, recurring over whirling cycles of time, pounding by, age after age, lifetimes that had no beginning and no end. Perhaps this was hell; to lie forever, immobilized, utterly alone, unable to call out, in the bottom of a white bowl filled to the brim with dark, dangerous waters, watching a dark spot of a dead fly inside a glass fixture that seemed always to be lit. Was she looking into a mirror? Was she the black, dead spot trapped inside the fixture? Panic such as she had never known began to beat in her temples and she knew she would never be able to call for help. Her

478

eyes opened, but her mouth was covered over, her hands unable to move. She had been buried alive.

"You're awake," said a man's voice, "good girl." A hand took her wrist, a thumb settled firmly on her pulse. It was salvation. She was not in hell. She was not doomed.

"Don't try to ask questions," the man's voice said the next time she woke up. "Your jaw is broken and wired together so it can heal. That's why you can't talk. I'll tell you everything you want to know. Don't waste your strength, you need it all. You're going to be as good as new, I promise you, but now you're very weak and I know that you're in pain. We're giving you as much medication for the pain as we can, but we can't stop all of it. I'm Doctor David Weitz. You're Freddy Long-bridge. You're at the Cedars of Lebanon Hospital. Your mother is here from France and she's taking care of your little girl. They're both fine. All you have to do is get better. You can't have any visitors for a while. You must try not to worry about anything. The world will take care of itself, I guarantee it. Just let yourself go and sleep. While you sleep, you'll be getting better. When you wake up, the nurse will call me wherever I am, and I'll come as soon as I can. You have private nurses and you'll never, ever be left alone, not for a minute. Don't worry, you're going to be fine. Sleep now, Mrs. Longbridge, just close your eyes and drift away. There's nothing to worry about. I'm here for you."

Freddy tried to thank him with her eyes. He looked down at her and smiled and she saw that he understood. She closed her eyes and slept.

"Maybe you can try to speak today," David Weitz suggested to Freddy. She had been fed intravenously for the three weeks in which she had been in a coma, and then fed through a straw until her jaw healed. Yesterday the wires had been removed, but she had been too afraid to try to talk.

"Annie?" she asked, without moving her lips, in a tiny voice that came from the back of her throat.

"She's terrific. She's at school right now. Your mother will be here later. How do you feel?"

"Better."

"You are. Much, much better."

"How . . . long?"

"How long have you been here? Over a month, but that's not the important thing. It won't seem as long now that you can talk."

"How much . . . more?"

"I just can't tell you for sure. You hit your head when you were thrown out of the plane. That caused what we call a closed head injury —an injury where there was no fracture of your skull but there was a sudden injury to your brain—like a severe bruise—which caused fluid to accumulate. That's why you were in a coma from the time you hit the ground. However, the coma lasted a relatively short time. When the fluid finally disappears, you can expect complete recovery, with, perhaps, some mild memory loss. However, we just don't know how long that will take. It's a slow business, and there's nothing we can do to rush it along. Meanwhile, you have a lot of other healing to finish. Two broken legs, one arm, one wrist, a broken nose, a broken cheekbone—fortunately there was no injury to your spine, and no pelvic fractures. You're doing very well."

David Weitz bent over her, peering intently through his glasses, his dark eyes magnified as she blinked at him, trying to understand all that he had just told her. "Don't think about the injuries," he said, reading her thoughts. "I'm proud of you—you're going to be truly fine. I want you to know that there are a lot of things we have to take care of, but nothing that's out of our control. Are you up to seeing your mother? Yes? All right, but I'll tell her not to stay for more than a few minutes. I'll be back later."

She had been glad to see her mother, Freddy thought, her eyelids closing again, but she felt exhausted after the short visit. She hadn't the strength to talk, except to the doctor. Until today, living through each minute had been the boundary of her life, both question and answer. "The world will take care of itself," David Weitz had said, and through pain, through the confusion in her head, through the terrible nights and fearful days, bandaged, her jaw wired shut, her limbs in casts, only one arm unbroken, she clung to the lifeline of his words. She repeated them to herself over and over; there was magic in them, some of his strength had been transferred to her. She abdicated her will, cast it aside, did as he bid her, because she trusted David Weitz absolutely. His devotion was abstract, to the cause of healing, and yet it was personal, because she was his patient.

Now, with Eve's coming, the real world had reentered her hospital room, a world she did not welcome. She was too frail, too broken, too sick to deal with it. She didn't want to think, to talk to people. Even to have to try to turn up the corners of her mouth in a smile was too much to be asked of her. She would tell her nurses that it was too soon for her to have visitors, Freddy decided. When, she wondered, would David Weitz be back, to check on her again?

"Your nurses tell me that you haven't asked for a mirror," David Weitz said to Freddy.

"No."

"It's not as bad as you think. With the help of reconstructive surgery you can expect to look the way you did before. Luckily, California is the world's capital of plastic surgeons. A few scars may remain, after the surgery, from the lacerations you sustained—it depends on how your skin heals—but you can cover most of them with your hair. However, about playing the cello—"

"Who said I played the cello? I've never touched one."

"That's a relief. It's the one function we can't promise to restore."

Freddy laughed for the first time since the crash. "Is that a doctor joke?"

"A classic."

"What if you told it to a cellist?"

"I wouldn't. I checked with Annie to be sure."

"Thank you for telling her how I was going to look. I was afraid that she'd be terrified when she saw me. She said you drew her sketches to show her what all the bandages and casts were about."

"She's a great kid."

"Do you have children?"

"No, I don't. I got divorced a long time ago, before I could afford them."

"I'm divorced too."

"So Annie told me."

"That must have been quite a conversation. What else did you talk about?"

"Her father, her schoolwork, her plans to learn to fly."

"Will I be out of here by the time Annie's summer vacation starts?"

"I don't think so. You're still not ready to get out of bed. When you are, your muscles will be very weak from lying here so long. You'll need a great deal of physical therapy."

"I'll send her to England, then. She can spend the summer at Longbridge Grange with her grandparents. Her father is probably there too."

"He is. I've talked to him a number of times on the phone. But not as often as I've talked to Mr. Hampton."

"Is he bothering you?"

481

"Not more than twice a day. Sometimes three times. He refuses to believe that you don't want any visitors. Are you sure you don't want to see him?"

"Absolutely. But I'll see Swede Castelli and make sure that Jock stops calling you," Freddy said with determination.

"Do you have any idea how much better you are, Mrs. Longbridge?"

"Thanks to you, Doctor Weitz."

"Nonsense. You're a fighter. Those first weeks . . . I was worried."

"I didn't worry. You said not to, so I didn't. You said you were here for me."

"So you remember that, Mrs. Longbridge?"

"Freddy. Won't you call me Freddy?"

"Of course. I'm David."

"I know."

"I have to go. I'll be back to see you later, before I leave for my office."

"Thank you, David."

"Jesus, Freddy, did you think you were still a stunt-double? What the hell is this?"

"I know, Swede. I'm told it looks worse than it is. I haven't bothered to inspect the damage. But I'm going to be fine . . . just a matter of time and patience. Don't worry. How's everything at Eagles?"

"Business is great. All the planes are flying, full loads in both directions, and we're making our stockholders very happy. However, morale is low at the head office."

"Meaning?"

"We miss you, the sight of your funny little face and the sound of your little footsteps and your snappy little ways of keeping us on our toes."

"Better get used to it, Swede. I'm not coming back."

"You're in no condition to make decisions. I don't believe you."

"Have it your own way. I don't care. Look, Swede, you've got to stop Jock from calling Doctor Weitz. He's a very busy man and he doesn't have time to take nuisance calls."

"That's a hell of a thing to say. Jock's in bad shape. Worse than you are, except for those plaster casts and bandages."

"I don't give a damn what kind of shape he's in. I simply don't want to see him. But he is not to bother Doctor Weitz. Will you get that through his skull?"

"I can try. But you know Jock."

"Unfortunately, yes. Much too well."

"Hell, Freddy, I didn't know you could sound so bitter."

"It's about time I learned to take care of myself, Swede."

"What's that supposed to mean?"

"Swede, old friend, I don't have much strength yet. Thanks for coming. I'm counting on you about Jock."

"Sure, Freddy. Take care of yourself. Jock's not the only one whose morale is low."

"Give me a kiss, Swede."

"Your big toes look pretty good to me."

"I knew you'd find a place."

Eve persuaded Freddy to take Annie out of school early, so that she could fly back to Europe with her granddaughter, and leave her with Tony in London, before she continued to Paris. Eve was badly needed back in Champagne, where the full cycle of hospitality couldn't properly begin without her. She had already spent far too much time away from Valmont.

Jock drove them to the airport to catch the plane for New York. While Annie explored the airport as they waited for their plane to board, Jock sat morosely with Eve, reluctant to see her go.

"Damn it, Eve, I'm going to really miss the hell out of you," he said, grabbing her hand and squeezing it.

"Darling Jock. All those dinners, all those movies, those weekend drives—what would Annie and I have done without you? You never let us feel alone for a minute. You're the most wonderful friend. You have a permanent invitation to come and stay with us in Champagne for as long as you like, whenever you like."

"Maybe someday. Eve, listen, about Freddy—"

"I tried, Jock, you know I did, several times, but she just doesn't want to see you. I thought . . . possibly she's waiting until she looks better. Maybe it's just vanity."

"How vain is Freddy? Come on, Eve, you know that couldn't have anything to do with it." Jock's insubordinate features were set in a mask of hopeless misery.

"You're probably right," Eve sighed. "But she wouldn't talk about it. I couldn't pry a single reason from her. Freddy doesn't tell me about a lot of things, we never had that sort of relationship . . . both of my daughters always kept a lot of secrets. And I . . . well, I had my secrets too. We're that kind of family. Now, with Delphine, it's different—we talk to each other a lot—but Freddy—" Eve shrugged her shoulders.

Freddy, even in her wounded, weakened state, wasn't one to confide in her mother.

"That bastard Weitz, I know he's going to try and make time with her," Jock said in gloomy suspicion. Even the golden hair that fell over his forehead seemed to have darkened with his mood of despair.

"Jock, really! Aren't you letting your imagination run away with you? Poor Freddy's hardly an object of desire at the moment."

"You're her mother, you can't understand about Freddy. It's her . . . her *spirit* . . . that's what he'll go for."

"Freddy is Doctor Weitz's patient. His interest is in making her well. Doctors don't 'make time' with every female patient in their care."

"She's different from every female. She always was. No other girl ever came close."

"I won't argue that with you, Jock. Look, once she's out of the hospital, once you can talk to her, things between the two of you can change. But whatever the problem is, you can't do anything about it now. Give it time."

"Do I have a choice?" he asked, resting his forehead on his hands and shaking his head.

No, thought Eve, no choice at all. Somehow you must have hurt her terribly, Jock, loving, generous, inarticulate, bumbling male creature that you are, without knowing what you were doing. Freddy gives her love so completely, so blindly, so unyieldingly and so *rarely*—but once she's cast you out of her life, there isn't much hope. Look at what happened to Tony. She'd never said a word about him. Just like that man McGuire—it's as if they'd both ceased to exist . . . had never existed. Eve looked at Jock sitting in a puddle of misery beside her and decided that her beloved, intractable, pigheaded daughter Marie-Frédérique must be certifiable as legally insane. If any man as thoroughly kind and decent as Jock, any man so disruptively—so almost ridiculously—good to look at had been in love with her for as long as she suspected that Jock had been in love with Freddy, she'd certainly give him a chance, no matter what he'd done. At the very least, *one* stingy, penurious chance. Why not make it a dozen? What was there to lose?

There could be no question that she looked all right now, Freddy admitted, looking in her hand mirror on an afternoon at the end of August. Except for one long, thin white scar that reached from her ear almost to the point of her chin, a scar that would never be hidden by makeup or suntan or an artful arrangement of her hair—she recognized herself. Her physical therapy at the hospital consumed most of her days. She could walk without a trace of a limp; her muscles had regained their former strength.

Why was she still in the hospital? She had no right to be taking up a bed in a private room, when there must be really sick people who needed it. Yet the thought of going home, to a big, lonely house, empty except for Helga and the maid, was chilling, frightening. Her parents had asked her to come to Valmont for the grape harvest. Delphine had invited her to come to St. Tropez, where she and Armand had bought a villa in which they would remain until October.

Even as she thought of these possibilities, Freddy shrank inside herself. She couldn't possibly venture as far as from her room to the lobby of the hospital, much less travel to Europe. Perhaps Annie could stay in England for the rest of the year. Yes, a year of school in England would be good for her, and she was perfectly happy with Penelope and Gerald and Tony. That way, Freddy thought, she wouldn't have to leave the hospital; she wouldn't have to leave her room.

She was safe here at Cedars. There was so hideously little safety in the world. Didn't Delphine and her mother realize that? Weren't they aware enough to understand danger? How could they expect her to visit them as if they lived around the corner? Didn't they know, as she did, that a person *had* to stay in a small, familiar space, a safe space where there were no responsibilities, no decisions, no worries, no terrors, no risks, no surprises? From her room to the physical therapy center of the hospital was as long a journey as she could force herself to take, and it was only the certainty that she could return to her safe room, to the safe hospital bed, that enabled her to make the trip down the long, busy hall and up and down the stairs. She hadn't used the elevator . . . she didn't want to take it . . . she would never take it, no matter how the stairs tired her . . . it was a bad place to be . . . a bad and evil place.

"How are you feeling today, Mrs. Longbridge?" the head floor nurse asked as she came into the room. "My, don't you look lovely!"

"I feel terrible," Freddy said. "I hurt all over. I don't know why I feel so bad. I won't have any dinner tonight, Mrs. Hill, I don't have the strength to eat it."

"I hear you've had a bad day," David Weitz said quietly. "No dinner?"

"Everything hurts," Freddy mumbled, curled up in her bed with the sheet drawn up to her chin.

"Absolutely everything? From head to toe?"

"Yes."

"I'm going to give you two aspirin and take you out for a drive. It's the only known specific when everything hurts."

"No!"

"You don't want to leave the hospital, do you, Freddy?"

"Don't be ridiculous!"

"Aha! The sure sign of a well patient. The minute you tell your doctor he's ridiculous, you're ready to leave this place. No doctor has ever been ridiculous in a hospital. It's against all rules. I'll give you five minutes to get dressed. We're going to the beach to see the sunset."

"I can't. I won't. I couldn't possibly put on my clothes. I feel too bad."

"Five minutes. Or you'll go in your nightgown and bathrobe."

"Don't you have anything better to do than to torment me?"

"Not right now."

"Shit!"

"You don't even need aspirin. Five minutes and counting."

"The lady will have chicken soup on the rocks and I'll have a vodka martini straight up," David told the barman at Jack's at the Beach, as they settled on the barstools facing the sunset.

"Make that two martinis," Freddy countered. "And make mine a double."

"My mother says chicken soup," David protested.

"Her son says I'm well enough to leave the hospital. Did your mother go to medical school?"

"All Jewish mothers are automatically qualified to practice medicine, even if their sons aren't doctors. Even if they only have daughters."

"I can drink liquor, can't I? It's not bad for me, is it? Your opinion, not your mother's."

"Of course. You can do everything you did before the accident."

"I was lucky, wasn't I?" she said soberly.

"Damn lucky."

"I still don't remember what happened."

"That's typical. A memory loss of the actual event often goes with a closed head injury. It may come back, or it may not. You can't control it."

Freddy was silent, looking straight through the enormous plate-glass window, where two men were busy lowering a sheet of thin gray plastic to dim the too-bright rays of the setting sun, as they did every night in

486

this famous seafood restaurant on the pier. At the left of the restaurant, in the distance, was an amusement park with an old roller coaster. She realized that she could clearly pick out the people holding on to the bars in front of their seats. There had been no diminution of her vision. She lowered her eyes quickly. Seeing that far and that distinctly had made her violently nervous. Freddy turned to David Weitz and started to look at him as intensely as he had been looking at her for all these months. Turn about was fair play. Dark hair, well cut, with one or two strands of gray; deep lines on either side of his mouth; a long distinguished face with something in it of a sad clown that disappeared entirely when he smiled, a wide, full mouth, professorial horn-rimmed glasses. She had never seen him without them.

"Do you wear those glasses all the time?" she asked.

"Only when I want to see. If I remember, I usually take them off in the shower, once I've located the soap."

"I don't know anything about you, except that the nurses think you're God, which is par for the course, I guess."

"They tend to exaggerate. Well . . . only a little."

"And what does God do when he's not working?"

"I'm unpredictable, complex, tightly wound, and mysteriously contradictory. Quite fascinating actually. I'm an ex-football player—voted most valuable quarterback in the Ivy League. I'm also a chess master. My hobby is polo and my string of ponies are summering in Argentina. I get my suits made to order on Savile Row and I have a serious collection of first-growth Burgundies in my air-conditioned wine cellar. I visit them from time to time so they won't feel neglected. I always read three pages of Sartre in French before I go to sleep, and I can recite from memory the complete works of Tolstoy, the *Kama Sutra*, Jane Austen and Henry Miller."

"Hmm."

"Actually I *was* a chess player . . . in high school. However, I've been known to play a fair game of Ping-Pong."

"What did you do during the war?"

"Medical Corps. Never got overseas."

"What do you do in your free time?"

"I have a house in Brentwood and I usually stay home when I get a chance. I read a little, listen to music a little, sometimes, on the weekend I might drive out here and walk on the beach, I see a few old friends, I have a few dates—restaurants, movies—mostly I work."

"If you're trying to make it sound dull, you haven't."

"Compared to what I've heard of your life, it sounds about as unadventurous and stodgy as a life can be—however, medicine is never dull, and that's what I do."

"Saving a patient every day?"

"Not quite, but it has its moments. What can I tell you?"

"You have. I'm starving." Freddy preened slightly, knowing that in her high-waisted, full lavender skirt and low-cut, white linen peasant blouse that Eve had hung in her closet before she left, she looked better than she had in many months.

"The specialty here is pompano baked in oiled paper, but I'm in the mood for a steamed lobster. Shall I ask the barman for a menu for you?"

"Lobster too, please," Freddy said, feeling pleased with herself. Doctors always knew everything about you, and you never knew anything about them, so you were always at a disadvantage. Finally, she thought, she had a few more details about David Weitz. She already knew so many of the important things: his kindness, his patience, his sensitivity to his patients which amounted to a degree of extrasensory perception, and his passion for his work. Now she could imagine him in a tree-shaded, cozy Brentwood house reading a book or walking in the sand at the edge of the waves, barefoot, with his pants legs rolled up. With his glasses on, of course, so he wouldn't get lost or fall over a starfish.

When their lobsters were ready they moved to a table and submitted to being enveloped in the large bib that every lobster customer was given whether he asked for it or not. The enormous, two-clawed Maine lobsters—lobsters, Freddy noted to herself, with no interest whatever, that had probably made their cross-country trip courtesy of Eagles—occupied their attention.

It is not possible to eat a lobster with another person with whom you do not feel comfortable, unless you're willing to settle fastidiously and wastefully for the mere center strips of easily extracted meat, and have no interest in the claws and the legs and all the little nooks and crannies that contain the most delicious morsels. This was Freddy's first lobster in almost a year, and she set about it with total concentration, using the shell crackers, the long, skinny, pointed fork, and, when all else failed, her fingers and her teeth. Twice she asked for more melted butter, but otherwise she had little to say except "Please pass the lemon."

When the lobsters were finished, Freddy heaved a great sigh of pleasure, and began to clean herself up with the help of fresh napkins and the large bowl of warm water with slices of lemon floating in it that had been set before each of them. When she was satisfied that she had scrubbed her face and her hands as well as possible, she untied her bib and emerged, her cheeks shining like those of a baby who had just had a bath. "Cheesecake?" she wondered aloud. "Or ice cream?"

"Both," David said, and leaned over and kissed her lips. Freddy gasped in surprise. "I like a girl who knows how to get the best from a lobster," he explained.

"So much that you kiss her?"

"Easily." He kissed her again, his glasses bumping into her nose. "Sorry about that," he said.

"Take off your glasses," she suggested.

"Then I couldn't see you."

"You know perfectly well what I look like."

"Not like this, not when you're happy. You are happy, aren't you, Freddy?"

"Yes," she said slowly, "yes, I am."

"But not entirely?"

"No . . . not entirely . . ." Freddy said, as she struggled to be completely honest about emotions she didn't understand, and could not, *would not*, force herself to think about. "There's nothing anyone can do about it—I guess I'm . . . a little depressed somewhere underneath . . . lots of reasons . . . it's complicated . . . I hope it will just go away by itself. It's probably a question of time. David, the thing is, I am happy for this particular moment, in fact I've been happy ever since we got here, and that's more happiness than I can remember feeling for a long, long time. The other . . . that unhappiness isn't your problem."

"But it is."

"Why would it be? You said I was ready to go home. You've pushed me out of the nest. After the way I attacked that lobster, there's no way I can pretend I'm too weak to cope. Do I still need a doctor's care?"

"Technically, no. But I want to keep on taking care of you."

"How?" said Freddy, puzzled.

"I want . . . I want you to marry me. Don't say no! Don't say anything at all! Don't tell me I don't know what I'm talking about, Freddy. Don't tell me you can't ask a girl to marry you after one date and two kisses. You can—I just did, and I haven't done anything impulsive before in my life. I know you better than you can dream I do. I also know it's much too soon, and I shouldn't have said anything—but I couldn't help it. I want you to know how I feel about you—I'm going to go on feeling that way; and you can take your time, and get to know me and decide . . . when you decide. That's all, not one more word."

"My goodness," Freddy said faintly. "What will we talk about on our second date?"

24

NEW Yorkers were always boasting about the glories of their city, and Bruno de Lancel found himself perfectly willing to agree with them. Was Manhattan more cultivated, more intellectual than London? Richer, more imperial than Rome? More dramatic, even more romantic than Paris? Yes, all of these and more. Whatever qualities they claimed, he accorded them freely, even half sincerely, as a taxi bore him toward the dinner that the John Allens were giving on a night in early October of 1951.

Marie de La Rochefoucauld had come back from her summer in the Loire Valley, as free, as unentangled as she had been when he'd seen her off on the *Ile de France* in June. Since her return, Bruno had managed to spend some time with her almost every weekend, although she still refused any dates other than afternoon excursions and quiet evenings in small restaurants. She told him that her family had been disappointed when unexpected business had prevented him from traveling to France during the entire summer.

"Maman said she would have liked to get to know you, from everything that I told her, and my brothers all counted on you for tennis . . . in short, you were missed, Bruno. You must not disappoint us again," Marie said with a mild, half-joking sweetness and a shy, darting look that Bruno, who was able to chronicle each half-degree of intimacy of her expressions, realized was the warmest she had ever given him.

The Allens' party tonight was to celebrate Marie's birthday, and Bruno had searched for a week before he found a present that she would find not too important to accept, yet which would be worthy of this sovereign girl. Finally he'd settled on a first edition of *Alice's Adventures in Wonderland,* a book she loved for reasons he had never been able to understand, although he'd read it with the careful attention of a man in love, as if it contained precious clues to her character. It had cost an astonishing amount of money, a fact he was certain she couldn't possibly realize, and, he reflected, it was always proper to give a book as a gift.

Bruno sat in the Allens' drawing room, in an agitated but well-concealed condition of anticipatory jealousy, for he knew that the guest list had been determined by Marie, not by Mrs. Allen. When he arrived, Sarah Allen greeted him, and explained that Marie was still dressing. "She got stuck in that awful subway on the way down from Columbia, tonight of all nights . . . what's more, here I am having a formal dinner and she only let me invite twelve of her friends besides you," she complained. "I do wish Marie had allowed me to give her a ball . . . she's made so many friends . . . but she didn't want a lot of fuss."

So there were to be twelve other people besides him, Bruno thought, as the guests arrived. Four were Marie's two favorite professors and their wives; one couple was the Allens' daughter, Joan, and her fiancé; two more couples were married friends she'd made among her fellow students. There was another unmarried man besides Bruno, but he brought a girl, a close friend of Marie's, with whom he was clearly involved. Bruno had met them all before. He was the only single, unattached man there, he realized with momentary disbelief. She'd chosen him . . . or had she made it possible for him to choose her? Or —and knowing Marie, it was distinctly probable—had she just innocently picked out the names of the people with whom she felt most at home in New York? Did his invitation mean nothing more significant than the fact that he was another friend, a friend on the same level as the other guests? He couldn't know, he realized. He might never know.

Bruno stood in a corner frowning, his dark yoke of eyebrows slashing across his brow, above his high-bridged, distinguished nose, his small, full mouth tight with anger that he should find himself so confused. Marie came into the room wearing a slim, floor-length, strapless dress of heavy white silk. Her long black hair had been braided into a coronet around her impeccably shaped head, enhancing the proud, slender shape of her neck. From her ears hung long pendant earrings, swaying sprays of old rose-cut diamonds with great cabochon rubies at their centers, and she had pinned a huge matching brooch in the center of her bodice, just at the point where the ivory skin of her shoulders rose from the top of her dress.

Marie's jewels were so magnificent that only inheritance could justify someone so young wearing them, yet she carried them with the same ease as she wore the inconspicuous gold earrings, the gold chain and watch that were the only other jewelry Bruno had ever seen her wear. He bit his lip in impotent emotion. As much in love as he was, he raged at the sight of Marie's unexpected and matter-of-fact possession of family jewels that had nothing to do with him. She should not be allowed to wear anything, not so much as a pair of shoes, that he didn't give her; she must never surprise him by appearing in an incarnation he did not expect, did not control, no matter how beautiful. *Oh, if he owned her, she'd learn!*

Dinner was a long, elaborate torture for Bruno, who found himself at the other end of the table from Marie. She sat between John Allen and one of her professors, looking happier and more animated than he had ever seen her. With sixteen people at the oval table, general conversation was impossible, and Bruno was forced to devote himself to his neighbors, while he tried to watch Marie, without being rude to either of the ladies at his right and left. She had not placed him next to her. Obviously she'd been in charge of the seating, just as she had been of the invitations. She had not even tried to catch his eye, he said to himself grimly, as they finished the birthday cake. The most accomplished flirt in the world could not have treated him with more cunning than the supposedly guileless Marie de La Rochefoucauld. *Oh, if he were her master, he'd teach her not to dare to play such tricks on him!*

After dinner, while coffee and brandy were served in the drawing room, Bruno tried to sit next to Marie, but found the other place on the love seat casually preempted by the younger of her two professors, the one who had not been seated by her at dinner. The man couldn't be more than thirty-five, Bruno thought, as he stood, balancing his demitasse and savagely studying this scholar who had chosen to make Chinese ceramics his life's work. He didn't have the fussy, dusty look that Bruno imagined a professional academic should have. He was obviously well bred and, judging by the elegance of his wife, must possess a substantial private income. The blond professor kept Marie laughing and parrying his irreverent remarks about the entire graduate school, until Bruno was forced to turn away in order to hide the grimace of vengeful jealousy he felt forming on his features.

Was it possible that here was the reason she had returned from the summer without accepting some French suitor? Was it conceivable that she was in love with this fellow who shared her deepest interests? Had she invited him tonight with his wife, to dispel suspicion? What a treasure of opportunities they could find to be together in the course of any day, Bruno thought, remembering how easy it had been for his mistresses to deceive their husbands. Did the two of them meet secretly in the stacks of the library, in the workrooms where fragments of ceramics were studied, did they have lunch together, and after lunch . . . No!

If Marie belonged to him, she would have no such vile liberty! He would dispose of her every minute, he would make sure that she had no intimate friends, no interests that he did not find suitable for her, not one aspect of her life that excluded him would be permitted. He would gain control of her nights and her days, slowly, moment by moment, with such dexterous care that she would never suspect how she was being trained, until it was far too late to struggle against it. La Vicomtesse Bruno de Saint-Fraycourt de Lancel would never be given leave to sit in a drawing room and giggle like a schoolgirl. She would learn what he would permit her to do, and she would not risk doing anything of which he did not approve.

"More coffee, Bruno?" Marie de La Rochefoucauld asked him, startling him because he had been so lost in thought that he hadn't seen her get up and come toward him. The light caught the green flecks in his brown eyes as he looked down at her.

"Thank you, Marie, no. I like your hair around your head that way. It makes you look almost fifteen."

"I think I look too dignified. Don't try to tease me," she commanded him, so calmly, so self-assuredly, yet so charmingly that his heart yearned as he looked at her, although his manner, powerful, easy, invisibly armored as ever, betrayed nothing. "Thank you for *Alice*," she continued, "it's the most enchanting present anyone has ever given me . . . how did you find it?"

"That's a secret."

"Bruno, do tell me," she insisted. "It's not the sort of book you can find in any bookstore. And I hate secrets, don't you?"

"You seem to have a few secrets of your own with that professor of yours," Bruno said lightly, gesturing vaguely in the direction of the blond academic.

"Joe? Isn't he amusing? I adore him, in fact everyone does. And his wife, Ellen, is one of the most charming women I've ever met—did you get a chance to talk to her? No? That's a shame—they've only been married for a year—she just told me that she's expecting a baby —it's wonderful to see two people so happy. Perhaps . . ."

"Perhaps what?"

"Joe and Ellen are giving a party for a group of students next week. Would it amuse you to come with me? I warn you, the other guests will all be from the Department of Oriental Art, but I think you'd like them and . . . I know they'd like you."

"What makes you think so?" Bruno asked. "I don't share their specialized interests."

"Bruno, sometimes you can be so . . . so obtuse! They'd like you because you're you and . . ." She hesitated, and, it seemed to Bruno, she had thought better of saying the words that came to her mind.

"And," he probed, "and what?"

"For heaven's sake, Bruno, they've . . . heard about you," Marie said, looking flustered. "I suppose they're . . . curious. Some of them don't think you exist, they think I've invented you."

"So you talk about me with your classmates?"

Marie tilted her head upward to meet his eyes squarely with her ineffably candid gaze, her calm self-assurance stripped away by her honesty. She spoke with a seriousness and a flame he had never seen in her.

"I can't help it, Bruno. How could I keep you to myself?"

"You are the most wonderfully law-abiding driver I've ever known," Freddy said to David, as he maneuvered his navy-blue Cadillac town car along the almost deserted stretch of Sunset Boulevard, where long, lusciously carved curves seemed to have been engineered to tempt drivers to swing and sway around them. "Did you ever go over the speed limit?"

"Probably, in college, but not on purpose, darling. When you see enough car crash injuries in the emergency room, you lose your interest in getting there a minute faster or passing the next guy on the right."

"I can certainly understand that," Freddy agreed. When she had first driven with David out to Jack's at the Beach, two months earlier, she'd imagined that his careful observance of the most detailed precautions known to the Department of Motor Vehicles had been due to his knowledge of her fear of venturing outside the world of the hospital. She'd assumed that he was taking special care of her, that he knew she was experiencing a shock of vertigo, a dizzy, phobic fear caused by the sheer openness of the world after the months she'd spent inside protecting walls. She thought that he was forcing himself to hold his powerful car down to a legal speed limit, which no other Californian she'd ever known had obeyed. Now, after two months during which she'd seen David at least three times a week, she realized that vehicular decorum was part of his personality.

Freddy smiled indulgently to herself. He was such a beautifully *organized* man. Would any woman dream that a doctor who did such daring things to people's nervous systems would be the kind of gourmet cook who followed every complicated recipe to the letter, never throwing in a pinch of this or a dash of that, without a debate as to the exact size of the pinch or dash? What patient of his, she wondered, who had been the recipient of his innovative, imaginative use of medical art, would suspect that in his own home he arranged the books in his library not just by author, but by title, as alphabetically as the words in a dictionary, and never, ever left one lying open, facedown, for even a few minutes, because it wasn't good for its binding? If he heard someone in a bookstore opening a new book and cracking the spine, David had to be restrained from protesting out loud. He was adorably boyish when he got all hot and bothered.

As for his phonograph records! He'd taught Freddy how to hold them always by the edges, with the palms of her hands, so that no fingerprints would mar their black, grooved surfaces; he explained why they had to be replaced in their protective paper sleeves before being put back inside the album covers, after they'd been meticulously wiped off with the special cloth that picked up every last speck of dust. Their only disagreement was whether a record, once on the phonograph, had to be kept there until it came to an end. Sometimes Freddy wanted to stop the music in the middle, for one reason or another, but David insisted that they wait till the arm of his Magnavox lifted the needle off the record mechanically. "It's virtually impossible to be sure that you won't scratch the record if you pick up the needle by hand," he'd explained, and she'd realized that he was absolutely right, shuddering at the memory of the shameful way she and Jane used to play snatches of one tune or another on their little, hand-wound machine, changing favorite records as casually as if they were playthings.

David had really shaped her up, Freddy reflected, as he slowed down far in advance for a red light, the Cadillac whispering to a stop so smooth that it couldn't be felt. She'd always had a small corner of disarray in her bedroom, her "rat's nest" where she would sling magazines, sweaters, letters, newspaper articles that she'd torn out, bills she wasn't ready to pay, shoes that needed to be reheeled, and snapshots she intended to put into her album someday, all mixed together in one awful mess that served as a surprisingly effective if informal filing cabinet. Whenever Freddy couldn't put her hands on something where it was supposed to be, she looked in the rat's nest and found it. But when she'd started to establish a small away-from-home rat's nest in David's bedroom, for she spent so much time with him, he'd been admirably firm.

"It's a minor bad habit, darling," he'd said. "It would be just as easy for you to put things away immediately or hang them up as soon as you take them off. I know it's a bore. I know I'm a monster about neatness —in an operating room, you'd have to know exactly where everything is at every second." She could understand his reasoning perfectly, Freddy thought, and, what's more, it hadn't been all that difficult to keep her things in order once she started reminding herself to do it. She still had a rat's nest at home, but now she felt guilty every time she rummaged in it. She'd soon get around to eliminating that lazy habit completely, she decided firmly.

In fact, IF they were going to get married, she thought, wrinkling her nose in perplexity, she'd better start in right away, and start riding herd on Annie too, who'd inherited the rat's-nest habit. Could it be genetic?

Once she'd left the hospital, Freddy realized that it was out of the question for Annie to stay in England for a year of school. She'd miss her far too much. Her daughter had been back home since the start of classes, although it wasn't easy to carry on a romance when an observant nine-year-old expected to have breakfast with her every day. She and David hadn't slept together for a single entire night; they'd never awakened in the same bed together, for he drove her home at a fairly respectable hour of the evening, particularly since he almost always had to be at Cedars early the next morning.

He was the most considerate lover a woman could dream of, she thought happily, glancing at his profile as he concentrated on the road ahead. Tender, sweet, gentle, as concerned with her pleasure as he was with his own . . . or more concerned? She only had two other lovers to whom she could compare David, and she couldn't remember if Tony, or Mac, all those years ago, had ever been as bent on making absolutely sure of her satisfaction as was David. Did David have a unique, built-in sensitivity to women, or was it his knowledge of her neurological responses? And wasn't she a little disgusting, even to be thinking this way, when she was always so fulfilled after he made love to her?

Would David never grab her and rip off a tumbled, hot-headed, ill-timed and delightful quickie, the sort that makes a sexy secret to share all through an evening, Freddy wondered, or was that too unlike him? Probably he would, once this courtship period was over, IF they got married—or was it just a question of when?

David had been as good as his word. He hadn't said another thing about marriage, just as he promised. He hadn't put the slightest pressure on her to make a decision. So why did she feel as if, somehow, there were some subtle invisible force that was causing her to lean toward saying yes to this man who was so good for her, who took such marvelous care of her, who showed his love in so many ways? Probably, Freddy told herself, it was because he was obviously a man any woman would be insane not to marry.

It was only this dinner tonight, she realized, that was making her nervous. Dinner with David's mother. It was an invitation she'd already wriggled out of twice, until finally she'd had to accept. Dinner with someone's mother was not a formal announcement of intention to wed, Freddy reminded herself. It was a compliment to be invited. Nothing more. Not pressure. After all, he hadn't taken her around to meet his sisters, although she imagined that having sisters was the reason that he was so good with Annie.

He'd assured her that tonight was nothing out of the ordinary, just the usual weekly dinner he'd been having with his mother for years. "I'm that ridiculously unfashionable thing known as a good son," David had told her, his dark eyes alive with self-mockery. "It's not my fault that she's a good little mother, is it?" She had a good little mother too, Freddy had reminded him, as well he knew, and if Eve didn't live six thousand miles away, she and her mother would no doubt be just as devoted as Eve and Delphine now were.

Susan Grunwald Weitz, widowed for three years, lived on one of the green and private streets of luxuriously secluded Bel Air, not very far east of Brentwood. They turned off Sunset and soon arrived at her house, a finely proportioned white mansion of Virginian elegance, lying well hidden behind tall gates.

"Hmm," observed Freddy, impressed and rather surprised. David's own house was bachelor-sized. "I thought your father was a doctor too?"

"His hobby was investing—oil and real estate. He managed to combine all his interests."

"What beautiful gardens," Freddy noticed, lagging behind, feeling just a little reluctant to commit herself to meeting David's mother, no matter how good, no matter how little.

"Mother's hobby. Come on, darling, she really won't eat you." He greeted the maid who opened the door and led them toward the living room. Freddy had a quick impression of a wealth of paintings and sculpture and bowls of massed flowers everywhere, before she realized that the living room seemed to contain more people than the one good little mother she had been prepared to meet.

Susan Weitz, who was almost as tall as her son, rose, composed and friendly, to greet them. There was not so much as a single streak of gray in her smooth, ash blond hair, her pearls were the best Freddy had ever seen, her blue dress simpler and more expensive than any that Freddy, who now could recognize these distinctions in one glance, had ever seen a Los Angeles woman wearing. Freddy's first thought was that she must have had her dress made in Paris. Her second was that Susan Weitz must have been the late doctor's second wife, for she certainly didn't look old enough to be David's mother.

However, as she was introduced to the other people in the room, Freddy had to admit that the women in their thirties, David's three married sisters, bore a family resemblance to Susan Weitz and to David himself. With their three husbands, they made an exceptionally tall, exceptionally lean, exceptionally attractive group, all cordial, yet not one degree overly cordial. They did not seem to be looking Freddy over in any covert or significant way. Just a simple little family dinner, she said to herself, assuming her Honorable Mrs. Longbridge smile. Everyone in the room absolutely *loomed* over her, for God's sake. She felt like a Munchkin.

"Mother, you didn't warn me that you were having the girls," David protested in surprise.

"Well, darling, your sisters were free and dying to come—you know I can never resist them."

"I told you about my little sisters, didn't I, darling?" he murmured to Freddy. "Sorry about this."

"They seem to have grown up since you mentioned them."

"Well, I'm the oldest, by light-years. Mother had me when she was eighteen. To me they'll always be kids," he said, giving her a drink.

The Weitzes, as Freddy thought of them, for she had caught none of the sisters' married names, carried on an easy discussion in which they included Freddy so naturally that she soon found herself feeling as if she were a normal-sized human being. Anyway, they looked shorter sitting down.

After the gay, chatter-filled dinner, they all went back to the living room, where Freddy was claimed by Barbara, who announced that she was the baby of the family.

"You have only the one sister, don't you?" Barbara asked, her kindness evident in her smile.

"Yes, and she lives so far away," Freddy said regretfully. The sight of the big, companionable Weitz family made her feel lonely for her own kin.

"I've seen a lot of her films. She's simply divine. David tells me that your daughter, Annie, looks a lot like your sister."

"Yes, it's startling. But they're different in many ways. I don't think Annie will ever be an actress."

"David says that Annie still wants to be a pilot. Are you happy about that? If I were her mother, I must say I wouldn't be entirely thrilled with her ambitions, particularly now that you've given it up yourself. It seems such a difficult life for a little girl, not really . . . well, not really feminine, if you know what I mean. But I imagine you can talk her out of it. David hopes you can, but he's probably told you, hasn't he? Channel her gently in another direction, as it were—golf, for instance. Or tennis. Those are such useful sports. Not something you have to do all alone, like flying. I'm an avid golfer myself. Do you play, Freddy? No? What a shame! Well, if you ever decide to learn, I can steer you right to the best pro in town. With your coordination, or whatever it is that pilots have, you'd be an absolute natural! I have an idea—why don't we lunch at the club and afterwards I'll introduce you to him? You might want to make a date for lessons. One way or another, I'll call you in a few days."

"That would be lovely," Freddy said, grinding out a smile. She didn't *choose* to fly, at the moment, for reasons she hadn't bothered to analyze, but that didn't mean she'd "given it up." And just what made Barbara think that you could talk anyone out of flying who really wanted to do it? Could any logic or persuasion, no matter how gentle—no matter how forceful—have stopped her? When you had that need, that urge to climb into the sky and make it your own, there was nothing a mother could do. Or should do. But Barbara was so warm, and she meant well.

"Move over, Babs," said Dianne, another sister who unceremoniously took Barbara's place. "Has she been telling you about her golf pro? Pay no attention. She's really far gone. She's the club champ, my dear, three years in a row. I think it's an appalling bore, all that dreary golfer's talk. But then I haven't got time for golf anyway, with five children and another on the way. Oh, I know, it doesn't show yet, but I hardly ever show until the sixth month . . . I'm lucky about that. You have only one child, I understand? That's too bad."

"Annie was born in the middle of the war. I had a job . . ." Freddy heard herself explaining.

"Bad luck! But then you're so young. Only thirty-one, David says. You have time to have a dozen more if you want them, don't you? Heavens, that does sound like a lot of work, doesn't it? You should see the look on your face! Really, Freddy, I was only joking. But naturally David's dying for children. That first marriage—well, they weren't married long enough to have babies—I'm sure he's told you about it. And you've stopped working, I hear. I have some friends with children who continue to cling to their careers, but I feel so sorry for them . . . there's always that appalling tug in both directions—they can never do real justice to their jobs or their babies, no matter how hard they try. Of course, most of them *want* to work, I can respect that, but I can't help thinking that they've made the wrong decision, and that they'll regret it later. What's your opinion?"

"I've never given it much thought," Freddy answered. "Annie was brought up by a working mother and she hasn't suffered as far as I can see. At least not yet."

"Oh no, of course not!" Dianne cried. "After all, there was the war and all. And then starting your business. You couldn't *help* it. But she must be so pleased that you're home for her now. And when she gets to be a teenager, she'll really need you. In fact, all your little ones are always going to need you, even when they're grown up. Didn't you just love being pregnant? I'm never so happy as when I am—I wonder why that is? Probably something primitive and atavistic. Now that you're not working, I hope you're free for lunch? I'll call you next week and make a date. I'd love you to have lunch with me at home, and see my children."

Who the hell had given Dianne the impression that she was never going to go back to work, Freddy wondered as she managed to return Dianne's warm, friendly look. She hadn't made a definite decision about Eagles. In a moment of physical weakness, she'd told Swede she wasn't coming back to work, and she hadn't changed her mind, but she was keeping her options open. Eagles was still . . . her baby. Oh well, Dianne was just an enthusiast. She must be a marvelous mother. And she meant well.

"I've come to rescue you," Bob, one of Dianne's brothers-in-law, said to Freddy, pulling Dianne to her feet and appropriating her chair. "Has she started on the joys of labor yet, or the ecstasy of contractions? No? You're lucky." He gave Dianne a gentle spank and sent her away. He turned toward Freddy. "I'm Elaine's husband—the middle sister—and she sent me over here when she saw you in Dianne's maternal clutches. I know what you're thinking, this family is overwhelming en masse—I had the same impression when I was first introduced to the Weitzes. I couldn't tell them apart . . . and the way they idolize David! He's a great guy, don't get me wrong, but not God Almighty. Just don't tell his sisters or his mother that! What's more, I hope you know that you won't have to put up with the girls and their interests or opinions if you don't choose to. Take us, for example—Elaine and I have only two children and no plans to have any more, we don't play golf or tennis—just a little swimming to stay in shape. We're the moderates of this family. We love chamber music, but we don't try to cram it down people's throats. If you like opera, so much the better, we say. If you prefer concerts, support the symphony. If ballet is your meat, well and good, and if you hate the ballet, there are plenty of other endeavors that need active patrons—the museum, UCLA, hospitals—whatever you feel passionate about. The main thing is to really *pour* yourself into a community project, don't you think, Freddy? The great thing about having enough time and enough money is to get involved with the community, to give, not just to take."

"I agree," said Freddy, blinking at this dynamic man. "Absolutely."

"Elaine and I had a feeling you would." Bob resonated with satisfaction. "We were hoping that you and David could come to dinner next week. We're having an interesting group, some of the music crowd, some of the art crowd—they're all dying to meet you. Elaine will telephone you tomorrow and give you the details. You'll be involved in something fascinating before you know it. And remember what I said about the Weitzes, even if we look alike, we're all very different sorts of people."

Oh no, thought Freddy, as Bob was replaced by Jimmy, another brother-in-law. You're all very much the same; good, kind, warmhearted, devoted to each other, happy, productive, hospitable, secure in who you are and what you want from life. You're enviable, a fortress of a family.

"Jimmy, everybody's had a chance to talk to Freddy but me," David's mother said as Jimmy stood up at her approach. "And she didn't come to visit you, she came to visit me—I should never have let the lot of you invite yourselves to dinner."

As Jimmy withdrew, Susan Weitz regarded Freddy frankly, her hazel eyes admiring. "They're all like children with a new puppy," she said. "I'm surprised that they haven't just jumped all over you and drooled and licked your pretty face. But they're so thrilled to see David happy that you can't blame them."

"The sun seems to rise and set on David in his sisters' eyes," Freddy ventured.

"To a point that even *I* notice it," David's mother agreed laughingly. "My husband used to tell me that I was the worst offender. But when you have only one son and three daughters, it's hard not to be partial. Especially when that son is David."

"Yes," agreed Freddy. "Especially David."

"I've wondered for years when he'd fall in love again. He used to say he was too busy—what nonsense! I knew that when the perfect girl came along he'd find time somehow. He was never meant to be a confirmed bachelor. Well! I don't want to make you blush any more than you're blushing already. But you will come back next week, won't you, Freddy? I promise that the girls won't be here—just the three of us, so that we can get to know each other. Do say you will!"

"I'll try," Freddy answered. "You have such wonderful paintings, Mrs. Weitz," she said, looking around the room.

"Thank you, Freddy. My husband and I started the collection, and after he died I kept on buying art—it keeps me busy."

Freddy picked up the silver bowl that stood on the small table by the side of her chair, lifted it to her nose and sniffed. "Did you make this yourself?" she asked.

"Why, Freddy!" Susan Weitz cried, delighted. "How ever did you know? I have my own, very, very special way of making potpourri. My mother's secret recipe, actually. But most people never realize—they think I've bought it. And none of the girls has the patience to make her own. If you like, I'll be so glad to show you how. It takes a long time, but it's worth it."

"Oh yes," said Freddy, "I do realize that."

The vines of champagne grapes sleep during the winter and do not wake until late February, when they begin to weep white sap from old wounds, wounds caused by the pruning of the vines the preceding March. The tears of the vine are like the sound of trumpets to a Champenois, for it is the signal that the growing season has begun. The irresistible rise of the pure, sticky sap forces buds to sprout on the branches of the bare vines. By the end of March, all the buds that will become clusters of grapes are open. The period from the weeping to the harvest, six or seven months in the future, is a time during which no one who grows champagne grapes, from the peasant with his few acres, to the proprietor of a *Grand Marque*, like Paul de Lancel, can ever be free of anxiety, threatened as they are daily, hourly, by the wide range of natural disasters that can affect the harvest.

By the end of October 1951, Paul and Eve de Lancel could finally take their ease. Paul had spent the summer watchfully supervising the entire Lancel enterprise, Eve running the château and caring for guests who charged in and out of Valmont with the regularity and relentlessness of a tide.

The harvest was completed all over Champagne; the army of ten thousand seasonal grape pickers, most of them miners and factory workers from other parts of France, some of them gypsies or itinerant agricultural workers, had finally departed, exhausted, satisfied, and good-natured, after ten days of labor during which they had slept in the dormitories that the big winegrowers built in the vineyards for their reception. They had eaten the five huge meals that were provided for them each day. They had drunk the pitchers of red wine that stood ready for them whenever they felt thirsty. They had sung and danced every night, and gone to the many fairs that beckoned throughout the area. When not eating, sleeping, drinking or socializing, the robust, strong-backed harvesters had worked without the slightest break from dawn to sunset, always bent in painful positions, doubled over, kneeling, crouching, even lying flat on the ground to pick the delicate fruit of the low-growing vines, never forgetting to take immense care not to bruise the skin of a single ripe grape and cause premature fermentation.

"I feel like a schoolgirl with all my exams over and nothing to worry about for almost five months," Eve said to Paul at breakfast. "It's most peculiar . . . I keep thinking that I should be worried about another week's menus."

"You look like a schoolgirl, but a rather tired one. What you should do is sleep really late. I want you to start to spoil yourself." He reached across his plate, took her hand and kissed it. He loved looking at Eve in the morning, before she had put on her makeup or arranged her hair for the day. To Paul, her private face, at fifty-five, looked fifteen years younger than it did when she was all done up and ready to deal with the public.

"The trouble with getting up so early for months is that it becomes a habit—I don't even need an alarm clock. As for spoiling myself, don't worry, dearest, I have plans for both of us. After Thanksgiving with Freddy in California, and Christmas and New Year's with Delphine and Armand in Barbados, we'll come back to Paris so that I can order my new wardrobe at Balenciaga—I've reserved a great big expensive suite at the Ritz, on the Vendôme side of course . . . theaters, museums, restaurants . . . I plan to spend all this year's profits—as long as you don't ask me to drink another drop of champagne until next spring, I'll be perfectly happy."

"The people who truly appreciate champagne say it's never better than before lunch—preferably for breakfast with poached eggs."

"That sounds like a hangover cure." Eve shuddered delicately, and poured herself another cup of tea.

"It only works for a hangover if you mix it half and half with stout . . . or with one-third orange juice, one-third cognac and two dashes of Cointreau and grenadine—or so I've heard."

"Let's not find out," Eve suggested.

"Agreed." Paul was a perfectly happy man as he sat back and looked toward the far horizon, over Lancel vineyards.

"Isn't it wonderful to have Valmont to ourselves?" Eve said. "When that last English wine writer left yesterday, I wanted to kiss him, I was so thrilled to see him go. I've arranged to have all the guest bedrooms repainted while we're away, and I've already chosen fabrics for new bedspreads and curtains. The rugs will do for another year."

"Don't you want to come out riding with me this morning? It's such perfect weather," Paul asked.

"No, I have a long-standing date to mulch my roses."

"Why can't one of the gardeners do that?"

"Anyone could, even a child. But I prefer doing it myself. Why should I let the gardeners have all the fun?" Eve asked.

"My mother always did her own mulching," Paul remembered. "She said if she covered her rosebushes and nourished them properly in the fall, she never worried about them, no matter how hard the winter, and she never trusted anyone to do the job as well as she did."

"And she was right, as always—or as almost always. I'm going to put on my gardening overalls. No more Balenciaga! Bliss!" Eve kissed him on top of his head, where his thick hair was still more blond than gray. "Have a good ride. See you at lunch, darling."

Three and a half hours later, when a portion of her rose garden was covered inches deep in mulch, Eve was in her bathroom, trying to scrub her nails clean before lunch. Suddenly the housekeeper knocked. The sound was urgent.

"Madame! Madame! Come to the stables, come quickly!"

"Lucie? What is it?" Eve demanded as she hurried down the stairs.

"I don't know, Madame. The stable boy told me to call you to come at once."

Eve raced toward the stables, running as fast as she could. A fall, she thought, a fall, it must be a fall. Even as good a horseman as Paul could always take a spill.

In front of the gaping stable doors, Paul lay with his head cushioned on a horse blanket, five or six men standing around him, looking toward her almost guiltily, as if they hadn't dared to move before she arrived.

"Have you telephoned the doctor?" she shouted, even before she was close enough to see what had happened.

The men, their caps in their hands, stood transfixed and silent. None of them nodded in assent to her command.

"Don't you have any sense! Quickly, *run* to the house! Telephone!"

No one answered her. No one moved. "Paul? Paul?" Eve cradled his head in her arms. She looked up at the oldest stable hand. "Emile, for the love of God! How did he fall?"

"Monsieur Paul, Madame—well—he rode up, he stopped, he told me he had a headache. He said that it struck him the moment he rode out of the woods. He pointed to the back of his head. He slid one foot out of the stirrup, took the reins in his hand, and then, before I could help him—he—he slipped off the horse and fell to the ground . . . like that, you see, like that. I put him on the blanket."

"Oh my God, why did you move him? You've hurt him!"

"No, Madame, I would never have moved him unless I knew . . . he was already . . ."

"Already? Already what! Are you crazy, Emile! Call the doctor!"

"I would have, Madame, I would have, but the doctor can't help . . . he is gone, Madame."

"Gone?"

"Yes, my poor Madame. He has left us."

The only decision Eve was able to make, in the hours of confusion that followed Paul's death, hours of such disbelief that she could not yet mourn, was that the funeral should not take place until all his children had gathered at Valmont. Delphine drove quickly from Paris and arrived within a few hours. It was she who took over the task of telephoning Bruno and Freddy. Eve was numb with shock as she wandered aimlessly, dry-eyed and wordless, from one room of the château to another, studying the views from different windows as if she were seeing them for the first time, caressing the carving of picture frames with cold fingertips, examining the patterns on needlepoint pillows, as if somehow she could break a mysterious code and find the unalterable clue that would explain to her what had happened to her life.

Freddy's flight would be a long one. She was to leave via TWA for New York from Los Angeles. In New York she would catch an Air

505

France flight to Paris, by way of the polar route, with stops at Gander and Shannon. In Paris, she would be met by Armand, who would drive her to Champagne.

Swede Castelli took Freddy to the airport. When the news had fallen on her, Freddy realized, in her grief, that Swede was the closest thing she had to family in Los Angeles . . . the one reliable constant in a world that had changed so quickly in the fifteen years they'd known each other.

"Listen, Freddy, try to get some sleep on the plane. You look beat," he said as they approached the boarding gate. Freddy looked out through the glass to where the huge, four-engine Lockheed Constellation stood waiting out on the tarmac. An open van of baggage was slowly being unloaded into its baggage compartment.

"Swede, is there a bar in this place?" she asked suddenly.

"There's always a bar in an airport. Shall we go find it?"

"Please."

Freddy and Swede each downed a scotch in silence. "Another?" Swede asked. Freddy nodded agreement.

"Why are bar drinks so ineffective? They might as well be water," she complained, as she finished the second drink.

"They're probably half water to begin with, and then they put in all those ice cubes. You've got about one-quarter of a normal drink in that glass. Let me order you another. Then you can be sure of sleeping on the flight."

"Good thought."

Swede had never seen Freddy put away three drinks in a row, even in a bar, and never before eleven in the morning, as she was now doing, but he assumed that it was her way of dealing with her emotions.

Freddy drank somberly and quickly. It was going to be a long, draining trip, and she knew that once she was airborne she was going to be offered more drink and food than she would want, but she felt an unaccustomed need for the effect of whiskey right now. If only she weren't traveling alone.

David, had he been able to leave his patients at a moment's notice, would have been a sturdy traveling companion, but she had forfeited that possibility when she had told him that she was certain that she would never marry him, no matter how much time he gave her. He'd thought that her decision had been caused by the impact of his family treating their marriage as a given, expecting her to fit into their closely organized lives.

"Don't you know that you could do anything you wanted? Don't you know that I'd never let them try to make you conform?" he had asked her in great pain. It had not been that, she'd had to tell him, for she could have coped easily with the Weitzes, even if there had been many more of them, after her experiences as a sixteenth Baroness Longbridge-in-training. When she understood that her future was taken for granted, she realized that she didn't love David *d'amour*. *Aimer d'amour*, "to love with love," that French phrase, which means romantic love, was not the way she loved him. Yet Freddy did indeed love David, and always would. She loved him as a good man, as a great doctor, as a loving friend—but not romantically. He would be a wonderful husband—she knew it rationally—but Freddy's gut told her that wasn't enough. Still, she wished he were with her now. Perhaps he would have been able to make her understand why her father, in perfect health, should have died from something called a cerebral aneurysm, a condition the French doctor had said was a weakened spot in an artery in the brain, which could strike at any time without previous symptoms.

"We'd better get back," Swede said. "They must have started boarding now."

Freddy looked at her watch. "What's the hurry? We have another ten minutes," she answered with belligerence. "What are they going to do, leave without me?"

"How long since you've flown commercial?" he asked mildly.

"Years. I don't even remember when."

"If they're planning to be on time, they just might leave without you. Come on, little lady, time to go."

"Little lady?"

"That just slipped out, ma'am. It won't happen again."

"It's all right. I don't mind." She took a peanut from the plate in front of her and chewed it thoughtfully.

"Freddy, will you get up? And get moving?"

"All in good time." Freddy carefully gathered up her coat and handbag, checked inside it for her ticket, as if she hadn't checked five minutes before, and finally followed him, lagging behind, Swede thought, like a child who was going to school for the first time.

Well, he didn't blame her. Even if she were traveling for fun, it was one hell of a trip, but to take the first step on the road to your father's funeral was rough. He hugged her hard at the gate and was astonished to feel how tightly she clung to him. Swede gave Freddy the flight bag he'd been carrying for her, and bodily pushed her out, past the ticket taker at the gate, onto the tarmac. She walked toward the Lockheed,

507

a lonely, drooping figure in the gusty wind, moving as slowly as if she had all the time in the world, although she was the last passenger to board.

Freddy sat stiffly in a window seat toward the front of the plane, refusing to surrender her coat to the stewardess. She felt chilled to the bone. In fact she was shaking with cold, although she realized that it couldn't be that chilly in the cabin. All around her she saw other passengers, most of them men, unbuttoning their jackets, loosening their ties and leaning back as they waited for the trip to begin.

Freddy discovered that she had two seats to herself. She rummaged in her flight bag for one of the books she'd brought to read on the endless trip. She fastened her seat belt, opened the book to the first page and read a few lines. They made absolutely no sense. She reread them carefully. There was nothing wrong with the words or the sentences. It was her mind that wouldn't translate them into the beginning of a story.

Freddy closed her eyes, and listened intently to the sound of the engines as they started. There didn't seem to be anything rough about their sound, she told herself. She turned and craned her neck backward, peering out the window. The wing was placed too far behind her for her to see the propellers. She had to assume that everything was in good order, she told herself, she had to assume that the mechanics who had done the maintenance work on this plane had been precise and careful and hadn't rushed through the job or neglected some small, not-quite-right detail that didn't seem worth taking extra time to investigate. She had to assume that the pilot and copilot and flight engineer were all experienced, competent men who knew their jobs and did them thoroughly, who remembered at all times that their safety was as much at risk as that of their passengers.

She knew too much, Freddy told herself severely, as, unnoticed, the book fell to the floor. If she didn't know all the things that could go wrong, she couldn't worry about them. That was why doctors weren't supposed to operate on members of their families. That was why lawyers didn't represent themselves in court cases. God, she needed a drink.

Freddy opened her eyes and saw that the stewardesses were strapped into their seats. The plane was still on the ground, poised at the end of the runway, while in the pilot's compartment the crew was going through the checklist for takeoff. In her mind she followed it, step by step. As the great machine began to gather speed for its takeoff run, she thought, *Too soon, too soon!* There hadn't been enough time spent on the checklist, she was certain of it, but there was no one she could tell. She wanted to scream it out loud at the top of her lungs, scream at the stupid oblivious attendants, at the passengers who didn't know the danger they were in, scream until the takeoff was aborted and the checklist was run through again. *Too soon!* But they had already taken off. Below them the ground fell smoothly away and they were circling into the departure pattern. The angle of the turn was too steep. Far, far too steep, dangerously too steep. A stall could happen at any second at that angle, didn't the cowboy who was flying this plane know that? The plane straightened out and started to climb to cruising altitude. Too quick a climb, much too quick a climb, what the fuck was his hurry, didn't he know that his angle of attack was too high, Freddy thought frantically. What kind of people did they let fly these things? What kind of training did they have? Probably some kid, some hotshot kid—all the older captains were being retired, she'd heard somewhere —some kid who hadn't been in a war, who hadn't enough hours in this particular aircraft to know what he was doing.

The seat-belt sign was turned off and she rang for a stewardess. "Could you bring me a double scotch, no ice, please?"

"Of course, Mrs. Longbridge. Is there anything else I can get you? Magazines, newspapers? It's an honor to have you aboard. We'll be serving lunch soon. I'll bring you a menu with your drink."

"No, thank you, just the drink." Shit! The damn woman knew who she was, Freddy thought, trying to make her fingers unclench around the arms of her seat. There was sweat trickling down her sides under her blouse, the roots of her hair were soaked, but she was still too cold to think of taking off her coat. Her heart was beating heavily, she couldn't manage to take a deep breath, and she felt as if she were about to be airsick for the first time in her life. *There was no air in here!* That was the trouble. Damn it, no air. No wonder she couldn't breathe. The big plane was totally sealed from the outside world, without any oxygen except for the pitiful stream that whistled down from the vents above the seat. How could they expect people to sit for hours without fresh air? God, she'd give anything to be able to punch her fist through the porthole and let some good clean air into this tightly sealed crate with its hideous interior, too big to be a flyable plane, too small to carry its weighty cargo of human souls.

The plane lumbered heavily through the sky, its four engines making a noise that sounded horribly wrong. Something was caught some-where, in one of the hundreds of vital parts, each one of which she could visualize and name, something was caught that must be freed or they were doomed.

Freddy rang again for the stewardess.

"Yes, Mrs. Longbridge?"

"I have to speak to the Captain. It's urgent. *Urgent.*"

"I don't know if he can come back to speak to you right now, but I'll go forward and ask him."

Years passed as Freddy listened for the defective engine, her eyes screwed shut so that she could hear better. There it was—a choke, a gasp, a hiccup, something any pilot would hear for himself, except one who didn't know what to listen for.

"Mrs. Longbridge?"

Freddy looked down at the pair of polished black shoes, at the blue uniform trousers. "Captain?"

"Yes, ma'am, what seems to be the trouble?"

"There's something wrong with one of your port engines. Can't you hear it?"

"No, ma'am, Mrs. Longbridge. They're all functioning perfectly. I just checked."

Was he deaf as well as dumb, Freddy asked herself furiously and peeked up at him. A man in early middle-age, without question a senior pilot, unmistakably competent, weathered, in charge. She didn't need more than a swift glance to tell her that. She would recognize the look of a man like that anywhere.

"Sorry, Captain. I guess I'm hearing things." She forced a laugh. He mustn't guess, he mustn't guess, she thought. It was too shameful.

"No problem, Mrs. Longbridge. We'd be delighted if you'd pay us a visit up front, after lunch, if you like."

"Thank you, Captain. I'll probably be sleeping."

"Anytime. Just let the stewardess know if you change your mind."

When her lunch was served, Freddy waved it away and asked for a blanket, a pillow and another drink. She must try to relax, she told the tiny crazed animal that was eating into her brain, a burrowing, tunneling animal, fleeing from a thousand dangers in a nightmare panic. But it was worse when she closed her eyes, she realized. When her eyes were open she could see people eating lunch with gusto, and as long as she could concentrate on them the plane would not fall from the sky, because if they were about to die, they wouldn't be eating, would they?

Freddy gave a sudden gasp of pure terror. The plane entered a cloud without warning. *Danger, there was danger here.*

Suddenly as the plane plowed deeper into the dirty whiteness, the lost memory of the minutes before her crash impaled themselves in her mind. She had checked her altimeter and seen that she had enough height to land on Catalina. But she had not radioed an airport tower in the neighborhood to find out if there had been a change in barometric pressure since her takeoff from Burbank. Any novice pilot would have known to take that utterly necessary step, given the lapse of time from takeoff and the changes in altitude she'd made while flying. Any pilot, any pilot at all, except one so cocky, so angry, so fed up with the world, so sure of herself, that she forgot to take the most elementary of precautions. If she could forget something so basic, so could that well-seasoned captain she had just talked to, so could the most senior pilot of any airline in the world, on the wrong day, in the wrong mood. There was no safety anywhere. *She must not scream!*

25

AFTER Paul de Lancel's funeral, the hundreds of people who had followed his coffin on foot to the village church returned to Valmont to pay their respects to his widow and his children. By midafternoon the last of them had finally gone, and Eve and her daughters sat down together, exhausted by the obligation to respond to so many saddened words, so many grieving faces, yet badly needing the comfort of being with each other.

Bruno stood beside them throughout the difficult day, his eyes cast down, his commanding, aquiline face serious and unreadable, a dark male presence who shook the offered hands and answered the words of condolence with precisely the degree of solemnity that the friends and neighbors of Paul de Lancel would expect. Delphine and he had greeted each other briskly but absently, as if they were the most distant of relatives. Their last interview, on the night of General von Stern's dinner party, was vivid in both their minds, but Delphine was so accomplished an actress, and Bruno so polished in deception, that each might have imagined it had been forgotten, although some things are never forgotten, as they were well aware. Never forgotten, never forgiven, never discussed.

To Eve, it was as if Bruno were invisible. She neither put out her hand to him when he arrived, nor did her eyes so much as pass over his face. She did not ignore him, because to ignore him would have been to admit his existence. She simply did not show, by any sign whatsoever, that he was present at this gathering, and she did it so skillfully that, except for Bruno, not one of them noticed.

Now that the formalities were over, Bruno escaped the château to go for a walk in the woods nearby. Armand Sadowski had left to drive Tony Longbridge and his parents, Penelope and Gerald, to Rheims, where they would catch a train for Paris. Jane, who was staying overnight, had gone upstairs to take a nap.

"Have you thought . . . yet . . . about what you're going to do?" Delphine finally ventured to ask Eve. Until her mother made some decision about her future, she couldn't possibly leave her here all alone, yet in a week she was due to begin work on a new film of Armand's.

"Yes, I have," Eve answered, her voice unexpectedly purposeful. Freddy and Delphine exchanged surprised glances. Until now, Eve had been wrapped in her heartbreak, as if it were a hooded cloak of solitude. She had not broken down and wept, as they had half expected, but refusing their company, she had spent a great deal of time alone in her rose garden, finishing the mulching she had started just before Paul's death.

"I'm going to follow the plans your father and I made for the winter," Eve said quietly. "If I had died, that's what I would have wanted him to do. I'll fly back to California with you, Freddy, and stay, as we planned, until I join Delphine and Armand in Barbados. After the Christmas vacation I'll return to Paris and do all the things we'd intended to do. The only change will be at the Ritz—I'll take a smaller suite. Early next spring, of course, I'll come back here where I'm needed. While the vines sleep I can travel; when they wake, I must be home."

"But . . . can you run the business . . . alone?" Delphine asked.

"I won't be alone, darling. Most of the men who were here when we arrived after the war are still well and working. Some who were sent to Germany didn't come back; some, like the cellarmen, the three Martin cousins, were executed by the Gestapo, but they've been replaced by members of their family. No one single man in the House of Lancel is indispensable, not even the *chef de cave*. Yet together they are the key to the growing of the grapes and the making of the wine. I'll have to hire someone to organize and supervise and oversee them, someone to run the House of Lancel as your father did. I'll find the best man in Champagne, even if I have to steal him away from my competition. Don't forget, I've learned more than a little about this business in the last six years—it was a crash course for me as well as for your father. If the house of any *Grand Marque* depended totally on certain particular people, how long do you think it would survive? Champagne makes strong widows, Delphine."

"Mother! How can you talk like that?"

"Because it's true. Read the history of the wine and you'll understand. It teaches you to be realistic. And next summer, I hope you'll all come and visit me and bring the children—after all, Valmont belongs to you now, not just to me." Eve's voice, although it was roughened with weeping, was strong and resolute. The denuded vines around

513

Valmont would bear fruit in the spring, as they had every year for centuries. This elemental, unchangeable process gave her courage to look ahead and imagine a future without Paul. Without the vines she would be lost—but she would never be without them.

"As far as I'm concerned," Freddy said, "Valmont doesn't belong to me at all. I can't imagine owning it."

"But it does. And after you, to Annie. When the notary comes tomorrow to read us the will, there shouldn't be any surprises. One-third will come to me, the other two-thirds, by law, must be divided among you, Delphine . . . and Bruno. When I die, the House of Lancel will belong to the three of you equally, and when you die, to all of your children. If none of you, or none of them, wants to be involved in the business, or if you disagree about how it should be run, remember that it can always be sold. Land in Champagne never lacks for buyers."

"Don't be morbid, Mother!" Delphine protested.

"It's not morbid to talk about death, darling. It's uncomfortable, because it forces you to realize that you won't live forever, but when land is concerned, it's never irrelevant. In any case, it will always be Lancel champagne that is made from our vines, no matter who owns the land. The name will be immortal so long as the grapes are tended."

Eve smiled gently at her daughters. She'd needed many hours in the rose garden to begin to face her life without Paul, and she knew that no matter how detailed her plans, they could not protect her from a never-ending loss. But that was the price you paid for a never-ending love. You could not have it both ways.

Bruno sat on a tree trunk in a clearing in the forest, in a place of deeply slanted light, aware, in a way that was entirely new to him, that he was at a moment in his life when he could say to himself, "This is the best it can be." The future held a parade of glorious events that rose before him as clearly as if this woodland were enchanted, but he had no urge to count them, no need to dwell on all the earthly delights that his father's death now made possible for him. It was enough, just for now, to think about Marie de La Rochefoucauld. Less than three weeks ago, on her birthday night, her admission that she talked about him with her friends had let him know that she loved him. A girl like Marie would never speak her heart more plainly than she had that night.

In the days following her party he had seen her frequently, and with his new understanding of her emotions, he could tell that in her demure, queenly, old-fashioned way she was waiting anxiously for him to respond to her. She hid her eagerness almost well enough so that if she had not already betrayed herself, he might still be in the condition of anxiety and self-doubt that had existed from the time he met her.

Marie de La Rochefoucauld was his for the asking, Bruno knew, as he stretched his legs and his arms, exhausted with so much joy. From the instant she had admitted that she could not keep him to herself, he had begun that training in obedience he had promised himself to impose on her. He kept her waiting, dangling, hoping, and uncertain, while he employed all his deliberate and powerful charm to make her fall more deeply in love with him. In the last week her glances had begun to reveal her state of mind. A questioning anguish escaped her clear gray eyes in certain moments during which Marie believed that he wasn't looking at her. Whenever Bruno spied that anguish, he became remote and superficially polite for a half hour, long enough to confuse and worry her, but not so long that she had reason to ask him what was wrong. Even before the news of Paul's death, Marie's universe began to be ruled by Bruno's moods. He had all the time in the world, he told himself in triumph, to bring her to the point of nervous despair, if he desired, but now that he knew it was possible, it was not yet necessary to test his power.

He would arrange their engagement, Bruno decided, as soon as he returned to New York, since nothing stood in the way of his return to France. They would fly back to Paris together in a few weeks' time, so that he could meet Marie's parents. Her mother would want to begin to plan the great wedding at which all the noble clans to which they belonged would gather to see them united. He imagined that the ceremony would take place in the spring—soon enough, since it was inevitable that in the fullness of time Marie was destined to become the peerless Vicomtesse Bruno de Saint-Fraycourt de Lancel. She would exist to please him; together they would found a dynasty.

But not here in Champagne. He never wanted to see Valmont again. Only this funeral, so bitterly delayed, so long-awaited, so prayed-for, could have brought him back to this province for even a day. Let whoever chose to live here do so, burdened with all the alarms and worries of a peasant. Let anyone maintain Valmont, so long as he himself received his fair share of the profits of the House of Lancel.

Perhaps it was time to go back to the château, Bruno thought, lazy distaste tainting his perfect happiness. He hated to get up and abandon his thoughts when everything he had ever wanted was finally within his grasp, but there was a damp chill in the forest air. "This is the best it can be," he repeated to himself, knowing that this moment would return again and again throughout his lifetime. A breeze sprung up as the leaves in the clearing started rustling behind him.

A hand, huge, rough, clapped over his mouth, forcing his head back. An arm, heavily muscled, tightened brutally around his neck. Other hands grabbed his arms, jerked them ferociously behind his back and fastened them tightly together. Hoisted to his feet, forced relentlessly forward, Bruno had to walk or fall. His captors marched behind him, so close that he felt their breath on his nape.

"You should never have come back," muttered a male voice that Bruno didn't recognize. "Never return to the scene of the crime. Don't you know that?"

"Remember the three Martins? Remember the men you denounced to the Gestapo? We are their younger brothers," a second voice whispered, barely audible over the crumbling of autumn leaves under their feet.

Now a third man spoke, almost as softly. "We were coming to find you the day your father arrived home from the war, but you disappeared."

"We intend to teach you a lesson," grunted the man who had spoken first. "Move!"

In his plunge into terror, Bruno was able to understand only that they were skirting the path toward the cellars. Not one human soul was visible anywhere in the landscape, as the late autumn light grew dimmer. The giant hand over his mouth kept him silent, grinding his lips painfully into his teeth.

"You thought you'd gotten away with it, didn't you? You thought that you had destroyed the only men who knew about Le Trésor."

Frantically, Bruno tried to shake his head.

"Don't deny it. We know it was you," the third voice muttered in his ear, its merciless edge only sharpened by its reined-in softness.

"There was another key," the second voice said in a hideous whisper. "The key belonged to my brother, Jacques, the oldest of the Martins. Your grandfather trusted him as he trusted the others. Except for your father, you had the only other key. There have never been more than three keys to Le Trésor in the history of Valmont.

"Jacques saw a German convoy one night, near the cellars. He followed, hid, and watched the soldiers carrying champagne into their trucks. The next day he went to Le Trésor and discovered that it was empty. He was afraid that someone might blame him or our brothers, until he understood that it could only be you who had sold the Germans the secret of Valmont. He told us everything, and gave us the key for safekeeping.

"When the Gestapo came for our brothers," the wolfish whisper continued, "we realized that you had had them murdered. We could not act because your Nazi friends protected you. After the war, your father never spoke to anyone of *Le Trésor*. He knew who the real thief was. We respected his shame. We respected his grief. We knew you'd return one day. He must have known it too."

Now they entered the huge, well-filled cellars, deserted by any workers, and hurried toward the far wall where the entrance to *Le Trésor* was hidden. Bruno struggled with insane strength, but he was as helpless as a piece of meat in the butcherly efficiency of their grip. One of them pressed on a chalk surface, and the wall swung open, the lock of the hidden door shining as brightly as it had when Bruno's grandfather first entrusted him with the secret of Valmont. A key was put in the lock, and the door of *Le Trésor* swung wide.

One of the Martins turned on the lights and closed the thick, hinged blocks of chalk behind them, muffling all noise.

The three men dragged Bruno through the vast, empty cellar. His feet scraped the ground. He had gone limp with knowledge, yet his eyes were still open, still aware, as they propped him up against the back wall. They moved quickly away from him under the battery of lights. The cousins unslung the rifles that hung from their shoulders, lifted them and took aim.

Three shots rang out. The Martins walked slowly toward the body on the cement floor. One of them turned Bruno over with his shoe, looking at the sightless eyes, the mouth that had been opened to scream. He had been dead before he hit the floor. Another of them took out a piece of paper on which he quickly scribbled the words, *Réglement de comptes.*

"Account paid in full," he said slowly, and laid the paper on Bruno's chest. They turned to leave, slipping their hunting rifles back over their shoulders.

As the door to *Le Trésor* swung shut behind them, one of the Martins said to the others, "Tomorrow we must send the key and arrange to let the police know where he is. There will be no further investigation . . . not when they read the note on his body. It would not be fair to Madame de Lancel, otherwise. There would be an endless search and he would never be found."

"His bones should not lie at Valmont. They desecrate it," said another of the cousins.

"I agree," the third Martin said. "Nor is it good for people to believe that there is no final accounting. That man lived too long."

Delphine and Armand persuaded Eve to rest before dinner, and went upstairs with her, while Freddy remained downstairs in a small salon with Jane, who had finished her nap. They were trying to catch up on the threads of their lives that were cut when Freddy and Tony had left for Los Angeles, five years earlier.

"I hated it bitterly when you two left," Jane complained. "What was the good of having snared you as a sister-in-law if you were going to live so far away?"

"Well, now you've got Tony back," Freddy said, "and, believe me, he looked a lot more fit today than the last time I saw him. Being a squire again has made a great difference. And that nice girl he says he's marrying . . . *and* giving up liquor. I'm happy for him."

"If I'd had a choice, I'd rather have kept *you*—I have plenty of other brothers. Oh dear, you did make a proper mess of it, the two of you. What a bloody balls-up! Wartime marriages—I wonder if they ever work? I'm so glad I had to wait." Jane gave Freddy the self-congratulatory smile of a woman who has made a total success of her life.

"Just imagine, Freddy, I would never have met darling Humphrey, I would never have had my darling children, I would never have been a marchioness, which is simply the most glorious game going, although you may never find anyone honest enough to admit it. The trick is not to worry about death duties. After all, they can't take it *all* away. Yes, it was a good thing that I wasn't a war bride too. It all worked out for the best."

"You never got remotely near being a war bride, Jane, as I remember perfectly well," Freddy protested, "so how can you sit there being sickeningly pleased with yourself for having escaped a fate that never threatened you?"

"If Jock had asked me, I'd have married him like a shot, and been dragged off to the desert sands of wildest California, just like poor old Tony."

"Come off it, Jane! You never had a romance with Jock!"

"Don't rub it in," Jane said with a touch of caustic asperity. A hint of future stateliness moderated the naughtiness of her brown eyes, but otherwise she was unchanged by her noble marriage.

"What are you talking about?" Freddy said, puzzled. It wasn't like Jane to have fantasy flings when she'd had so many real ones.

"You never guessed? No, I can see you didn't. But then I didn't want you to, or anybody else. It was horrible enough being ridiculously in love with someone who didn't know I was alive, without being an object of general pity."

"You were in *love* with Jock Hampton?"

"For years. And you don't have to sound so incredulous . . . that's a reflection on my taste, and my taste is excellent, if you please, Mrs. Longbridge! I was in love with that lovely man longer than I care to think about. I couldn't get over Jock, not properly, until I met Humphrey. I guess I'll always be a little in love with that beautiful blond Tarzan."

"That big *thug?* That over-the-hill cowboy? That derelict fullback, that only marginally intelligent lunkhead?" Freddy asked, bewildered and somehow angry. "No, Jane, say it wasn't so."

"Ah, but it was. And *how* it was! I doubt you've ever taken a good look at Jock. Never mind—it's a question of taste. But Freddy, don't you agree that once you've been truly in love, even when you fall in love with someone else, the first love will always remain alive inside you?" Jane inquired.

"I won't quarrel with that," Freddy said, her voice touched by a complicated nostalgia, the bittersweet memories of hours that could never return. "But why didn't you make a play for Jock . . . you never even flirted with him . . . you, the most shameless, infamous flirt in the British Empire? What was stopping you?"

"You," Jane said.

"Me?" Freddy objected, outraged. "That's the most unfair thing I've ever heard! How could I have stopped you? . . . *Why* would I have stopped you, for God's sake?"

"Not you yourself, silly—I meant that Jock was so entirely, head over heels, hopelessly in love with you that there was no way to even get his attention, much less flirt with him. He used to drag himself around looking at you—or worse, trying *not* to look at you—in a way that told me everything I needed to know. God, it was painful to watch him! Obviously I had to hang on to my pride, since it was all I had left. I found myself in the utterly mortifying position of watching him pining away for you while I pined away for him—and all the while Freddy and Tony, our two happy, self-absorbed young lovers, never even noticed a thing. Ah, love! But, as I said, it all worked out for the best—at least for me. And you know how truly sorry I was—I still am—that it didn't work out for you and Tony. As for Jock—how is he, anyway?"

"Jock? . . . Oh, you know Jock, he's . . . fine . . . going strong . . ."

"Poor Jock, still carrying that huge torch for you . . . a bit like the Statue of Liberty, isn't he? Tony told me he'd suspected it for years. But . . . when someone isn't one's type, one can't force it, can one?"

"Huh?"

"I said . . . no, never mind. Of course you're thinking about other things. Shall I make you a drink, poppet?"

"Who?"

"A drink? Do you want one? Freddy? Freddy? How many fingers am I holding up?"

"What?"

"I'll see to the drinks. You just sit there, it's been a long day. I'm glad I stayed over . . . you need someone to take care of you."

On the afternoon of the day following Paul de Lancel's funeral, four officers from the headquarters of the Epernay police arrived at Valmont. They asked the housekeeper to tell Madame de Lancel that they were unwilling to disturb her grief, yet they were obliged to investigate an anonymous letter they had received concerning one of her cellars.

"Go on, do your duty," Lucie had said with authority. "Madame de Lancel will tell you the same thing, but I don't intend to bother her with nonsense now."

The policemen left for the cellars, armed with the key and the map showing how to find the secret door to Le Trésor, which had been left at their headquarters by an unknown hand earlier in the day. Fifteen minutes later they stood in awe and astonishment as the door to Le Trésor swung open on a vast darkness. One of them groped about and found the light switch. The huge space was revealed to them under the brilliant lights, empty except for a body visible on the floor at the far side of the room. They approached it quickly. Even as they walked toward it, three of the four men, who had been in Epernay all through the war, recognized Bruno. Two of them swore softly, but without surprise. As they all stood over the corpse in a moment of hesitation, one of them, the senior officer, bent down to pick up the paper that had been left on Bruno's chest. He read it silently and passed it to the man standing next to him. Each of the policemen read the note in the same silence, and the three who had known Bruno gazed at each other in immediate understanding.

"What do we do now, Captain?" asked the youngest of the men.

"We bring the body to the château and we report the accident at headquarters, my boy."

"The *accident*, Captain?"

"You were not here during the war, Henri. Many people had reason to want this man dead. Who could possibly find out now who they were? Or how many of them there were? Who would go to that unnecessary trouble? It could not be done, Henri. It *should* not be done. Take my word for it, Henri, if you wish to learn something useful. This was an accident that was meant to happen."

"If you say so, Captain."

"I do, Henri. We all do."

"I *cannot* possibly understand why the police reported Bruno's death as a hunting accident," Freddy said. "I'm still in shock. Didn't they *have* to know that it was murder—finding him after they got an anonymous tip—what else could it have been? Yet they're not even going to investigate. I don't hold any particular grief for Bruno, but what's going on here? Doesn't anyone else but me think that it's simply unbelievable?"

Freddy, Eve, Delphine and Armand had just returned from the hurried formalities of Bruno's funeral, and were sitting outside on the terrace of Valmont, where the old stones still held the warmth of summer.

"It was neither an accident nor murder," Eve said, putting her arm around Freddy's shoulder. "It was an execution."

"*What!* An execution? What does *that* mean? And since when are private executions legal in France? Why aren't any of you more . . . I don't know exactly . . . more *surprised?* Yes, that's it! When they brought Bruno's body to the house, I think I was the only person in the family who was truly stunned. The rest of you seemed to almost accept it—in a way as if you had all . . . expected something like that to happen. But you *couldn't* have! What reason would anybody possibly have to imagine that Bruno was going to end up stone cold dead, a day after he left for a walk in the woods?"

"Darling, you've seen the monument in the center of Epernay, haven't you?" Eve asked.

"Yes, but what does that have to do with it?"

"It's not a tribute to dead soldiers, Freddy, it's engraved with the names of two hundred and eight men and women of this small region who died in the Resistance, some at the hands of the Gestapo, many in concentration camps. A number of them worked here at Valmont. The police understood that Bruno's death was connected to those deaths. He was a collaborator."

"You knew?" Delphine turned in astonishment, her hands flying to cover her mouth.

"Your father told me, but only me. He never wanted anyone else to know—the disgrace of the family name by his own son—it was to be hidden, even from you. However, we both realized that we knew only a part of the story. Who can tell what evil Bruno did here during the Occupation? He was alone at Valmont, after your grandfather died, for three dark years. Many people must have had good reason to bring him to justice."

"But the war's been over for six years," Freddy protested.

"It's easy to see that you've never lived in an occupied country, Freddy," Armand said. "Six years is nothing. If he'd come back here in ten years, twenty years, Bruno's executioners—whoever they were—would still have been waiting for him. They may even have been the police themselves, or people they knew, relatives or friends. The police have their own reasons not to want to investigate this death."

"Did you suspect anything, Delphine?" Freddy asked. "You were more or less in touch with Bruno during the war—do you have any idea what this could have been about?"

"No, nothing. Bruno was always . . . correct . . . with me," Delphine answered serenely, taking Armand's hand. Some things were far, far better buried. General von Stern's dinner party had never taken place. She had never begged Bruno for help. She had never agreed to put on her diamonds and go to ask a favor of the General at the house on the Rue de Lille. Whatever Bruno had been killed for, she was convinced that he had deserved his fate. No one, not Freddy or her mother, or even Armand himself, could ever fully understand what it had been like under the Occupation. If you were fortunate enough to have survived, it was wiser to forget. Thank heaven for the pragmatic French police.

"Now I truly can't wait to get away," Eve cried, a day later, after the notary left, flinging open her arms. "I crave a good dose of California sunshine after all that legal business."

"I was thinking, Mother—wouldn't it be great fun to go back by boat?" Freddy suggested. "I've never taken a sea voyage since I was a little kid, and the weather is still good. How about it?"

"That's the worst idea I've ever heard! First of all, you've been away from Annie for weeks as it is—much too long—and I'm dying to lay my hands on that delicious child. Second, I can't imagine anything more depressing than watching the ocean for five days on end, surrounded by strangers. You'd go out of your mind with the slowness of it, Freddy, and it's the last thing I need."

"I thought it might be . . . oh, you know . . . relaxing, calming, peaceful, luxurious. Sort of a rest cure."

"It's boring, it takes forever, and everybody eats too much. It's sweet of you to even consider it for my sake, darling, but I wouldn't dream of going any other way than by air. The only question is how soon we can start. I'm practically packed, I've had my last conferences with the housekeeper, the gardeners, the head of sales, and the *chef de cave*. I could leave today, much less tomorrow."

"I'll phone Paris and book your tickets," Armand volunteered, and set off in the direction of the phone.

"Swell," Freddy murmured. "Is he always so helpful, Delphine?"

"We absolutely have to get back to Paris. That might have something to do with it. No matter how difficult it is to get last-minute reservations, I bet he'll manage to get tickets for tomorrow."

"I can hardly wait," Freddy muttered to herself. Maybe, if Eve took the window seat, and they held hands a lot, it wouldn't be too bad. But they couldn't hold hands all the way to Los Angeles. She could put her head in her mother's lap and lie there with her eyes closed. But not all the way to Los Angeles. She could say she was airsick, but not all the way to Los Angeles. She couldn't drink herself into a stupor, with her mother sitting next to her. There was a new drug she'd heard about that was supposed to cure every kind of anxiety. What if . . . "Delphine, have you ever heard of something called Miltown?" Freddy asked.

"Miltown? No, never."

"What is Miltown, Freddy?" Eve asked.

"Some American invention. Nothing . . . important."

"I didn't expect to see the two of you till later!" Helga exclaimed as Freddy and Eve emerged from the taxi they'd taken from the airport.

"We had tailwinds, Helga," Freddy said. "The plane was early."

"Here, Madame de Lancel, let me help you with the bags," Helga said, bustling about in some confusion.

"It feels good to be back," Eve said, "but I'm bone tired. Freddy, I'm going straight upstairs to lie down. I don't even know what day it is, much less what time."

"When you wake up, come and find me, Mother, whatever time it is. I'll probably be awake anyway."

"I should certainly hope so, after the way you had your head buried under a blanket all the way home. I've never seen anyone sleep as long as you did. See you later, darling."

"Helga, where's Annie?" Freddy demanded, as soon as Eve started up the stairs.

"You just missed her, Mrs. Longbridge. She went out for a while."

"Out? Where did she go? When will she be back?" Freddy asked impatiently.

"I'm sure she'll be back by dark. It won't be more than a few hours," Helga said, sidling in the direction of the kitchen.

"Helga! Is Annie out all by herself?" Freddy inquired sharply. "What do you mean, 'back by dark,' you know I don't allow her to roam around unless we know who she's with."

"She's not alone, Mrs. Longbridge," Helga answered hastily. "She's with Mr. Hampton."

"Did he say where they were going?"

"Not exactly."

"*Helga!* Why are you looking so guilty? What the devil is going on?"

"Oh," Helga wailed, "it's supposed to be a surprise. They made me promise not to tell. Annie said you'd be so proud when you came home, she wanted to do it so badly, and Mr. Hampton told me that Annie was tall enough and smart enough, oh, Mrs. Longbridge, they talked me into it, the two of them, I just didn't have the heart to say no, not when they both got after me. Mr. Hampton . . . he's . . . giving her flying lessons . . . he's been out with her almost every afternoon since you've been gone . . . I honestly thought you wouldn't mind, I've heard all the stories you told Annie about how young you were when you had your first lesson . . . I should have stopped them, I suppose, but Mr. Hampton is such an experienced—after all, he's her godfather —and Annie was upset being all alone with you gone and her poor grandfather dead so suddenly—oh, Mrs. Longbridge . . . ."

"For heaven's sake, all right, all right, Helga, stop explaining, I understand what happened . . . stop crying and try to think. Where did they go?"

"Someplace called Santa Paula. Mr. Hampton said it was a good place to learn, not busy, not too big."

"Right." Freddy dashed up to her room two steps at a time, and threw off her travel clothes. Within minutes, still damp from a hasty shower, her hair dripping but clean after the long trip in stale air, she jumped into jeans, an old, faded blue work shirt and sneakers. She raced her car through the flats of the San Fernando Valley toward Santa Paula. All she had to do was to turn her back, and that bastard was busy corrupting her child, Freddy told herself. She'd waited till she was fifteen, for Christ's sake, to learn to fly, but Jock Hampton was *giving* lessons—Jock, who'd never flown a training plane in his life—to a child who wasn't even ten! What kind of a madman would do a thing like that, no matter how hard Annie begged him to teach her?

At the small, familiar airport, she rushed into the manager's shack outside of the main building.

"Have you seen a tall blond man with a dark-haired little girl?"

"Sure did. They just took off, in a Piper Cub. They landed for something to eat and went up again."

"Did they say when they'd be back?"

"I didn't talk to them. Try the girl at the lunch counter. Maybe she knows." Freddy ran out of his office and into the larger wooden building.

"You mean Jock and Annie? They had their usual, chocolate cake and milk, and took the plane up again," the counter waitress told Freddy. "She's a cute kid, Annie. Young for lessons, I thought, when they first showed up, but the kids around here . . . heck, they start younger every year, it seems to me. What'll you have?"

"Nothing! I'll just wait for them."

Freddy walked outside the building and impatiently scanned the empty sky. Across the single runway there was a deep, almost dry riverbed, and on the other side of the river stood a grove of well-remembered, gray-green trees—eucalyptus, pine, oak, all California natives—singing in the wind, the trees that had stood sentinel on the day she'd made her first cross-country flight with Mac and seen the Pacific from the air for the first time. The day she'd soloed. She threw herself down on the dry grass on the edge of the runway, in the gasoline-perfumed breeze, and prepared to wait.

For half an hour she sat cross-legged in the sun of early November. It was getting dark sooner now, Freddy noticed in spite of her fuming impatience. In less than two months it would be the shortest day of the year. On the other hand, after the depth of the winter solstice, the days would start growing longer, minute by minute, toward the summer solstice, if you wanted to look on the bright side. Considering that she'd spent the best part of the last two days in a plane cowering under a blanket, with only the fact that her mother was close at hand to keep her from falling apart with fear, Freddy saw no reason to look on the bright side. Not with her child up in a Piper Cub with a maniac.

She heard the faint drone of a small plane, and looking up with sky-wise eyes, Freddy spotted a small yellow Piper Cub, far, far away in the distance, flying steadily straight and level. Was it going on or was it going to land? She fixed it in her gaze and saw that it was getting set to enter the landing pattern, and none too snappily at that. She shook her head in disapproval. The angle of the plane was just off, nothing you didn't see every day, at any flying field, if you looked for it, but not up to Jock's standards. There was a slight wavering, a correction that was an overcorrection, followed by a new correction that took the angle a bit too far in the opposite direction. Jock was getting sloppy. And he'd never been sloppy. Other things, many other things, but not a sloppy pilot. Ever.

Annie was flying the plane! Freddy jumped to her feet and stood helplessly, riveted to the spot in the sudden terrified realization that her daughter was at the controls of the plane. She had nothing to wave, nothing with which to signal, no way to make Jock stop this insane experiment. Suddenly the uncertain wobbling of the plane was replaced by the smooth, gliding path of a perfect precision landing, and within a minute the Cub bled out its speed and touched down, like a large yellow butterfly lighting on a flower.

Freddy watched, motionless, as the plane taxied to a stop and the engine was shut off. The door opened and Annie climbed out carefully, Jock's hand firmly grasping her arm until she had one foot on the ground.

"Over here, Annie!" Freddy yelled, and the tall little girl turned and flew across the grass into her arms.

"Did you see me, Mom? Did you? Did you? " she shrieked, wild with excitement, kissing Freddy's face in twenty places.

"I saw you, all right. You—did fine, Annie."

"Oh, Mom! I did not! I was all over the place. That's what Jock said. But each time I get a little better. He still won't let me even try to land."

"That's . . . understandable."

"He says I have a lot to learn," Annie reported gravely. "Are you very surprised, Mommie? I wanted to do something wonderful for you because I knew how sad you were about Grandpa. It was all my idea, Mommie." Annie turned to the plane that was parked just off the edge of the runway. "I guess Jock thinks you're going to get mad because I made him give me lessons. It looks like he's not coming out of the plane."

"Why don't you go and wait for me at the lunch counter, Annie? I'll go say hello to Jock. We may be a while. Here's some money. Order anything you want."

Freddy stalked over to the Piper Cub, stepped up and thrust her head inside. Jock sat behind the right-hand wheel of the dual controls, his arms folded, staring fixedly into the distance. His stubborn jaw was set with the unmistakably defiant look of a man who knows he's in the wrong, but is trying not to admit it.

"Get out of there!" she ordered.

"Why should I?"

"So I can tell you what I think of you!"

"That's tempting, but no, thanks."

Goaded beyond fear, Freddy stepped up and perched gingerly on the edge of the seat inside the sturdy little Piper.

"How could you do it, Jock, how could you be so reckless with Annie? I'd like to tear you apart with my bare hands."

"I wasn't reckless. I was supremely careful, believe me. Listen, Freddy, I know perfectly well that I should have phoned you in France for permission. I came over to the house to keep Annie company while you were gone, and all of a sudden I heard myself agreeing to take her up just once, and then one thing led to another . . . she's such a natural, Freddy, I got drawn in against my better judgment."

"A mere child talked you into doing something you didn't want to do? Am I supposed to swallow that!"

"Annie can be even more persuasive than you ever were, but deep down, I guess—I really must have wanted to teach her." Jock turned. "I'm sorry, Freddy. I'm truly sorry you're upset, but you do know I wouldn't let her do anything dangerous, or even risky, don't you? Will you forgive me?"

Freddy looked him over, considering. She hadn't laid eyes on Jock in a year and she'd forgotten how big he was. He dwarfed the cockpit of the Piper Cub, leaning forward in his earnestness, as close to pitiful as she'd ever seen him. How could she stay angry, when he'd been so good to her mother and Annie in the last year?

"All right, Jock. I'll forgive you. But no more lessons until she's older. I'll explain that to her."

"Whatever you say." Jock drew a deep, relieved breath. "Say, why don't we take this little kite up, Freddy? I've always wanted to fly with you—you're such a beautiful pilot." How could he tell her that being close to her again made him feel as tentative as if he had captured a firefly, the one firefly in the world, and that if he released her now, he would never get her back?

"No." Freddy recoiled at his words, but tried to sound normal.

"Just for a few minutes? Look, it's the best time of the day. Come on, let's join the sunset." He reached over, slamming the door of the plane that she'd left open when she sat down.

"No! Jock, stop it!"

"Why not? Annie will understand when she sees us take off."

"I can't," she said numbly.

"I don't get it," he said, seeing her turn pale, her expression desolate, pain and fear carved clearly on her face.

"I've . . . oh, damn it, Jock, I've lost my nerve," Freddy blurted. "Since the accident I've avoided getting into a plane—I kidded myself that I just didn't feel like it, that I wasn't ready. Then, when I had to fly to France, I found out. It was a nightmare. I was in total panic, practically crazy with terror, and it didn't stop, not the whole time. The sweats, claustrophobia, expecting to crash every second—I'll never fly again, not ever. Nobody knows but you. I couldn't tell anyone —they wouldn't have understood. Please don't say anything . . . I don't want people to know."

"You're not *allowed* to lose your nerve, Freddy. Flying means too much to you. You've got to go up again—like a rider who's been thrown always gets back on the horse." He moved his hands deftly, turning the key in the ignition.

"Jock! Stop! Turn off the engine. Oh Christ, don't take off, you bastard!" Freddy screamed at him as he quickly swung the little plane around and headed toward the end of the empty runway.

"Just sit there and shut up! I've got the controls, you don't have to do anything!" he yelled at her over the sound of the motor. "Buckle your seat belt!"

Freddy obeyed. She couldn't jump out of a taxiing plane, and if she tried to wrestle his hands away from the controls she would surely kill them both. As the Piper sped down the runway, she squeezed her eyelids together tightly, balled up her fists, clamped her crossed arms over her breasts, jammed her chin down into her neck, shoulders raised to her ears, a frozen, contorted, blind figure with every muscle tensed for impact. When she felt the plane lift off the earth she screwed herself up even smaller, her heart about to explode in her chest.

"Breathe! You're turning blue," Jock shouted as the Piper gained altitude steadily. Freddy expelled the breath she'd been holding and gulped a mouthful of the fresh air that rushed into the cockpit.

"Better?" he asked.

"Take this thing down!"

"Not till you open your eyes."

"Jock, I beg you, don't do this to me!"

"I can't let you do it to yourself. Open your silly eyes and stop being such a dope."

Freddy lifted her lids a fraction. If he wouldn't land until she opened her eyes, she had to do what he said. She peeked through her lashes at her knees, and beyond her knees at the wheel, and behind the wheel the instrument panel, and a glimpse of Jock's hands on the other wheel.

"They're open. Now, God damn you, land!"

"They're open? I don't call that open. Your eyes will be open when you can see outside. When you look around you, when you look down at the earth and see that you're flying as high as a bird in the sky, and the world hasn't come to an end. When First Officer Marie-Frédérique de Lancel realizes that the laws of aerodynamics haven't been sus-pended on her account, then I shall consider that, to my satisfaction, her eyes are officially declared open."

"Oh, you're loving this, aren't you, you bastard? Torturing me is the most fun you've had in years. Why did I ever tell you anything, you smug, cocky, rotten, sneaky *fucker?* Why did I ever give you the small-est advantage over me?"

"Hey, you opened your eyes! I have a theory that it's impossible to stay angry with your eyes closed. You can't glare. Makes sense, doesn't it?"

"Save the theories for the ground. You made a promise," Freddy insisted.

"I said 'when you look around, when you look down'—so far, all you've looked at is the cockpit. You could be in a car."

Setting her teeth, Freddy warily moved her eyes around from one side to another, without relaxing the stiff set of her head on her neck. Then, without turning her body, she slowly leaned her entire torso sideways a few inches toward the window and glanced down. She im-mediately righted herself and fixed her gaze on the windshield.

"See anything interesting?"

"Very funny."

"Well? What'd you see?" he insisted.

"You bloody shit, I saw the same stuff I always see around here, what'd you expect, elephants?"

"You never know. It's pretty wild country, right on the edge of a desert—you could get lost before you knew it."

"You think I don't know that?"

"Familiar with the local landscape, are you?" Jock asked.

"You knew perfectly well I learned to fly in this area, that I soloed at a little airport right near here."

"I did not. Why would I know? Do you think I'm familiar with every little last detail of your past?"

"Obviously not." Freddy felt ridiculous. Of course he wouldn't know. Experienced pilots didn't talk about when and where they'd soloed unless they were sitting around reminiscing.

"I'll bet you don't know where I soloed, do you?" Jock asked.

"No, and I don't give a hoot in hell. I just want to go back down," Freddy demanded wrathfully.

"All right. O.K. In a minute. Just let me tell you about it. It was my sixteenth birthday, and my instructor knew, naturally, that I was dying to solo. I had nine hours, and I thought I was really hot stuff. This was at a little airport down near San Juan Capistrano, and it was after school and getting late and I thought it was then or never. Well, my instructor let me fly the pattern and do touch-and-goes for the whole hour's lesson without saying a word, not even a meaningful look. Then, when the hour was over, completely over, and it was practically dark out, this guy, God, I'll never forget him, says, 'Jock, taxi her over to the parking space,' and when we got there, he climbed down first as usual and he said, 'Well, kid, I'm going in for some coffee, you're too young to drink coffee, so you take her up and fly the pattern a few more times—see you later,' and he just walked away. Never looked back. Well, first I thought, does he want me to go up *alone* or what? And then I caught on and I gave this terrific yell and I just took her up and . . . well, you know how it feels, Freddy, you can't describe it. If you haven't done it, you haven't done it. If you have, you have. That's the thing of it. I didn't want to ever come down. I would have flown around all night, till I ran out of gas, if I hadn't seen the evening star, kind of blinking at me. Reminding me. Suddenly I realized that it was really getting dark, so I came in fast, not bumpy, just with all due speed . . . and it was over. Yeah—January 1936. Only it's never really over, thank God. Some days you think it's over, you think the thrill is gone, you think you're used to the wonder of it, but then it comes back. It always comes back. Like today, watching Annie put her little hands on the wheel—I thought of you, I was wishing you'd been there to see her face. Well—anyway. Story of my life. Pretty unusual, huh? Never happened to anyone else, I guess. A unique experience, unheard of in the annals of aviation." Jock yawned. "Wow, I'm sleepy, so sleepy . . . too many thrills for one day . . . think I'm getting old, Freddy, huh? You take her."

He stretched hugely, his long arms over his head, his hands flat against the top of the cockpit. Freddy automatically took the wheel, automatically her feet reached for the rudders, automatically she checked the instrument panel, automatically she flew the plane. Good, Jock, very good, you suckered me into it, *bored* me into it, smart, oh, very smart, and I didn't even see it coming.

She looked over at him. Jock was giving a very good imitation of a sleeping man. His eyes were definitely closed, no question of it, and his breathing was regular and seemed to be getting deeper. The sunlight in the cockpit gilded the blond hair of his bare, muscular forearms. His long, lean body slumped in the seat. Next thing you know, he'll begin to pretend to snore, she thought, and dismissed him from her mind.

Freddy was busy getting the feel of the Piper Cub, after a year away from flying. She did a few cautious turns, with a very gentle bank. The plane was light but it had plenty of horsepower. She'd flown it before, and knew its capacities. It handled so easily that a child could fly it. A child *had* flown it, she reminded herself.

She turned more steeply, sweeping immediately from one deeply angled turn directly into another in the graceful seraphic linkage that beginning students find so amazing, the heady, intoxicating dance any-one with any sense of balance at all can do with a plane, even if they don't know what keeps it flying or where it's going. Freddy looked around in every direction. There was no one in view. She took the Cub higher, until she'd reached four thousand feet. This was more like it. Oh, this felt—fine. This felt—*wonderful!* Tears came into her eyes as she understood that she felt not the slightest trace of fear. She deliberately thought about the details of her flights to Paris and back. She faced them, she tried to relive them, but all she could do was remember them. She knew in her gut that she'd never feel that way again. She had lost her nerve. Yes, indeed. Now she had it back. Yes, indeed. It could happen to anyone.

Freddy looked for a cloud to play with, but it was a cloudless day. The sun was getting low on the horizon, and Annie was waiting, patiently she hoped, back at the airport. Jock was not quite snoring, and not quite not snoring. She took the Piper Cub up another five hundred feet, looked around carefully once more in every direction and, without warning Jock, deliberately plunged the plane into a steep dive. The Piper, unbridled, roared toward the tapestry of the ground willingly, as if it had been waiting for her to do something interesting. Freddy watched the galloping needle on the instrument panel, trans-fixed with patient passion, until she'd picked up enough speed to begin her loop. Now she began to ease the throttle gently forward, coming out of the dive and beginning the upward climb, starting the circle that would take her over the top of the horizon, over the top of the world. As she climbed, she flicked an eye at Jock. He was still pretending to sleep, breathing easily, relaxed, almost—yes—almost smiling. Bastard!

She mounted relentlessly, higher and higher, her whole body eager for the magical thrill—higher, and higher—and *over!* Over the top, upside down, laughing, zooming, free to fly. Free, divinely free, master of the sky, queen of the horizon, keeper of the clouds, sister of the wind, cut loose from the humble, drudging reality of gravity in the only element that blesses mankind with such choice.

Freddy recovered from the loop and took her hands off the controls.

"Take her back, Jock," she said, "if you're awake."

Jock landed at Santa Paula and taxied slowly to the side of the landing strip. Neither of them started to leave the plane.

"Thanks, Jock," Freddy said, "you're a friend."

"It was nothing."

"It was everything."

"It was . . . what it was." He grinned at her, enchanted and tongue-tied. She was so hopelessly beautiful, with no makeup and her nutsy hair all over the place and a feisty look in her eyes that he hadn't seen in much too long.

"I've got to admit it, you cured me." Freddy shook her head in candid admiration. "Maybe—maybe you could do something about another problem that's been bothering me," she added thoughtfully. "It's the same kind of thing—strictly in my head."

"I'll try," he said eagerly.

"I'm suffering from some sort of amnesia. The doctors tell me it's common after an accident. They say I may never get that memory back —a whole important period of time out of my life! It's driving me bananas. The last thing I remember was singing old songs up on the bandstand at the hotel. I distinctly remember the last song, 'I'm Always Chasing Rainbows'—and the next thing I know, I was waking up in a hospital—*weeks* later, as it turned out. Obviously I'd gone up and crashed into a mountain, that much I know because they told me, but I don't remember anything after the bandstand."

"Nothing? Absolutely nothing?"

"Nope. I don't know what I did after I stopped singing. At least I assume I *must* have stopped singing or I couldn't have been flying a plane. Just look at the kind of connections I'm reduced to making! It's pathetic. I feel as if I'm only half here."

"Would the words 'Till We Meet Again' bring anything back?" He risked the question, a mesh of his blond hair flopping over his forehead, his eyes squinting apprehensively.

"Come on, Jock, that's the song my mother always told us was lucky, although she's never said exactly why. I sang that song for all of you at the Blue Swan because I felt a certain . . . magic . . . in it—I hoped it might bring you all back safely the next day. I didn't say I'd forgotten my *entire* life, just a part of it."

"So you don't remember anything from after 'Rainbows'—you don't even remember how you got home that night, you don't remember . . . anything . . . else?"

"How many times do I have to tell you that it's one big empty blank?"

"Hmm. Well, that *is* a problem."

"That's very helpful. At least you're convinced it's a problem. We're making progress. Very slowly, to be sure, but I suppose you could call it progress."

"I have an idea, if you'd stop laughing at me."

"I'm listening." Her frolicking smile was that of someone listening to the sound of bravos echoing in her ears, well-earned bravos.

"We should—re-create—the events of that night. I don't think it's necessary to hold another Eagle Squadron reunion, because you remember that, but there are other steps that could be taken. For instance, you could wear the same dress, that wild and disorderly red dress, if you still have it, and those jazzy red shoes, and your ATA wings, and we could go somewhere with a dance floor and music and we could have dinner the way we did, and dance the way we did, and I could tip the bandleader to play some of the old songs and . . . well, sort of take it from there. Something would be bound to happen that would trigger your memory."

"That sounds like an ingenious idea—as long as I don't have to sing. When can we do it?"

"Whenever you like. I'm available. I'm not going anywhere."

"How about tonight? Would tonight be too soon?" Freddy asked.

"Tonight would be—great. I don't have anything better to do. Do you?"

"No, Jock, nothing better."

Hastily, Freddy gave Jock a peck on the cheek and made ready to get out of the plane. If her memory was triggered any more powerfully than it had been as she sat so near him, she'd fall into Jock's arms and make an unseemly, unladylike, immodest spectacle of herself, right here inside the Piper Cub. He was going to have to work very hard to bring

533

back her memory. *Oh, yes!* Amnesia took a powerful lot of loving to cure, a powerful lot of kisses, a blizzard of hugs, an encyclopedia of words; all the loving Jock had, all the loving that had been waiting, stored up all these years for her. She wanted to hear him say it all over again. And again.

"Freddy—" Jock leaned toward her impulsively, such emotion blazing from his eyes that she almost tumbled out of the plane. What if he could read her mind? *Not so fast!* Amnesia, she had amnesia. Freddy clung to the thought as she forced herself to look blank. She blinked.

"Yes?" she asked innocently.

"I love you. Freddy, damn it, I'm so much in love with you I can't take it anymore!"

"Wait! Say that again!" Freddy commanded. She drew herself up, vulnerable no longer, needy no longer, ready to listen to her heart.

"Why, so you can gloat over me as usual?" He grinned again, suddenly sure of himself. She'd heard him the first time.

"No—it's what you just said—I think—I think maybe a little bit of my memory's coming back—something about . . . could it be a . . . a school prom? Something about going flyin' together? Hmm . . . doesn't it seem to you that we've already been flyin'?"

"Knock off that teasing. Tease me every day for the rest of your life, but now, let me give you a kiss."

"You don't want much, do you, Squadron Leader?"

"Oh, darling, I want it all. *All.* Starting with a kiss. Please, Freddy."

"I remember someone saying . . . yes . . . I remember it clearly . . . 'Only a jerk asks a girl's permission,' " Freddy said in an astonished voice as she reached out to Jock, lifting and opening her arms in a gesture that was half a surrender and wholly a promise.